D0896514

SONG OF SOLOMON

TAR BABY

SULA

Quality Paperback Book Club
New York

TONI MORRISON

SULA

Copyright © 1973 by Toni Morrison

SONG OF SOLOMON

Copyright © 1977 by Toni Morrison

TAR BABY

Copyright © 1981 by Toni Morrison

All rights reserved under International and Pan-American Copyright Conventions. Published in the United States by Alfred A. Knopf, Inc., New York, and simultaneously in Canada by Random House of Canada Limited, Toronto. Distributed by Random House Inc., New York.

No part of this book may be used or reproduced in any manner whatsoever without written permission of the publisher. For information, address Alfred A. Knopf, Inc., 201 East 50th Street, New York, NY 10022.

This volume was specially created for the Quality Paperback Book Club by arrangement with Alfred A. Knopf, Inc. This edition copyright © 1987 by Book-of-the-Month Club, Inc.

Printed in the United States of America

Quality Paperback Book Club®

SULA

SONG OF SOLOMON

TAR BABY

SULA

It is sheer good fortune to miss
somebody long before they leave you.
This book is for Ford and Slade, whom
I miss although they have not left me.

"*Nobody knew my rose of the world*
but me. . . . I had too much glory.
They don't want glory like that
in nobody's heart."

—The Rose Tattoo

PART ONE

In that place, where they tore the nightshade and blackberry patches from their roots to make room for the Medallion City Golf Course, there was once a neighborhood. It stood in the hills above the valley town of Medallion and spread all the way to the river. It is called the suburbs now, but when black people lived there it was called the Bottom. One road, shaded by beeches, oaks, maples and chestnuts, connected it to the valley. The beeches are gone now, and so are the pear trees where children sat and yelled down through the blossoms to passersby. Generous funds have been allotted to level the stripped and faded buildings that clutter the road from Medallion up to the golf course. They are going to raze the Time and a Half Pool Hall, where feet in long tan shoes once pointed down from chair rungs. A steel ball will knock to dust Irene's Palace of Cosmetology, where women used to lean their heads back on sink trays and doze while Irene lathered Nu Nile into their hair. Men in khaki work clothes will pry loose the slats of Reba's Grill, where the owner cooked in her hat because she couldn't remember the ingredients without it.

There will be nothing left of the Bottom (the footbridge that crossed the river is already gone), but perhaps it is just as well, since it wasn't a town anyway: just a neighborhood where on quiet days people in valley houses could hear singing sometimes, banjos sometimes, and, if a valley man happened to have business up in those hills—collecting rent or insurance payments—he might see a dark woman in a flowered dress doing a bit of cakewalk, a bit of black bottom, a bit of "messing around" to the lively notes of a mouth organ. Her bare feet would raise the saffron dust that floated down on the coveralls and bunion-split shoes of the man breathing music in and out of his harmonica. The black people watching her would laugh and rub their knees, and it would be easy for the valley man to hear the laughter and not notice the adult pain that rested somewhere under the eyelids, somewhere under their head rags and soft felt hats, somewhere in the palm of the hand, somewhere behind the frayed lapels, somewhere in the sinew's curve. He'd have to stand in the back of Greater Saint Matthew's and let the tenor's voice dress him in silk, or touch the hands of the spoon carvers (who had not worked in eight years) and let the fingers that danced on wood kiss his skin. Otherwise the pain would escape him even though the laughter was part of the pain.

A shucking, knee-slapping, wet-eyed laughter that could even describe and explain how they came to be where they were.

A joke. A nigger joke. That was the way it got started. Not the town, of course, but that part of town where the Negroes lived, the part they called the Bottom in spite of the fact that it was up in the hills. Just a nigger joke. The kind white folks tell when the mill closes down and they're looking for a little comfort somewhere. The kind colored folks tell on themselves when the rain doesn't come, or comes for weeks, and they're looking for a little comfort somehow.

A good white farmer promised freedom and a piece of bottom land to his slave if he would perform some very difficult chores. When the slave completed the work, he asked the farmer to keep his end of the bargain. Freedom was easy—the farmer had no objection to that. But he didn't want to give up any land. So he told the slave that he was very sorry that he had to give him valley land. He had hoped to give him a piece of the Bottom. The slave blinked and said he thought valley land was bottom land. The master said, "Oh, no! See those hills? That's bottom land, rich and fertile."

"But it's high up in the hills," said the slave.

"High up from us," said the master, "but when God looks down, it's the bottom. That's why we call it so. It's the bottom of heaven—best land there is."

So the slave pressed his master to try to get him some. He preferred it to the valley. And it was done. The nigger got the hilly land, where planting was backbreaking, where the soil slid down and washed away the seeds, and where the wind lingered all through the winter.

Which accounted for the fact that white people lived on the rich valley floor in that little river town in Ohio, and the blacks populated the hills above it, taking small consolation in the fact that every day they could literally look down on the white folks.

Still, it was lovely up in the Bottom. After the town grew and the farm land turned into a village and the village into a town and the streets of Medallion were hot and dusty with progress, those heavy trees that sheltered the shacks up in the Bottom were wonderful to see. And the hunters who went there sometimes wondered in private if maybe the white farmer was right after all. Maybe it was the bottom of heaven.

The black people would have disagreed, but they had no time to think about it. They were mightily preoccupied with earthly things—and each other, wondering even as early as 1920 what Shadrack was all about, what that little girl Sula who grew into a woman in their town was all about, and what they themselves were all about, tucked up there in the Bottom.

1919

Except for World War II, nothing ever interfered with the celebration of National Suicide Day. It had taken place every January third since 1920, although Shadrack, its founder, was for many years the only celebrant. Blasted and permanently astonished by the events of 1917, he had returned to Medallion handsome but ravaged, and even the most fastidious people in the town sometimes caught themselves dreaming of what he must have been like a few years back before he went off to war. A young man of hardly twenty, his head full of nothing and his mouth recalling the taste of lipstick, Shadrack had found himself in December, 1917, running with his comrades across a field in France. It was his first encounter with the enemy and he didn't know whether his company was running toward them or away. For several days they had been marching, keeping close to a stream that was frozen at its edges. At one point they crossed it, and no sooner had he stepped foot on the other side than the day was adangle with shouts and explosions. Shellfire was all around him, and though he knew that this was something called *it*, he could not muster up the proper feeling—the feeling that would accommodate *it*. He expected to be terrified or exhilarated—to feel *something* very strong. In fact, he felt only the bite of a nail in his boot, which pierced the ball of his foot whenever he came down on it. The day was cold enough to make his breath visible, and he wondered for a moment at the purity and whiteness of his own breath among the dirty, gray explosions surrounding him. He ran, bayonet fixed, deep in the great sweep of men flying across this field. Wincing at the pain in his foot, he turned his head a little to the right and saw the face of a soldier near him fly off. Before he could register shock, the rest of the soldier's head disappeared under the inverted soup bowl of his helmet. But stubbornly, taking no direction from the brain, the body of the headless soldier ran on, with energy and grace, ignoring altogether the drip and slide of brain tissue down its back.

When Shadrack opened his eyes he was propped up in a small bed. Before him on a tray was a large tin plate divided into three triangles. In one triangle was rice, in another meat, and in the third stewed tomatoes. A small round depression held a cup of whitish liquid. Shadrack stared at the soft colors that filled these triangles: the lumpy whiteness of rice, the quivering blood tomatoes, the grayish-brown meat. All their repugnance was contained in the neat balance of the triangles—a balance that soothed him, transferred some of its equilibrium to him. Thus reassured that the white, the red and the brown would stay where they were—would not explode or burst forth from their restricted zones—he suddenly felt hungry and looked around for his hands. His glance was cautious at first, for he had to be very careful—anything could be anywhere. Then he noticed two lumps beneath the beige blanket on either side of his hips. With extreme care he lifted one arm and was relieved to find his hand attached to his wrist. He tried the other and found it also. Slowly he directed one hand toward the cup and, just as he was about to spread his fingers, they began to grow in higgledy-piggledy fashion like Jack's beanstalk all over the tray and the bed. With a shriek he closed his eyes and thrust his huge growing hands under the covers. Once out of sight they seemed to shrink back to their normal size. But the yell had brought a male nurse.

"Private? We're not going to have any trouble today, are we? Are we, Private?"

Shadrack looked up at a balding man dressed in a green-cotton jacket and trousers. His hair was parted low on the right side so that some twenty or thirty yellow hairs could discreetly cover the nakedness of his head.

"Come on. Pick up that spoon. Pick it up, Private. Nobody is going to feed you forever."

Sweat slid from Shadrack's armpits down his sides. He could not bear to see his hands grow again and he was frightened of the voice in the apple-green suit.

"Pick it up, I said. There's no point to this . . ." The nurse reached under the cover for Shadrack's wrist to pull out the monstrous hand. Shadrack jerked it back and overturned the tray. In panic he raised himself to his knees and tried to fling off and away his terrible fingers, but succeeded only in knocking the nurse into the next bed.

When they bound Shadrack into a straitjacket, he was both relieved and grateful, for his hands were at last hidden and confined to whatever size they had attained.

Laced and silent in his small bed, he tried to tie the loose cords in his mind. He wanted desperately to see his own face and connect it with the word "private"—the word the nurse (and the others who helped bind him) had called him. "Private" he thought was something secret, and he wondered why they looked at him and called him a secret. Still, if his hands behaved as they had done, what might he expect from his face? The fear and longing were too much for him, so he began to think of other things. That is, he let his mind slip into whatever cave mouths of memory it chose.

He saw a window that looked out on a river which he knew was full of fish. Someone was speaking softly just outside the door...

Shadrack's earlier violence had coincided with a memorandum from the hospital executive staff in reference to the distribution of patients in high-risk areas. There was clearly a demand for space. The priority or the violence earned Shadrack his release, $217 in cash, a full suit of clothes and copies of very official-looking papers.

When he stepped out of the hospital door the grounds overwhelmed him: the cropped shrubbery, the edged lawns, the undeviating walks. Shadrack looked at the cement stretches: each one leading clearheadedly to some presumably desirable destination. There were no fences, no warnings, no obstacles at all between concrete and green grass, so one could easily ignore the tidy sweep of stone and cut out in another direction—a direction of one's own.

Shadrack stood at the foot of the hospital steps watching the heads of trees tossing ruefully but harmlessly, since their trunks were rooted too deeply in the earth to threaten him. Only the walks made him uneasy. He shifted his weight, wondering how he could get to the gate without stepping on the concrete. While plotting his course—where he would have to leap, where to skirt a clump of bushes—a loud guffaw startled him. Two men were going up the steps. Then he noticed that there were many people about, and that he was just now seeing them, or else they had just materialized. They were thin slips, like paper dolls floating down the walks. Some were seated in chairs with wheels, propelled by other paper figures from behind. All seemed to be smoking, and their arms and legs curved in the breeze. A good high wind would pull them up and away and they would land perhaps among the tops of the trees.

Shadrack took the plunge. Four steps and he was on the grass heading for the gate. He kept his head down to avoid seeing the paper people swerving and bending here and there, and he lost his way. When he looked up, he was standing by a low red building separated from the main building by a covered walkway. From somewhere came a sweetish smell which reminded him of something painful. He looked around for the gate and saw that he had gone directly away from it in his complicated journey over the grass. Just to the left of the low building was a graveled driveway that appeared to lead outside the grounds. He trotted quickly to it and left, at last, a haven of more than a year, only eight days of which he fully recollected.

Once on the road, he headed west. The long stay in the

hospital had left him weak—too weak to walk steadily on the gravel shoulders of the road. He shuffled, grew dizzy, stopped for breath, started again, stumbling and sweating but refusing to wipe his temples, still afraid to look at his hands. Passengers in dark, square cars shuttered their eyes at what they took to be a drunken man.

The sun was already directly over his head when he came to a town. A few blocks of shaded streets and he was already at its heart—a pretty, quietly regulated downtown.

Exhausted, his feet clotted with pain, he sat down at the curbside to take off his shoes. He closed his eyes to avoid seeing his hands and fumbled with the laces of the heavy high-topped shoes. The nurse had tied them into a double knot, the way one does for children, and Shadrack, long unaccustomed to the manipulation of intricate things, could not get them loose. Uncoordinated, his fingernails tore away at the knots. He fought a rising hysteria that was not merely anxiety to free his aching feet; his very life depended on the release of the knots. Suddenly without raising his eyelids, he began to cry. Twenty-two years old, weak, hot, frightened, not daring to acknowledge the fact that he didn't even know who or what he was . . . with no past, no language, no tribe, no source, no address book, no comb, no pencil, no clock, no pocket handkerchief, no rug, no bed, no can opener, no faded postcard, no soap, no key, no tobacco pouch, no soiled underwear and nothing nothing nothing to do . . . he was sure of one thing only: the unchecked monstrosity of his hands. He cried soundlessly at the curbside of a small Midwestern town wondering where the window was, and the river, and the soft voices just outside the door . . .

Through his tears he saw the fingers joining the laces, tentatively at first, then rapidly. The four fingers of each hand fused into the fabric, knotted themselves and zigzagged in and out of the tiny eyeholes.

By the time the police drove up, Shadrack was suffering from a blinding headache, which was not abated by the comfort he felt when the policemen pulled his hands away from what he thought was a permanent entanglement with his shoelaces. They took him to jail, booked him for vagrancy and intoxication, and locked him in a cell. Lying on a cot, Shadrack could only stare helplessly at the wall, so paralyzing was the pain in his head. He lay in this agony for a long while and then realized he was staring at the painted-over letters of a command to fuck himself. He studied the phrase as the pain in his head subsided.

Like moonlight stealing under a window shade an idea insinuated itself: his earlier desire to see his own face. He looked for a mirror; there was none. Finally, keeping his hands carefully behind his back he made his way to the toilet bowl and peeped in. The water was unevenly lit by the sun so he could make nothing out. Returning to his cot he took the blanket and covered his head, rendering the water dark enough to see his reflection. There in the toilet water he saw a grave black face. A black so definite, so unequivocal, it astonished him. He had been harboring a skittish apprehension that he was not real—that he didn't exist at all. But when the blackness greeted him with its indisputable presence, he wanted nothing more. In his joy he took the risk of letting one edge of the blanket drop and glanced at his hands. They were still. Courteously still.

Shadrack rose and returned to the cot, where he fell into

the first sleep of his new life. A sleep deeper than the hospital drugs; deeper than the pits of plums, steadier than the condor's wing; more tranquil than the curve of eggs.

The sheriff looked through the bars at the young man with the matted hair. He had read through his prisoner's papers and hailed a farmer. When Shadrack awoke, the sheriff handed him back his papers and escorted him to the back of a wagon. Shadrack got in and in less than three hours he was back in Medallion, for he had been only twenty-two miles from his window, his river, and his soft voices just outside the door.

In the back of the wagon, supported by sacks of squash and hills of pumpkins, Shadrack began a struggle that was to last for twelve days, a struggle to order and focus experience. It had to do with making a place for fear as a way of controlling it. He knew the smell of death and was terrified of it, for he could not anticipate it. It was not death or dying that frightened him, but the unexpectedness of both. In sorting it all out, he hit on the notion that if one day a year were devoted to it, everybody could get it out of the way and the rest of the year would be safe and free. In this manner he instituted National Suicide Day.

On the third day of the new year, he walked through the Bottom down Carpenter's Road with a cowbell and a hangman's rope calling the people together. Telling them that this was their only chance to kill themselves or each other.

At first the people in the town were frightened; they

knew Shadrack was crazy but that did not mean that he didn't have any sense or, even more important, that he had no power. His eyes were so wild, his hair so long and matted, his voice was so full of authority and thunder that he caused panic on the first, or Charter, National Suicide Day in 1920. The next one, in 1921, was less frightening but still worrisome. The people had seen him a year now in between. He lived in a shack on the riverbank that had once belonged to his grandfather long time dead. On Tuesday and Friday he sold the fish he had caught that morning, the rest of the week he was drunk, loud, obscene, funny and outrageous. But he never touched anybody, never fought, never caressed. Once the people understood the boundaries and nature of his madness, they could fit him, so to speak, into the scheme of things.

Then, on subsequent National Suicide Days, the grown people looked out from behind curtains as he rang his bell; a few stragglers increased their speed, and little children screamed and ran. The tetter heads tried goading him (although he was only four or five years older then they) but not for long, for his curses were stingingly personal.

As time went along, the people took less notice of these January thirds, or rather they thought they did, thought they had no attitudes or feelings one way or another about Shadrack's annual solitary parade. In fact they had simply stopped remarking on the holiday because they had absorbed it into their thoughts, into their language, into their lives.

Someone said to a friend, "You sure was a long time delivering that baby. How long was you in labor?"

And the friend answered, "'Bout three days. The pains

started on Suicide Day and kept up till the following Sunday. Was borned on Sunday. All my boys is Sunday boys."

Some lover said to his bride-to-be, "Let's do it after New Years, 'stead of before. I get paid New Year's Eve."

And his sweetheart answered, "OK, but make sure it ain't on Suicide Day. I ain't 'bout to be listening to no cowbells whilst the weddin's going on."

Somebody's grandmother said her hens always started a laying of double yolks right after Suicide Day.

Then Reverend Deal took it up, saying the same folks who had sense enough to avoid Shadrack's call were the ones who insisted on drinking themselves to death or womanizing themselves to death. "May's well go on with Shad and save the Lamb the trouble of redemption."

Easily, quietly, Suicide Day became a part of the fabric of life up in the Bottom of Medallion, Ohio.

1920

It had to be as far away from the Sundown House as possible. And her grandmother's middle-aged nephew who lived in a Northern town called Medallion was the one chance she had to make sure it would be. The red shutters had haunted both Helene Sabat and her grandmother for sixteen years. Helene was born behind those shutters, daughter of a Creole whore who worked there. The grandmother took Helene away from the soft lights and flowered carpets of the Sundown House and raised her under the dolesome eyes of a multicolored Virgin Mary, counseling her to be constantly on guard for any sign of her mother's wild blood.

So when Wiley Wright came to visit his Great Aunt Cecile in New Orleans, his enchantment with the pretty Helene became a marriage proposal—under the pressure of both women. He was a seaman (or rather a lakeman, for he was a ship's cook on one of the Great Lakes lines), in port only three days out of every sixteen.

He took his bride to his home in Medallion and put her in a lovely house with a brick porch and real lace curtains at the window. His long absences were quite bearable for Helene Wright, especially when, after some nine years of marriage, her daughter was born.

Her daughter was more comfort and purpose than she had ever hoped to find in this life. She rose grandly to the occasion of motherhood—grateful, deep down in her heart, that the child had not inherited the great beauty that was hers: that her skin had dusk in it, that her lashes were substantial but not undignified in their length, that she had taken the broad flat nose of Wiley (although Helene expected to improve it somewhat) and his generous lips.

Under Helene's hand the girl became obedient and polite. Any enthusiasms that little Nel showed were calmed by the mother until she drove her daughter's imagination underground.

Helene Wright was an impressive woman, at least in Medallion she was. Heavy hair in a bun, dark eyes arched in a perpetual query about other people's manners. A woman who won all social battles with presence and a conviction of the legitimacy of her authority. Since there was no Catholic church in Medallion then, she joined the most conservative black church. And held sway. It was Helene who never turned her head in church when latecomers arrived; Helene who established the practice of seasonal altar flowers; Helene who introduced the giving of banquets of welcome to returning Negro veterans. She lost only one battle—the pronunciation of her name. The people in the Bottom refused to say Helene. They called her Helen Wright and left it at that.

All in all her life was a satisfactory one. She loved her house and enjoyed manipulating her daughter and her husband. She would sigh sometimes just before falling asleep, thinking that she had indeed come far enough away from the Sundown House.

So it was with extremely mixed emotions that she read a letter from Mr. Henri Martin describing the illness of her grandmother, and suggesting she come down right away. She didn't want to go, but could not bring herself to ignore the silent plea of the woman who had rescued her.

It was November. November, 1920. Even in Medallion there was a victorious swagger in the legs of white men and a dull-eyed excitement in the eyes of colored veterans.

Helene thought about the trip South with heavy misgiving but decided that she had the best protection: her manner and her bearing, to which she would add a beautiful dress. She bought some deep-brown wool and three-fourths of a yard of matching velvet. Out of this she made herself a heavy but elegant dress with velvet collar and pockets.

Nel watched her mother cutting the pattern from newspapers and moving her eyes rapidly from a magazine model to her own hands. She watched her turn up the kerosene lamp at sunset to sew far into the night.

The day they were ready, Helene cooked a smoked ham, left a note for her lake-bound husband, in case he docked early, and walked head high and arms stiff with luggage ahead of her daughter to the train depot.

It was a longer walk than she remembered, and they saw the train steaming up just as they turned the corner. They ran along the track looking for the coach pointed out to them by the colored porter. Even at that they made a mistake. Helene and her daughter entered a coach peopled by some twenty white men and women. Rather than go back and down the three wooden steps again, Helene decided to spare herself some embarrassment and walk on through to the colored car. She carried two pieces of luggage and a string purse; her daughter carried a covered basket of food.

As they opened the door marked COLORED ONLY, they saw a white conductor coming toward them. It was a chilly day but a light skim of sweat glistened on the woman's face as she and the little girl struggled to hold the door open, hang on to their luggage and enter all at once. The conductor let his eyes travel over the pale yellow woman and then stuck his little finger into his ear, jiggling it free of wax. "What you think you doin', gal?"

Helene looked up at him.

So soon. So soon. She hadn't even begun the trip back. Back to her grandmother's house in the city where the red shutters glowed, and already she had been called "gal." All the old vulnerabilities, all the old fears of being somehow flawed gathered in her stomach and made her hands tremble. She had heard only that one word; it dangled above her wide-brimmed hat, which had slipped, in her exertion, from its carefully leveled placement and was now tilted in a bit of a jaunt over her eye.

Thinking he wanted her tickets, she quickly dropped both the cowhide suitcase and the straw one in order to search for them in her purse. An eagerness to please and an apology for living met in her voice. "I have them. Right here somewhere, sir . . ."

The conductor looked at the bit of wax his fingernail

had retrieved. "What was you doin' back in there? What was you doin' in that coach yonder?"

Helene licked her lips. "Oh . . . I . . ." Her glance moved beyond the white man's face to the passengers seated behind him. Four or five black faces were watching, two belonging to soldiers still in their shit-colored uniforms and peaked caps. She saw their closed faces, their locked eyes, and turned for compassion to the gray eyes of the conductor.

"We made a mistake, sir. You see, there wasn't no sign. We just got in the wrong car, that's all. Sir."

"We don't 'low no mistakes on this train. Now git your butt on in there."

He stood there staring at her until she realized that he wanted her to move aside. Pulling Nel by the arm, she pressed herself and her daughter into the foot space in front of a wooden seat. Then, for no earthly reason, at least no reason that anybody could understand, certainly no reason that Nel understood then or later, she smiled. Like a street pup that wags its tail at the very doorjamb of the butcher shop he has been kicked away from only moments before, Helene smiled. Smiled dazzlingly and coquettishly at the salmon-colored face of the conductor.

Nel looked away from the flash of pretty teeth to the other passengers. The two black soldiers, who had been watching the scene with what appeared to be indifference, now looked stricken. Behind Nel was the bright and blazing light of her mother's smile; before her the midnight eyes of the soldiers. She saw the muscles of their faces tighten, a movement under the skin from blood to marble. No change in the expression of the eyes, but a hard wetness that veiled them as they looked at the stretch of her mother's foolish smile.

As the door slammed on the conductor's exit, Helene walked down the aisle to a seat. She looked about for a second to see whether any of the men would help her put the suitcases in the overhead rack. Not a man moved. Helene sat down, fussily, her back toward the men. Nel sat opposite, facing both her mother and the soldiers, neither of whom she could look at. She felt both pleased and ashamed to sense that these men, unlike her father, who worshiped his graceful, beautiful wife, were bubbling with a hatred for her mother that had not been there in the beginning but had been born with the dazzling smile. In the silence that preceded the train's heave, she looked deeply at the folds of her mother's dress. There in the fall of the heavy brown wool she held her eyes. She could not risk letting them travel upward for fear of seeing that the hooks and eyes in the placket of the dress had come undone and exposed the custard-colored skin underneath. She stared at the hem, wanting to believe in its weight but knowing that custard was all that it hid. If this tall, proud woman, this woman who was very particular about her friends, who slipped into church with unequaled elegance, who could quell a roustabout with a look, if *she* were really custard, then there was a chance that Nel was too.

It was on that train, shuffling toward Cincinnati, that she resolved to be on guard—always. She wanted to make certain that no man ever looked at her that way. That no midnight eyes or marbled flesh would ever accost her and turn her into jelly.

For two days they rode; two days of watching sleet turn to rain, turn to purple sunsets, and one night knotted on the wooden seats (their heads on folded coats), trying not to hear the snoring soldiers. When they changed trains in Birmingham for the last leg of the trip, they discovered what luxury they had been in through Kentucky and Tennessee, where the rest stops had all had colored toilets. After Birmingham there were none. Helene's face was drawn with the need to relieve herself, and so intense was her distress she finally brought herself to speak about her problem to a black woman with four children who had got on in Tuscaloosa.

"Is there somewhere we can go to use the restroom?"

The woman looked up at her and seemed not to understand. "Ma'am?" Her eyes fastened on the thick velvet collar, the fair skin, the high-tone voice.

"The restroom," Helene repeated. Then, in a whisper, "The toilet."

The woman pointed out the window and said, "Yes, ma'am. Yonder."

Helene looked out of the window halfway expecting to see a comfort station in the distance; instead she saw gray-green trees leaning over tangled grass. "Where?"

"Yonder," the woman said. "Meridian. We be pullin' in direc'lin." Then she smiled sympathetically and asked, "Kin you make it?"

Helene nodded and went back to her seat trying to think of other things—for the surest way to have an accident would be to remember her full bladder.

At Meridian the women got out with their children. While Helene looked about the tiny stationhouse for a door that said COLORED WOMEN, the other woman stalked off to a field of high grass on the far side of the track. Some white men were leaning on the railing in front of the stationhouse. It was not only their tongues curling around toothpicks that kept Helene from asking information of them. She looked around for the other woman and, seeing just the top of her head rag in the grass, slowly realized where "yonder" was. All of them, the fat woman and her four children, three boys and a girl, Helene and her daughter, squatted there in the four o'clock Meridian sun. They did it again in Ellisville, again in Hattiesburg, and by the time they reached Slidell, not too far from Lake Pontchartrain, Helene could not only fold leaves as well as the fat woman, she never felt a stir as she passed the muddy eyes of the men who stood like wrecked Dorics under the station roofs of those towns.

The lift in spirit that such an accomplishment produced in her quickly disappeared when the train finally pulled into New Orleans.

Cecile Sabat's house leaned between two others just like it on Elysian Fields. A Frenchified shotgun house, it sported a magnificent garden in the back and a tiny wrought-iron fence in the front. On the door hung a black crepe wreath with purple ribbon. They were too late. Helene reached up to touch the ribbon, hesitated, and knocked. A man in a collarless shirt opened the door. Helene identified herself and he said he was Henri Martin and that he was there for the settin'-up. They stepped into the house. The

Virgin Mary clasped her hands in front of her neck three times in the front room and once in the bedroom where Cecile's body lay. The old woman had died without seeing or blessing her granddaughter.

No one other than Mr. Martin seemed to be in the house, but a sweet odor as of gardenias told them that someone else had been. Blotting her lashes with a white handkerchief, Helene walked through the kitchen to the back bedroom where she had slept for sixteen years. Nel trotted along behind, enchanted with the smell, the candles and the strangeness. When Helene bent to loosen the ribbons of Nel's hat, a woman in a yellow dress came out of the garden and onto the back porch that opened into the bedroom. The two women looked at each other. There was no recognition in the eyes of either. Then Helene said, "This is your . . . grandmother, Nel." Nel looked at her mother and then quickly back at the door they had just come out of.

"No. That was your great-grandmother. This is your grandmother. My . . . mother."

Before the child could think, her words were hanging in the gardenia air. "But she looks so young."

The woman in the canary-yellow dress laughed and said she was forty-eight, "an old forty-eight."

Then it was she who carried the gardenia smell. This tiny woman with the softness and glare of a canary. In that somber house that held four Virgin Marys, where death sighed in every corner and candles sputtered, the gardenia smell and canary-yellow dress emphasized the funeral atmosphere surrounding them.

The woman smiled, glanced in the mirror and said, throwing her voice toward Helene, "That your only one?"

"Yes," said Helene.

"Pretty. A lot like you."

"Yes. Well. She's ten now."

"Ten? Vrai? Small for her age, no?"

Helene shrugged and looked at her daughter's questioning eyes. The woman in the yellow dress leaned forward. "Come. Come, chere."

Helene interrupted. "We have to get cleaned up. We been three days on the train with no chance to wash or . . ."

"Comment t'appelle?"

"She doesn't talk Creole."

"Then you ask her."

"She wants to know your name, honey."

With her head pressed into her mother's heavy brown dress, Nel told her and then asked, "What's yours?"

"Mine's Rochelle. Well. I must be going on." She moved closer to the mirror and stood there sweeping hair up from her neck back into its halo-like roll, and wetting with spit the ringlets that fell over her ears. "I been here, you know, most of the day. She pass on yesterday. The funeral tomorrow. Henri takin' care." She struck a match, blew it out and darkened her eyebrows with the burnt head. All the while Helene and Nel watched her. The one in a rage at the folded leaves she had endured, the wooden benches she had slept on, all to miss seeing her grandmother and seeing instead that painted canary who never said a word of greeting or affection or . . .

Rochelle continued. "I don't know what happen to de

house. Long time paid for. You be thinkin' on it? Oui?" Her newly darkened eyebrows queried Helene.

"Oui." Helene's voice was chilly. "I be thinkin' on it."

"Oh, well. Not for me to say . . ."

Suddenly she swept around and hugged Nel—a quick embrace tighter and harder than one would have imagined her thin soft arms capable of.

"'Voir! 'Voir!" and she was gone.

In the kitchen, being soaped head to toe by her mother, Nel ventured an observation. "She smelled so nice. And her skin was so soft."

Helene rinsed the cloth. "Much handled things are always soft."

"What does 'vwah' mean?"

"I don't know," her mother said. "I don't talk Creole." She gazed at her daughter's wet buttocks. "And neither do you."

When they got back to Medallion and into the quiet house they saw the note exactly where they had left it and the ham dried out in the icebox.

"Lord, I've never been so glad to see this place. But look at the dust. Get the rags, Nel. Oh, never mind. Let's breathe awhile first. Lord, I never thought I'd get back here safe and sound. Whoo. Well, it's over. Good and over. Praise His name. Look at that. I told that old fool not to deliver any milk and there's the can curdled to beat all. What gets into people? I told him not to. Well, I got other things to worry 'bout. Got to get a fire started. I left it ready so I wouldn't have to do nothin' but light it. Lord, it's cold. Don't just sit there, honey. You could be pulling your nose..."

Nel sat on the red-velvet sofa listening to her mother but remembering the smell and the tight, tight hug of the woman in yellow who rubbed burned matches over her eyes.

Late that night after the fire was made, the cold supper eaten, the surface dust removed, Nel lay in bed thinking of her trip. She remembered clearly the urine running down and into her stockings until she learned how to squat properly; the disgust on the face of the dead woman and the sound of the funeral drums. It had been an exhilarating trip but a fearful one. She had been frightened of the soldiers' eyes on the train, the black wreath on the door, the custard pudding she believed lurked under her mother's heavy dress, the feel of unknown streets and unknown people. But she had gone on a real trip, and now she was different. She got out of bed and lit the lamp to look in the mirror. There was her face, plain brown eyes, three braids and the nose her mother hated. She looked for a long time and suddenly a shiver ran through her.

"I'm me," she whispered. "Me."

Nel didn't know quite what she meant, but on the other hand she knew exactly what she meant.

"I'm me. I'm not their daughter. I'm not Nel. I'm me. Me."

Each time she said the word *me* there was a gathering in her like power, like joy, like fear. Back in bed with her discovery, she stared out the window at the dark leaves of the horse chestnut.

"Me," she murmured. And then, sinking deeper into the

quilts, "I want . . . I want to be . . . wonderful. Oh, Jesus, make me wonderful."

The many experiences of her trip crowded in on her. She slept. It was the last as well as the first time she was ever to leave Medallion.

For days afterward she imagined other trips she would take, alone though, to faraway places. Contemplating them was delicious. Leaving Medallion would be her goal. But that was before she met Sula, the girl she had seen for five years at Garfield Primary but never played with, never knew, because her mother said that Sula's mother was sooty. The trip, perhaps, or her new found me-ness, gave her the strength to cultivate a friend in spite of her mother.

When Sula first visited the Wright house, Helene's curdled scorn turned to butter. Her daughter's friend seemed to have none of the mother's slackness. Nel, who regarded the oppressive neatness of her home with dread, felt comfortable in it with Sula, who loved it and would sit on the red-velvet sofa for ten to twenty minutes at a time—still as dawn. As for Nel, she preferred Sula's woolly house, where a pot of something was always cooking on the stove; where the mother, Hannah, never scolded or gave directions; where all sorts of people dropped in; where newspapers were stacked in the hallway, and dirty dishes left for hours at a time in the sink, and where a one-legged grandmother named Eva handed you goobers from deep inside her pockets or read you a dream.

1921

Sula Peace lived in a house of many rooms that had been built over a period of five years to the specifications of its owner, who kept on adding things: more stairways—there were three sets to the second floor—more rooms, doors and stoops. There were rooms that had three doors, others that opened out on the porch only and were inaccessible from any other part of the house; others that you could get to only by going through somebody's bedroom. The creator and sovereign of this enormous house with the four sickle-pear trees in the front yard and the single elm in the back yard was Eva Peace, who sat in a wagon on the third floor directing the lives of her children, friends, strays, and a constant stream of boarders. Fewer than nine people in the town remembered when Eva had two legs, and her oldest child, Hannah, was not one of them. Unless Eva herself introduced the subject, no one ever spoke of her disability; they pretended to ignore it, unless, in some mood of fancy, she began some fearful story about it—generally to entertain children. How the leg got up by itself one day and walked on off. How she hobbled after it but it ran too fast. Or how she had a corn on her toe and it just grew and grew and grew until her whole foot was a corn and then it traveled on up her leg and wouldn't stop growing until she put a red rag at the top but by that time it was already at her knee.

Somebody said Eva stuck it under a train and made them pay off. Another said she sold it to a hospital for $10,000—at which Mr. Reed opened his eyes and asked, "Nigger gal legs goin' for $10,000 a *piece?*" as though he could understand $10,000 a *pair*—but for *one?*

Whatever the fate of her lost leg, the remaining one was magnificent. It was stockinged and shod at all times and in all weather. Once in a while she got a felt slipper for Christmas or her birthday, but they soon disappeared, for Eva always wore a black laced-up shoe that came well above her ankle. Nor did she wear overlong dresses to disguise the empty place on her left side. Her dresses were mid-calf so that her one glamorous leg was always in view as well as the long fall of space below her left thigh. One of her men friends had fashioned a kind of wheelchair for her: a rocking-chair top fitted into a large child's wagon. In this contraption she wheeled around the room, from bedside to dresser to the balcony that opened out the north side of her room or to the window that looked out on the back yard. The wagon was so low that children who spoke to her standing up were eye level with her, and adults, standing or sitting, had to look down at her. But they didn't know it. They all had the impression that they were looking up at her, up into the open distances of her eyes, up into the soft black of her nostrils and up at the crest of her chin.

Eva had married a man named BoyBoy and had three

children: Hannah, the eldest, and Eva, whom she named after herself but called Pearl, and a son named Ralph, whom she called Plum.

After five years of a sad and disgruntled marriage BoyBoy took off. During the time they were together he was very much preoccupied with other women and not home much. He did whatever he could that he liked, and he liked womanizing best, drinking second, and abusing Eva third. When he left in November, Eva had $1.65, five eggs, three beets and no idea of what or how to feel. The children needed her; she needed money, and needed to get on with her life. But the demands of feeding her three children were so acute she had to postpone her anger for two years until she had both the time and the energy for it. She was confused and desperately hungry. There were very few black families in those low hills then. The Suggs, who lived two hundred yards down the road, brought her a warm bowl of peas, as soon as they found out, and a plate of cold bread. She thanked them and asked if they had a little milk for the older ones. They said no, but Mrs. Jackson, they knew, had a cow still giving. Eva took a bucket over and Mrs. Jackson told her to come back and fill it up in the morning, because the evening milking had already been done. In this way, things went on until near December. People were very willing to help, but Eva felt she would soon run her welcome out; winters were hard and her neighbors were not that much better off. She would lie in bed with the baby boy, the two girls wrapped in quilts on the floor, thinking. The oldest child,

Hannah, was five and too young to take care of the baby alone, and any housework Eva could find would keep her away from them from five thirty or earlier in the morning until dark—way past eight. The white people in the valley weren't rich enough then to want maids; they were small farmers and tradesmen and wanted hard-labor help if anything. She thought also of returning to some of her people in Virginia, but to come home dragging three young ones would have to be a step one rung before death for Eva. She would have to scrounge around and beg through the winter, until her baby was at least nine months old, then she could plant and maybe hire herself out to valley farms to weed or sow or feed stock until something steadier came along at harvest time. She thought she had probably been a fool to let BoyBoy haul her away from her people, but it had seemed so right at the time. He worked for a white carpenter and toolsmith who insisted on BoyBoy's accompanying him when he went West and set up in a squinchy little town called Medallion. BoyBoy brought his new wife and built them a one-room cabin sixty feet back from the road that wound up out of the valley, on up into the hills and was named for the man he worked for. They lived there a year before they had an outhouse.

Sometime before the middle of December, the baby, Plum, stopped having bowel movements. Eva massaged his stomach and gave him warm water. Something must be wrong with my milk, she thought. Mrs. Suggs gave her castor oil, but even that didn't work. He cried and fought so they couldn't get much down his throat anyway. He seemed in great pain and his shrieks were pitched high in outrage and suffering. At one point, maddened by his own crying, he gagged, choked and looked as though he was strangling to death. Eva rushed to him and kicked over the earthen slop jar, washing a small area of the floor with the child's urine. She managed to soothe him, but when he took up the cry again late that night, she resolved to end his misery once and for all. She wrapped him in blankets, ran her finger around the crevices and sides of the lard can and stumbled to the outhouse with him. Deep in its darkness and freezing stench she squatted down, turned the baby over on her knees, exposed his buttocks and shoved the last bit of food she had in the world (besides three beets) up his ass. Softening the insertion with the dab of lard, she probed with her middle finger to loosen his bowels. Her fingernail snagged what felt like a pebble; she pulled it out and others followed. Plum stopped crying as the black hard stools ricocheted onto the frozen ground. And now that it was over, Eva squatted there wondering why she had come all the way out there to free his stools, and what was she doing down on her haunches with her beloved baby boy warmed by her body in the almost total darkness, her shins and teeth freezing, her nostrils assailed. She shook her head as though to juggle her brains around, then said aloud, "Uh uh. Nooo." Thereupon she returned to the house and her bed. As the grateful Plum slept, the silence allowed her to think.

Two days later she left all of her children with Mrs. Suggs, saying she would be back the next day.

Eighteen months later she swept down from a wagon with two crutches, a new black pocketbook, and one leg. First she reclaimed her children, next she gave the surprised Mrs. Suggs a ten-dollar bill, later she started building a house on Carpenter's Road, sixty feet from BoyBoy's one-room cabin, which she rented out.

When Plum was three years old, BoyBoy came back to town and paid her a visit. When Eva got the word that he was on his way, she made some lemonade. She had no idea what she would do or feel during that encounter. Would she cry, cut his throat, beg him to make love to her? She couldn't imagine. So she just waited to see. She stirred lemonade in a green pitcher and waited.

BoyBoy danced up the steps and knocked on the door.

"Come on in," she hollered.

He opened the door and stood smiling, a picture of prosperity and good will. His shoes were a shiny orange, and he had on a citified straw hat, a light-blue suit, and a cat's-head stickpin in his tie. Eva smiled and told him to sit himself down. He smiled too.

"How you been, girl?"

"Pretty fair. What you know good?" When she heard those words come out of her own mouth she knew that their conversation would start off polite. Although it remained to be seen whether she would still run the ice pick through the cat's-head pin.

"Have some lemonade."

"Don't mind if I do." He swept his hat off with a satisfied gesture. His nails were long and shiny. "Sho is hot, and I been runnin' around all day."

Eva looked out of the screen door and saw a woman in a pea-green dress leaning on the smallest pear tree.

Glancing back at him, she was reminded of Plum's face when he managed to get the meat out of a walnut all by himself. Eva smiled again, and poured the lemonade.

Their conversation was easy: she catching him up on all the gossip, he asking about this one and that one, and like everybody else avoiding any reference to her leg. It was like talking to somebody's cousin who just stopped by to say howdy before getting on back to wherever he came from. BoyBoy didn't ask to see the children, and Eva didn't bring them into the conversation.

After a while he rose to go. Talking about his appointments and exuding an odor of new money and idleness, he danced down the steps and strutted toward the pea-green dress. Eva watched. She looked at the back of his neck and the set of his shoulders. Underneath all of that shine she saw defeat in the stalk of his neck and the curious tight way he held his shoulders. But still she was not sure what she felt. Then he leaned forward and whispered into the ear of the woman in the green dress. She was still for a moment and then threw back her head and laughed. A high-pitched big-city laugh that reminded Eva of Chicago. It hit her like a sledge hammer, and it was then that she knew what to feel. A liquid trail of hate flooded her chest.

Knowing that she would hate him long and well filled her with pleasant anticipation, like when you know you are going to fall in love with someone and you wait for the happy signs. Hating BoyBoy, she could get on with it, and have the safety, the thrill, the consistency of that hatred as long as she wanted or needed it to define and strengthen her or protect her from routine vulnerabilities.

(Once when Hannah accused her of hating colored people, Eva said she only hated one, Hannah's father BoyBoy, and it was hating him that kept her alive and happy.)

Happy or not, after BoyBoy's visit she began her retreat to her bedroom, leaving the bottom of the house more and more to those who lived there: cousins who were passing through, stray folks, and the many, many newly married couples she let rooms to with housekeeping privileges, and after 1910 she didn't willingly set foot on the stairs but once and that was to light a fire, the smoke of which was in her hair for years.

Among the tenants in that big old house were the children Eva took in. Operating on a private scheme of preference and prejudice, she sent off for children she had seen from the balcony of her bedroom or whose circumstances she had heard about from the gossipy old men who came to play checkers or read the *Courier*, or write her number. In 1921, when her granddaughter Sula was eleven, Eva had three such children. They came with woolen caps and names given to them by their mothers, or grandmothers, or somebody's best friend. Eva snatched the caps off their heads and ignored their names. She looked at the first child closely, his wrists, the shape of his head and the temperament that showed in his eyes and said, "Well. Look at Dewey. My my mymymy." When later that same year she sent for a child who kept falling down off the porch across the street, she said the same thing. Somebody said, "But, Miss Eva, you calls the other one Dewey."

"So? This here's another one."

When the third one was brought and Eva said "Dewey" again, everybody thought she had simply run out of names or that her faculties had finally softened.

"How is anybody going to tell them apart?" Hannah asked her.

"What you need to tell them apart for? They's all deweys."

When Hannah asked the question it didn't sound very bright, because each dewey was markedly different from the other two. Dewey one was a deeply black boy with a beautiful head and the golden eyes of chronic jaundice. Dewey two was light-skinned with freckles everywhere and a head of tight red hair. Dewey three was half Mexican with chocolate skin and black bangs. Besides, they were one and two years apart in age. It was Eva saying things like, "Send one of them deweys out to get me some Garret, if they don't have Garret, get Buttercup," or, "Tell them deweys to cut out that noise," or, "Come here, you dewey you," and, "Send me a dewey," that gave Hannah's question its weight.

Slowly each boy came out of whatever cocoon he was in at the time his mother or somebody gave him away, and accepted Eva's view, becoming in fact as well as in name a dewey—joining with the other two to become a trinity with a plural name . . . inseparable, loving nothing and no one but themselves. When the handle from the icebox fell off, all the deweys got whipped, and in dry-eyed silence watched their own feet as they turned their behinds high up into the air for the stroke. When the golden-eyed dewey was ready for school he would not go without the others. He was seven, freckled dewey was five, and Mexican dewey was only four. Eva solved the problem by having them all sent off together. Mr. Buckland Reed said, "But one of them's only four."

"How you know? They all come here the same year," Eva said.

"But that one there was one year old when he came, and that was three years ago."

"You don't know how old he was when he come here and neither do the teacher. Send 'em."

The teacher was startled but not unbelieving, for she had long ago given up trying to fathom the ways of the colored people in town. So when Mrs. Reed said that their names were Dewey King, that they were cousins, and all were six years old, the teacher gave only a tiny sigh and wrote them in the record book for the first grade. She too thought she would have no problem distinguishing among them, because they looked nothing alike, but like everyone else before her, she gradually found that she could not tell one from the other. The deweys would not allow it. They got all mixed up in her head, and finally she could not literally believe her eyes. They spoke with one voice, thought with one mind, and maintained an annoying privacy. Stouthearted, surly, and wholly unpredictable, the deweys remained a mystery not only during all of their lives in Medallion but after as well.

The deweys came in 1921, but the year before Eva had given a small room off the kitchen to Tar Baby, a beautiful, slight, quiet man who never spoke above a whisper. Most people said he was half white, but Eva said he was all white. That she knew blood when she saw it, and he didn't have none. When he first came to Medallion, the people called him Pretty Johnnie, but Eva looked at his milky skin and cornsilk hair and out of a mixture of fun and meanness called him Tar Baby. He was a mountain boy who stayed to himself, bothering no one, intent solely on drinking himself to death. At first he worked in a poultry market, and after wringing the necks of chickens all day, he came home and drank until he slept. Later he began to miss days at work and frequently did not have his rent money. When he lost his job altogether, he would go out in the morning, scrounge around for money doing odd jobs, bumming or whatever, and come home to drink. Because he was no bother, ate little, required nothing, and was a lover of cheap wine, no one found him a nuisance. Besides, he frequently went to Wednesday-night prayer meetings and sang with the sweetest hill voice imaginable "In the Sweet By-and-By." He sent the deweys out for his liquor and spent most of his time in a heap on the floor or sitting in a chair staring at the wall.

Hannah worried about him a little, but only a very little. For it soon became clear that he simply wanted a place to die privately but not quite alone. No one thought of suggesting to him that he pull himself together or see a doctor or anything. Even the women at prayer meeting who cried when he sang "In the Sweet By-and-By" never tried to get him to participate in the church activities. They just listened to him sing, wept and thought very graphically of their own imminent deaths. The people either accepted his own evaluation of his life, or were indifferent to it. There was, however, a measure of contempt in their indifference, for they had little patience with people who took themselves that seriously. Seriously enough to try to die. And it was natural that he, after all, became the first one to join Shadrack—Tar Baby and the deweys—on National Suicide Day.

Under Eva's distant eye, and prey to her idiosyncrasies, her own children grew up stealthily: Pearl married at fourteen and moved to Flint, Michigan, from where she posted frail letters to her mother with two dollars folded into the writing paper. Sad little nonsense letters about minor troubles, her husband's job and who the children favored. Hannah married a laughing man named Rekus who died when their daughter Sula was about three years old, at which time Hannah moved back into her mother's big house prepared to take care of it and her mother forever.

With the exception of BoyBoy, those Peace women loved all men. It was manlove that Eva bequeathed to her daughters. Probably, people said, because there were no men in the house, no men to run it. But actually that was not true. The Peace women simply loved maleness, for its own sake. Eva, old as she was, and with one leg, had a regular flock of gentleman callers, and although she did not participate in the act of love, there was a good deal of teasing and pecking and laughter. The men wanted to see her lovely calf, that neat shoe, and watch the focusing that sometimes swept down out of the distances in her eyes. They wanted to see the joy in her face as they settled down to play checkers, knowing that even when she beat them, as she almost always did, somehow, in her presence, it was they who had won something. They would read the newspaper aloud to her and make observations on its content, and Eva would listen feeling no obligation to agree and, in fact, would take them to task about their interpretation of events. But she argued with them with such an absence of bile, such a concentration of manlove, that they felt their convictions solidified by her disagreement.

With other people's affairs Eva was equally prejudiced about men. She fussed interminably with the brides of the newly wed couples for not getting their men's supper ready on time; about how to launder shirts, press them, etc. "Yo' man be here direc'lin. Ain't it 'bout time you got busy?"

"Aw, Miss Eva. It'll be ready. We just having spaghetti."

"Again?" Eva's eyebrows fluted up and the newlywed pressed her lips together in shame.

Hannah simply refused to live without the attentions of a man, and after Rekus' death had a steady sequence of lovers, mostly the husbands of her friends and neighbors. Her flirting was sweet, low and guileless. Without ever a pat of the hair, a rush to change clothes or a quick application of paint, with no gesture whatsoever, she rippled with sex. In her same old print wraparound, barefoot in the summer, in the winter her feet in a man's leather slippers with the backs flattened under her heels, she made men aware of her behind, her slim ankles, the dew-smooth skin and the incredible length of neck. Then the smile-eyes, the turn of the head—all so welcoming, light and playful. Her voice trailed, dipped and bowed; she gave a chord to the simplest words. Nobody, but nobody, could say "hey sugar" like Hannah. When he heard it, the man tipped his hat down a little over his eyes, hoisted his trousers and thought about the hollow place at the base of her neck. And all this without the slightest confusion about work and responsibilities. While Eva tested and argued with her men, leaving them feeling as though they had been in combat with a worthy, if amiable, foe, Hannah rubbed no edges, made no demands, made the man feel as though he were complete and wonderful just as he was—he didn't need fixing—and so he relaxed and swooned in the Hannah-light that shone on him simply because he was. If the man entered and Hannah was carrying a coal scuttle up from the basement, she handled it in such a way that it became a gesture of love. He made no move to help her with it simply because he wanted to see how her thighs looked when she bent to put it down, knowing that she wanted him to see them too.

But since in that crowded house there were no places for private and spontaneous lovemaking, Hannah would take the man down into the cellar in the summer where it was cool back behind the coal bin and the newspapers, or in the winter they would step into the pantry and stand up against the shelves she had filled with canned goods, or lie on the flour sack just under the rows of tiny green peppers. When those places were not available, she would slip into the seldom-used parlor, or even up to her bedroom. She liked the last place least, not because Sula slept in the room with her but because her love mate's tendency was always to fall asleep afterward and Hannah was fastidious about whom she slept with. She would fuck practically anything, but sleeping with someone implied for her a measure of trust and a definite commitment. So she ended up a daylight lover, and it was only once actually that Sula came home from school and found her mother in the bed, curled spoon in the arms of a man.

Seeing her step so easily into the pantry and emerge looking precisely as she did when she entered, only happier, taught Sula that sex was pleasant and frequent, but otherwise unremarkable. Outside the house, where children giggled about underwear, the message was different. So she watched her mother's face and the face of the men when they opened the pantry door and made up her own mind.

Hannah exasperated the women in the town—the "good" women, who said, "One thing I can't stand is a nasty woman"; the whores, who were hard put to find trade among black men anyway and who resented Hannah's generosity; the middling women, who had both husbands and affairs, because Hannah seemed too unlike them, having no passion attached to her relationships and being wholly incapable of jealousy. Hannah's friendships with women were, of course, seldom and short-lived, and the newly married couples whom her mother took in soon learned what a hazard she was. She could break up a marriage before it had even become one—she would make love to the new groom and wash his wife's dishes all in an afternoon. What she wanted, after Rekus died, and what she succeeded in having more often than not, was some touching every day.

The men, surprisingly, never gossiped about her. She was unquestionably a kind and generous woman and that, coupled with her extraordinary beauty and funky elegance of manner, made them defend her and protect her from any vitriol that newcomers or their wives might spill.

Eva's last child, Plum, to whom she hoped to bequeath everything, floated in a constant swaddle of love and affection, until 1917 when he went to war. He returned to the States in 1919 but did not get back to Medallion until 1920. He wrote letters from New York, Washington, D.C., and Chicago full of promises of homecomings, but there was obviously something wrong. Finally some two or three days after Christmas, he arrived with just the shadow of his old dip-down walk. His hair had been neither cut nor combed in months, his clothes were pointless and he had no socks. But he did have a black bag, a paper sack, and a sweet, sweet smile. Everybody welcomed him and gave him a warm room next to Tar Baby's and waited for him to tell them whatever it was he wanted them to know. They waited in vain for his telling but not long for the knowing. His habits were much like Tar Baby's but there were no bottles, and Plum was sometimes cheerful and animated. Hannah watched and Eva waited. Then he began to steal from them, take trips to Cincinnati and sleep for days in his room with the record player going. He got even thinner, since he ate only snatches of things at beginnings or endings of meals. It was Hannah who found the bent spoon black from steady cooking.

So late one night in 1921, Eva got up from her bed and put on her clothes. Hoisting herself up on her crutches, she was amazed to find that she could still manage them, although the pain in her armpits was severe. She practiced a few steps around the room, and then opened the door. Slowly, she manipulated herself down the long flights of stairs, two crutches under her left arm, the right hand grasping the banister. The sound of her foot booming in comparison to the delicate pat of the crutch tip. On each landing she stopped for breath. Annoyed at her physical condition, she closed her eyes and removed the crutches from under her arms to relieve the unaccustomed pressure. At the foot of the stairs she redistributed her weight between the crutches and swooped on through the front room, to the dining room, to the kitchen, swinging and swooping like a giant heron, so graceful sailing about in its own habitat but awkward and comical when it folded its wings and tried to walk. With a swing and a swoop she arrived at Plum's door and pushed it open with the tip of one crutch. He was lying in bed barely visible in the light coming from a single bulb. Eva swung over to the bed and propped her crutches at its foot. She sat down and gathered Plum into her arms. He woke, but only slightly.

"Hey, man. Hey. You holdin' me, Mamma?" His voice was drowsy and amused. He chuckled as though he had heard some private joke. Eva held him closer and began to rock. Back and forth she rocked him, her eyes wandering around his room. There in the corner was a half-eaten store-bought cherry pie. Balled-up candy wrappers and empty pop bottles peeped from under the dresser. On the floor by her foot was a glass of strawberry crush and a *Liberty* magazine. Rocking, rocking, listening to Plum's occasional chuckles, Eva let her memory spin, loop and fall. Plum in the tub that time as she leaned over him. He reached up and dripped water into her bosom and laughed. She was angry, but not too, and laughed with him.

"Mamma, you so purty. You so purty, Mamma."

Eva lifted her tongue to the edge of her lip to stop the tears from running into her mouth. Rocking, rocking. Later she laid him down and looked at him a long time. Suddenly she was thirsty and reached for the glass of strawberry crush. She put it to her lips and discovered it was blood-tainted water and threw it to the floor. Plum woke up and said, "Hey, Mamma, whyn't you go on back to bed? I'm all right. Didn't I tell you? I'm all right. Go on, now."

"I'm going, Plum," she said. She shifted her weight and pulled her crutches toward her. Swinging and swooping, she left his room. She dragged herself to the kitchen and made grating noises.

Plum on the rim of a warm light sleep was still chuckling. Mamma. She sure was somethin'. He felt twilight. Now there seemed to be some kind of wet light traveling over his legs and stomach with a deeply attractive smell. It wound itself—this wet light—all about him, splashing and running into his skin. He opened his eyes and saw what he imagined was the great wing of an eagle pouring a wet lightness over him. Some kind of baptism, some kind of blessing, he thought. Everything is going to be all right, it said. Knowing that it was so he closed his eyes and sank back into the bright hole of sleep.

Eva stepped back from the bed and let the crutches rest under her arms. She rolled a bit of newspaper into a tight stick about six inches long, lit it and threw it onto the bed where the kerosene-soaked Plum lay in snug delight.

Quickly, as the *whoosh* of flames engulfed him, she shut the door and made her slow and painful journey back to the top of the house.

Just as she got to the third landing she could hear Hannah and some child's voice. She swung along, not even listening to the voices of alarm and the cries of the deweys. By the time she got to her bed someone was bounding up the stairs after her. Hannah opened the door. "Plum! Plum! He's burning, Mamma! We can't even open the door! Mamma!"

Eva looked into Hannah's eyes. "Is? My baby? Burning?" The two women did not speak, for the eyes of each were enough for the other. Then Hannah closed hers and ran toward the voices of neighbors calling for water.

1922

It was too cool for ice cream. A hill wind was blowing dust and empty Camels wrappers about their ankles. It pushed their dresses into the creases of their behinds, then lifted the hems to peek at their cotton underwear. They were on their way to Edna Finch's Mellow House, an ice-cream parlor catering to nice folks—where even children would feel comfortable, you know, even though it was right next to Reba's Grill and just one block down from the Time and a Half Pool Hall. It sat in the curve of Carpenter's Road, which, in four blocks, made up all the sporting life available in the Bottom. Old men and young ones draped themselves in front of the Elmira Theater, Irene's Palace of Cosmetology, the pool hall, the grill and the other sagging business enterprises that lined the street. On sills, on stoops, on crates and broken chairs they sat tasting their teeth and waiting for something to distract them. Every passerby, every motorcar, every alteration in stance caught their attention and was commented on. Particularly they watched women. When a woman approached, the older men tipped their hats; the younger ones opened and closed their thighs. But all of them, whatever their age, watched her retreating view with interest.

Nel and Sula walked through this valley of eyes chilled by the wind and heated by the embarrassment of appraising stares. The old men looked at their stalklike legs, dwelled on the cords in the backs of their knees and remembered old dance steps they had not done in twenty years. In their lust, which age had turned to kindness, they moved their lips as though to stir up the taste of young sweat on tight skin.

Pig meat. The words were in all their minds. And one of them, one of the young ones, said it aloud. Softly but definitively and there was no mistaking the compliment. His name was Ajax, a twenty-one-year-old pool haunt of sinister beauty. Graceful and economical in every movement, he held a place of envy with men of all ages for his magnificently foul mouth. In fact he seldom cursed, and the epithets he chose were dull, even harmless. His reputation was derived from the way he handled the words. When he said "hell" he hit the *h* with his lungs and the impact was greater than the achievement of the most imaginative foul mouth in the town. He could say "shit" with a nastiness impossible to imitate. So, when he said "pig meat" as Nel and Sula passed, they guarded their eyes lest someone see their delight.

It was not really Edna Finch's ice cream that made them brave the stretch of those panther eyes. Years later their own eyes would glaze as they cupped their chins in remembrance of the inchworm smiles, the squatting haunches, the track-rail legs straddling broken chairs. The cream-colored trousers marking with a mere seam the place where the mystery curled. Those smooth vanilla crotches invited them; those lemon-yellow gabardines beckoned to them.

They moved toward the ice-cream parlor like tightrope walkers, as thrilled by the possibility of a slip as by the maintenance of tension and balance. The least sideways glance, the merest toe stub, could pitch them into those creamy haunches spread wide with welcome. Somewhere beneath all of that daintiness, chambered in all that neatness, lay the thing that clotted their dreams.

Which was only fitting, for it was in dreams that the two girls had first met. Long before Edna Finch's Mellow House opened, even before they marched through the chocolate halls of Garfield Primary School out onto the playground and stood facing each other through the ropes of the one vacant swing ("Go on." "No. You go."), they had already made each other's acquaintance in the delirium of their noon dreams. They were solitary little girls whose loneliness was so profound it intoxicated them and sent them stumbling into Technicolored visions that always included a presence, a someone, who, quite like the dreamer, shared the delight of the dream. When Nel, an only child, sat on the steps of her back porch surrounded by the high silence of her mother's incredibly orderly house, feeling the neatness pointing at her back, she studied the poplars and fell easily into a picture of herself lying on a flowered bed, tangled in her own hair, waiting for some fiery prince. He approached but never quite arrived. But always, watching the dream along with her, were some smiling sympathetic eyes. Someone as interested as she herself in the flow of her imagined hair, the thickness of the mattress of flowers, the voile sleeves that closed below her elbows in gold-threaded cuffs.

Similarly, Sula, also an only child, but wedged into a

household of throbbing disorder constantly awry with things, people, voices and the slamming of doors, spent hours in the attic behind a roll of linoleum galloping through her own mind on a gray-and-white horse tasting sugar and smelling roses in full view of a someone who shared both the taste and the speed.

So when they met, first in those chocolate halls and next through the ropes of the swing, they felt the ease and comfort of old friends. Because each had discovered years before that they were neither white nor male, and that all freedom and triumph was forbidden to them, they had set about creating something else to be. Their meeting was fortunate, for it let them use each other to grow on. Daughters of distant mothers and incomprehensible fathers (Sula's because he was dead; Nel's because he wasn't), they found in each other's eyes the intimacy they were looking for.

Nel Wright and Sula Peace were both twelve in 1922, wishbone thin and easy-assed. Nel was the color of wet sandpaper—just dark enough to escape the blows of the pitch-black truebloods and the contempt of old women who worried about such things as bad blood mixtures and knew that the origins of a mule and a mulatto were one and the same. Had she been any lighter-skinned she would have needed either her mother's protection on the way to school or a streak of mean to defend herself. Sula was a heavy brown with large quiet eyes, one of which featured a birthmark that spread from the middle of the lid toward the eyebrow, shaped something like a stemmed rose. It gave her otherwise plain face a broken excitement and blue-blade threat like the keloid scar of the razored man who sometimes played checkers with her grandmother. The birthmark was to grow darker as the years passed, but now it was the same shade as her gold-flecked eyes, which, to the end, were as steady and clean as rain.

Their friendship was as intense as it was sudden. They found relief in each other's personality. Although both were unshaped, formless things, Nel seemed stronger and more consistent than Sula, who could hardly be counted on to sustain any emotion for more than three minutes. Yet there was one time when that was not true, when she held on to a mood for weeks, but even that was in defense of Nel.

Four white boys in their early teens, sons of some newly arrived Irish people, occasionally entertained themselves in the afternoon by harassing black schoolchildren. With shoes that pinched and woolen knickers that made red rings on their calves, they had come to this valley with their parents believing as they did that it was a promised land—green and shimmering with welcome. What they found was a strange accent, a pervasive fear of their religion and firm resistance to their attempts to find work. With one exception the older residents of Medallion scorned them. The one exception was the black community. Although some of the Negroes had been in Medallion before the Civil War (the town didn't even have a name then), if they had any hatred for these newcomers it didn't matter because it didn't show. As a matter of fact, baiting them was the one activity that the white Protestant residents concurred in. In part their place in this world was secured only when they echoed the old residents' attitude toward blacks.

These particular boys caught Nel once, and pushed her from hand to hand until they grew tired of the frightened helpless face. Because of that incident, Nel's route home from school became elaborate. She, and then Sula, managed to duck them for weeks until a chilly day in November when Sula said, "Let's us go on home the shortest way."

Nel blinked, but acquiesced. They walked up the street until they got to the bend of Carpenter's Road where the boys lounged on a disused well. Spotting their prey, the boys sauntered forward as though there were nothing in the world on their minds but the gray sky. Hardly able to control their grins, they stood like a gate blocking the path. When the girls were three feet in front of the boys, Sula reached into her coat pocket and pulled out Eva's paring knife. The boys stopped short, exchanged looks and dropped all pretense of innocence. This was going to be better than they thought. They were going to try and fight back, and with a knife. Maybe they could get an arm around one of their waists, or tear . . .

Sula squatted down in the dirt road and put everything down on the ground: her lunchpail, her reader, her mittens, her slate. Holding the knife in her right hand, she pulled the slate toward her and pressed her left forefinger down hard on its edge. Her aim was determined but inaccurate. She slashed off only the tip of her finger. The four boys stared open-mouthed at the wound and the scrap of flesh, like a button mushroom, curling in the cherry blood that ran into the corners of the slate.

Sula raised her eyes to them. Her voice was quiet. "If I

can do that to myself, what you suppose I'll do to you?"

The shifting dirt was the only way Nel knew that they were moving away; she was looking at Sula's face, which seemed miles and miles away.

But toughness was not their quality—adventuresomeness was—and a mean determination to explore everything that interested them, from one-eyed chickens high-stepping in their penned yards to Mr. Buckland Reed's gold teeth, from the sound of sheets flapping in the wind to the labels on Tar Baby's wine bottles. And they had no priorities. They could be distracted from watching a fight with mean razors by the glorious smell of hot tar being poured by roadmen two hundred yards away.

In the safe harbor of each other's company they could afford to abandon the ways of other people and concentrate on their own perceptions of things. When Mrs. Wright reminded Nel to pull her nose, she would do it enthusiastically but without the least hope in the world.

"While you sittin' there, honey, go 'head and pull your nose."

"It hurts, Mamma."

"Don't you want a nice nose when you grow up?"

After she met Sula, Nel slid the clothespin under the blanket as soon as she got in the bed. And although there was still the hateful hot comb to suffer through each Saturday evening, its consequences—smooth hair—no longer interested her.

Joined in mutual admiration they watched each day as though it were a movie arranged for their amusement. The new theme they were now discovering was men. So they met regularly, without even planning it, to walk down the road to Edna Finch's Mellow House, even though it was too cool for ice cream.

Then summer came. A summer limp with the weight of blossomed things. Heavy sunflowers weeping over fences; iris curling and browning at the edges far away from their purple hearts; ears of corn letting their auburn hair wind down to their stalks. And the boys. The beautiful, beautiful boys who dotted the landscape like jewels, split the air with their shouts in the field, and thickened the river with their shining wet backs. Even their footsteps left a smell of smoke behind.

It was in that summer, the summer of their twelfth year, the summer of the beautiful black boys, that they became skittish, frightened and bold—all at the same time.

In that mercury mood in July, Sula and Nel wandered about the Bottom barefoot looking for mischief. They decided to go down by the river where the boys sometimes swam. Nel waited on the porch of 7 Carpenter's Road while Sula ran into the house to go to the toilet. On the way up the stairs, she passed the kitchen where Hannah sat with two friends, Patsy and Valentine. The two women were fanning themselves and watching Hannah put down some dough, all talking casually about one thing and another, and had gotten around, when Sula passed by, to the problems of child rearing.

"They a pain."

"Yeh. Wish I'd listened to mamma. She told me not to have 'em too soon."

"Any time atall is too soon for me."

"Oh, I don't know. My Rudy minds his daddy. He just wild with me. Be glad when he growed and gone."

Hannah smiled and said, "Shut your mouth. You love the ground he pee on."

"Sure I do. But he still a pain. Can't help loving your own child. No matter what they do."

"Well, Hester grown now and I can't say love is exactly what I feel."

"Sure you do. You love her, like I love Sula. I just don't like her. That's the difference."

"Guess so. Likin' them is another thing."

"Sure. They different people, you know . . ."

She only heard Hannah's words, and the pronouncement sent her flying up the stairs. In bewilderment, she stood at the window fingering the curtain edge, aware of a sting in her eye. Nel's call floated up and into the window, pulling her away from dark thoughts back into the bright, hot daylight.

They ran most of the way.

Heading toward the wide part of the river where trees grouped themselves in families darkening the earth below. They passed some boys swimming and clowning in the water, shrouding their words in laughter.

They ran in the sunlight, creating their own breeze, which pressed their dresses into their damp skin. Reaching a kind of square of four leaf-locked trees which promised cooling, they flung themselves into the four-cornered shade to taste their lip sweat and contemplate the wildness that had come upon them so suddenly. They lay in the grass, their foreheads almost touching, their bodies stretched away from each other at a 180-degree angle. Sula's head rested on her arm, an undone braid coiled around her wrist. Nel leaned on her elbows and worried long blades of grass with her fingers. Underneath their dresses flesh tightened and shivered in the high coolness, their small breasts just now beginning to create some pleasant discomfort when they were lying on their stomachs.

Sula lifted her head and joined Nel in the grass play. In concert, without ever meeting each other's eyes, they stroked the blades up and down, up and down. Nel found a thick twig and, with her thumbnail, pulled away its bark until it was stripped to a smooth, creamy innocence. Sula looked about and found one too. When both twigs were undressed Nel moved easily to the next stage and began tearing up rooted grass to make a bare spot of earth. When a generous clearing was made, Sula traced intricate patterns in it with her twig. At first Nel was content to do the same. But soon she grew impatient and poked her twig rhythmically and intensely into the earth, making a small neat hole that grew deeper and wider with the least manipulation of her twig. Sula copied her, and soon each had a hole the size of a cup. Nel began a more strenuous digging and, rising to her knee, was careful to scoop out the dirt as she made her hole deeper. Together they worked until the two holes were one and the same. When the depression was the size of a small dishpan, Nel's twig broke. With a gesture of disgust she threw the pieces into the hole they had made. Sula threw hers in too. Nel saw a bottle cap and tossed it in as well. Each then looked around for more debris to throw into the hole: paper, bits of glass, butts of cigarettes, until all of the small defiling things they could find were collected there. Carefully they replaced the soil and covered the entire grave with uprooted grass.

Neither one had spoken a word.

They stood up, stretched, then gazed out over the swift dull water as an unspeakable restlessness and agitation held them. At the same instant each girl heard footsteps in the grass. A little boy in too big knickers was coming up from the lower bank of the river. He stopped when he saw them and picked his nose.

"Your mamma tole you to stop eatin' snot, Chicken," Nel hollered at him through cupped hands.

"Shut up," he said, still picking.

"Come up here and say that."

"Leave him 'lone, Nel. Come here, Chicken. Lemme show you something."

"Naw."

"You scared we gone take your bugger away?"

"Leave him 'lone, I said. Come on, Chicken. Look. I'll help you climb a tree."

Chicken looked at the tree Sula was pointing to—a big double beech with low branches and lots of bends for sitting.

He moved slowly toward her.

"Come on, Chicken, I'll help you up."

Still picking his nose, his eyes wide, he came to where they were standing. Sula took him by the hand and coaxed him along. When they reached the base of the beech, she lifted him to the first branch, saying, "Go on. Go on. I got you." She followed the boy, steadying him, when he needed it, with her hand and her reassuring voice. When they were as high as they could go, Sula pointed to the far side of the river.

"See? Bet you never saw that far before, did you?"

"Uh uh."

"Now look down there." They both leaned a little and peered through the leaves at Nel standing below, squinting up at them. From their height she looked small and foreshortened.

Chicken Little laughed.

"Y'all better come on down before you break your neck," Nel hollered.

"I ain't never coming down," the boy hollered back.

"Yeah. We better. Come on, Chicken."

"Naw. Lemme go."

"Yeah, Chicken. Come on, now."

Sula pulled his leg gently.

"Lemme go."

"OK, I'm leavin' you." She started on.

"Wait!" he screamed.

Sula stopped and together they slowly worked their way down.

Chicken was still elated. "I was way up there, wasn't I? Wasn't I? I'm a tell my brovver."

Sula and Nel began to mimic him: "I'm a tell my brovver; I'm a tell my brovver."

Sula picked him up by his hands and swung him outward then around and around. His knickers ballooned and his shrieks of frightened joy startled the birds and the fat grasshoppers. When he slipped from her hands and sailed away out over the water they could still hear his bubbly laughter.

The water darkened and closed quickly over the place where Chicken Little sank. The pressure of his hard and tight little fingers was still in Sula's palms as she stood looking at the closed place in the water. They expected him to come back up, laughing. Both girls stared at the water.

Nel spoke first. "Somebody saw." A figure appeared briefly on the opposite shore.

The only house over there was Shadrack's. Sula glanced at Nel. Terror widened her nostrils. Had he seen?

The water was so peaceful now. There was nothing but the baking sun and something newly missing. Sula cupped her face for an instant, then turned and ran up to the little plank bridge that crossed the river to Shadrack's house. There was no path. It was as though neither Shadrack nor anyone else ever came this way.

Her running was swift and determined, but when she was close to the three little steps that led to his porch, fear crawled into her stomach and only the something newly missing back there in the river made it possible for her to walk up the three steps and knock at the door.

No one answered. She started back, but thought again of the peace of the river. Shadrack would be inside, just behind the door ready to pounce on her. Still she could not go back. Ever so gently she pushed the door with the tips of her fingers and heard only the hinges weep. More. And then she was inside. Alone. The neatness, the order startled her, but more surprising was the restfulness. Everything was so tiny, so common, so unthreatening. Perhaps this was not the house of the Shad. The terrible Shad who walked about with his penis out, who peed in front of ladies and girl-children, the only black who could curse white people and get away with it, who drank in the road from the mouth of the bottle, who shouted and shook in the streets. This cottage? This sweet old cottage? With its made-up bed? With its rag rug and wooden table? Sula stood in the middle of the little room and in her wonder forgot what she had come for until a sound at the door made her jump. He was there in the doorway looking at her. She had not heard his coming and now he was looking at her.

More in embarrassment than terror she averted her glance. When she called up enough courage to look back at him, she saw his hand resting upon the door frame. His fingers, barely touching the wood, were arranged in a graceful arc. Relieved and encouraged (no one with hands like that, no one with fingers that curved around wood so tenderly could kill her), she walked past him out of the door, feeling his gaze turning, turning with her.

At the edge of the porch, gathering the wisps of courage that were fast leaving her, she turned once more to look at him, to ask him . . . had he . . . ?

He was smiling, a great smile, heavy with lust and time to come. He nodded his head as though answering a question, and said, in a pleasant conversational tone, a tone of cooled butter, "Always."

Sula fled down the steps, and shot through the greenness and the baking sun back to Nel and the dark closed place in the water. There she collapsed in tears.

Nel quieted her. "Sh, sh. Don't, don't. You didn't mean

it. It ain't your fault. Sh. Sh. Come on, le's go, Sula. Come on, now. Was he there? Did he see? Where's the belt to your dress?"

Sula shook her head while she searched her waist for the belt.

Finally she stood up and allowed Nel to lead her away. "He said, 'Always. Always.' "

"What?"

Sula covered her mouth as they walked down the hill. Always. He had answered a question she had not asked, and its promise licked at her feet.

A bargeman, poling away from the shore, found Chicken late that afternoon stuck in some rocks and weeds, his knickers ballooning about his legs. He would have left him there but noticed that it was a child, not an old black man, as it first appeared, and he prodded the body loose, netted it and hauled it aboard. He shook his head in disgust at the kind of parents who would drown their own children. When, he wondered, will those people ever be anything but animals, fit for nothing but substitutes for mules, only mules didn't kill each other the way niggers did. He dumped Chicken Little into a burlap sack and tossed him next to some egg crates and boxes of wool cloth. Later, sitting down to smoke on an empty lard tin, still bemused by God's curse and the terrible burden his own kind had of elevating Ham's sons, he suddenly became alarmed by the thought that the corpse in this heat would have a terrible odor, which might get into the fabric of his woolen cloth. He dragged the sack away and hooked it over the side, so that the Chicken's body was half in and half out of the water.

Wiping the sweat from his neck, he reported his find to the sheriff at Porter's Landing, who said they didn't have no niggers in their county, but that some lived in those hills 'cross the river, up above Medallion. The bargeman said he couldn't go all the way back there, it was every bit of two miles. The sheriff said whyn't he throw it on back into the water. The bargeman said he never shoulda taken it out in the first place. Finally they got the man who ran the ferry twice a day to agree to take it over in the morning.

That was why Chicken Little was missing for three days and didn't get to the embalmer's until the fourth day, by which time he was unrecognizable to almost everybody who once knew him, and even his mother wasn't deep down sure, except that it just had to be him since nobody could find him. When she saw his clothes lying on the table in the basement of the mortuary, her mouth snapped shut, and when she saw his body her mouth flew wide open again and it was seven hours before she was able to close it and make the first sound.

So the coffin was closed.

The Junior Choir, dressed in white, sang "Nearer My God to Thee" and "Precious Memories," their eyes fastened on the songbooks they did not need, for this was the first time their voices had presided at a real-life event.

Nel and Sula did not touch hands or look at each other during the funeral. There was a space, a separateness, between them. Nel's legs had turned to granite and she expected the sheriff or Reverend Deal's pointing finger at any moment. Although she knew she had "done nothing," she felt convicted and hanged right there in the pew—two rows down from her parents in the children's section.

Sula simply cried. Soundlessly and with no heaving and gasping for breath, she let the tears roll into her mouth and slide down her chin to dot the front of her dress.

As Reverend Deal moved into his sermon, the hands of the women unfolded like pairs of raven's wings and flew high above their hats in the air. They did not hear all of what he said; they heard the one word, or phrase, or inflection that was for them the connection between the event and themselves. For some it was the term "Sweet Jesus." And they saw the Lamb's eye and the truly innocent victim: themselves. They acknowledged the innocent child hiding in the corner of their hearts, holding a sugar-and-butter sandwich. That one. The one who lodged deep in their fat, thin, old, young skin, and was the one the world had hurt. Or they thought of their son newly killed and remembered his legs in short pants and wondered where the bullet went in. Or they remembered how dirty the room looked when their father left home and wondered if that is the way the slim, young Jew felt, he who for them was both son and lover and in whose downy face they could see the sugar-and-butter sandwiches and feel the oldest and most devastating pain there is: not the pain of childhood, but the remembrance of it.

Then they left their pews. For with some emotions one has to stand. They spoke, for they were full and needed to say. They swayed, for the rivulets of grief or of ecstasy must be rocked. And when they thought of all that life and death locked into that little closed coffin they danced and screamed, not to protest God's will but to acknowledge it and confirm once more their conviction that the only way to avoid the Hand of God is to get in it.

In the colored part of the cemetery, they sank Chicken Little in between his grandfather and an aunt. Butterflies flew in and out of the bunches of field flowers now loosened from the top of the bier and lying in a small heap at the edge of the grave. The heat had gone, but there was still no breeze to lift the hair of the willows.

Nel and Sula stood some distance away from the grave, the space that had sat between them in the pews had dissolved. They held hands and knew that only the coffin would lie in the earth; the bubbly laughter and the press of fingers in the palm would stay aboveground forever. At first, as they stood there, their hands were clenched together. They relaxed slowly until during the walk back home their fingers were laced in as gentle a clasp as that of any two young girlfriends trotting up the road on a summer day wondering what happened to butterflies in the winter.

1923

The second strange thing was Hannah's coming into her mother's room with an empty bowl and a peck of Kentucky Wonders and saying, "Mamma, did you ever love us?" She sang the words like a small child saying a piece at Easter, then knelt to spread a newspaper on the floor and set the basket on it; the bowl she tucked in the space between her legs. Eva, who was just sitting there fanning herself with the cardboard fan from Mr. Hodges' funeral parlor, listened to the silence that followed Hannah's words, then said, "Scat!" to the deweys who were playing chain gang near the window. With the shoelaces of each of them tied to the laces of the others, they stumbled and tumbled out of Eva's room.

"Now," Eva looked up across from her wagon at her daughter. "Give me that again. Flat out to fit my head."

"I mean, did you? You know. When we was little."

Eva's hand moved snail-like down her thigh toward her stump, but stopped short of it to realign a pleat. "No. I don't reckon I did. Not the way you thinkin'."

"Oh, well. I was just wonderin'." Hannah appeared to be through with the subject.

"An evil wonderin' if I ever heard one." Eva was not through.

"I didn't mean nothing by it, Mamma."

"What you mean you didn't *mean* nothing by it? How you gone not mean something by it?"

Hannah pinched the tips off the Kentucky Wonders and snapped their long pods. What with the sound of the cracking and snapping and her swift-fingered movements, she seemed to be playing a complicated instrument. Eva watched her a moment and then said, "You gone can them?"

"No. They for tonight."

"Thought you was gone can some."

"Uncle Paul ain't brought me none yet. A peck ain't enough to can. He say he got two bushels for me."

"Triflin'."

"Oh, he all right."

"Sho he all right. Everybody all right. 'Cept Mamma. Mamma the only one ain't all right. Cause she didn't *love* us."

"Awww, Mamma."

"Awww, Mamma? Awww, Mamma? You settin' here with your healthy-ass self and ax me did I love you? Them big old eyes in your head would a been two holes full of maggots if I hadn't."

"I didn't mean that, Mamma. I know you fed us and all. I was talkin' 'bout something else. Like. Like. Playin' with us. Did you ever, you know, play with us?"

"Play? Wasn't nobody playin' in 1895. Just 'cause you got it good now you think it was always this good? 1895 was a killer, girl. Things was bad. Niggers was dying like flies. Stepping tall, ain't you? Uncle Paul gone bring me *two* bushels. Yeh. And they's a melon downstairs, ain't they? And I bake every Saturday, and Shad brings fish on Friday, and they's a pork barrel full of meal, and we float eggs in a crock of vinegar . . ."

"Mamma, what you talkin' 'bout?"

"I'm talkin' 'bout 18 and 95 when I set in that house five days with you and Pearl and Plum and three beets, you snake-eyed ungrateful hussy. What would I look like leapin' 'round that little old room playin' with youngins with three beets to my name?"

"I know 'bout them beets, Mamma. You told us that a million times."

"Yeah? Well? Don't that count? Ain't that love? You want me to tinkle you under the jaw and forget 'bout them sores in your mouth? Pearl was shittin' worms and I was supposed to play rang-around-the-rosie?"

"But Mamma, they had to be some time when you wasn't thinkin' 'bout . . ."

"No time. They wasn't no time. Not none. Soon as I got one day done here come a night. With you all coughin' and me watchin' so TB wouldn't take you off and if you was sleepin' quiet I thought, O Lord, they dead and put my hand over your mouth to feel if the breath was comin' what you talkin' 'bout did I love you girl I stayed alive for you can't you get that through your thick head or what is that between your ears, heifer?"

Hannah had enough beans now. With some tomatoes and hot bread, she thought, that would be enough for everybody, especially since the deweys didn't eat vegetables no how and Eva never made them and Tar Baby was living off air and music these days. She picked up the basket and stood with it and the bowl of beans over her mother. Eva's face was still asking her last question. Hannah looked into her mother's eyes.

"But what about Plum? What'd you kill Plum for, Mamma?"

It was a Wednesday in August and the ice wagon was coming and coming. You could hear bits of the driver's song. Now Mrs. Jackson would be tipping down her porch steps. "Jes a piece. You got a lil ole piece layin' 'round in there you could spare?" And as he had since the time of the pigeons, the iceman would hand her a lump of ice saying, "Watch it now, Mrs. Jackson. That straw'll tickle your pretty neck to death."

Eva listened to the wagon coming and thought about what it must be like in the icehouse. She leaned back a little and closed her eyes trying to see the insides of the icehouse. It was a dark, lovely picture in this heat, until it reminded her of that winter night in the outhouse holding her baby in the dark, her fingers searching for his asshole and the last bit of lard scooped from the sides of the can, held deliberately on the tip of her middle finger, the last bit of lard to keep from hurting him when she slid her finger in and all because she had broken the slop jar and the rags had frozen. The last food staple in the house she had rammed up her baby's behind to keep from hurting him too much when she opened up his bowels to pull the stools out. He had been screaming fit to kill, but when she found his hole at last and stuck her finger up in it, the shock was so great he was suddenly quiet. Even now on the hottest day anyone in Medallion could remember—a day so hot flies slept and cats were splaying their fur like quills, a day so hot pregnant wives leaned up against trees and cried, and women remembering some three-month-old hurt put ground glass in their lovers' food and the men looked at the food and wondered if there was glass in it and ate it anyway because it was too hot to resist eating it —even on this hottest of days in the hot spell, Eva shivered from the biting cold and stench of that outhouse.

Hannah was waiting. Watching her mother's eyelids. When Eva spoke at last it was with two voices. Like two people were talking at the same time, saying the same thing, one a fraction of a second behind the other.

"He give me such a time. Such a time. Look like he didn't even want to be born. But he come on out. Boys is hard to bear. You wouldn't know that but they is. It was such a carryin' on to get him born and to keep him alive. Just to keep his little heart beating and his little old lungs cleared and look like when he came back from that war he wanted to git back in. After all that carryin' on, just gettin' him out and keepin' him alive, he wanted to crawl back in my womb and well . . . I ain't got the room no more even if he could do it. There wasn't space for him in my womb. And he was crawlin' back. Being helpless and thinking baby thoughts and dreaming baby dreams and messing up his pants again and smiling all the time. I had room enough in my heart, but not in my womb, not no more. I birthed him once. I couldn't do it again. He was growed, a big old thing. Godhavemercy, I couldn't birth him twice. I'd be laying here at night and he be downstairs in that room, but when I closed my eyes I'd see him . . . six feet tall smilin' and crawlin' up the stairs quietlike so I wouldn't hear and opening the door soft so I wouldn't hear and he'd be creepin' to the bed trying to spread my legs trying to get back up in my womb. He was a man, girl, a big old growed-up man. I didn't have that much room. I kept on dreaming it. Dreaming it and I knowed it was true. One night it wouldn't be no dream. It'd be true and I would have done it, would have let him if I'd've had the room but a big man can't be a baby all wrapped up inside his mamma no more; he suffocate. I done everything I could to make him leave me and go on and live and be a man but he wouldn't and I had to keep him out so I just thought of a way he could die like a man not all scrunched up inside my womb, but like a man."

Eva couldn't see Hannah clearly for the tears, but she looked up at her anyway and said, by way of apology or explanation or perhaps just by way of neatness, "But I held him close first. Real close. Sweet Plum. My baby boy."

Long after Hannah turned and walked out of the room, Eva continued to call his name while her fingers lined up the pleats in her dress.

Hannah went off to the kitchen, her old man's slippers plopping down the stairs and over the hardwood floors. She turned the spigot on, letting water break up the tight knots of Kentucky Wonders and float them to the top of the bowl. She swirled them about with her fingers, poured the water off and repeated the process. Each time the green tubes rose to the surface she felt elated and collected whole handfuls at a time to drop in twos and threes back into the water.

Through the window over the sink she could see the deweys still playing chain gang; their ankles bound one to the other, they tumbled, struggled back to their feet and tried to walk single file. Hens strutted by with one suspicious eye on the deweys, another on the brick fireplace where sheets and mason jars were boiled. Only the deweys could play in this heat. Hannah put the Kentucky Wonders over the fire and, struck by a sudden sleepiness, she went off to lie down in the front room. It was even hotter there, for the windows were shut to keep out the sunlight. Hannah straightened the shawl that draped the couch and lay down. She dreamed of a wedding in a red bridal gown until Sula came in and woke her.

But before the second strange thing, there had been the wind, which was the first. The very night before the day Hannah had asked Eva if she had ever loved them, the wind tore over the hills rattling roofs and loosening doors. Everything shook, and although the people were frightened they thought it meant rain and welcomed it. Windows fell out and trees lost arms. People waited up half the night for the first crack of lightning. Some had even uncovered barrels to catch the rain water, which they loved to drink and cook in. They waited in vain, for no lightning no thunder no rain came. The wind just swept through, took what dampness there was out of the air, messed up the yards, and went on. The hills of the Bottom, as always, protected the valley part of town where the white people lived, and the next morning all the people were grateful because there was a dryer heat. So they set about their work early, for it was canning time, and who knew but what the wind would come back this time with a cooling rain. The men who worked in the valley got up at four thirty in the morning and looked at the sky where the sun was already rising like a hot white bitch. They beat the brims of their hats against their legs before putting them on and trudged down the road like old promises nobody wanted kept.

On Thursday, when Hannah brought Eva her fried tomatoes and soft scrambled eggs with the white left out for good luck, she mentioned her dream of the wedding in the red dress. Neither one bothered to look it up for they both knew the number was 522. Eva said she'd play it when Mr. Buckland Reed came by. Later she would remember it as the third strange thing. She had thought it odd even then, but the red in the dream confused her. But she wasn't certain that it was third or not because Sula was acting up, fretting the deweys and meddling the newly married couple. Because she was thirteen, everybody supposed her nature was coming down, but it was hard to put up with her sulking and irritation. The birthmark over her eye was getting darker and looked more and more like a stem and rose. She was dropping things and eating food that belonged to the newly married couple and started in to worrying everybody that the deweys needed a bath and she was going to give it to them. The deweys, who went wild at the thought of water, were crying and thundering all over the house like colts.

"We ain't got to, do we? Do we got to do what she says? It ain't Saturday." They even woke up Tar Baby, who came out of his room to look at them and then left the house in search of music.

Hannah ignored them and kept on bringing mason jars out of the cellar and washing them. Eva banged on the floor with her stick but nobody came. By noon it was quiet. The deweys had escaped, Sula was either in her room or gone off somewhere. The newly married couple, energized by their morning lovemaking, had gone to look for a day's work happily certain that they would find none.

The air all over the Bottom got heavy with peeled fruit and boiling vegetables. Fresh corn, tomatoes, string beans, melon rinds. The women, the children and the old men who had no jobs were putting up for a winter they understood so well. Peaches were stuffed into jars and black cherries (later, when it got cooler, they would put up jellies and preserves). The greedy canned as many as forty-two a day even though some of them, like Mrs. Jackson, who ate ice, had jars from 1920.

Before she trundled her wagon over to the dresser to get her comb, Eva looked out the window and saw Hannah bending to light the yard fire. And that was the fifth (or fourth, if you didn't count Sula's craziness) strange thing. She couldn't find her comb. Nobody moved stuff in Eva's room except to clean and then they put everything right back. But Eva couldn't find it anywhere. One hand pulling her braids loose, the other searching the dresser drawers, she had just begun to get irritated when she felt it in her blouse drawer. Then she trundled back to the window to catch a breeze, if one took a mind to come by, while she combed her hair. She rolled up to the window and it was then she saw Hannah burning. The flames from the yard fire were licking the blue cotton dress, making her dance. Eva knew there was time for nothing in this world other than the time it took to get there and cover her daughter's body with her own. She lifted her heavy frame up on her good leg, and with fists and arms smashed the windowpane. Using her stump as a support on the window sill, her good leg as a lever, she threw herself out of the window. Cut and bleeding she clawed the air trying to aim her body toward the flaming, dancing figure. She missed and came crashing down some twelve feet from Hannah's smoke. Stunned but still conscious, Eva dragged herself toward her firstborn, but Hannah, her senses lost, went flying out of the yard gesturing and bobbing like a sprung jack-in-the-box.

Mr. and Mrs. Suggs, who had set up their canning apparatus in their front yard, saw her running, dancing toward them. They whispered, "Jesus, Jesus," and together hoisted up their tub of water in which tight red tomatoes floated and threw it on the smoke-and-flame-bound woman. The water did put out the flames, but it also made steam, which seared to sealing all that was left of the beautiful Hannah Peace. She lay there on the wooden sidewalk planks, twitching lightly among the smashed tomatoes, her face a mask of agony so intense that for years the people who gathered 'round would shake their heads at the recollection of it.

Somebody covered her legs with a shirt. A woman unwrapped her head rag and placed it on Hannah's shoulder. Somebody else ran to Dick's Fresh Food and Sundries to call the ambulance. The rest stood there as helpless as sunflowers leaning on a fence. The deweys came and stepped in the tomatoes, their eyes raked with wonder. Two cats sidled through the legs of the crowd, sniffing the burned flesh. The vomiting of a young girl finally broke the profound silence and caused the women to talk to each other and to God. In the midst of calling Jesus they heard the hollow clang of the ambulance bell struggling up the hill, but not the "Help me, ya'll" that the dying woman whispered. Then somebody remembered to go and see about Eva. They found her on her stomach by the forsythia bushes calling Hannah's name and dragging her body through the sweet peas and clover that grew under the forsythia by the side of the house. Mother and daughter were placed on stretchers and carried to the ambulance. Eva was wide awake. The blood from her face cuts filled her eyes so she could not see, could only smell the familiar odor of cooked flesh.

Hannah died on the way to the hospital. Or so they said. In any case, she had already begun to bubble and blister so badly that the coffin had to be kept closed at the funeral and the women who washed the body and dressed it for death wept for her burned hair and wrinkled breasts as though they themselves had been her lovers.

When Eva got to the hospital they put her stretcher on the floor, so preoccupied with the hot and bubbling flesh of the other (some of them had never seen so extreme a burn case before) they forgot Eva, who would have bled to death except Old Willy Fields, the orderly, saw blood staining his just-mopped floors and went to find out where it was coming from. Recognizing Eva at once he shouted to a nurse, who came to see if the bloody one-legged black woman was alive or dead. From then on Willy boasted that he had saved Eva's life—an indisputable fact which she herself admitted and for which she cursed him every day for thirty-seven years thereafter and would have cursed him for the rest of her life except by then she was already ninety years old and forgot things.

Lying in the colored ward of the hospital, which was a

screened corner of a larger ward, Eva mused over the perfection of the judgment against her. She remembered the wedding dream and recalled that weddings always meant death. And the red gown, well that was the fire, as she should have known. She remembered something else too, and try as she might to deny it, she knew that as she lay on the ground trying to drag herself through the sweet peas and clover to get to Hannah, she had seen Sula standing on the back porch just looking. When Eva, who was never one to hide the faults of her children, mentioned what she thought she'd seen to a few friends, they said it was natural. Sula was probably struck dumb, as anybody would be who saw her own mamma burn up. Eva said yes, but inside she disagreed and remained convinced that Sula had watched Hannah burn not because she was paralyzed, but because she was interested.

1927

Old people were dancing with little children. Young boys with their sisters, and the church women who frowned on any bodily expression of joy (except when the hand of God commanded it) tapped their feet. Somebody (the groom's father, everybody said) had poured a whole pint jar of cane liquor into the punch, so even the men who did not sneak out the back door to have a shot, as well as the women who let nothing stronger than Black Draught enter their blood, were tipsy. A small boy stood at the Victrola turning its handle and smiling at the sound of Bert Williams' "Save a Little Dram for Me."

Even Helene Wright had mellowed with the cane, waving away apologies for drinks spilled on her rug and paying no attention whatever to the chocolate cake lying on the arm of her red-velvet sofa. The tea roses above her left breast had slipped from thc brooch that fastened them and were hanging heads down. When her husband called her attention to the children wrapping themselves into her curtains, she merely smiled and said, "Oh, let them be." She was not only a little drunk, she was weary and had been for weeks. Her only child's wedding—the culmination of all she had been, thought or done in this world—had dragged from her energy and stamina even she did not know she possessed. Her house had to be thoroughly cleaned, chickens had to be plucked, cakes and pies made, and for weeks she, her friends and her daughter had been sewing. Now it was all happening and it took only a little cane juice to snap the cords of fatigue and damn the white curtains that she had pinned on the stretcher only the morning before. Once this day was over she would have a lifetime to rattle around in that house and repair the damage.

A real wedding, in a church, with a real reception afterward, was rare among the people of the Bottom. Expensive for one thing, and most newlyweds just went to the courthouse if they were not particular, or had the preacher come in and say a few words if they were. The rest just "took up" with one another. No invitations were sent. There was no need for that formality. Folks just came, bringing a gift if they had one, none if they didn't. Except for those who worked in valley houses, most of them had never been to a big wedding; they simply assumed it was rather like a funeral except afterward you didn't have to walk all the way out to Beechnut Cemetery.

This wedding offered a special attraction, for the bridegroom was a handsome, well-liked man—the tenor of Mount Zion's Men's Quartet, who had an enviable reputation among the girls and a comfortable one among men. His name was Jude Greene, and with the pick of some eight or ten girls who came regularly to services to hear him sing, he had chosen Nel Wright.

He wasn't really aiming to get married. He was twenty then, and although his job as a waiter at the Hotel Medallion was a blessing to his parents and their seven other children, it wasn't nearly enough to support a wife. He had brought the subject up first on the day the word got out that the town was building a new road, tarmac, that would wind through Medallion on down to the river, where a great new bridge was to be built to connect Medallion to Porter's Landing, the town on the other side. The war over, a fake prosperity was still around. In a state of euphoria, with a hunger for more and more, the council of founders cast its eye toward a future that would certainly include trade from cross-river towns. Towns that needed more than a house raft to get to the merchants of Medallion. Work had already begun on the New River Road (the city had always meant to name it something else, something wonderful, but ten years later when the bridge idea was dropped for a tunnel it was still called the New River Road).

Along with a few other young black men, Jude had gone down to the shack where they were hiring. Three old colored men had already been hired, but not for the road work, just to do the picking up, food bringing and other small errands. These old men were close to feeble, not good for much else, and everybody was pleased they were taken on; still it was a shame to see those white men laughing with the grandfathers but shying away from the young black men who could tear that road up. The men like Jude who could do real work. Jude himself longed more than anybody else to be taken. Not just for the good money, more for the work itself. He wanted to swing the pick or kneel down with the string or shovel the gravel. His arms ached for something heavier than trays, for something dirtier than peelings; his feet wanted the heavy work shoes, not the thin-soled black shoes that the hotel required. More than anything he wanted the camaraderie of the road men: the lunch buckets, the hollering, the body movement that in the end produced something real, something he could point to. "I built that road," he could say. How much better sundown would be than the end of a day in the restaurant, where a good day's work was marked by the number of dirty plates and the weight of the garbage bin. "I built that road." People would walk over his sweat for years. Perhaps a sledge hammer would come crashing down on his foot, and when people asked him how come he limped, he could say, "Got that building the New Road."

It was while he was full of such dreams, his body already feeling the rough work clothes, his hands already curved to the pick handle, that he spoke to Nel about getting married. She seemed receptive but hardly anxious. It was after he stood in lines for six days running and saw the gang boss pick out thin-armed white boys from the Virginia hills and the bull-necked Greeks and Italians and heard over and over, "Nothing else today. Come back tomorrow," that he got the message. So it was rage, rage and a determination to take on a man's role anyhow that made him press Nel about settling down. He needed some of his appetites filled, some posture of adulthood recognized, but mostly he wanted someone to care about his hurt, to care very deeply. Deep enough to hold him, deep enough to rock him, deep enough to ask, "How you feel? You all right? Want some coffee?" And if he were to be a man, that someone could no longer be his mother. He chose the girl who had always been kind, who had never seemed hell-bent to marry, who made the whole venture seem like his idea, his conquest.

The more he thought about marriage, the more attractive it became. Whatever his fortune, whatever the cut of his garment, there would always be the hem—the tuck and fold that hid his raveling edges; a someone sweet, industrious and loyal to shore him up. And in return he would shelter her, love her, grow old with her. Without that someone he was a waiter hanging around a kitchen like a woman. With her he was head of a household pinned to an unsatisfactory job out of necessity. The two of them together would make one Jude.

His fears lest his burst dream of road building discourage her were never realized. Nel's indifference to his hints about marriage disappeared altogether when she discovered his pain. Jude could see himself taking shape in her eyes. She actually wanted to help, to soothe, and was it true what Ajax said in the Time and a Half Pool Hall? That "all they want, man, is they own misery. Ax em to die for you and they yours for life."

Whether he was accurate in general, Ajax was right about Nel. Except for an occasional leadership role with Sula, she had no aggression. Her parents had succeeded in rubbing down to a dull glow any sparkle or splutter she had. Only with Sula did that quality have free reign, but their friendship was so close, they themselves had difficulty distinguishing one's thoughts from the other's. During all of her girlhood the only respite Nel had had from her stern and undemonstrative parents was Sula. When Jude began to hover around, she was flattered—all the girls liked him—and Sula made the enjoyment of his attentions keener simply because she seemed always to want Nel to shine. They never quarreled, those two, the way some girlfriends did over boys, or competed against each other for them. In those days a compliment to one was a compliment to the other, and cruelty to one was a challenge to the other.

Nel's response to Jude's shame and anger selected her away from Sula. And greater than her friendship was this new feeling of being needed by someone who saw her singly. She didn't even know she had a neck until Jude remarked on it, or that her smile was anything but the spreading of her lips until he saw it as a small miracle.

Sula was no less excited about the wedding. She thought it was the perfect thing to do following their graduation from general school. She wanted to be the bridesmaid. No others. And she encouraged Mrs. Wright to go all out, even to borrowing Eva's punch bowl. In fact, she handled most of the details very efficiently, capitalizing on the fact that most people were anxious to please her since she had lost her mamma only a few years back and they still remembered the agony in Hannah's face and the blood on Eva's.

So they danced up in the Bottom on the second Saturday in June, danced at the wedding where everybody realized for the first time that except for their magnificent teeth, the deweys would never grow. They had been forty-eight inches tall for years now, and while their size was unusual it was not unheard of. The realization was based on the fact that they remained boys in mind. Mischievous, cunning, private and completely unhousebroken, their games and interests had not changed since Hannah had them all put into the first grade together.

Nel and Jude, who had been the stars all during the wedding, were forgotten finally as the reception melted into a dance, a feed, a gossip session, a playground and a love nest. For the first time that day they relaxed and looked at each other, and liked what they saw. They began to dance, pressed in among the others, and each one turned his thoughts to the night that was coming on fast. They had taken a housekeeping room with one of Jude's aunts (over the protest of Mrs. Wright, who had rooms to spare, but Nel didn't want to make love to her husband in her mother's house) and were getting restless to go there.

As if reading her thoughts, Jude leaned down and whispered, "Me too." Nel smiled and rested her cheek on his shoulder. The veil she wore was too heavy to allow her to feel the core of the kiss he pressed on her head. When she raised her eyes to him for one more look of reassurance, she saw through the open door a slim figure in blue, gliding, with just a hint of a strut, down the path toward the road. One hand was pressed to the head to hold down the large hat against the warm June breeze. Even from the rear Nel could tell that it was Sula and that she was smiling; that something deep down in that litheness was amused. It would be ten years before they saw each other again, and their meeting would be thick with birds.

PART TWO

1937

Accompanied by a plague of robins, Sula came back to Medallion. The little yam-breasted shuddering birds were everywhere, exciting very small children away from their usual welcome into a vicious stoning. Nobody knew why or from where they had come. What they did know was that you couldn't go anywhere without stepping in their pearly shit, and it was hard to hang up clothes, pull weeds or just sit on the front porch when robins were flying and dying all around you.

Although most of the people remembered the time when the sky was black for two hours with clouds and clouds of pigeons, and although they were accustomed to excesses in nature—too much heat, too much cold, too little rain, rain to flooding—they still dreaded the way a relatively trivial phenomenon could become sovereign in their lives and bend their minds to its will.

In spite of their fear, they reacted to an oppressive oddity, or what they called evil days, with an acceptance that bordered on welcome. Such evil must be avoided, they felt, and precautions must naturally be taken to protect themselves from it. But they let it run its course, fulfill itself, and never invented ways either to alter it, to annihilate it or to prevent its happening again. So also were they with people.

What was taken by outsiders to be slackness, slovenliness or even generosity was in fact a full recognition of the legitimacy of forces other than good ones. They did not believe doctors could heal—for them, none ever had done so. They did not believe death was accidental—life might be, but death was deliberate. They did not believe Nature was ever askew—only inconvenient. Plague and drought were as "natural" as springtime. If milk could curdle, God knows robins could fall. The purpose of evil was to survive it and they determined (without ever knowing they had made up their minds to do it) to survive floods, white people, tuberculosis, famine and ignorance. They knew anger well but not despair, and they didn't stone sinners for the same reason they didn't commit suicide—it was beneath them.

Sula stepped off the Cincinnati Flyer into the robin shit and began the long climb up into the Bottom. She was dressed in a manner that was as close to a movie star as anyone would ever see. A black crepe dress splashed with pink and yellow zinnias, foxtails, a black felt hat with the veil of net lowered over one eye. In her right hand was a black purse with a beaded clasp and in her left a red leather traveling case, so small, so charming—no one had seen anything like it ever before, including the mayor's wife and the music teacher, both of whom had been to Rome.

Walking up the hill toward Carpenter's Road, the heels and sides of her pumps edged with drying bird shit, she attracted the glances of old men sitting on stone benches in front of the courthouse, housewives throwing buckets of water on their sidewalks, and high school students on their way home for lunch. By the time she reached the Bottom, the news of her return had brought the black people out on their porches or to their windows. There were scattered hellos and nods but mostly stares. A little boy ran up to her saying, "Carry yo' bag, ma'am?" Before Sula could answer his mother had called him, "You, John. Get back in here."

At Eva's house there were four dead robins on the walk. Sula stopped and with her toe pushed them into the bordering grass.

Eva looked at Sula pretty much the same way she had looked at BoyBoy that time when he returned after he'd left her without a dime or a prospect of one. She was sitting in her wagon, her back to the window she had jumped out of (now all boarded up) setting fire to the hair she had combed out of her head. When Sula opened the door she raised her eyes and said, "I might have knowed them birds meant something. Where's your coat?"

Sula threw herself on Eva's bed. "The rest of my stuff will be on later."

"I should hope so. Them little old furry tails ain't going to do you no more good than they did the fox that was wearing them."

"Don't you say hello to nobody when you ain't seen them for ten years?"

"If folks let somebody know where they is and when they coming, then other folks can get ready for them. If they don't—if they just pop in all sudden like—then they got to take whatever mood they find."

"How you been doing, Big Mamma?"

"Gettin' by. Sweet of you to ask. You was quick enough when you wanted something. When you needed a little change or . . ."

"Don't talk to me about how much you gave me, Big Mamma, and how much I owe you or none of that."

"Oh? I ain't supposed to mention it?"

"OK. Mention it." Sula shrugged and turned over on her stomach, her buttocks toward Eva.

"You ain't been in this house ten seconds and already you starting something."

"Takes two, Big Mamma."

"Well, don't let your mouth start nothing that your ass can't stand. When you gone to get married? You need to have some babies. It'll settle you."

"I don't want to make somebody else. I want to make myself."

"Selfish. Ain't no woman got no business floatin' around without no man."

"You did."

"Not by choice."

"Mamma did."

"Not by choice, I said. It ain't right for you to want to stay off by yourself. You need . . . I'm a tell you what you need."

Sula sat up. "I need you to shut your mouth."

"Don't nobody talk to me like that. Don't nobody . . ."

"This body does. Just 'cause you was bad enough to cut

off your own leg you think you got a right to kick everybody with the stump."

"Who said I cut off my leg?"

"Well, you stuck it under a train to collect insurance."

"Hold on, you lyin' heifer!"

"I aim to."

"Bible say honor thy father and thy mother that thy days may be long upon the land thy God giveth thee."

"Mamma must have skipped that part. Her days wasn't too long."

"Pus mouth! God's going to strike you!"

"Which God? The one watched you burn Plum?"

"Don't talk to me about no burning. You watched your own mamma. You crazy roach! You the one should have been burnt!"

"But I ain't. Got that? I ain't. Any more fires in this house, I'm lighting them!"

"Hellfire don't need lighting and it's already burning in you..."

"Whatever's burning in me is mine!"

"Amen!"

"And I'll split this town in two and everything in it before I'll let you put it out!"

"Pride goeth before a fall."

"What the hell do I care about falling?"

"Amazing Grace."

"You sold your life for twenty-three dollars a month."

"You throwed yours away."

"It's mine to throw."

"One day you gone need it."

"But not you. I ain't never going to need you. And you know what? Maybe one night when you dozing in that wagon flicking flies and swallowing spit, maybe I'll just tip on up here with some kerosene and—who knows—you may make the brightest flame of them all."

So Eva locked her door from then on. But it did no good. In April two men came with a stretcher and she didn't even have time to comb her hair before they strapped her to a piece of canvas.

When Mr. Buckland Reed came by to pick up the number, his mouth sagged at the sight of Eva being carried out and Sula holding some papers against the wall, at the bottom of which, just above the word "guardian," she very carefully wrote Miss Sula Mae Peace.

⦿ ⦿ ⦿

Nel alone noticed the peculiar quality of the May that followed the leaving of the birds. It had a sheen, a glimmering as of green, rain-soaked Saturday nights (lit by the excitement of newly installed street lights); of lemon-yellow afternoons bright with iced drinks and splashes of daffodils. It showed in the damp faces of her children and the river-smoothness of their voices. Even her own body was not immune to the magic. She would sit on the floor to sew as she had done as a girl, fold her legs up under her or do a little dance that fitted some tune in her head. There were easy sun-washed days and purple dusks in which Tar Baby sang "Abide With Me" at prayer meetings, his lashes darkened by tears, his silhouette limp with regret against the whitewashed walls of Greater Saint Matthew's. Nel listened and was moved to smile. To smile at the sheer loveliness that pressed in from the windows and touched his grief, making it a pleasure to behold.

Although it was she alone who saw this magic, she did not wonder at it. She knew it was all due to Sula's return to the Bottom. It was like getting the use of an eye back, having a cataract removed. Her old friend had come home. Sula. Who made her laugh, who made her see old things with new eyes, in whose presence she felt clever, gentle and a little raunchy. Sula, whose past she had lived through and with whom the present was a constant sharing of perceptions. Talking to Sula had always been a conversation with herself. Was there anyone else before whom she could never be foolish? In whose view inadequacy was mere idiosyncrasy, a character trait rather than a deficiency? Anyone who left behind that aura of fun and complicity? Sula never competed; she simply helped others define themselves. Other people seemed to turn their volume on and up when Sula was in the room. More than any other thing, humor returned. She could listen to the crunch of sugar underfoot that the children had spilled without reaching for the switch; and she forgot the tear in the living-room window shade. Even Nel's love for Jude, which over the years had spun a steady gray web around her heart, became a bright and easy affection, a playfulness that was reflected in their lovemaking.

Sula would come by of an afternoon, walking along with her fluid stride, wearing a plain yellow dress the same way her mother, Hannah, had worn those too-big house dresses—with a distance, an absence of a relationship to clothes which emphasized everything the fabric covered. When she scratched the screen door, as in the old days, and stepped inside, the dishes piled in the sink looked as though they belonged there; the dust on the lamps sparkled; the hair brush lying on the "good" sofa in the living room did not have to be apologetically retrieved, and Nel's grimy intractable children looked like three wild things happily insouciant in the May shine.

"Hey, girl." The rose mark over Sula's eye gave her glance a suggestion of startled pleasure. It was darker than Nel remembered.

"Hey yourself. Come on in here."

"How you doin'?" Sula moved a pile of ironed diapers from a chair and sat down.

"Oh, I ain't strangled nobody yet so I guess I'm all right."

"Well, if you change your mind call me."

"Somebody need killin'?"

"Half this town need it."

"And the other half?"

"A drawn-out disease."

"Oh, come on. Is Medallion that bad?"

"Didn't nobody tell you?"

"You been gone too long, Sula."

"Not too long, but maybe too far."

"What's that supposed to mean?" Nel dipped her fingers into the bowl of water and sprinkled a diaper.

"Oh, I don't know."

"Want some cool tea?"

"Mmmm. Lots of ice, I'm burnin' up."

"Iceman don't come yet, but it's good and cold."

"That's fine."

"Hope I didn't speak too soon. Kids run in and out of here so much." Nel bent to open the icebox.

"You puttin' it on, Nel. Jude must be wore out."

"*Jude* must be wore out? You don't care nothin' 'bout my back, do you?"

"Is that where it's at, in your back?"

"Hah! Jude thinks it's everywhere."

"He's right, it is everywhere. Just be glad he found it, wherever it is. Remember John L.?"

"When Shirley said he got her down by the well and tried to stick it in her hip?" Nel giggled at the remembrance of that teen-time tale. "She should have been grateful. Have you seen her since you been back?"

"Mmm. Like a ox."

"That was one dumb nigger, John L."

"Maybe. Maybe he was just sanitary."

"Sanitary?"

"Well. Think about it. Suppose Shirley was all splayed out in front of you? Wouldn't you go for the hipbone instead?"

Nel lowered her head onto crossed arms while tears of laughter dripped into the warm diapers. Laughter that weakened her knees and pressed her bladder into action. Her rapid soprano and Sula's dark sleepy chuckle made a duet that frightened the cat and made the children run in from the back yard, puzzled at first by the wild free sounds, then delighted to see their mother stumbling merrily toward the bathroom, holding on to her stomach, fairly singing through the laughter: "Aw. Aw. Lord. Sula. Stop." And the other one, the one with the scary black thing over her eye, laughing softly and egging their mother on: "Neatness counts. You know what cleanliness is next to . . ."

"Hush." Nel's plea was clipped off by the slam of the bathroom door.

"What y'all laughing at?"

"Old time-y stuff. Long gone, old time-y stuff."

"Tell us."

"Tell *you?*" The black mark leaped.

"Uh huh. Tell us."

"What tickles us wouldn't tickle you."

"Uh huh, it would."

"Well, we was talking about some people we used to know when we was little."

"Was my mamma little?"

"Of course."

"What happened?"

"Well, some old boy we knew name John L. and a girl name . . ."

Damp-faced, Nel stepped back into the kitchen. She felt new, soft and new. It had been the longest time since she had had a rib-scraping laugh. She had forgotten how deep and down it could be. So different from the miscellaneous giggles and smiles she had learned to be content with these past few years.

"O Lord, Sula. You haven't changed none." She wiped her eyes. "What was all that about, anyway? All that scramblin' we did trying to do it and not do it at the same time?"

"Beats me. Such a simple thing."

"But we sure made a lot out of it, and the boys were dumber than we were."

"Couldn't nobody be dumber than I was."

"Stop lying. All of 'em liked you best."

"Yeah? Where are they?"

"They still here. You the one went off."

"Didn't I, though?"

"Tell me about it. The big city."

"Big is all it is. A big Medallion."

"No. I mean the life. The nightclubs, and parties . . ."

"I was in college, Nellie. No nightclubs on campus."

"Campus? That what they call it? Well. You wasn't in no college for—what—ten years now? And you didn't write to nobody. How come you never wrote?"

"You never did either."

"Where was I going to write to? All I knew was that you was in Nashville. I asked Miss Peace about you once or twice."

"What did *she* say?"

"I couldn't make much sense out of her. You know she been gettin' stranger and stranger after she come out the hospital. How is she anyway?"

"Same, I guess. Not so hot."

"No? Laura, I know, was doing her cooking and things. Is she still?"

"No. I put her out."

"Put her out? What for?"

"She made me nervous."

"But she was doing it for nothing, Sula."

"That's what you think. She was stealing right and left."

"Since when did you get froggy about folks' stealing?"

Sula smiled. "OK. I lied. You wanted a reason."

"Well, give me the real one."

"I don't know the real one. She just didn't belong in that house. Digging around in the cupboards, picking up pots and ice picks . . ."

"You sure have changed. That house was always full of people digging in cupboards and carrying on."

"That's the reason, then."

"Sula. Come on, now."

"You've changed too. I didn't used to have to explain everything to you."

Nel blushed. "Who's feeding the deweys and Tar Baby? You?"

"Sure me. Anyway Tar Baby don't eat and the deweys still crazy."

"I heard one of 'em's mamma came to take him back but didn't know which was hern."

"Don't nobody know."

"And Eva? You doing the work for her too?"

"Well, since you haven't heard it, let me tell you. Eva's real sick. I had her put where she could be watched and taken care of."

"Where would that be?"

"Out by Beechnut."

"You mean that home the white church run? Sula! That ain't no place for Eva. All them women is dirt poor with no people at all. Mrs. Wilkens and them. They got dropsy and can't hold their water—crazy as loons. Eva's odd, but she got sense. I don't think that's right, Sula."

"I'm scared of her, Nellie. That's why . . ."

"Scared? Of Eva?"

"You don't know her. Did you know she burnt Plum?"

"Oh, I heard that years ago. But nobody put no stock in it."

"They should have. It's true. I saw it. And when I got back here she was planning to do it to me too."

"Eva? I can't hardly believe that. She almost died trying to get to your mother."

Sula leaned forward, her elbows on the table. "You ever known me to lie to you?"

"No. But you could be mistaken. Why would Eva . . ."

"All I know is I'm scared. And there's no place else for me to go. We all that's left, Eva and me. I guess I should have stayed gone. I didn't know what else to do. Maybe I should have talked to you about it first. You always had better sense than me. Whenever I was scared before, you knew just what to do."

The closed place in the water spread before them. Nel put the iron on the stove. The situation was clear to her now. Sula, like always, was incapable of making any but the most trivial decisions. When it came to matters of grave importance, she behaved emotionally and irresponsibly and left it to others to straighten out. And when fear struck her, she did unbelievable things. Like that time with her finger. Whatever those hunkies did, it wouldn't have been as bad as what she did to herself. But Sula was so scared she had mutilated herself, to protect herself.

"What should I do, Nellie? Take her back and sleep with my door locked again?"

"No. I guess it's too late anyway. But let's work out a plan for taking care of her. So she won't be messed over."

"Anything you say."

"What about money? She got any?"

Sula shrugged. "The checks come still. It's not much, like it used to be. Should I have them made over to me?"

"Can you? Do it, then. We can arrange for her to have special comforts. That place is a mess, you know. A doctor don't never set foot in there. I ain't figured out yet how they stay alive in there as long as they do."

"Why don't I have the checks made over to you, Nellie? You better at this than I am."

"Oh no. People will say I'm scheming. You the one to do it. Was there insurance from Hannah?"

"Yes. Plum too. He had all that army insurance."

"Any of it left?"

"Well I went to college on some. Eva banked the rest. I'll look into it, though."

". . . and explain it all to the bank people."

"Will you go down with me?"

"Sure. It's going to be all right."

"I'm glad I talked to you 'bout this. It's been bothering me."

"Well, tongues will wag, but so long as we know the truth, it don't matter."

Just at that moment the children ran in announcing the entrance of their father. Jude opened the back door and walked into the kitchen. He was still a very good-looking man, and the only difference Sula could see was the thin pencil mustache under his nose, and a part in his hair.

"Hey, Jude. What you know good?"

"White man running it—nothing good."

Sula laughed while Nel, high-tuned to his moods, ignored her husband's smile saying, "Bad day, honey?"

"Same old stuff," he replied and told them a brief tale of some personal insult done him by a customer and his boss—a whiney tale that peaked somewhere between anger and a lapping desire for comfort. He ended it with the observation that a Negro man had a hard row to hoe in this world. He expected his story to dovetail into milkwarm commiseration, but before Nel could excrete it, Sula said she didn't know about that—it looked like a pretty good life to her.

"Say what?" Jude's temper flared just a bit as he looked at this friend of his wife's, this slight woman, not exactly plain, but not fine either, with a copperhead over her eye. As far as he could tell, she looked like a woman roaming the country trying to find some man to burden down with a lot of lip and a lot of mouths.

Sula was smiling. "I mean, I don't know what the fuss is about. I mean, everything in the world loves you. White men love you. They spend so much time worrying about your penis they forget their own. The only thing they want to do is cut off a nigger's privates. And if that ain't love and respect I don't know what is. And white women? They chase you all to every corner of the earth, feel for you under every bed. I knew a white woman wouldn't leave the house after 6 o'clock for fear one of you would snatch her. Now ain't that love? They think rape soon's they see you, and if they don't get the rape they looking for, they scream it anyway just so the search won't be in vain. Colored women worry themselves into bad health just trying to hang on to your cuffs. Even little children—white and black, boys and girls—spend all their childhood eating their hearts out 'cause they think you don't love them. And if that ain't enough, you love yourselves. Nothing in this world loves a black man more than another black man. You hear of solitary white men, but niggers? Can't stay away from one another a whole day. So. It looks to me like you the envy of the world."

Jude and Nel were laughing, he saying, "Well, if that's the only way they got to show it—cut off my balls and throw me in jail—I'd just as soon they left me alone." But thinking that Sula had an odd way of looking at things and that her wide smile took some of the sting from that rattlesnake over her eye. A funny woman, he thought, not that bad-looking. But he could see why she wasn't married; she stirred a man's mind maybe, but not his body.

⊙ ⊙ ⊙

He left his tie. The one with the scriggly yellow lines running lopsided across the dark-blue field. It hung over the top of the closet door pointing steadily downward while it waited with every confidence for Jude to return.

Could he be gone if his tie is still here? He will remember it and come back and then she would . . . uh. Then she could . . . tell him. Sit down quietly and tell him. "But Jude," she would say, "you *knew* me. All those days and years, Jude, you *knew* me. My ways and my hands and how my stomach folded and how we tried to get Mickey to nurse and how about that time when the landlord said . . . but you said . . . and I cried, Jude. You knew me and had listened to the things I said in the night, and heard me in the bathroom and laughed at my raggedy girdle and I laughed too because I knew you too, Jude. So how could you leave me when you knew me?"

But they had been down on all fours naked, not touching except their lips right down there on the floor where the tie is pointing to, on all fours like (uh huh, go on, say it) like dogs. Nibbling at each other, not even touching, not even looking at each other, just their lips, and when I opened the door they didn't even look for a minute and I thought the reason they are not looking up is because they are not doing that. So it's all right. I am just standing here. They are not doing that. I am just standing here and seeing it, but they are not really doing it. But then they did look up. Or you did. You did, Jude. And if only you had not looked at me the way the soldiers did on the train, the way you look at the children when they come in while you are listening to Gabriel Heatter and break your train of thought —not focusing exactly but giving them an instant, a piece of time, to remember what they are doing, what they are interrupting, and to go on back to wherever they were and let you listen to Gabriel Heatter. And I did not know how to move my feet or fix my eyes or what. I just stood there seeing it and smiling, because maybe there was some explanation, something important that I did not know about that would have made it all right. I waited for Sula to look up at me any minute and say one of those lovely college words like *aesthetic* or *rapport,* which I never understood but which I loved because they sounded so comfortable and firm. And finally you just got up and started putting on your clothes and your privates were hanging down, so soft, and you buckled your pants belt but forgot to button the fly and she was sitting on the bed not even bothering to put on her clothes because actually she didn't need to because somehow she didn't look naked to me, only you did. Her chin was in her hand and she sat like a visitor from out of town waiting for the hosts to get some quarreling done and over with so the card game could continue and me wanting her to leave so I could tell you privately that you had forgotten to button your fly because I didn't want to say it in front of her, Jude. And even when you began to talk, I couldn't hear because I was worried about you not knowing that your fly was open and scared too because your eyes looked like the soldiers' that time on the train when my mother turned to custard.

Remember how big that bedroom was? Jude? How when we moved here we said, Well, at least we got us a real big bedroom, but it was small then, Jude, and so shambly, and maybe it was that way all along but it would have been better if I had gotten the dust out from under the bed because I was ashamed of it in that small room. And then you walked past me saying, "I'll be back for my things." And you did but you left your tie.

The clock was ticking. Nel looked at it and realized that it was two thirty, only forty-five minutes before the children would be home and she hadn't even felt anything right or sensible and now there was no time or wouldn't be until nighttime when they were asleep and she could get into bed and maybe she could do it then. Think. But who could think in that bed where *they* had been and where they *also* had been and where only she was now?

She looked around for a place to be. A small place. The closet? No. Too dark. The bathroom. It was both small and bright, and she wanted to be in a very small, very bright place. Small enough to contain her grief. Bright enough to throw into relief the dark things that cluttered her. Once inside, she sank to the tile floor next to the toilet. On her knees, her hand on the cold rim of the bathtub, she waited for something to happen . . . inside. There was stirring, a movement of mud and dead leaves. She thought of the women at Chicken Little's funeral. The women who shrieked over the bier and at the lip of the open grave. What she had regarded since as unbecoming behavior seemed fitting to her now; they were screaming at the neck of God, his giant nape, the vast back-of-the-head that he had turned on them in death. But it seemed to her now that it was not a fist-shaking grief they were keening but rather a simple obligation to say something, do something, feel something about the dead. They could not let that heart-smashing event pass unrecorded, unidentified. It was poisonous, unnatural to let the dead go with a mere whimpering, a slight murmur, a rose bouquet of good taste. Good taste was out of place in the company of death, death itself was the essence of bad taste. And there must be much rage and saliva in its presence. The body must move and throw itself about, the eyes must roll, the hands should have no peace, and the throat should release all the yearning, despair and outrage that accompany the stupidity of loss.

"The real hell of Hell is that it is forever." Sula said

that. She said doing anything forever and ever was hell. Nel didn't understand it then, but now in the bathroom, trying to feel, she thought, "If I could be sure that I could stay here in this small white room with the dirty tile and water gurgling in the pipes and my head on the cool rim of this bathtub and never have to go out the door, I would be happy. If I could be certain that I never had to get up and flush the toilet, go in the kitchen, watch my children grow up and die, see my food chewed on my plate . . . Sula was wrong. Hell ain't things lasting forever. Hell is change." Not only did men leave and children grow up and die, but even the misery didn't last. One day she wouldn't even have that. This very grief that had twisted her into a curve on the floor and flayed her would be gone. She would lose that too.

"Why, even in hate here I am thinking of what Sula said."

Hunched down in the small bright room Nel waited. Waited for the oldest cry. A scream not for others, not in sympathy for a burnt child, or a dead father, but a deeply personal cry for one's own pain. A loud, strident: "Why me?" She waited. The mud shifted, the leaves stirred, the smell of overripe green things enveloped her and announced the beginnings of her very own howl.

But it did not come.

The odor evaporated; the leaves were still, the mud settled. And finally there was nothing, just a flake of something dry and nasty in her throat. She stood up frightened. There was something just to the right of her, in the air, just out of view. She could not see it, but she knew exactly what it looked like. A gray ball hovering just there. Just there. To the right. Quiet, gray, dirty. A ball of muddy strings, but without weight, fluffy but terrible in its malevolence. She knew she could not look, so she closed her eyes and crept past it out of the bathroom, shutting the door behind her. Sweating with fear, she stepped to the kitchen door and onto the back porch. The lilac bushes preened at the railing, but there were no lilacs yet. Wasn't it time? Surely it was time. She looked over the fence to Mrs. Rayford's yard. Hers were not in bloom either. Was it too late? She fastened on this question with enthusiasm, all the time aware of something she was not thinking. It was the only way she could get her mind off the flake in her throat.

She spent a whole summer with the gray ball, the little ball of fur and string and hair always floating in the light near her but which she did not see because she never looked. But that was the terrible part, the effort it took not to look. But it was there anyhow, just to the right of her head and maybe further down by her shoulder, so when the children went to a monster movie at the Elmira Theater and came home and said, "Mamma, can you sleep with us tonight?" she said all right and got into bed with the two boys, who loved it, but the girl did not. For a long time she could not stop getting in the bed with her children and told herself each time that they might dream a dream about dragons and would need her to comfort them. It was so nice to think about their scary dreams and not about a ball of fur. She even hoped their dreams would rub off on her and give her the wonderful relief of a nightmare so she could stop going around scared to turn her head this way or that lest she see it. That was the scary part—seeing it. It was not coming at her; it never did that, or tried to pounce on her. It just floated there for the seeing, if she wanted to, and O my God for the touching if she wanted to. But she didn't want to see it, ever, for if she saw it, who could tell but what she might actually touch it, or want to, and then what would happen if she actually reached out her hand and touched it? Die probably, but no worse than that. Dying was OK because it was sleep and there wasn't no gray ball in death, was there? Was there? She would have to ask somebody about that, somebody she could confide in and who knew a lot of things, like Sula, for Sula would know or if she didn't she would say something funny that would make it all right. Ooo no, not Sula. Here she was in the midst of it, hating it, scared of it, and again she thought of Sula as though they were still friends and talked things over. That was too much. To lose Jude and not have Sula to talk to about it because it was Sula that he had left her for.

Now her thighs were really empty. And it was then that what those women said about never looking at another man made some sense to her, for the real point, the heart of what they said, was the word *looked*. Not to promise never to make love to another man, not to refuse to marry another man, but to promise and know that she could never afford to look again, to see and accept the way in which their heads cut the air or see moons and tree limbs framed by their necks and shoulders . . . never to look, for now she could not risk looking—and anyway, so what? For now her thighs were truly empty and dead too, and it was Sula who had taken the life from them and Jude who smashed her heart and the both of them who left her with no thighs and no heart just her brain raveling away.

And what am I supposed to do with these old thighs now, just walk up and down these rooms? What good are they, Jesus? They will never give me the peace I need to get from sunup to sundown, what good are they, are you trying to tell me that I am going to have to go all the way through these days all the way, O my god, to that box with four handles with never nobody settling down between my legs even if I sew up those old pillow cases and rinse down the porch and feed my children and beat the rugs and haul the coal up out of the bin even then nobody, O Jesus, I could be a mule or plow the furrows with my hands if need be or hold these rickety walls up with my back if need be if I knew that somewhere in this world in the pocket of some night I could open my legs to some cowboy lean hips but you are trying to tell me no and O my sweet Jesus what kind of cross is that?

1939

When the word got out about Eva being put in Sunnydale, the people in the Bottom shook their heads and said Sula was a roach. Later, when they saw how she took Jude, then ditched him for others, and heard how he bought a bus ticket to Detroit (where he bought but never mailed birthday cards to his sons), they forgot all about Hannah's easy ways (or their own) and said she was a bitch. Everybody remembered the plague of robins that announced her return, and the tale about her watching Hannah burn was stirred up again.

But it was the men who gave her the final label, who fingerprinted her for all time. They were the ones who said she was guilty of the unforgivable thing—the thing for which there was no understanding, no excuse, no compassion. The route from which there was no way back, the dirt that could not ever be washed away. They said that Sula slept with white men. It may not have been true, but it certainly could have been. She was obviously capable of it. In any case, all minds were closed to her when that word was passed around. It made the old women draw their lips together; made small children look away from her in shame; made young men fantasize elaborate torture for her—just to get the saliva back in their mouths when they saw her.

Every one of them imagined the scene, each according to his own predilections—Sula underneath some white man—and it filled them with choking disgust. There was nothing lower she could do, nothing filthier. The fact that their own skin color was proof that it had happened in their own families was no deterrent to their bile. Nor was the willingness of black men to lie in the beds of white women a consideration that might lead them toward tolerance. They insisted that all unions between white men and black women be rape; for a black woman to be willing was literally unthinkable. In that way, they regarded integration with precisely the same venom that white people did.

So they laid broomsticks across their doors at night and sprinkled salt on porch steps. But aside from one or two unsuccessful efforts to collect the dust from her footsteps, they did nothing to harm her. As always the black people looked at evil stony-eyed and let it run.

Sula acknowledged none of their attempts at counter-conjure or their gossip and seemed to need the services of nobody. So they watched her far more closely than they watched any other roach or bitch in the town, and their alertness was gratified. Things began to happen.

First off, Teapot knocked on her door to see if she had any bottles. He was the five-year-old son of an indifferent mother, all of whose interests sat around the door of the Time and a Half Pool Hall. Her name was Betty but she was called Teapot's Mamma because being his mamma was precisely her major failure. When Sula said no, the boy turned around and fell down the steps. He couldn't get up right away and Sula went to help him. His mother, just then tripping home, saw Sula bending over her son's pained face. She flew into a fit of concerned, if drunken, motherhood, and dragged Teapot home. She told everybody that Sula had pushed him, and talked so strongly about it she was forced to abide by the advice of her friends and take him to the county hospital. The two dollars she hated to release turned out to be well spent, for Teapot did have a fracture, although the doctor said poor diet had contributed substantially to the daintiness of his bones. Teapot's Mamma got a lot of attention anyway and immersed herself in a role she had shown no inclination for: motherhood. The very idea of a grown woman hurting her boy kept her teeth on edge. She became the most devoted mother: sober, clean and industrious. No more nickels for Teapot to go to Dick's for a breakfast of Mr. Goodbars and soda pop: no more long hours of him alone or wandering the roads while she was otherwise engaged. Her change was a distinct improvement, although little Teapot did miss those quiet times at Dick's.

Other things happened. Mr. Finley sat on his porch sucking chicken bones, as he had done for thirteen years, looked up, saw Sula, choked on a bone and died on the spot. That incident, and Teapot's Mamma, cleared up for everybody the meaning of the birthmark over her eye; it was not a stemmed rose, or a snake, it was Hannah's ashes marking her from the very beginning.

She came to their church suppers without underwear, bought their steaming platters of food and merely picked at it—relishing nothing, exclaiming over no one's ribs or cobbler. They believed that she was laughing at their God.

And the fury she created in the women of the town was incredible—for she would lay their husbands once and then no more. Hannah had been a nuisance, but she was complimenting the women, in a way, by wanting their husbands. Sula was trying them out and discarding them without any excuse the men could swallow. So the women, to justify their own judgment, cherished their men more, soothed the pride and vanity Sula had bruised.

Among the weighty evidence piling up was the fact that Sula did not look her age. She was near thirty and, unlike them, had lost no teeth, suffered no bruises, developed no ring of fat at the waist or pocket at the back of her neck. It was rumored that she had had no childhood diseases, was never known to have chicken pox, croup or even a runny nose. She had played rough as a child—where were the scars? Except for a funny-shaped finger and that evil birthmark, she was free of any normal signs of vulnerability. Some of the men, who as boys had dated her, remembered that on picnics neither gnats nor mosquitoes would settle on her. Patsy, Hannah's one-time friend, agreed and said not only that, but she had witnessed the fact that when Sula drank beer she never belched.

The most damning evidence, however, came from Dessie, who was a big Daughter Elk and knew things. At one of the social meetings she revealed something to her friends.

"Yeh, well I noticed something long time ago. Ain't said nothing 'bout it 'cause I wasn't sure what it meant. Well . . . I did mention it to Ivy but not nobody else. I disremember how long ago. 'Bout a month or two I guess 'cause I hadn't put down my new linoleum yet. Did you see it, Cora? It's that kind we saw in the catalogue."

"Naw."

"Get on with it, Dessie."

"Well, Cora was with me when we looked in the catalogue..."

"We all know 'bout your linoleum. What we don't know is..."

"OK. Let me tell it, will you? Just before the linoleum come I was out front and seed Shadrack carryin' on as usual . . . up by the well . . . walkin' 'round it salutin' and carryin' on. You know how he does . . . hollerin' commands and..."

"Will you get on with it?"

"Who's tellin' this? Me or you?"

"You."

"Well, let me tell it then. Like I say, he was just cuttin' up as usual when Miss Sula Mae walks by on the other side of the road. And quick as that"—she snapped her fingers—"he stopped and cut on over 'cross the road, steppin' over to her like a tall turkey in short corn. And guess what? He tips his hat."

"Shadrack don't wear no hat."

"I know that but he tipped it anyway. You know what I mean. He acted like he had a hat and reached up for it and tipped it at her. Now you know Shadrack ain't civil to nobody!"

"Sure ain't."

"Even when you buyin' his fish he's cussin'. If you ain't got the right change he cussin' you. If you act like a fish ain't too fresh he snatch it out of your hand like he doin' you the favor."

"Well, everybody know he a reprobate."

"Yeh, so how come he tip his hat to Sula? How come he don't cuss her?"

"Two devils."

"Exactly!"

"What'd she do when he tipped it? Smile and give him a curtsey?"

"No, and that was the other thing. It was the first time I see her look anything but hateful. Like she smellin' you with her eyes and don't like your soap. When he tipped his hat she put her hand on her throat for a minute and *cut* out. Went runnin' on up the road to home. And him still standin' there tippin' away. And—this the point I was comin' to—when I went back in the house a big sty come on my eye. And I ain't never had no sty before. Never!"

"That's 'cause you saw it."

"Exactly."

"Devil all right."

"No two ways about it," Dessie said, and she popped the rubber band off the deck of cards to settle them down for a nice long game of bid whist.

Their conviction of Sula's evil changed them in accountable yet mysterious ways. Once the source of their personal misfortune was identified, they had leave to protect and love one another. They began to cherish their husbands and wives, protect their children, repair their homes and in general band together against the devil in their midst. In their world, aberrations were as much a part of nature as grace. It was not for them to expel or annihilate it. They would no more run Sula out of town than they would kill the robins that brought her back, for in their secret awareness of Him, He was not the God of three faces they sang about. They knew quite well that He had four, and that the fourth explained Sula. They had lived with various forms of evil all their days, and it wasn't that they believed God would take care of them. It was rather that they knew God had a brother and that brother hadn't spared God's son, so why should he spare them?

There was no creature so ungodly as to make them destroy it. They could kill easily if provoked to anger, but not by design, which explained why they could not "mob kill" anyone. To do so was not only unnatural, it was undignified. The presence of evil was something to be first recognized, then dealt with, survived, outwitted, triumphed over.

Their evidence against Sula was contrived, but their conclusions about her were not. Sula was distinctly different. Eva's arrogance and Hannah's self-indulgence merged in her and, with a twist that was all her own imagination, she lived out her days exploring her own thoughts and emotions, giving them full reign, feeling no obligation to please anybody unless their pleasure pleased her. As willing to feel pain as to give pain, to feel pleasure as to give pleasure, hers was an experimental life—ever since her mother's remarks sent her flying up those stairs, ever since her one major feeling of responsibility had been exorcised on the bank of a river with a closed place in the middle. The first experience taught her there was no other that you could count on; the second that there was no self to count on either. She had no center, no speck around which to grow. In the midst of a pleasant conversation with someone she might say, "Why do you chew with your mouth open?" not because the answer interested her but because she wanted to see the person's face change rapidly. She was completely free of ambition, with no affection for money, property or things, no greed, no desire to command attention or compliments—no ego. For that reason she felt no compulsion to verify herself—be consistent with herself.

She had clung to Nel as the closest thing to both an other and a self, only to discover that she and Nel were not one and the same thing. She had no thought at all of causing Nel pain when she bedded down with Jude. They had always shared the affection of other people: compared how a boy kissed, what line he used with one and then the other. Marriage, apparently, had changed all that, but having had no intimate knowledge of marriage, having lived in a house with women who thought all men available, and selected from among them with a care only for their tastes, she was ill prepared for the possessiveness of the one person she felt close to. She knew well enough what other women said and felt, or said they felt. But she and Nel had always seen through them. They both knew that those women were not jealous of other women; that they were only afraid of losing their jobs. Afraid their husbands would discover that no uniqueness lay between their legs.

Nel was the one person who had wanted nothing from her, who had accepted all aspects of her. Now she wanted everything, and all because of *that*. Nel was the first person who had been real to her, whose name she knew, who had seen as she had the slant of life that made it possible to stretch it to its limits. Now Nel was one of *them.* One of the spiders whose only thought was the next rung of the web, who dangled in dark dry places suspended by their own spittle, more terrified of the free fall than the snake's breath below. Their eyes so intent on the wayward stranger who trips into their net, they were blind to the cobalt on their own backs, the moonshine fighting to pierce their corners. If they were touched by the snake's breath, however fatal, they were merely victims and knew how to behave in that role (just as Nel knew how to behave as the wronged wife). But the free fall, oh no, that required—demanded—invention: a thing to do with the wings, a way of holding the legs and most of all a full surrender to the downward flight if they wished to taste their tongues or stay alive. But alive was what they, and now Nel, did not want to be. Too dangerous. Now Nel belonged to the town and all of its ways. She had given herself over to them, and the flick of their tongues would drive her back into her little dry corner where she would cling to her spittle high above the breath of the snake and the fall.

It had surprised her a little and saddened her a good deal when Nel behaved the way the others would have. Nel was one of the reasons she had drifted back to Medallion, that and the boredom she found in Nashville, Detroit, New Orleans, New York, Philadelphia, Macon and San Diego. All those cities held the same people, working the same mouths, sweating the same sweat. The men who took her to one or another of those places had merged into one large personality: the same language of love, the same entertainments of love, the same cooling of love. Whenever she introduced her private thoughts into their rubbings or goings, they hooded their eyes. They taught her nothing but love tricks, shared nothing but worry, gave nothing but money. She had been looking all along for a friend, and it took her a while to discover that a lover was not a comrade and could never be—for a woman. And that no one would ever be that version of herself which she sought to reach out to and touch with an ungloved hand. There was only her own mood and whim, and if that was all there was, she decided to turn the naked hand toward it, discover it and let others become as intimate with their own selves as she was.

In a way, her strangeness, her naïveté, her craving for the other half of her equation was the consequence of an idle imagination. Had she paints, or clay, or knew the discipline of the dance, or strings; had she anything to engage her tremendous curiosity and her gift for metaphor, she might have exchanged the restlessness and preoccupation with whim for an activity that provided her with all she yearned for. And like any artist with no art form, she became dangerous.

She had lied only once in her life—to Nel about the reason for putting Eva out, and she could lie to her only because she cared about her. When she had come back home, social conversation was impossible for her because she could not lie. She could not say to those old acquaintances, "Hey, girl, you looking good," when she saw how the years had dusted their bronze with ash, the eyes that had once opened wide to the moon bent into grimy sickles of concern. The narrower their lives, the wider their hips.

Those with husbands had folded themselves into starched coffins, their sides bursting with other people's skinned dreams and bony regrets. Those without men were like sour-tipped needles featuring one constant empty eye. Those with men had had the sweetness sucked from their breath by ovens and steam kettles. Their children were like distant but exposed wounds whose aches were no less intimate because separate from their flesh. They had looked at the world and back at their children, back at the world and back again at their children, and Sula knew that one clear young eye was all that kept the knife away from the throat's curve.

She was pariah, then, and knew it. Knew that they despised her and believed that they framed their hatred as disgust for the easy way she lay with men. Which was true. She went to bed with men as frequently as she could. It was the only place where she could find what she was looking for: misery and the ability to feel deep sorrow. She had not always been aware that it was sadness that she yearned for. Lovemaking seemed to her, at first, the creation of a special kind of joy. She thought she liked the sootiness of sex and its comedy; she laughed a great deal during the raucous beginnings, and rejected those lovers who regarded sex as healthy or beautiful. Sexual aesthetics bored her. Although she did not regard sex as ugly (ugliness was boring also), she liked to think of it as wicked. But as her experiences multiplied she realized that not only was it not wicked, it was not necessary for her to conjure up the idea of wickedness in order to participate fully. During the lovemaking she found and needed to find the cutting edge. When she left off cooperating with her body and began to assert herself in the act, particles of strength gathered in her like steel shavings drawn to a spacious magnetic center, forming a tight cluster that nothing, it seemed, could break. And there was utmost irony and outrage in lying under someone, in a position of surrender, feeling her own abiding strength and limitless power. But the cluster did break, fall apart, and in her panic to hold it together she leaped from the edge into soundlessness and went down howling, howling in a stinging awareness of the endings of things: an eye of sorrow in the midst of all that hurricane rage of joy. There, in the center of that silence was not eternity but the death of time and a loneliness so profound the word itself had no meaning. For loneliness assumed the absence of other people, and the solitude she found in that desperate terrain had never admitted the possibility of other people. She wept then. Tears for the deaths of the littlest things: the castaway shoes of children; broken stems of marsh grass battered and drowned by the sea; prom photographs of dead women she never knew; wedding rings in pawnshop windows; the tidy bodies of Cornish hens in a nest of rice.

When her partner disengaged himself, she looked up at him in wonder trying to recall his name; and he looked down at her, smiling with tender understanding of the state of tearful gratitude to which he believed he had brought her. She waiting impatiently for him to turn away and settle into a wet skim of satisfaction and light disgust, leaving her to the postcoital privateness in which she met herself, welcomed herself, and joined herself in matchless harmony.

At twenty-nine she knew it would be no other way for

her, but she had not counted on the footsteps on the porch, and the beautiful black face that stared at her through the blue-glass window. Ajax.

Looking for all the world as he had seventeen years ago when he had called her pig meat. He was twenty-one then, she twelve. A universe of time between them. Now she was twenty-nine, he thirty-eight, and the lemon-yellow haunches seemed not so far away after all.

She opened the heavy door and saw him standing on the other side of the screen door with two quarts of milk tucked into his arms like marble statues. He smiled and said, "I been lookin' all over for you."

"Why?" she asked.

"To give you these," and he nodded toward one of the quarts of milk.

"I don't like milk," she said.

"But you like bottles don't you?" He held one up. "Ain't that pretty?"

And indeed it was. Hanging from his fingers, framed by a slick blue sky, it looked precious and clean and permanent. She had the distinct impression that he had done something dangerous to get them.

Sula ran her fingernails over the screen thoughtfully for a second and then, laughing, she opened the screen door.

Ajax came in and headed straight for the kitchen. Sula followed slowly. By the time she got to the door he had undone the complicated wire cap and was letting the cold milk run into his mouth.

Sula watched him—or rather the rhythm in his throat—with growing interest. When he had had enough, he poured the rest into the sink, rinsed the bottle out and presented it to her. She took the bottle with one hand and his wrist with the other and pulled him into the pantry. There was no need to go there, for not a soul was in the house, but the gesture came to Hannah's daughter naturally. There in the pantry, empty now of flour sacks, void of row upon row of canned goods, free forever of strings of tiny green peppers, holding the wet milk bottle tight in her arm she stood wide-legged against the wall and pulled from his track-lean hips all the pleasure her thighs could hold.

He came regularly then, bearing gifts: clusters of black berries still on their branches, four meal-fried porgies wrapped in a salmon-colored sheet of the Pittsburgh *Courier*, a handful of jacks, two boxes of lime Jell-Well, a hunk of ice-wagon ice, a can of Old Dutch Cleanser with the bonneted woman chasing dirt with her stick; a page of Tillie the Toiler comics, and more gleaming white bottles of milk.

Contrary to what anybody would have suspected from just seeing him lounging around the pool hall, or shooting at Mr. Finley for beating his own dog, or calling filthy compliments to passing women, Ajax was very nice to women. His women, of course, knew it, and it provoked them into murderous battles over him in the streets, brawling thick-thighed women with knives disturbed many a Friday night with their bloodletting and attracted whooping crowds. On such occasions Ajax stood, along with the crowd, and viewed the fighters with the same golden-eyed indifference with which he watched old men playing checkers. Other than his mother, who sat in her shack with six younger sons working roots, he had never met an interesting woman in his life.

His kindness to them in general was not due to a ritual of seduction (he had no need for it) but rather to the habit he acquired in dealing with his mother, who inspired thoughtfulness and generosity in all her sons.

She was an evil conjure woman, blessed with seven adoring children whose joy it was to bring her the plants, hair, underclothing, fingernail parings, white hens, blood, camphor, pictures, kerosene and footstep dust that she needed, as well as to order Van Van, High John the Conqueror, Little John to Chew, Devil's Shoe String, Chinese Wash, Mustard Seed and the Nine Herbs from Cincinnati. She knew about the weather, omens, the living, the dead, dreams and all illnesses and made a modest living with her skills. Had she any teeth or ever straightened her back, she would have been the most gorgeous thing alive, worthy of her sons' worship for her beauty alone, if not for the absolute freedom she allowed them (known in some quarters as neglect) and the weight of her hoary knowledge.

This woman Ajax loved, and after her—airplanes. There was nothing in between. And when he was not sitting enchanted listening to his mother's words, he thought of airplanes, and pilots, and the deep sky that held them both. People thought that those long trips he took to large cities in the state were for some sophisticated good times they could not imagine but only envy; actually he was leaning against the barbed wire of airports, or nosing around hangars just to hear the talk of the men who were fortunate enough to be in the trade. The rest of the time, the time he was not watching his mother's magic or thinking of airplanes, he spent in the idle pursuits of bachelors without work in small towns. He had heard all the stories about Sula, and they aroused his curiosity. Her elusiveness and indifference to established habits of behavior reminded him of his mother, who was as stubborn in her pursuits of the occult as the women of Greater Saint Matthew's were in the search for redeeming grace. So when his curiosity was high enough he picked two bottles of milk off the porch of some white family and went to see her, suspecting that this was perhaps the only other woman he knew whose life was her own, who could deal with life efficiently, and who was not interested in nailing him.

Sula, too, was curious. She knew nothing about him except the word he had called out to her years ago and the feeling he had excited in her then. She had grown quite accustomed to the clichés of other people's lives as well as her own increasing dissatisfaction with Medallion. If she could have thought of a place to go, she probably would have left, but that was before Ajax looked at her through the blue glass and held the milk aloft like a trophy.

But it was not the presents that made her wrap him up in her thighs. They were charming, of course (especially the jar of butterflies he let loose in the bedroom), but her real pleasure was the fact that he talked to her. They had genuine conversations. He did not speak down to her or at her, nor content himself with puerile questions about her life or monologues of his own activities. Thinking she was possibly brilliant, like his mother, he seemed to expect brilliance from her, and she delivered. And in all of it, he listened more than he spoke. His clear comfort at being in her presence, his lazy willingness to tell her all about fixes and the powers of plants, his refusal to baby or protect her, his assumption that she was both tough and wise—all of that coupled with a wide generosity of spirit only occasionally erupting into vengeance sustained Sula's interest and enthusiasm.

His idea of bliss (on earth as opposed to bliss in the sky) was a long bath in piping-hot water—his head on the cool white rim, his eyes closed in reverie.

"Soaking in hot water give you a bad back." Sula stood in the doorway looking at his knees glistening just at the surface of the soap-gray water.

"Soaking in Sula give me a bad back."

"Worth it?"

"Don't know yet. Go 'way."

"Airplanes?"

"Airplanes."

"Lindbergh know about you?"

"Go 'way."

She went and waited for him in Eva's high bed, her head turned to the boarded-up window. She was smiling, thinking how like Jude's was his craving to do the white man's work, when two deweys came in with their beautiful teeth and said, "We sick."

Sula turned her head slowly and murmured, "Get well."

"We need some medicine."

"Look in the bathroom."

"Ajax in there."

"Then wait."

"We sick now."

Sula leaned over the bed, picked up a shoe and threw it at them.

"Cocksucker!" they screamed, and she leaped out of the bed naked as a yard dog. She caught the redheaded dewey by his shirt and held him by the heels over the banister until he wet his pants. The other dewey was joined by the third, and they delved into their pockets for stones, which they threw at her. Sula, ducking and tottering with laughter, carried the wet dewey to the bedroom and when the other two followed her, deprived of all weapons except their teeth, Sula had dropped the first dewey on the bed and was fishing in her purse. She gave each of them a dollar bill which they snatched and then scooted off down the stairs to Dick's to buy the catarrh remedy they loved to drink.

Ajax came sopping wet into the room and lay down on the bed to let the air dry him. They were both still for a long time until he reached out and touched her arm.

He liked for her to mount him so he could see her towering above him and call soft obscenities up into her face. As she rocked there, swayed there, like a Georgia pine on its knees, high above the slipping, falling smile, high above the golden eyes and the velvet helmet of hair, rocking, swaying, she focused her thoughts to bar the creeping disorder that was flooding her hips. She looked down, down from what seemed an awful height at the head of the man whose lemon-yellow gabardines had been the first sexual excitement she'd known. Letting her thoughts dwell on his face in order to confine, for just a while longer, the drift of her flesh toward the high silence of orgasm.

If I take a chamois and rub real hard on the bone, right on the ledge of your cheek bone, some of the black will disappear. It will flake away into the chamois and underneath there will be gold leaf. I can see it shining through the black. I know it is there ...

How high she was over his wand-lean body, how slippery was his sliding sliding smile.

And if I take a nail file or even Eva's old paring knife—that will do—and scrape away at the gold, it will fall away and there will be alabaster. The alabaster is what gives your face its planes, its curves. That is why your mouth smiling does not reach your eyes. Alabaster is giving it a gravity that resists a total smile.

The height and the swaying dizzied her, so she bent down and let her breasts graze his chest.

Then I can take a chisel and small tap hammer and tap away at the alabaster. It will crack then like ice under the pick, and through the breaks I will see the loam, fertile, free of pebbles and twigs. For it is the loam that is giving you that smell.

She slipped her hands under his armpits, for it seemed as though she would not be able to dam the spread of weakness she felt under her skin without holding on to something.

I will put my hand deep into your soil, lift it, sift it with my fingers, feel its warm surface and dewy chill below.

She put her head under his chin with no hope in the world of keeping anything at all at bay.

I will water your soil, keep it rich and moist. But how much? How much water to keep the loam moist? And how much loam will I need to keep my water still? And when do the two make mud?

He swallowed her mouth just as her thighs had swallowed his genitals, and the house was very, very quiet.

⊙ ⊙ ⊙

Sula began to discover what possession was. Not love, perhaps, but possession or at least the desire for it. She was astounded by so new and alien a feeling. First there was the morning of the night before when she actually wondered if Ajax would come by that day. Then there was an afternoon when she stood before the mirror finger-tracing the laugh lines around her mouth and trying to decide whether she was good-looking or not. She ended this deep perusal by tying a green ribbon in her hair. The green silk made a rippling whisper as she slid it into her hair—a whisper that could easily have been Hannah's chuckle, a soft slow nasal hiss she used to emit when something amused her. Like women sitting for two hours under the marcelling irons only to wonder two days later how soon they would need another appointment. The ribbon-tying was followed by other activity, and when Ajax came that evening, bringing her a reed whistle he had carved that morning, not only was the green ribbon still in her hair, but the bathroom was gleaming, the bed was made, and the table was set for two.

He gave her the reed whistle, unlaced his shoes and sat in the rocking chair in the kitchen.

Sula walked toward him and kissed his mouth. He ran his fingers along the nape of her neck.

"I bet you ain't even missed Tar Baby, have you?" he asked.

"Missed? No. Where is he?"

Ajax smiled at her delicious indifference. "Jail."

"Since when?"

"Last Saturday."

"Picked up for drunk?"

"Little bit more than that," he answered and went ahead to tell her about his own involvement in another of Tar Baby's misfortunes.

On Saturday afternoon Tar Baby had stumbled drunk into traffic on the New River Road. A woman driver swerved to avoid him and hit another car. When the police came, they recognized the woman as the mayor's niece and arrested Tar Baby. Later, after the word got out, Ajax and two other men went to the station to see about him. At first they wouldn't let them in. But they relented after Ajax and the other two just stood around for one hour and a half and repeated their request at regular intervals. When they finally got permission to go in and looked in at him in the cell, he was twisted up in a corner badly beaten and dressed in nothing but extremely soiled underwear. Ajax and the other men asked the officer why Tar Baby couldn't have back his clothes. "It ain't right," they said, "to let a grown man lay around in his own shit."

The policeman, obviously in agreement with Eva, who had always maintained that Tar Baby was white, said that if the prisoner didn't like to live in shit, he should come down out of those hills, and live like a decent white man.

More words were exchanged, hot words and dark, and the whole thing ended with the arraignment of the three black men, and an appointment to appear in civil court Thursday next.

Ajax didn't seem too bothered by any of it. More annoyed and inconvenienced than anything else. He had had several messes with the police, mostly in gambling raids, and regarded them as the natural hazards of Negro life.

But Sula, the green ribbon shining in her hair, was flooded with an awareness of the impact of the outside world on Ajax. She stood up and arranged herself on the arm of the rocking chair. Putting her fingers deep into the velvet of his hair, she murmured, "Come on. Lean on me."

Ajax blinked. Then he looked swiftly into her face. In her words, in her voice, was a sound he knew well. For the first time he saw the green ribbon. He looked around and saw the gleaming kitchen and the table set for two and detected the scent of the nest. Every hackle on his body rose, and he knew that very soon she would, like all of her sisters before her, put to him the death-knell question "Where you been?" His eyes dimmed with a mild and momentary regret.

He stood and mounted the stairs with her and entered the spotless bathroom where the dust had been swept from underneath the claw-foot tub. He was trying to remember the date of the air show in Dayton. As he came into the bedroom, he saw Sula lying on fresh white sheets, wrapped in the deadly odor of freshly applied cologne.

He dragged her under him and made love to her with the steadiness and the intensity of a man about to leave for Dayton.

Every now and then she looked around for tangible evidence of his having ever been there. Where were the butterflies? the blueberries? the whistling reed? She could find nothing, for he had left nothing but his stunning absence. An absence so decorative, so ornate, it was difficult for her to understand how she had ever endured, without falling dead or being consumed, his magnificent presence.

The mirror by the door was not a mirror by the door, it was an altar where he stood for only a moment to put on his cap before going out. The red rocking chair was a rocking of his own hips as he sat in the kitchen. Still, there was nothing of his—his own—that she could find. It was as if she were afraid she had hallucinated him and needed proof to the contrary. His absence was everywhere, stinging everything, giving the furnishings primary colors, sharp outlines to the corners of rooms and gold light to the dust collecting on table tops. When he was there he pulled everything toward himself. Not only her eyes and all her senses but also inanimate things seemed to exist because of him, backdrops to his presence. Now that he had gone, these things, so long subdued by his presence, were glamorized in his wake.

Then one day, burrowing in a dresser drawer, she found what she had been looking for: proof that he had been there, his driver's license. It contained just what she needed for verification—his vital statistics: Born 1901, height 5′11″, weight 152 lbs., eyes brown, hair black, color black. Oh yes, skin black. Very black. So black that only a steady careful rubbing with steel wool would remove it, and as it was removed there was the glint of gold leaf and under the gold leaf the cold alabaster and deep, deep down under the cold alabaster more black only this time the black of warm loam.

But what was this? Albert Jacks? His name was Albert Jacks? A. Jacks. She had thought it was Ajax. All those years. Even from the time she walked by the pool hall and looked away from him sitting astride a wooden chair, looked away to keep from seeing the wide space of intolerable orderliness between his legs; the openness that held no sign, no sign at all, of the animal that lurked in his trousers; looked away from the insolent nostrils and the smile that kept slipping and falling, falling, falling so she wanted to reach out with her hand to catch it before it fell to the pavement and was sullied by the cigarette butts and bottle caps and spittle at his feet and the feet of other men who sat or stood around outside the pool hall, calling, singing out to her and Nel and grown women too with lyrics like *pig meat* and *brown sugar* and *jailbait* and *O Lord, what have I done to deserve the wrath*, and *Take me, Jesus, I have seen the promised land*, and *Do, Lord, remember me* in voices mellowed by hopeless passion into gentleness. Even then, when she and Nel were trying hard not to dream of him and not to think of him when they touched the softness in their underwear or undid their braids as soon as they left home to let the hair bump and wave around their ears, or wrapped the cotton binding around their chests so the nipples would not break through their blouses and give him cause to smile his slipping, falling smile, which brought the blood rushing to their skin. And even later, when for the first time in her life she had lain in bed with a man and said his name involuntarily or said it truly meaning *him*, the name she was screaming and saying was not his at all.

Sula stood with a worn slip of paper in her fingers and said aloud to no one, "I didn't even know his name. And if I didn't know his name, then there is nothing I did know and I have known nothing ever at all since the one thing I wanted was to know his name so how could he help but leave me since he was making love to a woman who didn't even know his name.

"When I was a little girl the heads of my paper dolls came off, and it was a long time before I discovered that my own head would not fall off if I bent my neck. I used to walk around holding it very stiff because I thought a strong wind or a heavy push would snap my neck. Nel was the one who told me the truth. But she was wrong. I did not hold my head stiff enough when I met him and so I lost it just like the dolls.

"It's just as well he left. Soon I would have torn the flesh from his face just to see if I was right about the gold and nobody would have understood that kind of curiosity. They would have believed that I wanted to hurt him just like the little boy who fell down the steps and broke his leg and the people think I pushed him just because I looked at it."

Holding the driver's license she crawled into bed and fell into a sleep full of dreams of cobalt blue.

When she awoke, there was a melody in her head she could not identify or recall ever hearing before. "Perhaps I made it up," she thought. Then it came to her—the name of the song and all its lyrics just as she had heard it many times before. She sat on the edge of the bed thinking, "There aren't any more new songs and I have sung all the ones there are. I have sung them all. I have sung all the songs there are." She lay down again on the bed and sang a little wandering tune made up of the words *I have sung all the songs all the songs I have sung all the songs there are* until, touched by her own lullaby, she grew drowsy, and in the hollow of near-sleep she tasted the acridness of gold, left the chill of alabaster and smelled the dark, sweet stench of loam.

1940

"I heard you was sick. Anything I can do for you?"

She had practiced not just the words but the tone, the pitch of her voice. It should be calm, matter-of-fact, but strong in sympathy—for the illness though, not for the patient.

The sound of her voice as she heard it in her head betrayed no curiosity, no pride, just the inflection of any good woman come to see about a sick person who, incidentally, had such visits from nobody else.

For the first time in three years she would be looking at the stemmed rose that hung over the eye of her enemy. Moreover, she would be doing it with the taste of Jude's exit in her mouth, with the resentment and shame that even yet pressed for release in her stomach. She would be facing the black rose that Jude had kissed and looking at the nostrils of the woman who had twisted her love for her own children into something so thick and monstrous she was afraid to show it lest it break loose and smother them with its heavy paw. A cumbersome bear-love that, given any rein, would suck their breath away in its crying need for honey.

Because Jude's leaving was so complete, the full responsibility of the household was Nel's. There were no more fifty dollars in brown envelopes to count on, so she took to cleaning rather than fret away the tiny seaman's pension her parents lived on. And just this past year she got a better job working as a chambermaid in the same hotel Jude had worked in. The tips were only fair, but the hours were good—she was home when the children got out of school.

At thirty her hot brown eyes had turned to agate, and her skin had taken on the sheen of maple struck down, split and sanded at the height of its green. Virtue, bleak and drawn, was her only mooring. It brought her to Number 7 Carpenter's Road and the door with the blue glass; it helped her to resist scratching the screen as in days gone by; it hid from her the true motives for her charity, and, finally, it gave her voice the timbre she wanted it to have: free of delight or a lip-smacking "I told you so" with which the news of Sula's illness had been received up in the Bottom—free of the least hint of retribution.

Now she stood in Eva's old bedroom, looking down at that dark rose, aware of the knife-thin arms sliding back and forth over the quilt and the boarded-up window Eva had jumped out of.

Sula looked up and without a second's pause followed Nel's example of leaving out the greeting when she spoke.

"As a matter of fact, there is. I got a prescription. Nathan usually goes for me but he . . . school don't let out till three. Could you run it over to the drugstore?"

"Where is it?" Nel was glad to have a concrete errand. Conversation would be difficult. (Trust Sula to pick up a relationship exactly where it lay.)

"Look in my bag. No. Over there."

Nel walked to the dresser and opened the purse with the beaded clasp. She saw only a watch and the folded prescription down inside. No wallet, no change purse. She turned to Sula: "Where's your . . ."

But Sula was looking at the boarded-up window. Something in her eye right there in the corner stopped Nel from completing her question. That and the slight flare of the nostrils—a shadow of a snarl. Nel took the piece of paper and picked up her own purse, saying, "OK. I'll be right back."

As soon as the door was shut, Sula breathed through her mouth. While Nel was in the room the pain had increased. Now that this new pain killer, the one she had been holding in reserve, was on the way her misery was manageable. She let a piece of her mind lay on Nel. It was funny, sending Nel off to that drugstore right away like that, after she had not seen her to speak to for years. The drugstore was where Edna Finch's Mellow House used to be years back when they were girls. Where they used to go, the two of them, hand in hand, for the 18-cent ice-cream sundaes, past the Time and a Half Pool Hall, where the sprawling men said "pig meat," and they sat in that cool room with the marble-top tables and ate the first ice-cream sundaes of their lives. Now Nel was going back there alone and Sula was waiting for the medicine the doctor said not to take until the pain got really bad. And she supposed "really bad" was now. Although you could never tell. She wondered for an instant what Nellie wanted; why she had come. Did she want to gloat? Make up? Following this line of thought required more concentration than she could muster. Pain was greedy; it demanded all of her attention. But it was good that this new medicine, the reserve, would be brought to her by her old friend. Nel, she remembered, always thrived on a crisis. The closed place in the water; Hannah's funeral. Nel was the best. When Sula imitated her, or tried to, those long years ago, it always ended up in some action noteworthy not for its coolness but mostly for its being bizarre. The one time she tried to protect Nel, she had cut off her own finger tip and earned not Nel's gratitude but her disgust. From then on she had let her emotions dictate her behavior.

She could hear Nel's footsteps long before she opened the door and put the medicine on the table near the bed.

As Sula poured the liquid into a sticky spoon, Nel began the sickroom conversation.

"You look fine, Sula."

"You lying, Nellie. I look bad." She gulped the medicine.

"No. I haven't seen you for a long time, but you look . . ."

"You don't have to do that, Nellie. It's going to be all right."

"What ails you? Have they said?"

Sula licked the corners of her lips. "You want to talk about that?"

Nel smiled, slightly, at the bluntness she had forgotten. "No. No, I don't, but you sure you should be staying up here alone?"

"Nathan comes by. The deweys sometimes, and Tar Baby . . ."

"That ain't help, Sula. You need to be with somebody grown. Somebody who can . . ."

"I'd rather be here, Nellie."

"You know you don't have to be proud with me."

"Proud?" Sula's laughter broke through the phlegm. "What you talking about? I like my own dirt, Nellie. I'm not proud. You sure have forgotten me."

"Maybe. Maybe not. But you a woman and you alone."

"And you? Ain't you alone?"

"I'm not sick. I work."

"Yes. Of course you do. Work's good for you, Nellie. It don't do nothing for me."

"You never *had* to."

"I never would."

"There's something to say for it, Sula. 'Specially if you don't want people to have to do for you."

"Neither one, Nellie. Neither one."

"You can't have it all, Sula." Nel was getting exasperated with her arrogance, with her lying at death's door still smart-talking.

"Why? I can do it all, why can't I have it all?"

"You *can't* do it all. You a woman and a colored woman at that. You can't act like a man. You can't be walking around all independent-like, doing whatever you like, taking what you want, leaving what you don't."

"You repeating yourself."

"How repeating myself?"

"You say I'm a woman and colored. Ain't that the same as being a man?"

"I don't think so and you wouldn't either if you had children."

"Then I really would act like what you call a man. Every man I ever knew left his children."

"Some were taken."

"Wrong, Nellie. The word is 'left.' "

"You still going to know everything, ain't you?"

"I don't know everything, I just do everything."

"Well, you don't do what I do."

"You think I don't know what your life is like just because I ain't living it? I know what every colored woman in this country is doing."

"What's that?"

"Dying. Just like me. But the difference is they dying like a stump. Me, I'm going down like one of those redwoods. I sure did live in this world."

"Really? What have you got to show for it?"

"Show? To who? Girl, I got my mind. And what goes on in it. Which is to say, I got me."

"Lonely, ain't it?"

"Yes. But my lonely is *mine*. Now your lonely is somebody else's. Made by somebody else and handed to you. Ain't that something? A secondhand lonely."

Nel sat back on the little wooden chair. Anger skipped but she realized that Sula was probably just showing off. No telling what shape she was really in, but there was no point in saying anything other than what was the truth. "I always understood how you could take a man. Now I understand why you can't keep none."

"Is that what I'm supposed to do? Spend my life keeping a man?"

"They worth keeping, Sula."

"They ain't worth more than me. And besides, I never

loved no man because he was worth it. Worth didn't have nothing to do with it."

"What did?"

"My mind did. That's all."

"Well I guess that's it. You own the world and the rest of us is renting. You ride the pony and we shovel the shit. I didn't come up here for this kind of talk, Sula . . ."

"No?"

"No. I come to see about you. But now that you opened it up, I may as well close it." Nel's fingers closed around the brass rail of the bed. Now she would ask her. "How come you did it, Sula?"

There was a silence but Nel felt no obligation to fill it.

Sula stirred a little under the covers. She looked bored as she sucked her teeth. "Well, there was this space in front of me, behind me, in my head. Some space. And Jude filled it up. That's all. He just filled up the space."

"You mean you didn't even love him?" The feel of the brass was in Nel's mouth. "It wasn't even loving him?"

Sula looked toward the boarded-up window again. Her eyes fluttered as if she were about to fall off into sleep.

"But . . ." Nel held her stomach in. "But what about me? What about me? Why didn't you think about me? Didn't I count? I never hurt you. What did you take him for if you didn't love him and why didn't you think about me?" And then, "I was good to you, Sula, why don't that matter?"

Sula turned her head away from the boarded window. Her voice was quiet and the stemmed rose over her eye was very dark. "It matters, Nel, but only to you. Not to anybody else. Being good to somebody is just like being mean to somebody. Risky. You don't get nothing for it."

Nel took her hands from the brass railing. She was annoyed with herself. Finally when she had gotten the nerve to ask the question, the right question, it made no difference. Sula couldn't give her a sensible answer because she didn't know. Would be, in fact, the last to know. Talking to her about right and wrong was like talking to the deweys. She picked at the fringe on Sula's bedspread and said softly, "We were friends."

"Oh, yes. Good friends," Sula said.

"And you didn't love me enough to leave him alone. To let him love me. You had to take him away."

"What you mean take him away? I didn't kill him, I just fucked him. If we were such good friends, how come you couldn't get over it?"

"You laying there in that bed without a dime or a friend to your name having done all the dirt you did in this town and you still expect folks to love you?"

Sula raised herself up on her elbows. Her face glistened with the dew of fever. She opened her mouth as though to say something, then fell back on the pillows and sighed. "Oh, they'll love me all right. It will take time, but they'll love me." The sound of her voice was as soft and distant as the look in her eyes. "After all the old women have lain with the teen-agers; when all the young girls have slept with their old drunken uncles; after all the black men fuck all the white ones; when all the white women kiss all the black ones; when the guards have raped all the jailbirds and after all the whores make love to their grannies; after all the faggots get their mothers' trim; when Lindbergh sleeps with Bessie Smith and Norma Shearer makes it with Stepin Fetchit; after all the dogs have fucked all the cats and every weathervane on every barn flies off the roof to mount the hogs . . . then there'll be a little love left over for me. And I know just what it will feel like."

She closed her eyes then and thought of the wind pressing her dress between her legs as she ran up the bank of the river to four leaf-locked trees and the digging of holes in the earth.

Embarrassed, irritable and a little bit ashamed, Nel rose to go. "Goodbye, Sula. I don't reckon I'll be back."

She opened the door and heard Sula's low whisper. "Hey, girl." Nel paused and turned her head but not enough to see her.

"How you know?" Sula asked.

"Know what?" Nel still wouldn't look at her.

"About who was good. How you know it was you?"

"What you mean?"

"I mean maybe it wasn't you. Maybe it was me."

Nel took two steps out the door and closed it behind her. She walked down the hall and down the four flights of steps. The house billowed around her light then dark, full of presences without sounds. The deweys, Tar Baby, the newly married couples, Mr. Buckland Reed, Patsy, Valentine, and the beautiful Hannah Peace. Where were they? Eva out at the old folks' home, the deweys living anywhere, Tar Baby steeped in wine, and Sula upstairs in Eva's bed with a boarded-up window and an empty pocketbook on the dresser.

• • •

When Nel closed the door, Sula reached for more medicine. Then she turned the pillow over to its cool side and thought about her old friend. "So she will walk on down that road, her back so straight in that old green coat, the strap of her handbag pushed back all the way to the elbow, thinking how much I have cost her and never remember the days when we were two throats and one eye and we had no price."

Pictures drifted through her head as lightly as dandelion spores: the blue eagle that swallowed the E of the Sherman's Mellowe wine that Tar Baby drank; the pink underlid of Hannah's eye as she probed for a fleck of coal dust or a lash. She thought of looking out of the windows of all those trains and buses, looking at the feet and backs of all those people. Nothing was ever different. They were all the same. All of the words and all of the smiles, every tear and every gag just something to do.

"That's the same sun I looked at when I was twelve, the same pear trees. If I live a hundred years my urine will flow the same way, my armpits and breath will smell the same. My hair will grow from the same holes. I didn't mean anything. I never meant anything. I stood there watching her burn and was thrilled. I wanted her to keep on jerking like that, to keep on dancing."

Then she had the dream again. The Clabber Girl Baking Powder lady was smiling and beckoning to her, one hand under her apron. When Sula came near she disintegrated into white dust, which Sula was hurriedly trying to stuff into the pockets of her blue-flannel housecoat. The disintegration was awful to see, but worse was the feel of the powder—its starchy slipperiness as she tried to collect it by handfuls. The more she scooped, the more it billowed. At last it covered her, filled her eyes, her nose, her throat, and she woke gagging and overwhelmed with the smell of smoke.

Pain took hold. First a fluttering as of doves in her stomach, then a kind of burning, followed by a spread of thin wires to other parts of her body. Once the wires of liquid pain were in place, they jelled and began to throb. She tried concentrating on the throbs, identifying them as waves, hammer strokes, razor edges or small explosions. Soon even the variety of the pain bored her and there was nothing to do, for it was joined by fatigue so great she could not make a fist or fight the taste of oil at the back of her tongue.

Several times she tried to cry out, but the fatigue barely let her open her lips, let alone take the deep breath necessary to scream. So she lay there wondering how soon she would gather enough strength to lift her arm and push the rough quilt away from her chin and whether she should turn her cheek to the cooler side of the pillow now or wait till her face was thoroughly soaked and the move would be more refreshing. But she was reluctant to move her face for another reason. If she turned her head, she would not be able to see the boarded-up window Eva jumped out of. And looking at those four wooden planks with the steel rod slanting across them was the only peace she had. The sealed window soothed her with its sturdy termination, its unassailable finality. It was as though for the first time she was completely alone—where she had always wanted to be—free of the possibility of distraction. It would be here, only here, held by this blind window high above the elm tree, that she might draw her legs up to her chest, close her eyes, put her thumb in her mouth and float over and down the tunnels, just missing the dark walls, down, down until she met a rain scent and would know the water was near, and she would curl into its heavy softness and it would envelop her, carry her, and wash her tired flesh always. Always. Who said that? She tried hard to think. Who was it that had promised her a sleep of water always? The effort to recall was too great; it loosened a knot in her chest that turned her thoughts again to the pain.

While in this state of weary anticipation, she noticed that she was not breathing, that her heart had stopped completely. A crease of fear touched her breast, for any second there was sure to be a violent explosion in her brain, a gasping for breath. Then she realized, or rather she sensed, that there was not going to be any pain. She was not breathing because she didn't have to. Her body did not need oxygen. She was dead.

Sula felt her face smiling. "Well, I'll be damned," she thought, "it didn't even hurt. Wait'll I tell Nel."

1941

The death of Sula Peace was the best news folks up in the Bottom had had since the promise of work at the tunnel. Of the few who were not afraid to witness the burial of a witch and who had gone to the cemetery, some had come just to verify her being put away but stayed to sing "Shall We Gather at the River" for politeness' sake, quite unaware of the bleak promise of their song. Others came to see that nothing went awry, that the shallow-minded and small-hearted kept their meanness at bay, and that the entire event be characterized by that abiding gentleness of spirit to which they themselves had arrived by the simple determination not to let anything—anything at all: not failed crops, not rednecks, lost jobs, sick children, rotten potatoes, broken pipes, bug-ridden flour, third-class coal, educated social workers, thieving insurance men, garlic-ridden hunkies, corrupt Catholics, racist Protestants, cowardly Jews, slaveholding Moslems, jackleg nigger preachers, squeamish Chinamen, cholera, dropsy or the Black Plague, let alone a strange woman—keep them from their God.

In any case, both the raw-spirited and the gentle who came—not to the white funeral parlor but to the colored part of the Beechnut Cemetery—felt that either *because*

Sula was dead or just *after* she was dead a brighter day was dawning. There were signs. The rumor that the tunnel spanning the river would use Negro workers became an announcement. Planned, abandoned and replanned for years, this project had finally begun in 1937. For three years there were rumors that blacks would work it, and hope was high in spite of the fact that the River Road leading to the tunnel had encouraged similar hopes in 1927 but had ended up being built entirely by white labor—hillbillies and immigrants taking even the lowest jobs. But the tunnel itself was another matter. The craft work—no, they would not get that. But it was a major job, and the government seemed to favor opening up employment to black workers. It meant black men would not have to sweep Medallion to eat, or leave the town altogether for the steel mills in Akron and along Lake Erie.

The second sign was the construction begun on an old people's home. True, it was more renovation than construction, but the blacks were free, or so it was said, to occupy it. Some said that the very transfer of Eva from the ramshackle house that passed for a colored women's nursing home to the bright new one was a clear sign of the mystery of God's ways, His mighty thumb having been seen at Sula's throat.

So it was with a strong sense of hope that the people in the Bottom watched October close.

Then Medallion turned silver. It seemed sudden, but actually there had been days and days of no snow—just frost—when, late one afternoon, a rain fell and froze.

Way down Carpenter's Road, where the concrete sidewalks started, children hurried to the sliding places before shopkeepers and old women sprinkled stove ashes, like ancient onyx, onto the new-minted silver. They hugged trees simply to hold for a moment all that life and largeness stilled in glass, and gazed at the sun pressed against the gray sky like a worn doubloon, wondering all the while if the world were coming to an end. Grass stood blade by blade, shocked into separateness by an ice that held for days.

Late-harvesting things were ruined, of course, and fowl died of both chill and rage. Cider turned to ice and split the jugs, forcing the men to drink their cane liquor too soon. It was better down in the valley, since, as always, the hills protected it, but up in the Bottom black folks suffered heavily in their thin houses and thinner clothes. The ice-cold wind bled what little heat they had through windowpanes and ill-fitting doors. For days on end they were virtually housebound, venturing out only to coalbins or right next door for the trading of vital foodstuffs. Never to the stores. No deliveries were being made anyway, and when they were, the items were saved for better-paying white customers. Women could not make it down the icy slopes and therefore missed days of wages they sorely needed.

The consequence of all that ice was a wretched Thanksgiving of tiny tough birds, heavy pork cakes, and pithy sweet potatoes. By the time the ice began to melt and the first barge was seen shuddering through the ice skim on the river, everybody under fifteen had croup, or scarlet fever, and those over had chilblains, rheumatism, pleurisy, earaches and a world of other ailments.

Still it was not those illnesses or even the ice that marked the beginning of the trouble, that self-fulfilled prophecy that Shadrack carried on his tongue. As soon as the silvering began, long before the cider cracked the jugs, there was something wrong. A falling away, a dislocation was taking place. Hard on the heels of the general relief that Sula's death brought a restless irritability took hold. Teapot, for example, went into the kitchen and asked his mother for some sugar-butter-bread. She got up to fix it and found that she had no butter, only oleomargarine. Too tired to mix the saffron-colored powder into the hard cake of oleo, she simply smeared the white stuff on the bread and sprinkled the sugar over it. Teapot tasted the difference and refused to eat it. This keenest of insults that a mother can feel, the rejection by a child of her food, bent her into fury and she beat him as she had not done since Sula knocked him down the steps. She was not alone. Other mothers who had defended their children from Sula's malevolence (or who had defended their positions as mothers from Sula's scorn for the role) now had nothing to rub up against. The tension was gone and so was the reason for the effort they had made. Without her mockery, affection for others sank into flaccid disrepair. Daughters who had complained bitterly about the responsibilities of taking care of their aged mothers-in-law had altered when Sula locked Eva away, and they began cleaning those old women's spittoons without a murmur. Now that Sula was dead and done with, they returned to a steeping resentment of the burdens of old people. Wives uncoddled their husbands; there seemed no further need to reinforce their vanity. And even those Negroes who had moved down from Canada to Medallion, who remarked every chance they got that they had never been slaves, felt a loosening of the reactionary compassion for Southern-born blacks Sula had inspired in them. They returned to their original claims of superiority.

The normal meanness that the winter brought was compounded by the small-spiritedness that hunger and scarlet fever produced. Even a definite and witnessed interview of four colored men (and the promise of more in the spring) at the tunnel site could not break the cold vise of that lean and bitter year's end.

Christmas came one morning and haggled everybody's nerves like a dull ax—too shabby to cut clean but too heavy to ignore. The children lay wall-eyed on creaking beds or pallets near the stove, sucking peppermint and oranges in between coughs while their mothers stomped the floors in rage at the cakes that did not rise because the stove fire had been so stingy; at the curled bodies of men who chose to sleep the day away rather than face the silence made by the absence of Lionel trains, drums, crybaby dolls and rocking horses. Teen-agers sneaked into the Elmira Theater in the afternoon and let Tex Ritter free them from the recollection of their fathers' shoes, yawning in impotence under the bed. Some of them had a bottle of wine, which they drank at the feet of the glittering Mr. Ritter, making such a ruckus the manager had to put them out. The white people who came with Christmas bags of rock candy and old clothes were hard put to get a *Yes'm, thank you,* out of those sullen mouths.

Just as the ice lingered in October, so did the phlegm of December—which explained the enormous relief brought on by the first three days of 1941. It was as though the season had exhausted itself, for on January first the temperature shot up to sixty-one degrees and slushed the whiteness overnight. On January second drab patches of grass could be seen in the fields. On January third the sun came out—and so did Shadrack with his rope, his bell and his childish dirge.

He had spent the night before watching a tiny moon. The people, the voices that kept him company, were with him less and less. Now there were long periods when he heard nothing except the wind in the trees and the plop of buckeyes on the earth. In the winter, when the fish were too hard to get to, he did picking-up jobs for small businessmen (nobody would have him in or even near their homes), and thereby continued to have enough money for liquor. Yet the drunk times were becoming deeper but more seldom. It was as though he no longer needed to drink to forget whatever it was he could not remember. Now he could not remember that he had ever forgotten anything. Perhaps that was why for the first time after that cold day in France he was beginning to miss the presence of other people. Shadrack had improved enough to feel lonely. If he was lonely before, he didn't know it because the noise he kept up, the roaring, the busyness, protected him from knowing it. Now the compulsion to activity, to filling up the time when he was not happily fishing on the riverbank, had dwindled. He sometimes fell asleep before he got drunk; sometimes spent whole days looking at the river and the sky; and more and more he relinquished the military habits of cleanliness in his shack. Once a bird flew into his door—one of the robins during the time there was a plague of them. It stayed, looking for an exit, for the better part of an hour. When the bird found the window and flew away, Shadrack was grieved and actually waited and watched for its return. During those days of waiting, he did not make his bed, or sweep, or shake out the little rag-braid rug, and almost forgot to slash with his fish knife the passing day on his calendar. When he did return to housekeeping, it was not with the precision he had always insisted upon. The messier his house got, the lonelier he felt, and it was harder and harder to conjure up sergeants, and orderlies, and invading armies; harder and harder to hear the gunfire and keep the platoon marching in time. More frequently now he looked at and fondled the one piece of evidence that he once had a visitor in his house: a child's purple-and-white belt. The one the little girl left behind when she came to see him. Shadrack remembered the scene clearly. He had stepped into the door and there was a tear-stained face turning, turning toward him; eyes hurt and wondering; mouth parted in an effort to ask a question. She had wanted something—from him. Not fish, not work, but something only he could give. She had a tadpole over her eye (that was how he knew she was a friend—she had the mark of the fish he loved), and one of her braids had come undone. But when he looked at her face he had seen also the skull beneath, and thinking she saw it too—knew it was there and was afraid—he tried to think of something to say to comfort her, something to stop the hurt from spilling out of her eyes. So he had said "always," so she would not have to be afraid of the change—the falling away of skin, the drip and slide of blood, and the exposure of bone underneath. He had said "always" to convince her, assure her, of permanency.

It worked, for when he said it her face lit up and the hurt did leave. She ran then, carrying his knowledge, but her belt fell off and he kept it as a memento. It hung on a nail near his bed—unfrayed, unsullied after all those years, with only the permanent bend in the fabric made by its long life on a nail. It was pleasant living with that sign of a visitor, his only one. And after a while he was able to connect the belt with the face, the tadpole-over-the-eye-face that he sometimes saw up in the Bottom. His visitor, his company, his guest, his social life, his woman, his daughter, his friend—they all hung there on a nail near his bed.

Now he stared at the tiny moon floating high over the ice-choked river. His loneliness had dropped down somewhere around his ankles. Some other feeling possessed him. A feeling that touched his eyes and made him blink. He had seen her again months? weeks? ago. Raking leaves for Mr. Hodges, he had gone into the cellar for two bushel baskets to put them in. In the hallway he passed an open door leading to a small room. She lay on a table there. It was surely the same one. The same little-girl face, same tadpole over the eye. So he had been wrong. Terribly wrong. No "always" at all. Another dying away of someone whose face he knew.

It was then he began to suspect that all those years of rope hauling and bell ringing were never going to do any good. He might as well sit forever on his riverbank and stare out of the window at the moon.

By his day-slashed calendar he knew that tomorrow was the day. And for the first time he did not want to go. He wanted to stay with the purple-and-white belt. Not go. Not go.

Still, when the day broke in an incredible splash of sun, he gathered his things. In the early part of the afternoon, drenched in sunlight and certain that this would be the last time he would invite them to end their lives neatly and sweetly, he walked over the rickety bridge and on into the Bottom. But it was not heartfelt this time, not loving this time, for he no longer cared whether he helped them or not. His rope was improperly tied; his bell had a tinny unimpassioned sound. His visitor was dead and would come no more.

Years later people would quarrel about who had been the first to go. Most folks said it was the deweys, but one or two knew better, knew that Dessie and Ivy had been first. Said that Dessie had opened her door first and stood there shielding her eyes from the sun while watching Shadrack coming down the road. She laughed.

Maybe the sun; maybe the clots of green showing in the hills promising so much; maybe the contrast between Shadrack's doomy, gloomy bell glinting in all that sweet sunshine. Maybe just a brief moment, for once, of not feeling fear, of looking at death in the sunshine and being unafraid. She laughed.

Upstairs, Ivy heard her and looked to see what caused the thick music that rocked her neighbor's breasts. Then Ivy laughed too. Like the scarlet fever that had touched everybody and worn them down to gristle, their laughter infected Carpenter's Road. Soon children were jumping about giggling and men came to the porches to chuckle. By the time Shadrack reached the first house, he was facing a line of delighted faces.

Never before had they laughed. Always they had shut their doors, pulled down the shades and called their children out of the road. It frightened him, this glee, but he stuck to his habit—singing his song, ringing his bell and holding fast to his rope. The deweys with their magnificent teeth ran out from Number 7 and danced a little jig around the befuddled Shadrack, then cut into a wild aping of his walk, his song and his bell-ringing. By now women were holding their stomachs, and the men were slapping their knees. It was Mrs. Jackson, who ate ice, who tripped down off her porch and marched—actually marched—along behind him. The scene was so comic the people walked into the road to make sure they saw it all. In that way the parade started.

Everybody, Dessie, Tar Baby, Patsy, Mr. Buckland Reed, Teapot's Mamma, Valentine, the deweys, Mrs. Jackson, Irene, the proprietor of the Palace of Cosmetology, Reba, the Herrod brothers and flocks of teen-agers got into the mood and, laughing, dancing, calling to one another, formed a pied piper's band behind Shadrack. As the initial group of about twenty people passed more houses, they called to the people standing in doors and leaning out of windows to join them; to help them open further this slit in the veil, this respite from anxiety, from dignity, from gravity, from the weight of that very adult pain that had undergirded them all those years before. Called to them to come out and play in the sunshine—as though the sunshine would last, as though there really was hope. The same hope that kept them picking beans for other farmers; kept them from finally leaving as they talked of doing; kept them knee-deep in other people's dirt; kept them excited about other people's wars; kept them solicitous of white people's children; kept them convinced that some magic "government" was going to lift them up, out and away from that dirt, those beans, those wars.

Some, of course, like Helene Wright, would not go. She watched the ruckus with characteristic scorn. Others, who understood the Spirit's touch which made them dance, who understood whole families bending their backs in a field while singing as from one throat, who understood the ecstasy of river baptisms under suns just like this one, did not understand this curious disorder, this headless display and so refused also to go.

Nevertheless, the sun splashed on a larger and larger crowd that strutted, skipped, marched, and shuffled down the road. When they got down to where the sidewalk started, some of them stopped and decided to turn back, too embarrassed to enter the white part of town whooping like banshees. But except for three or four, the fainthearted were put to shame by the more aggressive and abandoned, and the parade danced down Main Street past Woolworth's and the old poultry house, turned right and moved on down the New River Road.

At the mouth of the tunnel excavation, in a fever pitch of excitement and joy, they saw the timber, the bricks, the steel ribs and the tacky wire gate that glittered under ice struck to diamond in the sun. It dazzled them, at first, and they were suddenly quiet. Their hooded eyes swept over the place where their hope had lain since 1927. There was the promise: leaf-dead. The teeth unrepaired, the coal credit cut off, the chest pains unattended, the school shoes unbought, the rush-stuffed mattresses, the broken toilets, the leaning porches, the slurred remarks and the staggering childish malevolence of their employers. All there in blazing sunlit ice rapidly becoming water.

Like antelopes they leaped over the little gate—a wire barricade that was never intended to bar anything but dogs, rabbits and stray children—and led by the tough, the enraged and the young they picked up the lengths of timber and thin steel ribs and smashed the bricks they would never fire in yawning kilns, split the sacks of limestone they had not mixed or even been allowed to haul; tore the wire mesh, tipped over wheelbarrows and rolled forepoles down the bank, where they sailed far out on the icebound river.

Old and young, women and children, lame and hearty, they killed, as best they could, the tunnel they were forbidden to build.

They didn't mean to go in, to actually go down into the lip of the tunnel, but in their need to kill it all, all of it, to wipe from the face of the earth the work of the thin-armed Virginia boys, the bull-necked Greeks and the knife-faced men who waved the leaf-dead promise, they went too deep, too far . . .

A lot of them died there. The earth, now warm, shifted; the first forepole slipped; loose rock fell from the face of the tunnel and caused a shield to give way. They found themselves in a chamber of water, deprived of the sun that had brought them there. With the first crack and whoosh of water, the clamber to get out was so fierce that others who were trying to help were pulled to their deaths. Pressed up against steel ribs and timber blocks young boys strangled when the oxygen left them to join the water. Outside, others watched in terror as ice split and earth shook beneath their feet. Mrs. Jackson, weighing less than 100 pounds, slid down the bank and met with an open mouth the ice she had craved all her life. Tar Baby, Dessie, Ivy, Valentine, the Herrod boys, some of Ajax's younger brothers and the deweys (at least it was supposed; their bodies were never found)—all died there. Mr. Buckland Reed escaped, so did Patsy and her two boys, as well as some fifteen or twenty who had not gotten close enough to fall, or whose timidity would not let them enter an unfinished tunnel.

And all the while Shadrack stood there. Having forgotten his song and his rope, he just stood there high up on the bank ringing, ringing his bell.

1965

Things were so much better in 1965. Or so it seemed. You could go downtown and see colored people working in the dime store behind the counters, even handling money with cash-register keys around their necks. And a colored man taught mathematics at the junior high school. The young people had a look about them that everybody said was new but which reminded Nel of the deweys, whom nobody had ever found. Maybe, she thought, they had gone off and seeded the land and growed up in these young people in the dime store with the cash-register keys around their necks.

They were so different, these young people. So different from the way she remembered them forty years ago.

Jesus, there were some beautiful boys in 1921! Look like the whole world was bursting at the seams with them. Thirteen, fourteen, fifteen years old. Jesus, they were fine. L. P., Paul Freeman and his brother Jake, Mrs. Scott's twins—and Ajax had a whole flock of younger brothers. They hung out of attic windows, rode on car fenders, delivered the coal, moved into Medallion and moved out, visited cousins, plowed, hoisted, lounged on the church steps, careened on the school playground. The sun heated them and the moon slid down their backs. God, the world was *full* of beautiful boys in 1921.

Nothing like these kids. Everything had changed. Even the whores were better then: tough, fat, laughing women with burns on their cheeks and wit married to their meanness: or widows couched in small houses in the woods with eight children to feed and no man. These modern-day whores were pale and dull before those women. These little clothes-crazy things were always embarrassed. Nasty but shamed. They didn't know what shameless was. They should have known those silvery widows in the woods who would get up from the dinner table and walk into the trees with a customer with as much embarrassment as a calving mare.

Lord, how time flies. She hardly recognized anybody in the town any more. Now there was another old people's home. Look like this town just kept on building homes for old people. Every time they built a road they built a old folks' home. You'd think folks was living longer, but the fact of it was, they was just being put out faster.

Nel hadn't seen the insides of this most recent one yet, but it was her turn in Circle Number 5 to visit some of the old women there. The pastor visited them regularly, but the circle thought private visits were nice too. There were just nine colored women out there, the same nine that had been in the other one. But a lot of white ones. White people didn't fret about putting their old ones away. It took a lot for black people to let them go, and even if somebody was old and alone, others did the dropping by, the floor washing, the cooking. Only when they got crazy and unmanageable were they let go. Unless it was somebody like Sula, who put Eva away out of meanness. It was true that Eva was foolish in the head, but not so bad as to need locking up.

Nel was more than a little curious to see her. She had been really active in church only a year or less, and that was because the children were grown now and took up less time and less space in her mind. For over twenty-five years since Jude walked out she had pinned herself into a tiny life. She spent a little time trying to marry again, but nobody wanted to take her on with three children, and she simply couldn't manage the business of keeping boyfriends. During the war she had had a rather long relationship with a sergeant stationed at the camp twenty miles down river from Medallion, but then he got called away and everything was reduced to a few letters—then nothing. Then there was a bartender at the hotel. But now she was fifty-five and hard put to remember what all that had been about.

It didn't take long, after Jude left, for her to see what the future would be. She had looked at her children and knew in her heart that that would be all. That they were all she would ever know of love. But it was a love that, like a pan of syrup kept too long on the stove, had cooked out, leaving only its odor and a hard, sweet sludge, impossible to scrape off. For the mouths of her children quickly forgot the taste of her nipples, and years ago they had begun to look past her face into the nearest stretch of sky.

In the meantime the Bottom had collapsed. Everybody who had made money during the war moved as close as they could to the valley, and the white people were buying down river, cross river, stretching Medallion like two strings on the banks. Nobody colored lived much up in the Bottom any more. White people were building towers for television stations up there and there was a rumor about a golf course or something. Anyway, hill land was more valuable now, and those black people who had moved down right after the war and in the fifties couldn't afford to come back even if they wanted to. Except for the few blacks still huddled by the river bend, and some undemolished houses on Carpenter's Road, only rich white folks were building homes in the hills. Just like that, they had changed their minds and instead of keeping the valley floor to themselves, now they wanted a hilltop house with a river view and a ring of elms. The black people, for all their new look, seemed awfully anxious to get to the valley, or leave town, and abandon the hills to whoever was interested. It was sad, because the Bottom had been a real place. These young ones kept talking about the community, but they left the hills to the poor, the old, the stubborn—and the rich white folks. Maybe it hadn't been a community, but it had been a place. Now there weren't any places left, just separate houses with separate televisions and separate telephones and less and less dropping by.

These were the same thoughts she always had when she walked down into the town. One of the last true pedestrians, Nel walked the shoulder road while cars slipped by. Laughed at by her children, she still walked wherever she wanted to go, allowing herself to accept rides only when the weather required it.

Now she went straight through the town and turned left at its farthest end, along a tree-lined walk that turned into a country road farther on and passed the cemetery, Beechnut Park.

When she got to Sunnydale, the home for the aged, it was already four o'clock and turning chill. She would be glad to sit down with those old birds and rest her feet.

A red-haired lady at the desk gave her a pass card and pointed to a door that opened onto a corridor of smaller doors. It looked like what she imagined a college dormitory to be. The lobby was luxurious—modern—but the rooms she peeped into were sterile green cages. There was too much light everywhere; it needed some shadows. The third door, down the hall, had a little name tag over it that read EVA PEACE. Nel twisted the knob and rapped a little on the door at the same time, then listened a moment before she opened it.

At first she couldn't believe it. She seemed so small, sitting at that table in a black-vinyl chair. All the heaviness had gone and the height. Her once beautiful leg had no stocking and the foot was in a slipper. Nel wanted to cry —not for Eva's milk-dull eyes or her floppy lips, but for the once proud foot accustomed for over a half century to a fine well-laced shoe, now stuffed gracelessly into a pink terrycloth slipper.

"Good evening, Miss Peace. I'm Nel Greene come to pay a call on you. You remember me, don't you?"

Eva was ironing and dreaming of stairwells. She had neither iron nor clothes but did not stop her fastidious lining up of pleats or pressing out of wrinkles even when she acknowledged Nel's greeting.

"Howdy. Sit down."

"Thank you." Nel sat on the edge of the little bed.

"You've got a pretty room, a real pretty room, Miss Peace."

"You eat something funny today?"

"Ma'am?"

"Some chop suey? Think back."

"No, ma'am."

"No? Well, you gone be sick later on."

"But I didn't have no chop suey."

"You think I come all the way over here for you to tell me that? I can't make visits too often. You should have some respect for old people."

"But Miss Peace, I'm visiting *you*. This is *your* room." Nel smiled.

"What you say your name was?"

"Nel Greene."

"Wiley Wright's girl?"

"Uh huh. You do remember. That makes me feel good, Miss Peace. You remember me and my father."

"Tell me how you killed that little boy."

"What? What little boy?"

"The one you threw in the water. I got oranges. How did you get him to go in the water?"

"I didn't throw no little boy in the river. That was Sula."

"You. Sula. What's the difference? You was there. You watched, didn't you? Me, I never would've watched."

"You're confused, Miss Peace. I'm Nel. Sula's dead."

"It's awful cold in the water. Fire is warm. How did you get him in?" Eva wet her forefinger and tested the iron's heat.

"Who told you all these lies? Miss Peace? Who told you? Why are you telling lies on me?"

"I got oranges. I don't drink they old orange juice. They puts something in it."

"Why are you trying to make out like I did it?"

Eva stopped ironing and looked at Nel. For the first time her eyes looked sane.

"You think I'm guilty?" Nel was whispering.

Eva whispered back, "Who would know that better than you?"

"I want to know who you been talking to." Nel forced herself to speak normally.

"Plum. Sweet Plum. He tells me things." Eva laughed a light, tinkly giggle—girlish.

"I'll be going now, Miss Peace." Nel stood.

"You ain't answered me yet."

"I don't know what you're talking about."

"Just alike. Both of you. Never was no difference between you. Want some oranges? It's better for you than chop suey. Sula? I got oranges."

Nel walked hurriedly down the hall, Eva calling after her, "Sula?" Nel couldn't see the other women today. That woman had upset her. She handed her pass back to the lady, avoiding her look of surprise.

Outside she fastened her coat against the rising wind. The top button was missing so she covered her throat with her hand. A bright space opened in her head and memory seeped into it.

Standing on the riverbank in a purple-and-white dress, Sula swinging Chicken Little around and around. His laughter before the hand-slip and the water closing quickly over the place. What had she felt then, watching Sula going around and around and then the little boy swinging out over the water? Sula had cried and cried when she came back from Shadrack's house. But Nel had remained calm.

"*Shouldn't we tell?*"

"*Did he see?*"

"*I don't know. No.*"

"*Let's go. We can't bring him back.*"

What did old Eva mean by *you watched?* How could she help seeing it? She was right there. But Eva didn't say *see*, she said *watched*. "I did not watch it. I just saw it." But it was there anyway, as it had always been, the old feeling and the old question. The good feeling she had had when Chicken's hands slipped. She hadn't wondered about that in years. "Why didn't I feel bad when it happened? How come it felt so good to see him fall?"

All these years she had been secretly proud of her calm, controlled behavior when Sula was uncontrollable, her compassion for Sula's frightened and shamed eyes. Now it seemed that what she had thought was maturity, serenity and compassion was only the tranquillity that follows a joyful stimulation. Just as the water closed peacefully over the turbulence of Chicken Little's body, so had contentment washed over her enjoyment.

She was walking too fast. Not watching where she placed her feet, she got into the weeds by the side of the road. Running almost, she approached Beechnut Park. Just over there was the colored part of the cemetery. She went in. Sula was buried there along with Plum, Hannah and now Pearl. With the same disregard for name changes by marriage that the black people of Medallion always showed, each flat slab had one word carved on it. Together they read like a chant: PEACE 1895–1921, PEACE 1890–1923, PEACE 1910–1940, PEACE 1892–1959.

They were not dead people. They were words. Not even words. Wishes, longings.

All these years she had been harboring good feelings about Eva; sharing, she believed, her loneliness and unloved state as no one else could or did. She, after all, was the only one who really understood why Eva refused to attend Sula's funeral. The others thought they knew; thought the grandmother's reasons were the same as their own—that to pay respect to someone who had caused them so much pain was beneath them. Nel, who did go, believed Eva's refusal was not due to pride or vengeance but to a plain unwillingness to see the swallowing of her own flesh into the dirt, a determination not to let the eyes see what the heart could not hold.

Now, however, after the way Eva had just treated her, accused her, she wondered if the townspeople hadn't been right the first time. Eva *was* mean. Sula had even said so. There was no good reason for her to speak so. Feebleminded or not. Old. Whatever. Eva knew what she was doing. Always had. She had stayed away from Sula's funeral and accused Nel of drowning Chicken Little for spite. The same spite that galloped all over the Bottom. That made every gesture an offense, every off-center smile a threat, so that even the bubbles of relief that broke in the chest of practically everybody when Sula died did not soften their spite and allow them to go to Mr. Hodges' funeral parlor or send flowers from the church or bake a yellow cake.

She thought about Nathan opening the bedroom door the day she had visited her, and finding the body. He said he knew she was dead right away not because her eyes were open but because her mouth was. It looked to him like a giant yawn that she never got to finish. He had run across the street to Teapot's Mamma, who, when she heard the news, said, "Ho!" like the conductor on the train when it was about to take off except louder, and then did a little dance. None of the women left their quilt patches in disarray to run to the house. Nobody left the clothes halfway through the wringer to run to the house. Even the men just said "uhn," when they heard. The day passed and no one came. The night slipped into another day and the body was still lying in Eva's bed gazing at the ceiling trying to complete a yawn. It was very strange, this stubbornness about Sula. For even when China, the most rambunctious whore in the town, died (whose black son and white son said, when they heard she was dying, "She ain't dead yet?"), even then everybody stopped what they were doing and turned out in numbers to put the fallen sister away.

It was Nel who finally called the hospital, then the mortuary, then the police, who were the ones to come. So the white people took over. They came in a police van and carried the body down the steps past the four pear trees and into the van for all the world as with Hannah. When the police asked questions nobody gave them any information. It took them hours to find out the dead woman's first name. The call was for a Miss Peace at 7 Carpenter's

Road. So they left with that: a body, a name and an address. The white people had to wash her, dress her, prepare her and finally lower her. It was all done elegantly, for it was discovered that she had a substantial death policy. Nel went to the funeral parlor, but was so shocked by the closed coffin she stayed only a few minutes.

The following day Nel walked to the burying and found herself the only black person there, steeling her mind to the roses and pulleys. It was only when she turned to leave that she saw the cluster of black folk at the lip of the cemetery. Not coming in, not dressed for mourning, but there waiting. Not until the white folks left—the gravediggers, Mr. and Mrs. Hodges, and their young son who assisted them—did those black people from up in the Bottom enter with hooded hearts and filed eyes to sing "Shall We Gather at the River" over the curved earth that cut them off from the most magnificent hatred they had ever known. Their question clotted the October air, Shall We Gather at the River? The beautiful, the beautiful river? Perhaps Sula answered them even then, for it began to rain, and the women ran in tiny leaps through the grass for fear their straightened hair would beat them home.

Sadly, heavily, Nel left the colored part of the cemetery. Further along the road Shadrack passed her by. A little shaggier, a little older, still energetically mad, he looked at the woman hurrying along the road with the sunset in her face.

He stopped. Trying to remember where he had seen her before. The effort of recollection was too much for him and he moved on. He had to haul some trash out at Sunnydale and it would be good and dark before he got home.

He hadn't sold fish in a long time now. The river had killed them all. No more silver-gray flashes, no more flat, wide, unhurried look. No more slowing down of gills. No more tremor on the line.

Shadrack and Nel moved in opposite directions, each thinking separate thoughts about the past. The distance between them increased as they both remembered gone things.

Suddenly Nel stopped. Her eye twitched and burned a little.

"Sula?" she whispered, gazing at the tops of trees. "Sula?"

Leaves stirred; mud shifted; there was the smell of overripe green things. A soft ball of fur broke and scattered like dandelion spores in the breeze.

"All that time, all that time, I thought I was missing Jude." And the loss pressed down on her chest and came up into her throat. "We was girls together," she said as though explaining something. "O Lord, Sula," she cried, "girl, girl, girlgirlgirl."

It was a fine cry—loud and long—but it had no bottom and it had no top, just circles and circles of sorrow.

A NOTE ON THE TYPE

This book was set on the Linotype in Janson, a recutting made direct from type cast from matrices long thought to have been made by the Dutchman Anton Janson, who was a practicing type founder in Leipzig during the years 1668–87. However, it has been conclusively demonstrated that these types are actually the work of Nicholas Kis (1650–1702), a Hungarian, who most probably learned his trade from the master Dutch type founder Dirk Voskens. The type is an excellent example of the influential and sturdy Dutch types that prevailed in England up to the time William Caslon developed his own comparable designs from them.

SONG OF SOLOMON

Daddy

The fathers may soar
And the children may know their names

Part I

Chapter 1

The North Carolina Mutual Life Insurance agent promised to fly from Mercy to the other side of Lake Superior at three o'clock. Two days before the event was to take place he tacked a note on the door of his little yellow house:

> At 3:00 p.m. on Wednesday the 18th of February, 1931, I will take off from Mercy and fly away on my own wings. Please forgive me. I loved you all.
>
> (signed) Robert Smith,
> Ins. agent

Mr. Smith didn't draw as big a crowd as Lindbergh had four years earlier—not more than forty or fifty people showed up—because it was already eleven o'clock in the morning, on the very Wednesday he had chosen for his flight, before anybody read the note. At that time of day, during the middle of the week, word-of-mouth news just lumbered along. Children were in school; men were at work; and most of the women were fastening their corsets and getting ready to go see what tails or entrails the butcher might be giving away. Only the unemployed, the self-employed, and the very young were available—deliberately available because they'd heard about it, or accidentally available because they happened to be walking at that exact moment in the shore end of Not Doctor Street, a name the post office did not recognize. Town maps registered the street as Mains Avenue, but the only colored doctor in the city had lived and died on that street, and when he moved there in 1896 his patients took to calling the street, which none of them lived in or near, Doctor Street. Later, when other Negroes moved there, and when the postal service became a popular means of transferring messages among them, envelopes from Louisiana, Virginia, Alabama, and Georgia began to arrive addressed to people at house numbers on Doctor Street. The post office workers returned these envelopes or passed them on to the Dead Letter Office. Then in 1918, when colored men were being drafted, a few gave their address at the recruitment office as Doctor Street. In that way, the name acquired a quasi-official status. But not for long. Some of the city legislators, whose concern for appropriate names and the maintenance of the city's landmarks was the principal part of their political life, saw to it that "Doctor Street" was never used in any official capacity. And since they knew that only Southside residents kept it up, they had notices posted in the stores, barbershops, and restaurants in that part of the city saying that the avenue running northerly and southerly from Shore Road fronting the lake to the junction of routes 6 and 2 leading to Pennsylvania, and also running parallel to and between Rutherford Avenue and Broadway, had always been and would always be known as Mains Avenue and not Doctor Street.

It was a genuinely clarifying public notice because it gave Southside residents a way to keep their memories alive and please the city legislators as well. They called it Not Doctor Street, and were inclined to call the charity hospital at its northern end No Mercy Hospital since it was 1931, on the day following Mr. Smith's leap from its cupola, before the first colored expectant mother was allowed to give birth inside its wards and not on its steps. The reason for the hospital's generosity to that particular woman was not the fact that she was the only child of this Negro doctor, for during his entire professional life he had never been granted hospital privileges and only two of his patients were ever admitted to Mercy, both white. Besides, the doctor had been dead a long time by 1931. It must have been Mr. Smith's leap from the roof over their heads that made them admit her. In any case, whether or not the little insurance agent's conviction that he could fly contributed to the place of her delivery, it certainly contributed to its time.

When the dead doctor's daughter saw Mr. Smith emerge as promptly as he had promised from behind the cupola, his wide blue silk wings curved forward around his chest, she dropped her covered peck basket, spilling red velvet rose petals. The wind blew them about, up, down, and into small mounds of snow. Her half-grown daughters scrambled about trying to catch them, while their mother moaned and held the underside of her stomach. The rose-petal scramble got a lot of attention, but the pregnant lady's moans did not. Everyone knew the girls had spent hour after hour tracing, cutting, and stitching the costly velvet, and that Gerhardt's Department Store would be quick to reject any that were soiled.

It was nice and gay there for a while. The men joined in trying to collect the scraps before the snow soaked through them—snatching them from a gust of wind or plucking them delicately from the snow. And the very young children couldn't make up their minds whether to watch the man circled in blue on the roof or the bits of red flashing around on the ground. Their dilemma was solved when a woman suddenly burst into song. The singer, standing at the back of the crowd, was as poorly dressed as the doctor's daughter was well dressed. The latter had on a neat gray coat with the traditional pregnant-woman bow at her navel, a black cloche, and a pair of four-button ladies' galoshes. The singing woman wore a knitted navy cap pulled far down over her forehead. She had wrapped herself up in an old quilt instead of a winter coat. Her head cocked to one side, her eyes fixed on Mr. Robert Smith, she sang in a powerful contralto:

O Sugarman done fly away
Sugarman done gone
Sugarman cut across the sky
Sugarman gone home. . . .

A few of the half a hundred or so people gathered there nudged each other and sniggered. Others listened as though it were the helpful and defining piano music in a silent movie. They stood this way for some time, none of them crying out to Mr. Smith, all of them preoccupied with one or the other of the minor events about them, until the hospital people came.

They had been watching from the windows–at first with mild curiosity, then, as the crowd seemed to swell to the very walls of the hospital, they watched with apprehension. They wondered if one of those things that racial-uplift groups were always organizing was taking place. But when they saw neither placards nor speakers, they ventured outside into the cold: white-coated surgeons, dark-jacketed business and personnel clerks, and three nurses in starched jumpers.

The sight of Mr. Smith and his wide blue wings transfixed them for a few seconds, as did the woman's singing and the roses strewn about. Some of them thought briefly that this was probably some form of worship. Philadelphia, where Father Divine reigned, wasn't all that far away. Perhaps the young girls holding baskets of flowers were two of his virgins. But the laughter of a gold-toothed man brought them back to their senses. They stopped daydreaming and swiftly got down to business, giving orders. Their shouts and bustling caused great confusion where before there had been only a few men and some girls playing with pieces of velvet and a woman singing.

One of the nurses, hoping to bring some efficiency into the disorder, searched the faces around her until she saw a stout woman who looked as though she might move the earth if she wanted to.

"You," she said, moving toward the stout woman. "Are these your children?"

The stout woman turned her head slowly, her eyebrows lifted at the carelessness of the address. Then, seeing where the voice came from, she lowered her brows and veiled her eyes.

"Ma'am?"

"Send one around back to the emergency office. Tell him to tell the guard to get over here quick. That boy there can go. That one." She pointed to a cat-eyed boy about five or six years old.

The stout woman slid her eyes down the nurse's finger and looked at the child she was pointing to.

"Guitar, ma'am."

"What?"

"Guitar."

The nurse gazed at the stout woman as though she had spoken Welsh. Then she closed her mouth, looked again at the cat-eyed boy, and lacing her fingers, spoke her next words very slowly to him.

"Listen. Go around to the back of the hospital to the guard's office. It will say 'Emergency Admissions' on the door. A-D-M-I-S-I-O-N-S. But the guard will be there. Tell him to get over here—on the double. Move now. Move!" She unlaced her fingers and made scooping motions with her hands, the palms pushing against the wintry air.

A man in a brown suit came toward her, puffing little white clouds of breath. "Fire truck's on its way. Get back inside. You'll freeze to death."

The nurse nodded.

"You left out a *s*, ma'am," the boy said. The North was new to him and he had just begun to learn he could speak up to white people. But she'd already gone, rubbing her arms against the cold.

"Granny, she left out a *s*."

"And a 'please.' "

"You reckon he'll jump?"

"A nutwagon do anything."

"Who is he?"

"Collects insurance. A nutwagon."

"Who is that lady singing?"

"That, baby, is the very last thing in pea-time." But she smiled when she looked at the singing woman, so the cat-eyed boy listened to the musical performance with at least as much interest as he devoted to the man flapping his wings on top of the hospital.

The crowd was beginning to be a little nervous now that the law was being called in. They each knew Mr. Smith. He came to their houses twice a month to collect one dollar and sixty-eight cents and write down on a little yellow card both the date and their eighty-four cents a week payment. They were always half a month or so behind, and talked endlessly to him about paying ahead—after they had a preliminary discussion about what he was doing back so soon anyway.

"You back in here already? Look like I just got rid of you."

"I'm tired of seeing your face. Really tired."

"I knew it. Soon's I get two dimes back to back, here you come. More regular than the reaper. Do Hoover know about you?"

They kidded him, abused him, told their children to tell him they were out or sick or gone to Pittsburgh. But they held on to those little yellow cards as though they meant something—laid them gently in the shoe box along with the rent receipts, marriage licenses, and expired factory identification badges. Mr. Smith smiled through it all, managing to keep his eyes focused almost the whole time on his customers' feet. He wore a business suit for his work, but his house was no better than theirs. He never had a woman that any of them knew about and said nothing in church but an occasional "Amen." He never beat anybody up and he wasn't seen after dark, so they thought he was probably a nice man. But he was heavily associated with illness and death, neither of which was distinguishable from the brown picture of the North Carolina Mutual Life Building on the back of their yellow cards. Jumping from the roof of Mercy was the most interesting thing he had done. None of them had suspected he had it in him. Just goes to show, they murmured to each other, you never really do know about people.

The singing woman quieted down and, humming the tune, walked through the crowd toward the rose-petal lady, who was still cradling her stomach.

"You should make yourself warm," she whispered to her, touching her lightly on the elbow. "A little bird'll be here with the morning."

"Oh?" said the rose-petal lady. "Tomorrow morning?"

"That's the only morning coming."

"It can't be," the rose-petal lady said. "It's too soon."

"No it ain't. Right on time."

The women were looking deep into each other's eyes when a loud roar went up from the crowd—a kind of wavy *oo* sound. Mr. Smith had lost his balance for a second, and was trying gallantly to hold on to a triangle of wood that jutted from the cupola. Immediately the singing woman began again:

O Sugarman done fly
O Sugarman done gone . . .

Downtown the firemen pulled on their greatcoats, but when they arrived at Mercy, Mr. Smith had seen the rose petals, heard the music, and leaped on into the air.

The next day a colored baby was born inside Mercy for the first time. Mr. Smith's blue silk wings must have left their mark, because when the little boy discovered, at four, the same thing Mr. Smith had learned earlier—that only birds and airplanes could fly—he lost all interest in himself. To have to live without that single gift saddened him and left his imagination so bereft that he appeared dull even to the women who did not hate his mother. The ones who did, who accepted her invitations to tea and envied the doctor's big dark house of twelve rooms and the green sedan, called him "peculiar." The others, who knew that the house was more prison than palace, and that the Dodge sedan was for Sunday drives only, felt sorry for Ruth Foster and her dry daughters, and called her son "deep." Even mysterious.

"Did he come with a caul?"

"You should have dried it and made him some tea from it to drink. If you don't he'll see ghosts."

"You believe that?"

"I don't, but that's what the old people say."

"Well, he's a deep one anyway. Look at his eyes."

And they pried pieces of baked-too-fast sunshine cake from the roofs of their mouths and looked once more into the boy's eyes. He met their gaze as best he could until, after a pleading glance toward his mother, he was allowed to leave the room.

It took some planning to walk out of the parlor, his back washed with the hum of their voices, open the heavy double doors leading to the dining room, slip up the stairs past all those bedrooms, and not arouse the attention of Lena and Corinthians sitting like big baby dolls before a table heaped with scraps of red velvet. His sisters made roses in the afternoon. Bright, lifeless roses that lay in peck baskets for months until the specialty buyer at Gerhardt's sent Freddie the janitor over to tell the girls that they could use another gross. If he did manage to slip by his sisters and avoid their casual malice, he knelt in his room at the window sill and wondered again and again why he had to stay level on the ground. The quiet that suffused the doctor's house then, broken only by the murmur of the women eating sunshine cake, was only that: quiet. It was not peaceful, for it was preceded by and would soon be terminated by the presence of Macon Dead.

Solid, rumbling, likely to erupt without prior notice, Macon kept each member of his family awkward with fear. His hatred of his wife glittered and sparked in every word he spoke to her. The disappointment he felt in his daughters sifted down on them like ash, dulling their buttery complexions and choking the lilt out of what should have been girlish voices. Under the frozen heat of his glance they tripped over doorsills and dropped the salt cellar into the yolks of their poached eggs. The way he mangled their grace, wit, and self-esteem was the single excitement of their days. Without the tension and drama he ignited, they might not have known what to do with themselves. In his absence his daughters bent their necks over blood-red squares of velvet and waited eagerly for any hint of him, and his wife, Ruth, began her days stunned into stillness by her husband's contempt and ended them wholly animated by it.

When she closed the door behind her afternoon guests, and let the quiet smile die from her lips, she began the preparation of food her husband found impossible to eat. She did not try to make her meals nauseating; she simply didn't know how not to. She would notice that the sunshine cake was too haggled to put before him and decide on a rennet dessert. But the grinding of the veal and beef for a meat loaf took so long she not only forgot the pork, settling for bacon drippings poured over the meat, she had no time to make a dessert at all. Hurriedly, then, she began to set the table. As she unfolded the white linen and let it billow over the fine mahogany table, she would look once more at the large water mark. She never set the table or passed through the dining room without looking at it. Like a lighthouse keeper drawn to his window to gaze once again at the sea, or a prisoner automatically searching out the sun as he steps into the yard for his hour of exercise, Ruth looked for the water mark several times during the day. She knew it was there, would always be there, but she needed to confirm its presence. Like the keeper of the lighthouse and the prisoner, she regarded it as a mooring, a checkpoint, some stable visual object that assured her that the world was still there; that this was life and not a dream. That she was alive somewhere, inside, which she acknowledged to be true only because a thing she knew intimately was out there, outside herself.

Even in the cave of sleep, without dreaming of it or thinking of it at all, she felt its presence. Oh, she talked endlessly to her daughters and her guests about how to get rid of it—what might hide this single flaw on the splendid wood: Vaseline, tobacco juice, iodine, a sanding followed by linseed oil. She had tried them all. But her glance was nutritious; the spot became, if anything, more pronounced as the years passed.

The cloudy gray circle identified the place where the bowl filled every day during the doctor's life with fresh flowers had stood. Every day. And when there were no flowers, it held a leaf arrangement, a gathering of twigs and berries, pussy willow, Scotch pine. . . . But always something to grace the dinner table in the evening.

It was for her father a touch that distinguished his own family from the people among whom they lived. For Ruth it was the summation of the affectionate elegance with which she believed her childhood had been surrounded. When Macon married her and moved into Doctor's house, she kept up the centerpiece-arranging. Then came the time she walked down to the shore through the roughest part of the city to get some driftwood. She had seen an arrangement of driftwood and dried seaweed in the homemakers section of the newspaper. It was a damp November day, and Doctor was paralyzed even then and taking liquid food in his bedroom. The wind had lifted her skirt from around her ankles and cut through her laced shoes. She'd had to rub her feet down with warm olive oil when she got back. At dinner, where just the two of them sat, she turned toward her husband and asked him how he liked the centerpiece. "Most people overlook things like that. They see it, but they don't see anything beautiful in it. They don't see that nature has already made it as perfect as it can be. Look at it from the side. It is pretty, isn't it?"

Her husband looked at the driftwood with its lacy beige seaweed, and without moving his head, said, "Your chicken is red at the bone. And there is probably a potato dish that is supposed to have lumps in it. Mashed ain't the dish."

Ruth let the seaweed disintegrate, and later, when its veins and stems dropped and curled into brown scabs on the table, she removed the bowl and brushed away the scabs. But the water mark, hidden by the bowl all these years, was exposed. And once exposed, it behaved as though it were itself a plant and flourished into a huge suede-gray flower that throbbed like fever, and sighed like the shift of sand dunes. But it could also be still. Patient, restful, and still.

But there was nothing you could do with a mooring except acknowledge it, use it for the verification of some idea you wanted to keep alive. Something else is needed to get from sunup to sundown: a balm, a gentle touch or nuzzling of some sort. So Ruth rose up and out of her guileless inefficiency to claim her bit of balm right after the preparation of dinner and just before the return of her husband from his office. It was one of her two secret indulgences—the one that involved her son—and part of the pleasure it gave her came from the room in which she did it. A damp greenness lived there, made by the evergreen that pressed against the window and filtered the light. It was just a little room that Doctor had called a study, and aside from a sewing machine that stood in the corner along with a dress form, there was only a rocker and tiny footstool. She sat in this room holding her son on her lap, staring at his closed eyelids and listening to the sound of his sucking. Staring not so much from maternal joy as from a wish to avoid seeing his legs dangling almost to the floor.

In late afternoon, before her husband closed his office and came home, she called her son to her. When he came into the little room she unbuttoned her blouse and smiled. He was too young to be dazzled by her nipples, but he was old enough to be bored by the flat taste of mother's milk, so he came reluctantly, as to a chore, and lay as he had at least once each day of his life in his mother's arms, and tried to pull the thin, faintly sweet milk from her flesh without hurting her with his teeth.

She felt him. His restraint, his courtesy, his indifference, all of which pushed her into fantasy. She had the distinct impression that his lips were pulling from her a thread of light. It was as though she were a cauldron issuing spinning gold. Like the miller's daughter—the one who sat at night in a straw-filled room, thrilled with the secret power Rumpelstiltskin had given her: to see golden thread stream from her very own shuttle. And that was the other part of her pleasure, a pleasure she hated to give up. So when Freddie the janitor, who liked to pretend he was a friend of the family and not just their flunky as well as their tenant, brought his rent to the doctor's house late one day and looked in the window past the evergreen, the terror that sprang to Ruth's eyes came from the quick realization that she was to lose fully half of what made her daily life bearable. Freddie, however, interpreted her look as simple shame, but that didn't stop him from grinning.

"Have mercy. I be damn."

He fought the evergreen for a better look, hampered more by his laughter than by the branches. Ruth jumped up as quickly as she could and covered her breast, dropping her son on the floor and confirming for him what he had begun to suspect—that these afternoons were strange and wrong.

Before either mother or son could speak, rearrange themselves properly, or even exchange looks, Freddie had run around the house, climbed the porch steps, and was calling them between gulps of laughter.

"Miss Rufie. Miss Rufie. Where you? Where you all at?" He opened the door to the green room as though it were his now.

"I be damn, Miss Rufie. When the last time I seen that? I don't even know the last time I seen that. I mean, ain't nothing wrong with it. I mean, old folks swear by it. It's just, you know, you don't see it up here much. . . ." But his eyes were on the boy. Appreciative eyes that communicated some complicity she was excluded from. Freddie looked the boy up and down, taking in the steady but secretive eyes and the startling contrast between Ruth's lemony skin and the boy's black skin. "Used to be a lot of womenfolk nurse they kids a long time down South. Lot of 'em. But you don't see it much no more. I knew a family—the mother wasn't too quick, though—nursed hers till the boy, I reckon, was near 'bout thirteen. But that's a bit much, ain't it?" All the time he chattered, he rubbed his chin and looked at the boy. Finally he stopped, and gave a long low chuckle. He'd found the phrase he'd been searching for. "A milkman. That's what you got here, Miss Rufie. A natural milkman if ever I seen one. Look out, womens. Here he come. Huh!"

Freddie carried his discovery not only into the homes in Ruth's neighborhood, but to Southside, where he lived and where Macon Dead owned rent houses. So Ruth kept close to home and had no afternoon guests for the better part of two months, to keep from hearing that her son had been rechristened with a name he was never able to shake and that did nothing to improve either one's relationship with his father.

Macon Dead never knew how it came about—how his only son acquired the nickname that stuck in spite of his own refusal to use it or acknowledge it. It was a matter that concerned him a good deal, for the giving of names in his family was always surrounded by what he believed to be monumental foolishness. No one mentioned to him the incident out of which the nickname grew because he was a difficult man to approach—a hard man, with a manner so cool it discouraged casual or spontaneous conversation. Only Freddie the janitor took liberties with Macon Dead, liberties he purchased with the services he rendered, and Freddie was the last person on earth to tell him. So Macon Dead neither heard of nor visualized Ruth's sudden terror, her awkward jump from the rocking chair, the boy's fall broken by the tiny footstool, or Freddie's amused, admiring summation of the situation.

Without knowing any of the details, however, he guessed, with the accuracy of a mind sharpened by hatred, that the name he heard schoolchildren call his son, the name he overheard the ragman use when he paid the boy three cents for a bundle of old clothes—he guessed that this name was not clean. Milkman. It certainly didn't sound like the honest job of a dairyman, or bring to his mind cold bright cans standing on the back porch, glittering like captains on guard. It sounded dirty, intimate, and hot. He knew that wherever the name came from, it had something to do with his wife and was, like the emotion he always felt when thinking of her, coated with disgust.

This disgust and the uneasiness with which he regarded his son affected everything he did in that city. If he could have felt sad, simply sad, it would have relieved him. Fifteen years of regret at not having a son had become the bitterness of finally having one in the most revolting circumstances.

There had been a time when he had a head full of hair and when Ruth wore lovely complicated underwear that he deliberately took a long time to undo. When all of his foreplay was untying, unclasping, unbuckling the snaps and strings of what must have been the most beautiful, the most delicate, the whitest and softest underwear on earth. Each eye of her corset he toyed with (and there were forty—twenty on each side); each grosgrain ribbon that threaded its pale-blue way through the snowy top of her bodice he unlaced. He not only undid the blue bow; he pulled it all the way out of the hem, so she had to rethread it afterward with a safety pin. The elastic bands that connected her perspiration shields to her slip he unsnapped and snapped again, teasing her and himself with the sound of the snaps and the thrill of his fingertips on her shoulders. They never spoke during these undressings. But they giggled occasionally, and as when children play "doctor," undressing of course was the best part.

When Ruth was naked and lying there as moist and crumbly as unbleached sugar, he bent to unlace her shoes. That was the final delight, for once he had undressed her feet, had peeled her stockings down over her ankles and toes, he entered her and ejaculated quickly. She liked it that way. So did he. And in almost twenty years during which he had not laid eyes on her naked feet, he missed only the underwear.

Once he believed that the sight of her mouth on the dead man's fingers would be the thing he would remember always. He was wrong. Little by little he remembered fewer and fewer of the details, until finally he had to imagine them, even fabricate them, guess what they must have been. The image left him, but the odiousness never did. For the nourishment of his outrage he depended on the memory of her underwear; those round, innocent corset eyes now lost to him forever.

So if the people were calling his son Milkman, and if she was lowering her eyelids and dabbing at the sweat on her top lip when she heard it, there was definitely some filthy connection and it did not matter at all to Macon Dead whether anyone gave him the details or not.

And they didn't. Nobody both dared enough and cared enough to tell him. The ones who cared enough, Lena and Corinthians, the living proof of those years of undressing his wife, did not dare. And the one person who dared to but didn't care to was the one person in the world he hated more than his wife in spite of the fact that she was his sister. He had not crossed the tracks to see her since his son was born and he had no intention of renewing their relationship now.

Macon Dead dug in his pocket for his keys, and curled his fingers around them, letting their bunchy solidity calm him. They were the keys to all the doors of his houses (only four true houses; the rest were really shacks), and he fondled them from time to time as he walked down Not Doctor Street to his office. At least he thought of it as his office, had even painted the word OFFICE on the door. But the plate-glass window contradicted him. In peeling gold letters arranged in a semicircle, his business establishment was declared to be Sonny's Shop. Scraping the previous owner's name off was hardly worth the trouble since he couldn't scrape it from anybody's mind. His storefront office was never called anything but Sonny's Shop, although nobody now could remember thirty years back, when, presumably, Sonny did something or other there.

He walked there now—strutted is the better word, for he had a high behind and an athlete's stride—thinking of names. Surely, he thought, he and his sister had some ancestor, some lithe young man with onyx skin and legs as straight as cane stalks, who had a name that was real. A name given to him at birth with love and seriousness. A name that was not a joke, nor a disguise, nor a brand name. But who this lithe young man was, and where his cane-stalk legs carried him from or to, could never be known. No. Nor his name. His own parents, in some mood of perverseness or resignation, had agreed to abide by a naming done to them by somebody who couldn't have cared less. Agreed to take and pass on to all their issue this heavy name scrawled in perfect thoughtlessness by a drunken Yankee in the Union Army. A literal slip of the pen handed to his father on a piece of paper and which he handed on to his only son, and his son likewise handed on to his; Macon Dead who begat a second Macon Dead who married Ruth Foster (Dead) and begat Magdalene called Lena Dead and First Corinthians Dead and (when he least expected it) another Macon Dead, now known to the part of the world that mattered as Milkman Dead. And as if that were not enough, a sister named Pilate Dead, who would never mention to her brother the circumstances or the details of this foolish misnaming of his son because the whole thing would have delighted her. She would savor it, maybe fold it too in a brass box and hang it from her other ear.

He had cooperated as a young father with the blind selection of names from the Bible for every child other than the first male. And abided by whatever the finger pointed to, for he knew every configuration of the naming of his sister. How his father, confused and melancholy over his wife's death in childbirth, had thumbed through the Bible, and since he could not read a word, chose a group of letters that seemed to him strong and handsome; saw in them a large figure that looked like a tree hanging in some princely but protective way over a row of smaller trees. How he had copied the group of letters out on a piece of brown paper; copied, as illiterate people do, every curlicue, arch, and bend in the letters, and presented it to the midwife.

"That's the baby's name."

"You want this for the baby's name?"

"I want that for the baby's name. Say it."

"You can't name the baby this."

"Say it."

"It's a man's name."
"Say it."
"Pilate."
"What?"
"Pilate. You wrote down Pilate."
"Like a riverboat pilot?"
"No. Not like no riverboat pilot. Like a Christ-killing Pilate. You can't get much worse than that for a name. And a baby girl at that."
"That's where my finger went down at."
"Well, your brain ain't got to follow it. You don't want to give this motherless child the name of the man that killed Jesus, do you?"
"I asked Jesus to save me my wife."
"Careful, Macon."
"I asked him all night long."
"He give you your baby."
"Yes. He did. Baby name Pilate."
"Jesus, have mercy."
"Where you going with that piece of paper?"
"It's going back where it came from. Right in the Devil's flames."
"Give it here. It come from the Bible. It stays in the Bible."

And it did stay there, until the baby girl turned twelve and took it out, folded it up into a tiny knot and put it in a little brass box, and strung the entire contraption through her left earlobe. Fluky about her own name at twelve, how much more fluky she'd become since then Macon could only guess. But he knew for certain that she would treat the naming of the third Macon Dead with the same respect and awe she had treated the boy's birth.

Macon Dead remembered when his son was born, how she seemed to be more interested in this first nephew of hers than she was in her own daughter, and even that daughter's daughter. Long after Ruth was up and about, as capable as she ever would be—and that wasn't much—of running the house again, Pilate continued to visit, her shoelaces undone, a knitted cap pulled down over her forehead, bringing her foolish earring and sickening smell into the kitchen. He had not seen her since he was sixteen years old, until a year before the birth of his son, when she appeared in his city. Now she was acting like an in-law, like an aunt, dabbling at helping Ruth and the girls, but having no interest in or knowledge of decent housekeeping, she got in the way. Finally she just sat in a chair near the crib, singing to the baby. That wasn't so bad, but what Macon Dead remembered most was the expression on her face. Surprise, it looked like, and eagerness. But so intense it made him uneasy. Or perhaps it was more than that. Perhaps it was seeing her all those years after they had separated outside that cave, and remembering his anger and her betrayal. How far down she had slid since then. She had cut the last thread of propriety. At one time she had been the dearest thing in the world to him. Now she was odd, murky, and worst of all, unkempt. A regular source of embarrassment, if he would allow it. But he would not allow it.

Finally he had told her not to come again until she could show some respect for herself. Could get a real job instead of running a wine house.

"Why can't you dress like a woman?" He was standing by the stove. "What's that sailor's cap doing on your head? Don't you have stockings? What are you trying to make me look like in this town?" He trembled with the thought of the white men in the bank—the men who helped him buy and mortgage houses—discovering that this raggedy bootlegger was his sister. That the propertied Negro who handled his business so well and who lived in the big house on Not Doctor Street had a sister who had a daughter but no husband, and that daughter had a daughter but no husband. A collection of lunatics who made wine and sang in the streets "like common street women! Just like common street women!"

Pilate had sat there listening to him, her wondering eyes resting on his face. Then she said, "I been worried sick about you too, Macon."

Exasperated, he had gone to the kitchen door. "Go 'head,

Pilate. Go on now. I'm on the thin side of evil and trying not to break through."

Pilate stood up, wrapped her quilt around her, and with a last fond look at the baby, left through the kitchen door. She never came back.

When Macon Dead got to the front door of his office he saw a stout woman and two young boys standing a few feet away. Macon unlocked his door, walked over to his desk, and settled himself behind it. As he was thumbing through his accounts book, the stout woman entered, alone.

"Afternoon Mr. Dead, sir. I'm Mrs. Bains. Live over at number three on Fifteenth Street."

Macon Dead remembered—not the woman, but the circumstances at number three. His tenant's grandmother or aunt or something had moved in there and the rent was long overdue.

"Yes, Mrs. Bains. You got something for me?"

"Well, that's what I come to talk to you about. You know Cency left all them babies with me. And my relief check ain't no more'n it take to keep a well-grown yard dog alive—half alive, I should say."

"Your rent is four dollars a month, Mrs. Bains. You two months behind already."

"I do know that, Mr. Dead, sir, but babies can't make it with nothing to put in they stomach."

Their voices were low, polite, without any hint of conflict.

"Can they make it in the street, Mrs. Bains? That's where they gonna be if you don't figure out some way to get me my money."

"No, sir. They can't make it in the street. We need both, I reckon. Same as yours does."

"Then you better rustle it up, Mrs. Bains. You got till"—he swiveled around to consult the calendar on the wall—"till Saturday coming. Saturday, Mrs. Bains. Not Sunday. Not Monday. Saturday."

If she had been younger and had more juice, the glitter in her eyes would have washed down onto her cheeks. Now, at her time of life, it simply gleamed. She pressed the flat of her hand on Macon Dead's desk and, holding the gleam steady in her eyes, pushed herself up from the chair. She turned her head a little to look out the plate-glass window, and then back at him.

"What's it gonna profit you, Mr. Dead, sir, to put me and them children out?"

"Saturday, Mrs. Bains."

Lowering her head, Mrs. Bains whispered something and walked slowly and heavily from the office. As she closed the door to Sonny's Shop, her grandchildren moved out of the sunlight into the shadow where she stood.

"What he say, Granny?"

Mrs. Bains put a hand on the taller boy's hair and fingered it lightly, absently searching with her nails for tetter spots.

"He must've told her no," said the other boy.

"Do we got to move?" The tall boy tossed his head free of her fingers and looked at her sideways. His cat eyes were gashes of gold.

Mrs. Bains let her hand fall to her side. "A nigger in business is a terrible thing to see. A terrible, terrible thing to see."

The boys looked at each other and back at their grandmother. Their lips were parted as though they had heard something important.

When Mrs. Bains closed the door, Macon Dead went back to the pages of his accounts book, running his fingertips over the figures and thinking with the unoccupied part of his mind about the first time he called on Ruth Foster's father. He had only two keys in his pocket then, and if he had let people like the woman who just left have their way, he wouldn't have had any keys at all. It was because of those keys that he could dare to walk over to that part of Not Doctor Street (it was still Doctor Street then) and approach the most important Negro in the city. To lift the lion's paw knocker, to entertain thoughts of marrying the doctor's daughter was possible because each key represented a house which he owned at the time. Without those keys he would have floated away at the doctor's first word: "Yes?" Or he would have melted like new wax under the heat of that pale eye. Instead he was able to say that he had been introduced to his daughter, Miss Ruth Foster, and would appreciate having the doctor's permission to keep her company now and then. That his intentions were honorable and that he himself was certainly worthy of the doctor's consideration as a gentleman friend for Miss Foster since, at twenty-five, he was already a colored man of property.

"I don't know anything about you," the doctor said, "other than your name, which I don't like, but I will abide by my daughter's preference."

In fact the doctor knew a good deal about him and was more grateful to this tall young man than he ever allowed himself to show. Fond as he was of his only child, useful as she was in his house since his wife had died, lately he had begun to chafe under her devotion. Her steady beam of love was unsettling, and she had never dropped those expressions of affection that had been so lovable in her childhood. The good-night kiss was itself a masterpiece of slow-wittedness on her part and discomfort on his. At sixteen, she still insisted on having him come to her at night, sit on her bed, exchange a few pleasantries, and plant a kiss on her lips. Perhaps it was the loud silence of his dead wife, perhaps it was Ruth's disturbing resemblance to her mother. More probably it was the ecstasy that always seemed to be shining in Ruth's face when he bent to kiss her—an ecstasy he felt inappropriate to the occasion.

None of that, of course, did he describe to the young man who came to call. Which is why Macon Dead still believed the magic had lain in the two keys.

In the middle of his reverie, Macon was interrupted by rapid tapping on the window. He looked up, saw Freddie peeping through the gold lettering, and nodded for him to enter. A gold-toothed bantamweight, Freddie was as much of a town crier as Southside had. It was this same rapid tapping on the window-pane, the same flash-of-gold smile that had preceded his now-famous scream to Macon: "Mr. Smith went splat!" It was obvious to Macon that Freddie now had news of another calamity.

"Porter gone crazy drunk again! Got his shotgun!"

"Who's he out for?" Macon began closing books and opening desk drawers. Porter was a tenant and tomorrow was collection day.

"Ain't out for nobody in particular. Just perched himself up in the attic window and commenced to waving a shotgun. Say he gotta kill him somebody before morning."

"He go to work today?"

"Yep. Caught the eagle too."

"Drunk it all up?"

"Not all of it. He only got one bottle, and he still got a fist fulla money."

"Who's crazy enough to sell him any liquor?"

Freddie showed a few gold teeth but said nothing, so Macon knew it was Pilate. He locked all his drawers save one—the one he unlocked and took a small .32 from.

"Police warn every bootlegger in the county, and he still gets it somehow." Macon went on with the charade, pretending he didn't know his sister was the one Porter and anybody else—adult, child, or beast—could buy wine from. He thought for the hundredth time that she needed to be in jail and that he would be willing to put her there if he could be sure she wouldn't loudmouth him and make him seem trashy in the eyes of the law—and the banks.

"You know how to use that thing, Mr. Dead, sir?"

"I know how."

"Porter's crazy when he drunk."

"I know what he is."

"How you aiming to get him down?"

"I ain't aiming to get him down. I'm aiming to get my money down. He can go on and die up there if he wants to. But if he don't toss me my rent, I'm going to blow him out of that window."

Freddie's giggle was soft, but his teeth strengthened its impact. A born flunky, he loved gossip and the telling of it. He was the ear that heard every murmur of complaint, every name-calling; and his was the eye that saw everything: the secret loving glances, the fights, the new dresses.

Macon knew Freddie as a fool and a liar, but a reliable liar. He was always right about his facts and always wrong about the motives that produced the facts. Just as now he was right about Porter having a shotgun, being in the attic window, and being drunk. But Porter was not waiting to kill somebody, meaning anybody, before morning. In fact he was very specific about whom he wanted to kill—himself. However, he did have a precondition which he shouted down, loud and clear, from the attic. "I want to fuck! Send me up somebody to fuck! Hear me? Send me up somebody, I tell ya, or I'ma blow my brains out!"

As Macon and Freddie approached the yard, the women from the rooming house were hollering answers to Porter's plea.

"What kinda bargain is that?"

"Kill yourself first and then we'll send you somebody."

"Do it have to be a woman?"

"Do it got to be human?"

"Do it got to be alive?"

"Can it be a piece of liver?"

"Put that thing down and throw me my goddam money!" Macon's voice cut through the women's fun. "Float those dollars down here, nigger, then blow yourself up!"

Porter turned and aimed his shotgun at Macon.

"If you pull that trigger," shouted Macon, "you better not miss. If you take a shot you better make sure I'm dead, cause if you don't I'm gonna shoot your balls up in your throat!" He pulled out his own weapon. "Now get the hell outta that window!"

Porter hesitated for only a second, before turning the barrel of the shotgun toward himself—or trying to. Its length made it difficult; his drunkenness made it impossible. Struggling to get the right angle, he was suddenly distracted. He leaned his shotgun on the window sill, pulled out his penis and in a high arc, peed over the heads of the women, making them scream and run in a panic that the shotgun had not been able to create. Macon rubbed the back of his head while Freddie bent double with laughter.

For more than an hour Porter held them at bay: cowering, screaming, threatening, urinating, and interspersing all of it with pleas for a woman.

He would cry great shoulder-heaving sobs, followed by more screams.

"I love ya! I love ya all. Don't act like that. You women. Stop it. Don't act like that. Don't you see I love ya? I'd die for ya, kill for ya. I'm saying I love ya. I'm telling ya. Oh, God have mercy. What I'm gonna do? What in this fuckin world am I gonna dooooo?"

Tears streamed down his face and he cradled the barrel of the shotgun in his arms as though it were the woman he had been begging for, searching for, all his life. "Gimme hate, Lord," he whimpered. "I'll take hate any day. But don't give me love. I can't take no more love, Lord. I can't carry it. Just like Mr. Smith. He couldn't carry it. It's too heavy. Jesus, *you* know. You know all about it. Ain't it heavy? Jesus? Ain't love heavy? Don't you see, Lord? You own son couldn't carry it. If it killed Him, what You think it's gonna do to me? Huh? Huh?" He was getting angry again.

"Come down outta there, nigger!" Macon's voice was still loud, but it was getting weary.

"And you, you baby-dicked baboon"—he tried to point at Macon—"you the worst. You need killin, you really *need* killin. You know why? Well, I'm gonna tell you why. I *know* why. Everybody . . ."

Porter slumped down in the window, muttering, "Everybody know why," and fell fast asleep. As he sank deeper into it, the shotgun slipped from his hand, rattled down the roof, and hit the ground with a loud explosion. The shot zipped past a bystander's shoe and blew a hole in the tire of a stripped Dodge parked in the road.

"Go get my money," Macon said.

"Me?" Freddie asked. "Suppose he . . ."

"Go get me my money."

Porter was snoring. Through the blast of the gun and the picking of his pocket he slept like a baby.

When Macon walked out of the yard, the sun had disappeared behind the bread company. Tired, irritable, he walked down Fifteenth Street, glancing up as he passed one of his other houses, its silhouette melting in the light that trembled between dusk and twilight. Scattered here and there, his houses stretched up beyond him like squat ghosts with hooded eyes. He didn't like to look at them in this light. During the day they were reassuring to see; now they did not seem to belong to him at all—in fact he felt as though the houses were in league with one another to make him feel like the outsider, the propertyless, landless wanderer. It was this feeling of loneliness that made him decide to take a shortcut back to Not Doctor Street, even though to do so would lead him past his sister's house. In the gathering darkness, he was sure his passing would be unnoticed by her. He crossed a yard and followed a fence that led into Darling Street where Pilate lived in a narrow single-story house whose basement seemed to be rising from rather than settling into the ground. She had no electricity because she would not pay for the service. Nor for gas. At night she and her daughter lit the house with candles and kerosene lamps; they warmed themselves and cooked with wood and coal, pumped kitchen water into a dry sink through a pipeline from a well and lived pretty much as though progress was a word that meant walking a little farther on down the road.

Her house sat eighty feet from the sidewalk and was backed by four huge pine trees, from which she got the needles she stuck into her mattress. Seeing the pine trees started him thinking about her mouth; how she loved, as a girl, to chew pine needles and as a result smelled even then like a forest. For a dozen years she had been like his own child. After their mother died, she had come struggling out of the womb without help from throbbing muscles or the pressure of swift womb water. As a result, for all the years he knew her, her stomach was as smooth and sturdy as her back, at no place interrupted by a navel. It was the absence of a navel that convinced people that she had not come into this world through normal channels; had never lain, floated, or grown in some warm and liquid place connected by a tissue-thin tube to a reliable source of human nourishment. Macon knew otherwise, because he was there and had seen the eyes of the midwife as his mother's legs collapsed. And heard as well her shouts when the baby, who they had believed was dead also, inched its way headfirst out of a still, silent, and indifferent cave of flesh, dragging her own cord and her own afterbirth behind her. But the rest was true. Once the new baby's lifeline was cut, the cord stump shriveled, fell off, and left no trace of having ever existed, which, as a young boy taking care of his baby sister, he thought no more strange than a bald head. He was seventeen years old, irreparably separated from her and already pressing forward in his drive for wealth, when he learned that there was probably not another stomach like hers on earth.

Now, nearing her yard, he trusted that the dark would keep anyone in her house from seeing him. He did not even look to his left as he walked by it. But then he heard the music. They were singing. All of them. Pilate, Reba, and Reba's daughter, Hagar. There was no one on the street that he could see; people were at supper, licking their fingers, blowing into saucers of coffee, and no doubt chattering about Porter's escapade and Macon's fearless confrontation of the wild man in the attic. There were no street lights in this part of town; only the moon directed the way of a pedestrian. Macon walked on, resisting as best he could the sound of the voices that followed him. He was rapidly approaching a part of the road where the music could not follow, when he saw, like a scene on the back of a postcard, a picture of where he was headed—his own home; his wife's narrow unyielding back; his daughters, boiled dry from years of yearning; his son, to whom he could speak only if his words held some command or criticism. "Hello, Daddy." "Hello, son, tuck your shirt in." "I found a dead bird, Daddy." "Don't bring that mess in this house. . . ." There was no music there, and tonight he wanted just a bit of music—from the person who had been his first caring for.

He turned back and walked slowly toward Pilate's house. They were singing some melody that Pilate was leading. A phrase that the other two were taking up and building on. Her powerful contralto, Reba's piercing soprano in counterpoint, and the soft voice of the girl, Hagar, who must be about ten or eleven now, pulled him like a carpet tack under the influence of a magnet.

Surrendering to the sound, Macon moved closer. He wanted no conversation, no witness, only to listen and perhaps to see the three of them, the source of that music that made him think of fields and wild turkey and calico. Treading as lightly as he could, he crept up to the side window where the candlelight flickered lowest, and peeped in. Reba was cutting her toenails with a kitchen knife or a switchblade, her long neck bent almost to her knees. The girl, Hagar, was braiding her hair, while Pilate, whose face he could not see because her back was to the window, was stirring something in a pot. Wine pulp, perhaps. Macon knew it was not food she was stirring, for she and her daughters ate like children. Whatever they had a taste for. No meal was ever planned or balanced or served. Nor was there any gathering at the table. Pilate might bake hot bread and each one of them would eat it with butter whenever she felt like it. Or there might be grapes, left over from the winemaking, or peaches for days on end. If one of them bought a gallon of milk they drank it until it was gone. If another got a half bushel of tomatoes or a dozen ears of corn, they ate them until they were gone too. They ate what they had or came across or had a craving for. Profits from their wine-selling evaporated like sea water in a hot wind—going for junk jewelry for Hagar, Reba's gifts to men, and he didn't know what all.

Near the window, hidden by the dark, he felt the irritability of the day drain from him and relished the effortless beauty of the women singing in the candlelight. Reba's soft profile, Hagar's hands moving, moving in her heavy hair, and Pilate. He knew her face better than he knew his own. Singing now, her face would be a mask; all emotion and passion would have left her features and entered her voice. But he knew that when she was neither singing nor talking, her face was animated by her constantly moving lips. She chewed things. As a baby, as a very young girl, she kept things in her mouth—straw from brooms, gristle, buttons, seeds, leaves, string, and her favorite, when he could find some for her, rubber bands and India rubber erasers. Her lips were alive with small movements. If you were close to her, you wondered if she was about to smile or was she merely shifting a straw from the baseline of her gums to her tongue. Perhaps she was dislodging a curl of rubber band from inside her cheek, or was she really smiling? From a distance she appeared to be whispering to herself, when she was only nibbling or splitting tiny seeds with her front teeth. Her lips were darker than her skin, wine-stained, blueberry-dyed, so her face had a cosmetic look—as though she had applied a very dark lipstick neatly and blotted away its shine on a scrap of newspaper.

As Macon felt himself softening under the weight of memory and music, the song died down. The air was quiet and yet Macon Dead could not leave. He liked looking at them freely this way. They didn't move. They simply stopped singing and Reba went on paring her toenails, Hagar threaded and unthreaded her hair, and Pilate swayed like a willow over her stirring.

Chapter 2

Only Magdalene called Lena and First Corinthians were genuinely happy when the big Packard rolled evenly and silently out of the driveway. They alone had a sense of adventure and were flagrant in their enjoyment of the automobile's plushness. Each had a window to herself and commanded an unobstructed view of the summer day flying past them. And each was both old enough and young enough to actually believe she was a princess riding in a regal chariot driven by a powerful coachman. In the back seat, away from the notice of Macon and Ruth, they slipped off their patent leather pumps, rolled their stockings down over their knees, and watched the men walking down the streets.

These rides that the family took on Sunday afternoons had become rituals and much too important for Macon to enjoy. For him it was a way to satisfy himself that he was indeed a successful man. It was a less ambitious ritual for Ruth, but a way, nevertheless, for her to display her family. For the little boy it was simply a burden. Pressed in the front seat between his parents, he could see only the winged woman careening off the nose of the car. He was not allowed to sit on his mother's lap during the drive—not because she wouldn't have it, but because his father objected to it. So it was only by kneeling on the dove gray seat and looking out the back window that he could see anything other than the laps, feet, and hands of his parents, the dashboard, or the silver winged woman poised at the tip of the Packard. But riding backward made him uneasy. It was like flying blind, and not knowing where he was going—just where he had been—troubled him. He did not want to see trees that he had passed, or houses and children slipping into the space the automobile had left behind.

Macon Dead's Packard rolled slowly down Not Doctor Street, through the rough part of town (later known as the Blood Bank because blood flowed so freely there), over the bypass downtown, and headed for the wealthy white neighborhoods. Some of the black people who saw the car passing by sighed with good-humored envy at the classiness, the dignity of it. In 1936 there were very few among them who lived as well as Macon Dead. Others watched the family gliding by with a tiny bit of jealousy and a whole lot of amusement, for Macon's wide green Packard belied what they thought a car was for. He never went over twenty miles an hour, never gunned his engine, never stayed in first gear for a block or two to give pedestrians a thrill. He never had a blown tire, never ran out of gas and needed twelve grinning raggle-tailed boys to help him push it up a hill or over to a curb. No rope ever held the door to its frame, and no teen-agers leaped on his running board for a lift down the street. He hailed no one and no one hailed him. There was never a sudden braking and backing up to shout or laugh with a friend. No beer bottles or ice cream cones poked from the open windows. Nor did a baby boy stand up to pee out of them. He never let rain fall on it if he could help it and he walked to Sonny's Shop—taking the car out only on these occasions. What's more, they doubted that he had ever taken a woman into the back seat, because rumor was that he went to "bad houses" or lay, sometimes, with a slack or lonely female tenant. Other than the bright and roving eyes of Magdalene called Lena and First Corinthians, the Packard had no real lived life at all. So they called it Macon Dead's hearse.

First Corinthians pulled her fingers through her hair. It was long, lightweight hair, the color of wet sand. "Are you going anyplace special, or are we just driving around?" She kept her eyes on the street, watching the men and women walking by.

"Careful, Macon. You always take the wrong turn here." Ruth spoke softly from the right side of the car.

"Do you want to drive?" Macon asked her.

"You know I don't drive," she answered.

"Then let me do it."

"All right, but don't blame me if . . ."

Macon pulled smoothly into the left fork of the road that led through downtown and into a residential area.

"Daddy? Are we going any special place?"

"Honoré," Macon said.

Magdalene called Lena pushed her stockings farther down on her legs. "On the lake? What's out there? There's nothing out there, nobody."

"There's a beach community out there, Lena. Your father wants to look at it." Ruth reasserted herself into the conversation.

"What for? Those are white people's houses," said Lena.

"All of it's not white people's houses. Some of it's nothing. Just land. Way over on the other side. It could be a nice summer place for colored people. Beach houses. You understand what I mean?" Macon glanced at his daughter through the rear-view mirror.

"Who's going to live in them? There's no colored people who can afford to have two houses," Lena said.

"Reverend Coles can, and Dr. Singleton," Corinthians corrected her.

"And that lawyer—what's his name?" Ruth looked around at Corinthians, who ignored her.

"And Mary, I suppose." Lena laughed.

Corinthians stared coldly at her sister. "Daddy wouldn't sell property to a barmaid. Daddy, would you let us live next to a barmaid?"

"She owns that place, Corinthians," Ruth said.

"I don't care what she owns. I care about what she is. Daddy?" Corinthians leaned toward her father for confirmation.

"You're going too fast, Macon." Ruth pressed the toe of her shoe against the floorboard.

"If you say one more thing to me about the way I drive, you're going to walk back home. I mean it."

Magdalene called Lena sat forward and put her hand on her mother's shoulder. Ruth was quiet. The little boy kicked his feet against the underside of the dashboard.

"Stop that!" Macon told him.

"I have to go to the bathroom," said his son.

Corinthians held her head. "Oh, Lord."

"But you went before we left," said Ruth.

"I have to *go!*" He was beginning to whine.

"Are you sure?" his mother asked him. He looked at her. "I guess we better stop," Ruth said to nobody in particular. Her eyes grazed the countryside they were entering.

Macon didn't alter his speed.

"Are *we* going to have a summer place, or are you just selling property?"

"I'm not selling anything. I'm thinking of buying and then renting," Macon answered her.

"But are *we*—"

"I have to go," said the little boy.

"—going to live there too?"

"Maybe."

"By ourselves? Who else?" Corinthians was very interested.

"I can't tell you that. But in a few years—five or ten—a whole lot of coloreds will have enough to afford it. A whole lot. Take my word for it."

Magdalene called Lena took a deep breath. "Up ahead you could pull over, Daddy. He might mess up the seat."

Macon glanced at her in the mirror and slowed down. "Who's going to take him?" Ruth fiddled with the door handle. "Not you," Macon said to her.

Ruth looked at her husband. She parted her lips but didn't say anything.

"Not me," said Corinthians. "I have on high heels."

"Come on," Lena sighed. They left the car, little boy and big sister, and disappeared into the trees that reared up off the shoulder of the road.

"You really think there'll be enough colored people—I mean nice colored people—in this city to live there?"

"They don't have to be from this city, Corinthians. People will drive to a summer house. White people do it all the time." Macon drummed his fingers on the steering wheel, which trembled a little as the car idled.

"Negroes don't like the water." Corinthians giggled.

"They'll like it if they own it," said Macon. He looked out the window and saw Magdalene called Lena coming out of the trees. A large colorful bouquet of flowers was in her hand, but her face was crumpled in anger. Over her pale-blue dress dark wet stains spread like fingers.

"He wet on me," she said. "He wet me, Mama." She was close to tears.

Ruth clucked her tongue.

Corinthians laughed. "I told you Negroes didn't like water."

He didn't mean it. It happened before he was through. She'd stepped away from him to pick flowers, returned, and at the sound of her footsteps behind him, he'd turned around before he was through. It was becoming a habit—this concentration on things behind him. Almost as though there were no future to be had.

But if the future did not arrive, the present did extend itself, and the uncomfortable little boy in the Packard went to school and at twelve met the boy who not only could liberate him, but could take him to the woman who had as much to do with his future as she had his past.

Guitar said he knew her. Had even been inside her house.

"What's it like in there?" Milkman asked him.

"Shiny," Guitar answered. "Shiny and brown. With a smell."

"A bad smell?"

"I don't know. Her smell. You'll see."

All those unbelievable but entirely possible stories about his father's sister—the woman his father had forbidden him to go near—had both of them spellbound. Neither wished to live one more day without finding out the truth, and they believed they were the legitimate and natural ones to do so. After all, Guitar already knew her, and Milkman was her nephew.

They found her on the front steps sitting wide-legged in a long-sleeved, long-skirted black dress. Her hair was wrapped in black too, and from a distance, all they could really see beneath her face was the bright orange she was peeling. She was all angles, he remembered later, knees, mostly, and elbows. One foot pointed east and one pointed west.

As they came closer and saw the brass box dangling from her ear, Milkman knew that what with the earring, the orange, and the angled black cloth, nothing—not the wisdom of his father nor the caution of the world—could keep him from her.

Guitar, being older and already in high school, had none of the reluctance that his young buddy still struggled with, and was the first one to speak.

"Hi."

The woman looked up. First at Guitar and then at Milkman.

"What kind of word is that?" Her voice was light but gravel-sprinkled. Milkman kept on staring at her fingers, manipulating the orange. Guitar grinned and shrugged. "It means hello."

"Then say what you mean."

"Okay. Hello."

"That's better. What you want?"

"Nothin. We just passin by."

"Look like you standin by."

"If you don't want us here, Miss Pilate, we'll go." Guitar spoke softly.

"I ain't the one with the wants. You the one want something."

"We wanna ask you something." Guitar stopped feigning indifference. She was too direct, and to keep up with her he had to pay careful attention to his language.

"Ask it."

"Somebody said you ain't got no navel."

"That the question?"

"Yes."

"Don't sound like a question. Sound like an answer. Gimme the question."

"Do you?"

"Do I what?"

"Do you have a navel?"

"No."

"What happened to it?"

"Beats me." She dropped a bright peeling into her lap and separated an orange section slowly. "Now do I get to ask a question?"

"Sure."

"Who's your little friend?"

"This here's Milkman."

"Do he talk?" Pilate swallowed a piece of the fruit.

"Yeah. He talk. Say something." Guitar shoved an elbow at Milkman without taking his eyes off Pilate.

Milkman took a breath, held it, and said, "Hi."

Pilate laughed. "You all must be the dumbest unhung Negroes on earth. What they telling you in them schools? You say 'Hi' to pigs and sheep when you want 'em to move. When you tell a human being 'Hi,' he ought to get up and knock you down."

Shame had flooded him. He had expected to feel it, but not that kind; to be embarrassed, yes, but not that way. She was the one who was ugly, dirty, poor, and drunk. The queer aunt whom his sixth-grade schoolmates teased him about and whom he hated because he felt personally responsible for her ugliness, her poverty, her dirt, and her wine.

Instead she was making fun of his school, of his teachers, of him. And while she looked as poor as everyone said she was, something was missing from her eyes that should have confirmed it. Nor was she dirty; unkempt, yes, but not dirty. The whites of her fingernails were like ivory. And unless he knew absolutely nothing, this woman was definitely not drunk. Of course she was anything but pretty, yet he knew he could have watched her all day: the fingers pulling thread veins from the orange sections, the berry-black lips that made her look as though she wore make-up, the earring. . . . And when she stood up, he all but gasped. She was as tall as his father, head and shoulders taller than himself. Her dress wasn't as long as he had thought; it came to just below her calf and now he could see her unlaced men's shoes and the silvery-brown skin of her ankles.

She held the peelings precisely as they had fallen in her lap, and as she walked up the steps she looked as though she were holding her crotch.

"Your daddy wouldn't like that. He don't like dumb peoples." Then she looked right at Milkman, one hand holding the peelings, the other on the doorknob. "I know your daddy. I know you too."

Again Guitar spoke up. "You his daddy's sister?"

"The only one he got. Ain't but three Deads alive."

Milkman, who had been unable to get one word out of his mouth after the foolish "Hi," heard himself shouting: "I'm a Dead! My mother's a Dead! My sisters. You and him ain't the only ones!"

Even while he was screaming he wondered why he was suddenly so defensive—so possessive about his name. He had always hated that name, all of it, and until he and Guitar became friends, he had hated his nickname too. But in Guitar's mouth it sounded clever, grown up. Now he was behaving with this strange woman as though having the name was a matter of deep personal pride, as though she had tried to expel him from a very special group, in which he not only belonged, but had exclusive rights.

In the heartbeat of silence that followed his shouts, Pilate laughed.

"You all want a soft-boiled egg?" she asked.

The boys looked at each other. She'd changed rhythm on them. They didn't want an egg, but they did want to be with her, to go inside the wine house of this lady who had one earring, no navel, and looked like a tall black tree.

"No, thanks, but we'd like a drink of water." Guitar smiled back at her.

"Well. Step right in." She opened the door and they followed her into a large sunny room that looked both barren and cluttered. A moss-green sack hung from the ceiling. Candles were stuck in bottles everywhere; newspaper articles and magazine pictures were nailed to the walls. But other than a rocking chair, two straight-backed chairs, a large table, a sink and stove, there was no furniture. Pervading everything was the odor of pine and fermenting fruit.

"You ought to try one. I know how to do them just right. I don't like my whites to move, you know. The yolk I want soft, but not runny. Want it like wet velvet. How come you don't just try one?"

She had dumped the peelings in a large crock, which like most everything in the house had been made for some other purpose. Now she stood before the dry sink, pumping water into a blue-and-white wash basin which she used for a saucepan.

"Now, the water and the egg have to meet each other on a kind of equal standing. One can't get the upper hand over the other. So the temperature has to be the same for both. I knock the chill off the water first. Just the chill. I don't let it get warm because the egg is room temperature, you see. Now then, the real secret is right here in the boiling. When the tiny bubbles come to the surface, when they as big as peas and just before they get big as marbles. Well, right then you take the pot off the fire. You don't just put the fire out; you take the pot off. Then you put a folded newspaper over the pot and do one small obligation. Like answering the door or emptying the bucket and bringing it in off the front porch. I generally go to the toilet. Not for a long stay, mind you. Just a short one. If you do all that, you got yourself a perfect soft-boiled egg.

"I remember the messes I used to make for my father when I cooked. Your father"—she directed a thumb at Milkman—"he couldn't cook worth poot. Once I made a cherry pie for him, or tried to. Macon was a nice boy and awful good to me. Be nice if you could have known him then. He would have been a real good friend to you too, like he was to me."

Her voice made Milkman think of pebbles. Little round pebbles that bumped up against each other. Maybe she was hoarse, or maybe it was the way she said her words, with both a drawl and a clip. The piny-winy smell was narcotic, and so was the sun streaming in, strong and unfettered because there were no curtains or shades at the windows that were all around the room, two in each of three walls, one on each side of the door, one on either side of the sink and the stove, and two on the farther wall. The fourth wall must back on the bedrooms, Milkman thought. The pebbly voice, the sun, and the narcotic wine smell weakened both the boys, and they sat in a pleasant semi-stupor, listening to her go on and on. . . .

"Hadn't been for your daddy, I wouldn't be here today. I would have died in the womb. And died again in the woods. Those woods and the dark would have surely killed me. But he saved me and here I am boiling eggs. Our papa was dead, you see. They blew him five feet up into the air. He was sitting on his fence waiting for 'em, and they snuck up from behind and blew him five feet into the air. So when we left Circe's big house we didn't have no place to go, so we just walked around and lived in them woods. Farm country. But Papa came back one day. We didn't know it was him at first, cause we both saw him blowed five feet into the air. We were lost then. And talking about dark! You think dark is just one color, but it ain't. There're five or six kinds of black. Some silky, some woolly.

Some just empty. Some like fingers. And it don't stay still. It moves and changes from one kind of black to another. Saying something is pitch black is like saying something is green. What kind of green? Green like my bottles? Green like a grasshopper? Green like a cucumber, lettuce, or green like the sky is just before it breaks loose to storm? Well, night black is the same way. May as well be a rainbow.

"Now, we lost and there was this wind and in front of us was the back of our daddy. We were some scared children. Macon kept telling me that the things we was scared of wasn't real. What difference do it make if the thing you scared of is real or not? I remember doing laundry for a man and his wife once, down in Virginia. The husband came into the kitchen one afternoon shivering and saying did I have any coffee made. I asked him what was it that had grabbed hold of him, he looked so bad. He said he couldn't figure it out, but he felt like he was about to fall off a cliff. Standing right there on that yellow and white and red linoleum, as level as a flatiron. He was holding on to the door first, then the chair, trying his best not to fall down. I opened my mouth to tell him wasn't no cliff in that kitchen. Then I remembered how it was being in those woods. I felt it all over again. So I told the man did he want me to hold on to him so he couldn't fall. He looked at me with the most grateful look in the world. 'Would you?' he said. I walked around back of him and locked my fingers in front of his chest and held on to him. His heart was kicking under his vest like a mule in heat. But little by little it calmed down."

"You saved his life," said Guitar.

"No such thing. His wife come in before it was time to let go. She asked me what I was doing and I told her."

"Told her what? What'd you say?"

"The truth. That I was trying to keep him from falling off a cliff."

"I bet he wished he had jumped off then. She believe you? Don't tell me she believed you."

"Not right away she didn't. But soon's I let go he fell dead-weight to the floor. Smashed his glasses and everything. Fell right on his face. And you know what? He went down so slow. I swear it took three minutes, three whole minutes to go from a standing upright position to when he mashed his face on the floor. I don't know if the cliff was real or not, but it took him three minutes to fall down it."

"Was he dead?" asked Guitar.

"Stone dead."

"Who shot your daddy? Did you say somebody shot him?" Guitar was fascinated, his eyes glittering with lights.

"Five feet into the air . . ."

"Who?"

"I don't know who and I don't know why. I just know what I'm telling you: what, when, and where."

"You didn't say where." He was insistent.

"I did too. Off a fence."

"Where was the fence?"

"On our farm."

Guitar laughed, but his eyes were too shiny to convey much humor. "Where was the farm?"

"Montour County."

He gave up on "where." "Well, when then?"

"When he sat there—on the fence."

Guitar felt like a frustrated detective. "What year?"

"The year they shot them Irish people down in the streets. Was a good year for guns and gravediggers, I know that." Pilate put a barrel lid on the table. Then she lifted the eggs from the wash basin and began to peel them. Her lips moved as she played an orange seed around in her mouth. Only after the eggs were split open, revealing moist reddish-yellow centers, did she return to her story. "One morning we woke up when the sun was nearly a quarter way cross the sky. Bright as anything. And blue. Blue like the ribbons on my mother's bonnet. See that streak of sky?" She pointed out the window. "Right behind them hickories. See? Right over there."

They looked and saw the sky stretching back behind the houses and the trees. "That's the same color," she said, as if she had discovered something important. "Same color as my mama's ribbons. I'd know her ribbon color anywhere, but I don't know her name. After she died Papa wouldn't let anybody say it. Well, before we could get the sand rubbed out of our eyes and take a good look around, we saw him sitting there on a stump. Right in the sunlight. We started to call him but he looked on off, like he was lookin at us and not lookin at us at the same time. Something in his face scared us. It was like looking at a face under water. Papa got up after a while and moved out of the sun on back into the woods. We just stood there looking at the stump. Shaking like leaves."

Pilate scraped the eggshells together into a little heap, her fingers fanning out over and over again in a gentle sweeping. The boys watched, afraid to say anything lest they ruin the next part of her story, and afraid to remain silent lest she not go on with its telling.

"Shaking like leaves," she murmured, "just like leaves."

Suddenly she lifted her head and made a sound like a hoot owl. "Ooo! Here I come!"

Neither Milkman nor Guitar saw or heard anyone approaching, but Pilate jumped up and ran toward the door. Before she reached it, a foot kicked it open and Milkman saw the bent back of a girl. She was dragging a large five-bushel basket of what looked like brambles, and a woman was pushing the other side of it, saying, "Watch the doorsill, baby."

"I got it," the girl answered. "Push."

"About time," said Pilate. "The light be gone before you know it."

"Tommy's truck broke down," the girl said, panting. When the two had managed to get the basket into the room, the girl stretched her back and turned around, facing them. But Milkman had no need to see her face; he had already fallen in love with her behind.

"Hagar." Pilate looked around the room. "This here's your brother, Milkman. And this is his friend. What's your name again, pretty?"

"Guitar."

"Guitar? You play any?" she asked.

"That ain't her brother, Mama. They cousins." The older woman spoke.

"Same thing."

"No it ain't. Is it, baby?"

"No," said Hagar. "It's different."

"See there. It's different."

"Well, what is the difference, Reba? You know so much."

Reba looked at the ceiling. "A brother is a brother if you both got the same mother or if you both—"

Pilate interrupted her. "I mean what's the difference in the way you act toward 'em? Don't you have to act the same way to both?"

"That's not the point, Mama."

"Shut up, Reba. I'm talking to Hagar."

"Yes, Mama. You treat them both the same."

"Then why they got two words for it 'stead of one, if they ain't no difference?" Reba put her hands on her hips and opened her eyes wide.

"Pull that rocker over here," said Pilate. "You boys have to give up your seats unless you gonna help."

The women circled the basket, which was full of blackberries still on their short, thorny branches.

"What we have to do?" Guitar asked.

"Get them little berries off them hateful branches without popping 'em. Reba, get that other crock."

Hagar looked around, all eyes and hair. "Why don't we pull a bed out the back room? Then we can all sit down."

"Floor's good enough for me," said Pilate, and she squatted down on her haunches and lifted a branch gently from the basket. "This all you got?"

"No." Reba was side-rolling a huge crock. "Two more outside."

"Better bring them in. Draw too many flies out there."

Hagar started for the door and motioned to Milkman. "Come on, brother. You can help."

Milkman jumped up, knocking his chair backward, and trotted after Hagar. She was, it seemed to him, as pretty a girl as he'd ever seen. She was much much older than he was. She must be as old as Guitar, maybe even seventeen. He seemed to be floating. More alive than he'd ever been, and floating. Together he and Hagar dragged two baskets up the porch stairs and into the house. She was as strong and muscular as he was.

"Careful, Guitar. Go slow. You keep on busting 'em."

"Leave him alone, Reba. He got to get the feel first. I asked you did you play any. That why they call you Guitar?"

"Not cause I do play. Because I wanted to. When I was real little. So they tell me."

"Where'd you ever see a guitar?"

"It was a contest, in a store down home in Florida. I saw it when my mother took me downtown with her. I was just a baby. It was one of those things where you guess how many beans in the big glass jar and you win a guitar. I cried for it, they said. And always asked about it."

"You should of called Reba. She'd get it for you."

"No, you couldn't buy it. You had to give the number of jellybeans."

"I heard you. Reba would of known how many. Reba wins things. She ain't never lost nothing."

"Really?" Guitar smiled, but he was doubtful. "She lucky?"

"Sure I'm lucky." Reba grinned. "People come from everywhere to get me to stand in for 'em at drawings and give them numbers to play. It works pretty well for them, and it always works for me. I win everything I try to win and lots of things I don't even try to win."

"Got to where won't nobody sell her a raffle ticket. They just want her to hold theirs."

"See this?" Reba put her hand down in the top of her dress and pulled out a diamond ring attached to a string. "I won this last year. I was the . . . what was it, Mama?"

"Five hundred thousandth."

"Five hundred . . . no it wasn't. That ain't what they said."

"Half a million is what they said."

"That's right. The half a millionth person to walk into Sears and Roebuck." Her laughter was gay and proud.

"They didn't want to give it to her," said Hagar, "cause she looked so bad."

Guitar was astonished. "I remember that contest, but I don't remember hearing nothing 'bout no colored person winning it." Guitar, a habitual street roamer, believed he knew every public thing going on in the city.

"Nobody did. They had picture-taking people and everything waiting for the next person to walk in the door. But they never did put my picture in the paper. Me and Mama looked, too, didn't we?" She glanced at Pilate for confirmation and went on. "But they put the picture of the man who won second prize in. He won a war bond. He was white."

"Second prize?" Guitar asked. "What kind of 'second prize'? Either you the half-millionth person or you ain't. Can't be no next-to-the-half-millionth."

"Can if the winner is Reba," Hagar said. "The only reason they got a second was cause she was the first. And the only reason they gave it to her was because of them cameras."

"Tell 'em why you was in Sears, Reba."

"Looking for a toilet." Reba threw her head back to let the laughter escape. Her hands were stained with blackberry juice, and when she wiped the tears from her eyes she streaked the purple from her nose to her cheekbone. Much lighter than Pilate or Hagar, Reba had the simple eyes of an infant. All of them had a guileless look about them, but complication and something more lurked behind Pilate's and Hagar's faces. Only Reba, with her light pimply skin and deferential manner, looked as though her simplicity might also be vacuousness.

"Ain't but two toilets downtown they let colored in: Mayflower Restaurant and Sears. Sears was closer. Good thing nature wasn't in a hurry. They kept me there fifteen minutes gettin my name and address to send the diamond over to me. But I wouldn't let 'em send it to me. I kept asking them, Is this a real contest? I don't believe you."

"It was worth a diamond ring to get you out of there. Drawing a crowd and getting ready to draw flies," said Hagar.

"What're you going to do with the ring?" Milkman asked her.

"Wear it. Seldom I win something I like."

"Everything she win, she give away," Hagar said.

"To a man," said Pilate.

"She don't never keep none of it. . . ."

"That's what she want to win—a man. . . ."

"Worse'n Santa Claus. . . ."

"Funny kind of luck ain't no luck at all. . . ."

"*He* comes just once a year. . . ."

Hagar and Pilate pulled the conversation apart, each yanking out some thread of comment more to herself than to Milkman or Guitar—or even Reba, who had dropped her ring back inside her dress and was smiling sweetly, and deftly separating the royal-purple berries from their twigs.

Milkman was five feet seven then but it was the first time in his life that he remembered being completely happy. He was with his friend, an older boy—wise and kind and fearless. He was sitting comfortably in the notorious wine house; he was surrounded by women who seemed to enjoy him and who laughed out loud. And he was in love. No wonder his father was afraid of them.

"When will this wine be ready?" he asked.

"This batch? Few weeks," Pilate said.

"You gonna let us have some?" Guitar smiled.

"Sure. You want some now? Plenty wine in the cellar."

"I don't want that. I want some of this. Some of the wine I made."

"You think you made this?" Pilate laughed at him. "You think this all there is to it? Picking a few berries?"

"Oh." Guitar scratched his head. "I forgot. We got to mash them in our bare feet."

"Feet? Feet?" Pilate was outraged. "Who makes wine with they feet?"

"Might taste good, Mama," said Hagar.

"Couldn't taste no worse," Reba said.

"Your wine any good, Pilate?" asked Guitar.

"Couldn't tell you."

"Why not?"

"Never tasted it."

Milkman laughed. "You sell wine you don't even taste?"

"Folks don't buy it for the taste. Buy it to get drunk."

Reba nodded. "Used to anyway. Ain't buying nothing now."

"Don't nobody want no cheap home brew. The Depression's over," Hagar said. "Everybody got work now. They can afford to buy Four Roses."

"Plenty still buy," Pilate told her.

"Where you get the sugar for it?" Guitar asked.

"Black market," said Reba.

"What 'plenty'? Tell the truth, Mama. If Reba hadn't won that hundred pounds of groceries, we'd have starved last winter."

"Would not." Pilate put a fresh piece of twig in her mouth.

"We *would* have."

"Hagar, don't contradict your mama," Reba whispered.

"Who was gonna feed us?" Hagar was insistent. "Mama can go for months without food. Like a lizard."

"Lizard live that long without food?" asked Reba.

"Girl, ain't nobody gonna let you starve. You ever had a hungry day?" Pilate asked her granddaughter.

"Course she ain't," said her mother.

Hagar tossed a branch to the heap on the floor and rubbed her fingers. The tips were colored a deep red. "Some of my days were hungry ones."

With the quickness of birds, the heads of Pilate and Reba shot up. They peered at Hagar, then exchanged looks.

"Baby?" Reba's voice was soft. "You been hungry, baby? Why didn't you say so?" Reba looked hurt. "We get you anything you want, baby. Anything. You *been* knowing that."

Pilate spit her twig into the palm of her hand. Her face went still. Without those moving lips her face was like a mask. It seemed to Milkman that somebody had just clicked off a light.

He looked at the faces of the women. Reba's had crumpled. Tears were streaming down her cheeks. Pilate's face was still as death, but alert as though waiting for some signal. Hagar's profile was hidden by her hair. She leaned forward, her elbows on her thighs, rubbing fingers that looked bloodstained in the lessening light. Her nails were very very long.

The quiet held. Even Guitar didn't dare break it.

Then Pilate spoke. "Reba. She don't mean food."

Realization swept slowly across Reba's face, but she didn't answer. Pilate began to hum as she returned to plucking the berries. After a moment, Reba joined her, and they hummed together in perfect harmony until Pilate took the lead:

O Sugarman don't leave me here
Cotton balls to choke me
O Sugarman don't leave me here
Buckra's arms to yoke me. . . .

When the two women got to the chorus, Hagar raised her head and sang too.

Sugarman done fly away
Sugarman done gone
Sugarman cut across the sky
Sugarman gone home.

Milkman could hardly breathe. Hagar's voice scooped up what little pieces of heart he had left to call his own. When he thought he was going to faint from the weight of what he was feeling, he risked a glance at his friend and saw the setting sun gilding Guitar's eyes, putting into shadow a slow smile of recognition.

Delicious as the day turned out to be for Milkman, it was even more so because it included secrecy and defiance, both of which dissipated within an hour of his father's return. Freddie had let Macon Dead know that his son had spent the afternoon "drinking in the wine house."

"He's lying! We didn't drink nothing. Nothing. Guitar didn't even get the glass of water he asked for."

"Freddie never lies. He misrepresents, but he never lies."

"He lied to you."

"About the wine-drinking? Maybe. But not about you being there, huh?"

"No, sir. Not about that." Milkman softened his tone a bit, but succeeded in keeping the edge of defiance in his voice.

"Now, what were your instructions from me?"

"You told me to stay away from there. To stay away from Pilate."

"Right."

"But you never told me why. They're our cousins. She's your own sister."

"And you're my own son. And you will do what I tell you to do. With or without explanations. As long as your feet are under my table, you'll do in this house what you are told."

At fifty-two, Macon Dead was as imposing a man as he had been at forty-two, when Milkman thought he was the biggest thing in the world. Bigger even than the house they lived in. But today he had seen a woman who was just as tall and who had made him feel tall too.

"I know I'm the youngest one in this family, but I ain't no baby. You treat me like I was a baby. You keep saying you don't have to explain nothing to me. How do you think that makes me feel? Like a baby, that's what. Like a twelve-year-old baby!"

"Don't you raise your voice to me."

"Is that the way your father treated you when you were twelve?"

"Watch your mouth!" Macon roared. He took his hands out of his pockets but didn't know what to do with them. He was momentarily confused. His son's question had shifted the scenery. He was seeing himself at twelve, standing in Milkman's shoes and feeling what he himself had felt for his own father. The numbness that had settled on him when he saw the man he loved and admired fall off the fence; something wild ran through him when he watched the body twitching in the dirt. His father had sat for five nights on a split-rail fence cradling a shotgun and in the end died protecting his property. Was that what this boy felt for him? Maybe it was time to tell him things.

"Well, did he?"

"I worked right alongside my father. Right alongside him. From the time I was four or five we worked together. Just the two of us. Our mother was dead. Died when Pilate was born. Pilate was just a baby. She stayed over at another farm in the daytime. I carried her over there myself in my arms every morning. Then I'd go back across the fields and meet my father. We'd hitch President Lincoln to the plow and . . . That's what we called her: President Lincoln. Papa said Lincoln was a good plow hand before he was President and you shouldn't take a good plow hand away from his work. He called our farm Lincoln's Heaven. It was a little bit a place. But it looked big to me then. I know now it must a been a little bit a place, maybe a hundred and fifty acres. We tilled fifty. About eighty of it was woods. Must of been a fortune in oak and pine; maybe that's what they wanted—the lumber, the oak and the pine. We had a pond that was four acres. And a stream, full of fish. Right down in the heart of a valley. Prettiest mountain you ever saw, Montour Ridge. We lived in Montour County. Just north of the Susquehanna. We had a four-stall hog pen. The big barn was forty feet by a hundred and forty—hip-roofed too. And all around in the mountains was deer and wild turkey. You ain't tasted nothing till you taste wild turkey the way Papa cooked it. He'd burn it real fast in the fire. Burn it black all over. That sealed it. Sealed the juices in. Then he'd let it roast on a spit for twenty-four hours. When you cut the black burnt part off, the meat underneath was tender, sweet, juicy. And we had fruit trees. Apple, cherry. Pilate tried to make me a cherry pie once."

Macon paused and let the smile come on. He had not said any of this for years. Had not even reminisced much about it recently. When he was first married he used to talk about Lincoln's Heaven to Ruth. Sitting on the porch swing in the dark, he would re-create the land that was to have been his. Or when he was just starting out in the business of buying houses, he would lounge around the barbershop and swap stories with the men there. But for years he hadn't had that kind of time, or interest. But now he was doing it again, with his son, and every detail of that land was clear in his mind: the well, the apple orchard, President Lincoln; her foal, Mary Todd; Ulysses S. Grant, their cow; General Lee, their hog. That was the way he knew what history he remembered. His father couldn't read, couldn't write; knew only what he saw and heard tell of. But he had etched in Macon's mind certain historical figures, and as a boy in school, Macon thought of the personalities of his horse, his hog, when he read about these people. His father may have called their plow horse President Lincoln as a joke, but Macon always thought of Lincoln with fondness since he had loved him first as a strong, steady, gentle, and obedient horse. He even liked General Lee, for one spring they slaughtered him and ate the best pork outside Virginia, "from the butt to the smoked ham to the ribs to the sausage to the jowl to the feet to the tail to the head cheese"—for eight months. And there was cracklin in November.

"General Lee was all right by me," he told Milkman, smiling. "Finest general I ever knew. Even his balls was tasty. Circe made up the best pot of maws she ever cooked. Huh! I'd forgotten that woman's name. That was it, Circe. Worked at a big farm some white people owned in Danville, Pennsylvania. Funny how things get away from you. For years you can't remember nothing. Then just like that, it all comes back to you. Had a dog run, they did. That was the big sport back then. Dog races. White people did love their dogs. Kill a nigger and comb their hair at the same time. But I've seen grown white men cry about their dogs."

His voice sounded different to Milkman. Less hard, and his speech was different. More southern and comfortable and soft. Milkman spoke softly too. "Pilate said somebody shot your father. Five feet into the air."

"Took him sixteen years to get that farm to where it was paying. It's all dairy country up there now. Then it wasn't. Then it was . . . nice."

"Who shot him, Daddy?"

Macon focused his eyes on his son. "Papa couldn't read, couldn't even sign his name. Had a mark he used. They tricked him. He signed something, I don't know what, and they told him they owned his property. He never read nothing. I tried to teach him, but he said he couldn't remember those little marks from one day to the next. Wrote one word in his life—Pilate's name; copied it out of the Bible. That's what she got folded up in that earring. He should have let me teach him. Everything bad that ever happened to him happened because he couldn't read. Got his name messed up cause he couldn't read."

"His name? How?"

"When freedom came. All the colored people in the state had to register with the Freedmen's Bureau."

"Your father was a slave?"

"What kind of foolish question is that? Course he was. Who hadn't been in 1869? They all had to register. Free and not free. Free and used-to-be-slaves. Papa was in his teens and went to sign up, but the man behind the desk was drunk. He asked Papa where he was born. Papa said Macon. Then he asked him who his father was. Papa said, 'He's dead.' Asked him who owned him, Papa said, 'I'm free.' Well, the Yankee wrote it all down, but in the wrong spaces. Had him born in Dunfrie, wherever the hell that is, and in the space for his name the fool wrote, 'Dead' comma 'Macon.' But Papa couldn't read so he never found out what he was registered as till Mama told him. They met on a wagon going North. Started talking about one thing and another, told her about being a freedman and showed off his papers to her. When she looked at his paper she read him out what it said."

"He didn't have to keep the name, did he? He could have used his real name, couldn't he?"

"Mama liked it. Liked the name. Said it was new and would wipe out the past. Wipe it all out."

"What was his real name?"

"I don't remember my mother too well. She died when I was four. Light-skinned, pretty. Looked like a white woman to me. Me and Pilate don't take nothing after her. If you ever have a doubt we from Africa, look at Pilate. She look just like Papa and he looked like all them pictures you ever see of Africans. A Pennsylvania African. Acted like one too. Close his face up like a door."

"I saw Pilate's face like that." Milkman felt close and confidential now that his father had talked to him in a relaxed and intimate way.

"I haven't changed my mind, Macon. I don't want you over there."

"Why? You still haven't said why."

"Just listen to what I say. That woman's no good. She's a snake, and can charm you like a snake, but still a snake."

"You talking about your own sister, the one you carried in your arms to the fields every morning."

"That was a long time ago. You seen her. What she look like to you? Somebody nice? Somebody normal?"

"Well, she . . ."

"Or somebody cut your throat?"

"She didn't look like that, Daddy."

"Well she *is* like that."

"What'd she do?"

"It ain't what she did; it's what she is."

"What is she?"

"A snake, I told you. Ever hear the story about the snake? The man who saw a little baby snake on the ground? Well, the man saw this baby snake bleeding and hurt. Lying there in the dirt. And the man felt sorry for it and picked it up and put it in his basket and took it home. And he fed it and took care of it till it was big and strong. Fed it the same thing he ate. Then one day, the snake turned on him and bit him. Stuck his poison tongue right in the man's heart. And while he was laying there dying, he turned to the snake and asked him, 'What'd you do that for?' He said, 'Didn't I take good care of you? Didn't I save your life?' The snake said, 'Yes.' 'Then what'd you do it for? What'd you kill me for?' Know what the snake said? Said, 'But you knew I was a snake, didn't you?' Now, I mean for you to stay out of that wine house and as far away from Pilate as you can."

Milkman lowered his head. His father had explained nothing to him.

"Boy, you got better things to do with your time. Besides, it's time you started learning how to work. You start Monday. After school come to my office; work a couple of hours there and learn what's real. Pilate can't teach you a thing you can use in this world. Maybe the next, but not this one. Let me tell you right now the one important thing you'll ever need to know: Own things. And let the things you own own other things. Then you'll own yourself and other people too. Starting Monday, I'm going to teach you how."

Chapter 3

Life improved for Milkman enormously after he began working for Macon. Contrary to what his father hoped, there was more time to visit the wine house. Running errands for Macon's rent houses gave him leave to be in Southside and get to know the people Guitar knew so well. Milkman was young and he was friendly—just the opposite of his father—and the tenants felt at ease enough with him to tease him, feed him, confide in him. But it was hard to see much of Guitar. Saturdays were the only days he was certain to find him. If Milkman got up early enough on Saturday morning, he could catch his friend before Guitar went roaming the streets and before he himself had to help Macon collect rents. But there were days in the week when they agreed to skip school and hang out, and on one of those days Guitar took him to Feather's pool hall on Tenth Street, right in the middle of the Blood Bank area.

It was eleven o'clock in the morning when Guitar pushed open the door and shouted, "Hey, Feather! Give us a couple of Red Caps."

Feather, a short squat man with sparse but curly hair, looked up at Guitar, then at Milkman, and frowned.

"Get him out of here."

Guitar stopped short and followed the little man's gaze to Milkman's face and back again. The half-dozen men there playing pool turned around at the sound of Feather's voice. Three of them were air force pilots, part of the 332nd Fighter Group. Their beautiful hats and gorgeous leather jackets were carefully arranged on chairs. Their hair was cut close to the skull; their shirt cuffs were turned neatly back on their forearms; their white scarves hung in snowy rectangles from their hip pockets. Silver chains glistened at their necks and they looked faintly amused as they worked chalk into the tips of their cues.

Guitar's face shone with embarrassment. "He's with me," he said.

"I said get him outta here."

"Come on, Feather, he's my friend."

"He's Macon Dead's boy, ain't he?"

"So what?"

"So get him outta here."

"He can't help who his daddy is." Guitar had his voice under control.

"Neither can I. Out."

"What his daddy do to you?"

"Nothing yet. That's why I want him outta here."

"He ain't like his daddy."

"He ain't got to be like him—*from* him is enough."

"I'll bc rcsponsible for—"

"Stop messing with me, Guitar. Get him out. He ain't old enough to have wet dreams."

The pilots laughed and a man in a gray straw hat with a white band said, "Aw, let the boy stay, Feather."

"You shut your mouth. I'm running this."

"What harm can he do? A twelve-year-old kid." He smiled at Milkman, who stopped himself from saying, No, thirteen.

"But it ain't your problem, is it?" asked Feather. "His daddy ain't your landlord, is he, and you ain't got no operating license to hang on to either. You ain't got nothing. . . ."

Feather turned on the man with the white hatband the same acid manner he'd used with the boys. Guitar took the opportunity offered by Feather's new target to shoot his hand out like a double-edged hatchet slamming into a tree, and shout, "Later for you, man. Come on. Let's shake this place." His voice now was loud and deep—loud enough and deep enough for two. Milkman slid his hands into his back pockets and followed his friend to the door. He stretched his neck a little to match the chilly height he hoped the soldiers had seen in his eyes.

Silently they ambled down Tenth Street until they reached a stone bench that jutted from the sidewalk near the curb. They stopped there and sat down, their backs to the eyes of two men in white smocks who were watching them. One of the men leaned in the doorway of a barbershop. The other sat in a chair tilted back to the plate-glass window of the shop. They were the owners of the barbershop, Railroad Tommy and Hospital Tommy. Neither boy spoke, not to the men nor to each other. They sat and watched the traffic go by.

"Have all the halls of academe crumbled, Guitar?" Hospital Tommy spoke from his chair. His eyes were milky, like those of very old people, but the rest of him was firm, lithe, and young-looking. His tone was casual but suggested authority nonetheless.

"No, sir." Guitar answered him over his shoulder.

"Then what, pray, are you doing out here in the streets at this time of day?"

Guitar shrugged. "We just took a day off, Mr. Tommy."

"And your companion? Is he on sabbatical too?"

Guitar nodded. Hospital Tommy talked like an encyclopedia and Guitar had to guess at most of his words. Milkman kept looking at the cars going by.

"Neither one of you appears to be having much fun on your holiday. You could have stayed in the halls of academe and looked evil."

Guitar fished for a cigarette and offered one to Milkman. "Feather made me mad is all."

"Feather?"

"Yeah. He wouldn't let us in. I go in there all the time. All the time and he don't say nothing. But today he throws us out. Said my friend here is too young. Can you beat that? Feather? Worrying about somebody's age?"

"I didn't know Feather had so much as a brain cell to worry with."

"He don't. Just showing off is all. He wouldn't even let me have a bottle of beer."

Railroad Tommy laughed softly from the doorway. "Is that all? He wouldn't let you have a beer?" He rubbed the back of his neck and then crooked a finger at Guitar. "Come over here, boy, and let me tell you about some other stuff you are not going to have. Come on over here."

Reluctantly they stood up and sidled closer to the laughing man.

"You think that's something? Not having a beer? Well, let me ask you something. You ever stood stock still in the galley of the Baltimore and Ohio dining car in the middle of the night when the kitchen closed down and everything's neat and ready for the next day? And the engine's highballing down the track and three of your buddies is waiting for you with a brand-new deck of cards?"

Guitar shook his head. "No, I never . . ."

"That's right, you never. And you never going to. That's one more thrill you not going to have, let alone a bottle of beer."

Guitar smiled. "Mr. Tommy," he began, but Tommy cut him off.

"You ever pull fourteen days straight and come home to a sweet woman, clean sheets, and a fifth of Wild Turkey? Eh?" He looked at Milkman. "Did you?"

Milkman smiled and said, "No, sir."

"No? Well, don't look forward to it, cause you not going to have that either."

Hospital Tommy drew a pinfeather toothpick from under his smock. "Don't tease the boy, Tommy."

"Who's teasing? I'm telling him the truth. He ain't going to have it. Neither one of 'em going to have it. And I'll tell you something else you not going to have. You not going to have no private coach with four red velvet chairs that swivel around in one place whenever you want 'em to. No. And you not going to have your own special toilet and your own special-made eight-foot bed either. And a valet and a cook and a secretary to travel with you and do everything you say. Everything: get the right temperature in your hot-water bottle and make sure the smoking tobacco in the silver humidor is fresh each and *every* day. That's something else you not going to have. You ever have five thousand dollars of cold cash money in your pocket and walk into a bank and tell the bank man you want such and such a house on such and such a street and he sell it to you right then? Well, you won't ever have it. And you not going to have a governor's mansion, or eight thousand acres of timber to sell. And you not going to have no ship under your command to sail on, no train to run, and you can join the 332nd if you want to and shoot down a thousand German planes all by yourself and land in Hitler's backyard and whip him with your own hands, but you never going to have four stars on your shirt front, or even three. And you not going to have no breakfast tray brought in to you early in the morning with a red rose on it and two warm croissants and a cup of hot chocolate. Nope. Never. And no pheasant buried in coconut leaves for twenty days and stuffed with wild rice and cooked over a wood fire so tender and delicate it make you cry. And no Rothschild '29 or even Beaujolais to go with it."

A few men passing by stopped to listen to Tommy's lecture. "What's going on?" they asked Hospital Tommy.

"Feather refused them a beer," he said. The men laughed.

"And *no* baked Alaska!" Railroad Tommy went on. "None! You never going to have that."

"No baked Alaska?" Guitar opened his eyes wide with horror and grabbed his throat. "You breaking my heart!"

"Well, now. That's something you will have—a broken heart." Railroad Tommy's eyes softened, but the merriment in them died suddenly. "And folly. A whole lot of folly. You can count on it."

"Mr. Tommy, suh," Guitar sang in mock humility, "we just wanted a bottle of beer is all."

"Yeah," said Tommy. "Yeah, well, welcome aboard."

"What's a baked Alaska?" They left the Tommys just as they had found them and continued down Tenth Street.

"Something sweet," answered Guitar. "A dessert."

"Taste good?"

"I don't know. I can't eat sweets."

"You can't?" Milkman was amazed. "Why not?"

"Makes me sick."

"You don't like nothing sweet?"

"Fruit, but nothing with sugar. Candy, cake, stuff like that. I don't even like to smell it. Makes me want to throw up."

Milkman searched for a physical cause. He wasn't sure he trusted anybody who didn't like sweets. "You must have sugar diabetes."

"You don't get sugar diabetes from not eating sugar. You get it from eating too much sugar."

"Then what is it, then?"

"I don't know. It makes me think of dead people. And white people. And I start to puke."

"Dead people?"

"Yeah. And white people."

"I don't get it."

Guitar said nothing, so Milkman continued, "How long you been like that?"

"Since I was little. Since my father got sliced up in a sawmill and his boss came by and gave us kids some candy. Divinity. A big sack of divinity. His wife made it special for us. It's sweet, divinity is. Sweeter than syrup. Real sweet. Sweeter than . . ." He stopped walking and wiped from his forehead the beads of sweat that were collecting there. His eyes paled and wavered. He spit on the sidewalk. "Ho—hold it," he whispered, and stepped into a space between a fried-fish restaurant and Lilly's Beauty Parlor.

Milkman waited on the sidewalk, staring at the curtained window of the beauty shop. Beauty shops always had curtains or shades up. Barbershops didn't. The women didn't want anybody on the street to be able to see them getting their hair done. They were ashamed.

When Guitar emerged, his eyes were teary from the effort of dry heaving. "Come on," he said. "Let's get us some weed. That's one thing I can have."

By the time Milkman was fourteen he had noticed that one of his legs was shorter than the other. When he stood barefoot and straight as a pole, his left foot was about half an inch off the floor. So he never stood straight; he slouched or leaned or stood with a hip thrown out, and he never told anybody about it—ever. When Lena said, "Mama, what is he walking like *that* for?" he said, "I'll walk any way I want to, including over your ugly face." Ruth said, "Be quiet, you two. It's just growing pains, Lena." Milkman knew better. It wasn't a limp—not at all—just the suggestion of one, but it looked like an affected walk, the strut of a very young man trying to appear more sophisticated than he was. It bothered him and he acquired movements and habits to disguise what to him was a burning defect. He sat with his left ankle on his right knee, never the other way around. And he danced each new dance with a curious stiff-legged step that the girls loved and other boys eventually copied. The deformity was mostly in his mind. Mostly, but not completely, for he did have shooting pains in that leg after several hours on a basketball court. He favored it, believed it was polio, and felt secretly connected to the late President Roosevelt for that reason. Even when everybody was raving about Truman because he had set up a Committee on Civil Rights,

Milkman secretly preferred FDR and felt very very close to him. Closer, in fact, to him than to his own father, for Macon had no imperfection and age seemed to strengthen him. Milkman feared his father, respected him, but knew, because of the leg, that he could never emulate him. So he differed from him as much as he dared. Macon was clean-shaven; Milkman was desperate for a mustache. Macon wore bow ties; Milkman wore four-in-hands. Macon didn't part his hair; Milkman had a part shaved into his. Macon hated tobacco; Milkman tried to put a cigarette in his mouth every fifteen minutes. Macon hoarded his money; Milkman gave his away. But he couldn't help sharing with Macon his love of good shoes and fine thin socks. And he did try, as his father's employee, to do the work the way Macon wanted it done.

Macon was delighted. His son belonged to him now and not to Ruth, and he was relieved at not having to walk all over town like a peddler collecting rents. It made his business more dignified, and he had time to think, to plan, to visit the bank men, to read the public notices, auctions, to find out what plots were going for taxes, unclaimed heirs' property, where roads were being built, what supermarkets, schools; and who was trying to sell what to the government for the housing projects that were going to be built. The quickie townlets that were springing up around war plants. He knew as a Negro he wasn't going to get a big slice of the pie. But there were properties nobody wanted yet, or little edges of property somebody didn't want Jews to have, or Catholics to have, or properties nobody knew were of any value yet. There was quite a bit of pie filling oozing around the edge of the crust in 1945. Filling that could be his. Everything had improved for Macon Dead during the war. Except Ruth. And years later when the war was over and that pie filling had spilled over into his very lap, had stickied his hands and weighed his stomach down into a sagging paunch, he still wished he had strangled her back in 1921. She hadn't stopped spending occasional nights out of the house, but she was fifty years old now and what lover could she have kept so long? What lover could there be that even Freddie didn't know about? Macon decided it was of no importance, and less and less often did he get angry enough to slap her. Particularly after the final time, which became final because his son jumped up and knocked him back into the radiator.

Milkman was twenty-two then and since he had been fucking for six years, some of them with the same woman, he'd begun to see his mother in a new light. She was no longer the person who worried him about galoshes and colds and food, who stood in the way of most of the little pleasures he could take at home because they all involved some form of dirt, noise, or disarray. Now he saw her as a frail woman content to do tiny things; to grow and cultivate small life that would not hurt her if it died: rhododendron, goldfish, dahlias, geraniums, imperial tulips. Because these little lives did die. The goldfish floated to the top of the water and when she tapped the side of the bowl with her fingernail they did not flash away in a lightning arc of terror. The rhododendron leaves grew wide and green and when their color was at its deepest and waxiest, they suddenly surrendered it and lapsed into limp yellow hearts. In a way she was jealous of death. Inside all that grief she felt when the doctor died, there had been a bit of pique too, as though he had chosen a more interesting subject than life—a more provocative companion than she was—and had deliberately followed death when it beckoned. She was fierce in the presence of death, heroic even, as she was at no other time. Its threat gave her direction, clarity, audacity. Regardless of what Macon had done, she'd always suspected that the doctor didn't have to die if he hadn't wanted to. And it may have been that suspicion of personal failure and rejection (plus a smidgen of revenge against Macon) that made her lead her husband down paths from which there was no exit save violence. Lena thought Macon's rages unaccountable. But Corinthians began to see a plan. To see how her mother had learned to bring her husband to a point, not of power (a nine-year-old girl could slap Ruth and get away with it), but of helplessness. She would begin by describing some incident in which she was a sort of honest buffoon. It began as a piece of pleasant dinner conversation, harmless on the surface because no one at the table was required to share her embarrassment; but all were able to admire her honesty and to laugh at her ignorance.

She had gone to the wedding of Mrs. Djvorak's granddaughter. Anna Djvorak was an old Hungarian woman who had been one of her father's patients. He'd had many working-class white patients and some middle-class white women who thought he was handsome. Anna Djvorak was convinced that the doctor had miraculously saved her son's life by not sending him to the tuberculosis sanatorium back in 1903. Almost everybody who did go to the "san," as they called it, died in it. Anna didn't know that the doctor had no practicing privileges there, just as he had none at Mercy. Nor did she know that the cure for tuberculosis in 1903 was precisely the one most detrimental to the patients. All she knew was that the doctor had prescribed a certain diet, hours of rest to be rigidly adhered to, and cod-liver oil twice a day. The boy survived. It was natural that she would want the miracle doctor's daughter at the wedding of this son's youngest daughter. Ruth went and when the congregation went to the altar to receive the host, she went also. Kneeling there with her head bowed, she was not aware that the priest was left with the choice of placing the wafer on her hat or skipping her. He knew immediately that she was not Catholic since she did not raise her head at his words and push out her tongue for the wafer to be carefully placed there.

"Corpus Domini Nostri Jesu Christi," said the priest, and then, to her, a sharp whisper: "Ssss. Raise your head!" She looked up, saw the wafer and the acolyte holding a little silver tray under it. "Corpus Domini Nostri Jesu Christi custodiat animam tuam . . ." The priest held the host toward her and she opened her mouth.

Later, at the reception, the priest asked her point-blank whether she was Catholic.

"No. I'm Methodist," she said.

"I see," he said. "Well, the sacraments of the Church are reserved for—" Just then old Mrs. Djvorak interrupted him.

"Father," she said, "I want you to meet one of my dearest

friends. Dr. Foster's daughter. Her father saved Ricky's life. Ricky wouldn't be here today if . . ."

Father Padrew smiled and shook Ruth's hand. "Very pleased to meet you, Miss Foster."

It was a simple occurrence, elaborately told. Lena listened and experienced each phrase of her mother's emotion from religious ecstasy to innocent confidence to embarrassment. Corinthians listened analytically, expectantly—wondering how her mother would develop this anecdote into a situation in which Macon would either lash out at her verbally or hit her. Milkman was only half listening.

" 'Are you Catholic?' he asked me. Well, I was embarrassed for a minute, but then I said, 'No. I'm Methodist.' And he started to tell me that only Catholics could take communion in a Catholic church. Well, I never heard of that. Anybody can take communion, I thought. At our church anybody can come up on the first Sunday. Well, before he could get it out, Anna came up and said, 'Father, I want you to meet one of my dearest friends. Dr. Foster's daughter.' Well, the priest was all smiles then. And shook my hand and said he was *very* pleased and honored to make my acquaintance. So it all turned out all right. But honestly, I didn't know. I went up there as innocent as a lamb."

"You didn't know that only Catholics take communion in a Catholic church?" Macon Dead asked her, his tone making it clear that he didn't believe her.

"No, Macon. How would I know?"

"You see them put up their own school, keep their kids out of public schools, and you still think their religious stuff is open to anybody who wants to drop in?"

"Communion is communion."

"You're a silly woman."

"Father Padrew didn't think so."

"You made a fool of yourself."

"Mrs. Djvorak didn't think so."

"She was just trying to keep the wedding going, keep you from fucking it up."

"Macon, please don't use that language in front of the children."

"What goddam children? Everybody in here is old enough to vote."

"There is no call for an argument."

"You make a fool of yourself in a Catholic church, embarrass everybody at the reception, and come to the table to gloat about how wonderful you were?"

"Macon . . ."

"And sit there lying, saying you didn't know any better?"

"Anna Djvorak wasn't the least bit—"

"Anna Djvorak don't even know your name! She called you *Dr. Foster's daughter!* I bet you one hundred dollars she still don't know your name! You by yourself ain't nobody. You your daddy's daughter!"

"That's so," said Ruth in a thin but steady voice. "I certainly am my daddy's daughter." She smiled.

Macon didn't wait to put his fork down. He dropped it on the table while his hand was on its way across the bread plate becoming the fist he smashed into her jaw.

Milkman hadn't planned any of it, but he had to know that one day, after Macon hit her, he'd see his mother's hand cover her lips as she searched with her tongue for any broken teeth, and discovering none, tried to adjust the partial plate in her mouth without anyone noticing—and that on that day he would not be able to stand it. Before his father could draw his hand back, Milkman had yanked him by the back of his coat collar, up out of his chair, and knocked him into the radiator. The window shade flapped and rolled itself up.

"You touch her again, one more time, and I'll kill you."

Macon was so shocked at being assaulted he could not speak. He had come to believe, after years of creating respect and fear wherever he put his foot down, after years of being the tallest man in every gathering, that he was impregnable. Now he crept along the wall looking at a man who was as tall as he was—and forty years younger.

Just as the father brimmed with contradictory feelings as he crept along the wall—humiliation, anger, and a grudging feeling of pride in his son—so the son felt his own contradictions. There was the pain and shame of seeing his father crumple before any man—even himself. Sorrow in discovering that the pyramid was not a five-thousand-year wonder of the civilized world, mysteriously and permanently constructed by generation after generation of hardy men who had died in order to perfect it, but that it had been made in the back room at Sears, by a clever window dresser, of papier-mâché, guaranteed to last for a mere lifetime.

He also felt glee. A snorting, horse-galloping glee as old as desire. He had won something and lost something in the same instant. Infinite possibilities and enormous responsibilities stretched out before him, but he was not prepared to take advantage of the former, or accept the burden of the latter. So he cock-walked around the table and asked his mother, "Are you all right?"

She was looking at her fingernails. "Yes, I'm fine."

Milkman looked at his sisters. He had never been able to really distinguish them (or their roles) from his mother. They were in their early teens when he was born; they were thirty-five and thirty-six now. But since Ruth was only sixteen years older than Lena, all three had always looked the same age to him. Now when he met his sisters' eyes over the table, they returned him a look of hatred so fresh, so new, it startled him. Their pale eyes no longer appeared to blur into their even paler skin. It seemed to him as though charcoal lines had been drawn around their eyes; that two drag lines had been smudged down their cheeks, and their rosy lips were swollen in hatred so full it was about to burst through. Milkman had to blink twice before their faces returned to the vaguely alarmed blandness he was accustomed to. Quickly he left the room, realizing there was no one to thank him—or abuse him. His action was his alone. It would change nothing between his parents. It would change nothing inside them. He had knocked his father down and perhaps there were some new positions on the chessboard, but the game would go on.

Sleeping with Hagar had made him generous. Or so he thought. Wide-spirited. Or so he imagined. Wide-spirited and generous enough to defend his mother, whom he almost never thought about, and to deck his father, whom he both feared and loved.

Back in his bedroom, Milkman fiddled with things on his dresser. There was a pair of silver-backed brushes his mother had given him when he was sixteen, engraved with his initials, the abbreviated degree designation of a doctor. He and his mother had joked about it and she hinted strongly that he ought to consider going to medical school. He'd foisted her off with "How would that look? M.D., M.D. If you were sick, would you go see a man called Dr. Dead?"

She laughed but reminded him that his middle name was Foster. Couldn't he use Foster as a last name? Dr. Macon Foster. Didn't that sound fine? He had to admit that it did. The silver-backed brushes were a constant reminder of what her wishes for him were—that he not stop his education at high school, but go on to college and medical school. She had as little respect for her husband's work as Macon had for college graduates. To Milkman's father, college was time spent in idleness, far away from the business of life, which was learning to own things. He was eager for his daughters to go to college—where they could have found suitable husbands—and one, Corinthians, did go. But it was pointless for Milkman, particularly since his son's presence was a real help to him in the office. So much so that he had been able to get his bank friends to speak to some of their friends and get his son moved out of 1-A draft classification and into a "necessary to support family" status.

Milkman stood before his mirror and glanced, in the low light of the wall lamp, at his reflection. He was, as usual, unimpressed with what he saw. He had a fine enough face. Eyes women complimented him on, a firm jaw line, splendid teeth. Taken apart, it looked all right. Even better than all right. But it lacked coherence, a coming together of the features into a total self. It was all very tentative, the way he looked, like a man peeping around a corner of someplace he is not supposed to be, trying to make up his mind whether to go forward or to turn back. The decision he made would be extremely important, but the way in which he made the decision would be careless, haphazard, and uninformed.

Standing there in the lamplight, trying not to think of how his father had looked creeping along the wall, he heard a knock at his door. He didn't want to see the face of Lena or Corinthians, nor to have any secret talk with his mother. But he was not any happier to see his father looming there in the hall. A line of blood was still visible in the thin cut at the corner of Macon's mouth. But he stood straight, and his eyes were steady.

"Look, Daddy," Milkman began, "I–"

"Don't say anything," Macon said, pushing past him. "Sit down."

Milkman moved toward the bed. "Look here, let's try to forget this. If you promise–"

"I told you to sit down. And down is what I mean." Macon's voice was low, but his face looked like Pilate's. He closed the door. "You a big man now, but big ain't nearly enough. You have to be a whole man. And if you want to be a whole man, you have to deal with the whole truth."

"You don't have to do any of this, you know. I don't need to know everything between you and Mama."

"I do have to do it and you do need to know it. If you're in the business of raising your fist at your father, you better have some intelligence behind that fist the next time you throw it. Nothing I'm about to say is by way of apology or excuse. It's just information.

"I married your mother in 1917. She was sixteen, living alone with her father. I can't tell you I was in love with her. People didn't require that as much as they do now. Folks were expected to be civilized to one another, honest, and–and clear. You relied on people being what they said they were, because there was no other way to survive. The important thing, when you took a wife, was that the two of you agreed on what was important.

"Your mother's father never liked me and I have to say I was very disappointed in him. He was just about the biggest Negro in this city. Not the richest, but the most respected. But a bigger hypocrite never lived. Kept all his money in four different banks. Always calm and dignified. I thought he was naturally that way until I found out he sniffed ether. Negroes in this town worshipped him. He didn't give a damn about them, though. Called them cannibals. He delivered both your sisters himself and each time all he was interested in was the color of their skin. He would have disowned you. I didn't like the notion of his being his own daughter's doctor, especially since she was also my wife. Mercy wouldn't take colored then. Anyway, Ruth wouldn't go to any other doctor. I tried to get a midwife for her, but the doctor said midwives were dirty. I told him a midwife delivered me, and if a midwife was good enough for my mother, a midwife was good enough for his daughter. Well, we had some words between us about it, and I ended up telling him that nothing could be nastier than a father delivering his own daughter's baby. That stamped it. We had very little to say after that, but they did it anyway. Both Lena and Corinthians. They let me do the naming by picking a word blind, but that was all. Your sisters are just a little over a year apart, you know. And both times he was there. She had her legs wide open and he was there. I know he was a doctor and doctors not supposed to be bothered by things like that, but he was a man before he was a doctor. I knew then they'd ganged up on me forever—the both of them—and no matter what I did, they managed to have things their way. They made sure I remembered whose house I was in, where the china came from, how he sent to England for the Waterford bowl, and again for the table they put it on. That table was so big they had to take it apart to get it in the door. He was always bragging about how he was the second man in the city to have a two-horse carriage.

"Where I'd come from, the farm we had, that was nothing to them. And what I was trying to do—they didn't have any interest in that. Buying shacks in shacktown, they called it.

'How's shacktown?' That's the way he'd greet me in the evenings.

"But it wasn't that. I could put up with that, because I knew what I wanted, and pretty much how to get it. So I could put up with that. Did put up with it. It was something else, something I couldn't put my finger on. I tried to get him to spend some of that money out of those four banks once. Some track land was going for a lot of money—railroad money. Erie Lackawanna was buying. I had a good hunch where the track would be laid. I walked all around over there, the Shore Road, the docks, the fork in routes 6 and 2. I figured out just where the tracks would have to go. And found land I could have got cheap and sold back to the railroad agents. He wouldn't lend me a dime. If he had, he would have died a rich man, instead of a fair-to-middling one. And I would have been way ahead. I asked your mother to talk him into it. I told her exactly where the Erie was headed. She said it had to be *his* decision; she couldn't influence him. She told me, her husband, that. Then I began to wonder who she was married to—me or him.

"Well, he took sick." Macon stopped, as though the mention of illness reminded him of his own frailty, and pulled a large white handkerchief out of his pocket. Gingerly he pressed it against the thin cut on his lip. He looked at the faint stain it made on his handkerchief. "All that ether," he said, "must have got in his blood. They had another name for it, but I know it was that ether. He just lay down and started swelling up. His body did; his legs and arms just wasted away. He couldn't see patients anymore, and for the first time in his life the pompous donkey found out what it was like to have to be sick and pay another donkey to make you well. One of them doctors, the one that was taking care of him—one of the same ones wouldn't let him set foot in their hospital, and who, if he had delivered *their* daughter's or wife's baby, had even thought of it, would have run him out of here on a rail—one of them, the ones he thought worth his attention, well, he came in here with some magic potion, Radiathor, and told him it would cure him. Ruth was all excited. And for a few days he was better. Then he got sicker. Couldn't move, holes were forming in his scalp. And he just lay there in that bed where your mother still sleeps and then he died there. Helpless, fat stomach, skinny arms and legs, looking like a white rat. He couldn't digest his food, you know. Had to drink all his meals and swallow something after every meal. I believe to this day that was ether too.

"The night he died, I'd been over on the other side of town, fixing a porch that fell down. Mr. Bradlee's house. Porch had been leaning for twenty years, and then just fell down, split clean away from the foundation. I got some men to help me and went over there to get it back up so the people wouldn't have to jump to get out the house and climb up three feet to get in it. Somebody tiptoed up to me and said, 'Doctor died.' Ruth, they said, was upstairs with him. I figured she was upset and went up right away to comfort her. I didn't have time to change clothes from working on the porch, but I went up anyway. She was sitting in a chair next to his bed, and the minute she saw me she jumped up and screamed at me, 'You dare come in here like that? Clean yourself! Clean up before you come in here!' It vexed me some, but I do respect the dead. I went and washed up. Took a bath, put on a clean shirt and collar, and went back in." Macon paused again and touched his cut lip as though that were where the pain that showed in his eyes was coming from.

"In the bed," he said, and stopped for so long Milkman was not sure he was going to continue. "In the bed. That's where she was when I opened the door. Laying next to him. Naked as a yard dog, kissing him. Him dead and white and puffy and skinny, and she had his fingers in her mouth.

"Now, I want you to know I had a terrible time after that. I started thinking all sorts of things. If Lena and Corinthians were my children. I come to know pretty quick they were, cause it was clear that bastard couldn't fuck nothing. Ether took care of whatever he had in that area long before I got there. And he wouldn't have been so worried about what color skin they had unless they were coming from me. Then I thought about his delivering Ruth's babies. I'm not saying that they had contact. But there's lots of things a man can do to please a woman, even if he can't fuck. Whether or not, the fact is she was in that bed sucking his fingers, and if she do that when he was dead, what'd she do when he was alive? Nothing to do but kill a woman like that. I swear, many's the day I regret she talked me out of killing her. But I wasn't looking forward to spending the rest of my days on some rock pile. But you see, Macon, sometimes I can't catch hold of myself quick enough. It just gets out. Tonight, when she said, 'Yes, I am my daddy's daughter,' and gave that little smirk . . ." Macon looked up at his son. The door of his face had opened; his skin looked iridescent. With only a minor break in his voice, he told him, "I am not a bad man. I want you to know that. Or believe it. No man ever took his responsibilities more seriously than I have. I'm not making claims to sainthood, but you have to know it all. I'm forty years older than you and I don't have another forty in me. Next time you take it into your head to jump me, I want you to think about the man you think you whipping. And think about the fact that next time I might not let you. Old as I am, I might not let you."

He stood up and pushed his handkerchief into his back pocket.

"Don't say anything now. But think about everything I've said."

Macon turned the doorknob, and without a backward glance, left the room.

Milkman sat on the edge of his bed; everything was still except for the light buzzing in his head. He felt curiously dis-associated from all that he had heard. As though a stranger that he'd sat down next to on a park bench had turned to him and begun to relate some intimacy. He was entirely sympathetic to the stranger's problems—understood perfectly his view of what had happened to him—but part of his sympathy came from the fact that he himself was not involved or in any way threatened by the stranger's story. It was quite the opposite from the feeling he'd had an hour or less ago. The alien who had just walked out of his room was also the man he felt passionately enough about to strike with all the fervor he could summon up. Even now he could feel the tingle in his shoulder that had signaled the uncontrollable urge to smash his father's face. On the way upstairs to his room he had felt isolated, but righteous. He was a man who saw another man hit a helpless person. And he had interfered. Wasn't that the history of the world? Isn't that what men did? Protected the frail and confronted the King of the Mountain? And the fact that the frail was his mother and the King of the Mountain his father made it more poignant, but did not change the essential facts. No. He would not pretend that it was love for his mother. She was too insubstantial, too shadowy for love. But it was her vaporishness that made her more needful of defense. She was not a maternal drudge, her mind pressed flat, her shoulders hunched under the burden of housework and care of others, brutalized by a bear of a man. Nor was she the acid-tongued shrew who defended herself with a vicious vocabulary and a fast lip. Ruth was a pale but complicated woman given to deviousness and ultra-fine manners. She seemed to know a lot and understand very little. It was an interesting train of thought, and new for him. Never had he thought of his mother as a person, a separate individual, with a life apart from allowing or interfering with his own.

Milkman put on his jacket and left the house. It was seven-thirty in the evening and not yet dark. He wanted to walk and breathe some other air. He wouldn't know what to feel until he knew what to think. And it was difficult thinking in that room where the silver-backed brushes with the M.D. initials shone in the light and where the chair his father had just sat in still held the imprint of his buttocks in the cushion. As the stars made themselves visible, Milkman tried to figure what was true and what part of what was true had anything to do with him. What was he supposed to do with this new information his father had dumped on him? Was it an effort to cop a plea? How was he supposed to feel about the two of them now? Was it *true*, first of all? Did his mother . . . had his mother made it with her own father? Macon had said no. That the doctor was impotent. How did he know? Well, he must have known what he was talking about, because he was much too eager for it to be true to let it go if there were any possibility it could have taken place. Still, he had admitted there were "other things" a man could do to please a woman. "Goddam," Milkman said aloud. "What the fuck did he tell me all that shit for?" He didn't want to know any of it. There was nothing he could do about it. The doctor was dead. You can't do the past over.

Milkman's confusion was rapidly turning to anger. "Strange motherfuckers," he whispered. "Strange." If he wanted me to lay off, he thought, why didn't he just say that? Just come to me like a man and say, Cool it. You cool it and I'll cool it. We'll both cool it. And I'd say, Okay, you got it. But no. He comes to me with some way-out tale about how come and why.

Milkman was heading toward Southside. Maybe he could find Guitar. A drink with Guitar would be just the thing. Or if he couldn't find Guitar, he'd go see Hagar. No. He didn't want to talk to Hagar, to any woman, just yet. Talk about strange. Now, that was a really strange bunch. His whole family was a bunch of crazies. Pilate singing all day and talking off the wall. Reba turning on for everything in pants. And Hagar . . . well, she was just fine, but still, she wasn't regular. She had some queer ways. But at least they were fun and not full of secrets.

Where would Guitar be? Never anywhere when you really needed him. A real pop-up. Popped up anywhere, anytime, but never on time. Milkman realized he was whispering every now and then and that people on the street were looking at him. Suddenly it seemed to him that there were a lot of people out for that time of day. Where the hell was everybody going? He made an effort not to vocalize his thoughts.

"You want to be a whole man, you have to deal with the whole truth," his father had said. Couldn't I be a whole man without knowing all that? "You better have some intelligence behind that fist." Okay. What intelligence? That my mama screwed her daddy. That my grandfather was a high-yellow nigger who loved ether and hated black skin. So what did he let you marry his daughter for? So he could screw her without the neighbors knowing it? Did you ever catch them doing it? No. You just felt something you couldn't put your finger on. His money, probably. He wouldn't let you put your finger on that, would he? And his daughter wouldn't help you, would she? So you figured they must be gettin it on the operating table. If he'd given you those four bankbooks to do what you liked, to buy up the Erie Lackawanna Railroad, he could have had her all he liked, right? He could have come right in your bed, and the three of you could have had a ball. He'd get one tit and you'd get . . . the . . . other. . . .

Milkman stopped dead in his tracks. Cold sweat broke out on his neck. People jostled him trying to get past the solitary man standing in their way. He had remembered something. Or believed he remembered something. Maybe he'd dreamed it and it was the dream he remembered. The picture was developing, of the two men in the bed with his mother, each nibbling on a breast, but the picture cracked and in the crack another picture emerged. There was this green room, a very small green room, and his mother was sitting in the green room and her breasts were uncovered and somebody was sucking them and the somebody was himself. So? So what? My mother nursed me. Mothers nurse babies. Why the sweat? He walked on, hardly noticing the people pushing past him, their annoyed, tight faces. He tried to see more of the picture, but couldn't. Then he heard something that he knew was related to the picture. Laughter. Somebody he couldn't see, in the room laughing . . . at him and at his mother, and his mother is ashamed. She lowers her eyes and won't look at him. "Look at me, Mama. Look at me." But she doesn't and the laughter is loud now. Everybody is laughing. Did he wet his pants? Is his mother ashamed because while he was nursing he wet his pants? What pants? He didn't wear pants then. He wore diapers. Babies always wet their diapers. Why does he think he has pants on? Blue pants with elastic around the calf. Little blue corduroy knickers. Why is he dressed that way?

Is that what the man is laughing at? Because he is a tiny baby dressed in blue knickers? He sees himself standing there. "Look at me, Mama," is all he can think of to say. "Please look at me." Standing? He is a tiny baby. Nursing in his mother's arms. He can't stand up.

"I couldn't stand up," he said aloud, and turned toward a shop window. There was his face leaning out of the upturned collar of his jacket, and he knew. "My mother nursed me when I was old enough to talk, stand up, and wear knickers, and somebody saw it and laughed and—and that is why they call me Milkman and that is why my father never does and that is why my mother never does, but everybody else does. And how did I forget that? And why? And if she did that to me when there was no reason for it, when I also drank milk and Ovaltine and everything else from a glass, then maybe she did other things with her father?"

Milkman closed his eyes and then opened them. The street was even more crowded with people, all going in the direction he was coming from. All walking hurriedly and bumping against him. After a while he realized that nobody was walking on the other side of the street. There were no cars and the street lights were on, now that darkness had come, but the sidewalk on the other side of the street was completely empty. He turned around to see where everybody was going, but there was nothing to see except their backs and hats pressing forward into the night. He looked again at the other side of Not Doctor Street. Not a soul.

He touched the arm of a man in a cap who was trying to get past him. "Why is everybody on this side of the street?" he asked him.

"Watch it, buddy," the man snapped, and moved on with the crowd.

Milkman walked on, still headed toward Southside, never once wondering why he himself did not cross over to the other side of the street, where no one was walking at all.

He believed he was thinking coldly, clearly. He had never

loved his mother, but had always known that she had loved him. And that had always seemed right to him, the way it should be. Her confirmed, eternal love of him, love that he didn't even have to earn or deserve, seemed to him natural. And now it was decomposing. He wondered if there was anyone in the world who liked him. Liked him for himself alone. His visits to the wine house seemed (before his talk with his father) an extension of the love he had come to expect from his mother. Not that Pilate or Reba felt the possessive love for him that his mother did, but they had accepted him without question and with all the ease in the world. They took him seriously too. Asked him questions and thought all his responses to things were important enough to laugh at or quarrel with him about. Everything he did at home was met with quiet understanding from his mother and his sisters (or indifference and criticism from his father). The women in the wine house were indifferent to nothing and understood nothing. Every sentence, every word, was new to them and they listened to what he said like bright-eyed ravens, trembling in their eagerness to catch and interpret every sound in the universe. Now he questioned them. Questioned everybody. His father had crept along the wall and then come upstairs with a terrible piece of news. His mother had been portrayed not as a mother who simply adored her only son, but as an obscene child playing dirty games with whatever male was near—be it her father or her son. Even his sisters, the most tolerant and accommodating of all the women he knew, had changed their faces and rimmed their eyes with red and charcoal dust.

Where was Guitar? He needed to find the one person left whose clarity never failed him, and unless he was out of the state, Milkman was determined to find him.

His first stop, Tommy's Barbershop, was fruitful. Guitar was there with several other men, leaning in various attitudes, but all listening to something.

As Milkman entered and spotted Guitar's back, he was so relieved he shouted, "Hey, Guitar!"

"Sh!" said Railroad Tommy. Guitar turned around and motioned him to come in but to be quiet. They were listening to the radio and muttering and shaking their heads. It was some time before Milkman discovered what they were so tense about. A young Negro boy had been found stomped to death in Sunflower County, Mississippi. There were no questions about who stomped him—his murderers had boasted freely—and there were no questions about the motive. The boy had whistled at some white woman, refused to deny he had slept with others, and was a Northerner visiting the South. His name was Till.

Railroad Tommy was trying to keep the noise down so he could hear the last syllable of the newscaster's words. In a few seconds it was over, since the announcer had only a few speculations and even fewer facts. The minute he went on to another topic of news, the barbershop broke into loud conversation. Railroad Tommy, the one who had tried to maintain silence, was himself completely silent now. He moved to his razor strop while Hospital Tommy tried to keep his customer in the chair. Porter, Guitar, Freddie the janitor, and three or four other men were exploding, shouting angry epithets all over the room. Apart from Milkman, only Railroad Tommy and Empire State were quiet—Railroad Tommy because he was preoccupied with his razor and Empire State because he was simple, and probably mute, although nobody seemed sure about that. There was no question whatever about his being simple.

Milkman tried to focus on the crisscrossed conversations.

"It'll be in the morning paper."

"Maybe it will, and maybe it won't," said Porter.

"It was on the radio! Got to be in the paper!" said Freddie.

"They don't put that kind of news in no white paper. Not unless he raped somebody."

"What you bet? What you bet it'll be in there?" said Freddie.

"Bet anything you can lose," Porter answered.

"You on for five."

"Wait a minute," Porter shouted. "Say where."

"What you mean, 'where'? I got five says it'll be in the morning paper."

"On the sports page?" asked Hospital Tommy.

"Or the funny papers?" said Nero Brown.

"No, man. Front page. I bet five dollars on front page."

"What the fuck is the difference?" shouted Guitar. "A kid is stomped and you standin round fussin about whether some cracker put it in the paper. He stomped, ain't he? Dead, ain't he? Cause he whistled at some Scarlett O'Hara cunt."

"What'd he do it for?" asked Freddie. "He knew he was in Mississippi. What he think that was? Tom Sawyer Land?"

"So he whistled! So what!" Guitar was steaming. "He supposed to die for that?"

"He from the North," said Freddie. "Acting big down in Bilbo country. Who the hell he think he is?"

"Thought he was a man, that's what," said Railroad Tommy.

"Well, he thought wrong," Freddie said. "Ain't no black men in Bilbo country."

"The hell they ain't," said Guitar.

"Who?" asked Freddie.

"Till. That's who."

"He dead. A dead man ain't no man. A dead man is a corpse. That's all. A corpse."

"A living coward ain't a man either," said Porter.

"Who you talking to?" Freddie was quick to get the personal insult.

"Calm down, you two," said Hospital Tommy.

"You!" shouted Porter.

"You calling me a coward?" Freddie wanted to get the facts first.

"If the shoe fits, put your rusty foot in it."

"You all gonna keep that up, you have to get out of my shop."

"Tell that nigger somethin," said Porter.

"I'm serious now," Hospital Tommy went on. "There is no cause for all this. The boy's dead. His mama's screaming. Won't let them bury him. That ought to be enough colored blood on the streets. You want to spill blood, spill the crackers' blood that bashed his face in."

"Oh, they'll catch them," said Walters.

"Catch 'em? Catch 'em?" Porter was astounded. "You out of your fuckin mind? They'll catch 'em, all right, and give 'em a big party and a medal."

"Yeah. The whole town planning a parade," said Nero.

"They got to catch 'em."

"So they catch 'em. You think they'll get any time? Not on your life!"

"How can they *not* give 'em time?" Walters' voice was high and tight.

"How? Just *don't*, that's how." Porter fidgeted with his watch chain.

"But everybody knows about it now. It's all over. Everywhere. The law is the law."

"You wanna bet? This is sure money!"

"You stupid, man. Real stupid. Ain't no law for no colored man except the one sends him to the chair," said Guitar.

"They say Till had a knife," Freddie said.

"They always say that. He could of had a wad of bubble gum, they'd swear it was a hand grenade."

"I still say he shoulda kept his mouth shut," said Freddie.

"You should keep yours shut," Guitar told him.

"Hey, man!" Again Freddie felt the threat.

"South's bad," Porter said. "Bad. Don't nothing change in the good old U.S. of A. Bet his daddy got his balls busted off in the Pacific somewhere."

"If they ain't busted already, them crackers will see to it. Remember them soldiers in 1918?"

"Ooooo. Don't bring all that up. . . ."

The men began to trade tales of atrocities, first stories they had heard, then those they'd witnessed, and finally the things that had happened to themselves. A litany of personal humiliation, outrage, and anger turned sicklelike back to themselves as humor. They laughed then, uproariously, about the speed with which they had run, the pose they had assumed, the ruse they had invented to escape or decrease some threat to their manliness, their humanness. All but Empire State, who stood, broom in hand and drop-lipped, with the expression of a very intelligent ten-year-old.

And Guitar. His animation had died down, leaving its traces in his eyes.

Milkman waited until he could get his attention. Then they both left, walking silently down the street.

"What is it? You looked pissed when you came in."

"Nothing," said Milkman. "Where can we get a drink?"

"Mary's?"

"Naw. Too many broads hasslin you."

"It's just eight-thirty. Cedar Lounge don't open till nine."

"Shit. *You* think. I'm tired."

"I got a taste at the pad," Guitar offered.

"Solid. Your box working?"

"Uh uh. Still broke."

"I need some music. Music and a taste."

"Then it'll have to be Miss Mary. I'll keep the ladies working elsewhere."

"Yeah? I want to see you tell those ladies what to do."

"Come on, Milk. This ain't New York; choices are limited."

"Okay. Mary's."

They walked a few blocks to the corner of Rye and Tenth streets. When they passed a tiny bakery, Guitar swallowed hard and quickened his steps. Mary's was the bar/lounge that did the best business in the Blood Bank—although each of the three other corners had a similar place—because of Mary herself, a pretty but overpainted barmaid/part-owner, who was sassy, funny, and good company for the customers. Whores worked her bar in safety; lonely drunks could drink there in peace; cruisers found chickens or hawks—whichever they preferred, even jailbait; restless housewives were flattered there and danced their heels off; teen-agers learned "life rules" there; and everybody found excitement there. For in Mary's the lights made everybody beautiful, or if not beautiful, then fascinating. The music gave tone and texture to conversations that would put you to sleep anywhere else. And the food and drink provoked people into behavior that resembled nothing less than high drama.

But all that began around eleven o'clock. It was practically empty at eight-thirty in the evening, when Guitar and Milkman arrived. They slid into a booth and ordered Scotch and water. Milkman drank his up quickly and ordered another before asking Guitar, "How come they call me Milkman?"

"How the fuck would I know? That's your name, ain't it?"

"My name is Macon Dead."

"You drag me all the way over here to tell me your name?"

"I need to know it."

"Aw, drink up, man."

"You know your name, don't you?"

"Cut the shit. What's on your mind?"

"I decked my old man."

"Decked?"

"Yeah. Hit him. Knocked him into the fuckin radiator."

"What'd he do to you?"

"Nothin."

"Nothin? You just up and popped him?"

"Yeah."

"For no reason?"

"He hit my mother."

"Oh."

"He hit her. I hit him."

"That's tough."

"Yeah."

"I mean it."

"I know." Milkman sighed heavily. "I know."

"Listen. I can understand how you feel."

"Uh uh. You can't understand. Unless it happens to you, you can't understand."

"Yes I can. You know I used to hunt a lot. When I was a kid down home—"

"Oh, shit, do we have to hear about Alabama again?"

"Not Alabama. Florida."

"Whatever."

"Just listen, Milkman. Listen to me. I used to hunt a lot. From the time I could walk almost and I was good at it. Everybody said I was a natural. I could hear anything, smell anything, and see like a cat. You know what I mean? A natural. And I was never scared—not of the dark or shadows or funny sounds, and I was never afraid to kill. Anything. Rabbit, bird, snakes, squirrels, deer. And I was little. It never bothered me. I'd take a shot at anything. The grown men used to laugh about it. Said I was a natural-born hunter. After we moved up here with my grandmother, that was the only thing about the South I missed. So when my grandmother used to send us kids back home in the summer, all I thought about was hunting again. They'd pile us on the bus and we'd spend the summer with my grandmother's sister, Aunt Florence. Soon's I got there I looked for my uncles, to go out in the woods. And one summer—I was about ten or eleven, I guess—we all went out and I went off on my own. I thought I saw deer tracks. It wasn't the season for deer, but that didn't bother me any. If I saw one I killed one. I was right about the tracks; it was a deer, but spaced funny—not wide apart like I thought they should be, but still a deer. You know they step in their own prints. If you never saw them before you'd think a two-legged creature was jumping. Anyway, I stayed on the trail until I saw some bushes. The light was good and all of a sudden I saw a rump between the branches. I dropped it with the first shot and finished it with the next. Now, I want to tell you I was feeling good. I saw myself showing my uncles what I'd caught. But when I got up to it—and I was going real slow because I thought I might have to shoot it again—I saw it was a doe. Not a young one; she was old, but she was still a doe. I felt . . . bad. You know what I mean? I killed a doe. A doe, man."

Milkman was gazing at Guitar with the wide steady eyes of a man trying to look sober.

"So I know how you felt when you saw your father hit your mother. It's like that doe. A man shouldn't do that. You couldn't help what you felt."

Milkman nodded his head, but it was clear to Guitar that nothing he had said had made any difference. Chances were Milkman didn't even know what a doe was, and whatever it was, it wasn't his mother. Guitar ran his finger around the rim of his glass.

"What'd she do, Milk?"

"Nothin. Smiled. He didn't like her smile."

"You're not making sense. Talk sense. And slow down. You know you can't hold liquor."

"What you mean, I can't hold liquor?"

" 'Scuse me. Help yourself."

"I'm trying to have a serious conversation and you talking shit, Guitar."

"I'm listening."

"And I'm talking."

"Yes, you talking, but what are you saying? Your papa clips your mama cause she smiles at him. You clip him cause he clipped her. Now, is that the way you all spend the evening in your house or is there something else you're trying to say?"

"Came up to talk to me afterwards."

"Who?"

"My old man."

"What'd he say?"

"Said I had to be a whole man and know the whole thing."

"Go on."

"He was gonna buy the Erie Lackawanna, but my mother wouldn't let him."

"Oh, yeah? Maybe she needs beatin."

"That's very funny, man."

"Why ain't you laughing, then?"

"I am laughing. Inside."

"Milk?"

"Yeah?"

"Your daddy slapped your mama, right?"

"Right. Right."

"You hit him, right?"

"Right."

"Nobody appreciates what you did. Right?"

"Hey, Guitar. You right again."

"Not your mother, not your sisters, and your daddy appreciates it least of all."

"Least of all. Right."

"So he bawls you out."

"Yep. No. No. He . . ."

"He talks quiet to you?"

"Right!"

"Explains things to you."

"Yeah."

"About why he hit her."

"Uh huh."

"And it's all about something that happened a long time ago? Before you were born?"

"You got it! You are a very smart little colored boy. And I am going to tell Oxford University about you."

"And you wish he'd kept it to himself because it don't concern you and you can't do nothin about it anyway."

"You have just passed the course. Guitar Bains, Ph.D."

"But it bothers you just the same?"

"Let me think." Milkman closed his eyes and tried to prop his chin on his hand, but it was too difficult. He was trying to get as drunk as possible as rapidly as possible. "Yes. Well, it did bother me. Before I came in here it did. I don't know, Guitar." He became serious and his face had the still and steady look of a grown man trying not to vomit . . . or cry.

"Forget it, Milk. Whatever it is, forget it. It ain't nothin. Whatever he told you, forget it."

"I hope I can. I sure hope I can."

"Listen, baby, people do funny things. Specially us. The cards are stacked against us and just trying to stay in the game, stay alive and in the game, makes us do funny things. Things we can't help. Things that make us hurt one another. We don't even know why. But look here, don't carry it inside and don't give it to nobody else. Try to understand it, but if you can't, just forget it and keep yourself strong, man."

"I don't know, Guitar. Things seem to be getting to me, you know?"

"Don't let 'em. Unless you got a plan. Look at Till. They got to him too. Now he's just an item on WJR's evening news."

"He was crazy."

"No. Not crazy. Young, but not crazy."

"Who cares if he fucks a white girl? Anybody can do that. What's he bragging for? Who cares?"

"Crackers care."

"Then they're crazier'n he is."

"Of course. But they're alive and crazy."

"Yeah, well, fuck Till. I'm the one in trouble."

"Did I hear you right, brother?"

"All right. I didn't mean that. I . . ."

"What's your trouble? You don't like your name?"

"No." Milkman let his head fall to the back of the booth. "No, I don't like my name."

"Let me tell you somethin, baby. Niggers get their names the way they get everything else—the best way they can. The best way they can."

Milkman's eyes were blurred now and so were his words. "Why can't we get our stuff the right way?"

"The best way is the right way. Come on. I'll take you home."

"No, I can't go back there."

"No? Where then?"

"Let me stay in your pad."

"Oh, man, you know my situation. One of us'll have to sleep on the floor. Besides . . ."

"I'll sleep on the floor."

"Besides, I may have company."

"No shit?"

"No shit. Come on, let's go."

"I ain't going home, Guitar. Hear me?"

"Want me to take you over to Hagar's?" Guitar motioned to the waitress for the check.

"Hagar's. Yeah. Sweet Hagar. Wonder what her name is."

"You just said it."

"I mean her last name. Her daddy's name."

"Ask Reba." Guitar paid their bar bill and helped Milkman negotiate to the door. The wind had risen and cooled. Guitar flapped his elbows against the cold.

"Ask anybody *but* Reba," said Milkman. "Reba don't know her own last name."

"Ask Pilate."

"Yeah. I'll ask Pilate. Pilate knows. It's in that dumb-ass box hanging from her ear. Her own name and everybody else's. Bet mine's in there too. I'm gonna ask her what my name is. Say, you know how my old man's daddy got his name?"

"Uh uh. How?"

"Cracker gave it to him."

"Sho 'nough?"

"Yep. And he took it. Like a fuckin sheep. Somebody should have shot him."

"What for? He was already Dead."

Chapter 4

Once again he did his Christmas shopping in a Rexall drugstore. It was late, the day before Christmas Eve, and he hadn't had the spirit or energy or presence of mind to do it earlier or thoughtfully. Boredom, which had begun as a mild infection, now took him over completely. No activity seemed worth the doing, no conversation worth having. The fluttery preparations at home seemed fake and dingy. His mother was going on as she did every year about the incredible price of trees and butter. As though their tree would be anything other than it had always been: the huge shadowy thing in a corner burdened with decorations she had had since she was a girl. As if her fruitcakes were edible, or her turkey done all the way to the bone. His father gave them all envelopes of varying amounts of money, never thinking that just once they might like something he actually went into a department store and selected.

The gifts Milkman had to buy were few and easily chosen in a drugstore. Cologne and dusting powder for Magdalene called Lena; a compact for Corinthians; a five-pound box of chocolates for his mother. And some shaving equipment for his father. In fifteen minutes he was done. The only problem gift was Hagar's. It was hard to select something hurriedly for her since she liked everything but preferred nothing. More important, he wasn't sure he wanted to keep it up. Keep up the whole business of "going with" Hagar. He seldom took her anywhere except to the movies and he never took her to parties where people of his own set danced and laughed and developed intrigues among themselves. Everybody who knew him knew about Hagar, but she was considered his private honey pot, not a real or legitimate girl friend—not someone he might marry. And only one or two of the various women he dated "seriously" ever put up a fight about her since they believed she was less than a rival.

Now, after more than a dozen years, he was getting tired of her. Her eccentricities were no longer provocative and the stupefying ease with which he had gotten and stayed between her legs had changed from the great good fortune he'd considered it, to annoyance at her refusal to make him hustle for it, work for it, do something difficult for it. He didn't even have to pay for it. It was so free, so abundant, it had lost its fervor. There was no excitement, no galloping of blood in his neck or his heart at the thought of her.

She was the third beer. Not the first one, which the throat receives with almost tearful gratitude; nor the second, that confirms and extends the pleasure of the first. But the third, the one you drink because it's there, because it can't hurt, and because what difference does it make?

Perhaps the end of the year was a good time to call it off. It wasn't going anywhere and it was keeping him lazy, like a pampered honey bear who had only to stick out his paw for another scoop, and so had lost the agility of the tree-climbers, the bee-fighters, but not the recollection of how thrilling the search had been.

He would buy her something for Christmas, of course, something nice to remember him by, but nothing that would give her any ideas about marriage. There was some costume jewelry on display. She might like that, but it would pale before the diamond ring Reba had stuck down in her dress. A Timex? She would never look at it. Staring at the glass tube that housed the watches, he found himself getting angry. All this indecision about what to get for Hagar was new. At Christmases past he simply chose (or had his sisters choose) from a long list of things that Hagar had mentioned specifically. Things quite out of place in her household: a navy-blue satin bathrobe (this for a woman who lived in a house that had no bathroom); a chubby; a snood with a velvet bow; a rhinestone bracelet with earrings to match; patent leather pumps; White Shoulders cologne. Milkman used to wonder at her specificity and her acquisitiveness until he reminded himself that Pilate and Reba celebrated no holidays. Yet their generosity was so wholehearted it looked like carelessness, and they did their best to satisfy every whim Hagar had. When he first took her in his arms, Hagar was a vain and somewhat distant creature. He liked to remember it that way—that he took her in his arms—but in truth it was she who called him back into the bedroom and stood there smiling while she unbuttoned her blouse.

From the time he first saw her, when he was twelve and she was seventeen, he was deeply in love with her, alternately awkward and witty in her presence. She babied him, ignored him, teased him—did anything she felt like, and he was grateful just to see her do anything or be any way. A good part of the enthusiasm with which he collected his father's rents was because of the time it gave him to visit the wine house and, hopefully, find Hagar there. He was free to drop in anytime and after school he tried to make sure he saw her.

Years passed and his puppy breath came as fast as ever in Hagar's presence. It slowed finally, after Guitar took him to his first Southside party, and after he found himself effortlessly popular with girls of his own age and in his own neighborhood. But while his breath was no longer that of a puppy, Hagar could still whip it into a pant when he was seventeen and she was twenty-two. Which she did on the dullest flattest day he could remember, a throw-away day in March when he drove his father's two-tone Ford over to her house for two bottles of wine. Milkman was much sought after and depended upon to secure the liquor he and his under-twenty-one friends believed vital to a party. When he got to Pilate's he walked in on a domestic crisis.

Reba's new man friend had asked her for a small loan and she had told him that she didn't have any money at all. The man, who had received two or three nice presents from her unasked, thought she was lying and was trying to tell him to shove off. They were quarreling in the backyard—that is, the man was quarreling. Reba was crying and trying to convince him that what she'd said was true. Just after Milkman opened the door, Hagar came running from the bedroom, where she'd been looking out the back window. She screamed to Pilate, "Mama! He's hitting her! I saw him! With his fist, Mama!"

Pilate looked up from a fourth-grade geography book she was reading and closed it. Slowly, it seemed to Milkman, she walked over to a shelf that hung over the dry sink, put the geography book on it, and removed a knife. Slowly still, she walked out the front door—there was no back door—and as soon as she did, Milkman could hear Reba's screams and the man's curses.

It didn't occur to him to stop Pilate—her mouth was not moving and her earring flashed fire—but he did follow her, as did Hagar, around to the back of the house, where, approaching the man from the back, she whipped her right arm around his neck and positioned the knife at the edge of his heart. She waited until the man felt the knife point before she jabbed it skillfully, about a quarter of an inch through his shirt into the skin. Still holding his neck, so he couldn't see but could feel the blood making his shirt sticky, she talked to him.

"Now, I'm not going to kill you, honey. Don't you worry none. Just be still a minute, the heart's right here, but I'm not going to stick it in any deeper. Cause if I stick it in any deeper, it'll go straight through your heart. So you have to be real still, you hear? You can't move a inch cause I might lose control. It's just a little hole now, honey, no more'n a pin scratch. You might lose about two tablespoons of blood, but no more. And if you're real still, honey, I can get it back out without no mistake. But before I do that, I thought we'd have a little talk."

The man closed his eyes. Sweat ran from his temples down the sides of his face. A few neighbors who had heard Reba's screams had gathered in Pilate's backyard. They knew right away that the man was a newcomer to the city. Otherwise he would have known a few things about Reba, one of which was that she gave away everything she had and if there was a case quarter in that house she'd have given it to him; and more important, he would have known not to fool with anything that belonged to Pilate, who never bothered anybody, was helpful to everybody, but who also was believed to have the power to step out of her skin, set a bush afire from fifty yards, and turn a man into a ripe rutabaga—all on account of the fact that she had no navel. So they didn't have much sympathy for him. They just craned their necks to hear better what Pilate was telling him.

"You see, darlin, that there is the only child I got. The first baby I ever had, and if you could turn around and see my face, which of course you can't cause my hand might slip, you'd know she's also the last. Women are foolish, you know, and mamas are the most foolish of all. And you know how mamas are, don't you? You got a mama, ain't you? Sure you have, so you know what I'm talking about. Mamas get hurt and nervous when somebody don't like they children. First real misery I ever had in my life was when I found out somebody—a little teeny tiny boy it was—didn't like my little girl. Made me so mad, I didn't know what to do. We do the best we can, but we ain't got the strength you men got. That's why it makes us so sad if a grown man start beating up on one of us. You know what I mean? I'd hate to pull this knife out and have you try some other time to act mean to my little girl. Cause one thing I know for sure: whatever she done, she's been good to *you*. Still, I'd hate to push it in more and have your mama feel like I do now. I confess, I don't know what to do. Maybe you can help me. Tell me, what should I do?"

The man struggled for breath and Pilate eased up on his throat but not his heart.

"Lemme go," he whispered.

"Hmmmmm?"

"Lemme go. I . . . won't never . . . put a hand on her. I promise."

"A real promise, sugar?"

"Yeah. I promise. You won't never see me no more."

Reba sat on the ground, her arms around her knees, staring through her unswollen eye at the scene as though she were at a picture show. Her lip was split and her cheek was badly bruised, and though her skirt and hands were stained with her effort to stop the blood pouring from her nose, a little still trickled down.

Pilate plucked the knife out of the man's shirt and took her arm away. He lurched a little, looked down at the blood on his clothes and up at Pilate, and licking his lips, backed all the way to the side of the house under Pilate's gaze. Her lips didn't start moving again until he was out of sight and running down the road.

All attention turned to Reba, who was having difficulty trying to stand up. She said she thought something was broken inside in the place where he'd kicked her. Pilate felt her ribs and said nothing was broken. But Reba said she wanted to go to the hospital. (It was her dream to be a patient in a hospital; she was forever trying to get admitted, since in her picture-show imagination, it was a nice hotel. She gave blood there as often as they would let her, and stopped only when the blood bank was moved to an office-type clinic some distance away from Mercy.) She was insistent now, and Pilate surrendered her judgment to Reba's. A neighbor offered to drive them and off they went, leaving Milkman to buy his wine from Hagar.

He was delighted with the performance and followed Hagar into the house to laugh and talk excitedly about it. She was as tranquil as he was agitated, as monosyllabic as he was garrulous.

"Was that something? Wow! She's two inches taller than he is, and she's talking about weak."

"We are weak."

"Compared to what? A B-52?"

"Every woman's not as strong as she is."

"I hope not. Half as strong is too much."

"Well, muscle strength is one thing. I meant women are weak in other ways."

"Name some. I want you to name some for me. Where are you weak?"

"I don't mean me. I mean other women."

"You don't have any weakness?"

"I haven't found any."

"I suppose you think you can whip me." It was the seventeen-year-old's constant preoccupation—who could whip him.

"Probably," said Hagar.

"Ha! Well, I guess I better not try to prove you wrong. Pilate might be back with her knife."

"Pilate scare you?"

"Yeah. Don't she scare you?"

"No. Nobody scares me."

"Yeah. You tough. I know you tough."

"Not tough. I just don't let people tell me what to do. I do what I want."

"Pilate tells you what to do."

"But I don't have to do it, if I don't want to."

"Wish I could say the same for my mother."

"Your mother boss you?"

"Well . . . not boss exactly." Milkman floundered for a word to describe the nagging he thought he was a victim of.

"How old are you now?" asked Hagar. She lifted her eyebrows like a woman mildly interested in the age of a small child.

"Seventeen."

"You old enough to be married." Hagar said it with the strong implication that he should not allow his mother to have any say about what he did.

"I'm waiting for you," he said, trying to regain (or acquire) some masculine flippancy.

"Be a long wait."

"Why?"

Hagar sighed as if her patience was being tried. "I'd like to be in love with the man I marry."

"Try me. You could learn if you'd try."

"You're too young for me."

"State of mind," he said.

"Uh huh. My mind."

"You're like all women. Waiting for Prince Charming to come trotting down the street and pull up in front of your door. Then you'll sweep down the steps and powie! Your eyes meet and he'll yank you up on his horse and the two of you ride off into the wind. Violins playing and 'courtesy of MGM' stamped on the horse's butt. Right?"

"Right," she said.

"What you going to do in the meantime?"

"Watch the lump grow in a little boy's pants."

Milkman smiled, but he was not amused. Hagar laughed. He jumped up to grab her, but she ran into the bedroom and shut the door. He rubbed his chin with the back of his hand and looked at the door. Then he shrugged and picked up the two bottles of wine.

"Milkman?" Hagar stuck her head out the door. "Come in here."

He turned around and put the bottles down on the table. The door was open, but he couldn't see her, could only hear her laughing, a low private laugh as though she had won a bet. He moved so quickly he forgot to duck the green sack hanging from the ceiling. A hickey was forming on his forehead by the time he got to her. "What you all got in there?" he asked her.

"That's Pilate's stuff. She calls it her inheritance." Hagar was unbuttoning her blouse.

"What'd she inherit? Bricks?" Then he saw her breasts.

"This is what I do in the meantime," she said.

Their tossing and giggling had been free and open then and they began to spend as much time in Guitar's room when he was at work as Guitar himself did when he was home. She became a quasi-secret but permanent fixture in his life. Very much a tease, sometimes accommodating his appetites, sometimes refusing. He never knew when or why she would do either. He assumed Reba and Pilate knew, but they never made any reference to the change in his relationship to Hagar. While he had lost some of his twelve-year-old's adoration of her, he was delighted to be sleeping with her and she was odd, funny, quirky company, spoiled, but artlessly so and therefore more refreshing than most of the girls his own age. There were months when Hagar would not see him, and then he'd appear one day and she was all smiles and welcome.

After about three years or so of Hagar's on-again-off-again passion, her refusals dwindled until finally, by the time he'd hit his father, they were nonexistent. Furthermore, she began to wait for him, and the more involved he got with the other part of his social life, the more reliable she became. She began to pout, sulk, and accuse him of not loving her or wanting to see her anymore. And though he seldom thought about his age, she was very aware of hers. Milkman had stretched his carefree boyhood out for thirty-one years. Hagar was thirty-six—and nervous. She placed duty squarely in the middle of their relationship; he tried to think of a way out.

He paid the clerk for the presents he had chosen and left the drugstore, having made up his mind to call it off.

I'll remind her that we are cousins, he thought. He would not buy her a present at all; instead he would give her a nice piece of money. Explain that he wanted her to get something really nice for herself, but that his gift-giving was compromising her. That he was not what she needed. She needed a steady man who could marry her. He was standing in her way. And since they were related and all, she should start looking for someone else. It hurt him, he would say, deeply hurt him, after all these years, but if you loved somebody as he did her, you had to think of them first. You couldn't be selfish with somebody you loved.

Having thought so carefully of what he would say to her, he felt as though he had already had the conversation and had settled everything. He went back to his father's office, got some cash out of the safe, and wrote Hagar a nice letter which ended: "Also, I want to thank you. Thank you for all you have meant to me. For making me happy all these years. I am signing this letter with love, of course, but more than that, with gratitude."

And he did sign it with love, but it was the word "gratitude" and the flat-out coldness of "thank you" that sent Hagar spinning into a bright blue place where the air was thin and it was silent all the time, and where people spoke in whispers or did not make sounds at all, and where everything was frozen except for an occasional burst of fire inside her chest that crackled away until she ran out into the streets to find Milkman Dead.

Long after he'd folded the money and the letter into an envelope, Milkman sat on at his father's desk. He added and re-added columns of figures, always eighty cents too little or eighty cents too much. He was still distracted and edgy, and all of it was not because of the problem of Hagar. He'd had a conversation with Guitar some time ago about the dragnet. A young boy, about sixteen years old, on his way home from school, had been strangled with what was believed to be a rope, and his head was bashed in. The state troopers cooperating with the local police said the way in which the boy had been killed was similar to the way another boy had been killed on New Year's Eve in 1953, and the way four grown men had been killed in 1955—the strangulation, the smashing of the face. In the poolrooms and in Tommy's Barbershop, the word was that Winnie Ruth Judd had struck again. The men laughed about it and repeated for the benefit of newcomers the story of how, in 1932, Winnie Ruth, a convicted murderer, who axed and dismembered her victims and stuffed them in trunks, was committed to a state asylum for the criminally insane, and escaped two or three times each year.

Once she had walked two hundred miles through two states before they caught her. Because there was a brutal killing in the city in December of that year, during the time Winnie Ruth was at large, Southside people were convinced that she had done it. From then on when some particularly nasty murder was reported, the Negroes said it was Winnie Ruth. They said that because Winnie Ruth was white and so were the victims. It was their way of explaining what they believed was white madness—crimes planned and executed in a truly lunatic manner against total strangers. Such murders could only be committed by a fellow lunatic of the race and Winnie Ruth Judd fit the description. They believed firmly that members of their own race killed one another for good reasons: violation of another's turf (a man is found with somebody else's wife); refusal to observe the laws of hospitality (a man reaches into his friend's pot of mustards and snatches out the meat); or verbal insults impugning their virility, honesty, humanity, and mental health. More important, they believed the crimes they committed were legitimate because they were committed in the heat of passion: anger, jealousy, loss of face, and so on. Bizarre killings amused them, unless of course the victim was one of their own.

They speculated about Winnie Ruth's motives for this recent murder. Somebody said she was raunchy from being cooped up and went looking for a lay. But she knew better than to expect a grown man to want her, so she went for a schoolboy. Another said she probably didn't like saddle shoes and when she got out of the loony bin and walked four hundred miles to safety, the first thing she saw was a kid wearing saddle shoes and she couldn't take it—ran amok.

Amid the jokes, however, was a streak of unspoken terror. The police said there had been a witness who thought he saw a "bushy-haired Negro" running from the schoolyard where the body was found.

"The same bushy-haired Negro they saw when Sam Sheppard axed his wife," said Porter.

"Hammered, man," said Guitar. "Twenty-seven hammer blows."

"Great Jesus. Why he do twenty-seven? That's a hard killin."

"Every killing is a hard killing," said Hospital Tommy. "Killing anybody is hard. You see those movies where the hero puts his hands around somebody's neck and the victim coughs a little bit and expires? Don't believe it, my friends. The human body is robust. It can gather strength when it's in mortal danger."

"You kill anybody in the war, Tommy?"

"I put my hand to a few."

"With your hands?"

"Bayonet, friend. The men of the Ninety-second used bayonets. Belleau Wood glittered with them. Fairly glittered."

"How'd it feel?"

"Unpleasant. Extremely unpleasant. Even when you know he'll do the same to you, it's still a very indelicate thing to do."

They laughed as usual at Tommy's proper way of speaking.

"That's because you didn't want to be in the army no way," said a fat man. "What about if you was roaming the streets and met up with Orval Faubus?"

"Boy, I'd love to kill that sucker," a heavy-set man said.

"Keep saying that. They'll soon have your ass downtown."

"My hair ain't bushy."

"They'll make it bushy."

"They'll take some brass knuckles and make your *head* bushy and call it hair."

Aside from Empire State's giggle, which was wholehearted, it had seemed to Milkman then that the laughter was wan and nervous. Each man in that room knew he was subject to being picked up as he walked the street and whatever his proof of who he was and where he was at the time of the murder, he'd have a very uncomfortable time being questioned.

And there was one more thing. For some time Milkman had been picking up hints that one or more of these murders had in fact been either witnessed or committed by a Negro. Some slip, someone knowing some detail about the victim. Like whether or not Winnie Ruth couldn't stand saddle shoes. Did the boy have on saddle shoes? Did the newspaper say so? Or was that just one of the fanciful details a good jokester would think of.

The two Tommys were cleaning up. "Closed," they said to a

man who poked his face in the door. "Shop's closing." The conversation died down and the men who were just hanging around seemed reluctant to go. Guitar too, but finally he slipped on his jacket, shadow-boxed with Empire State, and joined Milkman at the door. Southside shops were featuring feeble wreaths and lights, made more feeble by the tacky Yuletide streamers and bells the city had strung up on the lampposts. Only downtown were the lights large, bright, festive, and full of hope.

The two men walked down Tenth Street, headed for Guitar's room.

"Freaky," said Milkman. "Some freaky shit."

"Freaky world," said Guitar. "A freaky, fucked-up world."

Milkman nodded. "Railroad Tommy said the boy had on saddle shoes."

"Did he?" Guitar asked.

"Did he? You know he did. You were laughing right along with the rest of us."

Guitar glanced at him. "What you opening your nose for?"

"I know when I'm being put off."

"Then that's what it is, man. Nothing else. Maybe I don't feel like discussing it."

"You mean you don't feel like discussing it with me. You were full of discussion in Tommy's."

"Look, Milk, we've been tight a long time, right? But that don't mean we're not different people. We can't always think the same way about things. Can't we leave it like that? There are all kinds of people in this world. Some are curious, some ain't; some talk, some scream; some are kickers and other people are kicked. Take your daddy, now. He's a kicker. First time I laid eyes on him, he was kicking us out of our house. That was a difference right there between you and me, but we got to be friends anyway. . . ."

Milkman stopped and forced Guitar to stop too and turn around. "I know you're not going to give me a bullshit lecture."

"No lecture, man. I'm trying to tell you something."

"Well, tell me. Don't give me no fuckin bullshit lecture."

"What do you call a lecture?" asked Guitar. "When *you* don't talk for two seconds? When you have to listen to somebody else instead of talk? Is that a lecture?"

"A lecture is when somebody talks to a thirty-one-year-old man like he's a ten-year-old kid."

"You want me to talk or not?"

"Go ahead. Talk. Just don't talk to me in that funny tone. Like you a teacher and I'm some snot-nosed kid."

"That's the problem, Milkman. You're more interested in my tone than in what I'm saying. I'm trying to say that we don't have to agree on everything; that you and me are different; that–"

"You mean you got some secret shit you don't want me to know about."

"I mean there are things that interest me that don't interest you."

"How you know they don't interest me?"

"I know you. Been knowing you. You got your high-tone friends and your picnics on Honoré Island and you can afford to spend fifty percent of your brainpower thinking about a piece of ass. You got that red-headed bitch and you got a Southside bitch and no telling what in between."

"I don't believe it. After all these years you putting me down because of where I live?"

"Not where you live–where you hang out. You don't live nowhere. Not Not Doctor Street *or* Southside."

"You begrudge me–"

"I don't begrudge you a thing."

"You're welcome everywhere I go. I've tried to get you to come to Honoré–"

"Fuck Honoré! You hear me? The only way I'll go to that nigger heaven is with a case of dynamite and a book of matches."

"You used to like it."

"I never liked it! I went with you, but I never liked it. Never."

"What's wrong with Negroes owning beach houses? What

do you want, Guitar? You mad at every Negro who ain't scrubbing floors and picking cotton. This ain't Montgomery, Alabama."

Guitar looked at him, first in rage, and then he began to laugh. "You're right, Milkman. You have never in your life said a truer word. This definitely is not Montgomery, Alabama. Tell me. What would you do if it was? If this turned out to be another Montgomery?"

"Buy a plane ticket."

"Exactly. Now you know something about yourself you didn't know before: who you are and what you are."

"Yeah. A man that refuses to live in Montgomery, Alabama."

"No. A man that can't live there. If things ever got tough, you'd melt. You're not a serious person, Milkman."

"Serious is just another word for miserable. I know all about serious. My old man is serious. My sisters are serious. And nobody is more serious than my mother. She's so serious, she wasting away. I was looking at her in the backyard the other day. It was as cold as a witch's tit out there, but she had to get some bulbs in the ground before the fifteenth of December, she said. So there she was on her knees, digging holes in the ground."

"So? I miss the point."

"The point is that she wanted to put those bulbs in. She didn't have to. She likes to plant flowers. She really likes it. But you should have seen her face. She looked like the unhappiest woman in the world. The most miserable. So where's the fun? I've never in my whole life heard my mother laugh. She smiles sometimes, even makes a little sound. But I don't believe she has ever laughed out loud."

Without the least transition and without knowing he was going to, he began to describe to Guitar a dream he had had about his mother. He called it a dream because he didn't want to tell him it had really happened, that he had really seen it.

He was standing at the kitchen sink pouring the rest of his coffee down the drain when he looked through the window and saw Ruth digging in the garden. She made little holes and tucked something that looked like a small onion in them. As he stood there, mindlessly watching her, tulips began to grow out of the holes she had dug. First a solitary thin tube of green, then two leaves opened up from the stem—one on each side. He rubbed his eyes and looked again. Now several stalks were coming out of the ground behind her. Either they were bulbs she had already planted or they had been in the sack so long they had germinated. The tubes were getting taller and taller and soon there were so many of them they were pressing up against each other and up against his mother's dress. And still she didn't notice them or turn around. She just kept digging. Some of the stems began to sprout heads, bloody red heads that bobbed over and touched her back. Finally she noticed them, growing and nodding and touching her. Milkman thought she would jump up in fear—at least surprise. But she didn't. She leaned back from them, even hit out at them, but playfully, mischievously. The flowers grew and grew, until he could see only her shoulders above them and her flailing arms high above those bobbing, snapping heads. They were smothering her, taking away her breath with their soft jagged lips. And she merely smiled and fought them off as though they were harmless butterflies.

He knew they were dangerous, that they would soon suck up all the air around her and leave her limp on the ground. But she didn't seem to guess this at all. Eventually they covered her and all he could see was a mound of tangled tulips bent low over her body, which was kicking to the last.

He described all of that to Guitar as though the dream emphasized his point about the dangers of seriousness. He tried to be as light-hearted as possible in the telling, but at the end, Guitar looked him in the eyes and said, "Why didn't you go help her?"

"What?"

"Help her. Pull her out from underneath."

"But she liked it. She was having fun. She liked it."

"Are you sure?" Guitar was smiling.

"Sure I'm sure. It was my dream."

"It was *your* mother too."

"Aw, man, why you making something out of it that ain't there? You're making the whole thing into something superserious, just to prove your point. First I'm wrong for not living in Alabama. Then I'm wrong for not behaving right in my own dream. Now I'm wrong for dreaming it. You see what I mean? The least little thing is a matter of life and death to you. You're getting to be just like my old man. He thinks if a paper clip is in the wrong drawer, I should apologize. What's happening to everybody?"

"Looks like everybody's going in the wrong direction but you, don't it?"

Milkman swallowed. He remembered that long-ago evening after he hit his father how everybody was crammed on one side of the street, going in the direction he was coming from. Nobody was going his way. It was as though Guitar had been in that dream too.

"Maybe," he said. "But I know where I'm going."

"Where?"

"Wherever the party is."

Guitar smiled. His teeth were as white as the snowflakes that were settling on his jacket. "Merry Christmas," he said, "and Happy New Year." He waved his hand and cut around the corner to his street. He was lost in the snowy shadows of Southside before Milkman could ask him where he was going or tell him to wait.

Now he closed the accounts book in Sonny's Shop and gave up on the column of numbers. Something was happening to Guitar, had already happened to him. He was constantly chafing Milkman about how he lived, and that conversation was just one more example of how he'd changed. No more could Milkman run up the stairs to his room to drag him off to a party or a bar. And he didn't want to talk about girls or getting high. Sports were about the only things he was still enthusiastic about, and music. Other than that, he was all gloom and golden eyes. And politics.

It was that atmosphere of earnestness he provoked that led Milkman to talking about his family more than he would normally do and that also led him to defend with flippant remarks the kind of life he led. Pussy and Honoré parties. Guitar knew that wasn't all he was interested in, didn't he? He knew Milkman had other interests. Such as? he asked himself. Well, he was very good in his father's business, for one thing. Excellent, in fact. But he had to admit right away that real estate was of no real interest to him. If he had to spend the rest of his life thinking about rents and property, he'd lose his mind. But he was going to spend the rest of his life doing just that, wasn't he? That's what his father assumed and he supposed that was what he had assumed as well.

Maybe Guitar was right—partly. His life was pointless, aimless, and it was true that he didn't concern himself an awful lot about other people. There was nothing he wanted bad enough to risk anything for, inconvenience himself for. Still, what right had Guitar to talk? He didn't live in Montgomery either; all he did was work at that automobile factory and sneak off places—nobody knew where—and hang around Tommy's Barbershop. He never kept a woman more than a few months—the time span that he said was average before she began to make "permanent-arrangement-type noises."

He ought to get married, Milkman thought. Maybe I should too. Who? There were lots of women around and he was very much the eligible bachelor to the Honoré crowd. Maybe he'd pick one—the redhead. Get a nice house. His father would help him find one. Go into a real partnership with his father and . . . And what? There had to be something better to look forward to. He couldn't get interested in money. No one had ever denied him any, so it had no exotic attraction. Politics—at least barbershop politics and Guitar's brand—put him to sleep. He was bored. Everybody bored him. The city was boring. The racial problems that consumed Guitar were the most boring of all. He wondered what they would do if they didn't have black and white problems to talk about. Who would they be if they couldn't describe the insults, violence, and oppression that their lives (and the television news) were made up of? If they didn't have Kennedy or Elijah to quarrel about? They excused themselves for everything. Every job of work undone, every bill unpaid, every illness, every death was The Man's fault. And Guitar was becoming just like them—except he made no excuses for himself—just agreed, it seemed to Milkman, with every grievance he heard.

Milkman went into the bathroom, which served also as a pantry, and plugged in the hot plate to make himself some instant coffee. While he was there, he heard a rapid tapping on the windowpane. He stepped back into the office and saw Freddie's eyes through the lettering. Milkman unlocked the door.

"Hey, Freddie. What's up?"

"Looking for a warm spot. They got me runnin tonight. Christmas comin and all, all I do is run up and down the street." Freddie's janitor duties at the department store were supplemented by his function as a messenger and package deliverer.

"They give you a new truck yet?" Milkman asked him.

"You crazy? The engine have to fall out on the ground before they give me a decent one."

"I put some coffee water on. Have a cup?"

"Just what I'm lookin for. Saw your lights and thought there's got to be a hot cup a coffee in there. You wouldn't happen to have a little taste to go in it, would ya?"

"Just so happens I do."

"Atta boy."

Milkman went into the bathroom, lifted the lid from the toilet tank, and took out the half-pint bottle he kept hidden from Macon, who wouldn't have alcohol on the premises. He brought the bottle into the office, put it on the desk, and went back to make up two cups of coffee. When he reentered, Freddie was trying to look as though he hadn't already turned the pint up to his mouth. They laced their coffee and Milkman looked around for his cigarettes.

"Hard times, boy," Freddie said absently, after his first sip. "Hard times." Then, as though he noticed something missing, he asked, "Where's your buddy?"

"You mean Guitar?"

"Yeah. Guitar. Where's he?"

"Haven't seen him in a few days. You know Guitar. He'll disappear on you in a minute." Milkman noticed how white Freddie's hair was.

"How old are you, Freddie?"

"Who knows? They made dirt in the morning and me that afternoon." He giggled. "But I been around a long long time."

"You born here?"

"Naw. Down south. Jacksonville, Florida. Bad country, boy. Bad, bad country. You know they ain't even got an orphanage in Jacksonville where colored babies can go? They have to put 'em in jail. I tell people that talk about them sit-ins I was *raised* in jail, and it don't scare me none."

"I didn't know you were an orphan."

"Well, not a regular orphan. I had people and all, but my mama died and nobody would take me in. It was on account of the way she died that nobody would take me."

"How'd she die?"

"Ghosts."

"Ghosts?"

"You don't believe in ghosts?"

"Well"–Milkman smiled–"I'm willing to, I guess."

"You better believe, boy. They're here."

"Here?" Milkman didn't glance around the office, but he wanted to. The wind howled outside in the blackness and Freddie, looking like a gnome, flashed his gold teeth. "I don't mean in this room necessarily. Although they could be." He cocked his head and listened. "No. I mean they in the world."

"You've seen some?"

"Plenty. Plenty. Ghosts killed my mother. I didn't see that, of course, but I seen 'em since."

"Tell me about them."

"No I ain't. I don't do no talkin 'bout the ghosts I seen. They don't like that."

"Well, tell me about the one you didn't see. The one killed your mother."

"Oh. Well. That one. She was walking cross the yard with this neighbor friend of hers and they both looked up and saw a woman comin down the road. They stopped and waited to see who she was. When the woman got near, the neighbor called out howdy and soon's she said the word, the woman turned into a white bull. Right before their eyes. My mama fell down on the ground in labor pain right then and there. When I was born and they showed me to her, she screamed and passed out. Never *did* come to. My father died two months before I was born, and they couldn't get none of my people and nobody else to take a baby brought here by a white bull."

Milkman started laughing. He didn't mean to hurt Freddie's feelings, but he couldn't stop the laughter, and the more he tried, the more it came.

Freddie looked more surprised than hurt. "You don't believe me, do you?"

Milkman couldn't answer, he was laughing so hard.

"Okay," Freddie said, and threw up his hands. "Okay, laugh on. But they's a lot of strange things you don't know nothin about, boy. You'll learn. Lot of strange things. Strange stuff goin on right in this here town."

Milkman's laughter was under control now. "What? What strange stuff is happening in this town? I haven't seen any white bulls lately."

"Open your eyes. Ask your buddy. He knows."

"What buddy?"

"Your buddy Guitar. Ask him what strange stuff been happenin. Ask him how come he runnin round with Empire State all of a sudden."

"Empire State?"

"That's right. Empire State."

"Nobody runs around with Empire State. He's a nut. He just stands around with a broom, dribbling spit. He can't even talk."

"He *don't* talk. That don't mean he can't. Only reason he don't is cause he found his wife in bed with another man long time ago, and ain't found nothing to say since then."

"Well, what's Guitar doing with him?"

"Good question. Police would like to know the answer to that too."

"How'd you get from Empire State to the police?"

"You ain't heard? People say the police is lookin for a colored man what killed that white boy in the schoolyard."

"I know that. Everybody knows that."

"Well, the description fits State. And Guitar been takin him places. Hidin him, I believe."

"What's so strange about that? You know Guitar is like that. He'll hide anybody the law is looking for. He hates white people, especially cops, and anybody they're after can count on him for help."

"You don't understand. Him and State ain't actin like they just hidin him. They actin like he did it."

"You a little drunk, Freddie?"

"Yeah, I'm a little drunk, but that don't change nothin. Look here. Remember when Emmet Till was killed? Back in fifty-three? Well, right after that, a white boy was killed in the schoolyard, wasn't he?"

"I don't know. I can't remember the dates of murders I haven't committed."

"You don't know?" Freddie was incredulous.

"No. Are you saying State did it?"

"I'm sayin he acts like it and I'm sayin Guitar knows, and I'm sayin somethin strange is goin on. That's what I'm sayin."

He's mad at me, thought Milkman, because I laughed at his mother and that white bull story. So he's trying to get back at me.

"Keep your eyes open," Freddie went on. "Just keep them open." He looked in the pint bottle, saw it was empty, and got up to leave. "Yep. Some strange goings on round here. But don't put my name in it if you hear anything. Was just like this when that insurance man jumped off the roof. Ever hear tell of him?"

"Seems like I did."

"That must a been when you was a little bitty baby, 1931.

Well, it was some strange stuff then too." Freddie buttoned his coat and pulled his flap-eared cap down as far as it would go. "Well, thanks for the coffee, boy. Did me a lot of good. A lot of good." He took his gloves out of his pocket and moved to the door.

"You're welcome, Freddie. Merry Christmas if I don't see you before that."

"Same to you. And your folks. Tell Mr. Dead and your mother I said Merry Christmas." He was smiling again. When he reached the door he put on his gloves. Then he turned his head slowly and faced Milkman. "Tell you somebody else might know about what's goin on. Corinthians. Ask Corinthians."

He flashed his gold merrily and was gone.

Chapter 5

Nothing happened to the fear. He lay in Guitar's bed face-up in the sunlight, trying to imagine how it would feel when the ice pick entered his neck. But picturing a spurt of wine-red blood and wondering if the ice pick would make him cough didn't help. Fear lay like a pair of crossed paws on his chest.

He closed his eyes and threw his arm over his face to keep the light from overexposing his thoughts. In the darkness that his arm made he could see ice picks coming down faster than raindrops had when he tried as a little boy to catch them with his tongue.

Five hours ago, before he knocked on Guitar's door, he had stood on the top step, dripping in the summer rain that still patted the window, imagining that the drops were tiny steely picks. Then he knocked on the door.

"Yeah?" The voice was lightly aggressive; Guitar never opened his door to a knock anymore before finding out who it was.

"Me—Milkman," he answered, and waited for the clicking sounds of three locks being released.

Milkman walked in, hunching his shoulders under his wet suit jacket. "Anything to drink?"

"Now, you know better'n that." Guitar was smiling, his golden eyes dimmed for the moment. They had not seen much of each other since that argument about Honoré versus Alabama, but the quarrel had been cleansing for both of them. They were easy with each other now that they didn't have to pretend. When in conversation they came to the battleground of difference, their verbal sparring was full of good humor. Furthermore, their friendship had been tested in more immediate ways. The last six months had been dangerous for Milkman, and Guitar had come to his aid over and over again.

"Coffee, then," said Milkman. He sat on the bed with the heaviness of a very old man. "How long you gonna keep that up?"

"Forever. It's over, man. No booze. How about some tea?"

"Jesus."

"Loose too. Bet you thought tea grew in little bags."

"Oh, Christ."

"Like Louisiana cotton. Except the black men picking it wear diapers and turbans. All over India that's all you see. Bushes with little bitsy white tea bags blossoming. Right?"

"Gimme the tea, Guitar. Just the tea. No geography."

"No geography? Okay, no geography. What about some history in your tea? Or some sociopolitico– No. That's still geography. Goddam, Milk, I do believe my whole life's geography."

"Don't you wash pots out for people before you cook water in them?"

"For example, I live in the North now. So the first question come to mind is North of what? Why, north of the South. So North exists because South does. But does that mean North is different from South? No way! South is just south of North. . . ."

"You don't put the fuckin leaves in the boiling water. You pour the water *over* the leaves. In a pot, man. In a teapot!"

"But there is some slight difference worth noticing. Northerners, for example—born and bred ones, that is—are picky about their food. Well, not about the food. They actually don't give a shit about the food. What they're picky about is the trappings. You know what I mean? The pots and shit. Now, they're real funny about pots. But tea? They don't know Earl Grey from old man Lipton's instant."

"I want tea, man. Not won-ton shredded wheat."

"Old man Lipton dye him up some shredded *New York Times* and put it in a cute little white bag and northern Negroes run amok. Can't contain themselves. Ever notice that? How they love them little white bags?"

"Oh, Jesus."

"He's a Northerner too. Lived in Israel, but a Northerner in His heart. His bleeding heart. His cute little old bleeding red heart. Southerners think they own Him, but that's just because the first time they laid eyes on Him, He was strung up on a tree. They can relate to that, see. Both the stringer and the strung. But Northerners know better. . . ."

"Who you talking about? Black people or white people?"

"Black? White? Don't tell me you're one of those racial Negroes? Who said anything about black people? This is just a geography lesson." Guitar handed Milkman a steaming cup of tea.

"Yeah, well, if this is tea, I'm a soft-fried egg."

"See what I mean? Picky. Why you got to be a *soft*-fried egg? Why can't you be just a fried egg? Or just a plain old egg? And why a egg anyway? Negro's been a lotta things, but he ain't never been no egg."

Milkman began to laugh. Guitar had done it again. He'd come to the door sopping wet, ready to roll over and die, and now he was laughing, spilling tea, and choking out his reply: "How come? How come a nigger can't be a egg? He can be a egg if he wants to."

"Nope. Can't be no egg. It ain't in him. Something about his genes. His genes won't let him be no egg no matter how hard he tries. Nature says no. 'No, you can't be no egg, nigger. Now, you can be a crow if you wanna. Or a big baboon. But not no egg. Eggs is difficult, complicated. Fragile too. And white.' "

"They got brown eggs."

"Miscegenation. Besides, don't nobody want 'em."

"French people do."

"In France, yeah. But not in the Congo. Frenchman in the Congo won't touch a brown egg."

"Why won't he?"

"Scared of 'em. Might do something to his skin. Like the sun."

"French people love the sun. They're always trying to get in the sun. On the Riviera—"

"They try to get in the French sun, but not the Congo sun. In the Congo they hate the sun."

"Well, I got a right to be what I want to be, and I want to be a egg."

"Fried?"

"Fried."

"Then somebody got to bust your shell."

Quicker than a pulse beat, Guitar had changed the air. Milkman wiped his mouth, avoiding Guitar's eyes because he knew the phosphorus was back in them. The little room stood at attention in the quiet. It was a second-story porch walled in to make a room-for-rent so the landlady could get an income from it and have a watchman too. Its outside stairway made it perfect for a bachelor. Especially a secretive one like Guitar Bains.

"Can I have the pad tonight?" Milkman asked him. He examined his fingernails.

"To cop?"

Milkman shook his head.

Guitar didn't believe him. Didn't believe his friend really wanted to be alone the night before the day of his own murder. "That's scary, man. Very scary."

Milkman didn't answer.

"You're not obliged to go through no number, you know. Not for me. Everybody knows you're brave when you want to be."

Milkman looked up but still did not answer.

"Still and all," Guitar went on carefully, "you might get your heart cut out. Then you'll be just another brave nigger what got wasted."

Milkman reached for the Pall Mall package. It was empty, so he pulled a longish butt from the Planter's peanut butter jar top that was Guitar's ashtray for the day. He stretched out on the bed, letting his long fingers rub the pocket places in his clothes where matches might be. "Everything's cool," he said.

"Shit," said Guitar. "Ain't nothing cool. Nothing, nowhere. Even the North Pole ain't cool. You think so, go on up there and watch them fuckin glaciers ice your ass. And what the glaciers don't get the polar bears will." Guitar stood up, his head almost touching the ceiling. Annoyed by Milkman's indifference, he relieved his agitation by straightening up the room. He pulled an empty crate from underneath the straight-backed chair leaning in the corner, and started dumping trash into the box: dead matches from the window sill, pork bones from the barbecue he had eaten the day before. He crumpled the pleated paper cups that had been overflowing with cole slaw and fired them into the crate. "Every nigger I know wants to be cool. There's nothing wrong with controlling yourself, but can't nobody control other people." He looked sideways at Milkman's face, alert for any sign, any opening. This kind of silence was new. Something must have happened. Guitar was genuinely worried about his friend, but he also didn't want anything to happen in his room that would bring the police there. He picked up the peanut-butter-top ashtray.

"Wait. There's still some good butts in there." Milkman spoke softly.

Guitar dumped the whole ashtray into the box.

"What'd you do that for? You know we don't have no cigarettes."

"Then move your ass and go get some."

"Come on, Guitar. Cut the shit." Milkman rose from the bed and reached for the crate. He would have gotten it except Guitar stepped back and flung it all the way across the room, letting the mess settle right back where it came from. Graceful and economical as a cat, he arced his arm out of the swing and slammed his fist up against the wall, forming a barrier to any move Milkman might make.

"Pay attention." Guitar's voice was low. "Pay attention when I'm trying to tell you something."

Head to head, toe to toe they stood. Milkman's left foot hovered above the floor, and Guitar's eyes with their phosphorous lights singed his heart a little, but he took the stare. "And if I don't? What then, man? You gonna do me in? My name is Macon, remember? I'm already Dead."

Guitar didn't smile at the familiar joke, but there was enough recognition of it in his face to soften the glare in his eyes.

"Somebody ought to tell your murderer that," said Guitar.

Milkman gave a short laugh and moved back toward the bed. "You worry too much, Guitar."

"I worry just enough. But right now I need to know how come you ain't worried at all. You come up here knowing it's the thirtieth day. Knowing if anybody wants to find you they come here if not first then last. And you ask me to leave you by yourself. Just tell me what you doing."

"Look," Milkman said. "Out of all those times, I was scared just twice: the first time and the third. I've been handling it ever since, right?"

"Yeah, but something's funny this time."

"Ain't nothing funny."

"Yeah, it is. You. You funny."

"No I'm not. Just tired. Tired of dodging crazy people, tired of this jive town, of running up and down these streets getting nowhere. . . ."

"Well, you're home free if tired is all you are. Soon you'll have all the rest you ever need. Can't promise you the bed's comfortable, but morticians don't make mattresses."

"Maybe she won't come this time."

"She ain't missed in six months. You countin on her taking a holiday or something?"

"I can't hide from that bitch no more. I got to stop it. I don't want to go through this again a month from now."

"Why don't you get her people to do something?"

"I am her people."

"Listen, Milk, I'll split if you say so. But just listen to me a minute. That broad had a Carlson skinning knife last time. You know how sharp a Carlson skinning knife is? Cut you like a laser, man."

"I know."

"No, you don't know. You was up under the bar when me and Moon grabbed her."

"I know what she had."

"Won't be no Moon in this room tomorrow. And no Guitar either, if I listen to you. This time she might have a pistol."

"What fool is gonna give a colored woman a pistol?"

"Same fool that gave Porter a shotgun."

"That was years ago."

"It ain't even that that bothers me. It's the way you acting. Like you want it. Like you looking forward to it."

"Where'd you think that up?"

"Look at you. You all dressed up."

"I had to work in Sonny's Shop. You know my old man makes me dress up like this when I'm behind the desk."

"You had time to change. It's past midnight."

"Okay. So I'm clean. So I'm looking forward to it. I just got through telling you I don't want to hide no more. . . ."

"It's a secret, ain't it? You got yourself a secret."

"That makes two of us."

"Two? You and her?"

"No. You and me. You've been making some funny smoke screens lately." Milkman looked up at Guitar and smiled. "Just so you don't think I ain't noticed."

Guitar grinned back. Now that he knew there was a secret, he settled down into the groove of their relationship.

"Okay, Mr. Dead, sir. You on your own. Would you ask your visitor to kind of neaten things up a little before she goes? I don't want to come back and have to look through a pile of cigarette butts for your head. Be nice if it was laying somewhere I could spot it right off. And if it's her head that's left behind, well, there's some towels in the closet on the shelf in the back."

"Rest your mind, boy. Ain't nobody giving up no head."

They laughed then at the suitableness of the unintended pun, and it was in the sound of this laughter that Guitar picked up his brown leather jacket and started out the door.

"Cigarettes!" Milkman called after him. "Bring me some cigarettes before you disappear."

"Gotcha!" Guitar was halfway down the stairs. Already his thoughts had left Milkman and had flown ahead to the house where six old men waited for him.

He didn't come back that night.

Milkman lay quietly in the sunlight, his mind a blank, his lungs craving smoke. Gradually his fear of and eagerness for death returned. Above all he wanted to escape what he knew, escape the implications of what he had been told. And all he knew in the world about the world was what other people had told him. He felt like a garbage pail for the actions and hatreds of other people. He himself did nothing. Except for the one time he had hit his father, he had never acted independently, and that act, his only one, had brought unwanted knowledge too, as well as some responsibility for that knowledge. When his father told him about Ruth, he joined him in despising her, but he felt put upon; felt as though some burden had been given to him and that he didn't deserve it. None of that was his fault, and he didn't want to have to think or be or do something about any of it.

In that mood of lazy righteousness he wallowed in Guitar's bed, the same righteousness that had made him tail his mother like a secret agent when she left the house a week or so ago.

Returning home from a party, he had hardly pulled Macon's Buick up to the curb and turned off the car lights when he saw his mother walking a little ahead of him down Not Doctor Street. It was one-thirty in the morning, but in spite of the hour and her turned-up coat collar, there was no air of furtiveness about her at all. She was walking in what seemed to him a determined manner. Neither hurried nor aimless. Just the even-paced walk of a woman on her way to some modest but respectable work.

When Ruth turned the corner, Milkman waited a minute and started up the car. Creeping, not letting the engine slide into high gear, he drove around the corner. She was standing at the bus stop, so Milkman waited in the shadows until the bus came and she boarded it.

Surely this was no meeting of lovers. The man would have picked her up nearby somewhere. No man would allow a woman he had any affection for to come to him on public transportation in the middle of the night, especially a woman as old as Ruth. And what man wanted a woman over sixty anyway?

Following the bus was a nightmare; it stopped too often, too long, and it was difficult to tail it, hide, and watch to see if she got off. Milkman turned on the car radio, but the music, which he hoped would coat his nerve ends, only splayed them. He was very nervous and thought seriously about turning back.

Finally the bus pulled up at the intracounty train station. Its last stop. There, among the few remaining passengers, he saw her go into the lobby of the station. He believed he'd lost her. He'd never find out what train she was taking. He thought again of going back home. It was late, he was exhausted, and he wasn't sure he wanted to know any more about his mother. But having come this far, he realized it was foolish to turn back now and leave things forever up in the air. He parked in the lot and walked slowly toward the station. Maybe she's not taking a train, he thought. Maybe he meets her in the station.

He looked around carefully before pushing open the doors. There was no sign of her inside. It was a small, plain building. Old but well lit. Looming over the modest waiting room was the Great Seal of Michigan, in vivid Technicolor, painted, probably, by some high school art class. Two pink deer reared up on their hind legs, facing each other, and an eagle perched at eye level between them. The eagle's wings were open and looked like raised shoulders. Its head was turned to the left; one fierce eye bored into that of a deer. Purple Latin words stretched in a long ribbon beneath the seal: *Si Quaeris Peninsulam Amoenam Circumspice*. Milkman didn't understand the Latin and he didn't understand why the wolverine state had a buck painted on the seal. Or were they does? He remembered Guitar's story about killing one. "A man shouldn't do that." Milkman felt a quick beat of something like remorse, but he shook it off and resumed his search for his mother. He walked to the back of the station. Still no sight of her. Then he noticed that there was an upper platform, stairs leading to it, and an arrow with the words FAIRFIELD AND NORTHEASTERN SUBURBS painted on it. Perhaps she was up there. He moved cautiously toward the stairs, glancing up and all around lest he see her or miss her. A loudspeaker broke the silence, announcing the arrival of the two-fifteen train to Fairfield Heights, leaving from the upper platform. He dashed up the stairs then just in time to see Ruth step into a car, and to jump into another car himself.

The train made ten stops at about ten-minute intervals. He leaned out between the cars at each stop to see if she was getting off. After the sixth stop, he asked the conductor when the next train returned to the city. "Five forty-five a.m.," he said.

Milkman looked at his watch. It was already three o'clock. When the conductor called out, "Fairfield Heights. Last stop," a half hour later, Milkman looked out again and this time he saw her disembark. He darted behind the three-sided wooden structure that sheltered waiting passengers from the wind until he heard her wide rubber heels padding down the steps.

Beyond the shelter along the street below were stores—all closed now: newsstands, coffee shops, stationery shops, but no houses. The wealthy people of Fairfield did not live near a train station and very few of their houses could even be seen from the road. Nevertheless, Ruth walked in her even-paced way down the street and in just a few minutes was at the wide winding lane that led into Fairfield Cemetery.

As Milkman stared at the ironwork arched over the entrance, he remembered snatches of his mother's chatter about having looked so very carefully for a cemetery for the doctor's body—someplace other than the one where Negroes were all laid together in one area. And forty years ago Fairfield was farm country with a county cemetery too tiny for anybody to care whether its dead were white or black.

Milkman leaned against a tree and waited at the entrance. Now he knew, if he'd had any doubts, that all his father had told him was true. She was a silly, selfish, queer, faintly obscene woman. Again he felt abused. Why couldn't anybody in his whole family just be normal?

He waited for an hour before she came out.

"Hello, Mama," he said. He tried to make his voice sound as coolly cruel as he felt; just as he tried to frighten her by stepping out suddenly from behind the tree.

He succeeded. She stumbled in alarm and took a great gulp of air into her mouth.

"Macon! Is that you? You're here? Oh, my goodness. I . . ." She tried desperately to normalize the situation, smiling wanly and blinking her eyes, searching for words and manners and civilization.

Milkman stopped her. "You come to lay down on your father's grave? Is that what you've been doing all these years? Spending a night every now and then with your father?"

Ruth's shoulders seemed to slump, but she said in a surprisingly steady voice, "Let's walk toward the train stop."

Neither said a word during the forty-five minutes they waited in the little shelter for the train back to the city. The sun came up and pointed out the names of young lovers painted on the wall. A few men were walking up the stairs to the platform.

When the train backed in from its siding they still had not spoken. Only when the wheels were actually turning and the engine had cleared its throat did Ruth begin, and she began in the middle of a sentence as though she had been thinking it all through since she and her son left the entrance to Fairfield Cemetery.

". . . because the fact is that I am a small woman. I don't mean little; I mean small, and I'm small because I was pressed small. I lived in a great big house that pressed me into a small package. I had no friends, only schoolmates who wanted to touch my dresses and my white silk stockings. But I didn't think I'd ever need a friend because I had him. I was small, but he was big. The only person who ever really cared whether I lived or died. Lots of people were *interested* in whether I lived or died, but he cared. He was not a good man, Macon. Certainly he was an arrogant man, and often a foolish and destructive one. But he cared whether and he cared how I lived, and there was, and is, no one else in the world who ever did. And for that I would do anything. It was important for me to be in his presence, among his things, the things he used, had touched. Later it was just important for me to know that he was in the world. When he left it, I kept on reigniting that cared-for feeling that I got from him.

"I am not a strange woman. I am a small one.

"I don't know what all your father has told you about me down in that shop you all stay in. But I know, as well as I know my own name, that he told you only what was flattering to him. I know he never told you that he killed my father and that he tried to kill you. Because both of you took my attention away from him. I know he never told you that. And I know he never told you that he threw my father's medicine away, but it's true. And I couldn't save my father. Macon took away his medicine and I just didn't know it, and I wouldn't have been able to save you except for Pilate. Pilate was the one brought you here in the first place."

"Pilate?" Milkman was coming awake. He had begun listening to his mother with the dulled ear of someone who was about to be conned and knew it.

"Pilate. Old, crazy, sweet Pilate. Your father and I hadn't had physical relations since my father died, when Lena and Corinthians were just toddlers. We had a terrible quarrel. He threatened to kill me. I threatened to go to the police about what he had done to my father. We did neither. I guess my father's money was more important to him than the satisfaction of killing me. And I would have happily died except for my babies. But he did move into another room and that's the way things stayed until I couldn't stand it anymore. Until I thought I'd really die if I had to live that way. With nobody touching me, or even looking as though they'd like to touch me. That's when I started coming to Fairfield. To talk. To talk to somebody who wanted to listen and not laugh at me. Somebody I could trust. Somebody who trusted me. Somebody who was . . . interested in me. For my own self. I didn't care if that somebody was under the ground. You know, I was twenty years old when your father stopped sleeping in the bed with me. That's hard, Macon. Very hard. By the time I was thirty . . . I think I was just afraid I'd die that way.

"Then Pilate came to town. She came into this city like she owned it. Pilate, Reba, and Reba's little baby. Hagar. Pilate came to see Macon right away and soon as she saw me she knew what my trouble was. And she asked me one day, 'Do you want him?' 'I want somebody,' I told her. 'He's as good as anybody,' she said. 'Besides, you'll get pregnant and your baby ought to be his. He ought to have a son. Otherwise this be the end of us.'

"She gave me funny things to do. And some greenish-gray grassy-looking stuff to put in his food." Ruth laughed. "I felt like a doctor, like a chemist doing some big important scientific experiment. It worked too. Macon came to me for four days. He even came home from his office in the middle of the day to be with me. He looked puzzled, but he came. Then it was over. And two months later I was pregnant. When he found out about it, he immediately suspected Pilate and he told me to get rid of the baby. But I wouldn't and Pilate helped me stand him off. I wouldn't have been strong enough without her. She saved my life. And yours, Macon. She saved yours too. She watched you like you were her own. Until your father threw her out."

Milkman leaned his head against the cold handbar that was attached to the seat in front of him. He held it there, letting its chill circle his head. Then he turned to his mother. "Were you in the bed with your father when he was dead? Naked?"

"No. But I did kneel there in my slip at his bedside and kiss his beautiful fingers. They were the only part of him that wasn't . . ."

"You nursed me."

"Yes."

"Until I was . . . old. Too old."

Ruth turned toward her son. She lifted her head and looked deep into his eyes. "And I also prayed for you. Every single night and every single day. On my knees. Now you tell me. What harm did I do you on my knees?"

That was the beginning. Now it was all going to end. In a little while she would walk in the door and this time he would let her do it. Afterward there would be no remembrance of who he was or where. Of Magdalene called Lena and First Corinthians, of his father trying to stop him dead before he was born. Of the brilliant bitterness between his father and his mother, a bitterness as smooth and fixed as steel. And he wouldn't have those waking dreams or hear those awful words his mother had spoken to him: What harm? What harm did I do you on my knees?

He could hear her footsteps, and then the sound of the doorknob turning, sticking, and turning again. He knew, without uncovering his eyes, that she was right there, looking at him through the window.

Hagar. Killing, ice-pick-wielding Hagar, who, shortly after a Christmas thank-you note, found herself each month searching the barrels and cupboards and basement shelves for some comfortably portable weapon with which to murder her true love.

The "thank you" cut her to the quick, but it was not the

reason she ran scurrying into cupboards looking for weapons. That had been accomplished by the sight of Milkman's arms around the shoulders of a girl whose silky copper-colored hair cascaded over the sleeve of his coat. They were sitting in Mary's, smiling into glasses of Jack Daniel's on the rocks. The girl looked a little like Corinthians or Lena from the back, and when she turned, laughing, toward Milkman, and Hagar saw her gray eyes, the fist that had been just sitting in her chest since Christmas released its forefinger like the blade of a skinning knife. As regularly as the new moon searched for the tide, Hagar looked for a weapon and then slipped out of her house and went to find the man for whom she believed she had been born into the world. Being five years older than he was and his cousin as well did nothing to dim her passion. In fact her maturity and blood kinship converted her passion to fever, so it was more affliction than affection. It literally knocked her down at night, and raised her up in the morning, for when she dragged herself off to bed, having spent another day without his presence, her heart beat like a gloved fist against her ribs. And in the morning, long before she was fully awake, she felt a longing so bitter and tight it yanked her out of a sleep swept clean of dreams.

She moved around the house, onto the porch, down the streets, to the fruit stalls and the butchershop, like a restless ghost, finding peace nowhere and in nothing. Not in the first tomato off the vine, split open and salted lightly, which her grandmother put before her. Not the six-piece set of pink glass dishes Reba won at the Tivoli Theater. And not the carved wax candle that the two of them made for her, Pilate dipping the wick and Reba scratching out tiny flowers with a nail file, and put in a genuine store-bought candleholder next to her bed. Not even the high fierce sun at noon, nor the ocean-dark evenings. Nothing could pull her mind away from the mouth Milkman was not kissing, the feet that were not running toward him, the eye that no longer beheld him, the hands that were not touching him.

She toyed, sometimes, with her unsucked breasts, but at some point her lethargy dissipated of its own accord and in its place was wilderness, the focused meanness of a flood or an avalanche of snow which only observers, flying in a rescue helicopter, believed to be an indifferent natural phenomenon, but which the victims, in their last gulp of breath, knew was both directed and personal. The calculated violence of a shark grew in her, and like every witch that ever rode a broom straight through the night to a ceremonial infanticide as thrilled by the black wind as by the rod between her legs; like every fed-up-to-the-teeth bride who worried about the consistency of the grits she threw at her husband as well as the potency of the lye she had stirred into them; and like every queen and every courtesan who was struck by the beauty of her emerald ring as she tipped its poison into the old red wine, Hagar was energized by the details of her mission. She stalked him. Whenever the fist that beat in her chest became that pointing finger, when any contact with him at all was better than none, she stalked him. She could not get his love (and the possibility that he did not think of her at all was intolerable), so she settled for his fear.

On those days, her hair standing out from her head like a thundercloud, she haunted Southside and Not Doctor Street until she found him. Sometimes it took two days, or three, and the people who saw her passed the word along that Hagar "done took off after Milkman again." Women watched her out of their windows. Men looked up from their checker games and wondered if she'd make it this time. The lengths to which lost love drove men and women never surprised them. They had seen women pull their dresses over their heads and howl like dogs for lost love. And men who sat in doorways with pennies in their mouths for lost love. "Thank God," they whispered to themselves, "thank God I ain't never had one of them graveyard loves." Empire State himself was a good example of one. He'd married a white girl in France and brought her home. Happy as a fly and just as industrious, he lived with her for six years until he came home to find her with another man. Another black man. And when he discovered that his white wife loved not only him, not only this other black man, but the whole race, he sat down, closed his mouth, and never said another word. Railroad Tommy had given him a janitor's job to save him from the poorhouse, workhouse, or nuthouse, one.

So Hagar's forays were part and parcel of the mystery of having been "lifed" by love, and while the manifestation it took was a source of great interest to them, the consequences were not. After all, it served him right, messing with his own cousin.

Luckily for Milkman, she had proved, so far, to be the world's most inept killer. Awed (even in the midst of her anger) by the very presence of her victim, she trembled violently and her knife thrusts and hammer swings and ice-pick jabs were clumsy. As soon as the attempt had been thwarted by a wrist grab from behind or a body tackle from the front or a neat clip on the jaw, she folded up into herself and wept cleansing tears right there and later under Pilate's strap—to which she submitted with relief. Pilate beat her, Reba cried, and Hagar crouched. Until the next time. Like this time when she turned the doorknob of Guitar's little bachelor room.

It was locked. So she swung one leg over the porch railing and fiddled with the window. Milkman heard the noises, heard the window shake, but refused to move or take his arm away from his eyes. Even when he heard the tinkle and clatter of glass he did not move.

Hagar put her shoe back on before reaching into the window hole she had made and turning the catch. It took her the longest time to raise the window. She was hanging lopsided over the railing, one leg supporting her weight. The window slid in a crooked path up its jamb.

Milkman refused to look. Perspiration collected in the small of his back and ran out of his armpit down his side. But the fear was gone. He lay there as still as the morning light, and sucked the world's energy up into his own will. And willed her dead. Either she will kill me or she will drop dead. Either I am to live in this world on my terms or I will die out of it. If I am to live in it, then I want her dead. One or the other. Me or her. Choose.

Die, Hagar. Die. Die. Die.

But she didn't. She crawled into the room and walked over to the little iron bed. In her hand was a butcher knife, which she raised high over her head and brought down heavily toward the smooth neck flesh that showed above his shirt collar. The knife struck his collarbone and angled off to his shoulder. A small break in the skin began to bleed. Milkman jerked, but did not move his arm nor open his eyes. Hagar raised the knife again, this time with both hands, but found she could not get her arms down. Try as she might, the ball joint in her shoulders would not move. Ten seconds passed. Fifteen. The paralyzed woman and the frozen man.

At the thirtieth second Milkman knew he had won. He moved his arm and opened his eyes. His gaze traveled to her strung-up, held-up arms.

Oh, she thought, when she saw his face, I had forgotten how beautiful he is.

Milkman sat up, swung his legs over the side of the bed, and stood.

"If you keep your hands just that way," he said, "and then bring them down straight, straight and fast, you can drive that knife right smack in your cunt. Why don't you do that? Then all your problems will be over." He patted her cheek and turned away from her wide, dark, pleading, hollow eyes.

She stood that way for a long time, and it was an even longer time before anybody found her. They could have guessed where she was, though. If anybody missed her for a while they could guess. Even Ruth knew now. A week earlier she had learned from Freddie that Hagar had tried to kill Milkman six times in as many months. She stared at his golden teeth and said, "Hagar?" She hadn't laid eyes on her in years; had been to Pilate's house only once in her life—a very long time ago.

"Hagar?"

"Hagar. Shore Hagar."

"Does Pilate know?"

"Course she do. Whip her every time, but it don't do no good."

Ruth was relieved. For a moment she imagined that Pilate, who had brought her son to life in the first place, was now bound to see him dead. But right after that moment of relief, she felt hurt because Milkman had not told her himself. Then she realized that he really didn't tell her anything, and hadn't for years. Her son had never been a person to her, a separate real person. He had always been a passion. Because she had been so desperate to lie with her husband and have another baby by him, the son she bore was first off a wished-for bond between herself and Macon, something to hold them together and reinstate their sex lives. Even before his birth he was a strong feeling—a feeling about the nasty greenish-gray powder Pilate had given her to be stirred into rain water and put into food. But Macon came out of his few days of sexual hypnosis in a rage and later when he discovered her pregnancy, tried to get her to abort. Then the baby became the nausea caused by the half ounce of castor oil Macon made her drink, then a hot pot recently emptied of scalding water on which she sat, then a soapy enema, a knitting needle (she inserted only the tip, squatting in the bathroom, crying, afraid of the man who paced outside the door), and finally, when he punched her stomach (she had been about to pick up his breakfast plate, when he looked at her stomach and punched it), she ran to Southside looking for Pilate. She had never walked through that part of town, but she knew the street Pilate lived on, though not the house. Pilate had no telephone and no number on her house. Ruth had asked some passer-by where Pilate lived and was directed to a lean brown house set back from the unpaved road. Pilate was sitting on a chair; Reba was cutting Pilate's hair with a barber's clippers. That was the first time she saw Hagar, who was four or five years old then. Chubby, with four long braids, two like horns over each ear, two like tails at the back of her neck. Pilate comforted Ruth, gave her a peach, which Ruth could not eat because the fuzz made her sick. She listened to what Ruth said and sent Reba to the store for a box of Argo cornstarch. She sprinkled a little of it into her hand and offered it to Ruth, who obediently took a lump and put it in her mouth. As soon as she tasted it, felt its crunchiness, she asked for more, and ate half a box before she left. (From then on she ate cornstarch, cracked ice, nuts, and once in a fit she put a few tiny pebbles of gravel in her mouth. "When you expectin, you have to eat what the baby craves," Pilate said, " 'less it come in the world hongry for what you denied it." Ruth could not bite enough. Her teeth were on edge with the yearning. Like the impulse of a cat to claw, she searched for crunchy things, and when there was nothing, she would grind her teeth.)

Gnashing the cornstarch, Ruth let Pilate lead her into the bedroom, where the woman wrapped her in a homemade-on-the-spot girdle—tight in the crotch—and told her to keep it on until the fourth month and "don't take no more mess off Macon and don't ram another thing up in your womb." She also told her not to worry. Macon wouldn't bother her no more; she, Pilate, would see to it. (Years later Ruth learned that Pilate put a small doll on Macon's chair in his office. A male doll with a small painted chicken bone stuck between its legs and a round red circle painted on its belly. Macon knocked it out of the chair and with a yardstick pushed it into the bathroom, where he doused it with alcohol and burned it. It took nine separate burnings before the fire got down to the straw and cotton ticking of its insides. But he must have remembered the round fire-red stomach, for he left Ruth alone after that.)

When the baby was born the day after she stood in the snow, with cloth roses at her feet and a man with blue wings above her head, she regarded him as a beautiful toy, a respite, a distraction, a physical pleasure as she nursed him—until Freddie (again Freddie) caught her at it; then he was no longer her velveteened toy. He became a plain on which, like the cowboys and Indians in the movies, she and her husband fought. Each one befuddled by the values of the other. Each one convinced of his own purity and outraged by the idiocy he saw in the other. She was the Indian, of course, and lost her land, her customs, her integrity to the cowboy and became a spread-eagled footstool resigned to her fate and holding fast to tiny irrelevant defiances.

But who was this son of hers? This tall man who had flesh on the outside and feelings on the inside that she knew nothing of, but somebody did, knew enough about him to want to kill him. Suddenly, the world opened up for her like one of her imperial tulips and revealed its evil yellow pistil. She had been husbanding her own misery, shaping it, making of it an art and a Way. Now she saw a larger, more malevolent world outside her own. Outside the fourposter bed where Doctor had bubbled and rotted (all but his beautiful hands, which were the only things his grandson had inherited). Outside her garden and the fishbowl where her goldfish died. She had thought it was all done. That she had won out over the castor oil, and the pot of steam that had puckered and burned her skin so she could not bear to urinate or sit with her daughters at the table where they cut and sewed. She had had the baby anyway, and although it did nothing to close the break between herself and Macon, there he was, her single triumph.

Now Freddie was telling her that it wasn't done and over yet. Somebody was still trying to kill him. To deprive her of the one aggressive act brought to royal completion. And the person who was threatening his life was someone who shared Macon's blood.

"That hurts," she said aloud to Freddie as she folded into her pocket the rent money he handed her. "That hurts, you know."

She climbed the porch steps and went into the kitchen. Without knowing what her foot was planning to do, she kicked the cabinet door with the worn lock under the sink. It answered her kick with a tiny whine before it sneaked open again. Ruth looked at it and kicked it closed once more. Again it whined and opened right back up.

"I want you closed," she whispered. "Closed."

The door stayed open.

"Closed. You hear me? Closed. Closed. Closed." She was screaming by now.

Magdalene called Lena, hearing her shouts, ran down the stairs and into the kitchen. She found her mother staring at the sink and commanding it.

"Mother?" Lena was frightened.

Ruth looked up at her. "What is it?"

"I don't know. . . . I thought I heard you saying something."

"Get somebody to fix that door. I want it shut. Tight."

Lena stared as Ruth hurried past and when she heard her mother running up the stairs, she put her fingers to her lips in disbelief. Ruth was sixty-two years old. Lena had no idea she could move that fast.

Her passions were narrow but deep. Long deprived of sex, long dependent on self-manipulation, she saw her son's imminent death as the annihilation of the last occasion she had been made love to.

With the same determined tread that took her to the graveyard six or seven times a year, Ruth left the house and caught the number 26 bus and sat down right in back of the driver. She took her glasses off and wiped them on the hem of her skirt. She was serene and purposeful as always when death turned his attention to someone who belonged to her, as she was when death breathed in her father's wispy hair and blew the strands about. She had the same calmness and efficiency with which she cared for the doctor, putting her hand on death's chest and holding him back, denying him, keeping her father alive even past the point where he wanted to be alive, past pain on into disgust and horror at having to smell himself in his next breath. Past that until he was too sick to fight her efforts to keep him alive, lingering in absolute hatred of this woman who would not grant him peace, but kept her shining lightish eyes fixed on him like magnets holding him from the narrow earth he longed for.

Ruth wiped her glasses clean so she could see the street signs as they passed ("Eat cherries," Pilate had told her, "and you won't have to wear them little windows over your eyes"), her mind empty except for getting there—to Darling Street, where Pilate lived and where, she supposed, Hagar lived too. How had that chubby little girl weighed down with hair become a knife-wielding would-be killer out to get her son? Maybe Freddie lied. Maybe. She'd see.

When the banks disappeared and small shops in between rickety houses came into view, Ruth pulled the cord. She stepped down and walked toward the underpass that cut across Darling Street. It was a long walk and she was sweating by the time she got to Pilate's house. The door was open, but nobody was inside. The house smelled fruity and she remembered how the peach had nauseated her the last time she was there. Here was the chair she had collapsed in. There the candlemaker's rack, the pan where Pilate's homemade soap hardened into a yellowish-brown slab. This house had been a haven then, and in spite of the cold anger she felt now, it still looked like an inn, a safe harbor. A flypaper roll entirely free of flies curled down from the ceiling not far from a sack that hung there too. Ruth looked into the bedroom and saw three little beds, and like Goldilocks, she walked over to the nearest one and sat down. There was no back door to this two-room house, just a big room where they lived and this bedroom. It had a cellar that one could enter only from the outside under a metal door that slanted away from the house and opened onto stone stairs.

Ruth sat still, letting the anger and determination jell. She wondered whose bed it was and lifted up the blanket and saw only mattress ticking. The same was true of the next bed, but not of the third. It had sheets, a pillow, and a pillow slip. That would be Hagar's, she thought. The anger unjelled and flooded through her. She left the room, pressing her fury back so she would be able to wait and wait until somebody returned. Pacing the floor of the outer room, her elbows in the palms of her hands, she suddenly heard humming that seemed to be coming from the back of the house. Pilate, she thought. Pilate hummed and chewed things all the time. Ruth would ask her first if what Freddie said was true. She needed Pilate's calm view, her honesty and equilibrium. Then she would know what to do. Whether to unfold her arms and let the rage out to do whatever it might, or . . . She tasted again the Argo cornstarch and felt the marvelous biting and crunching it allowed her. Now she merely ground her teeth as she stepped out to the porch and made her way around the side of the house through the nicotiana growing all wild and out of control.

A woman sat on a bench, her hands clasped between her knees. It was not Pilate. Ruth stood still and looked at the woman's back. It didn't look like death's back at all. It looked vulnerable, soft, like an easily wounded shin, full of bone but susceptible to the slightest pain.

"Reba?" she said.

The woman turned around and fastened on her the most sorrowful eyes Ruth had ever seen.

"Reba's gone," she said, the second word sounding as if the going were permanent. "Can I do something for you?"

"I'm Ruth Foster."

Hagar stiffened. A lightning shot of excitement ran through her. Milkman's mother: the silhouette she had seen through the curtains in an upstairs window on evenings when she stood across the street hoping at first to catch him, then hoping just to see him, finally just to be near the things he was familiar with. Private vigils held at night, made more private because they were expressions of public lunacy. The outline she'd seen once or twice when the side door opened and a woman shook crumbs from a tablecloth or dust from a small rug onto the ground. Whatever Milkman had told her about his mother, whatever she had heard from Pilate and Reba, she could not remember, so overwhelmed was she in the presence of *his* mother. Hagar let her morbid pleasure spread across her face in a smile.

Ruth was not impressed. Death always smiled. And breathed. And looked helpless like a shinbone, or a tiny speck of black on the Queen Elizabeth roses, or film on the eye of a dead goldfish.

"You are trying to kill him." Ruth's voice was matter-of-fact. "If you so much as bend a hair on his head, so help me Jesus, I will tear your throat out."

Hagar looked surprised. She loved nothing in the world except this woman's son, wanted him alive more than anybody, but hadn't the least bit of control over the predator that lived inside her. Totally taken over by her anaconda love, she had no self left, no fears, no wants, no intelligence that was her own. So it was with a great deal of earnestness that she replied to Ruth. "I'll try not to. But I can't make you a for-certain promise."

Ruth heard the supplication in her words and it seemed to her that she was not looking at a person but at an impulse, a cell, a red corpuscle that neither knows nor understands why it is driven to spend its whole life in one pursuit: swimming up a dark tunnel toward the muscle of a heart or an eye's nerve end that it both nourished and fed from.

Hagar lowered her eyelids and gazed hungrily down the figure of the woman who had been only a silhouette to her. The woman who slept in the same house with him, and who could call him home and he would come, who knew the mystery of his flesh, had memory of him as long as his life. The woman who knew him, had watched his teeth appear, stuck her finger in his mouth to soothe his gums. Cleaned his behind, Vaselined his penis, and caught his vomit in a fresh white diaper. Had fed him from her own nipples, carried him close and warm and safe under her heart, and who had opened her legs far far wider than she herself ever had for him. Who even now could walk freely into his room if she wanted to and smell his clothes, stroke his shoes, and lay her head on the very spot where he had lain his. But what was more, so much more, this thin lemon-yellow woman knew with absolute certainty what Hagar would willingly have her throat torn out to know: that she would see him this very day. Jealousy loomed so large in her it made her tremble. Maybe you, she thought. Maybe it's you I should be killing. Maybe then he will come to me and let me come to him. He is my home in this world. And then, aloud, "He is my home in this world."

"And I am his," said Ruth.

"And he wouldn't give a pile of swan shit for either one of you."

They turned then and saw Pilate leaning on the window sill. Neither knew how long she'd been there.

"Can't say as I blame him neither. Two growed-up women

talkin 'bout a man like he was a house or needed one. He ain't a house, he's a man, and whatever he need, don't none of you got it."

"Leave me alone, Mama. Just leave me alone."

"You already alone. If you want more alone, I can knock you into the middle of next week, and leave you there."

"You're botherin me!" Hagar was shouting and digging her fingers in her hair. It was an ordinary gesture of frustration, but its awkwardness made Ruth know that there was something truly askew in this girl. That here was the wilderness of Southside. Not the poverty or dirt or noise, not just extreme unregulated passion where even love found its way with an ice pick, but the absence of control. Here one lived knowing that at any time, anybody might do anything. Not wilderness where there was system, or the logic of lions, trees, toads, and birds, but wild wilderness where there was none.

She had not recognized it in Pilate, whose equilibrium overshadowed all her eccentricities and who was, in any case, the only person she knew of strong enough to counter Macon. Although Ruth had been frightened of her the first time she saw her—when she knocked on the kitchen door way back then, looking, as she said, for her brother Macon. (Ruth was still frightened of her a little. Not just her short hair cut regularly like a man's, or her large sleepy eyes and busy lips, or the smooth smooth skin, hairless, scarless, and wrinkleless. For Ruth had actually seen it. The place on her stomach where a navel should have been and was not. Even if you weren't frightened of a woman who had no navel, you certainly had to take her very seriously.)

Now she held up her hand, imperiously, and silenced Hagar's whines.

"Sit down there. Sit down and don't leave this yard."

Hagar slumped and moved slowly back to her bench.

Pilate turned her eyes to Ruth. "Come on in. Rest yourself before you hop on that bus again."

They sat down at the table facing each other.

"Peaches kind of dried up on me in this heat," said Pilate, and she reached for a peck basket which held about a half dozen. "But there should be some good ones left in here. Can I slice you up some?"

"No, thank you," said Ruth. She was trembling a little now. After the tension, the anger, the bravado of her earlier state of mind, followed by the violence of Pilate's words to her granddaughter, this quiet social-tea tone disarmed her, threw her too soon and too suddenly back into the mannered dignity that was habitual for her. Ruth pressed her hands together in her lap to stop the shaking.

They were so different, these two women. One black, the other lemony. One corseted, the other buck naked under her dress. One well read but ill traveled. The other had read only a geography book, but had been from one end of the country to another. One wholly dependent on money for life, the other indifferent to it. But those were the meaningless things. Their similarities were profound. Both were vitally interested in Macon Dead's son, and both had close and supportive posthumous communication with their fathers.

"The last time I was here you offered me a peach. My visit was about my son then too."

Pilate nodded her head and with her right thumbnail slit the peach open.

"You won't never be able to forgive her. For just tryin to do it you won't never be able to forgive her. But it looks to me like you ought to be able to understand her. Think on it a minute. You ready now to kill her—well, maim her anyway—because she's tryin to take him away from you. She's the enemy to you because she wants to take him out of your life. Well, in her eyes there's somebody who wants to take him out of her life too—him. So he's her enemy. He's the one who's tryin to take himself out of her life. And she'll kill him before she lets him do that. What I'm sayin is that you both got the same idea.

"I do my best to keep her from it. She's my baby too, you know, but I tear her up every time she try. Just for the tryin, mind you, because I know one thing sure: she'll never pull it off. He come in the world tryin to keep from gettin killed. Layin in your stomach, his own papa was tryin to do it. And you helped some too. He had to fight off castor oil and knittin needles and being blasted with hot steam and I don't know what all you and Macon did. But he made it. When he was at his most helpless, he made it. Ain't nothin goin to kill him but his own ignorance, and won't no woman ever kill him. What's likelier is that it'll be a woman save his life."

"Nobody lives forever, Pilate."

"Don't?"

"Of course not."

"Nobody?"

"Of course, nobody."

"I don't see why not."

"Death is as natural as life."

"Ain't nothin natural about death. It's the most unnatural thing they is."

"You think people should live forever?"

"Some people. Yeah."

"Who's to decide? Which ones should live and which ones shouldn't?"

"The people themselves. Some folks want to live forever. Some don't. I believe they decide on it anyway. People die when they want to and if they want to. Don't nobody have to die if they don't want to."

Ruth felt a chill. She'd always believed that her father wanted to die. "I wish I could count on your faith as far as my son was concerned. But I think I'd be a really foolish woman if I did that. You saw your own father die, just like I did; you saw him killed. Do you think he wanted to die?"

"I saw Papa shot. Blown off a fence five feet into the air. I saw him wigglin on the ground, but not only did I not see him die, I seen him since he was shot."

"Pilate. You all buried him yourselves." Ruth spoke as if she were talking to a child.

"Macon did."

"It's the same thing."

"Macon seen him too. After he buried him, after he was blown off that fence. We both seen him. I see him still. He's helpful to me, real helpful. Tells me things I need to know."

"What things?"

"All kinds of things. It's a good feelin to know he's around. I tell you he's a person I can always rely on. I tell you somethin else. He's the *only* one. I was cut off from people early. You can't know what that was like. After my papa was blown off that fence, me and Macon wandered around for a few days until we had a fallin out and I went off on my own. I was about twelve, I think. When I cut out by myself, I headed for Virginia. I thought I remembered that was where my papa had people. Or my mother did. Seemed to me like I remembered somebody sayin that. I don't remember my mother because she died before I was born."

"*Before* you were born? How could she . . . ?"

"She died and the next minute I was born. But she was dead by the time I drew air. I never saw her face. I don't even know what her name was. But I do remember thinkin she come from Virginia. Anyways, that's where I struck out for. I looked around for somebody to take me in, give me a little work for a while so I could earn some money to get on down there. I walked for seven days before I found a place with a preacher's family. A nice place except they made me wear shoes. They sent me to school, though. A one-room place, where everybody sat. I was twelve, but since this was my first school I had to sit over there with the little bitty children. I didn't mind it too much; matter of fact, I liked a lot of it. I loved the geography part. Learning about that made me want to read. And the teacher was tickled at how much I liked geography. She let me have the book and I took it home with me to look at. But then the preacher started pattin on me. I was so dumb I didn't know enough to stop him. But his wife caught him at it, thumbin my breasts, and put me out. I took my geography book off with me.

I could of stayed in that town cause they was plenty of colored people to take me in. In them days, anybody too old to work kept the children. Grown folks worked and left their kids in other people's houses. But him being the preacher and all like that, I figured I ought to make tracks. I was broke as a haint cause the place didn't carry no wages. Just room and board. So I just took my geography book and a rock I picked up for a souvenir and lit out.

"It was a Sunday when I met up with some pickers. Folks call 'em migrants nowadays; then they was just called pickers. They took me in and treated me fine. I worked up in New York State pickin beans, then we'd move to another place and pick a different crop. Everyplace I went I got me a rock. They was about four or five families all together in the crew. All of them related one way or another. But they was good people and treated me fine. I stayed with them for three years, I believe, and the main reason I stayed on was a woman there I took to. A root worker. She taught me a lot and kept me from missin my own family, Macon and Papa. I didn't have a thought in my head of ever leavin them, but I did. I had to. After a while they didn't want me around no more." Pilate sucked a peach stone and her face was dark and still with the memory of how she was "cut off" so early from other people.

The boy. The nephew, or was it the cousin, of the woman who worked roots. When she was fifteen, and the rain was so heavy they had to stay in the shacks (those who had them—the others had tents) because nothing could be harvested in that pouring rain, the boy and Pilate lay down together. He was no older than she was and while everything about her delighted him, nothing about her surprised him. So it was with no malice whatsoever that one evening after supper he mentioned to some of the men (but within listening distance of the women) that he didn't know that some folks had navels and some didn't. The men and the women raised their eyes at his remark, and asked him to explain what he meant. He got it out, finally, after many false starts—he thought they were alarmed because he had taken the pretty girl with the single earring to bed—but he soon discovered that the navel thing was what bothered them.

The root woman was assigned the job of finding out if what he said was true or not. She called Pilate into her shack one day later. "Lay down," she said. "I want to check on something." Pilate lay down on the straw pallet. "Now lift up your dress," the woman said. "More. All the way up. Higher." And then her eyes flew open wide and she put her hand over her mouth. Pilate leaped up. "What? What is it?" She looked down at herself, thinking a snake or a poisonous spider had crawled over her legs.

"Nothin," the woman said. Then, "Child, where's your navel?"

Pilate had never heard the word "navel" and didn't know what the woman was talking about. She looked down at her legs, parted on the rough ticking. "Navel?" she asked.

"You know. This." And the woman pulled up her own dress and slipped the elastic of her bloomers down over her fat stomach. Pilate saw the little corkscrew thing right in the middle, the little piece of skin that looked like it was made for water to drain down into, like the little whirlpools along the edges of a creek. It was just like the thing her brother had on his stomach. He had one. She did not. He peed standing up. She squatting down. He had a penis like a horse did. She had a vagina like the mare. He had a flat chest with two nipples. She had teats like the cow. He had a corkscrew in his stomach. She did not. She thought it was one more way in which males and females were different. The boy she went to bed with had one too. But until now she had never seen another woman's stomach. And from the horror on the older woman's face she knew there was something wrong with not having it.

"What's it for?" she asked.

The woman swallowed. "It's for . . . it's for people who were born natural."

Pilate didn't understand that, but she did understand the conversation she had later with the root worker and some other women in the camp. She was to leave. They were very sorry, they liked her and all, and she was such a good worker and a big help to everybody. But she had to leave just the same.

"On account of my stomach?" But the women would not answer her. They looked at the ground.

Pilate left with more than her share of earnings, because the women did not want her to go away angry. They thought she might hurt them in some way if she got angry, and they also felt pity along with their terror of having been in the company of something God never made.

Pilate went away. Again she headed for Virginia. But now she knew how to harvest in a team and looked for another migrant crew, or a group of women who had followed their men to some seasonal work as brickmakers, iron workers, shipyard workers. In her three years picking, she had seen a number of these women, their belongings stuffed into wagons heading for the towns and cities that sought out and transported black men to various crafts that could be practiced only when the weather permitted. The companies did not encourage the women to come—they did not want an influx of poor colored settlers in those towns—but the women came anyway and took jobs as domestics and farm helpers in the towns, and lived wherever housing was free or dirt cheap. But Pilate did not want a steady job in a town where a lot of colored people lived. All her encounters with Negroes who had established themselves in businesses or trades in those small midwestern towns had been unpleasant. Their wives did not like the trembling unhampered breasts under her dress, and told her so. And though the men saw many raggedy black children, Pilate was old enough to disgrace them. Besides, she wanted to keep moving.

Finally she was taken on by some pickers heading home, stopping for a week's work here and there, wherever they could find it. Again she took a man to bed, and again she was expelled. Only this time there was no polite but firm pronouncement, nor any generous share of profits. They simply left her one day, moved out while she was in the town buying thread. She got back to campground to find nothing but a dying fire, a bag of rocks, and her geography book propped up on a tree. They even took her tin cup.

She had six copper pennies, five rocks, the geography book, and two spools of black thread—heavyweight No. 30. Right there she knew she must decide on whether to get to Virginia or settle in a town where she would probably have to wear shoes. So she did both—the latter to make the former possible. With the six pennies, the book, the rocks, and the thread, she walked back to town. Black women worked in numbers at two places in that town: the laundry and, across the street from it, the hotel/whorehouse. Pilate chose the laundry and walked in, saying to the three young girls elbow deep in water there, "Can I stay here tonight?"

"Nobody in here at night."

"I know. Can I stay?"

They shrugged. The next day Pilate was hired as a washerwoman at ten cents a day. She worked there, ate there, slept there, and saved her dimes. Her hands, well calloused from years of harvesting, were stripped of their toughness and became soft in the wash water. Before her hands could get the different but equally tough skin of a laundress, her knuckles split with the rubbing and wringing, and ran blood into the rinse tubs. She almost ruined an entire batch of sheets, but the other girls covered for her, giving the sheets a second rinse.

One day she noticed a train steaming away from the town. "Where does it go to?" she asked.

"South," they said.

"How much does it cost?"

They laughed. "They freight trains," they told her. Only two passenger cars, and no colored allowed.

"Well, how do colored people get where they want to go?"

"Ain't supposed to go nowhere," they said, "but if they do, have to go by wagon. Ask at the livery stable when the next wagon is going down. The livery people always know when somebody is getting ready to take off."

She did, and by the end of October, just before cold weather set in, she was on her way to West Virginia, which was close anyway, according to her geography book. When she got to Virginia itself, she realized that she didn't know in what part of the state to look for her people. There were more Negroes there than she'd ever seen, and the comfort she felt in their midst she kept all her life.

Pilate had learned, whenever she was asked her name, to give only her first name. The last name had a bad effect on people. Now she was forced to ask if anybody knew of a family called Dead. People frowned and said, "No, never heard of any such."

She was in Culpeper, Virginia, washing clothes in a hotel, when she learned that there was a colony of Negro farmers on an island off the coast of Virginia. They grew vegetables, had cattle, made whiskey, and sold a little tobacco. They did not mix much with other Negroes, but were respected by them and self-sustaining. And you could get to them only by boat. On a Sunday, she convinced the ferryman to take her there, when his work was done, in his skiff.

"What you want over there?" he asked.

"Work."

"You don't want to work over there," he said.

"Why not?"

"Them folks keep to theyselves too much."

"Take me. I'll pay."

"How much?"

"A nickel."

"Great Jesus! You on. Be here at nine-thirty."

There were twenty-five or thirty families on that island and when Pilate made it clear that she wasn't afraid of work, but didn't like the mainland and the confinement of town, she was taken in. She worked there for three months, hoeing, fishing, plowing, planting, and helping out at the stills. All she had to do, she thought, was keep her belly covered. And it was true. At sixteen now, she took a lover from one of the island families and managed to keep direct light from ever hitting her stomach. She also managed to get pregnant, and to the great consternation of the island women, who were convinced their menfolk were the most desirable on earth—which accounted for so much intermarrying among them—Pilate refused to marry the man, who was eager to take her for his wife. Pilate was afraid that she wouldn't be able to hide her stomach from a husband forever. And once he saw that uninterrupted flesh, he would respond the same way everybody else had. Yet, incredible as they found her decision, nobody asked her to leave. They watched over her and gave her fewer and lighter chores as her time drew near. When her baby was born, a girl, the two midwives in attendance were so preoccupied with what was going on between her legs they never even noticed her smooth balloon of a stomach.

The first thing the new mother looked for in her baby girl was the navel, which she was relieved to see. Remembering how she got the name that was folded in her ear, when the nine days' waiting was done she asked one of the women for a Bible. There was a hymnal, they said, but not a Bible on the island. Everybody who wanted to go to services had to go to the mainland.

"Can you tell me a nice name for a girl that's in the Bible?" Pilate asked.

"Oh, plenty," they said, and reeled off a score, from which she chose Rebecca and shortened it to Reba.

It was right after Reba was born that her father came to her again. Pilate had become extremely depressed and lonely after the birth. The baby's father was forbidden to see her, since she had not "healed" yet, and she spent some dark lonely hours along with the joyous ones with the baby. Clear as day, her father said, "Sing. Sing," and later he leaned in at the window and said, "You just can't fly on off and leave a body."

Pilate understood all of what he told her. To sing, which she did beautifully, relieved her gloom immediately. And she knew he was telling her to go back to Pennsylvania and collect what was left of the man she and Macon had murdered. (The fact that she had struck no blow was irrelevant. She was part of her brother's act, because, then, she and he were one.) When the child was six months old, she asked the mother of the baby's father to keep it, and left the island for Pennsylvania. They tried to discourage her because it was getting to be winter, but she paid them no attention.

A month later she returned with a sack, the contents of which she never discussed, which she added to her geography book and the rocks and the two spools of thread.

When Reba was two years old, Pilate was seized with restlessness. It was as if her geography book had marked her to roam the country, planting her feet in each pink, yellow, blue or green state. She left the island and began the wandering life that she kept up for the next twenty-some-odd years, and stopped only after Reba had a baby. No place was like the island ever again. Having had one long relationship with a man, she sought another, but no man was like that island man ever again either.

After a while, she stopped worrying about her stomach, and stopped trying to hide it. It occurred to her that although men fucked armless women, one-legged women, hunchbacks and blind women, drunken women, razor-toting women, midgets, small children, convicts, boys, sheep, dogs, goats, liver, each other, and even certain species of plants, they were terrified of fucking her—a woman with no navel. They froze at the sight of that belly that looked like a back; became limp even, or cold, if she happened to undress completely and walked straight toward them, showing them, deliberately, a stomach as blind as a knee.

"What are you? Some kinda *mer*maid?" one man had shouted, and reached hurriedly for his socks.

It isolated her. Already without family, she was further isolated from her people, for, except for the relative bliss on the island, every other resource was denied her: partnership in marriage, confessional friendship, and communal religion. Men frowned, women whispered and shoved their children behind them. Even a traveling side show would have rejected her, since her freak quality lacked that important ingredient—the grotesque. There was really nothing to see. Her defect, frightening and exotic as it was, was also a theatrical failure. It needed intimacy, gossip, and the time it took for curiosity to become drama.

Finally Pilate began to take offense. Although she was hampered by huge ignorances, but not in any way unintelligent, when she realized what her situation in the world was and would probably always be she threw away every assumption she had learned and began at zero. First off, she cut her hair. That was one thing she didn't want to have to think about anymore. Then she tackled the problem of trying to decide how she wanted to live and what was valuable to her. When am I happy and when am I sad and what is the difference? What do I need to know to stay alive? What is true in the world? Her mind traveled crooked streets and aimless goat paths, arriving sometimes at profundity, other times at the revelations of a three-year-old. Throughout this fresh, if common, pursuit of knowledge, one conviction crowned her efforts: since death held no terrors for her (she spoke often to the dead), she knew there was nothing to fear. That plus her alien's compassion for troubled people ripened her and—the consequence of the knowledge she had made up or acquired—kept her just barely within the boundaries of the elaborately socialized world of black people. Her dress might be outrageous to them, but her respect for other people's privacy—which they were all very intense about—was balancing. She stared at people, and in those days looking straight into another person's eyes was considered among black people the height of rudeness, an act acceptable only with and among children and certain kinds of outlaws—but she never made an impolite observation. And true to the palm oil that flowed in her veins, she never had a visitor to whom she did not offer food before one word of conversation—business or social—began. She laughed but never smiled and in 1963, when she was sixty-eight years old, she had not shed a tear since Circe had brought her cherry jam for breakfast.

She gave up, apparently, all interest in table manners or hygiene, but acquired a deep concern for and about human relationships. Those twelve years in Montour County, where she had been treated gently by a father and a brother, and where she herself was in a position to help farm animals under her care, had taught her a preferable kind of behavior. Preferable to that of the men who called her mermaid and the women who swept up her footprints or put mirrors on her door.

She was a natural healer, and among quarreling drunks and fighting women she could hold her own, and sometimes mediated a peace that lasted a good bit longer than it should have because it was administered by someone not like them. But most important, she paid close attention to her mentor—the father who appeared before her sometimes and told her things. After Reba was born, he no longer came to Pilate dressed as he had been on the woods' edge and in the cave, when she and Macon had left Circe's house. Then he had worn the coveralls and heavy shoes he was shot in. Now he came in a white shirt, a blue collar, and a brown peaked cap. He wore no shoes (they were tied together and slung over his shoulder), probably because his feet hurt, since he rubbed his toes a lot as he sat near her bed or on the porch, or rested against the side of the still. Along with winemaking, cooking whiskey became the way Pilate began to make her steady living. That skill allowed her more freedom hour by hour and day by day than any other work a woman of no means whatsoever and no inclination to make love for money could choose. Once settled in as a small-time bootlegger in the colored section of a town, she had only occasional police or sheriff problems, for she allowed none of the activities that often accompanied wine houses—women, gambling—and she more often than not refused to let her customers drink what they bought from her on the premises. She made and sold liquor. Period.

After Reba grew up and began to live from one orgasm to another, taking time out to produce one child, Hagar, Pilate thought it might be time for a change. Not because of Reba, who was quite content with the life her mother and she lived, but because of her granddaughter. Hagar was prissy. She hated, even as a two-year-old, dirt and disorganization. At three she was already vain and beginning to be proud. She liked pretty clothes. Astonished as Pilate and Reba were by her wishes, they enjoyed trying to fulfill them. They spoiled her, and she, as a favor to their indulgence, hid as best she could the fact that they embarrassed her.

Pilate decided to find her brother, if he was still alive, for the child, Hagar, needed family, people, a life very different from what she and Reba could offer, and if she remembered anything about Macon, he would be different. Prosperous, conventional, more like the things and people Hagar seemed to admire. In addition, Pilate wanted to make peace between them. She asked her father where he was, but he just rubbed his feet and shook his head. So for the first time, Pilate went voluntarily to the police, who sent her to the Red Cross, who sent her to the Salvation Army, who sent her to the Society of Friends, who sent her back to the Salvation Army, who wrote to their command posts in large cities from New York to St. Louis and from Detroit to Louisiana and asked them to look in the telephone directory, where in fact one captain's secretary found him listed. Pilate was surprised that they were successful, but the captain was not, because there could hardly be many people with such a name.

They made the trip in style (one train and two buses), for Pilate had a lot of money; the crash of 1929 had produced so many buyers of cheap home brew she didn't even need the collection the Salvation Army took up for her. She arrived with suitcases, a green sack, a full-grown daughter, and a granddaughter, and found her brother truculent, inhospitable, embarrassed, and unforgiving. Pilate would have moved on immediately except for her brother's wife, who was dying of lovelessness then, and seemed to be dying of it now as she sat at the table across from her sister-in-law listening to her life story, which Pilate was making deliberately long to keep Ruth's mind off Hagar.

Chapter 6

"I took her home. She was standing in the middle of the room when I got there. So I just took her home. Pitiful. Really pitiful."

Milkman shrugged. He didn't want to talk about Hagar, but it was a way to sit Guitar down and get around to asking him something else.

"What'd you do to her?" asked Guitar.

"What'd I do to *her?* You saw her with a butcher knife and you ask me that?"

"I mean before. That's a messed-up lady."

"I did what you do to some woman every six months—called the whole thing off."

"I don't believe you."

"It's the truth."

"No. It had to be something more."

"You calling me a liar?"

"Take it any way you want. But that girl's hurt—and the hurt came from you."

"What's the matter with you? You've been watching her try

to kill me for months and I never laid a hand on her. Now you sit there worried about her. All of a sudden you're police. You've been wearing a halo a lot lately. You got a white robe too?"

"What's that supposed to mean?"

"It means I'm tired of being criticized by you. I know we don't see eye to eye on a lot of things. I know you think I'm lazy—not serious, you say—but if we're friends . . . I don't meddle you, do I?"

"No. Not at all."

Several minutes passed while Milkman played with his beer and Guitar sipped tea. They were sitting in Mary's Place on a Sunday afternoon a few days after Hagar's latest attempt on his life.

"You're not smoking?" asked Milkman.

"No. I quit. Feel a hell of a lot better too." There was another pause before Guitar continued. "You ought to stop yourself."

Milkman nodded. "Yeah. If I stay around you I will. I'll stop smoking, fucking, drinking—everything. I'll take up a secret life and hanging out with Empire State."

Guitar frowned. "Now who's meddling?"

Milkman sighed and looked straight at his friend. "I am. I want to know why you were running around with Empire State last Christmas."

"He was in trouble. I helped him."

"That's all?"

"What else?"

"I don't know what else. But I know there is something else. Now, if it's something I can't know, okay, say so. But something's going on with you. And I'd like to know what it is."

Guitar didn't answer.

"We've been friends a long time, Guitar. There's nothing you don't know about me. I can tell you anything—whatever our differences, I know I can trust you. But for some time now it's been a one-way street. You know what I mean? I talk to you, but you don't talk to me. You don't think I can be trusted?"

"I don't know if you can or not."

"Try me."

"I can't. Other people are involved."

"Then don't tell me about other people; tell me about you."

Guitar looked at him for a long time. Maybe, he thought. Maybe I can trust you. Maybe not, but I'll risk it anyway because one day . . .

"Okay," he said aloud, "but you have to know that what I tell you can't go any further. And if it does, you'll be dropping a rope around my neck. Now do you still want to know it?"

"Yeah."

"You sure?"

"I'm sure."

Guitar poured some more hot water over his tea. He looked into his cup for a minute while the leaves settled slowly to the bottom. "I suppose you know that white people kill black people from time to time, and most folks shake their heads and say, 'Eh, eh, eh, ain't that a shame?' "

Milkman raised his eyebrows. He thought Guitar was going to let him in on some deal he had going. But he was slipping into his race bag. He was speaking slowly, as though each word had to count, and as though he were listening carefully to his own words. "I can't suck my teeth or say 'Eh, eh, eh.' I had to do something. And the only thing left to do is balance it; keep things on an even keel. Any man, any woman, or any child is good for five to seven generations of heirs before they're bred out. So every death is the death of five to seven generations. You can't stop them from killing us, from trying to get rid of us. And each time they succeed, they get rid of five to seven generations. I help keep the numbers the same.

"There is a society. It's made up of a few men who are willing to take some risks. They don't initiate anything; they don't even choose. They are as indifferent as rain. But when a Negro child, Negro woman, or Negro man is killed by whites and nothing is done about it by *their* law and *their* courts, this society selects a similar victim at random, and they execute him or her in a similar manner if they can. If the Negro was hanged, they hang; if a Negro was burnt, they burn; raped and murdered, they rape and murder. If they can. If they can't do it precisely in the same manner, they do it any way they can, but they do it. They call themselves the Seven Days. They are made up of seven men. Always seven and only seven. If one of them dies or leaves or is no longer effective, another is chosen. Not right away, because that kind of choosing takes time. But they don't seem to be in a hurry. Their secret is time. To take the time, to last. Not to grow; that's dangerous because you might become known. They don't write their names in toilet stalls or brag to women. Time and silence. Those are their weapons, and they go on forever.

"It got started in 1920, when that private from Georgia was killed after his balls were cut off and after that veteran was blinded when he came home from France in World War I. And it's been operating ever since. I am one of them now."

Milkman had held himself very still all the time Guitar spoke. Now he felt tight, shriveled, and cold.

"You? You're going to kill people?"

"Not people. White people."

"But why?"

"I just told you. It's necessary; it's got to be done. To keep the ratio the same."

"And if it isn't done? If it just goes on the way it has?"

"Then the world is a zoo, and I can't live in it."

"Why don't you just hunt down the ones who did the killing? Why kill innocent people? Why not just those who did it?"

"It doesn't matter who did it. Each and every one of them could do it. So you just get any one of them. There are no innocent white people, because every one of them is a potential nigger-killer, if not an actual one. You think Hitler surprised them? You think just because they went to war they thought he was a freak? Hitler's the most natural white man in the world. He killed Jews and Gypsies because he didn't have us. Can you see those Klansmen shocked by him? No, you can't."

"But people who lynch and slice off people's balls—they're crazy, Guitar, crazy."

"Every time somebody does a thing like that to one of us,

they say the people who did it were crazy or ignorant. That's like saying they were drunk. Or constipated. Why isn't cutting a man's eyes out, cutting his nuts off, the kind of thing you never get too drunk or ignorant to do? Too crazy to do? Too constipated to do? And more to the point, how come Negroes, the craziest, most ignorant people in America, don't get that crazy and that ignorant? No. White people are unnatural. As a race they are unnatural. And it takes a strong effort of the will to overcome an unnatural enemy."

"What about the nice ones? Some whites made sacrifices for Negroes. Real sacrifices."

"That just means there are one or two natural ones. But they haven't been able to stop the killing either. They are outraged, but that doesn't stop it. They might even speak out, but that doesn't stop it either. They might even inconvenience themselves, but the killing goes on and on. So will we."

"You're missing the point. There're not just one or two. There're a lot."

"Are there? Milkman, if Kennedy got drunk and bored and was sitting around a potbellied stove in Mississippi, he might join a lynching party just for the hell of it. Under those circumstances his unnaturalness would surface. But I know I wouldn't join one no matter how drunk I was or how bored, and I know you wouldn't either, nor any black man I know or ever heard tell of. Ever. In any world, at any time, just get up and go find somebody white to slice up. But they *can* do it. And they don't even do it for profit, which is why they do most things. They do it for fun. Unnatural."

"What about . . ." Milkman searched his memory for some white person who had shown himself unequivocally supportive of Negroes. "Schweitzer. Albert Schweitzer. Would he do it?"

"In a minute. He didn't care anything about those Africans. They could have been rats. He was in a laboratory testing *himself*—proving he could work on human dogs."

"What about Eleanor Roosevelt?"

"I don't know about the women. I can't say what their women would do, but I do remember that picture of those white mothers holding up their babies so they could get a good look at some black men burning on a tree. So I have my suspicions about Eleanor Roosevelt. But *none* about Mr. Roosevelt. You could've taken him and his wheelchair and put him in a small dusty town in Alabama and given him some tobacco, a checker-board, some whiskey, and a rope and he'd have done it too. What I'm saying is, under certain conditions they would *all* do it. And under the same circumstances we would not. So it doesn't matter that some of them *haven't* done it. I listen. I read. And now I know that they know it too. They know they are unnatural. Their writers and artists have been saying it for years. Telling them they are unnatural, telling them they are depraved. They call it tragedy. In the movies they call it adventure. It's just depravity that they try to make glorious, natural. But it ain't. The disease they have is in their blood, in the structure of their chromosomes."

"You can prove this, I guess. Scientifically?"

"No."

"Shouldn't you be able to prove it before you act on something like that?"

"Did they prove anything scientifically about us before they killed us? No. They killed us first and then tried to get some scientific proof about why we should die."

"Wait a minute, Guitar. If they are as bad, as unnatural, as you say, why do you want to be like them? Don't you want to be better than they are?"

"I am better."

"But now you're doing what the worst of them do."

"Yes, but I am reasonable."

"Reasonable? How?"

"I am not, one, having fun; two, trying to gain power or public attention or money or land; three, angry at anybody."

"You're not angry? You must be!"

"Not at all. I hate doing it. I'm afraid to do it. It's hard to do it when you aren't angry or drunk or doped up or don't have a personal grudge against the person."

"I can't see how it helps. I can't see how it helps anybody."

"I told you. Numbers. Balance. Ratio. And the earth, the land."

"I'm not understanding you."

"The earth is soggy with black people's blood. And before us Indian blood. Nothing can cure them, and if it keeps on there won't be any of us left and there won't be any land for those who are left. So the numbers have to remain static."

"But there are more of them than us."

"Only in the West. But still the ratio can't widen in their favor."

"But you should want everybody to know that the society exists. Then maybe that would help stop it. What's the secrecy for?"

"To keep from getting caught."

"Can't you even let other Negroes know about it? I mean to give us hope?"

"No."

"Why not?"

"Betrayal. The possibility of betrayal."

"Well, let *them* know. Let white people know. Like the Mafia or the Klan; frighten them into behaving."

"You're talking foolishness. How can you let one group know and not the other? Besides, we are not like them. The Mafia is unnatural. So is the Klan. One kills for money, the other kills for fun. And they have huge profits and protection at their disposal. We don't. But it's not about other people knowing. We don't even tell the victims. We just whisper to him, 'Your Day has come.' The beauty of what we do is its secrecy, its smallness. The fact that nobody needs the unnatural satisfaction of talking about it. Telling about it. We don't discuss it among ourselves, the details. We just get an assignment. If the Negro was killed on a Wednesday, the Wednesday man takes it; if he was killed on Monday, the Monday man takes that one. And we just notify one another when it's completed, not how or who. And if it ever gets to be too much, like it was for Robert Smith, we do *that* rather than crack and tell somebody. Like Porter. It was getting him down. They thought somebody would have to take over his day. He just needed a rest and he's okay now."

Milkman stared at his friend and then let the spasm he had been holding back run through him. "I can't buy it, Guitar."

"I know that."

"There's too much wrong with it."

"Tell me."

"Well, for one thing, you'll get caught eventually."

"Maybe. But if I'm caught I'll just die earlier than I'm supposed to—not better than I'm supposed to. And how I die or when doesn't interest me. What I die *for* does. It's the same as what I live for. Besides, if I'm caught they'll accuse me and kill me for one crime, maybe two, never for all. And there are still six other days in the week. We've been around for a long long time. And believe me, we'll be around for a long long time to come."

"You can't marry."

"No."

"Have children."

"No."

"What kind of life is that?"

"Very satisfying."

"There's no love in it."

"No love? No love? Didn't you hear me? What I'm doing ain't about hating white people. It's about loving us. About loving you. My whole life is love."

"Man, you're confused."

"Am I? When those concentration camp Jews hunt down Nazis, are they hating Nazis or loving dead Jews?"

"It's not the same thing."

"Only because they have money and publicity."

"No; because they turn them over to the courts. You kill and you don't kill the killers. You kill innocent people."

"I told you there are no—"

"And you don't correct a thing by—"

"We poor people, Milkman. I work at an auto plant. The rest

of us barely eke out a living. Where's the money, the state, the country to finance our justice? You say Jews try their catches in a court. Do we have a court? Is there one courthouse in one city in the country where a jury would convict them? There are places right now where a Negro still can't testify against a white man. Where the judge, the jury, the court, are legally bound to ignore anything a Negro has to say. What that means is that a black man is a victim of a crime only when a white man says he is. Only then. If there was anything like or near justice or courts when a cracker kills a Negro, there wouldn't have to be no Seven Days. But there ain't; so we are. And we do it without money, without support, without costumes, without newspapers, without senators, without lobbyists, and without illusions!"

"You sound like that red-headed Negro named X. Why don't you join him and call yourself Guitar X?"

"X, Bains—what difference does it make? I don't give a damn about names."

"You miss his point. His point is to let white people know you don't accept your slave name."

"I don't give a shit what white people know or even think. Besides, I do accept it. It's part of who I am. Guitar is *my* name. Bains is the slave master's name. And I'm all of that. Slave names don't bother me; but slave status does."

"And knocking off white folks changes your slave status?"

"Believe it."

"Does it do anything for my slave status?"

Guitar smiled. "Well, doesn't it?"

"Hell, no." Milkman frowned. "Am I going to live any longer because you all read the newspaper and then ambush some poor old white man?"

"It's not about you living longer. It's about how you live and why. It's about whether your children can make other children. It's about trying to make a world where one day white people will think before they lynch."

"Guitar, none of that shit is going to change how I live or how any other Negro lives. What you're doing is crazy. And something else: it's a habit. If you do it enough, you can do it to anybody. You know what I mean? A torpedo is a torpedo, I don't care what his reasons. You can off anybody you don't like. You can off me."

"We don't off Negroes."

"You hear what you said? *Negroes*. Not Milkman. Not 'No, I can't touch *you*, Milkman,' but 'We don't off Negroes.' Shit, man, suppose you all change your parliamentary rules?"

"The Days are the Days. It's been that way a long time."

Milkman thought about that. "Any other young dudes in it? Are all the others older? You the only young one?"

"Why?"

"Cause young dudes are subject to change the rules."

"You worried about yourself, Milkman?" Guitar looked amused.

"No. Not really." Milkman put his cigarette out and reached for another one. "Tell me, what's your day?"

"Sunday. I'm the Sunday man."

Milkman rubbed the ankle of his short leg. "I'm scared for you, man."

"That's funny. I'm scared for you too."

Chapter 7

Truly landlocked people know they are. Know the occasional Bitter Creek or Powder River that runs through Wyoming; that the large tidy Salt Lake of Utah is all they have of the sea and that they must content themselves with *bank*, *shore*, and *beach* because they cannot claim a coast. And having none, seldom dream of flight. But the people living in the Great Lakes region are confused by their place on the country's edge—an edge that is border but not coast. They seem to be able to live a long time believing, as coastal people do, that they are at the frontier where final exit and total escape are the only journeys left. But those five Great Lakes which the St. Lawrence feeds with memories of the sea are themselves landlocked, in spite of the wandering river that connects them to the Atlantic. Once the people of the lake region discover this, the longing to leave becomes acute, and a break from the area, therefore, is necessarily dream-bitten, but necessary nonetheless. It might be an appetite for other streets, other slants of light. Or a yearning to be surrounded by strangers. It may even be a wish to hear the solid click of a door closing behind their backs.

For Milkman it was the door click. He wanted to feel the heavy white door on Not Doctor Street close behind him and know that he might be hearing the catch settle into its groove for the last time.

"You'll own it all. All of it. You'll be free. Money is freedom, Macon. The only real freedom there is."

"I know, Daddy, I know. But I have to get away just the same. I'm not leaving the country; I just want to be on my own. Get a job on my own, live on my own. You did it at sixteen. Guitar at seventeen. Everybody. I'm still living at home, working for you—not because I sweated for the job, but because I'm your son. I'm over thirty years old."

"I need you here, Macon. If you were going to go, you should have gone five years ago. Now I've come to depend on you." It was difficult for him to beg, but he came as close to it as he could.

"Just a year. One year. Stake me for a year and let me go. When I come back, I'll work a year for nothing and pay you back."

"It's not the money. It's you being here, taking care of this. Taking care of all I'm going to leave you. Getting to know it, know how to handle it."

"Let me use some of it now, when I need it. Don't do like Pilate, put it in a green sack and hang it from the wall so nobody can get it. Don't make me wait until—"

"What did you say?" As suddenly as an old dog drops a shoe when he smells raw meat, Macon Dead dropped his pleading look and flared his nostrils with some new interest.

"I said give me a little bit—"

"No. Not that. About Pilate and a sack."

"Yeah. Her sack. You've seen it, haven't you? That green sack she got hanging from the ceiling? She calls it her inheritance. You can't get from one side of the room to the other without cracking your head on it. Don't you remember it?"

Macon was blinking rapidly, but he managed to calm himself and say, "I've never set foot in Pilate's house in my life. I looked in there once, but it was dark and I didn't see anything hanging down from the ceiling. When's the last time you saw it?"

"Maybe nine or ten months ago. What about it?"

"You think it's still there?"

"Why wouldn't it be?"

"You say it's green. You know for sure it's green?"

"Yeah, green. Grass green. What is it? What's bothering you?"

"She told you it was her inheritance, huh?" Macon was smiling, but so craftily that Milkman could hardly recognize it as a smile.

"No. She didn't; Hagar did. I was walking across the room toward the . . . uh . . . toward the other side and I'm tall enough for it to be in my way. I bumped my head on it. Made a hickey too. When I asked Hagar what it was she said, 'Pilate's inheritance.' "

"And it made a hickey on your head?"

"Yeah. Felt like bricks. What're you going to do, sue her?"

"You had any lunch?"

"It's ten-thirty, Daddy."

"Go to Mary's. Get us a couple of orders of barbecue. Meet me in the park across from Mercy. We'll eat lunch there."

"Daddy . . ."

"Go on now. Do what I say. Go on, Macon."

They met in the little public park across the street from Mercy Hospital. It was full of pigeons, students, drunks, dogs, squirrels, children, trees, and secretaries. The two colored men sat down on an iron bench a little away from the most crowded part, but not the edge. They were very well dressed, too well dressed to be eating pork out of a box, but on that warm September day it seemed natural, a perfect addition to the mellowness that pervaded the park.

Milkman was curious about his father's agitation, but not alarmed. So much had been going on, so many changes. Besides, he knew whatever was making his father fidget and look around to see if anyone was too near had to do with something his father wanted, not something he wanted himself. He could look at his father coolly now that he had sat on that train and listened to his mother's sad sad song. Her words still danced around in his head. "What harm did I do you on my knees?"

Deep down in that pocket where his heart hid, he felt used. Somehow everybody was using him for something or as something. Working out some scheme of their own on him, making him the subject of their dreams of wealth, or love, or martyrdom. Everything they did seemed to be about him, yet nothing he wanted was part of it. Once before he had had a long talk with his father, and it ended up with his being driven further from his mother. Now he had had a confidential talk with his mother, only to discover that before he was born, before the first nerve end had formed in his mother's womb, he was the subject of great controversy and strife. And now the one woman who claimed to love him more than life, more than her life, actually loved him more than *his* life, for she had spent half a year trying to relieve him of it. And Guitar. The one sane and constant person he knew had flipped, had ripped open and was spilling blood and foolishness instead of conversation. He was a fit companion for Empire State. So now he waited with curiosity, but without excitement or hope, for this latest claim.

"Listen to me. Just eat your meat and listen to me. Don't interrupt, because I might lose my train of thought.

"A long time ago, I told you about when I was a boy on the farm. About Pilate and me. About my father getting killed. I never finished the story; I never told you all of it. The part I left out was about me and Pilate. I tried to keep you away from her and said she was a snake. Now I'm going to tell you why."

A red ball rolled to his feet, and Macon picked it up and threw it back to a little girl. He made sure she was safely back in her mother's view before he began his story.

Six days after the first Macon Dead died, his children, a twelve-year-old Pilate and a sixteen-year-old Macon Dead, found themselves homeless. Bewildered and grieving, they went to the house of the closest colored person they knew: Circe, the midwife who had delivered them both and who was there when their mother died and when Pilate was named. She worked in a large house—a mansion—outside Danville, for a family of what was then called gentlemen farmers. The orphans called to Circe from the vegetable garden early in the morning as soon as they saw the smoke from the cook stove rising. Circe let them in, pressing her hands together with relief, and saying how glad she was to see them alive. She hadn't known what had happened to them after the killing. Macon explained that he had buried his father himself, down by that part of the stream on Lincoln's Heaven where they used to fish together, the place where he had caught that nine-pound trout. The grave was shallower than it ought to be, but he'd piled rocks there.

Circe told them to stay with her until they could all figure out what to do, someplace for them to go. She hid them in that house easily. There were rooms the family seldom went into, but if they weren't safe, she was prepared to share her own room (which was off limits to everybody in the house). It was small, though, so they agreed to stay in a pair of rooms on the third floor that were used only for storage. Circe would bring them food, water to wash in, and she would empty their slop jar.

Macon asked if they couldn't work there; would her mistress take them on as kitchen help, yard help, anything?

Circe bit her tongue trying to get the words out. "You crazy? You say you saw the men what killed him. You think they don't know you saw them? If they kill a growed man, what you think they do to you? Be sensible. We got to plan and figure this thing out."

Macon and Pilate stayed there two weeks, not a day longer. He had been working hard on a farm since he was five or six years old and she was born wild. They couldn't bear the stillness, the walls, the boredom of having nothing to do but wait for the day's excitement of eating and going to the toilet. Anything was better than walking all day on carpeting, than eating the soft bland food white people ate, than having to sneak a look at the sky from behind ivory curtains.

Pilate began to cry the day Circe brought her white toast and cherry jam for breakfast. She wanted her own cherries, from her own cherry tree, with stems and seeds; not some too-sweet mashed mush. She thought she would die if she couldn't hold her mouth under Ulysses S. Grant's teat and squirt the warm milk into her mouth, or pull a tomato off its vine and eat it where she stood. Craving certain specific foods had almost devastated her. That, plus the fact that her earlobe was sore from the operation she had performed on herself, had her near hysteria. Before they left the farm, she'd taken the scrap of brown paper with her name on it from the Bible, and after a long time trying to make up her mind between a snuffbox and a sunbonnet with blue ribbons on it, she took the little brass box that had belonged to her mother. Her miserable days in the mansion were spent planning how to make an earring out of the box which would house her name. She found a piece of wire, but couldn't get it through. Finally, after much begging and whining, Circe got a Negro blacksmith to solder a bit of gold wire to the box. Pilate rubbed her ear until it was numb, burned the end of the wire, and punched it through her earlobe. Macon fastened the wire ends into a knot, but the lobe was swollen and running pus. At Circe's instruction she put cobwebs on it to draw the pus out and stop the bleeding.

On the night of the day she cried so about the cherries, the two of them decided that when her ear got better, they would leave. It was too much of a hardship on Circe anyway for them to stay there, and if her white folks found out about them, they might let her go.

One morning Circe climbed all the way to the third floor with a covered plate of scrapple and found two empty rooms. They didn't even take a blanket. Just a knife and a tin cup.

The first day out was joyous for them. They ate raspberries and apples; they took off their shoes and let the dewy grass and sun-warmed dirt soothe their feet. At night they slept in a haystack, so grateful for open air even the field mice and the ticks were welcome bedmates.

The next day was pleasant but less exciting. They bathed in a curve of the Susquehanna and then wandered in a southerly direction, keeping to fields, woods, stream beds, and little-used paths, headed, they thought, for Virginia, where Macon believed they had people.

On the third day they woke to find a man that looked just like their father sitting on a stump not fifty yards away. He was not looking at them; he was just sitting there. They would have called out to him or run toward him except he was staring right past them with such distance in his eyes, he frightened them. So they ran away. All day long at various intervals they saw him: staring down into duck ponds; framed by the Y of a sycamore tree; shading his eyes from the sun as he peered over a rock at the wide valley floor beneath them. Each time they saw him they backed off and went in the opposite direction. Now the land itself, the only one they knew and knew intimately, began to terrify them. The sun was blazing down, the air was sweet, but every leaf that the wind lifted, every rustle of a pheasant hen in a clump of ryegrass, sent needles of fear through their veins. The cardinals, the gray squirrels, the garden snakes, the butterflies, the ground hogs and rabbits—all the affectionate things that had peopled their lives ever since they were born became ominous signs of a presence that was searching for them, following them. Even the river's babbling sounded like the call of a liquid throat waiting, just waiting for them. That was in the daylight. How much more terrible was the night.

Just before dark, when the sun had left them alone, when they were coming out of some woods looking around for the crest of the hill where they could see, perhaps, a farm, an abandoned shed—anyplace where they could spend the night—they saw a cave, and at its mouth stood their father. This time he motioned for them to follow him. Faced with the choice of the limitless nighttime woods and a man who looked like their father, they chose the latter. After all, if it was their father, he wouldn't hurt them, would he?

Slowly they approached the mouth of the cave, following their father's beckoning hand and his occasional backward glance.

They looked into the cave and saw nothing but a great maw of darkness. Their father had disappeared. If they stayed near the lip, they thought, it was as good a place as any to spend the night; perhaps he was simply looking out for them, showing them what to do and where to go. They made themselves as comfortable as they could on a rock formation that jutted out like a shelf from a hip-high mass of stone. There was nothing behind them that they could see and only the certainty of bats to disturb them. Yet it was nothing to that other darkness—outside.

Toward morning, Macon woke from a light and fitful sleep, with a terrific urge to relieve his bowels, the consequence of three days' diet of wild fruit. Without waking his sister, he climbed off the shelf, and shy of squatting on the crown of a hill in a new sun, he walked a little farther back into the cave. When he was finished, the darkness had disintegrated somewhat, and he saw, some fifteen feet in front of him, a man stirring in his sleep. Macon tried to button his pants and get away without waking him, but the leaves and twigs crunching under his feet pulled the man all the way out of his sleep. He raised his head, turned over, and smiled. Macon saw that he was very old, very white, and his smile was awful.

Macon stepped back, one hand outstretched behind him, thinking all the while of how his father's body had twitched and danced for whole minutes in the dirt. He touched the cave's wall and a piece of it gave way in his hand. Closing his fingers around it, he threw it at the grinning man's head, hitting him just above the eye. Blood spurted out and knocked the smile off the pale face, but did not stop the man from coming and coming, all the time wiping blood from his face and smearing it on his shirt.

Macon got hold of another rock, but missed that time. The man kept coming.

The scream that boomed down the cave tunnel and woke the bats came just when Macon thought he had taken his last living breath. The bleeding man turned toward the direction of the scream and looked at the colored girl long enough for Macon to pull out his knife and bring it down on the old man's back. He crashed forward, then turned his head to look up at them. His mouth moved and he mumbled something that sounded like "What for?" Macon stabbed him again and again until he stopped moving his mouth, stopped trying to talk, and stopped jumping and twitching on the ground.

Panting with the exertion of slashing through an old man's rib cage, Macon ran back to get the blanket the man had been sleeping on. He wanted the dead man to disappear, to be covered, hidden, to be gone. When he snatched the blanket, a large tarpaulin came with it and he saw three boards positioned across what looked like a shallow pit. He paused and then kicked the boards aside. Underneath were little gray bags, their necks tied with wire, arranged like nest eggs. Macon picked one of them up and was amazed at its weight.

"Pilate," he called. "Pilate."

But she was growing roots where she stood, and staring open-mouthed at the dead man. Macon had to pull her by the arm over to the hole where the bags lay. After some difficulty with the wire (he ended up having to use his teeth), he got one open and shook the gold nuggets it held out into the leaves and twigs that lay on the floor of the cave.

"Gold," he whispered, and immediately, like a burglar out on his first job, stood up to pee.

Life, safety, and luxury fanned out before him like the tail-spread of a peacock, and as he stood there trying to distinguish each delicious color, he saw the dusty boots of his father standing just on the other side of the shallow pit.

"It *is* Papa!" said Pilate. And as if in answer to her recognition, he took a deep breath, rolled his eyes back, and whispered, "Sing. Sing," in a hollow voice before he melted away again.

Pilate darted around the cave calling him, looking for him, while Macon piled the sacks of gold into the tarpaulin.

"Let's go, Pilate. Let's get out of here."

"We can't take that." She pointed a finger at his bundle.

"What? Not take it? You lost your mind?"

"That's stealing. We killed a man. They'll be after us, all over. If we take his money, then they'll think that's why we did it. We got to leave it, Macon. We can't get caught with no bags of money."

"This ain't money; it's gold. It'll keep us for life, Pilate. We can get us another farm. We can—"

"Leave it, Macon! Leave it! Let them find it just where it was!" Then she began to shout, "Papa! Papa!"

Macon slapped her and the little brass box dangled on her ear. She cupped it in her hands for a moment and then leaped on her brother like an antelope. They fought right there in front of the dead man's staring eyes. Pilate was almost as strong as Macon, but no real match for him, and he probably would have beaten her unconscious had she not got his knife, not yet dry from the old man's blood, and held it ready for his heart.

Macon stood very still and watched her eyes. He began calling her ugly names, but she didn't answer. He backed out of the cave and walked a little distance away.

All day he waited for her to come out. All day she stayed there. When night came he just sat, at the foot of a tree, unafraid of all the night things that had terrified him before, eyes wide open, waiting for her to stick her woolly head out of the cave. There was no sound from her direction and he waited the whole night. At dawn he crept forward a foot at a time, hoping he would catch her asleep. Just then he heard some dogs and knew hunters were walking nearby. He ran as fast as he could through the woods until he couldn't hear the dogs anymore.

Another day and a night he spent trying to work his way back to the cave and avoid the hunters if they were still about. Finally he got there, three days and two nights later. Inside the cave the dead man was still looking placidly up at him, but the tarpaulin and the gold were gone.

The secretaries went away. So did the children and the dogs. Only the pigeons, the drunks, and the trees were left in the little park.

Milkman had eaten almost none of his barbecue. He was watching his father's face, shining with perspiration and the emotions of memory.

"She took it, Macon. After all that, she took the gold."

"How do you know? You didn't see her take it," said Milkman.

"The tarpaulin was green." Macon Dead rubbed his hands together. "Pilate came to this city in 1930. Two years later they call back all the gold. I figured she spent it all in the twenty or so years since I'd seen her, since she was living like poor trash when she got here. It was natural for me to believe she'd got rid of it all. Now you tell me she got a green sack full of something hard enough to give you a hickey on your head when you bumped into it. That's the gold, boy. That's it!"

He turned to his son full face and licked his lips. "Macon, get it and you can have half of it; go wherever you want. Get it. For both of us. Please get it, son. Get the gold."

Chapter 8

Every night now Guitar was seeing little scraps of Sunday dresses—white and purple, powder blue, pink and white, lace and voile, velvet and silk, cotton and satin, eyelet and grosgrain. The scraps stayed with him all night and he remembered Magdalene called Lena and Corinthians bending in the wind to catch the heart-red pieces of velvet that had floated under the gaze of Mr. Robert Smith. Only Guitar's scraps were different. The bits of Sunday dresses that he saw did not fly; they hung in the air quietly, like the whole notes in the last measure of an Easter hymn.

Four little colored girls had been blown out of a church, and his mission was to approximate as best he could a similar death of four little white girls some Sunday, since he was the Sunday man. He couldn't do it with a piece of wire, or a switchblade. For this he needed explosives, or guns, or hand grenades. And that would take money. He knew that the assignments of the Days would more and more be the killing of white people in groups, since more and more Negroes were being killed in groups. The single, solitary death was going rapidly out of fashion, and the Days might as well prepare themselves for it.

So when Milkman came to him with a proposal to steal and share a cache of gold, Guitar smiled. "Gold?" He could hardly believe it.

"Gold."

"Nobody got gold, Milkman."

"Pilate does."

"It's against the law to have gold."

"That's why she got it. She can't use it, and she can't report its being stolen since she wasn't supposed to have it in the first place."

"How do we get rid of it—get greenbacks for it?"

"Leave that to my father. He knows bank people who know other bank people. They'll give him legal tender for it."

"Legal tender." Guitar laughed softly. "How much legal tender will it bring?"

"That's what we have to find out."

"What's the split?"

"Three ways."

"Your papa know that?"

"Not yet. He thinks it's two ways."

"When you gonna tell him?"

"Afterwards."

"Will he go for it?"

"How can he *not* go for it?"

"When do we get it?"

"Whenever we want to."

Guitar spread his palm. "My man." Milkman slapped his hand. "Legal tender. Legal tender. I love it. Sounds like a virgin bride." Guitar rubbed the back of his neck and lifted his face to the sun in a gesture of expansiveness and luxury.

"Now we have to come up with something. A way to get it," said Milkman.

"Be a breeze. A cool cool breeze," Guitar continued, smiling at the sun, his eyes closed as though to ready himself for the gold by trying out a little bit of the sun's.

"A breeze?" Now that Guitar was completely enthusiastic, Milkman's own excitement was blunted. Something perverse made him not want to hand the whole score to his friend on a platter. There should be some difficulty, some complication in this adventure. "We just walk over there and snatch it off the wall, right? And if Pilate or Reba say anything, we just knock them out the way. That what you have in mind?" He summoned as much irony as he could into his voice.

"Defeatism. That's what you got. Defeatism."

"Common sense is what I got."

"Come on, old dude. Your pappy give you a good thing and you want to fight it."

"I'm not fighting. I just want to get out alive and breathing so what I snatch does me some good. I don't want to have to give it to a brain surgeon to pull an ice pick out the back of my head."

"Can't no ice pick get through the back of your head, nigger."

"Can get through my heart."

"What you doin with a heart anyway?"

"Pumping blood. And I'd like to keep on pumping it."

"Okay. We got us a problem. A little bitty problem: how can two big men get a fifty-pound sack out of a house with three women in it—women who all together don't weigh three hundred pounds."

"What you have to weigh to pull a trigger?"

"What trigger? Nobody in that house got a gun."

"You don't know what Hagar's got."

"Look, Milk. She's been trying to kill you for almost a year. Used everything she could get her hands on and never once did she use a gun."

"So? Maybe she's thinking. Wait till next month."

"Next month she'll be too late, won't she?" Guitar leaned his head over to the side and smiled at Milkman, an engaging boyish smile. Milkman hadn't seen him this relaxed and cordial in a long

long time. He wondered if that's why he had let him in on it. Obviously he could pull it off alone, but maybe he wanted to see Guitar warm and joking again, his face open and smiling instead of with that grim reaper look.

They met again on Sunday on route 6 away from the colored part of town. A road consisting of used-car lots, Dairy Queens, and White Castle hamburger places. It was empty of shoppers that morning—nothing but the occasional sound of automobiles breaking the graveyard silence of the cars in the lots, lined up like tombstones.

Since that last conversation—the important one in which Guitar explained his work, not the brief chancy talks they'd had afterward—Milkman wished he had the nerve to ask Guitar the question that was bothering him. "Has he?" He could hardly phrase the question in his own mind, and certainly could never say it aloud. Guitar had impressed him with the seriousness and the dread of the work of the Days, and the danger. He had said that the Days never even talked about the details among themselves, so Milkman was sure any inquiry from him would only make Guitar sullen again. And cold. But the question was there. "Has he done it? Has he really killed somebody?" Like the old men on Tenth Street, now he bought the morning and evening papers, and once every two weeks the black newspaper, and read nervously, looking for reports of murders that appeared suspicious, pointless. When he found one, he followed the news stories until a suspect was found. Then he had to see if there were any black people murdered by someone other than their own.

"Did you do it yet?" He was like a teen-age girl wondering about the virginity of her friend, the friend who has a look, a manner newly minted—different, separate, focused somehow. "Did you do it yet? Do you know something both exotic and ordinary that I have not felt? Do you now know what it's like to risk your one and only self? How did it feel? Were you afraid? Did it change you? And if I do it, will it change me too?"

Maybe he could ask him one day, but not this day when it was so much like old times. Taking risks together the way they did when Milkman was twelve and Guitar was a teen-ager and they swaggered, haunched, leaned, straddled, ran all over town trying to pick fights or at least scare somebody: other boys, girls, dogs, pigeons, old women, school principals, drunks, ice cream vendors, and the horses of junkyard men. When they succeeded they rode the wind and covered their mouths to aggravate their laughter. And when they didn't, when somebody out-insulted them, or ignored them, or sent them running, they wisecracked and name-called until the sweat of embarrassment evaporated from the palms of their hands. Now they were men, and the terror they needed to provoke in others, if for no other reason than to feel it themselves, was rarer but not lighter. Dominion won by fear and secured by fear was still sweeter than any that could be got another way. (Except for women, whom they liked to win with charm but keep with indifference.)

It was like that again now, and Milkman didn't want to lose it.

There was something else too. Guitar had placed himself willingly and eagerly in a life cause that would always provide him with a proximity to knife-cold terror. Milkman knew his own needs were milder, for he could thrive in the presence of someone who inspired fear. His father, Pilate, Guitar. He gravitated toward each one, envious of their fearlessness now, even Hagar's, in spite of the fact that she was no longer a threat, but a fool who wanted not his death so much as his attention. Guitar could still create the sense of danger and life lived on the cutting edge. So Milkman had brought him into this scheme only partially for his help. Mostly because this escapade cried out for a cutting edge to go with its larklike quality. With Guitar as his co-conspirator, Milkman could look forward to both fun and fear.

They sauntered on down route 6, stopping frequently to examine the cars, gesticulating, bantering each other about the best way to burglarize a shack that, as Guitar said, "didn't have a door or window with a lock."

"But it's got people," Milkman insisted. "Three. All crazy."

"Women."

"Crazy women."

"Women."

"You're forgetting, Guitar, how Pilate got the gold in the first place. She waited in a cave with a dead man for three days to haul it out, and that was when she was twelve. If she did that at twelve to get it, what you think she'll do now when she's almost seventy to keep it?"

"We don't have to be rough. Cunning is all we need to be."

"Okay. Tell me how you gonna cunning them out of the house."

"Well, let's see now." Guitar stopped to scratch his back on a telephone pole. He closed his eyes, in either the ecstasy of relief or the rigors of concentration. Milkman stared off into the sky for inspiration, and while glancing toward the rooftops of the used-car places, he saw a white peacock poised on the roof of a long low building that served as headquarters for Nelson Buick. He was about to accept the presence of the bird as one of those waking dreams he was subject to whenever indecisiveness was confronted with reality, when Guitar opened his eyes and said, "Goddam! Where'd that come from?"

Milkman was relieved. "Must of come from the zoo."

"That raggedy-ass zoo? Ain't nothing in there but two tired monkeys and some snakes."

"Well, where then?"

"Beats me."

"Look–she's flying down." Milkman felt again his unrestrained joy at anything that could fly. "Some jive flying, but look at her strut."

"He."

"Huh?"

"He. That's a he. The male is the only one got that tail full of jewelry. Son of a bitch. Look at that." The peacock opened its tail wide. "Let's catch it. Come on, Milk," and Guitar started to run toward the fence.

"What for?" asked Milkman, running behind him. "What we gonna do if we catch him?"

"Eat him!" Guitar shouted. He swung easily over the double pipes that bordered the lot and began to circle the bird at a distance, holding his head a little to the side to fool the peacock, which was strutting around a powder-blue Buick. It closed its tail and let the tips trail in the gravel. The two men stood still, watching.

"How come it can't fly no better than a chicken?" Milkman asked.

"Too much tail. All that jewelry weighs it down. Like vanity. Can't nobody fly with all that shit. Wanna fly, you got to give up the shit that weighs you down."

The peacock jumped onto the hood of the Buick and once more spread its tail, sending the flashy Buick into oblivion.

"Faggot." Guitar laughed softly. "White faggot."

Milkman laughed too, and they watched a while more before leaving the used cars and the pure white peacock.

But the bird had set them up. Instead of continuing the argument about how they would cop, they began to fantasize about what the gold could buy when it became legal tender. Guitar, eschewing his recent asceticism, allowed himself the pleasure of waking up old dreams: what he would buy for his grandmother and her brother, Uncle Billy, the one who had come up from Florida to help raise them all after his father died; the marker he would buy for his father's grave, "pink with lilies carved on it"; then stuff for his brother and sisters, and his sisters' children. Milkman fantasized too, but not for the stationary things Guitar described. Milkman wanted boats, cars, airplanes, and the command of a large crew. He would be whimsical, generous, mysterious with his money. But all the time he was laughing and going on about what he would do and how he planned to live, he was aware of a falseness in his voice. He wanted the money—desperately, he believed—but other than making tracks out of the city, far away from Not Doctor Street, and Sonny's Shop, and Mary's Place, and Hagar, he could not visualize a life that much different from the one he had. New people. New places. Command. That was what he wanted in his life. And he couldn't get deep into Guitar's talk of elegant clothes for himself and his brother, sumptuous meals for Uncle Billy, and week-long card games in which the stakes would be a yard and a half and then a deuce and a quarter. He screamed and shouted "Wooeeeee!" at Guitar's list, but because his life was not unpleasant and even had a certain amount of luxury in addition to its comfort, he felt off center. He just wanted to beat a path away from his parents' past, which was also their present and which was threatening to become his present as well. He hated the acridness in his mother's and father's relationship, the conviction of righteousness they each held on to with both hands. And his efforts to ignore it, transcend it, seemed to work only when he spent his days looking for whatever was light-hearted and without grave consequences. He avoided commitment and strong feelings, and shied away from decisions. He wanted to know as little as possible, to feel only enough to get through the day amiably and to be interesting enough to warrant the curiosity of other people—but not their all-consuming devotion. Hagar had given him this last and more drama than he could ever want again. He'd always believed his childhood was sterile, but the knowledge Macon and Ruth had given him wrapped his memory of it in septic sheets, heavy with the odor of illness, misery, and unforgiving hearts. His rebellions, minor as they were, had all been in the company of, or shared with, Guitar. And this latest Jack and the Beanstalk bid for freedom, even though it had been handed to him by his father—assigned almost—stood some chance of success.

He had half expected his friend to laugh at him, to refuse with some biting comment that would remind Milkman that Guitar was a mystery man now, a man with blood-deep responsibilities. But when he watched Guitar's face as he described what could be had almost for the asking, he knew right away he hadn't guessed wrong. Maybe the professional assassin had had enough, or had changed his mind. Had he . . . ? "Did you . . . ?" As he listened to him go over each detail of meals, clothes, tombstones, he wondered if Guitar simply could not resist the lure of something he had never had—money.

Guitar smiled at the sun, and talked lovingly of televisions, and brass beds, and week-long card games, but his mind was on the wonders of TNT.

By the time they'd exhausted their imaginative spending, it was almost noon and they were back on the edge of Southside. They picked up where they'd left off in the discussion of the scheme. Guitar was ready now; Milkman was still cautious. Too cautious for Guitar.

"I don't understand you. You come running after me with a dynamite proposition, and for three days we talk about it, the best news I've had since pussy, but when we get down to business, you come up with some shit about how it can't be done. You shucking me or what?"

"What would I be shucking for? I didn't have to tell you about it."

"I don't know. I don't even know why you doing it. You know about me—you can guess why I'm in it. But money ain't never been what you needed or couldn't get."

Milkman ignored the reference to why Guitar was "in it," and said as calmly as he could, "I need it to get away. I told you, man. I got to get out of here. Be on my own."

"On *your* own? With a million-dollar wallet, you call that on your own?"

"Fuck you. What difference does it make why I want it?"

"Cause I'm not sure you do want it. At least not bad enough to go ahead and cop."

"I just want it right. No hassles. No . . . You know, burglary is a serious crime. I don't want to end up in—"

"What burglary? This ain't no burglary. This is Pilate."

"So?"

"So! They're your people."

"They're still people, and people scream."

"What's the worst? What's the worst thing can happen? We

bust in, right? Suppose all three of them are there. They're women. What can they do? Whip us?"

"Maybe."

"Come on! Who? Hagar? Right up in your face she blows it. Pilate? She loves you, boy. She wouldn't touch you."

"You believe that?"

"Yeah, I believe it! Look. You got qualms, tell me about them. Because you related? Your daddy's more related than you are, and it's his idea."

"It's not that."

"Then what?"

"They're crazy, Guitar. Nobody knows what they'll do; *they* don't even know."

"I know they're crazy. Anybody live like they do, selling fifty-cent wine and peeing in a bucket, with one million dollars hanging over their nappy heads, has to be. You scared of craziness? If you are, *you're* crazy."

"I don't want to be caught, that's all. I don't want to do time. I want to plan it so neither one happens. How come that's too much to ask? To plan."

"It don't look like planning. Looks like stalling."

"It is planning. Planning how to get them out the house. How to get us in the house. How to cut that sack off the ceiling and then get back out the house and on down the street. And it's hard to plan with them. They're not regular. They don't have regular habits. And then there's the wineheads. One of them liable to drop in any old time. They're not clock people, Guitar. I don't believe Pilate knows how to tell time except by the sun."

"They sleep at night."

"Anybody sleep can wake up."

"Anybody woke up can be knocked down."

"I don't want to knock nobody down. I want them gone when we hit."

"And what's gonna make them leave?"

Milkman shook his head. "An earthquake, maybe."

"Then let's make an earthquake."

"How?"

"Set the house on fire. Put a skunk in there. A bear. Something. Anything."

"Be serious, man."

"I'm trying, baby. I'm trying. Don't they go nowhere?"

"All together?"

"All together."

Milkman shrugged. "Funerals. They go to funerals. And circuses."

"Oh, man! We have to wait for somebody to die? Or for Ringling Brothers to come to town?"

"I'm trying to figure it out is all. At the moment we don't have a chance."

"Well, if a man don't *have* a chance, then he has to *take* a chance!"

"Be reasonable."

"Reasonable? You can't get no pot of gold being reasonable. Can't nobody get no gold being reasonable. You have to be unreasonable. How come you don't know that?"

"Listen to me. . . ."

"I just quit listening. You listen! You got a life? Live it! Live the motherfuckin life! Live it!"

Milkman's eyes opened wide. He tried hard not to swallow, but the clarion call in Guitar's voice filled his mouth with salt. The same salt that lay in the bottom of the sea and in the sweat of a horse's neck. A taste so powerful and necessary that stallions galloped miles and days for it. It was new, it was delicious, and it was his own. All the tentativeness, doubt, and inauthenticity that plagued him slithered away without a trace, a sound.

Now he knew what his hesitation had been all about. It was not to give an unnatural complexity to a simple job; nor was it to keep Guitar on hold. He had simply not believed in it before. When his father told him that long story, it really seemed like Jack and the Beanstalk . . . some fairy tale mess. He hadn't believed it was really there, or really gold, or that he could really have it just for the taking. It was too simple. But Guitar believed it, gave it a crisp concreteness, and what's more, made it into an act, an important, real, and daring thing to do. He felt a self inside himself emerge, a clean-lined definite self. A self that could join the chorus at Railroad Tommy's with more than laughter. He could tell this. The only other real confrontation he'd had was hitting his father, but that wasn't the kind of story that stirred the glitter up in the eyes of the old men in Tommy's.

Milkman didn't think through any of this clearly. He only tasted the salt and heard the hunter's horn in Guitar's voice.

"Tomorrow," he said. "Tomorrow night."

"What time?"

"One-thirty. I'll pick you up."

"Beautiful."

Far down the road, a long way from Milkman and Guitar, the peacock spread its tail.

On autumn nights, in some parts of the city, the wind from the lake brings a sweetish smell to shore. An odor like crystallized ginger, or sweet iced tea with a dark clove floating in it. There is no explanation for the smell either, since the lake, on September 19, 1963, was so full of mill refuse and the chemical wastes of a plastics manufacturer that the hair of the willows that stood near the shore was thin and pale. Carp floated belly up onto the beach, and the doctors at Mercy knew, but did not announce, that ear infections were a certainty for those who swam in those waters.

Yet there was this heavy spice-sweet smell that made you think of the East and striped tents and the *sha-sha-sha* of leg bracelets. The people who lived near the lake hadn't noticed the smell for a long time now because when air conditioners came, they shut their windows and slept a light surface sleep under the motor's drone.

So the ginger sugar blew unnoticed through the streets, around the trees, over roofs, until, thinned out and weakened a little, it reached Southside. There, where some houses didn't even have screens, let alone air conditioners, the windows were thrown wide open to whatever the night had to offer. And there the ginger smell was sharp, sharp enough to distort dreams and make the sleeper believe the things he hungered for were right at hand. To the Southside residents who were awake on such nights, it gave all their thoughts and activity a quality of being both intimate and far away. The two men standing near the pines on Darling Street—right near the brown house where wine drinkers went—could smell the air, but they didn't think of ginger. Each thought it was the way freedom smelled, or justice, or luxury, or vengeance.

Breathing the air that could have come straight from a marketplace in Accra, they stood for what seemed to them a very long time. One leaned against a tree, his foot hovering off the ground. Finally one touched the elbow of the other and they both moved toward an open window. With no trouble at all, they entered. Although they had stood deliberately in the dark of the pine trees, they were unprepared for the deeper darkness that met them there in that room. Neither had seen that kind of blackness, not even behind their own eyelids. More unsettling than the darkness, however, was the fact that in contrast to the heat outside (the slumbering ginger-laden heat that had people wiping sweat from their neck folds), it was as cold as ice in Pilate's house.

Suddenly the moon came out and shone like a flashlight right into the room. They both saw it at the same time. It hung heavy, hung green like the green of Easter eggs left too long in the dye. And like Easter, it promised everything: the Risen Son and the heart's lone desire. Complete power, total freedom, and perfect justice. Guitar knelt down before it and wove his fingers together into a footstep. Milkman hoisted himself up, one hand on Guitar's head, and shifted himself until he sat on Guitar's shoulders. Slowly Guitar stood up. Milkman felt upward along the sack until he found its neck. He thought the rope would have to be cut, and was annoyed to find the sack hung by wire instead.

He hoped the knife would be enough, because they hadn't figured on wire and had brought neither pincers nor a wire cutter. The sound of the grating knife filled the room. No one, he thought, could sleep through that. At last some few strands broke and it was only a moment before the entire blackness was severed. They'd figured on the weight of the sack being enough to tumble them the minute it was cut free, and planned that at a whispered signal, Guitar would bend his knees and sink down so Milkman's feet would hit the floor almost immediately. But there was no need for this graceful footwork; the bag was much lighter than they had anticipated, and Milkman made it down quite easily. As soon as they both regained balance, there was a huge airy sigh that each one believed was made by the other. Milkman handed his knife to Guitar, who closed it and tucked it in his back pocket. There was the deep sigh again and an even more piercing chill. Holding the sack by its neck and its bottom, Milkman followed Guitar to the window. Once Guitar had cleared the sill, he reached back to help Milkman over. The moonlight was playing tricks on him, for he thought he saw the figure of a man standing right behind his friend. Enveloped by the heat they'd left a few minutes earlier, they walked swiftly away from the house and out onto the road.

At another open window on the same side of the house, the one next to the sink where Hagar washed her hair and where Reba put pintos to soak, a woman's face appeared. "What the devil they want that for?" she wondered. Then she picked at the window sill until she had a splinter of wood and put it in her mouth.

Chapter 9

Amanuensis. That was the word she chose, and since it was straight out of the nineteenth century, her mother approved, relishing the blank stares she received when she told her lady guests what position her daughter had acquired with the State Poet Laureate. "She's Michael-Mary Graham's amanuensis." The rickety Latin word made the work her daughter did (she, after all, wasn't required to work) sound intricate, demanding, and totally in keeping with her education. And the women didn't dare ask for further details (they tried to remember its sound, but still couldn't find it in the dictionary), for they were suitably impressed by the name of Michael-Mary Graham. It was a lie, of course, even as the simpler word "secretary" was a lie, but Ruth repeated it with confidence because she believed it was true. She did not know then, and never found out, that Corinthians was Miss Graham's maid.

Unfit for any work other than the making of red velvet roses, she had a hard time finding employment befitting her degree. The three years she had spent in college, a junior year in France, and being the granddaughter of the eminent Dr. Foster should have culminated in something more elegant than the two uniforms that hung on Miss Graham's basement door. That all these advantages didn't was still incredible to her. It had been assumed that she and Magdalene called Lena would marry well—but hopes for Corinthians were especially high since she'd gone to college. Her education had taught her how to be an enlightened mother and wife, able to contribute to the civilization—or in her case, the civilizing—of her community. And if marriage was not achieved, there were alternative roles: teacher, librarian, or . . . well, something intelligent and public-spirited. When neither of these fates tapped her on the forehead right away, she simply waited. High toned and high yellow, she believed what her mother was also convinced of: that she was a prize for a professional man of color. So there were vacations and weekends in other cities as well as visits and teas in her own, where and when such men appeared. The first of the black doctors to move there, in the forties when she graduated, had a son five years her junior. The second, a dentist, had two infant girls; the third was a very old physician (rumored to be an alcoholic), whose two sons were already raising families. Then there were teachers, two lawyers, a mortician—but on the few occasions when eligible bachelors were among them, Corinthians was not their choice. She was pretty enough, pleasant enough, and her father had the money they could rely on if needed, but she lacked drive. These men wanted wives who could manage, who were not so well accustomed to middle-class life that they had no ambition, no hunger, no hustle in them. They wanted their wives to like the climbing, the acquiring, and the work it took to maintain status once it was achieved. They wanted wives who would sacrifice themselves and appreciate the hard work and sacrifice of their husbands. Corinthians was a little too elegant. Bryn Mawr in 1940. France in 1939. That was a bit much. Fisk, Howard, Talledega, Tougaloo—that was their hunting territory. A woman who spoke French and who had traveled on the *Queen Mary* might not have the proper attitude toward future patients or clients, and if the man was a teacher, he steered clear of a woman who had a better education than he did. At one point post office workers were even being considered suitable for Lena and Corinthians, but that was long after they had reached thirty-five, and after Ruth came to terms with the savage fact that her daughters were not going to marry doctors. It was a shock to them all, which they managed to withstand by not accepting a more complete truth: that they probably were not going to marry anybody.

Magdalene called Lena seemed resigned to her life, but when Corinthians woke up one day to find herself a forty-two-year-old maker of rose petals, she suffered a severe depression which lasted until she made up her mind to get out of the house. So her search for work—which was shock number two—was intense. The twenty-one years that she had been out of college worked against her for a teaching job. She had none of the "new" courses now required by the board of education. She considered going to the state teachers' school to take the required courses, even went to the administration building to register. But the sight of those torpedo breasts under fuzzy blue sweaters, the absolute nakedness of those young faces, drove her out of the building and off the campus like a leaf before a hailstorm. Which was too bad, because she had no real skills. Bryn Mawr had done what a four-year dose of liberal education was designed to do: unfit her for eighty percent of the useful work of the world. First, by training her for leisure time, enrichments, and domestic mindlessness. Second, by a clear implication that she was too good for such work. After graduation she returned to a work world in which colored girls, regardless of their background, were in demand for one and only one kind of work. And by 1963, Corinthians' main concern was simply that her family not know that she had been doing it for two years.

She avoided the other maids on the street, and those whom she saw regularly on the bus assumed that she had some higher household position than theirs since she came to work in high-heeled shoes and only a woman who didn't have to be on her feet all day could stand the pressure of heels on the long ride home. Corinthians was careful; she carried no shopping bag of shoes, aprons, or uniforms. Instead she had a book. A small gray book on which *Contes de Daudet* was printed in gold lettering on its cover. Once she was inside Miss Graham's house she changed into her uniform (which was a discreet blue anyway, not white) and put on a pair of loafers before she dropped to her knees with the pail of soapy water.

Miss Graham was delighted with Corinthians' dress and slightly uppity manners. It gave her house the foreign air she liked to affect, for she was the core, the very heartbeat, of the city's literary world. Michael-Mary Graham was very considerate of Corinthians. When she had large dinner parties, a Swedish cook was hired and the heavy work was done by the old white rummy she shared with the Goodwill Industries. Nor was she impatient with Corinthians' undistinguished everyday cooking, for Michael-Mary ate several small plain meals. It was also a pleasure and a relief to have a maid who read and who seemed to be acquainted with some of the great masters of literature. So nice to give a maid a copy of *Walden* for Christmas rather than that dreary envelope, and to be able to say so to her friends. In the world Michael-Mary Graham inhabited, her mild liberalism, a residue of her Bohemian youth, and her posture of sensitive lady poet passed for anarchy.

Corinthians was naïve, but she was not a complete fool. She never let her mistress know she had ever been to college or Europe or could recognize one word of French that Miss Graham had not taught her (*entrez*, for example). Actually, the work Corinthians did was good for her. In that house she had what she never had in her own: responsibility. She flourished in a way, and exchanged arrogance occasionally for confidence. The humiliation of wearing a uniform, even if it was blue, and deceiving people was tempered by the genuine lift which came of having her own money rather than receiving an allowance like a child. And she was surprised to discover that the amount of neatly folded bills Michael-Mary handed her each Saturday at noon was within two dollars of the amount real secretaries took home each week.

Other than scrubbing the kitchen tile and keeping a hard shine on the wooden floors, the work was not hard. The poetess lived alone and shaped her time and activities carefully in order to meet the heavy demands of artistic responsibility. Being a poet she could, of course, do little else. Marriage, children—all had been sacrificed to the Great Agony and her home was a tribute to the fastidiousness of her dedication (and the generosity of her father's will). Colors, furnishings, and appointments had been selected for their inspirational value. And she was fond of saying, in deprecating some item, "I couldn't write a line with *that* in the house." *That* might be a vase, the new toilet bowl the plumbers hauled in, a plant, or even the Christmas wreath St. John's third-grade class presented to her in gratitude for the moving reading she'd given at their holiday assembly. Every morning between ten and noon she wrote, and every afternoon between three and four-fifteen. Evenings were often given over to discussions and meetings with local poets, painters, musicians, and writers of fiction, at which they praised or condemned other artists, scorned the marketplace and courted it. Of this group Michael-Mary Graham was the queen, for her poetry had been published—first in 1938, in a volume called *Seasons of My Soul;* there was a second collection in 1941, called *Farther Shores.* What was more, her poems had appeared in at least twenty small literary magazines, two "slicks," six college journals, and the Sunday supplements of countless newspapers. She was also the winner, between 1938 and 1958, of nine Poet of the Year awards, culminating finally in the much-coveted State Poet Laureateship. At the ceremony, her most famous poem, "Watchword," was performed by the Choral Speech Society of St. John's High School. None of that, however, had mitigated the reluctance of her publishers to bring out her complete collected works (tentatively called *The Farthest Shore*). But there was no question in her mind that they would come around.

When Miss Graham first saw Corinthians, she was not at all

impressed with her. First, because the prospective employee came ten minutes early for the interview and Michael-Mary, who adhered to her schedule to the minute, was forced to answer the door in a print peignoir. Already irritated by this lapse, she was further disenchanted by the woman's delicate frame. Obviously she could not put up the screens, take down the storm windows, or endure any sustained heavy cleaning. But when she learned the woman's name, Michael-Mary was so charmed by the sound of "Corinthians Dead," she hired her on the spot. As she told friends later, her poetic sensibility overwhelmed her good judgment.

They got on well together, mistress and maid, and by the sixth month of her stay, Michael-Mary suggested that she learn how to type. So Corinthians was almost on her way to becoming an amanuensis after all.

Shortly after Miss Graham encouraged her to take typing so she might be helpful with some of her mistress's work, a black man sat down next to Corinthians on the bus. She took little notice of him—only that he was ill-dressed and appeared elderly. But soon she became aware that he was staring at her. A quick corner-of-the-eye peek to verify this was met by his radiant smile. Corinthians turned her head and kept it so until he got off.

The next day he was there again. Once more she made her disdain clear. The rest of the week passed without his watchful eyes. But on the following Monday he was back, looking at her with an expression that stopped just short of a leer. These occasional meetings went on for a month or so. Corinthians thought she should be afraid of him, for something in his manner suggested waiting—a confident, assured waiting. Then one morning he dropped a white envelope on the seat beside her just before he got off the bus. She let it lie there all the way to her stop, but couldn't resist scooping it up as surreptitiously as possible when she stood to pull the cord.

Standing at the stove, waiting for Michael-Mary's milk to skim, she opened the envelope and withdrew a greeting card.

Raised letters of the word "Friendship" hung above a blue and yellow bouquet of flowers and were repeated inside above a verse.

Friendship is an outstretched hand,
A smile of warm devotion.
I offer both to you this day,
With all the heart's emotion.

A white hand of no particular sex held another, smaller, blue and yellow bouquet. There was no signature.

Corinthians threw it in the brown paper bag opened for the day's garbage. It stayed there all day, but it also stayed on her mind. When evening came, she reached down through the grapefruit rind, the tea leaves, and the salami casing to find it, brush it clean, and transfer it to her purse. She couldn't explain to herself why. The man was a complete nuisance and his flirtation an insult. But no one, not anyone at all, had made any attempt (any serious attempt) to flirt with her in a long time. At the very least the card was good for conversation. She wished he had signed it, not because she wanted to know his name, but so it would look more authentic—otherwise somebody might think she bought it herself.

For two weeks afterward the man was not on the bus. When he did appear, it was hard for Corinthians not to speak or acknowledge his presence. As they neared the place where he usually got off, he leaned over to her and said, "I truly hope you didn't mind." She looked up, gave him a small smile, and shook her head. He said nothing more.

But on subsequent days they did exchange greetings and finally they began to talk. In a while they were chatting (carefully, guardedly) and she, at least, was looking forward to his being there. By the time she knew that his name was Henry Porter and that he had occasional yard work in that part of town, she was glad she had never shown or mentioned either the card or the man to anyone.

Pleasant as their conversations were, they were also curious.

Each took care not to ask the other certain questions—for fear he or she would have to volunteer the same information. What part of town do you live in? Do you know Mr. So-and-so?

Eventually Mr. Porter offered to pick Corinthians up after work. He didn't own a car, he said, but borrowed a friend's sometimes. Corinthians agreed, and the result was a pair of middle-aged lovers who behaved like teen-agers—afraid to be caught by their parents in a love relationship they were too young for. He took her for rides in an old gray Oldsmobile—to the country, to drive-in movies—and they sat over bad coffee in certain dime stores where they were not likely to be recognized.

Corinthians knew she was ashamed of him, that she would have to add him to the other secret, the nature of her work, that he could never set foot in her house. And she hated him a lot for the shame she felt. Hated him sometimes right in the middle of his obvious adoration of her, his frequent compliments about her looks, her manners, her voice. But those swift feelings of contempt never lasted long enough for her to refuse those drive-in movie sessions where she was the sole object of someone's hunger and satisfaction.

At some point Corinthians began to suspect that Porter's discretion was not only in deference to who she was (her position and all), but also because he too didn't want to be discovered. Her first thought was that he was married. His denials, accompanied by a wistful smile which she interpreted as a sly one, only aggravated her suspicions. Finally, to prove his bachelorhood as well as to indulge himself in a real bed, he invited her to his room. She declined immediately and repeatedly for several days until he accused her of the very thing that was absolutely true: that she was ashamed of him.

"Ashamed of you?" Her eyes and mouth went wide with surprise (genuine surprise, because she never thought he would guess it). "If I were ashamed I wouldn't see you at all, let alone *this* way." Her hand pointed toward the world outside the car they sat in: the row upon row of automobiles in the hot drive-in movie lot.

Porter traced her cheek line with his knuckle. "Well, then? The things you tell me can't be true and not true at the same time."

"I've never told you anything except what was true. I thought we both knew . . . understood . . . the problem."

"Maybe," he said. "Let's hear it, Corrie." His knuckles stroked her jaw line. "Let's hear the problem."

"My father. It's only my father . . . the way he is."

"How is he?"

Corinthians shrugged. "You know as well as I do. He never wanted us to mix with . . . people. He's very strict."

"And that's the reason you won't come home with me?"

"I'm sorry. I have to live there. I can't let him know about us. Not yet." But when? she thought. If not at forty-four, then when? If not now, when even my pubic hair is turning gray and when my breasts have dropped of their own accord—then when?

Porter spoke her own question aloud. "When, then?" And she could not answer him right away. She put her fingers to her forehead and said, "I don't know. I honestly don't know."

It was such a fake gesture to go along with her fake feelings of moral and filial commitment that she knew right away how foolish she seemed. The things they did in that old car, the things she'd let her tongue say, as recently as five minutes ago . . . and now to caress her temples and say in Michael-Mary's reading voice, "I don't know," embarrassed her and must have disgusted Porter, for he took his hand from her face and put it on the steering wheel. Right at the beginning of the second feature, he started the car and moved it slowly down the gravel aisle.

Neither spoke until the car entered downtown traffic. It was ten-thirty. She'd told her mother she would be typing manuscript for Miss Graham until very late. "In this heat?" was all her mother said. Corinthians sat quietly, feeling shame but not thinking the word, until she realized that he was driving her to the bus stop where he always let her out to walk home the way she normally would. In a sudden flash she knew he was never going to see her again, and the days rolled out before her like a dingy gray carpet in an unfurnished, unpeopled hall-for-rent.

"Are you taking me home?" She succeeded in keeping the anxiety out of her voice—succeeded too well, for her words sounded arrogant and careless.

He nodded and said, "I don't want a doll baby. I want a woman. A grown-up woman that's not scared of her daddy. I guess you don't want to be a grown-up woman, Corrie."

She stared through the windshield. A grown-up woman? She tried to think of some. Her mother? Lena? The dean of women at Bryn Mawr? Michael-Mary? The ladies who visited her mother and ate cake? Somehow none of them fit. She didn't know any grown-up women. Every woman she knew was a doll baby. Did he mean like the women who rode on the bus? The other maids, who were not hiding what they were? Or the black women who walked the streets at night?

"You mean like those women on the bus? You can have one of *them*, you know. Why don't you drop a greeting card in one of *their* laps?" His words had hit home; she had been compared—unfavorably, she believed—with the only people she knew for certain she was superior to. "They'd love to have a greeting card dropped in their lap. Just love it. But oh, I forgot. You couldn't do that, could you, because they wouldn't be able to read it. They'd have to take it home and wait till Sunday and give it to the preacher to read it to them. Of course when they heard it they might not know what it meant. But it wouldn't matter—they'd see the flowers and the curlicues all over the words and they'd be happy. It wouldn't matter a bit that it was the most ridiculous, most clichéd, most commercial piece of tripe the drugstore world has to offer. They wouldn't know mediocrity if it punched them right in their fat faces. They'd laugh and slap their fat thighs and take you right on into their kitchens. Right up on the breakfast table. But you wouldn't give them a fifteen-cent greeting card, would you?—no matter how silly and stupid it was—because they're grown-up women and you don't have to court *them*. You can just come right out and say, 'Hello there, come on to my room tonight.' Right? Isn't that so? Isn't that so?" She was close to screaming. "But no. You wanted a lady. Somebody who knows how to sit down, how to dress, how to eat the food on her plate. Well, there is a difference between a woman and a lady, and I know you know which one I am."

Porter pulled the car over to the curb, and without shutting off the motor, leaned across her and opened the door. Corinthians got out and did her best to slam it, but the rusty hinges of the borrowed Oldsmobile did not accommodate her. She had to settle for the gesture.

By the time she reached number 12 Not Doctor Street, her trembling had become uncontrollable. Suddenly the shaking stopped and she froze at the steps. Two seconds later she turned on her heel and ran back down the street to where Porter had stopped the car. The moment she had put her foot on the step leading up to the porch, she saw her ripeness mellowing and rotting before a heap of red velvet scraps on a round oak table. The car was still there, its motor purring. Corinthians ran toward it faster than she had ever run in her life, faster than she'd cut across the grass on Honoré Island when she was five and the whole family went there for a holiday. Faster even than the time she flew down the stairs having seen for the first time what the disease had done to her grandfather. She put her hand on the door handle and found it locked. Porter was sitting pretty much the way he was when she'd tried to slam the door. Bending down, she rapped on the window. Porter's profile did not move. She rapped again, louder, mindless of who might see her under the gray beech tree just around the corner from home. So close and yet so far, she felt as though she were in a dream; there, but not there, within a hair's breadth but not reaching it.

She was First Corinthians Dead, daughter of a wealthy property owner and the elegant Ruth Foster, granddaughter of the magnificent and worshipped Dr. Foster, who had been the second man in the city to have a two-horse carriage, and a woman who had turned heads on every deck of the *Queen Mary* and had Frenchmen salivating all over Paris. Corinthians Dead, who had held herself pure all these years (well, almost all, and almost pure), was now banging on the car-door window of a yardman. But she would bang forever to escape the velvet. The red velvet that had flown all over the snow that day when she and Lena and her mother had walked past the hospital on their way to the department store. Her mother was pregnant—a fact that had embarrassed Corinthians when first she learned of it. All she could think of was how her friends would laugh when they found out she had a pregnant mother. Her relief was sweet when she discovered that it was too soon to show. But by February her mother was heavy and needed to get out of the house, to exercise a little. They'd walked slowly through the snow, watching carefully for icy places. Then as they passed Mercy, there was a crowd watching a man on the roof. Corinthians had seen him before her mother did, but when Ruth looked up she was so startled she dropped the basket, scattering the roses everywhere. Corinthians and Lena busied themselves picking them up, wiping the snow from the cloth on their coats, all the while peeping at the man in blue wings on the hospital roof. They were laughing, Lena and she; collecting the roses, looking up at the man, and laughing from fear, embarrassment, and giddiness. It was all mixed together—the red velvet, the screams, and the man crashing down on the pavement. She had seen his body quite clearly, and to her astonishment, there was no blood. The only red in view was in their own hands and in the basket. Her mother's moans were getting louder and she seemed to be sinking into the ground. A stretcher came at last for the doll-broken body (all the more doll-like because there was no blood), and finally a wheelchair for her mother, who was moving straight into labor.

Corinthians continued to make roses, but she hated that stupid hobby and gave Lena any excuse to avoid it. They spoke to her of death. First the death of the man in the blue wings. Now her own. For if Porter did not turn his head and lean toward the door to open it for her, Corinthians believed she would surely die. She banged her knuckles until they ached to get the attention of the living flesh behind the glass, and would have smashed her fist through the window just to touch him, feel his heat, the only thing that could protect her from a smothering death of dry roses.

He did not move. In a panic, lest he shift gears and drive away, leaving her alone in the street, Corinthians climbed up on the fender and lay full out across the hood of the car. She didn't look through the windshield at him. She just lay there, stretched across the car, her fingers struggling for a grip on steel. She thought of nothing. Nothing except what her body needed to do to hang on, to never let go. Even if he drove off at one hundred miles an hour, she would hang on. Her eyes were shut tight with the effort of clinging to the hood, and she didn't hear the door open and shut, nor Porter's footsteps as he moved around to the front of the car. She screamed at first when he put his hand on her shoulders and began pulling her gently into his arms. He carried her to the passenger's side of the car, stood her on her feet while he opened the door and helped her ease into the seat. In the car, he pressed her head onto his shoulder and waited for her soft crying to wane before he left the driver's seat to pick up the purse she had let fall on the sidewalk. He drove away then to number 3 Fifteenth Street, a house owned by Macon Dead, where sixteen tenants lived, and where there was an attic window, from which this same Henry Porter had screamed, wept, waved a shotgun, and urinated over the heads of the women in the yard.

It was not yet midnight and hot—hot enough to make people angry, had it not been for a pleasant smell in the air, like sweet ginger. Corinthians and Porter entered the hall that opened off the front door. Except for a hem of light under the kitchen door, where a card game was in progress, there was no sign of any other tenant.

Corinthians saw only the bed, an iron bed painted hospital white. She sank down on it as soon as she got into the room and stretched out, feeling bathed, scoured, vacuumed, and for the first time simple. Porter undressed after she did and lay down beside her. They were quiet for a minute, then he turned over and parted her legs with his.

Corinthians looked down at him. "Is this for me?" she asked.

"Yes," he said. "Yes, this is for you."

"Porter."

"This is . . . for you. Instead of roses. And silk underwear and bottles of perfume."

"Porter."

"Instead of chocolate creams in a heart-shaped box. Instead of a big house and a great big car. Instead of long trips . . ."

"Porter."

". . . in a clean white boat."

"No."

"Instead of picnics . . ."

"No."

". . . and fishing . . ."

"No."

". . . and being old together on a porch."

"No."

"This is for you, girl. Oh, yes. This is for you."

They woke at four o'clock in the morning, or rather she did. When she opened her eyes she saw him staring at her and those were either tears in his eyes or sweat. It was very hot in that room in spite of the open window.

"The bathroom," she murmured. "Where is the bathroom?"

"Down the hall," he said. Then, apologetically, "Can I get you something?"

"Oh." She pushed a few strands of matted damp hair from her forehead. "Something to drink, please. Something cold."

He dressed quickly, leaving off his shirt and his socks, and left the room. Corinthians got up too and began to put her clothes on. Since there seemed to be no mirror in the room, she stood in front of the open window and used the upper part of the pane, dark enough to show her reflection, to smooth her hair. Then she noticed the walls. What she had assumed to be wallpaper as she entered and fell on the bed was in fact calendars. Row after row of calendars: S. &. J. Automobile Parts, featuring a 1939 Hudson; the Cuyahoga River Construction Company ("We build to please—We're pleased to build"); Lucky Hart Beauty Products (a wavy-haired lady smiling out of a heavily powdered face); the *Call and Post* newspaper. But most of them were from the North Carolina Mutual Life Insurance Company. They literally covered the walls, each one turned to December. It was as though he'd kept every calendar since 1939. Some of them were large cards displaying all twelve months and on those she noticed circles drawn around dates.

Porter came in while she was gazing at them. He held a glass of iced water, the cubes jammed to the rim.

"Why do you keep calendars?" she asked.

He smiled. "Passes the time. Here. Drink your drink. It'll cool you."

She took the glass and sipped a little from it, trying to keep the ice from touching her teeth as she looked at him over the rim. Standing there, barefoot, her hair damp with sweat and sticking to her cheeks like paint, she felt easy. In place of vanity she now felt a self-esteem that was quite new. She was grateful to him, this man who rented a tiny room from her father, who ate with a knife and did not even own a pair of dress shoes. A perfect example of the men her parents had kept her from (and whom she had also kept herself from) all her life because such a man was known to beat his woman, betray her, shame her, and leave her. Corinthians moved close to him, tilted his chin up with her fingers, and planted a feathery kiss on his throat. He held her head in his hands until she closed her eyes and tried to set the glass down on a tiny table.

"Uh uh. It'll be light soon. Gotta get you home."

She obeyed and finished dressing herself. They walked as softly as possible down the stairs and past the wide triangle of light that lay on the floor in front of the kitchen door. The men were still at their card game, but the door was partially open now. Porter and Corinthians moved quickly past, just out of the light.

Still a voice called, "Who that? Mary?"

"No. Just me. Porter."

"Porter?" The voice was incredulous. "What shift you on?"

"Catch you later," said Porter and opened the front door before the speaker's curiosity could propel him into the hall.

Corinthians slid as close to Porter as the floor gear of the car allowed, her head resting on the seat back. She closed her eyes once more and took deep breaths of the sweet air her brother had been inhaling three hours ago.

"Hadn't you better fix your hair?" Porter asked. He thought she was beautiful like that, girlish, but he didn't want her excuse to her parents, if they were still awake, to sound ridiculous.

She shook her head. She wouldn't have collected her hair into a ball at her nape now for anything in the world.

Porter parked under the same tree where Corinthians had thrown herself across the hood of the car. Now, after a whispered confession, she walked the four blocks, no longer afraid to mount the porch steps.

As soon as she closed the door she heard voices and instinctively touched her loose hair. The voices came from beyond the dining room, from behind the closed kitchen door. Men's voices. Corinthians blinked. She had just come from a house in which men sat in a lit kitchen talking in loud excited voices, only to meet an identical scene at home. She wondered if this part of the night, a part she was unfamiliar with, belonged, had always belonged, to men. If perhaps it was a secret hour in which men rose like giants from dragon's teeth and, while the women slept, clustered in their kitchens. On tiptoe she approached the door. Her father was speaking.

"You still haven't explained to me why you brought him along."

"What difference does it make now?" That was her brother's voice.

"He knows about it," said her father. "That's what difference."

"About what? There's nothing to know. It was a bust." Milkman's voice swelled like a blister.

"It was a mistake, not a bust. It just means it's somewhere else. That's all."

"Yeah. The mint. You want me to go to the mint?"

"No!" Macon struck the table. "It's got to be there. It's got to."

Corinthians couldn't make sense out of what they were talking about with so much passion, and she didn't want to stay there and learn, lest it distract her from the contentment she was feeling. She left them and climbed the stairs to her own bed.

Downstairs in the kitchen, Milkman folded his arms on the table and put his head down. "I don't care. I don't care where it is."

"It was just a mistake," said his father. "One little mess-up. That don't mean we have to pull out."

"You call being thrown in jail a little mess-up?"

"You out, ain't you? You was only there twenty minutes."

"Two hours."

"Wouldn't have been two minutes if you had called me soon's you got there. Sooner. Should have called me soon's they picked you up."

"Police cars don't have telephones in them." Milkman was weary. He lifted his head and let it rest in his hand, directing his words into his shirt sleeve.

"They would have let you, if it had just been you. Soon as you told them your name they would have let you go. But you was with that Southside nigger. That's what did it."

"That is *not* what did it. It was riding around with a sack of rocks and human bones that did it. Human bones. Which is, if you're a halfway intelligent cop, a hint that there must have been a human being connected to them bones at one time."

"Of course at one time. But not tonight. There couldn't have been a human attached to the bones yesterday. It takes time for a body to be a skeleton. They know that. And don't tell me it wasn't Guitar they was suspicious of. That yellow-eyed nigger looks like he might do anything."

"They didn't see his eyes when they told us to pull over. They didn't see nothing. They just sideswiped us, and told us to get out. Now, what was that for? What'd they stop us for? We wasn't speeding. Just driving along." Milkman searched for cigarettes. He got angry again when he thought about bending over the car, his legs spread, his hands on the hood, while the policeman fingered his legs, his back, his ass, his arms. "What business they got stopping cars that ain't speeding?"

"They stop anybody they want to. They saw you was colored, that's all. And they're looking for the Negro that killed that boy."

"Who said it was a Negro?"

"Paper said it."

"They always say that. Every time . . ."

"What difference does it make? If you'd been alone and told them your name they never would have hauled you in, never would have searched the car, and never would have opened that sack. They know me. You saw how they acted when I got there."

"They didn't act any different when you got there. . . ."

"What?"

"They acted different when you took that sucker off in the corner and opened your wallet."

"You better be thankful I got a wallet."

"I am. God knows I am."

"And that would have been the end of it, except for that Southside nigger. Hadn't been for him, they wouldn't of had to get Pilate down there." Macon rubbed his knees. The idea of having to depend on Pilate to get his son out of jail humiliated him. "Raggedy bootlegging bitch."

"She's still a bitch?" Milkman began to chuckle. Exhaustion and the slow release of tension made him giddy. "You thought she stole it. All these years . . . all these years you've been holding that against her." He was laughing out right now. "How she sneaked out of some cave with a big bag of gold that must have weighed a hundred pounds over her shoulder, all over the country for fifty years and didn't spend none of it, just hung it from the ceiling like a fuckin sack of onions." Milkman put his head back and let the laughter fill the kitchen. Macon was silent. "Fifty years . . . You been thinking about that gold for fifty years! Oh, shit. This is some crazy shit. . . ." Tears of laughter were running from his eyes. "Crazy. All of you. Just straight-out, laid-back crazy. I should of known. The whole thing was crazy; everything about it was crazy—the whole idea."

"What's crazier? Her hauling a sack of gold around all this time, or hauling a dead man's bones around? Huh? Which one?" Macon asked.

"I don't know. I really don't know."

"If she do one, she could do the other. She's the one they should have kept. When you all told them the bones belonged to her, they should have locked her up soon's she walked in the door."

Milkman wiped the tears on his sleeve. "Lock her up for what? After that story she told?" He started laughing again. "She came in there like Louise Beaver and Butterfly McQueen all rolled up in one. 'Yassuh, boss. Yassuh, boss. . . .' "

"She didn't say that."

"Almost. She even changed her voice."

"I told you she was a snake. Drop her skin in a split second."

"She didn't even look the same. She looked short. Short and pitiful."

"That's cause she wanted it back. She wanted them to let her have the bones back."

"Her poor husband's bones, that she didn't have no money to bury. Pilate got a husband somewhere?"

"Does the Pope?"

"Well, she got 'em back. They gave 'em to her."

"She knew what she was doing, all right."

"Yeah, she knew. But how did she know so fast? I mean she came in there . . . you know . . . prepared. She had it all together when she got there. Cop must have told her everything when he picked her up and brought her to the station."

"Uh uh. They don't do that."

"Then how did she know?"

"Who knows what Pilate knows?"

Milkman shook his head. "Only The Shadow knows." He was still amused, but earlier, when he and Guitar had sat handcuffed on a wooden bench, his neck skin had crawled with fear.

"White man's bones," Macon said. He stood up and yawned. The dark of the sky was softened now. "Nigger bitch roaming around with a white man's bones." He yawned again. "I'll never understand that woman. I'm seventy-two years old and I'm going to die not understanding one thing about her." Macon walked toward the kitchen door and opened it. Then he turned around and said to Milkman, "But you know what that means, don't you? If she took the white man's bones and left the gold, then the gold must still be there." He shut the door before his son could protest.

Well, it would rot there, thought Milkman. If anybody even mentions the word "gold," I'm going to have to take his teeth out. He sat on there in the kitchen, wishing for more coffee, but too tired to get up and fix it. In a minute his mother would be downstairs; she had got up when he and Macon had come in, but Macon sent her back upstairs. Milkman fished for another cigarette and watched dawn eclipse the electric light over the sink. It was a cheery sun, which suggested another hot day. But the stronger it got, the more desolate he became. Alone, without Macon, he let the events of the night come back to him—he remembered little things, details, and yet he wasn't sure these details had really happened. Perhaps he made them up. Pilate *had* been shorter. As she stood there in the receiving room of the jail, she didn't even come up to the sergeant's shoulder—and the sergeant's head barely reached Milkman's own chin. But Pilate was as tall as he was. When she whined to the policeman, verifying Milkman's and Guitar's lie that they had ripped off the sack as a joke on an old lady, she had to look up at him. And her hands were shaking as she described how she didn't know the sack was gone until the officer woke her up; that she couldn't imagine why anybody would want to run off with her husband's bones; that her husband had been lynched in Mississippi fifteen years ago, and that they wouldn't let her cut him down, and that she left town then and that when she went back the body had dropped off the rope of its own accord, so she collected it and tried to bury it, but the "funeral peoples" wanted fifty dollars for a coffin, and the carpenter wanted twelve-fifty for a pine box and she just didn't have no twelve dollars and fifty cents so she just carried what was left of Mr. Solomon (she always called him Mr. Solomon cause he was such a dignified colored man) and put it in a sack and kept it with her. "Bible say what so e'er the Lord hath brought together, let no man put asunder—Matthew Twenty-one: Two. We was bony fide and legal wed, suh," she pleaded. Even her eyes, those big sleepy old eyes, were small as she went on: "So I thought I just as well keep him near me and when I die they can put him in the same hole as me. We'll raise up to Judgment Day together. Hand in hand."

Milkman was astonished. He thought Pilate's only acquaintance with the Bible was the getting of names out of it, but she quoted it, apparently, verse and chapter. Furthermore, she had looked at Milkman and Guitar and Macon like she didn't know who exactly they were. In fact, when asked if she knew them, she pointedly said, "Not this man, here," looking at her brother, "but I do believe I've noticed this fella around the neighborhood." Here she motioned toward Guitar, who sat there like marble with the eyes of a dead man. Later, as Macon drove them all home—Pilate sitting in front, Guitar and himself in the back—Guitar never said a word. His anger was like heat shimmering out of his skin, making the hot air blowing in through the open window seem refreshing by comparison.

And again there was a change. Pilate was tall again. The top of her head, wrapped in a silk rag, almost touched the roof of the car, as did theirs. And her own voice was back. She spoke, but to Macon only, and nobody else spoke at all. In a conversational tone, like somebody picking up a story that had been interrupted in the telling, she told her brother something quite different from what she told the policemen.

"I spent that whole day and night in there, and when I looked out the next morning you was gone. I was scared I would run into you, but I didn't see hide nor hair of you. It was three years or more 'fore I went back. The winter it was. Snow was everywhere and I couldn't hardly find my way. I looked up Circe first, then went looking for the cave. It was a hard trek, I can tell you, and I was in frail condition. Snow piled up every which way. But you should of known better than to think I'd go back there for them little old bags. I wasn't stuttin 'em when I first laid eyes on 'em, I sure wasn't thinking about them three years later. I went cause Papa told me to. He kept coming to see me, off and on. Tell me things to do. First he just told me to sing, to keep on singing. 'Sing,' he'd whisper. 'Sing, sing.' Then right after Reba was born he came and told me outright: 'You just can't fly on off and leave a body,' he tole me. A human life is precious. You shouldn't fly off and leave it. So I knew right away what he meant cause he was right there when we did it. He meant that if you take a life, then you own it. You responsible for it. You can't get rid of nobody by killing them. They still there, and they yours now. So I had to go back for it. And I did find the cave. And there he was. Some wolves or something must have drug it cause it was right in the mouth of the cave, laying up, sitting up almost, on that very rock we slept on. I put him in my sack, piece by piece. Some cloth was still on him, but his bones was clean and dry. I've had it every since. Papa told me to, and he was right, you know. You can't take a life and walk off and leave it. Life is life. Precious. And the dead you kill is yours. They stay with you anyway, in your mind. So it's a better thing, a more better thing to have the bones right there with you wherever you go. That way, it frees up your mind."

Fucks up your mind, thought Milkman, fucks it up for good. He pulled himself up from the table. He had to get some sleep before he went looking for Guitar.

Staggering up the stairs, he remembered Pilate's back as she got out of the Buick—not bent at all under the weight of the sack. And he remembered how Guitar glared at her as she walked away from the car. When Macon dropped him off, he neither answered nor turned his head at Milkman's "See y' later."

Milkman woke at noon. Somebody had come into his room and placed a small fan on the floor near the foot of his bed. He listened to the whirring for a long time before he got up and went into the bathroom to fill the tub. He lay there in lukewarm water, still sweating, too hot and tired to soap himself. Every now and then he flicked water on his face, letting it wet his two-day-old beard. He wondered if he could shave without slicing his chin open. The tub was uncomfortable, too short for him to stretch out, though he remembered when he could almost swim in it. Now he looked down at his legs. The left one looked just as long as the other. His eyes traveled up his body. The touch of the policeman's hand was still there—a touch that made his flesh jump like the tremor of a horse's flank when flies light on it. And something more. Something like shame stuck to his skin. Shame at being spread-eagled, fingered, and handcuffed. Shame at having stolen a skeleton, like a kid on a Halloween trick-or-treat prank rather than a grown man making a hit. Shame at needing both his father and his aunt to get him off. Then more shame at seeing his father—with an accommodating "we all understand how it is" smile—buckle before the policemen. But nothing was like the shame he felt as he watched and listened to Pilate. Not just her Aunt Jemima act, but the fact that she was both adept at it and willing to do it—for him. For the one who had just left her house carrying what he believed was her inheritance. It didn't matter that he also believed she had "stolen" it. . . . From whom? From a dead man? From his father, who was also stealing it? Then and now? He had stolen it too, and what's more, he had been prepared—at least he told himself he had been prepared—to knock her down if she had come into the room while he was in the act of stealing it. To knock down an old black lady who had cooked him his first perfect egg, who had shown him the sky, the blue of it, which was like her mother's ribbons, so that from then on when he looked at it, it had no distance, no remoteness, but was intimate, familiar, like a room that he lived in, a place where he belonged. She had told him stories, sung him songs, fed him bananas and corn bread and, on the first cold day of the year, hot nut soup. And if his mother was right, this old black lady—in her late sixties, but with the skin and agility of a teen-aged girl—had brought him into the world when only a miracle could have. It was this woman, whom he would have knocked senseless, who shuffled into the police station and did a little number for the cops—opening herself up wide for their amusement, their pity, their scorn, their mockery, their disbelief, their meanness, their whimsy, their annoyance, their power, their anger, their boredom—whatever would be useful to her and to himself.

Milkman sloshed his legs in the water. He thought again of how Guitar had looked at Pilate—the jeweled hatred in his eyes. He had no right to that look. Suddenly, Milkman knew the answer to the question he had never been able to ask Guitar. Guitar could kill, would kill, and probably had killed. The Seven Days was the consequence of this ability, but not its origin. No. He had no cause to look at her like that, Milkman thought, and heaving himself upright in the tub, he soaped himself hurriedly.

The September heat blasted him as soon as he got outside, and wiped out the pleasant effects of his bath. Macon had taken the Buick—age forced him to walk less—so Milkman went on foot to Guitar's house. As he rounded the corner, he noticed a familiar-looking gray Oldsmobile, a jagged crack in the rear window, parked in front of the house. Several men were inside and two were standing outside: Guitar and Railroad Tommy. Milkman slowed his steps. Tommy was talking, while Guitar nodded his head. Then the two men shook hands—a handshake Milkman had never seen before: first Tommy held Guitar's hand in both his own, then Guitar held Tommy's hand in his two. Tommy got in the car and Guitar dashed around the house to the side stairs that led to his room. The Oldsmobile—Milkman figured it was a 1953 or 1954 model—made a tight U-turn and headed toward him. When it passed by, all the occupants looked straight ahead. Porter was driving, with Empire State in the middle and Railroad Tommy on the far side, and in the back seat was Hospital Tommy and a man named Nero. Milkman didn't know the other man.

That must be *them*, he thought. His heart beat wildly. Six men, one of them Porter, and Guitar. Those are the Days. And that car. That was the car that let Corinthians off near the house sometimes. Milkman had first assumed his sister had an occasional lift home from her job. Later, since she never mentioned it, and also because she seemed quieter and rounder lately, he decided she was seeing some man on the sly. He thought it funny, sweet and a little sad. But now he knew that whoever she was seeing belonged to that car and belonged to the Seven Days. Foolish woman, he thought. Of all the people to pick. She was so silly. So silly. Jesus!

He wasn't up to Guitar now. He would see him later.

People behaved much better, were more polite, more understanding when Milkman was drunk. The alcohol didn't change him at all, but it had a tremendous impact on whomever he saw while he was under its influence. They looked better, never spoke above a whisper, and when they touched him, even to throw him out of the house party because he had peed in the kitchen sink, or when they picked his pockets as he dozed on a bench at the bus station, they were gentle, loving.

He stayed that way, swaying from light buzz to stoned, for two days and a night, and would have extended it to at least another day but for a sobering conversation with Magdalene called Lena, to whom he had not said more than four consecutive sentences since he was in the ninth grade.

She was waiting for him at the top of the stairs when he came home early one morning. Wrapped in a rayon robe and without her glasses, she looked unreal yet kind, like the man who had picked his pocket a short while ago.

"Come here. I want to show you something. Can you come in here for a minute?" She was whispering.

"Can't it wait?" He was kind too; and he was proud of the civility in his voice, considering how tired he was.

"No," she said. "No. You have to see it now. Today. Just look at it."

"Lena, I'm really beat out . . ." he began in sweet reasonableness.

"It won't take more'n a minute. It's important."

He sighed and followed her down the hall into her bedroom. She walked to the window and pointed. "Look down there."

In what seemed to him like elegant if slow motion, Milkman went to the window, parted the curtain, and followed her pointing finger with his eyes. All he saw was the lawn at the side of the house. Not a thing was moving there, but in the light of early day he thought he might have missed it.

"What?"

"That little maple. Right there." She pointed to a tiny maple tree about four feet high. "The leaves should be turning red now. September is almost over. But they're not; they're just shriveling and falling down green."

He turned to her and smiled. "You said it was important." He was not angry, not even irritated, and he enjoyed his equanimity.

"It is important. Very important." Her voice was soft; she kept on staring at the tree.

"Then tell me. I've got to go to work in a few minutes."

"I know. But you can spare me a minute, can't you?"

"Not to stare at a dead bush, I can't."

"It's not dead yet. But it will be soon. The leaves aren't turning this year."

"Lena, you been in the sherry?"

"Don't make fun of me," she said, and there was a hint of steel in her voice.

"But you have, haven't you?"

"You're not paying any attention to me."

"I am. I'm standing here listening to you tell me the news of the day—that a bush is dying."

"You don't remember it, do you?"

"Remember it?"

"You peed on it."

"I what?"

"You peed on it."

"Lena, maybe we can discuss this later. . . ."

"And on me."

"Uh . . . Lena, I have done some things in my life. Some things I don't feel too good about. But I swear to God I never peed on you."

"It was summer. The year Daddy had that Packard. We went for a ride and you had to go to the bathroom. Remember?"

Milkman shook his head. "No. I don't remember that."

"I took you. We were in the country and there was no place else to go. So they made me take you. Mama wanted to, but Daddy wouldn't let her. And he wouldn't go himself. Corinthians turned up her nose and refused outright, so they made me go. I had on heels too. I was a girl too, but they made me go. You and I had to slide down a little slope off the shoulder of the road. It was pretty back in there. I unbuttoned your pants and turned away so you could be private. Some purple violets were growing all over the grass, and wild jonquil. I picked them and took some twigs from a tree. When I got home I stuck them in the ground right down there." She nodded toward the window. "Just made a hole and stuck them in. I always liked flowers, you know. I was the one who started making artificial roses. Not Mama. Not Corinthians. Me. I loved to do it. It kept me . . . quiet. That's why they make those people in the asylum weave baskets and make rag rugs. It keeps them quiet. If they didn't have the baskets they might find out what's really wrong and . . . do something. Something terrible. After you peed on me, I wanted to kill you. I even tried to once or twice. In little ways:

leaving soap in your tub, things like that. But you never slipped and broke your neck, or fell down the stairs or anything." She laughed a little. "But then I saw something. The flowers I'd stuck in the ground, the ones you peed on—well, they died, of course, but not the twig. It lived. It's that maple. So I wasn't mad about it anymore—the pee, I mean—because the tree was growing. But it's dying now, Macon."

Milkman rubbed the corner of his eye with his ring finger. He was so sleepy. "Yeah, well, that was a helluva piss, wouldn't you say? You want me to give it another shot?"

Magdalene called Lena drew one hand out of the pocket of her robe and smashed it across his mouth. Milkman stiffened and made an incomplete gesture toward her. She ignored it and said, "As surely as my name is Magdalene, you are the line I will step across. I thought because that tree was alive that it was all right. But I forgot that there are all kinds of ways to pee on people."

"You listen here." Milkman was sober now and he spoke as steadily as he could. "I'm going to make some allowance for your sherry—up to a point. But you keep your hands off me. What is all this about peeing on people?"

"You've been doing it to us all your life."

"You're crazy. When have I ever messed over anybody in this house? When did you ever see me telling anybody what to do or giving orders? I don't carry no stick; I live and let live, you know that."

"I know you told Daddy about Corinthians, that she was seeing a man. Secretly. And—"

"I *had* to. I'd love for her to find somebody, but I *know* that man. I—I've been around him. And I don't think he . . ." Milkman stopped, unable to explain. About the Days, about what he suspected.

"Oh?" Her voice was thick with sarcasm. "You have somebody else in mind for her?"

"No."

"No? But he's Southside, and not good enough for her? It's good enough for you, but not for her, right?"

"Lena . . ."

"What do you know about somebody not being good enough for somebody else? And since when did you care whether Corinthians stood up or fell down? You've been laughing at us all your life. Corinthians. Mama. Me. Using us, ordering us, and judging us: how we cook your food; how we keep your house. But now, all of a sudden, you have Corinthians' welfare at heart and break her up from a man you don't approve of. Who are you to approve or disapprove anybody or anything? I was breathing air in the world thirteen years before your lungs were even formed. Corinthians, twelve. You don't know a single thing about either one of us—we made roses; that's all you knew—but now you know what's best for the very woman who wiped the dribble from your chin because you were too young to know how to spit. Our girlhood was spent like a found nickel on you. When you slept, we were quiet; when you were hungry, we cooked; when you wanted to play, we entertained you; and when you got grown enough to know the difference between a woman and a two-toned Ford, everything in this house stopped for you. You have yet to wash your own underwear, spread a bed, wipe the ring from your tub, or move a fleck of your dirt from one place to another. And to this day, you have never asked one of us if we were tired, or sad, or wanted a cup of coffee. You've never picked up anything heavier than your own feet, or solved a problem harder than fourth-grade arithmetic. Where do you get the *right* to decide our lives?"

"Lena, cool it. I don't want to hear it."

"I'll tell you where. From that hog's gut that hangs down between your legs. Well, let me tell you something, baby brother: you will need more than that. I don't know where you will get it or who will give it to you, but mark my words, you will need more than that. He has forbidden her to leave the house, made her quit her job, evicted the man, garnisheed his wages, and it is all because of you. You are exactly like him. Exactly. I didn't go to college because of him. Because I was afraid of what he might do to Mama. You think because you hit him once that we all believe you were protecting her. Taking her side. It's a lie. You were taking over, letting us know you had the right to tell her and all of us what to do."

She stopped suddenly and Milkman could hear her breathing. When she started up again, her voice had changed; the steel was gone and in its place was a drifting, breezy music. "When we were little girls, before you were born, he took us to the ice-house once. Drove us there in his Hudson. We were all dressed up, and we stood there in front of those sweating black men, sucking ice out of our handkerchiefs, leaning forward a little so as not to drip water on our dresses. There were other children there. Barefoot, naked to the waist, dirty. But we stood apart, near the car, in white stockings, ribbons, and gloves. And when he talked to the men, he kept glancing at us, us and the car. The car and us. You see, he took us there so they could see us, envy us, envy him. Then one of the little boys came over to us and put his hand on Corinthians' hair. She offered him her piece of ice and before we knew it, *he* was running toward us. He knocked the ice out of her hand into the dirt and shoved us both into the car. First he displayed us, then he splayed us. All our lives were like that: he would parade us like virgins through Babylon, then humiliate us like whores in Babylon. Now he has knocked the ice out of Corinthians' hand again. And you are to blame." Magdalene called Lena was crying. "You are to blame. You are a sad, pitiful, stupid, selfish, hateful man. I hope your little hog's gut stands you in good stead, and that you take good care of it, because you don't have anything else. But I want to give you notice." She pulled her glasses out of her pocket and put them on. Her eyes doubled in size behind the lenses and were very pale and cold. "I don't make roses anymore, and you have pissed your last in this house."

Milkman said nothing.

"Now," she whispered, "get out of my room."

Milkman turned and walked across the room. It was good advice, he thought. Why not take it? He closed the door.

Part II

Chapter 10

When Hansel and Gretel stood in the forest and saw the house in the clearing before them, the little hairs at the nape of their necks must have shivered. Their knees must have felt so weak that blinding hunger alone could have propelled them forward. No one was there to warn or hold them; their parents, chastened and grieving, were far away. So they ran as fast as they could to the house where a woman older than death lived, and they ignored the shivering nape hair and the softness in their knees. A grown man can also be energized by hunger, and any weakness in his knees or irregularity in his heartbeat will disappear if he thinks his hunger is about to be assuaged. Especially if the object of his craving is not gingerbread or chewy gumdrops, but gold.

Milkman ducked under the boughs of black walnut trees and walked straight toward the big crumbling house. He knew that an old woman had lived in it once, but he saw no signs of life there now. He was oblivious to the universe of wood life that did live there in layers of ivy grown so thick he could have sunk his arm in it up to the elbow. Life that crawled, life that slunk and crept and never closed its eyes. Life that burrowed and scurried, and life so still it was indistinguishable from the ivy stems on which it lay. Birth, life, and death—each took place on the hidden side of a leaf. From where he stood, the house looked as if it had been eaten by a galloping disease, the sores of which were dark and fluid.

One mile behind him were macadam and the reassuring sounds of an automobile or two—one of which was Reverend Cooper's car, driven by his thirteen-year-old nephew.

Noon, Milkman had told him. Come back at noon. He could just as easily have said twenty minutes, and now that he was alone, assaulted by what city people regard as raucous silence, he wished he had said five minutes. But even if the boy hadn't had chores to do, it would be foolish to be driven fifteen miles outside Danville on "business" and stay a hot minute.

He should never have made up that elaborate story to disguise his search for the cave; somebody might ask him about it. Besides, lies should be very simple, like the truth. Excessive detail was simply excess. But he was so tired after the long bus ride from Pittsburgh, coming right after the luxury of the flight, he was afraid he wouldn't be convincing.

The airplane ride exhilarated him, encouraged illusion and a feeling of invulnerability. High above the clouds, heavy yet light, caught in the stillness of speed ("Cruise," the pilot said), sitting in intricate metal become glistening bird, it was not possible to believe he had ever made a mistake, or could. Only one small thought troubled him—that Guitar was not there too. He would have loved it—the view, the food, the stewardesses. But Milkman wanted to do this by himself, with no input from anybody. This one time he wanted to go solo. In the air, away from real life, he felt free, but on the ground, when he talked to Guitar just before he left, the wings of all those other people's nightmares flapped in his face and constrained him. Lena's anger, Corinthians' loose and uncombed hair, matching her slack lips, Ruth's stepped-up surveillance, his father's bottomless greed, Hagar's hollow eyes—he did not know whether he deserved any of that, but he knew he was fed up and he knew he had to leave quickly. He told Guitar of his decision before he told his father.

"Daddy thinks the stuff is still in the cave."

"Could be." Guitar sipped his tea.

"Anyway, it's worth checking out. At least we'll know once and for all."

"I couldn't agree more."

"So I'm going after it."

"By yourself?"

Milkman sighed. "Yeah. Yeah. By myself. I need to get out of here. I mean I really have to go away somewhere."

Guitar put his cup down and folded his hands in front of his mouth. "Wouldn't it be easier with the two of us? Suppose you have trouble?"

"It might be easier, but it might look more suspicious with two men instead of one roaming around the woods. If I find it, I'll haul it back and we'll split it up just like we agreed. If I don't, well, I'll be back anyway."

"When you leaving?"

"Tomorrow morning."

"What's your father say about you going alone?"

"I haven't told him yet. You're the only one knows so far." Milkman stood up and went to the window that looked out on Guitar's little porch. "Shit."

Guitar was watching him carefully. "What's the matter?" he asked. "Why you so low? You don't act like a man on his way to the end of the rainbow."

Milkman turned around and sat on the sill. "I hope it *is* a rainbow, and nobody has run off with the pot, cause I need it."

"Everybody needs it."

"Not as bad as me."

Guitar smiled. "Look like you really got the itch now. More than before."

"Yeah, well, everything's worse than before, or maybe it's the same as before. I don't know. I just know that I want to live my own life. I don't want to be my old man's office boy no more. And as long as I'm in this place I will be. Unless I have my own money. I have to get out of that house and I don't want to owe anybody when I go. My family's driving me crazy. Daddy wants me to be like him and hate my mother. My mother wants me to think like her and hate my father. Corinthians won't speak to me; Lena wants me out. And Hagar wants me chained to her bed or dead. Everybody wants something from me, you know what I mean? Something they think they can't get anywhere else. Something they think I got. I don't know what it is—I mean what it is they really want."

Guitar stretched his legs. "They want your life, man."

"My life?"

"What else?"

"No. Hagar wants my life. My family . . . they want—"

"I don't mean that way. I don't mean they want your dead life; they want your living life."

"You're losing me," said Milkman.

"Look. It's the condition our condition is in. Everybody wants the life of a black man. Everybody. White men want us dead or quiet—which is the same thing as dead. White women, same thing. They want us, you know, 'universal,' human, no 'race consciousness.' Tame, except in bed. They like a little racial loincloth in the bed. But outside the bed they want us to be individuals. You tell them, 'But they lynched my papa,' and they say, 'Yeah, but you're better than the lynchers are, so forget it.' And black women, they want your whole self. Love, they call it, and understanding. 'Why don't you *understand* me?' What they mean is, Don't love anything on earth except me. They say, 'Be responsible,' but what they mean is, Don't go anywhere where I ain't. You try to climb Mount Everest, they'll tie up your ropes. Tell them you want to go to the bottom of the sea—just for a look—they'll hide your oxygen tank. Or you don't even have to go that far. Buy a horn and say you want to play. Oh, they love the music, but only after you pull eight at the post office. Even if you make it, even if you stubborn and mean and you get to the top of Mount Everest, or you do play and you good, real good—that still ain't enough. You blow your lungs out on the horn and they want what breath you got left to hear about how you love them. They want your full attention. Take a risk and they say you not for real. That you don't love them. They won't even let you risk your own life, man, your *own* life—unless it's over them. You can't even die unless it's about them. What good is a man's life if he can't even choose what to die for?"

"Nobody can choose what to die for."

"Yes you can, and if you can't, you can damn well try to."

"You sound bitter. If that's what you feel, why are you playing your numbers game? Keeping the racial ratio the same and all? Every time I ask you what you doing it for, you talk about love. Loving Negroes. Now you say—"

"It *is* about love. What else but love? Can't I love what I criticize?"

"Yeah, but except for skin color, I can't tell the difference between what the white women want from us and what the colored women want. You say they all want our life, our living life. So if a colored woman is raped and killed, why do the Days rape and kill a white woman? Why worry about the colored woman at all?"

Guitar cocked his head and looked sideways at Milkman. His nostrils flared a little. "Because she's *mine*."

"Yeah. Sure." Milkman didn't try to keep disbelief out of his voice. "So everybody wants to kill us, except black men, right?"

"Right."

"Then why did my father—who is a very black man—try to kill me before I was even born?"

"Maybe he thought you were a little girl; I don't know. But I don't have to tell you that your father is a very strange Negro. He'll reap the benefits of what we sow, and there's nothing we can do about that. He behaves like a white man, thinks like a white man. As a matter of fact, I'm glad you brought him up. Maybe you can tell me how, after losing everything his own father worked for to some crackers, after *seeing* his father shot down by them, how can he keep his knees bent? Why does he love them so? And Pilate. She's worse. She saw it too and, first, goes back to get a cracker's bones for some kind of crazy self-punishment, and second, leaves the cracker's gold right where it was! Now, is that voluntary slavery or not? She slipped into those Jemima shoes cause they fit."

"Look, Guitar. First of all, my father doesn't care whether a white man lives or swallows lye. He just wants what they have. And Pilate is a little nuts, but she wanted us out of there. If she hadn't been smart, both our asses would be cooling in the joint right now."

"My ass. Not yours. She wanted you out, not me."

"Come on. That ain't even fair."

"No. Fair is one more thing I've given up."

"But to Pilate? What for? She knew what we did and still she bailed us out. Went down for us, clowned and crawled for us. You saw her face. You ever see anything like it in your life?"

"Once. Just once," said Guitar. And he remembered anew how his mother smiled when the white man handed her the four ten-dollar bills. More than gratitude was showing in her eyes. More than that. Not love, but a willingness to love. Her husband was sliced in half and boxed backward. He'd heard the mill men tell how the two halves, not even fitted together, were placed cut side down, skin side up, in the coffin. Facing each other. Each eye looking deep into its mate. Each nostril inhaling the breath the other nostril had expelled. The right cheek facing the left. The right elbow crossed over the left elbow. And he had worried then, as a child, that when his father was wakened on Judgment Day his first sight would not be glory or the magnificent head of God—or even the rainbow. It would be his own other eye.

Even so, his mother had smiled and shown that willingness to love the man who was responsible for dividing his father up throughout eternity. It wasn't the divinity from the foreman's wife that made him sick. That came later. It was the fact that instead of life insurance, the sawmill owner gave his mother forty dollars "to tide you and them kids over," and she took it happily and bought each of them a big peppermint stick on the very day of the funeral. Guitar's two sisters and baby brother sucked away at the bone-white and blood-red stick, but Guitar couldn't. He held it in his hand until it stuck there. All day he held it. At the graveside, at the funeral supper, all the sleepless night. The others made fun of what they believed was his miserliness, but he could not eat it or throw it away, until finally, in the outhouse, he let it fall into the earth's stinking hole.

"Once," he said. "Just once." And felt the nausea all over again. "The crunch is here," he said. "The big crunch. Don't let them Kennedys fool you. And I'll tell you the truth: I hope your daddy's right about what's in that cave. And I sure hope you don't have no second thoughts about getting it back here."

"What's that supposed to mean?"

"It means I'm nervous. Real nervous. I need the bread."

"If you're in a hurt, I can let you have—"

"Not *me*. *Us*. We have work to do, man. And just recently"—Guitar squinted his eyes at Milkman—"just recently one of us was put out in the streets, by somebody I don't have to name. And his wages were garnisheed cause this somebody said two months rent was owing. This somebody needs two months rent on a twelve-by-twelve hole in the wall like a fish needs side pockets. Now we have to take care of this man, get him a place to stay, pay the so-called back rent, and—"

"That was my fault. Let me tell you what happened. . . ."

"No. Don't tell me nothing. You ain't the landlord and you didn't put him out. You may have handed him the gun, but you didn't pull the trigger. I'm not blaming you."

"Why not? You talk about my father, my father's sister, and you'll talk about my sister too if I let you. Why you trust me?"

"Baby, I hope I never have to ask myself that question."

It ended all right, that gloomy conversation. There was no real anger and nothing irrevocable was said. When Milkman left, Guitar opened his palm as usual and Milkman slapped it. Maybe it was fatigue, but the touching of palms seemed a little weak.

At the Pittsburgh airport he discovered that Danville was 240 miles northeast, and not accessible by any public transportation other than a Greyhound bus. Reluctantly, unwilling to give up the elegance he had felt on the flight, he taxied from the airport to the bus station and settled himself for two idle hours before the Greyhound left. By the time he boarded, the inactivity, the picture magazines he'd read, the strolls in the streets near the station, had exhausted him. He fell asleep fifteen minutes outside Pittsburgh. When he woke it was late in the afternoon, with an hour more to go before he reached Danville. His father had raved about the beauty of this part of the country, but Milkman saw it as merely green, deep into its Indian summer but cooler than his own city, although it was farther south. The mountains, he thought, must make for the difference in temperature. For a few minutes he tried to enjoy the scenery running past his window, then the city man's boredom with nature's repetition overtook him. Some places had lots of trees, some did not; some fields were green, some were not, and the hills in the distance were like the hills in every distance. Then he watched signs—the names of towns that lay twenty-two miles ahead, seventeen miles to the east, five miles to the northeast. And the names of junctions, counties, crossings, bridges, stations, tunnels, mountains, rivers, creeks, landings, parks, and lookout points. Everybody had to do his act, he thought, for surely anybody who was interested in Dudberry Point already knew where it was.

He had two bottles of Cutty Sark in his suitcase, along with two shirts and some underwear. The large suitcase, he thought, would have its real load on the return trip. Now he wished he had not checked it under the bus, for he wanted a drink right then. According to his watch, the gold Longines his mother had given him, it would be another twenty minutes before a stop. He lay back on the headrest and tried to fall asleep. His eyes were creasing from the sustained viewing of uneventful countryside.

In Danville he was astonished to learn that the bus depot was a diner on route 11 where the counterman sold bus tickets, hamburgers, coffee, cheese and peanut butter crackers, cigarettes, candy and a cold-cut plate. No lockers, no baggage room, no taxi, and now he realized no men's room either.

Suddenly he felt ridiculous. What was he supposed to do? Put his suitcase down and ask the man: Where is the cave near the farm where my father lived fifty-eight years ago? He knew nobody, had no names except the first name of an old lady who was now dead. And rather than call any more attention to himself in this tiny farming town than his beige three-piece suit, his button-down light-blue shirt and black string tie, and his beautiful Florsheim shoes had already brought, he asked the counterman if he could check his bag there. The man gazed at the suitcase and seemed to be turning the request over in his mind.

"I'll pay," said Milkman.

"Leave 'er here. Back a the pop crates," the man said. "When you wanna pick 'er up?"

"This evening," he said.

"Fine. She'll be right here."

Milkman left the diner/bus station with a small satchel of shaving things and walked out into the streets of Danville, Pennsylvania. He'd seen places like this in Michigan, of course, but he never had to do anything in them other than buy gas. The three stores on the street were closing up for the night. It was five-fifteen and about a dozen people, all told, were walking on the sidewalks. One of them was a Negro. A tall man, elderly, with a brown peaked cap and an old-fashioned collar. Milkman followed him for a while, then caught up to him and said, "Say, I wonder if you could help me." He smiled as he spoke.

The man turned around but did not answer. Milkman wondered if he had offended him in some way. Finally the man nodded and said, "Do what I can." He had a slight country lilt, like that of the white man at the counter.

"I'm looking for . . . Circe, a lady named Circe. Well, not

her, but her house. Do you know where she used to live? I'm from out of town. I just got off the bus. I have some business to take care of here, an insurance policy, and I need to check on some property out there."

The man was listening and apparently not going to interrupt him, so Milkman ended his sentence lamely with: "Can you help me?"

"Reverend Cooper would know," said the man.

"Where can I find him?" Milkman felt something missing from the conversation.

"Stone Lane. Follow this here street till you come to the post office. Go on around the post office and that'll be Windsor. The next street is Stone Lane. He lives in there."

"Will there be a church there?" Milkman assumed a preacher lived next door to his church.

"No. No. Church ain't got no parsonage. Reverend Cooper lives in Stone Lane. Yella house, I believe."

"Thanks," said Milkman. "Thanks a lot."

"Mighty welcome," said the man. "Good evenin'." And he walked away.

Milkman considered whether to go back for his suitcase, abandoned the idea, and followed the directions given him. An American flag identified the post office, a frame structure next to a drugstore that served also as the Western Union office. He turned left at the corner, but noticed there were no street signs anywhere. How could he find Windsor or Stone Lane if there were no signs? He walked through a residential street, another and another, and he was just about to go back to the drugstore and look under "A.M.E." or "A.M.E. Zion" in the telephone directory when he saw a yellow-and-white house. Maybe this is it, he thought. He climbed the steps, determined to mind his manners. A thief should be polite and win goodwill.

"Good evening. Is Reverend Cooper here?"

A woman was standing in the doorway. "Yes, he's here. Would you like to come in? I'll call him."

"Thank you." Milkman entered a tiny hall and waited.

A short chubby man appeared, fingering his glasses. "Yes, sir? You wanted to see me?" His eyes ran rapidly over Milkman's clothes, but his voice betrayed no excessive curiosity.

"Yes. Uh . . . how are you?"

"Fine. Fine. And you?"

"Pretty good." Milkman felt as awkward as he sounded. He had never had to try to make a pleasant impression on a stranger before, never needed anything from a stranger before, and did not remember ever asking anybody in the world how they were. I might as well say it all, he thought. "I could use your help, sir. My name is Macon Dead. My father is from around–"

"Dead? Macon Dead, you say?"

"Yes." Milkman smiled apologetically for the name. "My father–"

"Well, I'll be." Reverend Cooper took off his glasses. "Well, I'll be! Esther!" He threw his voice over his shoulder without taking his eyes off his guest. "Esther, come here!" Then to Milkman: "I know your people!"

Milkman smiled and let his shoulders slump a little. It was a good feeling to come into a strange town and find a stranger who knew your people. All his life he'd heard the tremor in the word: "I live here, but my *people* . . ." or: "She acts like she ain't got no *people*," or: "Do any of your *people* live there?" But he hadn't known what it meant: links. He remembered Freddie sitting in Sonny's Shop just before Christmas, saying, "None of my people would take me in." Milkman beamed at Reverend Cooper and his wife. "You do?"

"Sit on down here, boy. You the son of the Macon Dead I knew. Oh, well, now, I don't mean to say I knew him all that well. Your daddy was four or five years older than me, and they didn't get to town much, but everybody round here remembers the old man. Old Macon Dead, your granddad. My daddy and him was good friends. A blacksmith, my daddy was. I'm the only one got the call. Well well well." Reverend Cooper grinned and massaged his knees. "Oh, Lord, I'm forgetting myself. You must be hungry. Esther, get him something to fill himself up on."

"Oh, no. No, thank you, sir. Maybe a little something to drink. I mean if you do drink, that is."

"Sure. Sure. Nothing citified, I'm sorry to say, but– Esther!" She was on her way to the kitchen. "Bring some glasses and get that whiskey out the cupboard. This here's Macon Dead's boy and he's tired and needs a drink. Tell me, how'd you find me? Don't tell me your daddy remembered me?"

"He probably does, but I met a man in the street and he told me how to find you."

"You asked him for me?" Reverend Cooper wanted to get all the facts straight. Already he was framing the story for his friends: how the man came to his house first, how he asked for him. . . .

Esther returned with a Coca-Cola tray, two glasses, and a large mayonnaise jar of what looked like water. Reverend Cooper poured it warm and neat into the two glasses. No ice, no water–just pure rye whiskey that almost tore Milkman's throat when he swallowed it.

"No. I didn't ask for you by name. I asked him if he knew where a woman named Circe used to live."

"Circe? Yes. Lord, old Circe!"

"He told me to talk to you."

Reverend Cooper smiled and poured more whiskey. "Everybody round here knows me and I know everybody."

"Well, I know my father stayed with her awhile, after they . . . when they . . . after his father died."

"They had a fine place. Mighty fine. Some white folks own it now. Course that's what they wanted. That's why they shot him. Upset a lot of people here, a whole lot of people. Scared 'em too. But didn't your daddy have a sister name of Pilate?"

"Yes, sir. Pilate."

"Still living, is she?"

"Oh, yes. Very much living."

"Issat so? Pretty girl, real pretty. My daddy was the one made the earring for her. That's how we knew they was alive. After Old Macon Dead was killed, nobody knew whether the children was dead too or what. Then a few weeks passed and Circe came to my daddy's shop. Right across from where the post office is now—that's where my daddy's blacksmith shop was. She came in there with this little metal box with a piece of paper bag folded up in it. Pilate's name was written on it. Circe didn't tell Daddy anything, but that he was to make a earring out of it. She stole a brooch from the folks she worked for. My daddy took the gold pin off it and soldered it to the box. So we knew they was alive and Circe was taking care of 'em. They'd be all right with Circe. She worked for the Butlers—rich white folks, you know—but she was a good midwife in those days. Delivered everybody. Me included."

Maybe it was the whiskey, which always made other people gracious when he drank it, but Milkman felt a glow listening to a story come from this man that he'd heard many times before but only half listened to. Or maybe it was being there in the place where it happened that made it seem so real. Hearing Pilate talk about caves and woods and earrings on Darling Street, or his father talk about cooking wild turkey over the automobile noise of Not Doctor Street, seemed exotic, something from another world and age, and maybe not even true. Here in the parsonage, sitting in a cane-bottomed chair near an upright piano and drinking homemade whiskey poured from a mayonnaise jar, it was real. Without knowing it, he had walked right by the place where Pilate's earring had been fashioned, the earring that had fascinated him when he was little, the fixing of which informed the colored people here that the children of the murdered man were alive. And this was the living room of the son of the man who made the earring.

"Did anybody ever catch the men who did it—who killed him?"

Reverend Cooper raised his eyebrows. "Catch?" he asked, his face full of wonder. Then he smiled again. "Didn't have to catch 'em. They never went nowhere."

"I mean did they have a trial; were they arrested?"

"Arrested for what? Killing a nigger? Where did you say you was from?"

"You mean nobody did anything? Didn't even try to find out who did it?"

"Everybody knew who did it. Same people Circe worked for—the Butlers."

"And nobody did anything?" Milkman wondered at his own anger. He hadn't felt angry when he first heard about it. Why now?

"Wasn't nothing to do. White folks didn't care, colored folks didn't dare. Wasn't no police like now. Now we got a county sheriff handles things. Not then. Then the circuit judge came through just once or twice a year. Besides, the people what did it owned half the county. Macon's land was in their way. Folks just was thankful the children escaped."

"You said Circe worked for the people who killed him. Did she know that?"

"Course she did."

"And she let them stay there?"

"Not out in the open. She hid them."

"Still, they were in the same house, right?"

"Yep. Best place, I'd say. If they came to town somebody'd see 'em. Nobody would think of looking there."

"Did Daddy—did my father know that?"

"I don't know what he knew, if Circe ever told him. I never saw him after the murder. None of us did."

"Where are they? The Butlers. They still live here?"

"Dead now. Every one of 'em. The last one, the girl Elizabeth, died a couple years back. Barren as a rock and just as old. Things work out, son. The ways of God are mysterious, but if you live it out, just live it out, you see that it always works out. Nothing they stole or killed for did 'em a bit a good. Not one bit."

"I don't care whether it did them good. The fact is they did somebody else harm."

Reverend Cooper shrugged. "White folks different up your way?"

"No, I guess not. . . . Sometimes, though, you can do something."

"What?" The preacher looked genuinely interested.

Milkman couldn't answer except in Guitar's words, so he said nothing.

"See this here?" The reverend turned around and showed Milkman a knot the size of a walnut that grew behind his ear. "Some of us went to Philly to try and march in an Armistice Day parade. This was after the First World War. We were invited and had a permit, but the people, the white people, didn't like us being there. They started a fracas. You know, throwing rocks and calling us names. They didn't care nothing 'bout the uniform. Anyway, some police on horseback came—to quiet them down, we thought. They ran *us* down. Right under their horses. This here's what a hoof can do. Ain't that something?"

"Jesus God."

"You wouldn't be here to even things up, would you?" The preacher leaned over his stomach.

"No. I'm passing through, that's all. Just thought I'd look around. I wanted to see the farm. . . ."

"Cause any evening up left to do, Circe took care of."

"What'd she do?"

"Hah! What didn't she do?"

"Sorry I didn't come out here long time ago. I would have liked to meet her. She must have been a hundred years old when she died."

"Older. Was a hundred when I was a boy."

"Is the farm nearby?" Milkman appeared mildly interested.

"Not too far."

"I sort of wanted to see where it was since I'm out this way. Daddy talked so much about it."

"It's right back of the Butler place, about fifteen miles out. I can take you there. My old piece of car's in the shop, but it was supposed to be ready yesterday. I'll check on it."

Milkman waited four days for the car to be ready. Four days at Reverend Cooper's house as his guest, and the purpose of long visits from every old man in the town who remembered his father or his grandfather, and some who'd only heard. They all repeated various aspects of the story, all talked about how beautiful Lincoln's Heaven was. Sitting in the kitchen, they looked at Milkman with such rheumy eyes, and spoke about his grandfather with such awe and affection, Milkman began to miss him too. His own father's words came back to him: "I worked right alongside my father. Right alongside him." Milkman thought then that his father was boasting of his manliness as a child. Now he knew he had been saying something else. That he loved his father; had an intimate relationship with him; that his father loved him, trusted him, and found him worthy of working "right alongside" him. "Something went wild in me," he'd said, "when I saw him on the ground."

His was the genuine feeling that Milkman had faked when Reverend Cooper described the hopelessness of "doing anything." These men remembered both Macon Deads as extraordinary men. Pilate they remembered as a pretty woods-wild girl "that couldn't nobody put shoes on." Only one of them remembered his grandmother. "Good-lookin, but looked like a white woman. Indian, maybe. Black hair and slanted-up eyes. Died in childbirth, you know." The more the old men talked—the more he heard about the only farm in the county that grew peaches, real peaches like they had in Georgia, the feasts they had when hunting was over, the pork kills in the winter and the work, the backbreaking work of a going farm—the more he missed something in his life. They talked about digging a well, fashioning traps, felling trees, warming orchards with fire when spring weather was bad, breaking young horses, training dogs. And in it all was his own father, the second Macon Dead, their contemporary, who was strong as an ox, could ride bareback and barefoot, who, they agreed, outran, outplowed, outshot, outpicked, outrode them all. He could not recognize that stern, greedy, unloving man in the boy they talked about, but he loved the boy they described and loved that boy's father, with his hip-roofed barn, his peach trees, and Sunday break-of-dawn fishing parties in a fish pond that was two acres wide.

They talked on and on, using Milkman as the ignition that gunned their memories. The good times, the hard times, things that changed, things that stayed the same—and head and shoulders above all of it was the tall, magnificent Macon Dead, whose death, it seemed to him, was the beginning of their own dying even though they were young boys at the time. Macon Dead was the farmer they wanted to be, the clever irrigator, the peach-tree grower, the hog slaughterer, the wild-turkey roaster, the man who could plow forty in no time flat and sang like an angel while he did it. He had come out of nowhere, as ignorant as a hammer and broke as a convict, with nothing but free papers, a Bible, and a pretty black-haired wife, and in one year he'd leased ten acres, the next ten more. Sixteen years later he had one of the best farms in Montour County. A farm that colored their lives like a paintbrush and spoke to them like a sermon. "You see?" the farm said to them. "See? See what you can do? Never mind you can't tell one letter from another, never mind you born a slave, never mind you lose your name, never mind your daddy dead, never mind nothing. Here, this here, is what a man can do if he puts his mind to it and his back in it. Stop sniveling," it said. "Stop picking around the edges of the world. Take advantage, and if you can't take advantage, take disadvantage. We live here. On this planet, in this nation, in this county right here. *No*where else! We got a home in this rock, don't you see! Nobody starving in my home; nobody crying in my home, and if I got a home you got one too! Grab it. Grab this land! Take it, hold it, my brothers, make it, my brothers, shake it, squeeze it, turn it, twist it, beat it, kick it, kiss it, whip it, stomp it, dig it, plow it, seed it, reap it, rent it, buy it, sell it, own it, build it, multiply it, and pass it on—can you hear me? Pass it on!"

But they shot the top of his head off and ate his fine Georgia peaches. And even as boys these men began to die and were dying still. Looking at Milkman in those nighttime talks, they yearned for something. Some word from him that would rekindle the dream and stop the death they were dying. That's why Milkman began to talk about his father, the boy they knew, the son of the fabulous Macon Dead. He bragged a little and they came alive. How many houses his father owned (they grinned); the new car every two years (they laughed); and when he told them how his father tried to buy the Erie Lackawanna (it sounded better that way), they hooted with joy. That's him! That's Old Macon Dead's boy, all right! They wanted to know everything and Milkman found himself rattling off assets like an accountant, describing deals, total rents income, bank loans, and this new thing his father was looking into—the stock market.

Suddenly, in the midst of his telling, Milkman wanted the gold. He wanted to get up right then and there and go get it. Run to where it was and snatch every grain of it from under the noses of the Butlers, who were dumb enough to believe that if they killed one man his whole line died. He glittered in the light of their adoration and grew fierce with pride.

"Who'd your daddy marry?"

"The daughter of the richest Negro doctor in town."

"That's him! That's Macon Dead!"

"Send you all to college?"

"Sent my sisters. I work right alongside him in our office."

"Hah! Keep you home to get that money! Macon Dead gonna always make him some money!"

"What kinda car he drive?"

"Buick. Two-twenty-five."

"Great God, a deuce and a quarter! What year?"

"This year!"

"That's him! That's Macon Dead! He gonna buy the Erie Lackawanna! If he want it, he'll get it! Bless my soul. Bet he worry them white folks to death. Can't nobody keep him down! Not no Macon Dead! Not in this world! And not in the next! Haw! Goddam! The Erie Lacka*wan*na!"

• •

After all the waiting, Reverend Cooper couldn't go. His preaching income was supplemented by freightyard work and he was called for an early shift. His nephew, called Nephew since he was their only one, was assigned to drive Milkman out to the farm—as close as they could get. Nephew was thirteen and barely able to see over the steering wheel.

"Does he have a license?" Milkman asked Mrs. Cooper.

"Not yet," she said, and when she saw his consternation she explained that farm kids drove early—they had to.

Milkman and Nephew started out right after breakfast. It took them the better part of an hour because the roads were curving two-lanes and they spent twenty minutes behind a light truck they couldn't pull around. Nephew spoke very little. He seemed interested only in Milkman's clothes, which he took every opportunity to examine. Milkman decided to give him one of his shirts, and asked him to stop by the bus station to pick up the suitcase he'd left there.

Finally Nephew slowed down on a stretch of road that showed no houses at all. He stopped.

"What's the matter? You want me to drive?"

"No, sir. This is it."

"What's it? Where?"

"Back in there." He pointed to some bushes. "The road to the Butler place is in there and the farm's back behind it. You got to walk it. Car won't make it."

Nothing was truer; as it turned out, Milkman's feet could hardly make it over the stony road covered with second growth. He had asked Nephew to wait, thinking he would survey the area quickly and come back later on his own. But the boy had chores, he said, and would be back whenever Milkman wanted him to be there.

"An hour," said Milkman.

"Take me an hour just to get back to town," said Nephew.

"Reverend Cooper said you were to take me. Not leave me stranded."

"My mama whip me, I don't do my chores."

Milkman was annoyed, but because he didn't want the boy to think he was nervous about being left out there alone, he agreed to having him come back at—he glanced at his heavy, overdesigned watch—at noon. It was nine o'clock then.

His hat had been knocked off by the first branches of the old walnut trees, so he held it in his hand. His cuffless pants were darkened by the mile-long walk over moist leaves. The quiet fairly roared in his ears. He was uncomfortable and a little anxious, but the gold loomed large in his mind, as did the faces of the men he'd drunk with last night, and he stepped firmly onto the gravel and leaves of the driveway which circled the biggest house he'd ever seen.

This is where they stayed, he thought, where Pilate cried when given cherry jam. He stood still a moment. It must have been beautiful, must have seemed like a palace to them, but neither had ever spoken of it in any terms but how imprisoned they felt, how difficult it was to see the sky from their room, how repelled they were by the carpets, the draperies. Without knowing who killed their father, they instinctively hated the murderers' house. And it did look like a murderer's house. Dark, ruined, evil. Never, not since he knelt by his window sill wishing he could fly, had he felt so lonely. He saw the eyes of a child peer at him over the sill of the one second-story window the ivy had not covered. He smiled. Must be myself I'm seeing—thinking about how I used to watch the sky out the window. Or maybe it's the light trying to get through the trees. Four graceful columns supported the portico, and the huge double door featured a heavy, brass knocker. He lifted it and let it fall; the sound was soaked up like a single raindrop in cotton. Nothing stirred. He looked back down the path and saw the green maw out of which he had come, a greenish-black tunnel, the end of which was nowhere in sight.

The farm, they said, was right in back of the Butler place, but knowing how different their concept of distance was, he thought he'd better get moving. If he found what he was looking for he would have to come back at night—with equipment, of course, but also with some familiarity with the area. On impulse he reached out his hand and tried to turn the doorknob. It didn't budge. Half turning to leave—literally as an afterthought—he pushed the door and it swung open with a sigh. He leaned in. The smell prevented him from seeing anything more than the absence of light did. A hairy animal smell, ripe, rife, suffocating. He coughed and looked for somewhere to spit, for the odor was in his mouth, coating his teeth and tongue. He pulled a handkerchief from his back pocket, held it over his nose, backed away from the open door, and had just begun to spill the little breakfast he'd eaten when the odor disappeared and, quite suddenly, in its place was a sweet spicy perfume. Like ginger root—pleasant, clean, seductive. Surprised and charmed by it, he retraced his steps and went inside. After a second or two he was able to see the hand-laid and hand-finished wooden floor in a huge hall, and at its farther end a wide staircase spiraling up into the dark. His eyes traveled up the stairs.

He had had dreams as a child, dreams every child had, of the witch who chased him down dark alleys, between lawn trees, and finally into rooms from which he could not escape. Witches in black dresses and red underskirts; witches with pink eyes and green lips, tiny witches, long rangy witches, frowning witches, smiling witches, screaming witches and laughing witches, witches that flew, witches that ran, and some that merely glided on the ground. So when he saw the woman at the top of the stairs there was no way for him to resist climbing up toward her outstretched hands, her fingers spread wide for him, her mouth gaping open for him, her eyes devouring him. In a dream you climb the stairs. She grabbed him, grabbed his shoulders and pulled him right up against her and tightened her arms around him. Her head came to his chest and the feel of that hair under his chin, the dry bony hands like steel springs rubbing his back, her floppy mouth babbling into his vest, made him dizzy, but he knew that always, always at the very instant of the pounce or the gummy embrace he would wake with a scream and an erection. Now he had only the erection.

Milkman closed his eyes, helpless to pull away before the completion of the dream. What made him surface from it was a humming sound around his knees. He looked down and there, surrounding him, was a pack of golden-eyed dogs, each of which had the intelligent child's eyes he had seen from the window. Abruptly the woman let him go and he looked down at her too. Beside the calm, sane, appraising eyes of the dogs, her eyes looked crazy. Beside their combed, brushed gun-metal hair, hers was wild and filthy.

She spoke to the dogs. "Go on away. Helmut, go on. Horst, move." She waved her hands and the dogs obeyed.

"Come, come," she said to Milkman. "In here." She took his hand in both of hers, and he followed her—his arm outstretched, his hand in hers—like a small boy being dragged reluctantly to bed. Together they weaved among the bodies of the dogs that floated around his legs. She led him into a room, made him sit on a gray velvet sofa, and dismissed all the dogs but two that lay at her feet.

"Remember the Weimaraners?" she asked, settling herself, pulling her chair close to him.

She was old. So old she was colorless. So old only her mouth and eyes were distinguishable features in her face. Nose, chin, cheekbones, forehead, neck all had surrendered their identity to the pleats and crochetwork of skin committed to constant change.

Milkman struggled for a clear thought, so hard to come by in a dream: Perhaps this woman is Circe. But Circe is dead. This woman is alive. That was as far as he got, because although the woman was talking to him, she might in any case still be dead—as a matter of fact, she *had* to be dead. Not because of the wrinkles, and the face so old it could not be alive, but because out of the toothless mouth came the strong, mellifluent voice of a twenty-year-old girl.

"I knew one day you would come back. Well, that's not entirely true. Some days I doubted it and some days I didn't think about it at all. But you see, I was right. You did come."

It was awful listening to that voice come from that face. Maybe something was happening to his ears. He wanted to hear the sound of his own voice, so he decided to take a chance on logic.

"Excuse me. I'm his son. I'm Macon Dead's son. Not the one you knew."

She stopped smiling.

"My name is Macon Dead too, but I'm thirty-two years old. You knew my father and his father too." So far, so good. His voice was the same. Now he needed only to know if he had assessed the situation correctly. She did not answer him. "You're Circe, aren't you?"

"Yes; Circe," she said, but she seemed to have lost all interest in him. "My name is Circe."

"I'm just visiting," he said. "I spent a couple of days with Reverend Cooper and his wife. They're the ones brought me out here."

"I thought you were him. I thought you came back to see me. Where is he? *My* Macon?"

"Back home. He's alive. He told me about you. . . ."

"And Pilate. Where is she?"

"There too. She's fine."

"Well, you look like him. You really do." But she didn't sound convinced.

"He's seventy-two years old now," said Milkman. He thought that would clear things up, make her know he couldn't be the Macon she knew, who was sixteen when she last saw him. But all she said was "Uhn," as though seventy-two, thirty-two, any age at all, meant nothing whatsoever to her. Milkman wondered how old she really was.

"Are you hungry?" she asked.

"No. Thank you. I ate breakfast."

"So you've been staying with that little Cooper boy?"

"Yes, ma'am."

"A runt. I told him not to smoke, but children don't listen."

"Do you mind if I do?" Milkman was relaxing a little and he hoped the cigarette would relax him more.

She shrugged. "Do what you like. Everybody does what he likes nowadays anyway."

Milkman lit the cigarette and the dogs hummed at the sound of the match, their eyes glittering toward the flame.

"Ssh!" whispered Circe.

"Beautiful," said Milkman.

"What's beautiful?"

"The dogs."

"They're not beautiful, they're strange, but they keep things away. I'm completely worn out taking care of 'em. They belonged to Miss Butler. She bred them, crossbred them. Tried for years to get them in the AKC. They wouldn't permit it."

"What did you call them?"

"Weimaraners. German."

"What do you do with them?"

"Oh, I keep some. Sell some. Till we all die in here together." She smiled.

She had dainty habits which matched her torn and filthy clothes in precisely the way her strong young cultivated voice matched her wizened face. Her white hair—braided, perhaps; perhaps not—she touched as though replacing a wayward strand from an elegant coiffure. And her smile—an opening of flesh like celluloid dissolving under a drop of acid—was accompanied by a press of fingers on her chin. It was this combination of daintiness and cultivated speech that misled Macon and invited him to regard her as merely foolish.

"You should get out once in a while."

She looked at him.

"Is this your house now? Did they will you this? Is that why you have to stay here?"

She pressed her lips over her gums. "The only reason I'm here alone is because she died. She killed herself. All the money was gone, so she killed herself. Stood right there on the landing where you were a minute ago and threw herself off the banister. She didn't die right away, though; she lay in the bed a week or two and there was nobody here but us. The dogs were in the kennel then. I brought her in the world, just like I did her mother and her grandmother before that. Birthed just about everybody in the county, I did. Never lost one either. Never lost nobody but your mother. Well, grandmother, I guess she was. Now I birth dogs."

"Some friend of Reverend Cooper said she looked white. My grandmother. Was she?"

"No. Mixed. Indian mostly. A good-looking woman, but fierce, for the young woman I knew her as. Crazy about her husband too, overcrazy. You know what I mean? Some women love too hard. She watched over him like a pheasant hen. Nervous. Nervous love."

Milkman thought about this mixed woman's great-granddaughter, Hagar, and said, "Yes. I know what you mean."

"But a good woman. I cried like a baby when I lost her. Like a baby. Poor Sing."

"What?" He wondered if she lisped.

"I cried like a baby when I—"

"No. I mean what did you call her?"

"Sing. Her name was Sing."

"Sing? Sing Dead. Where'd she get a name like that?"

"Where'd you get a name like yours? White people name Negroes like race horses."

"I suppose so. Daddy told me how they got their name."

"What'd he tell you?"

Milkman told her the story about the drunken Yankee.

"Well, he didn't have to keep the name. She made him. She made him keep that name," Circe said when he was through.

"She?"

"Sing. His wife. They met on a wagon going North. Ate pecans all the way, she told me. It was a wagonful of ex-slaves going to the promised land."

"Was she a slave too?"

"No. No indeed. She always bragged how she was never a slave. Her people neither."

"Then what was she doing on that wagon?"

"I can't answer you because I don't know. Never crossed my mind to ask her."

"Where were they coming from? Georgia?"

"No. Virginia. Both of them lived in Virginia, her people and his. Down around Culpeper somewhere. Charlemagne or something like that."

"I think that's where Pilate was for a while. She lived all over the country before she came to us."

"Did she ever marry that boy?"

"What boy?"

"The boy she had the baby by."

"No. She didn't marry him."

"Didn't think she would. She was too ashamed."

"Ashamed of what?"

"Her stomach."

"Oh, that."

"Borned herself. I had very little to do with it. I thought they were both dead, the mother and the child. When she popped out you could have knocked me over. I hadn't heard a heartbeat anywhere. She just came on out. Your daddy loved her. Hurt me to hear they broke away from one another. So it does me good to hear they're back together again." She had warmed up talking about the past and Milkman decided not to tell her that Macon and Pilate just lived in the same city. He wondered how she knew about their split, and if she knew what they broke apart about.

"You knew about their quarrel?" he asked quietly, nonchalantly.

"Not the substance. Just the fact. Pilate came back here just after her baby was born. One winter. She told me they split up when they left here and she hadn't seen him since."

"Pilate told me they lived in a cave for a few days after they left this house."

"Is that right? Must have been Hunters Cave. Hunters used it to rest up in there sometimes. Eat. Smoke. Sleep. That's where they dumped Old Macon's body."

"They who? I thought . . . My father said he buried him. Down by a creek or a river someplace where they used to fish."

"He did. But it was too shallow and too close to the water. The body floated up at the first heavy rain. Those children hadn't been gone a month when it floated up. Some men were fishing down there and saw this body, a Negro. So they knew who it was. Dumped it in the cave, and it was summer too. You'd think they would have buried a body in the summer. I told Mrs. Butler I thought it was a disgrace."

"Daddy doesn't know that."

"Well, don't tell him. Let him have his peace. It's hard enough with a murdered father; he don't need to know what happened to the body."

"Did Pilate tell you why she came back here?"

"Yes. She said her father told her to. She had visits from him, she said."

"I'd like to see that cave. Where he's . . . where they put him."

"Won't be anything left to see now. That's been a long time ago."

"I know, but maybe there's something I can bury properly."

"Now, that's a thought worth having. The dead don't like it if they're not buried. They don't like it at all. You won't have trouble finding it. You go back out the road you came in on. Go north until you come to a stile. It's falling down, but you'll see it's a stile. Right in there the woods are open. Walk a little way in and you'll come to a creek. Cross it. There'll be some more woods, but ahead you'll see a short range of hills. The cave is right on the face of those hills. You can't miss it. It's the only one there. Tell your daddy you buried him properly, in a graveyard. Maybe with a headstone. A nice headstone. I hope they find me soon enough and somebody'll take pity on me." She looked at the dogs. "Hope they find me soon and don't let me lay in here too long."

Milkman swallowed as her thought touched his mind. "People come to see you, don't they?"

"Dog buyers. They come every now and then. They'll find me, I guess."

"Reverend Cooper . . . They think you're dead."

"Splendid. I don't like those Negroes in town. Dog people come and the man that delivers the dog food once a week. They come. They'll find me. I just hope it's soon."

He loosened his collar and lit another cigarette. Here in this dim room he sat with the woman who had helped deliver his father and Pilate; who had risked her job, her life, maybe, to hide them both after their father was killed, emptied their slop jars, brought them food at night and pans of water to wash. Had even sneaked off to the village to have the girl Pilate's name and snuffbox made into an earring. Then healed the ear when it got infected. And after all these years was thrilled to see what she believed was one of them. Healer, deliverer, in another world she would have been the head nurse at Mercy. Instead she tended Weimaraners and had just one selfish wish: that when she died somebody would find her before the dogs ate her.

"You should leave this place. Sell the damn dogs. I'll help you. You need money? How much?" Milkman felt a flood of pity and thought gratitude made her smile at him. But her voice was cold.

"You think I don't know how to walk when I want to walk? Put your money back in your pocket."

Rebuffed from his fine feelings, Milkman matched her cold tone: "You loved those white folks that much?"

"Love?" she asked. "Love?"

"Well, what are you taking care of their dogs for?"

"Do you know why she killed herself? She couldn't stand to see the place go to ruin. She couldn't live without servants and money and what it could buy. Every cent was gone and the taxes took whatever came in. She had to let the upstairs maids go, then the cook, then the dog trainer, then the yardman, then the chauffeur, then the car, then the woman who washed once a week. Then she started selling bits and pieces–land, jewels, furniture. The last few years we ate out of the garden. Finally she couldn't take it anymore. The thought of having no help, no money—well, she couldn't take that. She had to let everything go."

"But she didn't let you go." Milkman had no trouble letting his words snarl.

"No, she didn't let me go. She killed herself."

"And you still loyal."

"You don't listen to people. Your ear is on your head, but it's not connected to your brain. I said she killed herself rather than do the work I'd been doing all my life!" Circe stood up, and the dogs too. "Do you hear me? She saw the work I did all her days and *died*, you hear me, *died* rather than live like me. Now, what do you suppose she thought I was! If the way I lived and the work I did was so hateful to her she killed herself to keep from having to do it, and you think I stay on here because I loved her, then you have about as much sense as a fart!"

The dogs were humming and she touched their heads. One stood on either side of her. "They loved this place. Loved it. Brought pink veined marble from across the sea for it and hired men in Italy to do the chandelier that I had to climb a ladder and clean with white muslin once every two months. They loved it. Stole for it, lied for it, killed for it. But I'm the one left. Me and the dogs. And I will never clean it again. Never. Nothing. Not a speck of dust, not a grain of dirt, will I move. Everything in this world they lived for will crumble and rot. The chandelier already fell down and smashed itself to pieces. It's down there in the ballroom now. All in pieces. Something gnawed through the cords. Ha! And I want to see it all go, make sure it does go, and that nobody fixes it up. I brought the dogs in to make sure. They keep strangers out too. Folks tried to get in here to steal things after she died. I set the dogs on them. Then I just brought them all right in here with me. You ought to see what they did to her bedroom. Her walls didn't have wallpaper. No. Silk brocade that took some Belgian women six years to make. She loved it—oh, how much she loved it. Took thirty Weimaraners one day to rip it off the walls. If I thought the stink wouldn't strangle you, I'd show it to you." She looked at the walls around her. "This is the last room."

"I wish you'd let me help you," he said after a while.

"You have. You came in here and pretended it didn't stink and told me about Macon and my sweet little Pilate."

"Are you sure?"

"Never surer."

They both stood and walked down the hall. "Mind how you step. There's no light." Dogs came from everywhere, humming. "Time for their feeding," she said. Milkman started down the stairs. Halfway down, he turned and looked up at her.

"You said his wife made him keep the name. Did you ever know his real name?"

"Jake, I believe."

"Jake what?"

She shrugged, a Shirley Temple, little-girl-helpless shrug. "Jake was all she told me."

"Thanks," he called back, louder than he needed to, but he wanted his gratitude to cut through the stink that was flooding back over the humming of the dogs.

But the humming and the smell followed him all the way back down the tunnel to the macadam road. When he got there it was ten-thirty. Another hour and a half before Nephew would be back. Milkman paced the shoulder of the road, making plans. When should he return? Should he try to rent a car or borrow the preacher's? Had Nephew got his suitcase? What equipment would he need? Flashlight and what else? What story should be in his mind in case he was discovered? Of course: looking for his grandfather's remains—to collect them and take them for a proper burial. He paced further, and then began to stroll in the direction Nephew would be coming from. After a few minutes, he wondered if he was going the right way. He started back, but just then saw the ends of two or three wooden planks sticking out of the brush. Maybe this was the stile Circe had described to him. Not exactly a stile, but the remains of one. Circe had not left that house in years, he thought. Any stile she knew of would have to be in disrepair now. And if her directions were accurate, he might make it there and back before twelve. At least he would be able to check it out in the daylight.

Gingerly, he parted the brush and walked a little way into the woods. He didn't see even a trace of a track. But as he kept on a bit, he heard water and followed the sound, which seemed to be just ahead of the next line of trees. He was deceived. He walked for fifteen minutes before he came to it. "Cross it," she'd said, and he thought there would be a bridge of some sort. There was none. He looked across and saw hills. It must be there. Right there. He calculated that he could just make it in the hour or so left before he should be back on the road. He sat down, took off his shoes and socks, stuffed the socks in his pocket, and rolled up his pants. Holding his shoes in his hand, he waded in. Unprepared for the coldness of the water and the slimy stones at the bottom, he slipped to one knee and soaked his shoes trying to break his fall. He righted himself with difficulty and poured the water out of his shoes. Since he was already wet, there was no point in turning back; he waded on out. After half a minute, the creek bed dropped six inches and he fell again, only now he went completely under and got a glimpse of small silvery translucent fish as his head went down. Snorting water, he cursed the creek, which was too shallow to swim and too rocky to walk. He should have pulled a stick to check depth before he put his foot down, but his excitement had been too great. He went on, feeling with his toes for firm footing before he put his weight down. It was slow moving—the water was about two or three feet deep and some twelve yards wide. If he hadn't been so eager, maybe he could have found a narrower part to cross. Thoughts of what he should have done instead of just plunging in, fruitless as they were, irritated him so that they kept him moving until he made it to the other side. He threw his shoes on the dry ground and hoisted himself up and out on the bank. Breathless, he reached for his cigarettes and found them soaked. He lay back on the grass and let the high sunshine warm him. He opened his mouth so the clear air could bathe his tongue.

After a while he sat up and put on the wet socks and shoes. He looked at his watch to check the time. It ticked, but the face was splintered and the minute hand was bent. Better move, he thought, and struck out for the hills, which, deceptive as the sound of the creek, were much farther away than they seemed. He had no idea that simply walking through trees, bushes, on untrammeled ground could be so hard. Woods always brought to his mind City Park, the tended woods on Honoré Island where he went for outings as a child and where tiny convenient paths led you through. "He leased ten acres of virgin woods and cleared it all," said the men describing the beginning of Old Macon Dead's farm. Cleared this? Chopped down this? This stuff he could barely walk through?

He was sweating into his wet shirt and just beginning to feel the result of sharp stones on his feet. Occasionally he came to a clear space and he'd alter his direction as soon as the low hills came back into view.

Finally flat ground gave way to a gentle upward slope of bushes, saplings, and rock. He walked along its edge, looking for an opening. As he moved southward, the skirts of the hills were rockier and the saplings fewer. Then he saw, some fifteen to twenty feet above him, a black hole in the rock which he could get to by a difficult, but not dangerous, climb, made more difficult by the thin smooth soles of his shoes. He wiped sweat from his forehead on his coat sleeve, slipped off the narrow black tie that hung open around his collar and put it in his pocket.

The salt taste was back in his mouth and he was so agitated by what he believed, hoped, he would find there, he had to put his hands on warm stone to dry them. He thought of the pitiful hungry eyes of the old men, their eagerness for some word of defiant success accomplished by the son of Macon Dead; and of the white men who strutted through the orchards and ate the Georgia peaches after they shot his grandfather's head off. Milkman took a deep breath and began to negotiate the rocks.

As soon as he put his foot on the first stone, he smelled money, although it was not a smell at all. It was like candy and sex and soft twinkling lights. Like piano music with a few strings in the background. He'd noticed it before when he waited under the pines near Pilate's house; more when the moon lit up the green sack that hung like a kept promise from her ceiling; and most when he tumbled lightly to the floor, sack in hand. Las Vegas and buried treasure; numbers dealers and Wells Fargo wagons; race track pay windows and spewing oil wells; craps, flushes, and sweepstakes tickets. Auctions, bank vaults, and heroin deals. It caused paralysis, trembling, dry throats, and sweaty palms. Urgency, and the feeling that "they" had been mastered or were on your side. Quiet men stood up and threw a queen down on the table hard enough to break her neck. Women sucked their bottom lips and put little red disks down in numbered squares. Lifeguards, A-students, eyed cash registers and speculated on how far away the door was. To win. There was nothing like it in the world.

Milkman became agile, pulling himself up the rock face, digging his knees into crevices, searching with his fingers for solid earth patches or ledges of stone. He left off thinking and let his body do the work. He stood up, finally, on level ground twenty feet to the right of the mouth of the cave. There he saw a crude footpath he might have found earlier if he had not been so hasty. That was the path the hunters used and that Pilate and his father had also used. None of them tore their clothes as he had, climbing twenty feet of steep rock.

He entered the cave and was blinded by the absence of light. He stepped back out and reentered, cupping his eyes. After a while, he could distinguish the ground from the wall of the cave. There was the ledge of rock where they'd slept, much larger than he had pictured. And worn places on the floor where fires had once burned, and several boulders standing around the entrance—one with a kind of V-shaped crown. But where were the bones? Circe said they dumped him in here. Farther back, probably, back where the shallow pit was. Milkman had no flashlight and his matches were certainly wet, but he tried to find a dry one anyway. Only one or two even sputtered. The rest were dead. Still, his eyes were getting used to the dark. He pulled a branch from a bush that grew near the entrance and bending forward, let it graze the ground before him as he walked. He had gone thirty or forty feet when he noticed the cave's walls were closer together. He could not see the roof at all. He stopped and began to move slowly sideways, the branch tip scratching a yard or so ahead. The side of his hand grazed rock and he flung the dry bat shit off it and moved to the left. The branch struck air. He stopped again, and lowered the tip until it touched ground again. Raising it up and down, and pressing it back and around, he could tell that he had found the pit. It was about two feet deep and maybe eight feet wide. Frantically he scraped the branch around the bottom. It hit something hard, again something else hard. Milkman swallowed and dropped to his knees. He squinted his eyes as hard as he could, but he couldn't see a thing. Suddenly he remembered a lighter in his vest pocket. He dropped the branch and fumbled for it, almost faint from the money smell—the twinkling lights, the piano music. He pulled it out, praying it would light. On the second try, it burst into flame and he peered down. The lighter went out. He snapped it back and held his hand over its fragile flame. At the bottom of the hole he saw rocks, boards, leaves, even a tin cup, but no gold. Stretched out on his stomach, holding the lighter in one hand, he swept the bottom with the other, clawing, pulling, fingering, poking. There were no fat little pigeon-breasted bags of gold. There was nothing. Nothing at all. And before he knew it, he was hollering a long, *awwww* sound into the pit. It triggered the bats, which swooped suddenly and dived in the darkness over his head. They startled him and he leaped to his feet, whereupon the sole of his right shoe split away from the soft cordovan leather. The bats drove him out in a lopsided run, lifting his foot high to accommodate the flopping sole.

In the sunlight once more, he stopped for breath. Dust, tears, and too bright light were in his eyes, but he was too angry and disgusted to rub them. He merely threw the lighter in a wide high arc into the trees at the foot of the hills and limped down the footpath, paying no attention to the direction he was going. He put his feet down wherever was most convenient. Quite suddenly, it seemed to him, he was at the creek again, but upstream where the crossing—about twelve feet here and so shallow he could see the stony bottom—was laid across with boards. He sat down and lashed the sole of his shoe to its top with his black string tie, then walked across the homemade bridge. The woods on the other side had a pathway.

Milkman began to shake with hunger. Real hunger, not the less than top-full feeling he was accustomed to, the nervous desire to taste something good. Real hunger. He believed if he didn't get something to eat that instant he would pass out. He examined the bushes, the branches, the ground for a berry, a nut, anything. But he didn't know what to look for, nor how they grew. Trembling, his stomach in a spasm, he tore off a few leaves and put them in his mouth. They were as bitter as gall, but he chewed them anyway, spit them out, and got others. He thought of the breakfast food Mrs. Cooper had put before him, which had disgusted him then. Fried eggs covered with grease, fresh-squeezed orange juice with seed and pulp floating in it, thick hand-cut bacon, a white-hot mound of grits and biscuits. It was her best effort, he knew, but perhaps because of the whiskey he'd drunk the night before, he could only bring himself to drink two cups of black coffee and eat two biscuits. The rest had nauseated him, and what he did eat he had left at Circe's door.

Some brush closed in on him and when he swept it angrily aside, he saw a stile and the road in front of him. Macadam, automobiles, fence posts, civilization. He looked at the sky to gauge the hour. The sun was a quarter of the way down from what even he knew was high noon. About one o'clock, he guessed. Nephew would have come and gone. He felt in his back pocket for his wallet. It was discolored at the edges from the water, but the contents were dry. Five hundred dollars, his driver's license, phone numbers on slips of paper, social security card, airline ticket stub, cleaners receipts. He looked up and down the road. He had to get food, and started walking south, where he believed Danville lay, hoping to hitch as soon as a car came by. He was not only ravenous; his feet hurt. The third car to pass stopped—a 1954 Chevrolet—and the driver, a black man, showed the same interest in Milkman's clothes that Nephew had shown. He seemed not to notice or care about the rip at the knee or under the arm, the tie-tied shoe, the leaves in Milkman's hair, or the dirt all over the suit.

"Where you headed, partner?"

"Danville. As close as I can get."

"Hop on in, then. Little out my way. I cut over to Buford, but I'll get you closer than you was."

" 'Preciate it," answered Milkman. He loved the car seat, loved it. And sank his weary back into its nylon and sighed.

"Good cut of suit," the man said. "I guess you ain't from here'bouts."

"No. Michigan."

"Sure 'nough? Had a aunt move out there. Flint. You know Flint?"

"Yeah. I know Flint." Milkman's feet were singing, the tender skin of the ball louder than the heels. He dared not spread his toes, lest the singing never stop.

"What kinda place is it, Flint?"

"Jive. No place you'd want to go to."

"Thought so. Name sounds good, but I thought it'd be like that."

Milkman had noticed a six-bottle carton of Coca-Cola on the back seat when he got in the car. It was on his mind.

"Could I buy one of those Coca-Colas from you? I'm kinda thirsty."

"It's warm," said the man.

"Long as it's wet."

"Help yourself."

Milkman reached around and pulled a bottle out of its case.

"Got a bottle opener?"

The man took the bottle from him and put its head in his mouth and slowly pried the top off. Foam shot all over his chin and his lap before Milkman could take it from him.

"Hot." The man laughed and wiped himself with a navy-and-white handkerchief.

Milkman gulped the Coke, foam and all, in three or four seconds.

"Like another?"

He did but he said no. Just a cigarette.

"Don't smoke," said the man.

"Oh," said Milkman, and struggled against and lost to a long belch.

"Bus station's right around the bend there." They were just outside Danville. "You can make it easy."

"I really do thank you." Milkman opened the door. "What do I owe you? For the Coke and all?"

The man was smiling, but his face changed now. "My name's Garnett, Fred Garnett. I ain't got much, but I can afford a Coke and a lift now and then."

"I didn't mean . . . I . . ."

But Mr. Garnett had reached over and closed the door. Milkman could see him shaking his head as he drove off.

Milkman's feet hurt him so, he could have cried, but he made it to the diner/bus station and looked for the man behind the counter. He wasn't there, but a woman offered to help. There followed a long discussion in which he discovered that the bag was not there, the man was not there, she didn't know if a colored boy had picked it up or not, they didn't have a checkroom and she was mighty sorry but he could look at the stationmaster's if the boy didn't have it, and was there anything else she could do?

"Hamburgers," he said. "Give me some hamburgers and a cup of coffee."

"Yes, sir. How many?"

"Six," he said, but his stomach cramped on the fourth and bent him double with a pain that lasted off and on all the way to Roanoke. But before he left, he telephoned Reverend Cooper. His wife answered and told him that her husband was still at the freightyard and he could catch him there if he hurried. Milkman thanked her and hung up. Walking like a pimp in delicate shoes, he managed to get to the yard, which was fairly close to the bus station. He entered the gate and asked the first man he saw if Reverend Cooper was still there.

"Coop?" the man said. "I think he went on over to the station house. See it? Right over there."

Milkman followed his finger, and hobbled over the gravel and ties to the station house.

It was empty save for an old man dragging a crate.

"Excuse me," Milkman said. "Is Rev–is Coop still here?"

"Just left. If you run you can catch him," the man said. He wiped the sweat of exertion from his forehead.

Milkman thought about running anywhere on his tender feet and said, "Oh, well. I'll try to catch him another time." He turned to go.

"Say," said the man. "If you ain't gonna try to catch him, could you give me a hand with this?" He pointed down to the huge crate at his feet. Too tired to say no or explain, Milkman nodded. The two of them grunted and groaned over the box, and finally got it up on a dolly, where they could push it to the weighing platform. Milkman slumped over the crate and caught his breath, barely able to nod to the old man's thank yous. Then he went out of the station into the street.

He was tired now. Really tired. He didn't want to see Reverend Cooper and his success-starved friends again. And he certainly didn't want to explain anything to his father or Guitar just yet. So he hobbled back to the bus station and asked for the next bus leaving that was going south. It had to be south. And it had to be Virginia. Because now he thought he knew how to find out what had happened to the gold.

.   .

Full of hamburgers, sore of foot, sick to his stomach, but at least sitting down, he couldn't even feel the disappointment that lay in the pit in the cave. He slept heavily for several hours on the bus, woke and daydreamed, napped a little more, woke again at a rest stop and ate a bowl of pea soup. He went into a drugstore and replaced the shaving equipment and toilet articles he'd left at Reverend Cooper's, and decided to wait and get his shoe fixed (it was sealed with chewing gum now), his suit mended, and a new shirt in Virginia.

The Greyhound bus made a sound like the hum of the Weimaraners as it sped down the road, and Milkman shivered a little, the way he had when Circe glanced at them, sitting in the "last room," wondering if she would outlive them. But there were over thirty of them and reproducing all the time.

The low hills in the distance were no longer scenery to him. They were real places that could split your thirty-dollar shoes. More than anything in the world he'd wanted it to be there, for row upon row of those little bags to turn their fat pigeon chests up to his hands. He thought he wanted it in the name of Macon Dead's Georgia peaches, in the name of Circe and her golden-eyed dogs, and especially in the name of Reverend Cooper and his old-timey friends who began to die before their facial hair was out when they saw what happened to a black man like them—"ignorant as a hammer and broke as a convict"—who had made it anyway. He also thought he wanted it in the name of Guitar, to erase what looked like doubt in his face when Milkman left, the "I-know-you-gonna-fuck-up" look. There wasn't any gold, but now he knew that all the fine reasons for wanting it didn't mean a thing. The fact was he wanted the gold because it was gold and he wanted to own it. Free. As he had sat chomping the hamburgers in the bus station, imagining what going home would be like now—not only to have to say there was no gold, but also to know he was trapped there—his mind had begun to function clearly.

Circe said that Macon and Sing had boarded that wagon in Virginia, where they both came from. She also said Macon's body rose up from the ground at the first heavy rain, and that the Butlers, or somebody, dumped it in the hunters' cave one summer night. One summer night. And it was a body, a corpse, when they hauled it away, because they recognized him as a Negro. Yet Pilate said it was winter when she was there, and there were only bones. She said she went to see Circe and visited the cave four years later, in the snow, and took the white man's bones. Why didn't she see her father's bones? There should have been two skeletons. Did she step over one and collect the other? Surely Circe had told her the same thing she told him—that her father's body was in the cave. Did Pilate tell Circe that they had killed a man in there? Probably not, since Circe didn't mention it. Pilate said she took the white man's bones and didn't even look for the gold. But she lied. She had not mentioned the second skeleton because it wasn't there when she got to the cave. She didn't come back four years later—or if she did, it was her *second* trip. She came back *before* they dumped the Negro they found in the cave. She took the bones, all right; Milkman had seen them on the table in the jailhouse. But that's not all she took. She took the gold. To Virginia. And maybe somebody in Virginia would know.

Milkman followed in her tracks.

Chapter 11

The women's hands were empty. No pocketbook, no change purse, no wallet, no keys, no small paper bag, no comb, no handkerchief. They carried nothing. Milkman had never in his life seen a woman on the street without a purse slung over her shoulder, pressed under her arm, or dangling from her clenched fingers. These women walked as if they were going somewhere, but they carried nothing in their hands. It was enough to let him know he was really in the backwoods of Virginia, an area the signs kept telling him was the Blue Ridge Mountains. Danville, with its diner/bus station and its post office on the main street was a thriving metropolis compared to this no-name hamlet, a place so small nothing financed by state funds or private enterprise reared a brick there. In Roanoke, Petersburg, Culpeper he'd asked for a town named Charlemagne. Nobody knew. The coast, some said. Tidewater. A valley town, said others. He ended up at an AAA office, and after a while they discovered it and its correct name: Shalimar. How do I get there? Well, you can't walk it, that's for sure. Buses go there? Trains? No. Well, not very near. There is one bus, but it just goes to . . . He ended up buying a fifty-dollar car for seventy-five dollars out of a young man's yard. It broke down before he could get to the gas station and fill the tank. And when he got pushed to the station, he spent $132 on a fan belt, brake lining, oil filter, gas line filter, two retreads, and a brand-new oil pan, which he didn't need but bought before the mechanic told him the gasket was broken. It was a hard and bitter price to pay. Not because it wasn't worth it, and not because it had to be in cash since the garage owner looked at his Standard Oil credit card like it was a three-dollar bill, but because he had got used to prices in the South: socks two pairs for a quarter, resoled shoes thirty cents, shirt $1.98, and the two Tommys needed to know that he got a shave *and* a haircut for fifty cents.

By the time he bought the car, his morale had soared and he was beginning to enjoy the trip: his ability to get information and help from strangers, their attraction to him, their generosity (Need a place to stay? Want a good place to eat?). All that business about southern hospitality was for real. He wondered why black people ever left the South. Where he went, there wasn't a white face around, and the Negroes were as pleasant, wide-spirited, and self-contained as could be. He earned the rewards he got here. None of the pleasantness was directed at him because of his father, as it was back home, or his grandfather's memory, as it was in Danville. And now, sitting behind a steering wheel, he felt even better. He was his own director—relieving himself when he wanted to, stopping for cold beer when he was thirsty, and even in a seventy-five-dollar car the sense of power was strong.

He'd had to pay close attention to signs and landmarks, because Shalimar was not on the Texaco map he had, and the AAA office couldn't give a nonmember a charted course—just the map and some general information. Even at that, watching as carefully as he could, he wouldn't have known he had arrived if the fan belt hadn't broken again right in front of Solomon's General Store, which turned out to be the heart and soul of Shalimar, Virginia.

He headed for the store, nodding at the four men sitting outside on the porch, and side-stepping the white hens that were strolling about. Three more men were inside, in addition to the man behind the counter, who he assumed was Mr. Solomon himself. Milkman asked him for a cold bottle of Red Cap, please.

"No beer for sale on Sunday," the man said. He was a light-skinned Negro with red hair turning white.

"Oh. I forgot what day it was." Milkman smiled. "Pop, then. I mean soda. Got any on ice?"

"Cherry smash. That suit you?"

"Fine. Suit me fine."

The man walked over to the side of the store and slid open the door of an ancient cooler. The floor was worn and wavy with years of footsteps. Cans of goods on the shelf were sparse, but the sacks, trays, and cartons of perishables and semiperishables were plentiful. The man pulled a bottle of red liquid from the cooler and wiped it dry on his apron before handing it to Milkman.

"A nickel if you drink it here. Seven cents if you don't."

"I'll drink it here."

"Just get in?"

"Yeah. Car broke down. Is there a garage nearby?"

"Naw. Five miles yonder is one, though."

"Five miles?"

"Yep. What's the trouble? Mebbe one a us can fix it. Where you headed?"

"Shalimar."

"You standin in it."

"Right here? This is Shalimar?"

"Yes, suh. Shalimar." The man pronounced it *Shalleemone*.

"Good thing I broke down. I would have missed it for sure." Milkman laughed.

"Your friend almost missed it too."

"My friend? What friend?"

"The one lookin for you. Drove in here early this mornin and axed for ya."

"Asked for me by name?"

"No. He never mentioned your name."

"Then how do you know he was looking for me?"

"Said he was lookin for his friend in a three-piece beige suit. Like that." He pointed to Milkman's chest.

"What'd he look like?"

"Dark-skinned man. 'Bout your complexion. Tall. Thin. What's a matter? Y'all get your wires crossed?"

"Yeah. No. I mean . . . what was his name?"

"Didn't say. Just asked for you. He come a long way to meet you, though. I know that. Drove a Ford with Michigan tags."

"Michigan? You sure Michigan?"

"Sure I'm sure. Was he supposed to meet you in Roanoke?"

When Milkman looked wild-eyed, the man said, "I seen your tags."

Milkman sighed with relief. And then said, "I wasn't sure where we were going to meet up. And he didn't say his name?"

"Naw. Just said to give you some good-luck message if I was to see you. Lemme see . . ."

"Good luck?"

"Yeah. Said to tell you your day was sure coming or your day . . . something like that . . . your day is here. But I know it had a day in it. But I ain't sure if he said it was comin or was already here." He chuckled. "Wish mine was here. Been waitin fifty-seven years and it ain't come yet."

The other men in the store laughed congenially, while Milkman stood frozen, everything in him quiet but his heart. There was no mistaking the message. Or the messenger. Guitar was looking for him, was following him, and for professional reasons. Unless . . . Would Guitar joke about that phrase? That special secret word the Seven Days whispered to their victims?

"The drink abuse you?" Mr. Solomon was looking at him. "Sweet soda water don't agree with me."

Milkman shook his head and swallowed the rest hurriedly. "No," he said. "I'm just . . . car weary. I think I'll sit outside awhile." He started toward the door.

"You want me to see 'bout your car for you?" Mr. Solomon sounded slightly offended.

"In a minute. I'll be right back."

Milkman pushed the screen door and stepped outside on the porch. The sun was blazing. He took off his jacket and held it on his forefinger over his shoulder. He gazed up and down the dusty road. Shotgun houses with wide spaces between them, a few dogs, chickens, children, and the women with nothing in their hands. They sat on porches, and walked in the road swaying their hips under cotton dresses, bare-legged, their unstraightened hair braided or pulled straight back into a ball. He wanted one of them bad. To curl up in a cot in that one's arms, or that one, or that. That's the way Pilate must have looked as a girl, looked even now, but out of place in the big northern city she had come to. Wide sleepy eyes that tilted up at the corners, high cheekbones, full lips blacker than their skin, berry-stained, and long long necks. There must be a lot of intermarriage in this place, he thought. All the women looked alike, and except for some light-skinned red-headed men (like Mr. Solomon), the men looked very much like the women. Visitors to Shalimar must be rare, and new blood that settled here nonexistent.

Milkman stepped off the porch, scattering the hens, and walked down the road toward a clump of trees near a building that looked like a church or clubhouse of some sort. Children were playing behind the trees. Spreading his jacket on the burnt grass, he sat down and lit a cigarette.

Guitar was here. Had asked for him. But why was he afraid? They were friends, close friends. So close he had told him all about the Seven Days. There was no trust heavier than that. Milkman was a confidant, almost an accomplice. So why was he afraid? It was senseless. Guitar must have left that particular message so Milkman could know who was looking for him without his giving his name. Something must have happened back home. Guitar must be running, from the police, maybe, and decided to run toward his friend—the only one other than the Days who would know what it was all about and whom he could trust. Guitar needed to find Milkman and he needed help. That was it. But if Guitar knew Milkman was headed for Shalimar, he must have found that out in Roanoke, or Culpeper—or maybe even in Danville. And if he knew that, why didn't he wait? Where was he now? Trouble. Guitar was in trouble.

Behind him the children were singing a kind of ring-around-the-rosy or Little Sally Walker game. Milkman turned to watch. About eight or nine boys and girls were standing in a circle. A boy in the middle, his arms outstretched, turned around like an airplane, while the others sang some meaningless rhyme:

Jay the only son of Solomon
Come booba yalle, come booba tambee
Whirl about and touch the sun
Come booba yalle, come booba tambee . . .

They went on with several verses, the boy in the middle doing his imitation of an airplane. The climax of the game was a rapid shouting of nonsense words accompanied by more rapid twirling: "Solomon rye balaly *shoo*; yaraba medina hamlet *too*"—until the last line. "Twenty-one children the last one *Jay!*" At which point the boy crashed to earth and the others screamed.

Milkman watched the children. He'd never played like that as a child. As soon as he got up off his knees at the window sill, grieving because he could not fly, and went off to school, his velvet suit separated him from the other children. White and black thought he was a riot and went out of their way to laugh at him and see to it that he had no lunch to eat, nor any crayons, nor ever got through the line to the toilet or the water fountain. His mother finally surrendered to his begging for corduroy knickers or straights, which helped a little, but he was never asked to play those circle games, those singing games, to join in anything, until Guitar pulled those four boys off him. Milkman smiled, remembering how Guitar grinned and whooped as the four boys turned on him. It was the first time Milkman saw anybody really enjoy a fight. Afterward Guitar had taken off his baseball cap and handed it to Milkman, telling him to wipe the blood from his nose. Milkman bloodied the cap, returned it, and Guitar slapped it back on his head.

Remembering those days now, Milkman was ashamed of having been frightened or suspicious of Guitar's message. When he turned up, he would explain everything and Milkman would do what he could to help. He stood up and brushed his jacket. A black rooster strutted by, its blood-red comb draped forward like a wicked brow.

Milkman walked back toward Solomon's store. He needed a place to stay, some information, and a woman, not necessarily in that order. He would begin wherever the beginning was. In a way it was good Guitar had asked for him. Along with waiting for him and waiting for some way to get a new fan belt, he had a legitimate reason to dawdle. Hens and cats gave up their places on the steps as he approached them.

"Feelin better, are ya?" asked Mr. Solomon.

"Much better. Just needed a stretch, I guess." He jutted his chin toward the window. "Nice around here. Peaceful. Pretty women too."

A young man sitting on a chair tilted to the wall pushed his hat back from his forehead and let the front legs of the chair hit the floor. His lips were open, exposing the absence of four front teeth. The other men moved their feet. Mr. Solomon smiled but didn't say anything. Milkman sensed that he'd struck a wrong note. About the women, he guessed. What kind of place was this where a man couldn't even ask for a woman?

He changed the subject. "If my friend, the one who stopped by this morning, was going to wait for me here, where would he be likely to find a place to stay? Any rooming houses around here?"

"Rooming houses?"

"Yeah. Where a man can spend the night."

Mr. Solomon shook his head. "Nothin like that here."

Milkman was getting annoyed. What was all the hostility for? He looked at the men sitting around the store. "You think maybe one of them could help with the car?" he asked Mr. Solomon. "Maybe get another belt somewhere?"

Mr. Solomon kept his eyes on the counter. "Guess I could ask them." His voice was soft; he spoke as if he was embarrassed about something. There was none of the earlier chattiness he'd been full of when Milkman arrived.

"If they can't find one, let me know right away. I may have to buy another car to get back home."

Every one of the faces of the men turned to look at him, and Milkman knew he had said something else wrong, although he didn't know what. He only knew that they behaved as if they'd been insulted.

In fact they had been. They looked with hatred at the city Negro who could buy a car as if it were a bottle of whiskey because the one he had was broken. And what's more, who had said so in front of them. He hadn't bothered to say his name, nor ask theirs, had called them "them," and would certainly despise their days, which should have been spent harvesting their own crops, instead of waiting around the general store hoping a truck would come looking for mill hands or tobacco pickers in the flatlands that belonged to somebody else. His manner, his clothes were reminders that they had no crops of their own and no land to speak of either. Just vegetable gardens, which the women took care of, and chickens and pigs that the children took care of. He was telling them that they weren't men, that they relied on women and children for their food. And that the lint and tobacco in their pants pockets where dollar bills should have been was the measure. That thin shoes and suits with vests and smooth smooth hands were the measure. That eyes that had seen big cities and the inside of airplanes were the measure. They had seen him watching their women and rubbing his fly as he stood on the steps. They had also seen him lock his car as soon as he got out of it in a place where there couldn't be more than two keys twenty-five miles around. He hadn't found them fit enough or good enough to want to know their names, and believed himself too good to tell them his. They looked at his skin and saw it was as black as theirs, but they knew he had the heart of the white men who came to pick them up in the trucks when they needed anonymous, faceless laborers.

Now one of them spoke to the Negro with the Virginia license and the northern accent.

"Big money up North, eh?"

"Some," Milkman answered.

"Some? I hear tell everybody up North got big money."

"Lotta people up North got nothing." Milkman made his voice pleasant, but he knew something was developing.

"That's hard to believe. Why would anybody want to stay there if they ain't no big money?"

"The sights, I guess." Another man answered the first. "The sights and the women."

"You kiddin," said the first man in mock dismay. "You mean to tell me pussy different up North?"

"Naw," said the second. "Pussy the same everywhere. Smell like the ocean; taste like the sea."

"Can't be," said a third. "Got to be different."

"Maybe the pricks is different." The first man spoke again.

"Reckon?" asked the second man.

"So I hear tell," said the first man.

"How different?" asked the second man.

"Wee little," said the first man. "Wee, wee little."

"Naw!" said the second man.

"So they tell me. That's why they pants so tight. That true?" The first man looked at Milkman for an answer.

"I wouldn't know," said Milkman. "I never spent much time smacking my lips over another man's dick." Everybody smiled, including Milkman. It was about to begin.

"What about his ass hole? Ever smack your lips over that?"

"Once," said Milkman. "When a little young nigger made me mad and I had to jam a Coke bottle up his ass."

"What'd you use a bottle for? Your cock wouldn't fill it?"

"It did. After I took the Coke bottle out. Filled his mouth too."

"Prefer mouth, do you?"

"If it's big enough, and ugly enough, and belongs to a ignorant motherfucker who is about to get the livin shit whipped out of him."

The knife glittered.

Milkman laughed. "I ain't seen one of those since I was fourteen. Where I come from *boys* play with knives—if they scared they gonna lose, that is."

The first man smiled. "That's me, motherfucker. Scared to death I'm gonna lose."

Milkman did the best he could with a broken bottle, but his face got slit, so did his left hand, and so did his pretty beige suit, and he probably would have had his throat cut if two women hadn't come running in screaming, "Saul! Saul!"

The store was full of people by then and the women couldn't get through. The men tried to shush them, but they kept on screaming and provided enough lull for Mr. Solomon to interrupt the fight.

"All right. All right. That's enough of that."

"Shut your mouth, Solomon."

"Get them women outta here."

"Stick him, Saul, stick that cocksucker."

But Saul had a jagged cut over his eye and the blood pouring from it made it hard to see. It was difficult but not impossible for Mr. Solomon to pull him away. He left cursing Milkman, but his fervor was gone.

Milkman backed up against the counter, waiting to see if anybody else was going to jump him. When it looked as if no one was, and when the people were drifting outside to watch Saul scuffling and cursing at the men pulling him away, he slumped a little and wiped his face. When the entire store save for the owner was empty, Milkman hurled the broken bottle into a corner. It careened by the cooler and bounced off the wall before splintering on the floor. He walked outside, still panting, and looked around. Four older men still sat on the porch, as though nothing had happened. Blood was streaming down Milkman's face, but it had dried on his hand. He kicked at a white hen and sat down on the top step, wiping the blood with his handkerchief. Three young women with nothing in their hands stood in the road looking at him. Their eyes were wide but noncommittal. Children joined them, circling the women like birds. Nobody said anything. Even the four men on the porch were quiet. Nobody came toward him, offered him a cigarette or a glass of water. Only the children and the hens walked around. Under the hot sun, Milkman was frozen with anger. If he'd had a weapon, he would have slaughtered everybody in sight.

"You pretty good with a bottle. How you with a shotgun?" One of the older men had sidled up to him. The smile on his face was faint. It was as though now that the young men had had their chance, with unsatisfactory results, the older men would take over. Their style, of course, would be different. No name-calling toilet contest for them. No knives either, or hot breath and knotted neck muscles. They would test him, match and beat him, probably, on some other ground.

"Best shot there is," Milkman lied.

"That so?"

"Yeah, it's so."

"Some of us is going huntin later on. Care to join us?"

"That toothless motherfucker going too?"

"Saul? No."

"Cause I might have to knock the rest of them out."

The man laughed. "Sheriff took the others—with the butt of a gun."

"Yeah? Good."

"Well, you comin?"

"Sure I'm coming. Just get me the gun."

He laughed again. "Name's Omar."

"Macon Dead."

Omar blinked at the name, but didn't comment on it. He merely told him to come by King Walker's, a gas station about two miles up the road, right around sundown. "It's straight up yonder. Ain't no way in the world you can miss it."

"I won't miss it." Milkman stood up and walked to his car. He fumbled for the car keys, opened the door, and slid into the seat. He rolled down all four windows, found a towel in the back seat, and stretched out, using his jacket for a pillow and the towel as a bandage for his face. His feet stuck out the open door. Fuck 'em. Who were all these people roaming the world trying to kill him? His own father had tried while he was still in his mother's stomach. But he'd lived. And he had lived the last year dodging a woman who came every month to kill him, and he had lain just like this, with his arm over his eyes, wide open to whatever she had in her hand. He'd lived through that too. Then a witch had stepped out of his childhood nightmares to grab him, and he'd lived through that. Some bats had driven him out of a cave—and he'd lived through that. And at no time did he have a weapon. Now he walked into a store and asked if somebody could fix his car and a nigger pulled a knife on him. And he still wasn't dead. Now what did these black Neanderthals think they were going to do? Fuck 'em. My name's Macon; I'm already dead. He had thought this place, this Shalimar, was going to be home. His original home. His people came from here, his grandfather and his grandmother. All the way down South people had been nice to him, generous, helpful. In Danville they had made him the object of hero worship. In his own home town his name spelled dread and grudging respect. But here, in his "home," he was unknown, unloved, and damn near killed. These were some of the meanest unhung niggers in the world.

He slept, unmolested by everything and everybody except a dream in which he thought he saw Guitar looking down on him. When he woke he bought two cans of pineapple and a box of crackers from Mr. Solomon. He ate on the porch with the hens. The men were gone, and the sun was leaving. Only the children stayed to watch him eat. When he poured the last of the pineapple juice down his throat, one of the children stepped forward to ask, "Can we have your can, mister?" He held it out and they snatched the can and ran off to fashion some game out of it.

He started out for King Walker's. Even if he could have come up with a way to get out of the hunt, he wouldn't have taken it, in spite of the fact that he had never handled a firearm in his life. He had stopped evading things, sliding through, over, and around difficulties. Before he had taken risks only with Guitar. Now he took them alone. Not only had he let Hagar stab him; he had let the nightmare witch catch him and kiss him. To a man surviving that, anything else was a joke.

King Walker was nothing like his name suggested. He was a small man, bald, with a left cheek bulging with tobacco. Years ago he'd been a star pitcher in one of the black baseball leagues and the history of his career was nailed and pasted all over his shop. They had not lied when they said no garage or mechanic on duty was nearer than five miles. King Walker's station had obviously gone broke a long time ago. The pumps were dry; there wasn't even a can of oil in the place. Now it seemed to be used as a kind of clubhouse for the men and Walker lived in the back of the station. In addition to King Walker, who wasn't going, there was Omar and another man who had also been on the porch and who introduced himself as Luther Solomon—no relation to the grocery store Solomon. They were waiting for some others, who came soon after Milkman got there, driving an old Chevy. Omar introduced them as Calvin Breakstone and Small Boy.

Calvin seemed to be the most congenial of them, and followed the introductions with a command to King Walker to "get this city boy some shoes for his feet." King rummaged around, spitting tobacco, and came up with some mud-caked brogans. They outfitted Milkman completely, laughing all the while at his underwear, fingering his vest—Small Boy tried to get his wrestler's arms into Milkman's jacket—and wondering what had happened to his feet. Bits of skin still peeled from his toes because of the two days he had spent in wet shoes and socks. King Walker made him sprinkle Arm & Hammer soda on them before he put on the thick socks they gave him. When Milkman was dressed in World War II army fatigues with a knit cap on his head, they opened some Falstaff beer and began to talk about guns. At which point the revelry mixed with meanness abated and King Walker handed Milkman his Winchester .22.

"Ever use a twenty-two?"

"Not in a good while," Milkman said.

The five men piled into the Chevy and drove off into the lessening light. From what Milkman could tell, after fifteen minutes or so they were going up to high ground. As the car swerved through narrow roads, the conversation picked up again and they talked about other trips, game, kills, misses. Soon the only light came from the moon and it was getting cool enough for Milkman to be grateful for his knit cap. The car pulled ahead and around some sharp bends. In the rear-view mirror Milkman thought he glimpsed the headlights of another car and wondered briefly if they were being met by others. The sky was dark enough now for stars.

"Better make time, Calvin. Coon be done ate and gone on home."

Calvin pulled over and stopped the car.

"Let 'em rip," he said, and handed the car keys to Small Boy, who walked around to the back and unlocked the trunk. Three hounds leaped out, sniffing and wagging their tails. But they didn't make a sound.

"You brought Becky?" asked Luther. "Oh, man! We gonna get some coon tonight!"

The dogs' nervousness, their eagerness to hear the signal that would allow them to race off into the trees, made Milkman jittery. What was he supposed to do? Two feet in any direction from the headlights was black night.

Omar and Small Boy hauled equipment from the trunk: four lamps, one flashlight, rope, shells, and a pint bottle of liquor. When all four lamps were ablaze, they asked Milkman if he wanted to use a lamp or a flashlight. He hesitated, and Calvin said, "He can run with me. Give him the torch."

Milkman put it in his back pocket.

"Take that change out your pocket," said Calvin. "Makes too much noise."

Milkman did as he was told and took King's shotgun, a piece of rope, and a deep swig from the bottle they were passing around.

The dogs padded about, silent, panting, almost faint with excitement. But still they made no sound. Calvin and Omar both loaded their double-gauge shotguns with .22 shells in one barrel and buckshot in the other. Small Boy clapped his hands once, and the three hounds sped screaming into the night. The men didn't take off after them at once, as Milkman had supposed they would. Instead they stood quietly and listened for a while. Small Boy laughed lightly, shaking his head. "Becky's leadin. Let's go. Calvin, you and Macon go off to the right. We'll head this a way, and circle over by the gulch. Don't shoot no bears, now."

"Shoot him if I see him," said Calvin as he and Milkman moved away.

As they left the Chevy, the car that Milkman had noticed sped past them. Obviously, there were no others in the hunting party. Calvin was ahead, the burning lamp swinging low from his hand. Milkman flicked on his flashlight.

"Better save it," said Calvin. "You don't need it now."

They plodded on in a direction that may have been toward the screaming dogs, but Milkman couldn't tell.

"Any bears out here?" he asked in what he hoped was an interested but not anxious voice.

"Just us, and we got the guns." Calvin laughed and was suddenly swallowed up by the dark, only the low swinging lamp marking his path. Milkman watched the lamp until he realized that focusing on it kept him from seeing anything else. If he was to grow accustomed to the dark, he would have to look at what it was possible to see. A long moan sailed up through the trees somewhere to the left of where they were. It sounded like a woman's voice, sobbing, and mingling with the dogs' yelps and the men's shouts. A few minutes later, the distant screaming of the dogs and the calls of the three men stopped. There was only the soughing wind and his and Calvin's footsteps. It took Milkman a while to figure out how to pick up his feet and miss the roots and stones; to distinguish a tree from a shadow; to keep his head down and away from the branches that swept back from Calvin's hand into his face. They were walking upland. Every now and then Calvin stopped, threw his lamplight on a tree, and examined it closely from about three feet off the ground to up as far as his arm could go. Other times he lowered the lamp over the ground, and squatting down on his haunches, peered into the dirt. Each time he seemed to be whispering. Whatever he discovered he kept to himself and Milkman didn't ask him. All he wanted to do was keep up, be ready to shoot whatever the game was when it appeared, and look out for an attempt any of them might make on his life. Within an hour after arriving in Shalimar, a young man had tried to kill him in public. What these older men, under cover of night, were capable of he could only guess.

He heard the sound of the sobbing woman again and asked Calvin, "What the hell is that?"

"Echo," he said. "Ryna's Gulch is up ahead. It makes that sound when the wind hits a certain way."

"Sounds like a woman crying," said Milkman.

"Ryna. Folks say a woman name Ryna is cryin in there. That's how it got the name."

Calvin stopped, but so suddenly that Milkman, deep in thought about Ryna, bumped into him. "Hush!" Calvin closed his eyes and tilted his head into the wind. All Milkman could hear was the dogs again, yelping, but more rapidly, he thought, than before. Calvin whistled. A faint whistle came back to them.

"Son of a fuckin bitch!" Calvin's voice broke with agitation. "Bobcat! Come on, man!" He literally sprang away and Milkman did the same. Now they moved at double time, still on land that sloped upward. It was the longest trek Milkman had ever made in his life. Miles, he thought; we must be covering miles. And hours; it must be two hours now since he whistled. On they walked, and Calvin never broke his stride for anything except an occasional shout and an occasional pause to listen to the sound that came back.

The light was changing and Milkman was getting very tired. The distance between himself and Calvin's lamp was getting wider and wider. He was twenty years younger than Calvin, but found himself unable to keep up the pace. And he was getting clumsy—stepping over big stones rather than around them, dragging his feet and catching them in humped roots, and now that Calvin was not directly in front, he had to push the branches away from his face himself. The doubling down and under branches and pushing things out of his way were as exhausting as the walk. His breath was coming in shorter and shorter gasps and he wanted to sit down more than anything in the world. He believed they were circling now, for it seemed to him that this was the third time he had seen that double-humped rock in the distance. Should they be circling? he wondered. Then he thought he remembered hearing that certain prey circled when it was being stalked. Did bobcat? He didn't even know what a bobcat looked like.

At last he surrendered to his fatigue and made the mistake of sitting down instead of slowing down, for when he got up again, the rest had given his feet an opportunity to hurt him and the pain in his short leg was so great he began to limp and hobble. Soon it wasn't possible for him to walk longer than five minutes at a time without pausing to lean against a sweet gum tree. Calvin was a pinpoint of light bobbing ahead in and out of the trees. Finally Milkman could take no more; he had to rest. At the next tree he sank down to the ground and put his head back on its bark. Let them laugh if they wanted to; he would not move until his heart left from under his chin and went back down into his chest where it belonged. He spread his legs, pulled the flashlight out of his hip pocket, and put his Winchester down near his right leg. At rest now, he could feel the blood pulsing in his temple and the cut on his face stinging in the night wind from the leaf juice and tree sap the branches had smeared on it.

When he was breathing almost normally, he began to wonder what he was doing sitting in the middle of a woods in Blue Ridge country. He had come here to find traces of Pilate's journey, to find relatives she might have visited, to find anything he could that would either lead him to the gold or convince him that it no longer existed. How had he got himself involved in a hunt, involved in a knife-and-broken-bottle fight in the first place? Ignorance, he thought, and vanity. He hadn't been alert early enough, hadn't seen the signs jutting out everywhere around him. Maybe this was a mean bunch of black folk, but he should have guessed it, sensed it, and part of the reason he hadn't was the easy, good treatment he had received elsewhere. Or had he? Maybe the glow of hero worship (twice removed) that had bathed him in Danville had also blinded him. Perhaps the eyes of the men in Roanoke, Petersburg, Newport News, had not been bright with welcome and admiration. Maybe they were just curious or amused. He hadn't stayed in any place long enough to find out. A meal here, gas there–the one real contact was the buying of the car, and the seller needing a buyer would naturally be friendly under those circumstances. The same thing held when he'd had to have those elaborate repairs. What kind of savages were these people? Suspicious. Hot-tempered. Eager to find fault and despise any outsider. Touchy. Devious, jealous, traitorous, and evil. He had done nothing to deserve their contempt. Nothing to deserve the explosive hostility that engulfed him when he said he might have to buy a car. Why didn't they respond the way the man in Roanoke did when he bought the car? Because in Roanoke he did not have a car. Here he had one and wanted another, and perhaps it was that that upset them. Furthermore, he hadn't even suggested that he would trade the old one in. He had hinted that he would abandon the "broken" one and just get another. But so what? What business was it of theirs what he did with his money? He didn't deserve . . .

It sounded old. *Deserve*. Old and tired and beaten to death. Deserve. Now it seemed to him that he was always saying or thinking that he didn't deserve some bad luck, or some bad treatment from others. He'd told Guitar that he didn't "deserve" his family's dependence, hatred, or whatever. That he didn't even "deserve" to hear all the misery and mutual accusations his parents unloaded on him. Nor did he "deserve" Hagar's vengeance. But why shouldn't his parents tell him their personal problems? If not him, then who? And if a stranger could try to kill him, surely Hagar, who knew him and whom he'd thrown away like a wad of chewing gum after the flavor was gone—she had a right to try to kill him too.

Apparently he thought he deserved only to be loved—from a distance, though—and given what he wanted. And in return he would be . . . what? Pleasant? Generous? Maybe all he was really saying was: I am not responsible for your pain; share your happiness with me but not your unhappiness.

They were troublesome thoughts, but they wouldn't go away. Under the moon, on the ground, alone, with not even the sound of baying dogs to remind him that he was with other people, his self—the cocoon that was "personality"—gave way. He could barely see his own hand, and couldn't see his feet. He was only his breath, coming slower now, and his thoughts. The rest of him had disappeared. So the thoughts came, unobstructed by other people, by things, even by the sight of himself. There was nothing here to help him—not his money, his car, his father's reputation, his suit, or his shoes. In fact they hampered him. Except for his broken watch, and his wallet with about two hundred dollars, all he had started out with on his journey was gone: his suitcase with the Scotch, the shirts, and the space for bags of gold; his snap-brim hat, his tie, his shirt, his three-piece suit, his socks, and his shoes. His watch and his two hundred dollars would be of no help out here, where all a man had was what he was born with, or had learned to use. And endurance. Eyes, ears, nose, taste, touch—and some other sense that he knew he did not have: an ability to separate out, of all the things there were to sense, the one that life itself might depend on. What did Calvin see on the bark? On the ground? What was he saying? What did he hear that made him know something unexpected had happened some two miles—perhaps more—away, and that that something was a different kind of prey, a bobcat? He could still hear them—the way they had sounded the last few hours. Signaling one another. What were they saying? "Wait up?" "Over here?" Little by little it fell into place. The dogs, the men—none was just hollering, just signaling location or pace. The men and the dogs were talking to each other. In distinctive voices they were saying distinctive, complicated things. That long *yah* sound was followed by a specific kind of howl from one of the dogs. The low *howm howm* that sounded like a string bass imitating a bassoon meant something the dogs understood and executed. And the dogs spoke to the men: single-shot barks—evenly spaced and widely spaced—one every three or four minutes, that might go on for twenty minutes. A sort of radar that indicated to the men where they were and what they saw and what they wanted to do about it. And the men agreed or told them to change direction or to come back. All those shrieks, those rapid tumbling barks, the long sustained yells, the tuba sounds, the drumbeat sounds, the low liquid *howm howm*, the reedy whistles, the thin *eeeee*'s of a cornet, the *unh unh unh* bass chords. It was all language. An extension of the click people made in their cheeks back home when they wanted a dog to follow them. No, it was not language; it was what there was before language. Before things were written down. Language in the time when men and animals did talk to one another, when a man could sit down with an ape and the two converse; when a tiger and a man could share the same tree, and each understood the other; when men ran *with* wolves, not from or after them. And he was hearing it in the Blue Ridge Mountains under a sweet gum tree. And if they could talk to animals, and the animals could talk to them, what didn't they know about human beings? Or the earth itself, for that matter. It was more than tracks Calvin was looking for—he whispered to the trees, whispered to the ground, touched them, as a blind man caresses a page of Braille, pulling meaning through his fingers.

Milkman rubbed the back of his head against the bark. This was what Guitar had missed about the South—the woods, hunters, killing. But something had maimed him, scarred him like Reverend Cooper's knot, like Saul's missing teeth, and like his own father. He felt a sudden rush of affection for them all, and out there under the sweet gum tree, within the sound of men tracking a bobcat, he thought he understood Guitar now. Really understood him.

Down either side of his thighs he felt the sweet gum's surface roots cradling him like the rough but maternal hands of a grandfather. Feeling both tense and relaxed, he sank his fingers into the grass. He tried to listen with his fingertips, to hear what, if anything, the earth had to say, and it told him quickly that someone was standing behind him and he had just enough time to raise one hand to his neck and catch the wire that fastened around his throat. It cut like a razor into his fingers, tore into the skin so deeply he had to let go. The wire pressed into his neck then and took his breath. He thought he heard himself gurgling and saw a burst of many-colored lights dancing before his eyes. When the music followed the colored lights, he knew he had just drawn the last sweet air left for him in the world. Exactly the way he'd heard it would be, his life flashed before him, but it consisted of only one image: Hagar bending over him in perfect love, in the most intimate sexual gesture imaginable. In the midst of that picture he heard the voice of the someone holding the wire say, "Your Day has come," and it filled him with such sadness to be dying, leaving this world at the fingertips of his friend, that he relaxed and in the instant it took to surrender to the overwhelming melancholy he felt the cords of his struggling neck muscles relax too and there was a piece of a second in which the wire left him room enough to gasp, to take another breath. But it was a living breath this time, not a dying one. Hagar, the lights, the music, disappeared, and Milkman grabbed the Winchester at his side, cocked it, and pulled the trigger, shooting into the trees in front of him. The blast startled Guitar, and the wire slipped again. Guitar pulled it back, but Milkman knew his friend would need both hands to keep it that way. He turned the shotgun backward as far as he could and managed awkwardly, to pull the trigger again, hitting only branches and dirt. He was wondering if there was another blast in the gun when he heard right up close the wild, wonderful sound of three baying dogs who he knew had treed a bobcat. The wire dropped and he heard Guitar breaking into a fast run through the trees. Milkman stood up and grabbed his flashlight, pointing it in the direction of the sound of running feet. He saw nothing but branches resettling themselves. Rubbing his neck, he moved toward the sound of the dogs. Guitar did not have a gun, otherwise he would have used it, so Milkman felt secure heading for the dogs with the gun in his hand even though it had no more shot. He didn't miss; his sense of direction was accurate and he came upon Calvin, Small Boy, Luther, and Omar crouching on the ground a few feet away from the dogs and the glistening night eyes of a bobcat in a tree.

The dogs were trying their best to get up into the tree, and the men were considering whether to shoot the bobcat down, shoot a limb and make him jump down and fight the dogs, or what. They decided to try and kill the cat where he lay. Omar stood up and took his lamp over to the left. The cat crept a little ways out, following the light. Then Small Boy took aim and put a bullet just under the left foreleg and the bobcat dropped through the branches into the jaws of Becky and her companions.

There was a lot of life in the cat; he fought well until Calvin hollered the dogs away and shot it again, and once more, and then it was still.

They held the lamps over the carcass and groaned with pleasure at the size, the ferocity, the stillness of it. All four got down on their knees, pulling rope and knives, cutting a branch the width of a wrist, tying it and binding it for the long walk back.

They were so pleased with themselves it was some time before anybody remembered to ask Milkman what he was shooting at back there. Milkman hoisted the stake he was carrying a little higher and said, "I dropped the gun. I tripped and it went off. Then when I picked it up it went off again."

They burst into laughter. "Tripped? What'd you have the safety off for? Was you scared?"

"Scared to death," said Milkman. "Scared to death."

They hooted and laughed all the way back to the car, teasing Milkman, egging him on to tell more about how scared he was. And he told them. Laughing too, hard, loud, and long. Really laughing, and he found himself exhilarated by simply walking the earth. Walking it like he belonged on it; like his legs were stalks, tree trunks, a part of his body that extended down down down into the rock and soil, and were comfortable there—on the earth and on the place where he walked. And he did not limp.

They met dawn in King Walker's gas station for a rehash of the night they had spent. Milkman was the butt of their humor, but it was good-humored humor, quite unlike the laughter the trip had begun with. "Lucky to be alive. Cat wasn't the problem; this here nigger was the problem. Blastin away at us while we got a mean cat gettin ready to chew us and the dogs up both. Shootin all through the woods. Could have blown his own head off. Don't you city boys know how to handle yourself?"

"You country niggers got it all over us," Milkman answered.

Omar and Small Boy slapped him on the shoulders. Calvin hollered to Luther, "Go get Vernell. Tell her to get breakfast ready. Soon's we skin this cat, we comin in there with a appetite and she better be ready to meet it!"

Milkman went with them to the back of the station, where, on a small cemented area covered by a corrugated tin roof, the dead bobcat lay. Milkman's neck had swollen so it was difficult for him to lower his chin without pain.

Omar sliced through the rope that bound the bobcat's feet. He and Calvin turned it over on its back. The legs fell open. Such thin delicate ankles.

"Everybody wants a black man's life."

Calvin held the forefeet open and up while Omar pierced the curling hair at the point where the sternum lay. Then he sliced all the way down to the genitals. His knife pointed upward for a cleaner, neater incision.

"Not his dead life; I mean his living life."

When he reached the genitals he cut them off, but left the scrotum intact.

"*It's the condition our condition is in.*"

Omar cut around the legs and the neck. Then he pulled the hide off.

"*What good is a man's life if he can't even choose what to die for?*"

The transparent underskin tore like gossamer under his fingers.

"*Everybody wants the life of a black man.*"

Now Small Boy knelt down and slit the flesh from the scrotum to the jaw.

"*Fair is one more thing I've given up.*"

Luther came back and, while the others rested, carved out the rectal tube with the deft motions of a man coring an apple.

"*I hope I never have to ask myself that question.*"

Luther reached into the paunch and lifted the entrails. He dug under the rib cage to the diaphragm and carefully cut around it until it was free.

"*It* is *about love. What else but love? Can't I love what I criticize?*"

Then he grabbed the windpipe and the gullet, eased them back, and severed them with one stroke of his little knife.

"*It* is *about love. What else?*"

They turned to Milkman. "You want the heart?" they asked him. Quickly, before any thought could paralyze him, Milkman plunged both hands into the rib cage. "Don't get the lungs, now. Get the heart."

"*What else?*"

He found it and pulled. The heart fell away from the chest as easily as yolk slips out of its shell.

"*What else? What else? What else?*"

Now Luther went back into the stomach cavity and yanked the entrails out altogether. They sucked up like a vacuum through the hole that was made at the rectum. He slipped the entrails into a paper bag while the others began cleaning up, hosing down, salting, packing, straightening, and then they turned the cat over to let the blood drain down on its own hide.

"What are you going to do with it?" asked Milkman.

"Eat him!"

A peacock soared away and lit on the hood of a blue Buick.

Milkman looked at the bobcat's head. The tongue lay in its mouth as harmless as a sandwich. Only the eyes held the menace of the night.

Hungry as he was, he couldn't eat much of Vernell's breakfast, so he pushed the scrambled eggs, hominy, fried apples around in the plate, gulped coffee and talked a lot. And, somehow, he had to get around to the purpose of his visit to Shalimar.

"You know, my grandfather came from somewhere near here. My grandmother too."

"Did? From around here? What's their name?"

"I don't know her maiden name, but her first name was Sing. Any of you ever know anybody with a name like that?"

They shook their heads. "Sing? No. Never heard of nobody name that."

"I had an aunt live down this way too. Name of Pilate. Pilate Dead. Ever hear of her?"

"Ha! Sound like a newspaper headline: Pilot Dead. She do any flying?"

"No. *P-i-l-a-t-e*, Pilate."

"*P-i-l-a-t-e*. That spell *Pie-late*," Small Boy said.

"Naw, nigger. Not no *Pie-late*. Pilate like in the Bible, dummy."

"He don't read the Bible."

"He don't read nothin."

"He can't read nothin."

They teased Small Boy until Vernell interrupted them. "You all hush. You say Sing?" she asked Milkman.

"Yeah. Sing."

"I believe that was the name of a girl my gran used to play with. I remember the name cause it sounded so pretty. Gran used to talk about her all the time. Seem like her folks didn't like her to play with the colored children from over this way, so her and my gran used to sneak off and go fishin and berry-pickin. You know what I mean? She'd have to meet her in secret." Vernell eyed Milkman carefully. "This Sing girl was light-skinned, with straight black hair."

"That's her!" Milkman said. "She was mixed or Indian, one."

Vernell nodded. "Indian. One of old Heddy's children. Heddy was all right, but she didn't like her girl playin with coloreds. She was a Byrd."

"A what?"

"A Byrd. Belonged to the Byrd family over by the ridge. Near Solomon's Leap."

"Oh, yeah?" said one of the men. "One of Susan Byrd's people?"

"That's right. One of them. They never was too crazy 'bout colored folks. Susan either."

"Do they still live there?" asked Milkman.

"Susan do. Right behind the ridge. Only house back in there with a brick front. She by herself now. All the others moved out so they could pass."

"Can I walk it?" he asked.

"Most folks could, I reckon," said Omar. "But after last night I don't recommend it for you." He laughed.

"Can you drive a car through?"

"Part of the way you can. But the road is narrow and messy back up in there," said Vernell. "Horse, maybe, but not no car."

"I'll make it. Might take me a week, but I'll make it," said Milkman.

"Just don't carry no guns"—Calvin cooled his coffee in his saucer—"and you'll be all right." They all laughed again.

Milkman thought about that. Guitar was out there someplace, and since he seemed to know everything Milkman was doing or getting ready to do, he'd also know he was going out to some ridge. He touched his swollen neck. He didn't want to go anywhere alone without a gun.

"You ought to have a rest before you go trottin off anywhere," Omar said, looking at him. "There's a nice lady up the road a ways. She'd be proud to take you in." The look in his eyes was unmistakable. "Pretty woman too. Real pretty." Vernell grunted and Milkman smiled. Hope she's got a gun, he thought.

She didn't, but she had indoor plumbing and her smile was just like her name, Sweet, as she nodded her head to Milkman's query about whether he could take a bath. The tub was the newest feature in the tiny shotgun house and Milkman sank gratefully into the steaming water. Sweet brought him soap and a boar's-bristle brush and knelt to bathe him. What she did for his sore feet, his cut face, his back, his neck, his thighs, and the palms of his hands was so delicious he couldn't imagine that the lovemaking to follow would be anything but anticlimactic. If this bath and this woman, he thought, are all that come out of this trip, I will rest easy and do my duty to God, country, and the Brotherhood of Elks for the rest of my life. I will walk hot coals with a quart of kerosene in my hand for this. I will walk every railroad tie from here to Cheyenne and back for this. But when the lovemaking came, he decided he would crawl.

Afterward he offered to bathe her. She said he couldn't because the tank was small and there wasn't enough water for another hot bath.

"Then let me give you a cool one," he said. He soaped and rubbed her until her skin squeaked and glistened like onyx. She put salve on his face. He washed her hair. She sprinkled talcum on his feet. He straddled her behind and massaged her back. She put witch hazel on his swollen neck. He made up the bed. She gave him gumbo to eat. He washed the dishes. She washed his clothes and hung them out to dry. He scoured her tub. She ironed his shirt and pants. He gave her fifty dollars. She kissed his mouth. He touched her face. She said please come back. He said I'll see you tonight.

Chapter 12

At four o'clock he knocked on the door of the only house back of the ridge with a brick front. Fresh and shining in the army fatigues Sweet had washed and pressed, he had tramped along feeling ready for anything. But he didn't think Guitar would jump him in the daytime on a winding path (which they called a road) that cut through hilly land that was nevertheless tilled and had a smattering of houses and people. If he did confront him (with anything other than a gun) Milkman was sure he could take him, but it would be best to get back before nightfall. He didn't know what was on Guitar's mind, but he knew it had something to do with the gold. If he knows I'm here and where I have been and what I did in each place, then he must know that I'm trying to get it, doing just what I said I would do. Why would he try to kill me before I got it or even found out what happened to it? Most of it was a total mystery to him, but the part that was clear was enough to keep him alert and jittery all the way.

The Byrd house sat on a neat lawn separated by a white picket fence from the field grass on either side of the property. A child's swing dangled from a cedar tree; four little steps painted blue led up to the porch, and from the window, between fluttering curtains, came the smell of gingerbread baking.

A woman who looked to be about his mother's age answered the door.

"Miss Byrd?" Milkman asked her.

"Yes?"

"How are you? My name is, uh, Macon, and I'm visiting here for a few days. I'm from Michigan and I think some of my people lived here a long time ago. I was hoping you'd be able to help me."

"Help you what?" She sounded arch and Milkman had the distinct impression that this lady did not like the color of his skin.

"Find them. I mean find out about them. We're all split up, my family, and some folks in town thought you might know some of them."

"Who's that, Susan?" Another woman's voice came from behind her.

"Somebody to see *me*, Grace."

"Well, why don't you ask him in? Don't make him state his business on the steps."

Miss Byrd sighed. "Please come in, Mr. Macon."

Milkman followed her into a pleasant living room full up with sunshine. "Excuse me," she said. "I didn't mean to be rude. Please have a seat." She motioned to a gray velvet wing-back chair. A woman in a two-piece print dress came into the room, clutching a paper napkin in her hand and chewing on something.

"Who'd you say?" She addressed her question to Miss Byrd, but ran inquisitive eyes over Milkman.

Miss Byrd held out a hand. "This is a friend of mine—Miss Long. Grace Long—Mr. . . ."

"How do you do?" Grace held out her hand to him.

"Fine, thank you."

"Mr. Macon, is it?"

"Yes."

"Susan, perhaps Mr. Macon would like some refreshment." Miss Long smiled and sat on the sofa facing the gray chair.

"Well, he just stepped foot in the door, Grace. Give me time." Miss Byrd turned to Milkman. "Would you like a cup of coffee or some tea?"

"Sure. Thanks."

"Which one?"

"Coffee's all right."

"You've got butter cookies, Susan. Give him some of those butter cookies."

Miss Byrd gave her friend a tired frown. "I'll just be a minute," she said to Milkman, and left the room.

"Yes, well. Did I hear you say you were visiting in these parts? We don't see too many visitors." Grace crossed her ankles. Like Susan Byrd, she wore black laced shoes and cotton stockings. As she made herself comfortable, she inched her dress up a little.

"Yes, visiting."

"You in the service?"

"Ma'am? Oh, no. I was hunting last night. Some friends lent me these." He smoothed the seam Sweet had made in the fatigues.

"Hunting? Oh, Lord, don't tell me you're one of them. I can't stand those hunting people. They make me sick, always prowling round other people's property. Day and night they're shooting up the world. I tell my students—I'm a schoolteacher, you know, I teach over at the normal school. Have you seen it yet?"

"No, not yet."

"Well, there's nothing to see, really. Just a school, like any other. But you're welcome to stop by. We'd be pleased to have you. Where you from again?"

"Michigan."

"I thought so. Susan!" She turned around. "He's from up North." Then back to Milkman: "Where are you staying?"

"Well, nowhere yet. I just met a few people in town and . . ."

Susan Byrd came in with a tray of coffee cups and a plate of wide pale cookies.

"He's from Michigan," said Grace.

"I heard him. How do you take your coffee?"

"Black."

"Black? No cream or sugar at all?" asked Grace. "Wish I could do that; maybe I could get back into a twelve. But it's never going to happen now." She pressed one hand on her hip and smiled at Milkman.

"What did you want to see me about?" Susan Byrd placed a mild but clear stress on the word "me."

"I'm trying to locate anybody who might have known my grandmother. Her name was Sing."

Grace clapped her hands to her mouth and gave a little squeal. "Relatives! You all are relatives!" Milkman put his cup down. "Well, I'll be!" Grace's eyes were lit and dancing.

"You've come to the right place," said Susan, "but I doubt if I can help you any."

"What are you talking about, Susan? Your mother was named Sing, wasn't she?"

"No, she wasn't, Grace, and if you let me finish a sentence you might learn something you don't know too."

"I thought you said—"

"My mother's name was Mary. *M-a-r-y*, Mary."

"Well, excuse *me*."

Susan turned to Milkman. "My father, Crowell Byrd, had a sister named Sing."

"That must be her! My grandmother! Sing. Did she marry a man named—"

"I knew there was somebody in your family named Sing!"

"She didn't marry anybody that I know of." Susan interrupted them both.

"Oh, this is really something. A stranger walks right into your house and he's your own . . . what? Cousin? I hate to say it, but this is a small world. Isn't it? You have got to visit my class, Mr. Macon."

Milkman joined Susan Byrd in ignoring Grace Long. "Where did she live?" he asked her.

"The last time my father saw her, she was on a wagon headed for Massachusetts to a private school up there. A Quaker school."

"Your people Quakers? You never told me that. See, Mr. Macon, what your friends hide from you? I bet she'd hide you too."

"And she never married?" Milkman couldn't take the time to acknowledge Grace's attentions.

"Not anybody we heard of. After she went to that Quaker school they lost track of her. I believe they tried to locate her, mostly because my grandmother—her name was Heddy—she was so torn up about it. I always believed the same thing my father believed: that she didn't want to be found after she left that school."

"You know darn well she didn't," said Grace. "She probably started passing like the rest of 'em, that's what." She leaned toward Milkman. "There used to be a lot of that. A lot of it. Not so much nowadays, but there used to be a lot of 'em did it—if they could." She shot a glance at Susan. "Like your cousins, Susan. They're passing now. Lilah, John. I know John is, and he knows I know he is."

"Everybody knows that, Grace."

"Mr. Macon doesn't know it. I saw John on the street in Mayville—"

"Mr. Macon doesn't need to know it. He's not even interested."

"How do you know he's not?"

"Because he said the woman he's looking for was his grandmother, and if she's his grandmother she'd be too dark to . . ." Susan Byrd hesitated. "Well, too dark to pass. Wouldn't she?" She flushed a little.

Milkman ignored the question. "And you say she lived in Massachusetts, right?"

"Yes. Boston."

"I see." It looked like a dead end, so he decided to follow another line. "Did you ever know or hear of a woman around here named Pilate?"

"Pilate. No. Never. Have you, Grace?"

Grace shook her head. "No, and I've been here most of my life."

"I've been here *all* of mine," said Susan. "Both my parents were born here and so was I. Never been farther away than St. Phillips County. I have people in South Carolina, but I've never even been to visit them."

"That's because they're passing too. Just like John. You couldn't visit them if you wanted to." Grace leaned over the plate of cookies and selected one.

"They're not the only family I have left." Susan was indignant.

"I hope not. It's a sad thing, Mr. Macon, when you're left without any people to claim you. I keep up with my family. I'm not married, you know, not yet anyway, but my family is *very* close." She gave him a meaningful look. Milkman turned his wrist and looked down to see what time it was.

"Oh, look at that." Grace pointed to his hand. "What a good-looking watch. May I see it?" Milkman stood up to hand it to her and remained standing. "Look, Susan, it doesn't have a single number on it. Just dots. Now, how can anybody figure out what time it is from those dots?"

Susan rose too. "You ever been down here before, Mr. Macon?"

"No. This is my first visit."

"Well, I hope it won't be your last. How long will you be here?"

"Oh, I think I'll get on back tonight or tomorrow at the latest." He looked out the window. The sun was dropping.

"That soon?" asked Grace. "Why don't you give him something to take with him, Susan? Would you like to take some butter cookies with you, Mr. Macon?"

"No, thank you."

"You'll be happy to have them later." The woman was wearing him down. He smiled, though, and said, "If you like."

"I'll fix a little package for you. Okay, Susan?" She fled from the room.

Susan managed a small smile. "Wish you could stay and visit with us awhile." Her words were as mechanical as her smile.

"So do I," he said, "but, well, maybe I'll be back."

"That'd be nice. Sorry I couldn't be of any help to you."

"You have been."

"Have I?"

"Oh, sure. You have to know what's wrong before you can find what's right."

She smiled a genuine smile then. "It's important to you, is it, to find your people?"

Milkman thought about it. "No. Not really. I was just passing through, and it was just—just an idea. It's not important."

Grace returned with a little parcel wrapped in white paper napkins. "Here you are," she said. "You'll appreciate this later on."

"Thank you. Thank you both."

"Nice meeting you."

"And you."

He left the house feeling tired and off center. I'll spend one more night here and then leave, he thought. The car should be fixed by now. There's nothing here to know, no gold or any traces of it. Pilate lived in Virginia, but not in this part of the state. Nobody at all has heard of her. And the Sing that lived here went to Boston, not Danville, Pennsylvania, and passed for white. His grandmother would have been "too dark to pass." She had actually blushed. As though she'd discovered something shameful about him. He was both angry and amused and wondered what Omar and Sweet and Vernell thought of Miss Susan Byrd.

He was curious about these people. He didn't feel close to

them, but he did feel connected, as though there was some cord or pulse or information they shared. Back home he had never felt that way, as though he belonged to anyplace or anybody. He'd always considered himself the outsider in his family, only vaguely involved with his friends, and except for Guitar, there was no one whose opinion of himself he cared about. Once, long ago, he had cared what Pilate and Hagar thought of him, but having conquered Hagar and having disregarded Pilate enough to steal from her, all that was gone. But there was something he felt now—here in Shalimar, and earlier in Danville—that reminded him of how he used to feel in Pilate's house. Sitting in Susan Byrd's living room, lying with Sweet, eating with those men at Vernell's table, he didn't have to get over, to turn on, or up, or even out.

And there was something more. It wasn't true what he'd said to Susan Byrd: that it wasn't important to find his people. Ever since Danville, his interest in his own people, not just the ones he met, had been growing. Macon Dead, also known as Jake somebody. Sing. Who were they, and what were they like? The man who sat for five nights on a fence with a gun, waiting. Who named his baby girl Pilate, who tore a farm out of a wilderness. The man who ate pecans on a wagon going North. Did he have brothers or sisters whom he left behind? Who was his mother, his father? And his wife. Was she the Boston Sing? If so, what was she doing on a wagon? Why would she go off to a northern private school on a wagon? Not a carriage or a train, but a wagon—full of ex-slaves. Maybe she never got to Boston. Maybe she didn't pass. She could have changed her mind about school and run off with the boy she ate pecans with. And whoever she was, why did she want her husband to keep that awful name? To wipe out the past? What past? Slavery? She was never a slave. *His* slave past? And why didn't his own father, and Pilate, know any of their own relatives? Wasn't there any family to notify when the father died? Macon didn't ever try to get to Virginia. Pilate headed straight for it.

Milkman opened the parcel Grace had fixed for him and took

out a cookie. A little piece of paper fluttered to the ground. He picked it up and read: "Grace Long 40 Route 2 three houses down from the Normal School." He smiled. That's why it took her so long to wrap up four cookies. He bit into one of them and sauntered along, crumpling the napkins and Grace's invitation into a wad. The questions about his family still knocked around in his head like billiard balls. If his grandfather, this Jake, was born in the same place his wife was, in Shalimar, why did he tell the Yankee he was born in Macon, thereby providing him with the raw material for the misnaming? And if he and his wife were born in the same place, why did Pilate and his father and Circe all say they "met" on that wagon? And why did the ghost tell Pilate to sing? Milkman chuckled to himself. That wasn't what he was telling her at all; maybe the ghost was just repeating his wife's name, Sing, and Pilate didn't know it because she never knew her mother's name. After she died Macon Dead wouldn't let anybody say it aloud. That was funny. He wouldn't speak it after she died, and after he died that's all he ever said—her name.

Jesus! Here he was walking around in the middle of the twentieth century trying to explain what a ghost had done. But why not? he thought. One fact was certain: Pilate did not have a navel. Since that was true, anything could be, and why not ghosts as well?

He was near the road leading to the town now, and it was getting dark. He lifted his wrist to look at his watch and remembered that Grace had not given it back to him. "Damn," he murmured aloud. "I'm losing everything." He stood still, trying to make up his mind whether to go back for it now or later. If he went now, he'd be forced to return in deep darkness. Totally defenseless before a hit from Guitar. But it would be a real bother to have to come all the way back here—where no car could make it—tomorrow when he was going to leave. But Guitar might be—

"I can't let him direct and determine what I do, where I go or when. If I do that now I'll do it all my life and he'll run me off the earth."

He didn't know what to do, but decided finally that a watch was not worth worrying about. All it could do was tell him the time of day and he really wasn't interested. Wiping cookie crumbs from his mustache, he turned into the main road, and there, outlined in cobalt blue, stood Guitar. Leaned, rather, against a persimmon tree. Milkman stopped, surprised at the calm, steady beat of his heart—the complete absence of fear. But then, Guitar was cleaning his fingernails with a harmless match stick. Any weapon he had would have to be hidden in his denim jacket or pants.

They looked at each other for a minute. No, less. Just long enough for the heart of each man to adjust its throb to the downbeat of the other. Guitar spoke first.

"My man."

Milkman ignored the greeting. "Why, Guitar? Just tell me why."

"You took the gold."

"What gold? There wasn't any gold."

"You took the gold."

"The cave was empty, man. I got down on my stomach and looked in that pit. I put my hands—"

"You took the gold."

"You're crazy, Guitar."

"Angry. Never crazy."

"There wasn't any gold!" Milkman tried hard not to shout.

"I saw you, motherfucker."

"Saw me what?"

"Take the gold."

"Where?"

"In Danville."

"You saw me with gold in Danville?"

"I saw you with gold in Danville."

"You've got to be kidding. What was I doing with it?"

"Shipping it."

"Shipping it?"

"Yeah. Why the game, man? You just greedy, like your old

man? Or what?" Guitar's eyes rested on the last butter cookie in Milkman's hand. He frowned and began to breathe through his lips.

"Guitar, I didn't ship no gold. There wasn't any gold to ship. You couldn't have seen me."

"I saw you, baby. I was in the station."

"What fuckin station?"

"The freight station in Danville."

Milkman remembered then, going to look for Reverend Cooper, looking all over for him. Then going into the station house to see if he'd gone, and there helping a man lift a huge crate onto the weighing platform. He started to laugh. "Oh, shit. Guitar, that wasn't no gold. I was just helping that man lift a crate. He asked me to help him. Help him lift a big old crate. I did and then I split."

Guitar looked at the cookie again, then back into Milkman's eyes. Nothing changed in his face. Milkman knew it sounded lame. It was the truth, but it sounded like a lie. A weak lie too. He also knew that in all his life, Guitar had never seen Milkman give anybody a hand, especially a stranger; he also knew that they'd even discussed it, starting with Milkman's not coming to his mother's rescue in a dream he had. Guitar had accused him of selfishness and indifference; told him he wasn't serious, and didn't have any fellow feeling—none whatsoever. Now he was standing there saying that he willingly, spontaneously, had helped an old white man lift a huge, heavy crate. But it was true. It was true. And he'd prove it.

"Guitar, why am I here? If I was shipping gold back home, why am I here dressed like this? Would I be roaming around in the country like a fool with a crate of gold off somewhere? Would I? What the fuck would I do that for and then come here?"

"Maybe you shipped the gold *here*, you jive-ass."

"What the fuck are you talking about?"

"I looked! I saw it! You hear me? I drove down there, followed you there, because I had a funny feeling that you were pulling a fast one. I wasn't sure, but I felt it. If I was wrong, I'd help you get it. But I wasn't wrong. I got into Danville that afternoon. I drove right past the freight depot and there you were in your little beige suit. I parked and followed you into the station. When I got there I saw you shipping it. Giving it to the man. I waited until you left, and I went back in and asked the cracker if my friend"—he slurred the word—"had shipped a crate to Michigan. The man said no. Just one crate on the load, he said. Just one crate. And when I asked him where it was going, all he could remember was Virginia." Guitar smiled. "The bus you caught wasn't headed for Michigan. It was headed for Virginia. And here you are."

Milkman felt whipped. There was nothing to do but let it play.

"Was my name on the crate?"

"I didn't look."

"Would I send a crate of gold to Virginia—*gold*, man."

"You might. You did."

"Is that why you tried to kill me?"

"Yes."

"Because I ripped you off?"

"Because you ripped *us* off! You are fuckin with our work!"

"You're wrong. Dead wrong."

"The 'dead' part is you."

Milkman looked down at the cookie in his hand. It looked foolish and he started to throw it away, but changed his mind. "So my Day has come?"

"Your Day has come, but on *my* schedule. And believe it: I will run you as long as there is ground. Your name is Macon, but you ain't dead yet."

"Tell me something. When you saw me in the station, with the crate, why did you back off and hide? Why didn't you just walk up to me? It could have been settled there."

"I told you. I had this funny funny feeling."

"That I was going to cut you out?"

"Cut *us* out. Yes."

"And you believe I did?"

"Yes."

"Back there in the woods you were angry."

"Yes."

"Now you're going to wait till the gold comes."

"Yes."

"And I pick it up."

"You won't be able to pick it up."

"Do me a favor. When it gets here. Check it first to see if there's gold in it."

"First?"

"Or last. But before you haul it all the way back home."

"Don't worry yourself about it."

"One more thing. Why the message? Why'd you warn me with a message at the store?"

"You're my friend. It's the least I could do for a friend."

"My man. I want to thank you."

"You're welcome, baby."

Milkman slipped into Sweet's bed and slept the night in her perfect arms. It was a warm dreamy sleep all about flying, about sailing high over the earth. But not with arms stretched out like airplane wings, nor shot forward like Superman in a horizontal dive, but floating, cruising, in the relaxed position of a man lying on a couch reading a newspaper. Part of his flight was over the dark sea, but it didn't frighten him because he knew he could not fall. He was alone in the sky, but somebody was applauding him, watching him and applauding. He couldn't see who it was.

When he awoke the next morning and set about seeing to the repair of his car, he couldn't shake the dream, and didn't really want to. In Solomon's store he found Omar and Solomon shaking sacks of okra into peck baskets and he still felt the sense of lightness and power that flying had given him.

"Got a belt for your car," said Omar. "Ain't new, but it ought to fit."

"Hey, that's good. Thanks, Omar."

"You leavin us right away?"

"Yeah, I have to get on back."

"You see that Byrd woman all right?"

"Yeah, I saw her."

"She help you any?" Omar wiped the okra fuzz from his hands onto his trousers.

"No. Not much."

"Well, King Walker say he be down this morning and put the belt on. You probably ought to get a good checkup on that car once you get on the road."

"I plan to."

"Sweet give you any breakfast?" asked Solomon.

"She tried, but I wanted to get over here early to see about the car."

"What about a cup a coffee; there's a full pot in back."

"No, thanks. I think I'll walk around a little till he comes."

It was six-thirty in the morning and the town was bustling as though it were high noon. Life and business began early in the South so the coolest part of the day could be taken advantage of. People had already eaten, women had already washed clothes and were spreading them on bushes, and in a few days, when the school in the next town opened, children at this hour would already be walking, running over the roads and fields to class. Now they were sauntering about, doing chores, teasing cats, throwing bread to stray chickens, and some of them were playing their endless round games. Milkman could hear them singing and wandered off toward them and the huge cedar that reared up over their heads. Again their sweet voices reminded him of the gap in his own childhood, as he leaned against the cedar to watch them. The boy in the middle of the circle (it seemed always to be a boy) spun around with his eyes closed and his arm stretched out, pointing. Round and round he went until the song ended with a shout and he stopped, his finger pointing at a child Milkman could not see. Then they all dropped to their knees and he was surprised to hear them begin another song at this point, one he had heard off and on all his life. That old blues song Pilate sang all the time: "O Sugarman don't leave me here," except the children sang, "Solomon don't leave me here."

Milkman smiled, remembering Pilate. Hundreds of miles away, he was homesick for her, for her house, for the very people he had been hell-bent to leave. His mother's quiet, crooked, apologetic smile. Her hopeless helplessness in the kitchen. The best years of her life, from age twenty to forty, had been celibate, and aside from the consummation that began his own life, the rest of her life had been the same. He hadn't thought much of it when she'd told him, but now it seemed to him that such sexual deprivation would affect her, hurt her in precisely the way it would affect and hurt him. If it were possible for somebody to force him to live that way, to tell him, "You may walk and live among women, you may even lust after them, but you will not make love for the next twenty years," how would he feel? What would he do? Would he continue as he was? And suppose he were married and his wife refused him for fifteen years. His mother had been able to live through that by a long nursing of her son, some occasional visits to a graveyard. What might she have been like had her husband loved her?

And his father. An old man now, who acquired things and used people to acquire more things. As the son of Macon Dead the first, he paid homage to his own father's life and death by loving what that father had loved: property, good solid property, the bountifulness of life. He loved these things to excess because he loved his father to excess. Owning, building, acquiring—that was his life, his future, his present, and all the history he knew. That he distorted life, bent it, for the sake of gain, was a measure of his loss at his father's death.

As Milkman watched the children, he began to feel uncomfortable. Hating his parents, his sisters, seemed silly now. And the skim of shame that he had rinsed away in the bathwater after having stolen from Pilate returned. But now it was as thick and as tight as a caul. How could he have broken into that house—

the only one he knew that achieved comfort without one article of comfort in it. No soft worn-down chair, not a cushion or a pillow. No light switch, no water running free and clear after a turn of a tap handle. No napkins, no tablecloth. No fluted plates or flowered cups, no circle of blue flame burning in a stove eye. But peace was there, energy, singing, and now his own remembrances.

His mind turned to Hagar and how he had treated her at the end. Why did he never sit her down and talk to her? Honestly. And what ugly thing was it he said to her the last time she tried to kill him? And God, how hollow her eyes had looked. He was never frightened of her; he never actually believed that she would succeed in killing him, or that she really wanted to. Her weapons, the complete lack of cunning or intelligence even of conviction, in her attacks were enough to drain away any fear. Oh, she could have accidentally hurt him, but he could have stopped her in any number of ways. But he hadn't wanted to. He had used her—her love, her craziness—and most of all he had used her skulking, bitter vengeance. It made him a star, a celebrity in the Blood Bank; it told men and other women that he was one bad dude, that he had the power to drive a woman out of her mind, to destroy her, and not because she hated him, or because he had done some unforgivable thing to her, but because he had fucked her and she was driven wild by the absence of his magnificent joint. His hog's gut, Lena had called it. Even the last time, he used her. Used her imminent arrival and feeble attempt at murder as an exercise of his will against hers—an ultimatum to the universe. "Die, Hagar, die." Either this bitch dies or I do. And she stood there like a puppet strung up by a puppet master who had gone off to some other hobby.

O Solomon don't leave me here.

The children were starting the round again. Milkman rubbed the back of his neck. Suddenly he was tired, although the morning was still new. He pushed himself away from the cedar and sank to his haunches.

Jay the only son of Solomon
Come booba yalle, come . . .

Everybody in this town is named Solomon, he thought wearily. Solomon's General Store, Luther Solomon (no relation), Solomon's Leap, and now the children were singing "*Solomon* don't leave me" instead of "*Sugarman.*" Even the name of the town sounded like Solomon: Shalimar, which Mr. Solomon and everybody else pronounced *Shalleemone.*

Milkman's scalp began to tingle. Jay the only son of Solomon? Was that *Jake* the only son of Solomon? Jake. He strained to hear the children. That was one of the people he was looking for. A man named Jake who lived in Shalimar, as did his wife, Sing.

He sat up and waited for the children to begin the verse again. "Come booba yalle, come booba tambee," it sounded like, and didn't make sense. But another line—"Black lady fell down on the ground"—was clear enough. There was another string of nonsense words, then "Threw her body all around." Now the child in the center began whirling, spinning to lyrics sung in a different, faster tempo: "Solomon 'n' Reiner Belali Shalut . . ."

Solomon again, and Reiner? Ryna? Why did the second name sound so familiar? Solomon and Ryna. The woods. The hunt. Solomon's Leap and Ryna's Gulch, places they went to or passed by that night they shot the bobcat. The gulch was where he heard that noise that sounded like a woman crying, which Calvin said came from Ryna's Gulch, that there was an echo there that folks said was "a woman name Ryna" crying. You could hear her when the wind was right.

But what was the rest: Belali . . . Shalut . . . Yaruba? If Solomon and Ryna were names of people, the others might be also. The verse ended in another clear line. "Twenty-one children, the last one *Jake!*" And it was at the shout of *Jake* (who was also, apparently, "the only son of Solomon") that the twirling boy stopped. Now Milkman understood that if the child's finger pointed at nobody, missed, they started up again. But if it pointed directly to another child, that was when they fell to their knees and sang Pilate's song.

Milkman took out his wallet and pulled from it his airplane ticket stub, but he had no pencil to write with, and his pen was in his suit. He would just have to listen and memorize it. He closed his eyes and concentrated while the children, inexhaustible in their willingness to repeat a rhythmic, rhyming action game, performed the round over and over again. And Milkman memorized all of what they sang.

Jake the only son of Solomon
Come booba yalle, come booba tambee
Whirled about and touched the sun
Come konka yalle, come konka tambee

Left that baby in a white man's house
Come booba yalle, come booba tambee
Heddy took him to a red man's house
Come konka yalle, come konka tambee

Black lady fell down on the ground
Come booba yalle, come booba tambee
Threw her body all around
Come konka yalle, come konka tambee

Solomon and Ryna Belali Shalut
Yaruba Medina Muhammet too.
Nestor Kalina Saraka cake.
Twenty-one children, the last one Jake!

O Solomon don't leave me here
Cotton balls to choke me
O Solomon don't leave me here
Buckra's arms to yoke me

Solomon done fly, Solomon done gone
Solomon cut across the sky, Solomon gone home.

He almost shouted when he heard "Heddy took him to a red man's house." Heddy was Susan Byrd's grandmother on her father's side, and therefore Sing's mother too. And "red man's house" must be a reference to the Byrds as Indians. Of course! Sing was an Indian or part Indian and her name was Sing Byrd or, more likely, Sing Bird. No—Singing Bird! That must have been her name originally—Singing Bird. And her brother, Crowell Byrd, was probably Crow Bird, or just Crow. They had mixed their Indian names with American-sounding names. Milkman had four people now that he could recognize in the song: Solomon, Jake, Ryna and Heddy, and a veiled reference to Heddy's Indianness. All of which seemed to put Jake and Sing together in Shalimar, just as Circe had said they were. He couldn't be mistaken. These children were singing a story about his own people! He hummed and chuckled as he did his best to put it all together.

Jake's father was Solomon. Did Jake whirl about and touch the sun? Did Jake leave a baby in a white man's house? No. If the "Solomon don't leave me" line was right, Solomon was the one who left, who "flew away"—meaning died or ran off—not Jake. Maybe it was the baby, or Jake himself, who was begging him to stay. But who was the "black lady" who fell down on the ground? Why did she throw her body all around? It sounded like she was having a fit. Was it because somebody took her baby first to a white man's house, then to an Indian's house? Ryna? Was Ryna the black lady still crying in the gulch? Was Ryna Solomon's daughter? Maybe she had an illegitimate child, and her father— No. It's Solomon she is crying for, not a baby. "Solomon don't leave me." He must have been her lover.

Milkman was getting confused, but he was as excited as a child confronted with boxes and boxes of presents under the skirt of a Christmas tree. Somewhere in the pile was a gift for him.

Yet there were many many missing pieces. Susan Byrd, he thought—she would have to know more than she had told him. Besides, he had to get his watch back.

He ran back to Solomon's store and caught a glimpse of himself in the plate-glass window. He was grinning. His eyes were shining. He was as eager and happy as he had ever been in his life.

Chapter 13

It was a long time after he left, that warm September morning, that she was able to relax enough to drop the knife. When it clattered to the linoleum, she brought her arms down, oh, so slowly, and cradled her breasts as though they were two mangoes thumbed over in the marketplace and pushed aside. She stood that way in the little rented room with the sunshine pouring in until Guitar came home. He could not get her to speak or move, so he picked her up in his arms and carried her downstairs. He sat her on the bottom step while he went to borrow a car to drive her home.

Terrible as he thought the whole business was, and repelled as he was by mindlessness in love, he could not keep the deep wave of sorrow from engulfing him as he looked at this really rather pretty woman sitting straight as a pole, holding her breasts, and staring in front of her out of hollow eyes.

The engine of the old car he'd borrowed roared, but Guitar spoke softly to her. "You think because he doesn't love you that you are worthless. You think because he doesn't want you anymore that he is right—that his judgment and opinion of you are correct. If he throws you out, then you are garbage. You think he belongs to you because you want to belong to him. Hagar, don't. It's a bad word, 'belong.' Especially when you put it with somebody you love. Love shouldn't be like that. Did you ever see the way the clouds love a mountain? They circle all around it; sometimes you can't even see the mountain for the clouds. But you know what? You go up top and what do you see? His head. The clouds never cover the head. His head pokes through, because the clouds let him; they don't wrap him up. They let him keep his head up high, free, with nothing to hide him or bind him. Hear me, Hagar?" He spoke to her as he would to a very young child. "You can't own a human being. You can't lose what you don't own. Suppose you did own him. Could you really love somebody who was absolutely nobody without you? You really want somebody like that? Somebody who falls apart when you walk out the door? You don't, do you? And neither does he. You're turning over your whole life to him. Your whole life, girl. And if it means so little to you that you can just give it away, hand it to him, then why should it mean any more to him? He can't value you more than you value yourself." He stopped. She did not move or give any sign that she had heard him.

Pretty woman, he thought. Pretty little black-skinned woman. Who wanted to kill for love, die for love. The pride, the conceit of these doormat women amazed him. They were always women who had been spoiled children. Whose whims had been taken seriously by adults and who grew up to be the stingiest, greediest people on earth and out of their stinginess grew their stingy little love that ate everything in sight. They could not believe or accept the fact that they were unloved; they believed that the world itself was off balance when it appeared as though they were not loved. Why did they think they were so lovable? Why did they think their brand of love was better than, or even as good as, anybody else's? But they did. And they loved their love so much they would kill anybody who got in its way.

He looked at her again. Pretty. Pretty little black girl. Pretty little black-skinned girl. What had Pilate done to her? Hadn't anybody told her the things she ought to know? He thought of his two sisters, grown women now who could deal, and the litany of their growing up. Where's your daddy? Your mama know you out here in the street? Put something on your head. You gonna catch your death a cold. Ain't you hot? Ain't you cold? Ain't you scared you gonna get wet? Uncross your legs. Pull up your socks. I thought you was goin to the Junior Choir. Your slip is showin. Your hem is out. Come back in here and iron that collar. Hush your mouth. Comb your head. Get up from there and make that bed. Put on the meat. Take out the trash. Vaseline get rid of that ash.

Neither Pilate nor Reba knew that Hagar was not like them. Not strong enough, like Pilate, nor simple enough, like Reba, to make up her life as they had. She needed what most colored girls needed: a chorus of mamas, grandmamas, aunts, cousins, sisters, neighbors, Sunday school teachers, best girl friends, and what all to give her the strength life demanded of her—and the humor with which to live it.

Still, he thought, to have the object of your love, worthy or not, despise you, or leave you . . .

"You know what, Hagar? Everything I ever loved in my life left me. My father died when I was four. That was the first leaving I knew and the hardest. Then my mother. There were four of us and she just couldn't cut it when my father died. She ran away. Just ran away. My aunt took care of us until my grandmother could get there. Then my grandmother took care of us. Then Uncle Billy came. They're both close to dead now. So it was hard for me to latch on to a woman. Because I thought if I loved anything it would die. But I did latch on. Once. But I guess once is all you can manage." Guitar thought about it and said, "But I never wanted to kill her. *Him*, yeah. But not her." He smiled, but Hagar wasn't looking, wasn't even listening, and when he led her out of the car into Reba's arms her eyes were still empty.

. .

All they knew to do was love her and since she would not speak, they brought things to please her. For the first time in life Reba *tried* to win things. And, also for the first time, couldn't. Except for a portable television set, which they couldn't connect because they had no electricity, Reba won nothing. No raffle ticket, no Bingo, no policy slip, no clearing-house number, no magazine sweepstakes, no, nor any unpierced carnival balloon succumbed to her magic. It wore her down. Puzzled and luckless, she dragged herself home clutching stalks of anything that blossomed along the edges of lots and other people's gardens. These she presented to her daughter, who sat in a chair by the window or lay in bed fingering, fingering her hair.

They cooked special things for her; searched for gifts that they hoped would break the spell. Nothing helped. Pilate's lips were still and Reba's eyes full of panic. They brought her lipstick and chocolate milk, a pink nylon sweater and a fuchsia bed jacket. Reba even investigated the mysteries of making jello, both red and green. Hagar didn't even look at it.

One day Pilate sat down on Hagar's bed and held a compact before her granddaughter's face. It was trimmed in a goldlike metal and had a pink plastic lid.

"Look, baby. See here?" Pilate turned it all around to show it off and pressed in the catch. The lid sprang open and Hagar saw a tiny part of her face reflected in the mirror. She took the compact then and stared into the mirror for a long while.

"No wonder," she said at last. "Look at that. No wonder. No wonder."

Pilate was thrilled at the sound of Hagar's voice. "It's yours, baby," she said. "Ain't it pretty?"

"No wonder," said Hagar. "No wonder."

"No wonder what?" asked Pilate.

"Look at how I look. I look awful. No wonder he didn't want me. I look terrible." Her voice was calm and reasonable, as though the last few days hadn't been lived through at all. "I need to get up from here and fix myself up. No *wonder!*" Hagar threw back the bedcover and stood up. "Ohhh. I smell too. Mama, heat me some water. I need a bath. A long one. We got any bath salts left? Oh, Lord, my head. Look at that." She peered into the compact mirror again. "I look like a ground hog. Where's the comb?"

Pilate called Reba and together they flew through the house to find the comb, but when they found it Hagar couldn't get the teeth through her roped and matted hair.

"Wash it," said Reba. "Wash it and we'll comb it while it's wet."

"I need shampoo, then. Real shampoo. I can't use Mama's soap."

"I'll go get some." Reba was trembling a little. "What kind?"

"Oh, any kind. And get some hair oil, Reba. Posner's, and some . . . Oh, never mind. Just that. Mama? Have you seen my . . . Oh, my God. No wonder. No wonder."

Pilate pulled a piece of string from Hagar's bedspread and put it in her mouth. "I'll heat up the water," she said.

When Reba got back she washed Hagar's hair, brushed it, and combed it gently.

"Just make me two braids, Reba. I'm going to have to go to the beauty shop. Today. Oh, and I need something to wear." Hagar stood at the door of the little cardboard closet, running her hands over the shoulders of dresses. "Everything's a mess in here. A mess. All wrinkled . . ."

"Water's hot. Where you want the tub?"

"Bring it in here."

"You think you should be taking a bath so soon?" Reba asked. "You just got up."

"Hush, Reba," said Pilate. "Let the child take care of herself."

"But she's been in the bed three days."

"All the more reason."

"I can't put these things on. Everything's a mess." Hagar was almost in tears.

Reba looked at Pilate. "I hope you right. I don't approve of getting up too fast and jumping right in some water."

"Help me with this tub and stop grumbling."

"All wrinkled. What am I going to wear?"

"That ain't enough water to cover her feet."

"It'll grow when she sits down."

"Where's my yellow dress? The one that buttons all the way down?"

"Somewhere in there, I reckon."

"Find it for me and press it, would you? I know it's a mess. Everything's a mess."

Reba found and pressed the yellow dress. Pilate helped Hagar bathe. Finally a clean and clothed Hagar stood before the two women and said, "I have to buy some clothes. New clothes. Everything I have is a mess."

They looked at each other. "What you need?" asked Pilate.

"I need everything," she said, and everything is what she got. She shopped for everything a woman could wear from the skin out, with the money from Reba's diamond. They had seventy-five cents between them when Hagar declared her needs, and six dollars owed to them from customers. So the two-thousand-dollar two-carat diamond went to a pawnshop, where Reba traded it for thirty dollars at first and then, accompanied by storming Pilate, she went back and got one hundred and seventy more for it. Hagar stuffed two hundred dollars and seventy-five cents into her purse and headed downtown, still whispering to herself every now and then, "No wonder."

She bought a Playtex garter belt, I. Miller No Color hose, Fruit of the Loom panties, and two nylon slips—one white, one pink—one pair of Joyce Fancy Free and one of Con Brio ("Thank heaven for little Joyce heels"). She carried an armful of skirts and an Evan-Picone two-piece number into the fitting room. Her little yellow dress that buttoned all the way down lay on the floor as she slipped a skirt over her head and shoulders, down to her waist. But the placket would not close. She sucked in her stomach and pulled the fabric as far as possible, but the teeth of the zipper would not join. A light sheen broke out on her forehead as she huffed and puffed. She was convinced that her whole life depended on whether or not those aluminum teeth would meet. The nail of her forefinger split and the balls of her thumbs ached as she struggled with the placket. Dampness became sweat and her breath came in gasps. She was about to weep when the saleswoman poked her head through the curtain and said brightly, "How are you doing?" But when she saw Hagar's gnarled and frightened face, the smile froze.

"Oh, my," she said, and reached for the tag hanging from the skirt's waist. "This is a five. Don't force it. You need, oh, a nine or eleven, I should think. Please. Don't force it. Let me see if I have that size."

She waited until Hagar let the plaid skirt fall down to her ankles before disappearing. Hagar easily drew on the skirt the woman brought back, and without further search, said she would take it and the little two-piece Evan-Picone.

She bought a white blouse next and a nightgown—fawn trimmed in sea foam. Now all she needed was make-up.

The cosmetics department enfolded her in perfume, and she read hungrily the labels and the promise. Myrurgia for primeval woman who creates for him a world of tender privacy where the only occupant is you, mixed with Nina Ricci's L'Air du Temps. Yardley's Flair with Tuvaché's Nectaroma and D'Orsay's Intoxication. Robert Piguet's Fracas, and Calypso and Visa and Bandit. Houbigant's Chantilly. Caron's Fleurs de Rocaille and Bellodgia. Hagar breathed deeply the sweet air that hung over the glass counters. Like a smiling sleepwalker she circled. Round and round the diamond-clear counters covered with bottles, wafer-thin disks, round boxes, tubes, and phials. Lipsticks in soft white hands darted out of their sheaths like the shiny red penises of puppies. Peachy powders and milky lotions were grouped in front of poster after cardboard poster of gorgeous grinning faces. Faces in ecstasy. Faces somber with achieved seduction. Hagar believed she could spend her life there among the cut glass, shimmering in peaches and cream, in satin. In opulence. In luxe. In love.

It was five-thirty when Hagar left the store with two shopping bags full of smaller bags gripped in her hands. And she didn't put them down until she reached Lilly's Beauty Parlor.

"No more heads, honey." Lilly looked up from the sink as Hagar came in.

Hagar stared. "I have to get my hair done. I have to hurry," she said.

Lilly looked over at Marcelline. It was Marcelline who kept the shop prosperous. She was younger, more recently trained, and could do a light press that lasted. Lilly was still using red-hot irons and an ounce of oil on every head. Her customers were loyal but dissatisfied. Now she spoke to Marcelline. "Can you take her? I can't, I know."

Marcelline peered deeply into her customer's scalp. "Hadn't planned on any late work. I got two more coming. This is my eighth today."

No one spoke. Hagar stared.

"Well," said Marcelline. "Since it's you, come on back at eight-thirty. Is it washed already?"

Hagar nodded.

"Okay," said Marcelline. "Eight-thirty. But don't expect nothing fancy."

"I'm surprised at you," Lilly chuckled when Hagar left. "You just sent two people away."

"Yeah, well, I don't feel like it, but I don't want no trouble with that girl Hagar. No telling what she might do. She jump that cousin of hers, no telling what she might do to me."

"That the one going with Macon Dead's boy?" Lilly's customer lifted her head away from the sink.

"That's her. Ought to be shamed, the two of them. *Cousins*."

"Must not be working out if she's trying to kill him."

"I thought he left town."

"Wouldn't you?"

"Well, I know I don't want to truck with her. Not me."

"She don't bother nobody but him."

"Well, Pilate, then. Pilate know I turned her down, she wouldn't like it. They spoil that child something awful."

"Didn't you order fish from next door?"

"All that hair. I hope she don't expect nothing fancy."

"Call him up again. I'm getting hungry."

"Be just like her. No appointment. No nothing. Come in here all late and wrong and want something fancy."

She probably meant to wait somewhere. Or go home and return to Lilly's at eight-thirty. Yet the momentum of the thing held her—it was all of a piece. From the moment she looked into the mirror in the little pink compact she could not stop. It was as though she held her breath and could not let it go until the energy and busyness culminated in a beauty that would dazzle him. That was why, when she left Lilly's, she looked neither right nor left but walked on and on, oblivious of other people, street lights, automobiles, and a thunderous sky. She was thoroughly soaked before she realized it was raining and then only because one of the shopping bags split. When she looked down, her Evan-Picone white-with-a-band-of-color skirt was lying in a neat half fold on the shoulder of the road, and she was far far from home. She put down both bags, picked the skirt up and brushed away the crumbs of gravel that stuck to it. Quickly she refolded it, but when she tried to tuck it back into the shopping bag, the bag collapsed altogether. Rain soaked her hair and poured down her neck as she stooped to repair the damage. She pulled out the box of Con Brios, a smaller package of Van Raalte gloves, and another containing her fawn-trimmed-in-sea-foam shortie nightgown. These she stuffed into the other bag. Retracing her steps, she found herself unable to carry the heavier bag in one hand, so she hoisted it up to her stomach and hugged it with both arms. She had gone hardly ten yards when the bottom fell out of it. Hagar tripped on Jungle Red (Sculptura) and Youth Blend, and to her great dismay, saw her box of Sunny Glow toppling into a puddle. She collected Jungle Red and Youth Blend safely, but Sunny Glow, which had tipped completely over and lost its protective disk, exploded in light peach puffs under the weight of the raindrops. Hagar scraped up as much of it as she could and pressed the wilted cellophane disk back into the box.

Twice before she got to Darling Street she had to stop to retrieve her purchases from the ground. Finally she stood in Pilate's doorway, limp, wet, and confused, clutching her bundles in whatever way she could. Reba was so relieved to see her that she grabbed her, knocking Chantilly and Bandit to the floor. Hagar stiffened and pulled away from her mother.

"I have to hurry," she whispered. "I have to hurry."

Loafers sluicing, hair dripping, holding her purchases in her arms, she made it into the bedroom and shut the door. Pilate and Reba made no move to follow her.

Hagar stripped herself naked there, and without taking time to dry her face or hair or feet, she dressed herself up in the white-with-a-band-of-color skirt and matching bolero, the Maidenform brassiere, the Fruit of the Loom panties, the no color hose, the Playtex garter belt and the Joyce con brios. Then she sat down to attend to her face. She drew charcoal gray for the young round eye through her brows, after which she rubbed mango tango on her cheeks. Then she patted sunny glow all over her face. Mango tango disappeared under it and she had to put it on again. She pushed out her lips and spread jungle red over them. She put baby clear sky light to outwit the day light on her eyelids and touched bandit to her throat, earlobes, and wrists. Finally she poured a little youth blend into her palm and smoothed it over her face.

At last she opened the door and presented herself to Pilate and Reba. And it was in their eyes that she saw what she had not seen before in the mirror: the wet ripped hose, the soiled white dress, the sticky, lumpy face powder, the streaked rouge, and the wild wet shoals of hair. All this she saw in their eyes, and the sight filled her own with water warmer and much older than the rain. Water that lasted for hours, until the fever came, and then it stopped. The fever dried her eyes up as well as her mouth.

She lay in her little Goldilocks'-choice bed, her eyes sand dry and as quiet as glass. Pilate and Reba, seated beside the bed, bent over her like two divi-divi trees beaten forward by a wind always blowing from the same direction. Like the trees, they offered her all they had: love murmurs and a protective shade.

"Mama." Hagar floated up into an even higher fever.

"Hmmm?"

"Why don't he like my hair?"

"Who, baby? Who don't like your hair?"

"Milkman."

"Milkman does too like your hair," said Reba.

"No. He don't. But I can't figure out why. Why he never liked my hair."

"Of course he likes it. How can he not like it?" asked Pilate.

"He likes silky hair." Hagar was murmuring so low they had to bend down to hear her.

"Silky hair? Milkman?"

"He don't like hair like mine."

"Hush, Hagar."

"Silky hair the color of a penny."

"Don't talk, baby."

"Curly, wavy, silky hair. He don't like mine."

Pilate put her hand on Hagar's head and trailed her fingers through her granddaughter's soft damp wool. "How can he not love your hair? It's the same hair that grows out of his own armpits. The same hair that crawls up out his crotch on up his stomach. All over his chest. The very same. It grows out of his nose, over his lips, and if he ever lost his razor it would grow all over his face. It's all over his head, Hagar. It's his hair too. He got to love it."

"He don't love it at all. He hates it."

"No he don't. He don't know what he loves, but he'll come around, honey, one of these days. How can he love himself and hate your hair?"

"He loves silky hair."

"Hush, Hagar."

"Penny-colored hair."

"Please, honey."
"And lemon-colored skin."
"Shhh."
"And gray-blue eyes."
"Hush now, hush."
"And thin nose."
"Hush, girl, hush."
"He's never going to like my hair."
"Hush. Hush. Hush, girl, hush."

The neighbors took up a collection because Pilate and Reba had spent everything getting Hagar the things needed to fix herself up. It didn't amount to much, though, and it was touch and go whether she'd have a decent funeral until Ruth walked down to Sonny's Shop and stared at Macon without blinking. He reached into his cash drawer and pulled out two twenty-dollar bills and put them down on the desk. Ruth didn't stretch out her hand to pick them up, or even shift her feet. Macon hesitated, then wheeled around in his chair and began fiddling with the combination to his safe. Ruth waited. Macon dipped into the safe three separate times before Ruth unclasped her hands and reached for the money. "Thank you," she said, and marched off to Linden Chapel Funeral Home to make the fastest arrangements possible.

Two days later, halfway through the service, it seemed as though Ruth was going to be the lone member of the bereaved family there. A female quartet from Linden Baptist Church had already sung "Abide with Me"; the wife of the mortician had read the condolence cards and the minister had launched into his "Naked came ye into this life and naked shall ye depart" sermon, which he had always believed suitable for the death of a young woman; and the winos in the vestibule who came to pay their respects to "Pilate's girl," but who dared not enter, had begun to sob, when the door swung open and Pilate burst in, shouting, "Mercy!" as though it were a command. A young man stood up and moved toward her. She flung out her right arm and almost knocked him down. "I want mercy!" she shouted, and began walking toward the coffin, shaking her head from side to side as though somebody had asked her a question and her answer was no.

Halfway up the aisle she stopped, lifted a finger, and pointed. Then slowly, although her breathing was fast and shallow, she lowered her hand to her side. It was strange, the languorous, limp hand coming to rest at her side while her breathing was coming so quick and fast. "Mercy," she said again, but she whispered it now. The mortician scurried toward her and touched her elbow. She moved away from him and went right up to the bier. She tilted her head and looked down. Her earring grazed her shoulder. Out of the total blackness of her clothes it blazed like a star. The mortician tried to approach her again, and moved closer, but when he saw her inky, berry-black lips, her cloudy, rainy eyes, the wonderful brass box hanging from her ear, he stepped back and looked at the floor.

"Mercy?" Now she was asking a question. "Mercy?"

It was not enough. The word needed a bottom, a frame. She straightened up, held her head high, and transformed the plea into a note. In a clear bluebell voice she sang it out—the one word held so long it became a sentence—and before the last syllable had died in the corners of the room, she was answered in a sweet soprano: "I hear you."

The people turned around. Reba had entered and was singing too. Pilate neither acknowledged her entrance nor missed a beat. She simply repeated the word "Mercy," and Reba replied. The daughter standing at the back of the chapel, the mother up front, they sang.

In the nighttime.
Mercy.
In the darkness.
Mercy.
In the morning.
Mercy.

At my bedside.
Mercy.
On my knees now.
Mercy. Mercy. Mercy. Mercy.

They stopped at the same time in a high silence. Pilate reached out her hand and placed three fingers on the edge of the coffin. Now she addressed her words to the woman bordered in gray satin who lay before her. Softly, privately, she sang to Hagar the very same reassurance she had promised her when she was a little girl.

Who's been botherin my sweet sugar lumpkin?
Who's been botherin my baby?
Who's been botherin my sweet sugar lumpkin?
Who's been botherin my baby girl?

Somebody's been botherin my sweet sugar lumpkin.
Somebody's been botherin my baby.
Somebody's been botherin my sweet sugar lumpkin.
Some*body's been botherin my baby girl.*

I'll find who's botherin my sweet sugar lumpkin.
I'll find who's botherin my baby.
I'll find who's botherin my sweet sugar lumpkin.
I'll find who's botherin my baby girl.

"My baby girl." The three words were still pumping in her throat as she turned away from the coffin. Looking about at the faces of the people seated in the pews, she fastened on the first pair of eyes that were directed toward her. She nodded at the face and said, "My baby girl." She looked for another pair of eyes and told him also, "My baby girl." Moving back down the aisle, she told each face turned toward her the same piece of news. "My baby girl. That's my baby girl. My baby girl. My baby girl. My baby girl."

Conversationally she spoke, identifying Hagar, selecting her away from everybody else in the world who had died. First she spoke to the ones who had the courage to look at her, shake their heads, and say, "Amen." Then she spoke to those whose nerve failed them, whose glance would climb no higher than the long black fingers at her side. Toward them especially she leaned a little, telling in three words the full story of the stumped life in the coffin behind her. "My baby girl." Words tossed like stones into a silent canyon.

Suddenly, like an elephant who has just found his anger and lifts his trunk over the heads of the little men who want his teeth or his hide or his flesh or his amazing strength, Pilate trumpeted for the sky itself to hear, "And she was *loved!*"

It startled one of the sympathetic winos in the vestibule and he dropped his bottle, spurting emerald glass and jungle-red wine everywhere.

Chapter 14

Perhaps it was because the sun had hit the rim of the horizon, but Susan Byrd's house looked different. The cedar tree was a silvery gray and its bark crinkled all the way up. It looked to Milkman like the leg of an ancient elephant. And now he noticed that the ropes that held the swing were frayed and the picket fence that had looked so bright and perky before was really flaked, peeling, even leaning to the left. The blue steps leading to the porch were faded into a watery gray. In fact the whole house looked seedy.

He lifted his hand to knock on the door and noticed the doorbell. He rang it and Susan Byrd opened the door.

"Hello again," he said.

"Well," she said, "you're as good as your word."

"I'd like to talk to you some more, if you don't mind. About Sing. May I come in?"

"Of course." She stood back from the door and the odor of another batch of gingerbread wafted out. Again they sat in the living room—he in the gray wing-back chair, she on the sofa this time. Miss Long was nowhere in sight.

"I know you don't know who Sing married or if she married, but I was wondering—"

"Of course I know who she married. That is if they *did* marry. She married Jake, that black boy her mother took care of."

Milkman felt dizzy. Everybody kept changing right in front of him. "But yesterday you said nobody heard from her after she left."

"Nobody did. But they knew who she left with!"

"Jake?"

"Jake. Black Jake. Black as coal."

"Where—where did they live? Boston?"

"I don't know where they ended up. North, I guess. We never heard."

"I thought you said she went to a private school in Boston."

She dismissed the whole notion with a wave of her hand. "I just said that in front of *her*, Grace. She talks so much, you know. Carries tales all over the county. It's true she was supposed to go to some school, but she didn't. She left on that double-team wagon with that black boy, Jake. A whole lot of slaves got together. Jake was driving. Can you imagine it? Riding off with a wagonload of slaves?"

"What was Jake's last name? Can you tell me?"

She shrugged. "I don't think he had one. He was one of those flying African children. They must all be dead a long time now."

"Flying African children?"

"Um hm, one of Solomon's children. Or Shalimar. Papa said Heddy always called him Shalimar."

"And Heddy was . . ."

"My grandmother. Sing's mother and Papa's too. An Indian woman. She was the one who took care of Jake when his father left them all. She found him and took him home and raised him. She didn't have any boy children then. My father, Crowell, came later." She leaned forward and whispered, "She didn't have a husband, Heddy. I didn't want to go into all of that with Grace. You can imagine what she'd do with that information.

You're a stranger, so it doesn't matter. But Grace . . ." Susan Byrd looked pleadingly at the ceiling. "This Jake was a baby she found, and he and Sing grew up together, and I guess rather than be packed off to some Quaker school, she ran away with him. You know colored people and Indians mixed a lot, but sometimes, well, some Indians didn't like it—the marrying, I mean. But neither one of them knew their own father, Jake nor Sing. And my own father didn't know his. Heddy never said. I don't know to this day if he was white, red, or—well—*what*. Sing's name was Singing Bird. And my father's name was Crow at first. Later he changed it to Crowell Byrd. After he took off his buckskin." She smiled.

"Why did you call Solomon a flying African?"

"Oh, that's just some old folks' lie they tell around here. Some of those Africans they brought over here as slaves could fly. A lot of them flew back to Africa. The one around here who did was this same Solomon, or Shalimar—I never knew which was right. He had a slew of children, all over the place. You may have noticed that everybody around here claims kin to him. Must be over forty families spread in these hills calling themselves Solomon something or other. I guess he must have been hot stuff." She laughed. "But anyway, hot stuff or not, he disappeared and left everybody. Wife, everybody, including some twenty-one children. And they say they all saw him go. The wife saw him and the children saw him. They were all working in the fields. They used to try to grow cotton here. Can you imagine? In these hills? But cotton was king then. Everybody grew it until the land went bad. It was cotton even when I was a girl. Well, back to this Jake boy. He was supposed to be one of Solomon's original twenty-one—all boys and all of them with the same mother. Jake was the baby. The baby and the wife were right next to him when he flew off."

"When you say 'flew off' you mean he ran away, don't you? Escaped?"

"No, I mean flew. Oh, it's just foolishness, you know, but according to the story he wasn't running away. He was flying.

He flew. You know, like a bird. Just stood up in the fields one day, ran up some hill, spun around a couple of times, and was lifted up in the air. Went right on back to wherever it was he came from. There's a big double-headed rock over the valley named for him. It like to killed the woman, the wife. I guess you could say 'wife.' Anyway she's supposed to have screamed out loud for days. And there's a ravine near here they call Ryna's Gulch, and sometimes you can hear this funny sound by it that the wind makes. People say it's the wife, Solomon's wife, crying. Her name was Ryna. They say she screamed and screamed, lost her mind completely. You don't hear about women like that anymore, but there used to be more—the kind of woman who couldn't live without a particular man. And when the man left, they lost their minds, or died or something. Love, I guess. But I always thought it was trying to take care of children by themselves, you know what I mean?"

She talked on and on while Milkman sat back and listened to gossip, stories, legends, speculations. His mind was ahead of hers, behind hers, with hers, and bit by bit, with what she said, what he knew, and what he guessed, he put it all together.

Sing had said she was going to a Quaker school, but she joined Jake on his wagonful of ex-slaves heading for Boston or somewhere. They must have dropped their passengers all along the way. And then Jake, at the reins, took a wrong turn, because he couldn't read, and they ended up in Pennsylvania.

"But there's a children's game they play around here. And in the game they sing, 'Jake the *only* son of Solomon.' *Only*." He looked at her, hoping she wouldn't mind the interruption.

"Well, they're wrong. He wasn't the only son. There were twenty others. But he was the only one Solomon tried to take with him. Maybe that's what it means. He lifted him up, but dropped him near the porch of the big house. That's where Heddy found him. She used to come over there and help with the soapmaking and the candlemaking. She wasn't a slave, but she worked over at the big house certain times of year. She was melting tallow when she looked up and saw this man holding a baby and flying toward the ridge. He brushed too close to a tree and the baby slipped out of his arms and fell through the branches to the ground. He was unconscious, but the trees saved him from dying. Heddy ran over and picked him up. She didn't have any male children, like I said, just a little bitty girl, and this one just dropped out of the sky almost in her lap. She never named him anything different; she was afraid to do that. She found out the baby was Ryna's, but Ryna was out of her mind. Heddy lived a good ways off from the place Solomon and them others worked on. She tried to keep the girl away from that place too. And you can imagine how she felt when both of them ran off. Just my father was left."

"Did Jake have to register at the Freedmen's Bureau before he left the state?"

"Everybody did. Everybody who had been slaves, that is. Whether they left the state or not. But we were never slaves, so–"

"You told me that. Weren't any of Jake's brothers registering too?"

"I couldn't say. Those must have been some times, back then. Some bad times. It's a wonder anybody knows who anybody is."

"You've helped me a lot, Miss Byrd. I'm grateful." He thought then about asking her if she had a photo album. He wanted to see Sing, Crowell, even Heddy. But he decided against it. She might start asking him questions, and he didn't want to trouble her with a new-found relative who was as black as Jake.

"Now, that's not the woman you're looking for, is it? Pilate?"

"No," he said. "Couldn't be." He made motions of departure and then remembered his watch.

"By the way, did I leave my watch here? I'd like it back."

"Watch?"

"Yes. Your friend wanted to see it. Miss Long. I handed it to her but I forgot–" Milkman stopped. Susan Byrd was laughing out loud.

“Well, you can say goodbye to it, Mr. Macon. Grace will go to dinner all over the county telling people about the watch you gave her.”

“What?”

“Well, you know. She doesn’t mean any real harm, but it’s a quiet place. We don’t have many visitors, especially young men who wear gold watches and have northern accents. I’ll get it back for you.”

“Never mind. Never mind.”

“You’ll just have to forgive her otherwise. This is a dull place, Mr. Macon. There’s absolutely nothing in the world going on here. Not a thing.”

Chapter 15

The fan belt didn't last long enough for him to get to the next gasoline station. It broke on the edge of a little town called Jistann, the needle trembling at H. Milkman sold it to the tow-truck man for twenty dollars and caught the first bus out. It was probably best that way, for over the humming wheels, his legs folded in the little space in front of his seat, he had time to come down from the incredible high that had begun as soon as he slammed the Byrd woman's door.

He couldn't get back to Shalimar fast enough, and when he did get there, dusty and dirty from the run, he leaped into the car and drove to Sweet's house. He almost broke her door down. "I want to swim!" he shouted. "Come on, let's go swimming. I'm dirty and I want waaaaater!"

Sweet smiled and said she'd give him a bath.

"Bath! You think I'd put myself in that tight little porcelain box? I need the sea! The whole goddam sea!" Laughing, hollering, he ran over to her and picked her up at the knees and ran around the room with her over his shoulder. "The sea! I have to swim in the sea. Don't give me no itty bitty teeny tiny tub, girl. I need the whole entire complete deep blue sea!"

He stood her on her feet. "Don't you all swim around here?"

"Over at the quarry is where the kids go sometimes."

"Quarry? You all don't have no sea? No ocean?"

"Naw; this hill country."

"Hill country. Mountain country. Flying country."

"A man was here to see you."

"Oh, yeah? That would be Mr. Guitar Bains."

"He didn't give his name."

"He don't have to! He's Guitar Bains. *Gi*tar, *Gi*tar, Gitar Bains!" Milkman did a little dance and Sweet covered her mouth, laughing.

"Come on, Sweet, tell me where the sea is."

"They some water comin down below the ridge on the other side. Real deep; wide too."

"Then let's go! Come on!" He grabbed her arm and pulled her out to the car. He sang all the way: " 'Solomon 'n Ryna Belali Shalut . . .' "

"Where you learn that?" she asked him. "That's a game we used to play when we was little."

"Of course you did. Everybody did. Everybody but me. But I can play it now. It's my game now."

The river in the valley was wide and green. Milkman took off his clothes, climbed a tree and dived into the water. He surfaced like a bullet, iridescent, grinning, splashing water. "Come on. Take them clothes off and come on in here."

"Naw. I don't wanna swim."

"Come in here, girl!"

"Water moccasins in there."

"Fuck 'em. Get in here. Hurry up!"

She stepped out of her shoes, pulled her dress over her head and was ready. Milkman reached up for her as she came timidly down the bank, slipping, stumbling, laughing at her own awkwardness, then squealing as the cold river water danced up her legs, her hips, her waist. Milkman pulled her close and kissed her mouth, ending the kiss with a determined effort to pull her under the water. She fought him. "Oh, my hair! My hair's gonna get wet."

"No it ain't," he said, and poured a handful right in the middle of her scalp. Wiping her eyes, spluttering water, she turned to wade out, shrieking all the way. "Okay, okay," he bellowed. "Leave me. Leave me in here by myself. I don't care. I'll play with the water moccasins." And he began to whoop and dive and splash and turn. "He could fly! You hear me? My great-granddaddy could fly! Goddam!" He whipped the water with his fists, then jumped straight up as though he too could take off, and landed on his back and sank down, his mouth and eyes full of water. Up again. Still pounding, leaping, diving. "The son of a bitch could fly! You hear me, Sweet? That motherfucker could fly! Could fly! He didn't need no airplane. Didn't need no fuckin tee double you ay. He could fly his own self!"

"Who you talkin 'bout?" Sweet was lying on her side, her cheek cupped in her hand.

"Solomon, that's who."

"Oh, him." She laughed. "You belong to that tribe of niggers?" She thought he was drunk.

"Yeah. That tribe. That flyin motherfuckin tribe. Oh, man! He didn't need no airplane. He just took off; got fed up. *All the way up!* No more cotton! No more bales! No more orders! No more shit! He flew, baby. Lifted his beautiful black ass up in the sky and flew on home. Can you dig it? Jesus God, that must have been something to see. And you know what else? He tried to take his baby boy with him. My grandfather. Wow! Woooee! Guitar! You hear that? Guitar, my great-granddaddy could flyyyyyy and the whole damn town is named after him. Tell him, Sweet. Tell him my great-granddaddy could fly."

"Where'd he go, Macon?"

"Back to Africa. Tell Guitar he went back to Africa."

"Who'd he leave behind?"

"Everybody! He left everybody down on the ground and he sailed on off like a black eagle. 'O-o-o-o-o-o Solomon done fly,

Solomon done gone /Solomon cut across the sky, Solomon gone home!' "

He could hardly wait to get home. To tell his father, Pilate; and he would love to see Reverend Cooper and his friends. "You think Macon Dead was something? Huh. Let me tell you about *his* daddy. You ain't heard nothin yet."

Milkman turned in his seat and tried to stretch his legs. It was morning. He'd changed buses three times and was now speeding home on the last leg of his trip. He looked out the window. Far away from Virginia, fall had already come. Ohio, Indiana, Michigan were dressed up like the Indian warriors from whom their names came. Blood red and yellow, ocher and ice blue.

He read the road signs with interest now, wondering what lay beneath the names. The Algonquins had named the territory he lived in Great Water, *michi gami*. How many dead lives and fading memories were buried in and beneath the names of the places in this country. Under the recorded names were other names, just as "Macon Dead," recorded for all time in some dusty file, hid from view the real names of people, places, and things. Names that had meaning. No wonder Pilate put hers in her ear. When you know your name, you should hang on to it, for unless it is noted down and remembered, it will die when you do. Like the street he lived on, recorded as Mains Avenue, but called Not Doctor Street by the Negroes in memory of his grandfather, who was the first colored man of consequence in that city. Never mind that he probably didn't deserve their honor—they knew what kind of man he was: arrogant, color-struck, snobbish. They didn't care about that. They were paying their respect to whatever it was that made him *be* a doctor in the first place, when the odds were that he'd be a yardman all of his life. So they named a street after him. Pilate had taken a rock from every state she had lived in—because she *had* lived there. And having lived there, it was hers—and his, and his father's, his grandfather's, his grandmother's. Not Doctor Street, Solomon's Leap, Ryna's Gulch, Shalimar, Virginia.

He closed his eyes and thought of the black men in Shalimar, Roanoke, Petersburg, Newport News, Danville, in the Blood Bank, on Darling Street, in the pool halls, the barbershops. Their names. Names they got from yearnings, gestures, flaws, events, mistakes, weaknesses. Names that bore witness. Macon Dead, Sing Byrd, Crowell Byrd, Pilate, Reba, Hagar, Magdalene, First Corinthians, Milkman, Guitar, Railroad Tommy, Hospital Tommy, Empire State (he just stood around and swayed), Small Boy, Sweet, Circe, Moon, Nero, Humpty-Dumpty, Blue Boy, Scandinavia, Quack-Quack, Jericho, Spoonbread, Ice Man, Dough Belly, Rocky River, Gray Eye, Cock-a-Doodle-Doo, Cool Breeze, Muddy Waters, Pinetop, Jelly Roll, Fats, Leadbelly, Bo Diddley, Cat-Iron, Peg-Leg, Son, Shortstuff, Smoky Babe, Funny Papa, Bukka, Pink, Bull Moose, B.B., T-Bone, Black Ace, Lemon, Washboard, Gatemouth, Cleanhead, Tampa Red, Juke Boy, Shine, Staggerlee, Jim the Devil, Fuck-Up, and *Dat* Nigger.

Angling out from these thoughts of names was one more—the one that whispered in the spinning wheels of the bus: "Guitar is biding his time. Guitar is biding his time. Your day has come. Your day has come. Guitar is biding his time. Guitar is a very good Day. Guitar is a very good Day. A very good Day, a very good Day, and biding, biding his time."

In the seventy-five-dollar car, and here on the big Greyhound, Milkman felt safe. But there were days and days ahead. Maybe if Guitar was back in the city now, among familiar surroundings, Milkman could defuse him. And certainly, in time, he would discover his foolishness. There was no gold. And although things would never be the same between them, at least the man-hunt would be over.

Even as he phrased the thought in his mind, Milkman knew it was not so. Either Guitar's disappointment with the gold that was not there was so deep it had deranged him, or his "work" had done it. Or maybe he simply allowed himself to feel about

Milkman what he had always felt about Macon Dead and the Honoré crowd. In any case, he had snatched the first straw, limp and wet as it was, to prove to himself the need to kill Milkman. The Sunday-school girls deserved better than to be avenged by that hawk-headed raven-skinned Sunday man who included in his blood sweep four innocent white girls and one innocent black man.

Perhaps that's what all human relationships boiled down to: Would you save my life? or would you take it?

"Everybody wants a black man's life."

Yeah. And black men were not excluded. With two exceptions, everybody he was close to seemed to prefer him out of this life. And the two exceptions were both women, both black, both old. From the beginning, his mother and Pilate had fought for his life, and he had never so much as made either of them a cup of tea.

Would you save my life or would you take it? Guitar was exceptional. To both questions he could answer yes.

"Should I go home first, or go to Pilate's first?" Out in the street, late at night with autumn air blowing cold off the lake, he tried to make up his mind. He was so eager for the sight of Pilate's face when he told her what he knew, he decided to see her first. He'd have a long time at his own house. He took a taxi to Darling Street, paid the driver, and bounded up the stairs. He pushed the door open and saw her standing over a tub of water, rinsing out the green bottles she used for her wine.

"Pilate!" he shouted. "Have I got stuff to tell you!"

She turned around. Milkman opened his arms wide so he could hold all of her in a warm embrace. "Come here, sweetheart," he said, grinning. She came and broke a wet green bottle over his head.

When he came to, he was lying on his side in the cellar. He opened one eye and considered the option of not coming to for a little while more. For a long time now he knew that anything could appear to be something else, and probably was. Nothing could be taken for granted. Women who loved you tried to cut your throat, while women who didn't even know your name scrubbed your back. Witches could sound like Katharine Hepburn and your best friend could try to strangle you. Smack in the middle of an orchid there might be a blob of jello and inside a Mickey Mouse doll, a fixed and radiant star.

So he lay on the cool damp floor of the cellar and tried to figure out what he was doing there. What did Pilate knock him out for? About the theft of her sack of bones? No. She'd come to his rescue immediately. What could it be, what else could he have done that would turn her against him? Then he knew. Hagar. Something had happened to Hagar. Where was she? Had she run off? Was she sick or . . . Hagar was dead. The cords of his neck tightened. How? In Guitar's room, did she . . . ?

What difference did it make? He had hurt her, left her, and now she was dead—he was certain of it. He had left her. While he dreamt of flying, Hagar was dying. Sweet's silvery voice came back to him: "Who'd he leave behind?" He left Ryna behind and twenty children. Twenty-one, since he dropped the one he tried to take with him. And Ryna had thrown herself all over the ground, lost her mind, and was still crying in a ditch. Who looked after those twenty children? Jesus Christ, he left twenty-one children! Guitar and the Days chose never to have children. Shalimar left his, but it was the children who sang about it and kept the story of his leaving alive.

Milkman rolled his head back and forth on the cellar floor. It was his fault, and Pilate knew it. She had thrown him in the cellar. What, he wondered, did she plan to do with him? Then he knew that too. Knew what Pilate's version of punishment was when somebody took another person's life. Hagar. Something of Hagar's must be nearby. Pilate would put him someplace near something that remained of the life he had taken, so he could *have* it. She would abide by this commandment from her father herself, and make him do it too. "You just can't fly on off and leave a body."

Suddenly Milkman began to laugh. Curled up like a Polish sausage, a rope cutting his wrists, he laughed.

"Pilate!" he called. "Pilate! That's not what he meant. Pilate! He didn't mean that. He wasn't talking about the man in the cave. Pilate! He was talking about himself. His own father flew away. He was the 'body.' The body you shouldn't fly off and leave. Pilate! Pilate! Come here. Let me tell you what your father said. Pilate, he didn't even tell you to sing, Pilate. He was calling for his wife—your mother. Pilate! Get me out of here!"

Light exploded in his face. The cellar door opened over his head. Pilate's feet appeared on the stone steps, and paused.

"Pilate," said Milkman, softly now, "that's not what he meant. I know what he meant. Come, let me tell you. And Pilate, those bones. They're not that white man's bones. He probably didn't even die. I went there. I saw. He wasn't there and the gold wasn't there either. Somebody found it and found him too. They must have, Pilate. Long before you got there. But, Pilate . . ."

She descended a few steps.

"Pilate?"

She came all the way down and he looked in her eyes and at her still mouth. "Pilate, your father's body floated up out of the grave you all dug for him. One month later it floated up. The Butlers, somebody, put his body in the cave. Wolves didn't drag the white man to the front of the cave and prop him on a rock. That was your father you found. You've been carrying your father's bones—all this time."

"Papa?" she whispered.

"Yes. And, Pilate, you have to bury him. He wants you to bury him. Back where he belongs. On Solomon's Leap."

"Papa?" she asked again.

Milkman did not speak; he watched her long fingers travel up her dress, to rest like the wing of a starling on her face. "I've been carryin Papa?" Pilate moved toward Milkman, stopped and looked at him for a while. Then her eyes turned to a rickety wooden table that stood against the stone wall of the cellar. It was in a part of the room so dark he had not even seen it. She walked over to the table and lifted from it a green-and-white shoe box, its cover held down with a rubber band. "Joyce," it said on the box. "Thank heaven for little Joyce heels."

"If I bury Papa, I guess I ought to bury this too—somewhere." She looked back at Milkman.

"No," he said. "No. Give it here."

When he went home that evening, he walked into the house on Not Doctor Street with almost none of the things he'd taken with him. But he returned with a box of Hagar's hair.

She wouldn't set foot on an airplane, so he drove. She seemed happy now. Her lips mobile again, she sat next to him in Macon's Buick, a mink stole Reba had won wrapped around her shoulders over her old black dress. The knit cap was pulled down on her forehead and her shoes still had no laces. Every now and then she glanced at the back seat to check on the sack. Peace circled her.

Milkman felt it too. His return to Not Doctor Street was not the triumph he'd hoped it would be, but there was relief in his mother's crooked smile. And Lena, though unforgiving as ever, was civil to him, since Corinthians had moved to a small house in Southside, which she shared with Porter. The Seven Days, Milkman guessed, would be looking for a new recruit, as they had to when Robert Smith jumped off the roof of Mercy. But there were long rambling talks with his father, who could not hear it enough—the "boys" who remembered him in Danville; his mother's running off with his father; the story about his father and his grandfather. He wasn't a bit interested in the flying part, but he liked the story and the fact that places were named for his people. Milkman softened his description of Circe, saying simply that she was alive, and taking care of the dogs.

"I ought maybe to take me a trip down there," said Macon.

"Virginia?" Milkman asked him.

"Danville. I ought to go by and see some of those boys before these legs stop moving. Let Freddie pick up the rents, maybe."

It was nice. No reconciliation took place between Pilate and Macon (although he seemed pleased to know that they were going to bury their father in Virginia), and relations between Ruth and Macon were the same and would always be. Just as the consequences of Milkman's own stupidity would remain, and regret would always outweigh the things he was proud of having done. Hagar was dead and he had not loved her one bit. And Guitar was . . . somewhere.

In Shalimar there was general merriment at his quick return, and Pilate blended into the population like a stick of butter in a churn. They stayed with Omar's family, and on the second and last evening, Milkman and Pilate walked up the road to the path that led to Solomon's Leap. It was the higher of two outcroppings of rock. Both flat-headed, both looking over a deep valley. Pilate carried the sack, Milkman a small shovel. It was a long way to the top, but neither stopped for breath. At the very top, on the plateau, the trees that could stand the wind at that height were few. They looked a long time for an area of earth among the rock faces large enough for the interment. When they found one, Pilate squatted down and opened the sack while Milkman dug. A deep sigh escaped from the sack and the wind turned chill. Ginger, a spicy sugared ginger smell, enveloped them. Pilate laid the bones carefully into the small grave. Milkman heaped dirt over them and packed it down with the back of his shovel.

"Should we put a rock or a cross on it?" Milkman asked.

Pilate shook her head. She reached up and yanked her earring from her ear, splitting the lobe. Then she made a little hole with her fingers and placed in it Sing's snuffbox with the single word Jake ever wrote. She stood up then, and it seemed to Milkman that he heard the shot after she fell. He dropped to his knees and cradled her lolling head in the crook of his arm, barking at her, "You hurt? You hurt, Pilate?"

She laughed softly and he knew right away that she was reminded of the day he first met her and said the most stupid thing there was to say.

The twilight had thickened and all around them it was getting dark. Milkman moved his hand over her chest and stomach, trying to find the place where she might be hit. "Pilate? You okay?" He couldn't make out her eyes. His hand under her head was sweating like a fountain. "Pilate?"

She sighed. "Watch Reba for me." And then, "I wish I'd a knowed more people. I would of loved 'em all. If I'd a knowed more, I would a loved more."

Milkman bent low to see her face and saw darkness staining his hand. Not sweat, but blood oozing from her neck down into his cupped hand. He pressed his fingers against the skin as if to force the life back in her, back into the place it was escaping from. But that only made it flow faster. Frantically he thought of tourniquets and could even hear the rip of cloth he should have been tearing. He shifted his weight and was about to lay her down, the better to wrap her wound, when she spoke again.

"Sing," she said. "Sing a little somethin for me."

Milkman knew no songs, and had no singing voice that anybody would want to hear, but he couldn't ignore the urgency in her voice. Speaking the words without the least bit of a tune, he sang for the lady. "Sugargirl don't leave me here/ Cotton balls to choke me/Sugargirl don't leave me here/ Buckra's arms to yoke me." The blood was not pulsing out any longer and there was something black and bubbly in her mouth. Yet when she moved her head a little to gaze at something behind his shoulder, it took a while for him to realize that she was dead. And when he did, he could not stop the worn old words from coming, louder and louder as though sheer volume would wake her. He woke only the birds, who shuddered off into the air. Milkman laid her head down on the rock. Two of the birds circled round them. One dived into the new grave and scooped something shiny in its beak before it flew away.

Now he knew why he loved her so. Without ever leaving the ground, she could fly. "There must be another one like you," he whispered to her. "There's got to be at least one more woman like you."

Even as he knelt over her, he knew there wouldn't be another mistake; that the minute he stood up Guitar would try to blow his head off. He stood up.

"Guitar!" he shouted.

Tar tar tar, said the hills.

"Over here, brother man! Can you see me?" Milkman cupped his mouth with one hand and waved the other over his head. "Here I am!"

Am am am am, said the rocks.

"You want me? Huh? You want my life?"

Life life life life.

Squatting on the edge of the other flat-headed rock with only the night to cover him, Guitar smiled over the barrel of his rifle. "My man," he murmured to himself. "My main man." He put the rifle on the ground and stood up.

Milkman stopped waving and narrowed his eyes. He could just make out Guitar's head and shoulders in the dark. "You want my life?" Milkman was not shouting now. "You need it? Here." Without wiping away the tears, taking a deep breath, or even bending his knees—he leaped. As fleet and bright as a lodestar he wheeled toward Guitar and it did not matter which one of them would give up his ghost in the killing arms of his brother. For now he knew what Shalimar knew: If you surrendered to the air, you could *ride* it.

A Note on the Type

This book was set on the Linotype in Janson, a recutting made direct from type cast from matrices long thought to have been made by the Dutchman Anton Janson, who was a practicing type founder in Leipzig during the years 1668–87. However, it has been conclusively demonstrated that these types are actually the work of Nicholas Kis (1650–1702), a Hungarian, who most probably learned his trade from the master Dutch type founder Dirk Voskens. The type is an excellent example of the influential and sturdy Dutch types that prevailed in England up to the time William Caslon developed his own incomparable designs from them.

TAR BABY

FOR

Mrs. Caroline Smith

Mrs. Millie MacTeer

Mrs. Ardelia Willis

Mrs. Ramah Wofford

Mrs. Lois Brooks

— and each of their sisters,

all of whom knew

their true and ancient

properties

For it hath been declared
unto me of you, my brethren, by them
which are of the house of
Chloe, that there are
contentions among you.

I Corinthians 1:11

HE BELIEVED he was safe. He stood at the railing of H.M.S. *Stor Konigsgaarten* and sucked in great gulps of air, his heart pounding in sweet expectation as he stared at the harbor. Queen of France blushed a little in the lessening light and lowered her lashes before his gaze. Seven girlish white cruisers bobbed in the harbor but a mile or so down current was a deserted pier. Carefully casual, he went below to the quarters he shared with the others, who had gone on shore leave, and since he had no things to gather—no book of postage stamps, no razor blade or key to any door—he merely folded more tightly the blanket corners under the mattress of his bunk. He took off his shoes and knotted the laces of each one through the belt hoop of his pants. Then, after a leisurely look around, he ducked through the passageway and returned to the top deck. He swung one leg over the railing, hesitated and considered diving headfirst, but, trusting what his feet could tell him more than what his hands could, changed his mind and simply stepped away from the ship. The water was so soft and warm that it was up to his armpits before he realized he was in it. Quickly he brought his knees to his chest and shot forward. He swam well. At each fourth stroke he turned skyward and lifted his head to make sure his course was parallel to the shore but away. Although his skin blended well with the dark waters, he was careful not to lift his arms too high above the waves. He gained on the pier and was gratified that his shoes still knocked softly against his hips.

After a while he thought it was time to head inland—toward the pier. As he scissored his legs for the turn, a bracelet of water circled them and yanked him into a wide, empty tunnel. He struggled to rise out of it and was turned three times. Just before the urge to breathe water became unmanageable, he was tossed up into the velvet air and laid smoothly down on the surface of the sea. He trod water for several minutes while he regulated his breathing, then he struck out once more for the pier. Again the bracelet tightened around his ankles and the wet throat swallowed him. He went down, down, and found himself not at the bottom of the sea, as he expected, but whirling in a vortex. He thought nothing except, I am going counterclockwise. No sooner had he completed the thought than the sea flattened and he was riding its top. Again he trod water, coughed, spat and shook his head to free his ears of water. When he'd rested he decided to swim butterfly and protect his feet from the sucking that had approached him both times from his right side. But when he tore open the water in front of him, he felt a gentle but firm pressure along his chest, stomach, and down his thighs. Like the hand of an insistent woman it pushed him. He fought hard to break through, but couldn't. The hand was forcing him away from the shore. The man turned his head to see what lay behind him. All he saw was water, blood-tinted by a sun sliding into it like a fresh heart. Far away to his right was *Stor Konigsgaarten,* lit fore and aft.

His strength was leaving him and he knew he should not waste it fighting the current. He decided to let it carry him for a while. Perhaps it would disappear. In any case, it would give him time to regain strength. He floated as best he could in water that heaved and pulsed in the ammonia-scented air and was getting darker all the time. He knew he was in a part of the world that had never known and would never know twilight and that very soon he might be zooming toward the horizon in a pitch-black sea. Queen of France was already showing lights scattered like teardrops from a sky pierced to weeping by the blade tip of an early star. Still the water-lady cupped him in the palm of her hand, and nudged him out to sea. Suddenly he saw new lights—four of them—to his left. He could not judge the distance, but knew they had just been turned on aboard a small craft. Just as suddenly the water-lady removed her hand and the man swam toward the boat anchored in blue water and not the green.

As he neared it, he circled. He heard nothing and saw no one. Moving port side, he made out *Seabird II* and a three-foot rope ladder gently tapping the bow. He grabbed a rung and hoisted himself up and aboard. Panting lightly he padded across the deck. There was no trace of the sun and his canvas shoes were gone.

He sidled along the deck, his back against the walls of the wheelhouse, and looked into its curved windows. No one was there, but he heard music from below and smelled food cooked with a heavy dose of curry. He had nothing in mind to say if anyone suddenly appeared. It was better not to plan, not to have a ready-made story because, however tight, prepared stories sounded most like a lie. The sex, weight, the demeanor of whomever he encountered would inform and determine his tale.

He made his way aft and cautiously descended a short flight of stairs. The music was louder there and the smell of curry stronger. The farthest door stood ajar and from it came the light, the music and the curry. Nearer to him were two closed doors. He chose the first; it opened into a dark closet. The man stepped into it and closed the door softly after him. It smelled heavily of citrus and oil. Nothing was clear so he squatted where he was and listened to what seemed to be radio or record-player music. Slowly he moved his hand forward in the dark and felt nothing as far as his arm could reach. Moving it to the right he touched a wall. He duck-waddled closer to it and sank to the floor, his back against the wall.

He was determined to remain alert at all costs, but the water-lady brushed his eyelids with her knuckles. He dropped into sleep like a rock.

The engine did not wake him—he had slept with the noise of heavier ones for years. Nor did the boat's list. Before the engines was the forgotten sound of a woman's voice—so new and welcoming it broke his dream life apart. He woke thinking of a short street of yellow houses with white doors which women opened wide and called out, "Come on in here, you honey you," their laughter sprawling like a quilt over the command. But nothing sprawled in this woman's voice.

"I'm never lonely," it said. "Never."

The man's scalp tingled. He licked his lips and tasted the salt caked in his mustache.

"Never?" It was another woman's voice—lighter, half in doubt, half in awe.

"Not at all," said the first woman. Her voice seemed warm on the inside, cold at the edges. Or was it the other way around?

"I envy you," said the second voice, but it was farther away now, floating upward and accompanied by footsteps on stairs and the swish of cloth—corduroy against corduroy, or denim against denim—the sound only a woman's thighs could make. A delicious autumn invitation to come in out of the rain and curl up by the stove.

The man could not hear the rest of their talk—they were topside now. He listened awhile longer and then stood up slowly, carefully, and reached for the doorknob. The passageway was brightly lit—the music and curry smell gone. Through the space between doorjamb and door he saw a porthole and in it, deep night. Something crashed to the deck and a moment later rolled to the door saddle where it stopped in a finger of light at his foot. It was a bottle and he could just make out Bain de Soleil on the label. He did not move. His mind was blank but on call. He had not heard anyone descend, but now a woman's hand came into view. Beautifully shaped, pink nail polish, ivory fingers, wedding rings. She picked up the bottle and he could hear her soft grunt as she stooped. She stood and her hand disappeared. Her feet made no sound on the teak boards, but after a few seconds had passed he heard a door—to the galley, perhaps—open and close.

He was the only man aboard. He felt it—a minus something, which eased him. The two or three—he didn't know how many—women who were handling the boat would soon dock at a private pier where there would be no customs inspector stamping passports and furrowing his brow with importance.

The light from the passage allowed him to examine the closet. It was a shelved storage room with a mixture of snorkeling and fishing gear and ship's supplies. A topless crate took up most of the room on the floor. In it were twelve miniature orange trees, all bearing fruit. The man pulled off one of the tiny oranges no bigger than a good-sized strawberry and ate it. The meat was soft, fiberless and bitter. He ate another. And another. And as he ate a wide surgical hunger opened up in him. He had not eaten since the night before, but the hunger that cut through him now was as unaccounted for as it was sudden.

The boat was under way and it did not take him long to realize that they were headed out, not for Queen of France after all. But not very far, he thought. Women with polished fingernails who needed suntan oil would not sail off into the night if they were going very far. So he chewed bitter oranges and waited on his haunches in the closet. When the boat finally drew along and the engine was cut, his hunger was no longer formal; it made him squeeze his fingers together to keep from bolting out of the closet toward the kitchen. But he waited—until the light footsteps were gone. Then he stepped into the passageway spotted in two places by moonlight. Topside he watched two figures moving behind the beam of a heavy-duty flashlight. And when he heard a car's engine start up, he went below. Quickly he found the galley, but because lights would not do, he patted counter surfaces for matches. There weren't any and the stove was electric. He opened a little refrigerator and discovered its bottled water and half a lime. Elsewhere, in refrigerator light, he located a jar of Dijon mustard, but nothing of the curry food. The dishes were rinsed and so was a white carton. The women had not *cooked*—they had warmed up carry-out food that they'd brought aboard. The man ran his finger deep into corners of the white carton and up its sides. Whatever had been left, they must have given to the gulls. He looked in the cupboards: glasses, cups, dishes, a blender, candles, plastic straws, multicolored toothpicks and at last a box of Norwegian flat bread. He covered the bread with mustard, ate it and drank all that was left of the bottled water before going back on deck. There he saw the stars and exchanged stares with the moon, but he could see very little of the land, which was just as well because he was gazing at the shore of an island that, three hundred years ago, had struck slaves blind the moment they saw it.

1

THE END of the world, as it turned out, was nothing more than a collection of magnificent winter houses on Isle des Chevaliers. When laborers imported from Haiti came to clear the land, clouds and fish were convinced that the world was over, that the sea-green green of the sea and the sky-blue sky of the sky were no longer permanent. Wild parrots that had escaped the stones of hungry children in Queen of France agreed and raised havoc as they flew away to look for yet another refuge. Only the champion daisy trees were serene. After all, they were part of a rain forest already two thousand years old and scheduled for eternity, so they ignored the men and continued to rock the diamondbacks that slept in their arms. It took the river to persuade them that indeed the world was altered. That never again would the rain be equal, and by the time they realized it and had run their roots deeper, clutching the earth like lost boys found, it was too late. The men had already folded the earth where there had been no fold and hollowed her where there had been no hollow, which explains what happened to the river. It crested, then lost its course, and finally its head. Evicted from the place where it had lived, and forced into unknown turf, it could not form its pools or waterfalls, and ran every which way. The clouds gathered together, stood still and watched the river scuttle around the forest floor, crash headlong into the haunches of hills with no notion of where it was going, until exhausted, ill and grieving, it slowed to a stop just twenty leagues short of the sea.

The clouds looked at each other, then broke apart in confusion. Fish heard their hooves as they raced off to carry the news of the scatterbrained river to the peaks of hills and the tops of the champion daisy trees. But it was too late. The men had gnawed through the daisy trees until, wild-eyed and yelling, they broke in two and hit the ground. In the huge silence that followed their fall, orchids spiraled down to join them.

When it was over, and houses instead grew in the hills, those trees that had been spared dreamed of their comrades for years afterward and their nightmare mutterings annoyed the diamondbacks who left them for the new growth that came to life in spaces the sun saw for the first time. Then the rain changed and was no longer equal. Now it rained not just for an hour every day at the same time, but in seasons, abusing the river even more. Poor insulted, brokenhearted river. Poor demented stream. Now it sat in one place like a grandmother and became a swamp the Haitians called Sein de Veilles. And witch's tit it was: a shriveled fogbound oval seeping with a thick black substance that even mosquitoes could not live near.

But high above it were hills and vales so bountiful it made visitors tired to look at them: bougainvillea, avocado, poinsettia, lime, banana, coconut and the last of the rain forest's champion trees. Of the houses built there, the oldest and most impressive was L'Arbe de la Croix. It had been designed by a brilliant Mexican architect, but the Haitian laborers had no union and therefore could not distinguish between craft and art, so while the panes did not fit their sashes, the windowsills and door saddles were carved lovingly to perfection. They sometimes forgot or ignored the determination of water to flow downhill so the toilets and bidets could not always produce a uniformly strong swirl of water. But the eaves were so wide and deep that the windows could be left open even in a storm and no rain could enter the rooms—only wind, scents and torn-away leaves. The floor planks were tongue-in-groove, but the hand-kilned tiles from Mexico, though beautiful to behold, loosened at a touch. Yet the doors were plumb and their knobs, hinges and locks secure as turtles.

It was a wonderful house. Wide, breezy and full of light. Built in the days when plaster was taken for granted and with the sun and the airstream in mind, it needed no air conditioning. Graceful landscaping kept the house just under a surfeit of beauty. Every effort had been made to keep it from looking "designed." Almost nothing was askew and the few things that were had charm: the little island touches here and there (a washhouse, a kitchen garden, for example) were practical. At least that was the judgment of discriminating visitors. They all agreed that except for the unfortunate choice of its name it was "the most handsomely articulated and blessedly unrhetorical house in the Caribbean." One or two had reservations—wondered whether all that interior sunlight wasn't a little too robust and hadn't the owner gone rather overboard with the recent addition of a greenhouse? Valerian Street was mindful of their criticism, but completely indifferent to it. His gray eyes drifted over the faces of such guests like a four o'clock shadow on its way to twilight. They reminded him of the Philadelphia widows who, when they heard he was going to spend the whole first year of his retirement in his island house, said, "You'll be back. Six months and you will be bored out of your mind." That was four Decembers ago, and the only things he missed were hydrangeas and the postman. The new greenhouse made it possible to reproduce the hydrangea but the postman was lost to him forever. The rest of what he loved he brought with him: some records, garden shears, a sixty-four-bulb chandelier, a light blue tennis shirt and the Principal Beauty of Maine. Ferrara Brothers (Domestic and International) took care of the rest, and with the help of two servants, the Principal Beauty and mounds of careful correspondence he was finally installed for the year on a hill high enough to watch the sea from three sides. Not that he was interested. Beyond its providing the weather that helped or prevented the steamers bringing mail, he never gave the sea a thought. And whatever he did think about, he thought it privately in his greenhouse. In the late afternoons, when the heat had to be taken seriously, and early in the morning, he was there. Long before the Principal Beauty had removed her sleeping mask, he turned the switch that brought the "Goldberg" Variations into the greenhouse. At first he'd experimented with Chopin and some of the Russians, but the Magnum Rex peonies, overwhelmed by all that passion, whined and curled their lips. He settled finally on Bach for germination, Haydn and Liszt for strong sprouting. After that all of the plants seemed content with Rampal's Rondo in D. By the time he sugared his breakfast coffee, the peonies, the anemones and all their kind had heard forty or fifty minutes of music which nourished them but set Sydney the butler's teeth on edge although he'd heard some variety of it every day for forty years. What made it bearable now was that the music was confined to the greenhouse and not swarming all through the house as it often did back in Philadelphia. He could hear it only thinly now as he wiped moisture beads from a glass of iced water with a white napkin. He set it near the cup and saucer and noticed how much the liver spots had faded on his employer's hand. Mr. Street thought it was the lotion he rubbed on nightly, but Sydney thought it was the natural tanning of the skin in this place they had all come to three years ago.

Except for the kitchen, which had a look of permanence, the rest of the house had a hotel feel about it—a kind of sooner or later leaving appearance: a painting or two hung in an all right place but none was actually stationed or properly lit; the really fine china was still boxed and waiting for a decision nobody was willing to make. It was hard to serve well in the tentativeness. No crystal available (it too was closed away in Philadelphia) so a few silver trays had to do for everything from fruit to petits fours. Every now and then, the Principal Beauty, on one of her trips, brought back from the States another carton chock-full of something Sydney asked for: the blender, the cademon stone, two more tablecloths. These items had to be carefully selected because they were exchanged for other items that she insisted on taking back to Philadelphia. It was her way of keeping intact the illusion that they still lived in the States but were wintering near Dominique. Her husband encouraged her fantasy by knotting every loose string of conversation with the observation "It can wait till we get home." Six months after they'd arrived Sydney told his wife that periodic airing of trunk luggage in the sunlight was more habit than intention. They would have to tear down that greenhouse to get him off the island because as long as it was there, he'd be there too. What the devil does he do in there, she had asked him.

"Relaxes a little, that's all. Drinks a bit, reads, listens to his records."

"Can't nobody spend every day in a shed for three years without being up to some devilment," she said.

"It's not a shed," said Sydney. "It's a greenhouse I keep telling you."

"Whatever you call it."

"He grows hydrangeas in there. And dahlias."

"If he wants hydrangeas he should go back home. He hauls everybody down to the equator to grow Northern flowers?"

"It's not just that. Remember how he liked his study back at the house? Well, it's like that, except it's a greenhouse kind of a study."

"Anybody build a greenhouse on the equator ought to be shame."

"This is not the equator."

"Could of fooled me."

"Nowhere near it."

"You mean there's some place on this planet hotter than this?"

"I thought you liked it here."

"Love it."

"Then stop complaining."

"It's because I do love it that I'm complaining. I'd like to know if it's permanent. Living like this you can't figure nothing. He might pack up any minute and trot off someplace else."

"He'll be here till he dies," Sydney told her. "Less that greenhouse burns up."

"Well, I'll pray nothing happens to it," she said, but she needn't have. Valerian took very good care of the greenhouse for it was a nice place to talk to his ghosts in peace while he transplanted, fed, air-layered, rooted, watered, dried and thinned his plants. He kept a small refrigerator of Blanc de Blancs and read seed catalogs while he sipped the wine. Sometimes he gazed through the little greenhouse panes at the washhouse. Other times he checked catalogs, brochures and entered into ringing correspondence with nurseries from Tokyo to Newburgh, New York. He read only mail these days, having given up books because the language in them had changed so much—stained with rivulets of disorder and meaninglessness. He loved the greenhouse and the island, but not his neighbors. Luckily there was a night, three years ago, after he'd first settled into tropic life, when he woke up with a toothache so brutal it lifted him out of bed and knocked him to his knees. He knelt on the floor clutching the Billy Blass sheets and thinking, This must be a stroke. No tooth could do this to me. Directly above the waves of pain his left eye was crying while his right went dry with rage. He crawled to the night table and pressed the button that called Sydney. When he arrived, Valerian insisted on being taken to Queen of France at once, but there was no way to get there. At that hour fishermen had not even begun to stir and the launch was twice a week. They owned no boat and even if they had neither Sydney nor anyone else could handle it. So the quick-witted butler telephoned the neighbors Valerian hated and got both the use of a fifty-six-foot Palaos called *Seabird II* and the boat skills of the Filipino houseboy. After a daring jeep ride in the dark, an interminable boat ride and a taxi ride that was itself a memory, they arrived at Dr. Michelin's door at

2:00 a.m. Sydney banged while the Filipino chatted with the taxi driver. The dentist roared out the second floor window. He had been run out of Algeria and thought his door was being assaulted by local Blacks—whose teeth he would not repair. At last, Valerian, limp and craven, sat in the dentist's chair where he gave himself up to whatever the Frenchman had in mind. Dr. Michelin positioned a needle toward the roof of Valerian's mouth but seemed to change his mind at the last minute, for Valerian felt the needle shoot straight into his nostril on up to the pupil of his eye and out his left temple. He stretched his hand toward the doctor's trousers, hoping that his death grip—the one they always had to pry loose—would be found to contain the crushed balls of a D.D.S. But before he could get a grip under the plaid bathrobe, the pain disappeared and Valerian wept outright, grateful for the absence of all sensation in his head. Dr. Michelin didn't do another thing. He just sat down and poured himself a drink, eyeing his patient in silence.

This encounter, born in encouraged hatred, ended in affection. The good doctor let Valerian swallow a little of his brandy through a straw and against his better judgment, and Valerian recognized a man who took his medical oaths seriously. They got good and drunk together that night, and the combination of Novocain and brandy gave Valerian an expansiveness he had not felt in years. They visited each other occasionally and whenever Valerian thought of that first meeting he touched the place where the abscess had been and smiled. It had a comic book quality about it: two elderly men drunk and quarreling about Pershing (whom Valerian had actually seen), neither one mentioning then or ever the subject of exile or advanced years which was what they had in common. Both felt as though they had been run out of their homes. Robert Michelin expelled from Algeria; Valerian Street voluntarily exiled from Philadelphia.

Both had been married before and the long years of a second

marriage had done nothing to make either forget his first. The memory of those years of grief in the wake of a termagant was still keen. Michelin had remarried within a year of his divorce, but Valerian stayed a bachelor for a long time and on purpose until he went out for an after lunch stroll on a wintry day in Maine, a stroll he hoped would get rid of the irritable boredom he'd felt among all those food industry appliance reps. His walk from the inn had taken him only two blocks to the main street when he found himself in the middle of a local Snow Carnival Parade. He saw the polar bear and then he saw her. The bear was standing on its hind feet, its front ones raised in benediction. A rosy-cheeked girl was holding on to one of the bear's forefeet like a bride. The plastic igloo behind them threw into dazzling relief her red velvet coat and the ermine muff she waved to the crowd. The moment he saw her something inside him knelt down.

Now he sat in the December sunlight watching his servant pour coffee into his cup.

"Has it come?"

"Sir?"

"The salve."

"Not yet." Sydney removed the lid from a tiny box of saccharin tablets and edged it toward his employer.

"They take their sweet time."

"Mail's cut back to twice a week I told you."

"It's been a month."

"Two weeks. Still botherin you?"

"Not right this minute, but they'll start up again." Valerian reached for the sugar cubes.

"You could be a little less hardheaded about those shoes. Sandals or a nice pair of huaraches all day would clear up every one of them bunions."

"They're not bunions. They're corns." Valerian plopped the cubes into his cup.

"Corns too."

"When you get your medical degree call me. Ondine bake these?"

"No. Mrs. Street brought them back yesterday."

"She uses that boat like it's a bicycle. Back and forth; back and forth."

"Why don't you get one of your own? That thing's too big for her. Can't water-ski with it. Can't even dock it in the town. They have to leave it in one place and get in another little boat just to land."

"Why should I buy her a boat and let it sit ten months out of a year? If those nitwits don't mind her using theirs, it's fine with me."

"Maybe she'd stay the whole year if she had one."

"Not likely. And I prefer she should stay because her husband's here, not because a boat is. Anyway, tell Ondine not to serve them anymore."

"No good?"

"One of the worst things about being old is eating. First you have to find something you can eat and second you have to try not to drop it all over yourself."

"I wouldn't know about that."

"Of course not. You're fifteen minutes younger than I am. Nevertheless, tell Ondine no more of these. Too flaky. They fly all over no matter what you do."

"Croissant supposed to be flaky. That's as short a dough as you can make."

"Just tell her, Sydney."

"Yes, sir."

"And find out if the boy can straighten those bricks. They are popping up all over the place."

"He needs cement he said."

"No. No cement. He's to pack them down properly. The soil will hold them if he does it right."

"Yes, sir."

"Mrs. Street awake?"

"I believe so. Anything else special you going to want for the holidays?"

"No. Just the geese. I won't be able to eat a bit of it, but I want to see it on the table anyway. And some more thalomide."

"You want Yardman to bring you thalomide? He can't even pronounce it."

"Write a note. Tell him to give it to Dr. Michelin."

"All right."

"And tell Ondine that half Postum and half coffee is revolting. Worse than Postum alone."

"Okay. Okay. She thought it would help."

"I know what she thought, but the help is worse than the problem."

"That might not be what the trouble is, you know."

"You are determined to make me have an ulcer. I don't have an ulcer. You have an ulcer. I have occasional irregularity."

"I *had* an ulcer. It's gone now and Postum helped it go."

"I'm delighted. Did you say she was awake?"

"She was. Could have gone back to sleep, though."

"What did she want?"

"Want?"

"Yes. Want. The only way you could know she was awake is if she rang you up there. What did she want?"

"Towels, fresh towels."

"Sydney."

"She did. Ondine forgot to—"

"What were the towels wrapped around?"

"Why you keep thinking that? Everything she drinks you see her drink. A little dinner wine, that's all and hardly more than a glass of that. She never was a drinker. You the one. Why you always trying to make her into one?"

"I'll speak to Jade."

"What could Jade know that I don't?"

"Nothing, but she's as honest as they come."

"Come on, now, Mr. Street. It's the truth."

Valerian held a pineapple quarter with his fork and began cutting small regular pieces from it.

"All right," said Sydney, "I'll tell you. She wanted Yardman to stop by the airport before he comes Thursday."

"What for, pray?"

"A trunk. She's expecting a trunk. It's been shipped already, she said, and ought to be here by then."

"What an idiot."

"Sir?"

"Idiot. Idiot."

"Mrs. Street, sir?"

"Mrs. Street, Mr. Street, you, Ondine. Everybody. This is the first time in thirty years I've been able to enjoy this house. Really live in it. Not for a month or a weekend but for a while, and everybody is conspiring to ruin it for me. Coming and going, going and coming. It's beginning to feel like Thirtieth Street Station. Why can't everybody settle down, relax, have a nice simple Christmas. Not a throng, just a nice simple Christmas dinner."

"She gets a little bored, I guess. Got more time than she can use."

"Insane. Jade's here. They get on like schoolgirls, it seems to me. Am I wrong?"

"No, you're right. They get along fine, like each other's company, both of them."

"They don't like it enough to let it go at that. Apparently we are expecting *more* company, and since I am merely the owner and operator of this hotel, there is no reason to let me know about it."

"Can I get you some toast?"

"And you. You have finally surprised me. What else have you been keeping from me?"

"Eat your pineapple."

"I am eating it."

"I can't stand here all morning. You got corns—I got bunions."

"If you won't take my advice, bunions are the consequence."

"I know my work. I'm a first-rate butler and I can't be first-rate in slippers."

"You know your work, but I know your feet. Thom McAn will be the death of you."

"I never wore Thom McAns in my life. Never. In nineteen twenty-nine I didn't wear them."

"I distinctly recall at least four pairs of decent shoes I've given you."

"I prefer my bunions to your corns."

"Ballys don't cause corns. If anything they prevent them. It's the perspiration that causes them. When—"

"See? Gotcha. That's exactly what I been tellin you. Philadelphia shoes don't work in the tropics. Make your feet sweat. You need some nice huaraches. Make your feet feel good. Free em up, so they can breathe."

"The day I spend in huaraches is the day I spend in a straitjacket."

"You keep on hacking away at your toes with a razor and you'll beg for a straitjacket."

"Well, you won't know about it because your Thom McAn bunions are going to put you in a rocker for the rest of your life."

"Suit me fine."

"And me. Maybe then I could hire somebody who wouldn't keep things from me. Sneak Postum into a good pot of coffee, saccharin in the lime pie. And don't think I don't know about the phony salt."

"Health is the most important thing at our age, Mr. Street."

"Not at all. It's the least important. I have no intention of staying alive just so I can wake up and skip down the stairs to a cup of Postum in the morning. Look in the cabinet and get me a drop of medicine for this stuff."

"Cognac's not medicine." Sydney moved toward the sideboard and bent to open one of its doors.

"At seventy everything's medicine. Tell Ondine to quit it. It's not doing a thing for me."

"Sure don't help your disposition none."

"Exactly. Now. Very quietly and very quickly, tell me who this company is."

"No company, Mr. Street."

"Don't antagonize an old man reduced to Postum."

"It's your son. Michael's not company."

Valerian put his cup carefully onto the saucer. "She told you that? That Michael was coming?"

"No. Not exactly. But so Yardman would know what to look for she told me where the trunk was coming from and what color it was."

"Then it's coming from California."

"It's coming from California."

"And it's red."

"And it's red. Fire red."

"With 'Dick Gregory for President' stickers pasted on the sides."

"And a bull's-eye painted on the lid."

"And a lock that only closes if you kick it, but opens with a hairpin and the key is . . ." Valerian stopped and looked up at Sydney. Sydney looked at Valerian. They said it together. ". . . at the top of Kilimanjaro."

"Some joke," said Valerian.

"Pretty good for a seven-year-old."

They were quiet for a while, Valerian chewing pineapple, Sydney leaning against the sideboard. Then Valerian said, "Why do you suppose he hangs on to it? A boy's camp footlocker."

"Keep his clothes in."

"Foolish. All of it. The trunk, him and this visit. Besides, he won't show."

"She thinks so this time."

"She's not thinking. She's dreaming, poor baby. Are you sure there was nothing between those towels?"

"Here comes the lady. Ask her yourself."

A light clicking of heels on Mexican tile was getting louder.

"When the boy goes to the airport," whispered Valerian, "tell him to pick up some Maalox on the way back." "Well," he said to his wife, "what have we here? Wonder Woman?"

"Please," she said, "it's too hot. Good morning, Sydney."

"Morning, Mrs. Street."

"Then what is that between your eyebrows?"

"Frownies."

"Beg pardon?"

"Frownies."

Sydney walked around the table, tilted the pot and poured coffee soundlessly into her cup.

"You have trouble frowning?" asked her husband.

"Yes."

"And that helps?"

"Supposed to." She held the cup in front of her lips and closed her eyes. The steam floated into her face while she inhaled.

"I am confused. Not senile, mind you. Just confused. Why would you want to frown?"

Margaret took another breath of coffee steam and opened her eyes very slowly. She looked at her husband with the complete dislike of a natural late-sleeper for a cheerful early-riser.

"I don't want to frown. Frownies don't make you frown. They erase the consequences of frowning."

Valerian opened his mouth but said nothing for a moment. Then: "But why don't you just stop frowning? Then you won't need to paste your face with little pieces of tape."

Margaret sipped more coffee and returned the cup to its saucer. Lifting the neckline of her dress away from her she blew gently into her bosom and looked at the pale wedges

Sydney placed before her. Ondine had left the spiky skin on the underside deliberately—just to hurt and confuse her. "I thought we'd have . . . mangoes." Sydney removed the fruit and hurried to the swinging doors. "What gets into everybody? The same thing every morning?"

"I wanted pineapple. If you don't, tell Sydney at night what you'd like for breakfast the next morning. That way he can—"

"She knows I hate fresh pineapple. The threads get in my teeth. I like canned. Is that so terrible?"

"Yes. Terrible."

"They tell *us* what to eat. Who's working for who?"

"Whom. If you give Ondine menus for the whole week—that is exactly what she will prepare."

"Really? You've been doing that for thirty years and you can't even get her to fix you a cup of coffee. She makes you drink Postum."

"That's different."

"Sure."

Sydney returned with a bowl of crushed ice in which a mango stood. The peeling had been pulled back from the shiny fruit in perfect curls. The slits along the pulp were barely visible. Valerian yawned behind his fist, then said, "Sydney, can I or can I not order a cup of coffee and get it?"

"Yes, sir. 'Course you can." He put down the mango and filled Valerian's cup.

"See, Margaret. And there's your mango. Four hundred and twenty-five calories."

"What about your croissant?"

"One twenty-seven."

"God." Margaret closed her eyes, her blue-if-it's-a-boy blue eyes and put down her fork.

"Have a grapefruit."

"I don't want grapefruit. I want mango."

Valerian shrugged. "Slurp away. But you had three helpings of mousse last night."

"Two, I had two. Jade had three."

"Oh, well, only two . . ."

"Well, what do we have a cook for? Even I can slice grapefruit."

"To wash the dishes."

"Who needs dishes? According to you, all I need is a teaspoon."

"Well, someone has to wash your teaspoon."

"And your shovel."

"Funny. Very funny."

"It's true." Margaret held her breath and stuck her fork into the mango. She exhaled slowly as the section came away on the tines. She glanced at Valerian before putting the slice in her mouth. "I've never seen anyone eat as much as you and not gain an ounce—ever. I think she adds things to my food. Wheat germs or something. At night she sneaks in with one of those intravenous things and pumps me full of malts."

"Nobody pumps you full of anything."

"Or whipped cream maybe."

Sydney had left them discussing calories and now he was back with a silver tray on which wafer-thin slices of ham tucked into toast baskets held a poached egg. He went to the sideboard and lifted them onto plates. He laid stems of parsley on the right rim and two tomato slices to the left of each plate. He whisked away the fruit bowls, careful not to spill the water from the ice, and then leaned forward with the hot dish. Margaret frowned at the dish and waved it away. Sydney returned to the sideboard, put the rejected dish down and picked up the other. Valerian accepted it enthusiastically and Sydney edged the salt and pepper mill an inch or two out of his reach.

"I suppose you are decorating the house with guests for Christmas. Push that salt over here, will you?"

"Why would you suppose that?" Margaret stretched out a hand, a beautifully manicured hand, and passed him the salt and pepper. Her little victory with the mango strengthened her enough to concentrate on what her husband was saying.

"Because I asked you not to. It follows therefore that you would defy me."

"Have it your way. Let's just spend the holidays all alone in the cellar."

"We haven't got a cellar, Margaret. You should take a look around this place. You might like it. Come to think of it, I don't believe you've seen the kitchen yet, have you? We've got two, two kitchens. One is—"

"Valerian. Please shut up."

"But this is exciting. We've been coming here for only thirty years and already you've discovered the dining room. That's three whole rooms. One every decade. First you found the bedroom. That is I assume you did. It's hard to tell when a wife sleeps separately from her mate. Then in nineteen sixty-five I think it was, you located the living room. Remember that? Those cocktail parties? Those were good times. Heights, I'd say. You not only knew the airport and the dock and the bedroom, but the living room as well."

"Yes. I am having guests for Christmas."

"Then the dining room. Speak of a find! Dinner for ten, twenty, thirty. Think what's before you in one kitchen, let alone two. We could entertain hundreds, thousands."

"Michael's coming."

"I wouldn't put it off any longer if I were you. If we hurry by the time I'm eighty we can invite Philadelphia."

"And a friend of his. That's all."

"He won't come."

"I've never had more than twelve people in this house at any one time."

"His friend will show and he won't. Again."

"And I am not a cook and I never have been. I don't want to see the kitchen. I don't like kitchens."

"Why work yourself up this way every year? You know he'll disappoint you."

"I was a child bride, remember? I hadn't time to learn to cook before you put me in a house that already had one plus a kitchen fifty miles from the front door."

"Seems to me you did once. You and Ondine giggling away in the kitchen is one of my clearest and fondest memories."

"Why do you say that? You always say that."

"It's true. I'd come home and you'd be—"

"Not that! About Michael, I mean. That he won't show up."

"Because he never has."

"He never has *here*. Down here in this jungle with nothing to do. No young people. No fun. No music . . ."

"No *music?*"

"I mean his kind of music."

"You surprise me."

"And so he won't be bored to death, I've invited a friend of his—" She stopped and pressed a finger to the frownie between her eyes. "I haven't invited anybody down here in years because of you. You hate everybody."

"I don't hate anybody."

"Three years it's been. What's the matter with you? Don't you want to see your son anymore? I know you don't want to see anybody else—but your own son. You pay more attention to that fat dentist than you do Michael. What are you trying to prove down here? Why do you cut yourself off from everybody, everything?"

"It's just that I'm undergoing this very big change in my life called dying."

"Retirement isn't death."

"A distinction without a difference."

"Well, I am not dying. I am living."

"A difference without distinction."

"And I'm going back with him."

"Sounds terminal."

"It might be."

"Christmas isn't the best time to make decisions like that, Margaret. It's a sentimental holiday full of foolish—"

"Look. I'm going."

"I don't advise it."

"I don't care."

"He's not a little boy anymore. The knapsack, I know, is confusing, but Margaret, he'll soon be thirty."

"So what?"

"So what makes you think he'll want you to live with him?"

"He will."

"You're going to travel with him? Go to snake dances?"

"I'm going to live near him. Not with him, near him."

"It won't work."

"Why not?"

Valerian put his palms down on either side of his plate. "He doesn't care all that much for us, Margaret."

"You," she said, "he doesn't care all that much for you."

"Whatever you say."

"Then I can go?"

"We'll see. When he gets here, ask him. Ask him if he wants his mother next door to the reservation in a condominium."

"He's through with that. The school closed. He's not with them anymore."

"Oh? He's done the Hopis? Gone on to the Choctaws, I suppose. No, wait a minute. *C* comes before *H*. Let me see, Navajos, right?"

"He's not with any tribe. He's studying."

"What, pray?"

"Environmental something. He wants to be an environmental lawyer."

"Does he now?"

"Yes."

"Well, why not? A band manager, shepherd, poet-in-residence, film producer, lifeguard ought to study law, the more environmental the better. An advantage really, since he's certainly had enough environments to choose from. And what will you do? Design no-nuke stickers?"

"You can't make me change my mind."

"It's not a matter of changing it. It's a matter of using it. Let him alone, Margaret. Let him be. You can't do it over. What you want is crazy."

"No. *This* is crazy. I live in airplanes now. Nowhere. Not in Philadelphia where I at least have friends. Not here boiling under a palm tree with nobody to talk to. You keep saying next month, next month, next month. But you never do it. You never leave."

"But you do—whenever you like. Lots of people live in two places."

"I want to live in one—just one. In October you said after New Year's, you'll come back. Then when New Year's comes you'll say after carnival. If I want to live with you I have to do it your way—here. I can't keep flying back and forth across the ocean wondering where I left the Kotex. Anyway. I'm going back with Michael. For a while. Make a home for him."

"You'll have to eat corncakes. Three hundred and twenty-five per serving."

"I told you he's not there anymore. He's applied at U.C. Berkeley, I think."

"Marijuana cookies then. Two hundred—"

"You will not listen."

"Margaret, promise me something."

"What?"

"That you won't go unless he agrees to it."

"But—"

"Promise."

She studied him for a moment for she never knew if he was teasing her, patronizing her or simply lying. But now he looked deadly earnest so she nodded saying, "All right. All right. That's no risk."

"What about Jade, then?" asked Valerian.

"What about her? She can stay as long as she likes."

"She thinks she's working for you."

"Let her work for you while I'm gone."

"Oh dear."

"Or just relax. She wanted to spend the winter here is all. Why, I can't think."

"Getting over an affair, I thought."

"At her age it takes three days, not three months."

"You don't like her anymore?"

"I love her. But I'm not going to give up going back with Michael just to help her cool off for another month or two. Besides, look what she has to go back to."

"What?"

"Everything. Europe. The future. The world. Why are you frowning? Does she need money?"

"No. No. Not that I know of. She signed on with some agency or something in New York, or is about to."

"There. She doesn't need the pretense of working for me."

Valerian swallowed the last bit of egg and ham and tapped the toast basket with his fork. "Clever. Very clever."

"Jade?"

"No, Ondine. This is really good. I think she served something like this in the States."

"Talk about calories. You're eating like a horse already and the day has just started."

"Pique."

"Pique. Why?"

"The nursery, Stateside, sent a defective order. Completely ruined."

"Shame." Margaret reached toward a croissant, changed her mind and withdrew her hand.

"Have it," said her husband. "It wasn't four twenty-five, that mango. Not even a hundred."

"You liar. I should have known. I was going to ask Jade about that."

"She wants to open up a little shop of some sort," he said.

"You're mumbling."

"Shop. She wants to be a model a little longer, then open up a shop."

"Wonderful. She has a head. You'll help her, won't you? Won't you?"

"Of course."

"Well, why the long face?"

"I was thinking of Sydney and Ondine."

"As usual. What about them?"

"They like her here."

"We all do."

"She's their family. All they have of a family left."

"And you. You're as much family to them as she is. They've known you longer than they have her."

"It's not the same."

"What is it? What are you thinking?"

"Nothing."

"Something."

"Sydney's very excited about that shop idea," Valerian said. "Ondine too."

"Oh?"

"Nothing definite. At the dreaming stage still."

"Now who's worked up?"

"It's a possibility, that's all. An attractive one for them, I suppose."

"That's selfish, Valerian."

"Perhaps, but I don't think so. I don't think so."

"You're worrying about nothing. They won't leave you and the situation they have here to go into the retail business. At this time of life, never."

"Yes?"

"Of course yes. Look at you." She laughed. "You're scared. Scared Kingfish and Beulah won't take care of you."

"I have always taken care of them."

"And they will do the same for you. God knows they will. You couldn't pry them out of here. With or without Jade. They are yours for life."

"Don't snarl. Your frownie is coming loose."

"I'm not snarling. They're loyal people and they should be."

"I've never understood your jealousy."

"That's just like you to call it jealousy."

"When we were first married I used to have to pull you away from Ondine. Guests in the house and you'd prefer gossiping in the kitchen with her."

"Well, you sure put a stop to that, didn't you?"

"I put a stop to a hostess neglecting guests. I didn't put a stop to—"

"I was shy."

"But I didn't want you to turn around and be outright hateful to her. She would have quit even then if I hadn't—"

"I know. I know, and then Sydney the Precious would have left too. Don't dwell on it. They're here and they always will be. I can guarantee it."

"But you won't be."

"I said for a while."

"*If* Michael comes."

"He will."

"We'll see."

"Then it's all set? I can go?"

"Don't push me into my last and final hour, Margaret. Let me saunter toward it."

"You are sweet."

"Not sweet, helpless."

"You? Valerian Street, the Candy King? You've never been stronger, or more beautiful."

"Stop. You got your way."

"You *are* beautiful. Slim. Trim. Distingue."

"Forgive her, Larousse."

"Distingue?"

"Distingué."

"Joueaux Noël."

"Dear God."

"Joyoux Noël, Sydney."

"Ma'am?"

"Did you tell the boy about the trunk?"

"He hasn't come yet, ma'am. As soon as he does . . ."

"And turkey. Ondine will do a turkey. Sydney?"

"Ah, yes, ma'am, if you like."

"I like. I really like."

"I've ordered geese, Margaret."

"Geese?" She stared at Valerian for suddenly she could not imagine it. Like a blank frame in a roll of film, she lost the picture that should have accompanied the word. Turkey she saw, but geese . . . "We have to have turkey for Christmas. This is a family Christmas, an old-fashioned family Christmas, and Michael has to have turkey."

"If Tiny Tim could eat goose, Margaret, Michael can eat goose."

"Turkey!" she said. "Roast turkey with the legs sticking up and a shiny brown top." She was moving her hands to show them how it looked. "Little white socks on the feet."

"I'll mention it to Ondine, ma'am."

"You will not mention it! You will tell her!"

"Yes, ma'am."

"And apple pies."

"Apple, ma'am?"

"Apple. And pumpkin."

"We are in the Caribbean, Margaret."

"No! I said no! If we can't have turkey and apple pie for Christmas then maybe we shouldn't be here at all!"

"Hand me some of my medicine, Sydney."
"Yes, sir."
"Sydney?"
"Ma'am?"
"Will we have turkey and apple pies for Christmas dinner?"
"Yes, ma'am. I'll see to it."
"Thank you. Is Jade down yet?"
"Not yet, ma'am."
"When she is, tell her I'll be ready at ten."
"Yes, ma'am."

Margaret Lenore stood up so suddenly her chair careened for a brief moment before righting itself. Quickly she was gone.

"Everything all right, Mr. Street?"
"I am going to kill you, Sydney."
"Yes, sir."

BEYOND the doors through which Sydney had been gliding all morning was the first kitchen. A large sunny room with two refrigerators, two steel sinks, one stove, rows of open cabinets and a solid oak table that seated six. Sydney sat down and immediately the place he took at the perfectly round table was its head. He looked out the windows and then at his wife's arm. The flesh trembled as she wire-whisked a bowl of eggs.

"Mango all right?" she asked without turning her head.

"She ate a mouthful," said Sydney.

"Contrary," murmured his wife. She poured the eggs into a shallow buttered pan, and stirred them slowly with a wooden spoon.

"It's all right, Ondine. Lucky you had one."

"I'll say. Even the colored people down here don't eat mangoes."

"Sure they do." Sydney slipped a napkin from its ring. The pale blue linen complemented his mahogany hands.

"Yardmen," said Ondine. "And beggars." She poured the eggs

into a frying pan of chicken livers. She was seventeen years her husband's junior, but her hair, braided across the crown of her head, was completely white. Sydney's hair was not as black as it appeared, but certainly not snow white like Ondine's. She bent to check on the biscuits in the oven.

"What's the Principal Beauty hollering about?"

"Turkey."

Ondine looked at her husband over her shoulder. "Don't fool with me this morning."

"And apple pie."

"You better get me a plane ticket out of here." She straightened.

"Calm down, girl."

"She want it, she can come in here and cook it. After she swim on back up to New York and get the ingredients. Where she think she is?"

"It's for the boy."

"God help us."

"She wants an old-fashioned Christmas."

"Then she can bring her old-fashioned butt in here and cook it up."

"Pumpkin pie, too."

"Is any of this serious?"

"I told you. The boy is coming."

"He's always coming. Ain't got here yet."

"Then you know as much as I do. Every year the same. She'll walk on a hot tin roof till he wires saying he can't. Then look out!"

"You can't be serious about apples. Surely."

"I can't be certain, Ondine. Looks like he might make it this time. He's already shipped his trunk. That old red footlocker, remember? Yardman supposed to pick it up Thursday."

"She don't know that. He call her and say so? Ain't been no mail come in here from him, has it?"

"She called him, I believe. This morning. Making sure of the time difference."

"That's what she rang you up for?"

"I didn't have time to tell you."

"When's he due?"

"Soon, I reckon." Sydney dropped two sugar cubes into his Postum.

"I thought all he ate was sunflowers and molasses these days."

Sydney shrugged. "Last time I saw him he ate a mighty lot of steak."

"And fresh coconut cake. The whole cake as I recall."

"That's your fault. You spoiled him stupid."

"You can't spoil a child. Love and good food never spoiled nobody."

"Then maybe he'll fly in here for sure this time just to get some more of it."

"No way. Not down here, he won't. He hates this place, coconuts and all. Always did."

"Liked it when he was younger."

"Well, he's grown now and sees with grown-up eyes, like I do."

"I still say you ruined him. He can't fix his mind on nothing."

"I ain't ruined him. I gave him what any child is due."

"Uh-huh."

"You really believe that? That I ruined him?"

"Oh, I don't know, girl. Just talking. But between you and the Principal Beauty, he never wanted for affection."

"Bitch."

"You have to stop that, Ondine. Every time she comes down here you act out. I'm getting tired of refereeing everybody."

"The Principal Beauty of Maine is the main bitch of the prince."

"You worry me. Cut the fire out from under that pan and bring me my breakfast."

"I just want you to know I am not fooled by all that turkey and apple pie business. Fact is he don't want to be nowhere near her. And I can't say as I blame him, mother though she be."

"You making up a life that nobody is living. She sees him all the time in the States and he don't complain."

"Visits. Visits he can't do nothing about, but he never comes to see her."

"He writes her sweet letters."

"That's what he studied in school."

"Letters?"

"Poems."

"Don't think he don't love her. He does."

"I didn't say he didn't love her; I said he don't want to be near her. Sure he love her. That's only natural. He's not the one who's not natural. She is."

"You and Mr. Street just alike. Always thinking evil about that girl."

"When she get to be a girl?"

"She was a girl when I first saw her. Seventeen."

"So was I."

"Aw, the devil. Everybody's going crazy in this house. Everybody. Mr. Street hollering about Postum and putting cognac in his cup—she's hollering about mangoes and turkeys and I don't know what all and now you denying her her own son."

"I'm not denying her nothin. She can have him. He turned out to be a different breed of cat anyway after he went to all those schools. He was a sweet boy. Now I suppose he'll be wanting mangoes too. Well, he can have em if he'll stop coming in my kitchen to liberate me every minute."

"He means well, Ondine."

"What's this about the Postum?"

"He says no more diet stuff. Regular coffee, real salt, all such as that."

"He'll rue it."

"It's his life."

"Okay by me. It's bothersome trying to cook with all those concoctions. Fake this. Fake that. Tears up a meal if you ask me. That plus everything temporary like this. Seems like everything I need to cook with is back in Philadelphia. I was just going by what the doctor told him three years ago. He leave that liquor alone he could eat like regular people. Is he still constipated?"

"Nope. Other people get constipated. He gets occasional irregularity. But he wants some Maalox just in case. Tell Yardman to bring a bottle out next time."

"He the one should be eating mangoes. Open him right up. Other than for that, I can't think of a soul in this world eat mangoes for breakfast."

"I do."

They hadn't heard her come in. She stood before the swinging doors, hands on hips, toes pointing in, and smiling. Sydney and Ondine looked around, their faces bright with pleasure.

"Here she is!" said Sydney, and reached out a hand to hug her waist. She came forward and kissed his forehead. Then Ondine's.

"Sleep well, sugar?"

"Well and late." She sat down and locked her arms over her head in a deep yawn. "The air. The night air is incredible. It's like food."

"You weren't serious, were you?" asked Ondine. "About wanting a mango?"

"No. Yes. I don't know." Jadine dug her fingernails into her hair and scratched.

"I've got some nice liver. Sautéed just right. With eggs."

"What kind of liver?"

"Chicken."

"The chicken's eggs and its liver? Is there anything inside a chicken we don't eat?"

"Jadine, we're still at the table," said Sydney. "Don't talk like that." He patted her knee.

"Pineapple," she said. "I'll have some pineapple."

"Well," said Ondine, "thank God somebody in this house got some sense. That hussy sure don't."

"Let up, woman. She's got something to deal with."

"So has he."

"Yeah, well, I've known him practically all his life and I'll tell you this: he gets his way. Even when he was a little boy, he got his way."

Jadine looked up. "Valerian was a little boy? You sure?"

"Hush up." Sydney wiped his mouth with the pale blue napkin. "You be around all day today?"

"Most of it. But I may have to take the boat back to town."

"What for? More Christmas shopping?"

"Yep."

"You sure you won't have some livers?"

"No, thanks, Nanadine, but could I have a cup of chocolate?"

"In this heat?" asked Sydney. He raised his eyebrows, but Ondine smiled. She loved it when her niece called her that—a child's effort to manage "Aunt Ondine." "Sure you can," she said, and went immediately to the nickel-plated door that opened on a hallway. At the end, four steps descended to the second kitchen where supplies were kept and which was equipped like a restaurant kitchen.

Back in the first kitchen Sydney grumbled in the sunlight. "Air conditioning in the shed, but none in the house. I swear. All that money."

Jadine licked sweet wet juice from her fingertips. "I love it. Makes the nights so much better. As soon as the sun goes down it's cool anyway."

"I work in the daytime, girl."

"So do I."

"You still calling that work?"

"It is work."

Sydney sucked his teeth. "Exercising. Cutting pictures out of magazines. Going to the store."

"I type," she said. "And going to the store is a twenty-three-mile boat trip, *after* driving through jungle, swamp . . ."

"You better not let him hear you call anything on this island jungle."

"Well, what does he call it? The Tuileries?"

"You know what he calls it," said Sydney, digging in his vest pocket for a toothpick. "L'Arbe de la Croix."

"I hope he's wrong." Jadine laughed.

Ondine entered, limping a little from the few stairs and frowning. "There's something in this house that loves bitter-sweet chocolate. I had six eight-ounce boxes, now there's two."

"Rats?" asked Sydney. He looked concerned. Mr. Street and the other families had pooled money to have mongooses shipped to the island to get rid of snakes and rats.

"If rats fold wrappers, then yes, rats."

"Well, who then? Couldn't be over fifteen people on the whole island. The Watts are gone; so are the Broughtons," said Sydney.

"Maybe it's one of the new staff over at Deauville. All Filipinos again, I heard. Four of them."

"Come on, Nanadine. Why would they walk all the way over here to steal a piece of chocolate?" Her niece swirled a napkin ring on her finger.

Ondine poured a tiny bit of water into a saucepan and plopped a chocolate square into it. "Well, somebody is. And not just chocolate either. The Evian, too. Half a case."

"Must be Yardman," said Sydney, "or one of them Marys."

"Couldn't be. He don't step foot inside the house unless I'm behind him and I can't get them Marys further in than the screen door."

"You don't know that, Ondine," said Sydney. "You not in here every minute."

"I do know that and I know my kitchens. Better than I know my face."

Jadine loosened the straps of her halter and fanned her neck. "Well, let me tell you your face is prettier than your kitchens."

Ondine smiled. "Look who's talking. The girl who modeled for Karen."

"Caron, Nanadine. Not Karen."

"Whatever. My face wasn't in every magazine in Paris. Yours was. Prettiest thing I ever saw. Made those white girls disappear. Just disappear right off the page." She stirred milk into the chocolate paste and chuckled. "Your mother would have loved to see that."

"You think you'll ever do that again?" Sydney asked her.

"Maybe, but once is plenty. I want my own business now."

Once more they looked at her, pleasure shining in their faces. Ondine brought the chocolate and set it down. She touched Jadine's hair and said softly to her, "Don't you ever leave us, baby. You all we got."

"Whipped cream?" asked Jadine, smiling. "Any whipped cream?"

Ondine looked in the refrigerator for cream while Sydney and Jadine turned to the window as they heard footsteps on the gravel. Yardman came alone on Saturdays, pulling his own oars in his own mud-colored boat with *Prix de France* fading in blue on the prow. Today being Saturday and no dinner party or special work to be done, he did not bring a Mary who, according to Sydney, might be his wife, his mother, his daughter, his sister, his woman, his aunt or even a next-door neighbor. She looked a little different to the occupants of L'Arbe de la Croix each time, except for her Greta Garbo hat. They all referred to her as Mary and couldn't ever be wrong about it because all the baptized black women on the island had Mary among their names. Once in a while Yardman brought a small-boned girl too. Fourteen, perhaps, or twenty, depending on what she chose to do with her eyes.

Sydney would go down to the little dock then, in the Willys jeep, and return with the whole crew, driving through beautiful terrain, then through Sein de Veilles saying nothing for he preferred their instructions to come from his wife. Yardman sometimes ventured a comment or two, but the Mary and the small-boned girl never said anything at all. They just sat in the jeep quietly hiding their hair from the eyes of malevolent strangers. Sydney may have maintained a classy silence, but Ondine talked to them constantly. Yardman answered her but the Mary never did except for a quiet "Oui, madame" if she felt pressed. Ondine tried, unsuccessfully, for months to get a Mary who would work inside. With no explicit refusal or general explanation each Mary took the potatoes, the pot, the paper sack and the paring knife outdoors to the part of the courtyard the kitchen opened onto. It enraged Ondine because it gave the place a nasty, common look. But when, at her insistence, Yardman brought another Mary, she too took the pail of shrimp outside to shell and devein them. One of them even hauled the ironing board and the basket of Vera sheets out there. Ondine made her bring it all back and from then on they had the flat linen done in Queen of France along with the fine.

Yardman, however, was accommodating. Not only did he run errands for them in the town, he swept, mowed, trimmed, clipped, transplanted, moved stones, hauled twigs and leaves, sprayed and staked as well as washed windows, reset tiles, resurfaced the drive, fixed locks, caught rats—all manner of odd jobs. Twice a year a professional maintenance crew came. Four young men and an older one, all white, in a launch with machines. They cleaned draperies, waxed and polished floors, scrubbed walls and tile, checked the plumbing and the wiring, varnished and sealed the shutters, cleaned the gutters and downspouts. The money they made from the fifteen families on the island alone was enough for a thriving business, but they worked other private and semiprivate islands year-round and were able to drive Mercedeses and Yamahas all over Queen of France.

Now all three looked out the kitchen window at the old man as though they could discover with their eyes an uncontrolled craving for chocolate and bottled water in his. Yardman's face was nothing to enjoy, but his teeth were a treat. Stone-white and organized like a drugstore sample of what teeth ought to be.

Ondine sighed pointedly and walked to the door. She wished he could read, then she wouldn't have to recite a list of chores and errands three times over so he would not forget: a red footlocker, a bottle of Maalox, the Christmas tree, thalomide, putting down bricks—but she'd be damned if she'd mention a turkey.

2

A HOUSE of sleeping humans is both closed and wide open. Like an ear it resists easy penetration but cannot brace for attack. Luckily in the Caribbean there is no fear. The unsocketed eye that watches sleepers is not threatening—it is merely alert, which anyone can tell for it has no lid and cannot wax or wane. No one speaks of a quarter or half moon in the Caribbean. It is always full. Always adrift and curious. Unastonished but never bored by the things it beholds: a pair of married servants sleeping back to back. The man without pajama tops in deference to the heat; his wife up to her neck in percale to defy it. There is safety in those backs. Each one feels it radiating from the other, knows that the steady, able spine of its partner is a hip turn away. Then their sleep is tranquil, earned, unlike the sleep of the old man upstairs in cotton pajamas. He has napped so frequently in his greenhouse during the day that night sleep eludes him. Sometimes he needs a half balloon of brandy to find it, and even then he chats the night away, whispering first to his wrist, then to the ceiling the messages he has received that need telling. And when he has got it straight—the exact wording, even the spelling of the crucial words—he is happy and laughs lightly like a sweet boy. His wife, in another room, has carefully climbed the steps to sleep and arrived at its door with luggage packed and locked: buffered nails, lightly oiled skin, hair pinned, teeth brushed—all her tips in shining order. Her breathing is still rapid, for she has just done twelve minutes of Canadian Air Force exercises. Eventually it slows, and under her sleeping mask two cotton balls soaked in witch hazel nestle against peaceful eyelids. She is hopeful in sleep for this may be the night she will dream the dream she ought to. Next to her bedroom, adjacent to it with a connecting door (she is not in this house year-round and has chosen a guest room rather than the master bedroom as her own), a young woman barely twenty-five years old is wide-awake. Again. She fell asleep immediately when first she lay down, but after an hour she woke rigid and frightened from a dream of large hats. Large beautiful women's hats like Norma Shearer's and Mae West's and Jeanette MacDonald's although the dreamer is too young to have seen their movies or remembered them if she had. Feathers. Veils. Flowers. Brims flat, brims drooping, brims folded, and rounded. Hat after lovely sailing hat surrounding her until she is finger-snapped awake. She lay there under the eye of the moon wondering why the hats had shamed and repelled her so. As soon as she gave up looking for the center of the fear, she was reminded of another picture that was not a dream. Two months ago, in Paris, the day she went grocery shopping. One of the happiest days of her life—full of such good weather and such good news she decided to throw a party to celebrate. She telephoned all the people she loved and some she did not and then drove all the way to the Supra Market in the 19ème arrondissement. Everything on her list was sure to be there, and no substitutes or compromises were necessary: Major Grey's chutney, real brown rice, fresh pimiento, tamarind rinds, coconut and the split breasts of two young lambs. There were Chinese mushrooms and arugula; palm hearts and Bertolli's Tuscany olive oil. If you had just been chosen for the cover of *Elle,* and there were three count three gorgeous and raucous men to telephone you or screech up to your door in Yugoslavian touring cars with Bordeaux Blanc and sandwiches and a little C, and when you have a letter from a charming old man saying your orals were satisfactory to the committee—well, then you go to the Supra Market for your dinner ingredients and plan a rich and tacky menu of dishes Easterners thought up for Westerners in order to indispose them, but which were printed in *Vogue* and *Elle* in a manner impressive to a twenty-five-year-old who could look so much younger when she chose that she didn't even have to lie to the agencies, and they gave what they believed was a nineteen-year-old face the eyes and mouth of a woman of three decades.

Under such benevolent circumstances, knowing she was intelligent and lucky, everything on her list would of course be there. And when the vision materialized in a yellow dress Jadine was not sure it was not all part of her list—an addition to the coconut and tamarind, a kind of plus to go with the limes and pimiento. Another piece of her luck. The vision itself was a woman much too tall. Under her long canary yellow dress Jadine knew there was too much hip, too much bust. The agency would laugh her out of the lobby, so why was she and everybody else in the store transfixed? The height? The skin like tar against the canary yellow dress? The woman walked down the aisle as though her many-colored sandals were pressing gold tracks on the floor. Two upside-down *V*'s were scored into each of her cheeks, her hair was wrapped in a gelée as yellow as her dress. The people in the aisles watched her without embarrassment, with full glances instead of sly ones. She had no arm basket or cart. Just her many-colored sandals and her yellow robe. Jadine turned her cart around and went back down the aisle telling herself she wanted to reexamine the vegetables. The woman leaned into the dairy section and opened a carton from which she selected three eggs. Then she put her right elbow into the palm of her left hand and held the eggs aloft between earlobe and shoulder. She looked up then and they saw something in her eyes so powerful it had burnt away the eyelashes.

She strolled along the aisle, eggs on high, to the cashier, who tried to tell her that eggs were sold by the dozen or half-dozen—not one or two or three or four—but she had to look up into those eyes too beautiful for lashes to say it. She swallowed and was about to try again when the woman reached into the pocket of her yellow dress and put a ten-louis piece on the counter and walked away, away, gold tracking the floor and leaving them all behind. Left arm folded over her waist, right hand holding three chalk-white eggs in the air, and what will she do with her hands when she reaches the door? they wondered. Take her elbow out of the palm of her hand and push it open? Turn around and ask for a paper bag? Drop the eggs in a pocket? Each one of them begged in his heart that it would not happen. That she would float through the glass the way a vision should. She did of course and they needn't have worried—the door always opened when you stepped on the mat before it, but they had forgotten that or had taken it for granted so long they had not really seen it until that woman approached it with the confidence of transcendent beauty and it flew open in silent obedience.

She would deny it now, but along with everybody else in the market, Jadine gasped. Just a little. Just a sudden intake of air. Just a quick snatch of breath before that woman's woman—that mother/sister/she; that unphotographable beauty—took it all away.

Jadine followed her profile, then her back as she passed the store window—followed her all the way to the edge of the world where the plate glass stopped. And there, just there—a moment before the cataclysm when all loveliness and life and breath in the world was about to disappear—the woman turned her head sharply around to the left and looked right at Jadine. Turned those eyes too beautiful for eyelashes on Jadine and, with a small parting of her lips, shot an arrow of saliva between her teeth down to the pavement and the hearts below. Actually it didn't matter. When you have fallen in love, rage is superfluous; insult impossible. You mumble "bitch," but the hunger never moves, never closes. It is placed, open and always ready for another canary-yellow dress, other tar-black fingers holding three white eggs; or eyes whose force has burnt away their lashes.

Jadine's luck continued. The dinner party was memorable and

nowhere had anything begun to spoil. Like the arugula leaf, life was green and nicely curved. Nothing was limp. There were no tears or brown spots. The items on her shopping list were always there. The handsome raucous men wanted to marry, live with, support, fund and promote her. Smart and beautiful women wanted to be her friend, confidante, lover, neighbor, guest, playmate, host, servant, student or simply near. A lucky girl—why leave the show? cable to old relatives? write a cheery request-type, offer-type letter to a rich old pushover and split to Dominique on whatever Air France had to offer when everything on her shopping list was right there in Paris? Nothing was absent, not even the spit of an African woman whose eyes had burnt away their lashes.

Jadine slipped out of bed and went to the window. She knelt on the floor, and, folding her arms on the sill, rested her head on the pane. She lifted the back of her hand to her mouth and squeezed the soft flesh with her teeth. She couldn't figure out why the woman's insulting gesture had derailed her—shaken her out of proportion to incident. Why she had wanted that woman to like and respect her. It had certainly taken the zing out of the magazine cover as well as her degree. Beyond the window etched against the light of a blazing moon she could see the hills at the other side of the island where one hundred horsemen rode one hundred horses, so Valerian said. That was how the island got its name. He had pointed the three humps of hills out to her, but Margaret, who had accompanied them on the tour of the grounds when Jadine first arrived, said no such thing. One rider. Just one. Therefore Isle de *le* Chevalier. One French soldier on a horse, not a hundred. She'd gotten the story from a neighbor—the first family Valerian had sold to. Valerian stuck to his own story, which he preferred and felt was more accurate because he had heard it from Dr. Michelin, who lived in town and knew all about it. "They're still there," he said. "And you can see them if you go over there at night. But I don't suppose we'll ever meet. If they've been riding for as long as the story is old, they must be as tired as I am, and I don't want to meet anybody older or more tired than I am."

Maybe they're not old, Jadine thought, staring out the window. Maybe they're still young, still riding. One hundred men on one hundred horses. She tried to visualize them, wave after wave of chevaliers, but somehow that made her think of the woman in yellow who had run her out of Paris. She crawled back into bed and tried to fix the feeling that had troubled her.

The woman had made her feel lonely in a way. Lonely and inauthentic. Perhaps she was overreacting. The woman appeared simply at a time when she had a major decision to make: of the three raucous men, the one she most wanted to marry and who was desperate to marry her was exciting and smart and fun and sexy . . . so? I guess the person I want to marry is him, but I wonder if the person he wants to marry is me or a black girl? And if it isn't me he wants, but any black girl who looks like me, talks and acts like me, what will happen when he finds out that I hate ear hoops, that I don't have to straighten my hair, that Mingus puts me to sleep, that sometimes I want to get out of my skin and be only the person inside—not American—not black —just me? Suppose he sleeps with somebody else after we're married? Will I feel the way I did when he took Nina Fong away for the weekend? He was amazed, he said, at my reaction. Weren't we always to be honest with each other? He didn't want a relationship with lies. Did I? And then we made up, set the date—no wedding, just a marriage—he got rid of his old mattress and bought a new one, a new one for us to grow old on, he said.

Then the magazine cover, and then her degree assured and then, the woman in yellow. And then she ran away because Ryk is white and the woman spit at her and she had to come to see her aunt and uncle to see what they would feel, think, say. White but European which was not as bad as white and American; they would understand that, or would they? Had they ever said? They liked her being in Paris, the schools she'd gone to, the friends she'd had there. They were always boasting about it. And it was not like she needed their views on anything. After her mother died they were her people—but she never lived with them except summers at Valerian's house when she was very young. Less and then never, after college. They were family; they had gotten Valerian to pay her tuition while they sent her the rest, having no one else to spend it on. Nanadine and Sydney mattered a lot to her but what they thought did not. She had sought them out to touch bases, to sort out things before going ahead with, with, with anything. So far she had been playful with them, had not said anything definite about her plans. When they asked her was she serious about this Ryk fellow who telephoned and who sent letters every week, she pretended it was nothing. That she was thinking of going back to Paris only to get her things. There was a small assignment in New York; she would take it and then she wanted to see about opening a business of her own, she'd told them, a gallery, or a boutique or a . . . she'd looked at their faces then . . . well, something they could all do together so they could live together like a family at last. They smiled generously, but their eyes made her know they were happy to play store with her, but nothing would pull them away from the jobs they had had for thirty years or more.

Jadine kicked off the sheet and buried her head under the pillow to keep the moonlight out of her eyes, and the woman in yellow out of her mind.

WHEN JADINE had gotten out of bed to stare at the hills, Valerian woke up. He had finished chatting to the ceiling and into his wrist the exact spelling of the message: *These iceboxes are brown broken perspective v-i-o-l-i-a-x is something more and can't be coal note.* He had sipped the brandy rather quickly, annoyed by the day's turn of events, and had lain for a while thinking how impossible it was that, unlike other men, he had been pushed into a presidency but had to fight for his retirement.

When he was thirty-nine he swore that he would quit at exactly sixty-five before he started spending his days traveling from the executive toilet back to his desk where the ballpoint pens mounted on marble had gone dry and his pencils were always long and sharp. That he would never permit himself to become the industrial nuisances his uncles had: stubborn, meddlesome, hanging on to their desks with their fingernails; flourishing once or twice a year when a crisis occurred with an old client or a new F.D.A. official that needed their familiarity or style or some other antiquated company charm. His uncles had been good to him. Their mother (Valerian's grandmother) had four sons each of whom had married a woman who had only girls. Except Valerian's mother who delivered one girl and one boy, who was the future of the family. When his father died and Valerian was seven, the uncles gathered to steady everybody and take over the education of their dead brother's son since it was, they said, "self-understood" that he would inherit the candy factory. And just to show how much they loved and anticipated him, they named a candy after him. *Valerians.* Red and white gumdrops in a red and white box (mint-flavored, the white ones; strawberry-flavored, the red). Valerians turned out to be a slow but real flop, although not a painful one financially for it was made from the syrup sludge left over from their main confection—Teddy Boys.

"What's the matter with them?" asked the uncles.

"Faggoty," said the sales reps.

"Faggoty?"

"Yeah. Like Valentines. Can you see a kid sitting on a curb tossing those fairy candies in his mouth? Seasonal is all we can do. Valentine's Day. Give us something with nuts, why don't you?"

Nobody in the East or Midwest touched them. They sat in movie house display cases and on candy store shelves until they were hard as marbles and stuck together like grapes.

"But somebody's buying them," the uncles said.

"Jigs," said the salesmen. "Jigs buy 'em. Maryland, Florida, Mississippi. Close the line. Nobody can make a dollar selling faggot candy to jigs."

"But when they move north, don't they ask for what they got in Mississippi?"

"Hell, no. They're *leaving* the South. When they move out they want to leave that stuff behind. They don't want to be reminded. Alaga syrup is dead in New York. So is Gold Dust Soap and so are Valerians. Close it out."

But they didn't close it out. Not right away, at least. The uncles let the item sell itself in the South until the sugar shortage of the early forties and even then they fought endlessly to keep it on: they went to the bathroom, to lunch, read food industry literature and held caucuses among themselves about whether to manufacture a nickel box of Valerians in Mississippi where beet sugar was almost free and the labor too. "Ooooh. Valerian!!" said the box. And that was all. Not even a picture of the candy or a happy face eating it. Valerian appreciated their efforts but recognized them as sentimental and not professional and swore again he would retire exactly at sixty-five if not before and would not let his ownership position keep him there making an ass of himself. After all he was the first partner with a college education and a love of other things. And it was because of these other things—music, books—that all the way through a nine-year childless marriage to a woman who disliked him; all the way through a hateful, shoddy, interminable divorce; all the way into and out of the military service, he could be firm. After the war he went to a convention of industrial food appliance sales in Maine and stepped out for a breath of winter air. There on a float with a polar bear he saw Miss Maine. She was so young and so unexpectedly pretty he swallowed air and had a coughing fit. She was all red and white, like the Valerians. So already at thirty-nine he was showing signs of the same sentimentality his uncles had. It made his resolve even firmer; out of respect for the company, the industry, he would do what they required the Swedes and Germans who worked for them to do—retire at sixty-five. After all, it was a family shop. They had taken a little bit of sugar and a little bit of cocoa and made a good living—for themselves and ninety others, and the people who lived in the factory's neighborhood stayed there and loved it there largely because of the marvelous candy odor that greeted them in the morning and bid them goodnight. Smelling it was almost like having it and they could have it too, way back then, because damaged lots of Teddy Boys were regularly given to children and homeless men. And when the homeless men found themselves on a train in Oregon or a camp in Boulder, Colorado, they remembered the delicious smell of Philadelphia with far more pleasure than they remembered its women. The childhood of the children growing up in that candy air never quite left, and may have been why they never quite grew up. They moved to Dallas and Altoona and listened to other people's stories of childhood politely but without envy. They seldom tried to describe their own, because how could you make another person know what it was like? All you could say was "there was a candy factory in our neighborhood and it smelled so good." So they kept it to themselves and kept their childhood longer than they should have in Dallas and Altoona and Newport News.

And the Street Brothers Candy Company never left the neighborhood or forgot the workers. It expanded, but right on the block and behind the original building; they hired more salesmen and even when they bought machines to do what the Swedish and German women had done they kept them on in other capacities although it was clear they had no need for them—out of respect for Grandmother Stadt and out of respect for the industry. They had six good items by the time Valerian took over and all the women were dead but not the uncles and it was because of this same respect for the industry and its legendary place in the neighborhood and the hearts of those who lived there that he was determined to retire at sixty-five—before he got foolish.

He married Miss Maine and when she had a baby boy he was as relieved as the uncles, but resisted the temptation to introduce a new confection named after his son. By that time they had reduced the size of the Teddy Boys' hats which nobody connected anymore to Theodore Roosevelt. (An error the uncles encouraged since the candy had been made first by their workaholic mother as a treat for Theodore, her youngest son, and later on to sell for pin money. Hers were big, chocolatey things, like gingerbread boys, but when they went into business they were much smaller.) Now you couldn't even see the Teddy Boys' buttons. Through it all Valerian never swerved from his sixty-five timetable. He prepared for it. Bought an island in the Caribbean for almost nothing; built a house on a hill away from the mosquitoes and vacationed there when he could and when his wife did not throw a fit to go elsewhere. Over the years he sold off parts of it, provided the parcels were large and the buyers discreet, but he kept his distance and his dream of getting out of the way at sixty-five, and letting his son take over. But the son was not charmed by Teddy Boys or island retreats. Valerian's disappointment was real, so he agreed to the company's sale to one of the candy giants who could and did triple the volume in two years. Valerian turned his attention to refining the house, its grounds, mail service to the island, measuring French colonial taxes against American residential ones, killing off rats, snakes and other destructive animal life, adjusting the terrain for comfortable living. When he knew for certain that Michael would always be a stranger to him, he built the greenhouse as a place of controlled ever-flowering life to greet death in. It seemed a simple, modest enough wish to him. Normal, decent—like his life. Fair, generous—like his life. Nobody except Sydney and Ondine seemed to understand that. He had never abused himself, but he thought keeping fit inelegant somehow, and vain. His claims to decency were human: he had never cheated anybody. Had done the better thing whenever he had a choice and sometimes when he did not. He had never been miserly or a spendthrift, and his politics were always rational and often humane. He had played his share of tennis and golf but it was more for business reasons than pleasure. And he'd had countless discussions with friends and clients about the house he was building in the Caribbean, about land value, tax credit, architects, designers, space, line, color, breeze, tamarind trees, hurricanes, cocoa, banana and *fleur de fuego*. There had been two or three girls who had helped him enter the fifties (lovely, lovely). Nothing to worry Margaret had she known. Merely life preservers in the post-fifty ocean, helping him make it to shore. There was a moment during the war when he thought some great event was in store for him, but it never happened. He was never sent with the message the world was waiting for. He knew the message was not his, that he had not thought it up, but he believed he was worthy of delivering it. Nothing of the sort befell him, so he returned to civilian life a bachelor, intact. Until he saw Miss Maine (whom a newspaper, published by the envious grandfather of a runner-up, called "a principal beauty of Maine"), looking like the candy that had his name. His youth lay in her red whiteness, a snowy Valentine Valerian. And Bride of Polar Bear became his bride. The disgust of the aunts at his marriage to a teenager from a family of nobodies dissolved with the almost immediate birth of his son. Valerian didn't need a youth then, the boy was that. Now the boy was a grown man, but perpetually childlike so Valerian wanted his own youth again and a place to spend it. His was taken from him when his father died and his mother and aunts all changed from hearty fun-loving big sisters to grave, *serioso mammas* who began their duties by trying to keep him from grieving over his father's death. Luckily a drunken woman did their laundry. And although he stayed on one year past sixty-five to make some changes and another year past that to make sure the changes held, he did manage to retire at sixty-eight to L'Arbe de la Croix and sleep the deep brandy sleep he deserved.

MARGARET was not dreaming nor was she quite asleep, although the moon looking at her face believed she was. She was experiencing the thing insomniacs dread—not being awake but the ticky-tacky thoughts that fill in the space where sleep ought to be. Rags and swatches; draincloths and crumpled paper napkins. Old griefs and embarrassments; jealousies and offense. Just common ignoble scraps not deep enough for dreaming and not light enough to dismiss. Yet she was hopeful that sleep would come, that she would have the dream she ought to for maybe that would dispel the occasional forgetfulness that plagued her when she forgot the names and uses of things. It happened mostly at meals, and once, years ago, with the Princess telephone which she picked up with her car keys and address book and tried to stuff in her purse. They were rare moments, but dark and windy enough to last. After lunch with friends you could go to the powder room, twist the lipstick out of its tube and wonder suddenly if it was for licking or writing your name. And because you never knew when it would come back, a thin terror accompanied you always—except in sleep. So there was peace and hope on the face of this beautiful woman born to two ordinary-looking people, Joseph and Leonora Lordi, who had looked at their beautiful redheaded child with shock and amazement. Of course there was no thought of adultery (Leonora was sixty before she showed the world her two bare legs), but the hair bothered Joe—caught his eye at the dinner table and ruined his meals. He looked at little Margarette's skin as delicate as the shell of a robin's egg and almost as blue and stroked his thumb. Leonora shrugged and covered her head with lace older than Maine itself. She was as puzzled as her husband but not as alarmed, although it did look funny at the nine-thirty mass:

Margarette's head glowing like an ember among the coal-dark heads of her other children. She couldn't explain it and didn't try, but Joe never left off stroking his thumb and staring at his little girl's blue-if-it's-a-boy blue eyes. He stroked his thumb and stroked his thumb until he smashed his temple with his fist having just remembered Buffalo. The Buffalo great-aunts Celestina and Alicia—twins with hair the color of saffron and the white skin of the north. He roared and began to tell people about his Buffalo aunts whom he had not seen since he was six. And, although his brothers shouted yeah, yeah, when he reminded them, he thought he saw doubt in the eyes of his friends. Thus began a series of letters to Buffalo inviting the twins to South Suzanne. They were flattered by his letters, but could not understand the sudden affection from a great-nephew they did not remember. For a year they declined to pay a visit on account of advanced age, until Joe offered to pay their bus fare. "Where?" asked Leonora, "where will they sleep?" and Joe touched his fingers: Adolphe, Campi, Estella, Cesare, Nick, Nuzio, Mickelena or any of the other Lordis scattered around the county. Leonora looked at the ceiling, covered her head with lace older than Maine itself and went to mass to beg for sanity, Madre de Dio, if not peace in her house.

The aunts came and when Joe picked them up at the bus station and saw that the saffron had turned to garlic he smashed his temple again. It turned out better than nothing however for he was able to regale them in the presence of company about losing their flaming hair, and they smiled and acknowledged that it had certainly been lost—which was proof enough for everyone that such hair and such skin had existed at one time and therefore could legitimately reappear four generations later on the tiny head of Margarette Lenore. Still it left its mark on her—being *that* pretty with *that* coloring. Joe and Leonora left her alone after the Buffalo aunts went home. Maybe her beauty scared them a little; maybe they just felt, well, at least she has that. She won't have to worry. And they stepped back and let her be. They gave her care, but they withdrew attention. Their strength they gave to the others who were not beautiful; their knowledge, what information they had they did not give to this single beautiful one. They saved it, distributed it instead to those whose characters had to be built. The rest of their energies they used on the problems of surviving in a county that did not want them there. During the months when the earth permitted it, Joe and his brothers dug a hole in the ground. They cinder-blocked it, topped it and put in a toilet and a gas line. Little by little the Lordis moved out of their trailer across the yard into the cinder-block basement. They lived huddled and quite warm there, considering what Maine winters were like. Then Joe started the first floor walls and by 1935 all six of them were in a seven-room house the Lordi brothers had built with their own hands. Leonora rented the trailer, but kept its back yard for peppers, corn, fat squash and the columbine she loved beyond reason. But Margarette always loved the trailer best for there the separateness she felt had less room to grow in. In the hand-built house, and later in the big brick house on Chester Street, after her father and uncles bought two trucks and began Lordi Brothers, the loneliness was only partially the look in the eyes of the uncles and the nuns. Much of it was the inaccessibility of the minds (not the hearts) of Leonora and Joseph Lordi. So when she got married eight months out of high school, she did not have to leave home, she was already gone; she did not have to leave them; they had already left her. And other than money gifts to them and brief telephone calls, she was still gone. It was always like that: she was gone and other people were where they belonged. She was going up or down stairs; other people seemed to be settled somewhere. She was on the two concrete steps of the trailer; the six wooden steps of the hand-built house; the thirty-seven steps at the stadium when she was crowned; and a million wide steps in the house of Valerian Street. It was just her luck to fall in love with and marry a man who had a house bigger than her elementary school. A house of three stories with pearl-gray *S*'s everywhere—on cups, saucers, glasses, silverware, and even in their bed. When she and Valerian lay snug in bed, facing each other and touching toes, the pearl-gray *S* on the sheet hems and pillow slips coiled at her and she stiffened like Joan Fontaine in *Rebecca* until she learned from her husband that his ex-wife had nothing to do with it. His grandmother had had some of the monograms done and his mother the rest. Margaret's relief was solid but it did nothing to keep her from feeling drowned when he was not there in the spaciousness of that house with only a colored couple with unfriendly faces to save her. Alone in the house, peeping into a room, it looked all right, but the minute she turned her back she heard the afterboom, and who could she tell that to? Not the coloreds. She was seventeen and couldn't even give them orders the way she was supposed to. It must be like room service, she thought, and she asked them to bring her things and they did but when she said thank you and sipped the Coca-Cola, they smiled a private smile she hated. The woman Ondine cooked and did the cleaning; the man too, and he also had morning chats with Valerian, brushed his clothes, sent some to the laundry, some to the cleaners, some disappeared altogether. There was nothing in that line for her to do but amuse herself in solitude and, awful as that was, the dinners with Valerian's friends were worse. There men talked about music and money and the Marshall Plan. She knew nothing about any of it, but she was never stupid enough to pretend she did or try to enter the conversation. The wives talked around the edge of such matters or dropped amusing bits into the conversations like the green specks in cannoli filling. Once a wife whom she showed to the downstairs powder room asked her where she had gone to school and she said South Suzanne. What's there? asked the woman. South Suzanne High School, said Margaret. The woman gave her a wide generous grin for a long time, then patted Margaret's stomach. "Get to work, fast, sweetheart."

Margaret lived for the concerts Valerian took her to, and the dinners for two at restaurants and even alone at home. Otherwise it was solitude with the colored couple floating mysteriously through the house. In the fourth month of her marriage she sat on the screened porch listening to "Search for Tomorrow" when Ondine passed by with a can of linseed oil and said, "Excuse me. Did they arrest Joan Barron yet?" Margaret said No, but they must be about to. "Oo," said Ondine, and began to fill her in on the cast of characters. Margaret was not a regular listener but she became one with Ondine and a maiden friendship flowered. Margaret was not afraid anymore (although it was some time before Sydney did not inspire her with awe). She looked forward to the chats with Ondine whose hair was black then and "dressed" as she called it, once a month. They talked about Valerian's family and South Suzanne and Baltimore, where Ondine was from. Ondine was just about to show her how to make crust (and Margaret by then knew the honor of the offer, since Ondine didn't like sharing recipes or kitchen space) when Valerian put a stop to it saying she should guide the servants, not consort with them. The next thing you know they'd be going to movies together, which hurt Margaret a lot because taking in a movie with Ondine was definitely on her mind. They quarreled about it. Not because Margaret thought Valerian was wrong: she had never known him to be and doubted if he could be in error about anything. Not him, not with those calm eyes or that crisp quiet voice that reassured and poked fun at you at the same time. And although the theme of her defense in the argument was that Ondine (if not all colored people) was just as good as they were, she didn't believe it, and besides that wasn't the point of the disagreement anyway. Valerian was never rude to Ondine or Sydney, in fact he pampered them. No. The point was not consorting with Negroes, the point was her ignorance and her origins. It was a nasty quarrel and their first in which they said regrettable things to each other that resulted in not touching toes in the night. It frightened Margaret—the possibility of losing him. And though she abandoned the movie idea, and still sneaked into Ondine's kitchen of an afternoon, she took the advice of the lady in the powder room and "got to work, fast." When the baby was born everything changed except the afterboom which got louder and louder and even when she carried her baby through the rooms it was there as soon as she turned her back. It had been a horror and a pleasure to teach little Michael how to count by walking him up those wide stairs flashing white like piano keys. One, two, three . . . his little hand in hers repeating the numbers as they mounted each tread. No one would believe that she loved him. That she was not one of those women in the *National Enquirer*. That she was never an overprotective or designing parent with unfulfilled dreams. Now that Michael was an adult, of all the people she knew in the world, he seemed to her the best. The smartest and the nicest. She liked his company, to talk to him, to be around him. Not because he is my son, she told herself, my only child, but because he is interesting and he thinks I am interesting too. I am special to him. Not as a mother, but as a person. Just as he is to me.

In wanting to live near him she was not behaving like a brood hen. Quite the contrary. She had cut the cord decisively and was enjoying her son as an individual. He was simply better society than her women friends. Younger, freer, more fun. And he was better company than the men of her acquaintance who either wanted to seduce, lecture or bore her to death. She felt natural, easy, unafraid with Michael. There was no competition with him, no winning, no preening, no need to be anybody but who she was, and in his presence she did not forget the names and uses of things. It wasn't always that way. When he was an infant he seemed to want everything of her, and she didn't know what to give. She loved him even then. But no one would believe it. They would think she was one of those mothers in the *National Enquirer*. And since she was not anything like them, she fell asleep finally, but did not have the dream she ought to.

DOWN BELOW, where the moon couldn't get to, in the servants' quarters, Sydney and Ondine made alternate trips to the bathroom and went quickly back to sleep. Ondine dreaming of sliding into water, frightened that her heavy legs and swollen ankles will sink her. But still asleep she turns over and touches her husband's back—the dream dissolves and with it the anxiety. He is in Baltimore now as usual and because it was always a red city in his mind—red brick, red sun, red necks and cardinals—his dream of it now was rust-colored. Wagons, fruit stands, all rust-colored. He had left that city to go to Philadelphia and there he became one of those industrious Philadelphia Negroes—the proudest people in the race. That was over fifty years ago, and still his most vivid dreams were the red rusty Baltimore of 1921. The fish, the trees, the music, the horses' harnesses. It was a tiny dream he had each night that he would never recollect from morning to morning. So he never knew what it was exactly that refreshed him.

They were all asleep now. Nothing disturbed them. Not the moon certainly and certainly no footsteps in the dark.

3

FOG CAME to that place in wisps sometimes, like the hair of maiden aunts. Hair so thin and pale it went unnoticed until masses of it gathered around the house and threw back one's own reflection from the windows. The sixty-four bulbs in the dining room chandelier were no more than a rhinestone clip in the hair of the maiden aunts. The gray of it, the soil and swirl of it, was right in the room, moistening the table linen and clouding the wine. Salt crystals clung to each other. Oysters uncurled their fringes and sank to the bottom of the tureen. Patience was difficult to come by in that fuzzy caul and breathing harder still. It was then that the word "island" had meaning.

Jadine and Margaret touched their cheeks and temples to dry the places the maiden aunts were kissing. Sydney (unbidden but right on time) circled the table with steps as felt as blackboard erasers. He kept his eyes on the platter, or the table setting, or his feet, or the hands of those he was serving, and never made eye contact with any of them, including his niece. With a practiced sidelong glance he caught Valerian pressing his thumb to the edge of the soup plate, pushing it an inch or so away. Instantly Sydney retraced his felt steps to clear the plates for the next course. Just before he reached Margaret, who had not yet touched anything, she dipped her spoon into the bisque and began to eat. Sydney hesitated and then stepped back.

"You're dawdling, Margaret," said Valerian.

"Sorry," she murmured. The maiden aunts stroked her cheek and she wiped away the dampness their fingers left.

"There is a rhythm to a meal. I've always told you that."

"I said sorry. I'm not a fast eater."

"Speed has nothing to do with it. Pace does," Valerian answered.

"So my pace is different from yours."

"It's the soufflé, Margaret," Jadine interrupted. "Valerian knows there's a soufflé tonight."

Margaret put her spoon down. It clicked against the china. Sydney floated to her elbow.

She was usually safe with soup, anything soft or liquid that required a spoon, but she was never sure when the confusion would return: when she would scrape her fork tines along the china trying to pick up the painted blossoms at its center, or forget to unwrap the Amaretti cookie at the side of her plate and pop the whole thing into her mouth. Valerian would squint at her, but say nothing, convinced that she was stewed. Lobster, corn on the cob—all problematic. It came. It went. And when it left sometimes for a year, she couldn't believe how stupid it was. Still she was careful at table, watching other people handle their food—just to make sure that never again would she pick up the knife instead of the celery stalk or pour water from her glass over the prime ribs instead of the meat's own juices. Now it was coming back. Right after she managed to eat the correct part of the mango, in spite of the fact that Ondine tried to trick her by leaving the skin on and propping it up in ice, she had dug in her fork recklessly, and a slice came away. Right after that Sydney presented her with a plate of something shaped like a cardboard box. Now she had hesitated to see if the little white pebbles floating in her bowl were to be eaten or not. It came to her in a flash—oysterettes!—and she had dipped her spoon happily into the soup but had hardly begun when Valerian complained. Now Jade was announcing a new obstacle: soufflé. Margaret prayed she would recognize it.

"Mushroom?" she asked.

"I don't know," said Jadine. "I think so."

"I hate mushrooms."

"I'm not sure; maybe it's plain."

"I like it when it's hot, plain and fluffy," said Margaret.

"Well, let's hope that's what we get. Omelet's more likely in this weather." Valerian was fidgety and signaled for more wine. "The only thing I dislike about this island is the fog."

"It may not be good for eggs, but it's doing a good job of souffléing my hair," said Jadine. "I should have had it cut like yours, Margaret." She pressed her hair down with both palms, but as soon as she removed them her hair sprang back into a rain cloud.

"Oh, no. Mine's so stringy now," said Margaret.

"But it still looks okay. That's why that haircut's so popular, you know? Uncombed, even wet, it's got a shape that suits the face. This shaggy-dog style I wear has to be worked on, and I mean *worked* on."

Margaret laughed. "It's very becoming, Jade. It makes you look like what was her name in *Black Orpheus?* Eurydice."

"Chee, Margaret, chee," said Valerian. "Eurydi-chee."

"Remember her hair when she was hanging from the wires in that streetcar garage?" Margaret continued to address Jadine.

"You mean the hair in her armpits?" Jadine asked. She was uncomfortable with the way Margaret stirred her into blackening up or universaling out, always alluding to or ferreting out what she believed were racial characteristics. She ended by resisting both, but it kept her alert about things she did not wish to be alert about.

Margaret's blue-if-it's-a-boy blue eyes crinkled with laughter. "No, I mean the hair on her head. It was lovely. Who noticed her armpits?"

"I would like to stay well through dessert, ladies, if you please. Could we find another topic?"

"Valerian, could you for once, just once—"

"Say," Jadine broke in. "What about Christmas? That's a topic we need to talk about. We haven't even begun to plan.

Any guests?" She picked up the salad utensils from the bowl of many-colored greens Sydney held near her. "Oh, I meant to tell you, the von Brandts sent a note . . ."

"Brandt, Jade. Just plain Brandt. The 'von' is imaginary," Valerian said.

Margaret took hold of the long wooden handles poking out of the salad bowl that Sydney held toward her. Carefully she transferred the greens to her plate. Nothing spilled. She took another helping and it arrived safely also. She sighed and was about to tell Jade to decline the Brandts' invitation when Valerian shouted, "What the hell is the matter with you?"

Startled, Margaret looked around. He was glaring at her. Jade was looking at her plate while Sydney leaned near her wrist. "What?" she said. "What?"—looking down at her plate. It was all right, nothing spilled, nothing broken: lettuce, tomatoes, cucumber all there. Then Sydney set the bowl on the table and picked up the salad spoon and fork. She had left them on the table.

"Oh, I'm sorry," she whispered, but she was angry. What was so awful about that? They had looked at her as though she'd wet her pants. Then quickly they pretended it had not happened; Jadine was chirping again.

"Well anyway, they want you both for dinner. Small, she says. But the Hatchers are having a big weekend thing. And they want—" She paused for half a heartbeat. Their faces were closed, snapped shut like the lids of jewelry boxes. "They thought you'd like to come for the entire weekend. Christmas Eve, a dinner party; then breakfast, then some boating in the afternoon, then, then a cocktail party with dancing. The Journeymen from Queen of France are playing. Well, they're not really *from* there. New Jersey, I think, but they've been playing at Chez Marin—" She couldn't go on in that silence. "What's the matter, Margaret?"

"Let's go back to armpits," Margaret said.

The maiden aunts smiled and tossed their maiden aunt hair.

"We'll do nothing of the sort. You were saying, Jade?" Valerian drained his wineglass.

Jadine shrugged. "Are you planning Christmas here—or where?"

"Here. Quietly. Although we may have a guest or two."

"Oh? Who?"

"Tell her, Margaret."

"Michael is coming. For Christmas." Margaret's smile was shy.

"But that's wonderful," said Jadine.

"Valerian thinks he won't. He will though, because I promised him this really terrific present."

"What? Can you tell me?"

"A poet," said Valerian. "She's giving him his favorite poet for Christmas. Isn't that so, love?"

"You make everything I do sound stupid."

"I thought I described it fairly."

"It's not the words; it's the tone." Margaret turned her head to Jadine. "I've invited B. J. Bridges for the holidays and he said he'd come. He used to be Michael's teacher."

"And Michael doesn't know?"

"Not exactly. But he'll guess. I gave him a hint—a big one—so he could. I used a line from one of Bridges's poems in my letter. 'And he glittered when he walked.' "

"Then you may as well have your nervous breakdown right now," said Valerian. "He won't come. You've misled him entirely."

"What are you talking about? He's on his way. His trunk's already been shipped."

"That is not a line from anything Bridges ever wrote. Michael will think you're dotty."

"It is. I have the poem right upstairs. I underlined it myself. It was the one Michael used to recite."

"Then Bridges is not only a mediocrity, he's a thief."

"Perhaps he was using it as a quotation, or an allusion—" Jadine fiddled with her hair.

"He'll think you're batty and . . ."

"Valerian, please."

". . . and go snake dancing."

"Then I'll go with him."

"We've been all through this, Margaret."

"When will you know for sure?" Jadine's voice affected lightness.

"She already knows for sure. The rest is hope and a determination to irritate me."

"Irritating you doesn't have to be determined. All anybody has to do is breathe a slice of your air—"

"Must you always speak in food measurements? The depression is over. You are free to leave something on your plate. There's more. There really is more."

"I don't have to sit here and listen to this. You're trying to ruin it for me, but you're not going to. I tear my life apart and come down here for the winter and all I ask in return is a normal Christmas that includes my son. You won't come to us—we have to come to you and it's not fair. You know it's not. This whole thing is getting to be too much!"

"Is that a problem for you? Having too much?"

"That's not what I mean."

"I know what you mean, but is it a problem for you? Because if it is I can arrange for less. I could certainly do with less myself. Less hysteria, less shouting, less drama . . ."

Jadine, unable to think of anything to do or say, .watched tomato seeds slide into the salad dressing, and set about applying the principles of a survey course in psychology. During the two months she'd been there, Valerian and Margaret frequently baited one another and each had a dictionary of complaints against the other, entries in which, from time to time, they showed her. Just a May and December marriage, she thought, at its crucial stage. He's seventy; she's knocking fifty. He is waning, shutting up, closing in. She's blazing with the fire of a soon to be setting sun. Naturally they bickered and taunted one another. Naturally. Normally, even. For they were decent people. Over and above their personal generosity to her and their solicitude for her uncle and aunt, they seemed decent. Decent like Sydney and Nanadine were decent, and this house full of decent folk situated in the pure sea air was exactly where she wanted to be right now. This vacation with light but salaried work was what she needed to pull herself together. Listening to Margaret and Valerian fight was a welcome distraction, just as playing daughter to Sydney and Nanadine was.

But recently (a few days ago, last night, and again tonight) flecks of menace lay in these quarrels. They no longer seemed merely the tiffs of long-married people who alone knew the physics of their relationship. Who like two old cats clawed each other, used each other to display a quarrelsomeness neither took seriously, quarreling because they thought it was expected of them, quarreling simply to exchange roles now and then for their own private amusement: the heavy would appear abused in public, the aggressive and selfish one would appear the eye and heart of restraint before an audience. And most of the time, like now, the plain of their battle was a child, and the weapons public identification of human frailty. Still, this was a little darker than what she had come to expect from them. Bits of blood, tufts of hair seemed to stick on those worn claws. Maybe she had misread their rules. Or maybe (most likely) she wasn't an audience anymore. Maybe she was family now—or nobody. No, she thought, it must be this place. The island exaggerated everything. Too much light. Too much shadow. Too much rain. Too much foliage and much too much sleep. She'd never slept so deeply in her life. Such tranquillity in sleep made for wildness during the waking hours. That's what it was: the wilderness creeping into Valerian and Margaret's seasoned and regulated arguments, subverting the rules so that they looked at each other under the tender light of a seventy-year-old chandelier, bought by Valerian's father in celebration of his wife's first pregnancy, lifted their lips and bared their teeth.

". . . she never liked me," Margaret was saying. "From the very beginning she hated me."

"How could she hate you from the beginning? She didn't even know you." Valerian lowered his voice in an effort to calm her.

"That's what I'd like to know."

"She was perfectly polite and gracious to you in the beginning."

"She was awful to me, Valerian. Awful!"

"That was later when you wouldn't let Michael visit her."

"Wouldn't let? I couldn't make him go. He hated her; he'd shrink at the very—"

"Margaret, stick to the facts, Michael was two or three. He couldn't have hated anybody, let alone his aunt."

"He did, and if you had any feelings you would have hated her too."

"My own sister?"

"Or at least told her off."

"For what, for God's sake. For having a private wedding instead of a circus? You never invite them down here and she's probably upset about it, that's all. And this is her way of—"

"Dear God. You have screamed at me for years for having too many people. Now you want me to invite Cissy and Frank. I don't believe—"

"I didn't *say* that. I don't want her here any more than you do. I am only trying to explain why they didn't let us know about the wedding. From what I gather—"

"What do you mean *us*? She invited Michael! But not me!"

"Stacey's idea."

"Do you think if Michael got married I would invite Stacey and not her parents?"

"Margaret, I don't give one goddamn—"

"She's always treated me that way. You know what she did to me the first day I met her."

"I suppose I should but I don't."

"You don't?"

"No. Sorry."

"What she said to me that first day?"

"It's been some time."

"About my cross?"

"Your what?"

"My cross. The cross I wore. My first communion present. She said for me to take it off. That only whores wore crosses."

Valerian laughed. "That sounds like her."

"You think it's funny."

"In a way."

"That your own sister . . . my God."

"Margaret, you didn't have to do it—take it off. Why didn't you tell her to go to hell?"

"Why didn't you?"

"I don't remember."

"Because you agreed with her, that's why."

"That my bride was a whore?"

"You know what I mean."

"All I know is that you let her get under your skin and she's still there after thirty years. You don't give a gnat's ass about the wedding. You just wanted to be anywhere Michael is. You can't stand for him to be wherever you're not."

"That's not true."

"You wanted to crash some fatheaded wedding because Michael was there. You are too stupid to live."

"I don't have to sit here and be called names!"

"Idiot. I married an idiot!"

"And I married an old fool!"

"Of course you did. Who else but an old fool would marry a high school dropout off the back of a truck!"

"A *float!*" Margaret shouted, and when the wineglass bounced from the centerpiece of calla lilies and rolled toward him he didn't even look at it. He simply watched his wife's face crumple and her boy-blue eyes well up.

"Oh," said Jadine. "This is . . . maybe . . . Margaret? Would you like to . . ." But Margaret was gone, leaving the oak door swinging behind her and the maiden aunts cowering in the corners of the room.

Sydney (unbidden but right on time) removed the glass and placed a fresh white napkin over the wine spot. Then he collected the salad plates, replacing them with warm white china with a single band of gold around the edges. Each plate he handled with a spotlessly white napkin and was careful, as he slipped it from the blue quilted warmer, not to make a sound. When the plates were in position, he disappeared for a few seconds and returned with a smoking soufflé. He held it near Valerian a moment for inspection, and then proceeded to the sideboard to slice it into flawless, frothy wedges.

Jadine considered her soufflé while Valerian signaled for more wine. It seemed a long time before he murmured to her, "Sorry."

Jadine smiled or tried to and said, "You shouldn't tease her like that."

"No, I suppose not," he answered, but his voice held no conviction and his twilight gaze was muddy.

"Is it because she wants to go away?" asked Jadine.

"Of course not. Not at all."

"Michael?"

"Yes. Michael."

He said nothing more so Jadine decided to exit as quickly as she could manage it. She was folding her napkin when suddenly he spoke. "She's nervous. Afraid he won't show. I'm nervous. Afraid he will."

There was another silence as Jadine struggled to think of something purposeful—even relevant—to say. She couldn't think of a thing so she gave up and said the obvious. "I remember Michael. He's . . . nice." She recalled an eighteen-year-old boy with red hair and cut-off jeans.

"Quite," said Valerian. "Quite nice."

"If he does come, as well as his friend, how can it hurt?"

"I don't know. It depends."

"On what?"

"Things outside my control. I can't be responsible for things outside my control." He pushed away his plate and drank his wine.

Jadine sighed. She wanted to leave the table, but didn't know how. Does he want me to stay or doesn't he? she wondered. Does he want me to talk or doesn't he? All I can do is ask polite questions and urge him to talk if he feels like it. Maybe I should go to Margaret, or change the subject, or have my head examined for coming here. "No one asks you to be," she said softly.

"That's not the point, whether I'm asked or not. A lot of life *is* outside and frequently it's the part that most needs control." He covered his lips with his napkin for a while then uncovered them and said, "Margaret thinks this is some sort of long lazy vacation for me, designed to hurt her. In fact I'm doing just the opposite. I intend to go back at some point. I will go back but actually it's for Michael that I stay. His protection."

"You make him sound weak, the way you say that. I don't remember him that way at all."

"You did know him, didn't you?" Valerian looked at her with surprise.

"Well, not really *know* him. I met him twice. The last time when you invited me to spend the summer in Orange County. Remember?" Jadine perked up, animated by her own memory. "My first year at college? He was there and we used to talk. He was . . . oh . . . clearheaded—independent it seemed to me. Actually we didn't talk; we quarreled. About why I was studying art history at that snotty school instead of—I don't know what. Organizing or something. He said I was abandoning my history. My people."

"Typical," said Valerian. "His idea of racial progress is All Voodoo to the People."

"I think he wanted me to string cowrie beads or sell Afro combs. The system was all fucked up he said and only a return to handicraft and barter could change it. That welfare mothers could do crafts, pottery, clothing in their homes, like the lace-makers of Belgium and *voilà!* dignity and no more welfare." Jadine smiled.

"That's exactly what the world is waiting for: two billion African pots," said Valerian.

"His intentions were good."

"They were not good. He wanted a race of exotics skipping around being picturesque for him. What were those welfare mothers supposed to put in those pots? Did he have any suggestions about that?"

"They'd trade them for other goods."

"Really? Two thousand calabashes for a week of electricity? It's been tried. It was called the Dark Ages."

"Well, the pottery wasn't to be utilitarian." Jadine was laughing. "It'd be art."

"Oh, I see. Not the Dark Ages, the Renaissance."

"It was a long time ago, Valerian. Eight years? Nine? He was just a kid then. So was I."

"You've grown. He hasn't. His vocabulary, perhaps, but not his mind. It's still in the grip of that quisling *Little Prince*. Do you know it?"

"Know what?"

"That book. *The Little Prince*."

"No. I never read it."

"Saint-Exupéry. Read it some time. And pay attention not to what it says, but what it means."

Jadine nodded. It seemed like a perfect exit line to her, since she didn't know what he was talking about and didn't want to pursue his thoughts if they were anything like his eyes at this moment. Without melanin, they were all reflection, like mirrors, chamber after chamber, corridor after corridor of mirrors, each one taking its shape from the other and giving it back as its own until the final effect was color where no color existed at all. Once more she stirred to rise from the table and once more he stopped her, not irritably this time but with compassion.

"Did they trouble you—the things he said that summer?"

"For a while."

"You knew better?"

"I knew the life I was leaving. It wasn't like what he thought: all grits and natural grace. But he did make me want to apologize for what I was doing, what I felt. For liking 'Ave Maria' better than gospel music, I suppose."

Nothing on Sydney's face showed his disappointment that the soufflé had not been completely eaten up by either one of them. He collected the dishes with his look of alert serenity, and stepped through the hair of the maiden aunts with an easy silent tread. He was perfect at those dinners when his niece sat down with his employers, as perfect as he was when he served Mr. Street's friends. The silver tray of walnuts, the equally silver bowl of peaches he brought in, and a jiffy later, the coffee—all were exactly and surreptitiously placed on the table. One hardly knew if he left the room or stood in some shadowy corner of it.

Jadine leaned her cheek on her fist. "Picasso *is* better than an Itumba mask. The fact that he was intrigued by them is proof of *his* genius, not the mask-makers'. I wish it weren't so, but . . ." She gave a tiny shrug. Little matches of embarrassment burned even now in her face as she thought of all those black art shows mounted two or three times a year in the States. The junior high school sculpture, the illustration-type painting. Eighty percent ludicrous and ten percent derivative to the point of mimicry. But the American Blacks were at least honestly awful; the black artists in Europe were a scandal. The only thing more pitiful than their talent was their pretensions. There was just one exception: a Stateside Black whose work towered over the weeds like a sequoia. But you could hardly find his stuff anywhere.

"You look sad," said Valerian. "He must really have made

you suffer. You should have mentioned it to me. I wanted that summer to be an especially pleasant one for you."

"It was. Actually it was good he made me think about myself that way, at that place. He might have convinced me if we'd had that talk on Morgan Street. But in Orange County on a hundred and twenty acres of green velvet?" She laughed softly. "Can you believe it? He wanted us to go back to Morgan Street and be thrilling."

"Us? He was going with you?"

"Just to get us started. He meant us Blacks: Sydney, Ondine and me."

"Sydney? A potter?" Valerian turned his gaze toward his butler and laughed.

Jadine smiled but did not look at her uncle.

"You can see how much he knows about Sydney. And I haven't given you one-thousandth of what I gave him, of what I made available to him. And you have fifty times the sense he does, I don't mind telling you." Valerian's sentences changed tempo. They were slower, and it was taking him longer to blink his eyes. "Margaret did that. She made him think poetry was incompatible with property. She made a perpetual loser of one of the most beautiful, the brightest boy in the land." He held his forehead for a moment. To Jadine he seemed terribly close to tears and she was relieved when he merely repeated himself. "The most beautiful, the brightest boy in the land."

"He didn't turn out the way you wanted?"

"No."

"You want him to be something else?"

"I want him to be something at all."

"Maybe he is."

"Yes. An adolescent. A kitten. But not playful. Complaining. A complaining kitten. Always mewing. Meow. Meow. Meow."

"You shouldn't hate him, though. He's your son."

Valerian took his hand from his forehead and stared deep into the peaches nestled in their silver bowl. "I don't hate him. I love him. Margaret thinks I don't. But I do. I think about him all the time. You know . . . this isn't going to sound right . . . but I never was convinced that she did. Perhaps she did. In her way. I don't know. But she wasn't ready for him. She just wasn't ready. Now, now she's ready. When it's over. Now she wants to bake him cookies. See him off to school. Tie his shoelaces. Take care of him. Now. Absurd. I don't believe it. I don't believe her. When he was just a little thing I came home one day and went into the bathroom. I was standing there and I heard this humming—singing—coming from somewhere in the room. I looked around and then I found it. In the cabinet. Under the sink. He was crouched in there singing. That was the first time, but not the last. Every now and then I'd come home, he'd be under the sink. Humming to himself. When I'd pull him out, ask him what he was doing there, he'd say he liked the soft. He was two, I think, two years old, looking in the dark for something—soft. Now imagine how many soft, cuddly things he had in his room. Bunny rabbits, slippers, panda bears. I used to try to be it for him, but I wasn't there during the day. She was though. I sometimes had the feeling that she didn't talk to him very much, then it would go away. The feeling, I mean. She'd change, she'd get interested in him, read to him, take him to shows, parks. Months would pass. Then I'd come home and he'd be under the sink again, humming that little, I can't tell you how lonely, *lonely* song. I wasn't imagining it; it was lonely. Well, he got older and she'd go hot and cold, in and out. But he seemed to miss her so, need her so that when she was attentive he was like a slave to her. Then she'd lose interest again. When he was twelve he went to boarding school and things were better. Until he came to visit. She would do things—odd things—to get his attention and keep it. Anything to keep his eyes on her. She'd make up things, threats to herself, attacks, insults—anything to see him fly into a rage and show how willing he was to defend her. I watched, and tried to play it down or prove, *prove* she was making it up. I always checked, it was always nothing. All I ended up doing was making him angry with me. I thought another child—but she said no. Absolutely refused. I have until this day never understood that. When he left for college I was relieved. It was already too late, but I still hoped he'd get out from under her. In a way he has, I suppose. Never visits, seldom writes. Calls sometimes. Complains. About Indians. About water. About chemicals. Meow. Meow. Meow. But he is on his own, I guess. On his own. But now—" Valerian turned to Jadine and stared right at her chin. "Now she wants to get hold of him again. Tempting him with some fake poet. And she wants to go back with him, live near him. For a while she says. Know what that means? A 'while'? It means as soon as he trusts her again, needs her again, counts on her, she'll change her mind, leave him. I haven't seen him for three years, and the last couple of times I didn't like him, or even know him. But I loved him. Just like I loved the boy under the sink, humming. That beautiful boy. With a smile like . . . like Sunday."

The maiden aunts, huddled in the corners of the room, were smiling in their sleep. Jadine flared her nostrils in an effort not to yawn. Another cup of coffee, another glass of port—nothing could bring her alive to the memories of an old man. I ought to be saying something, she thought. I ought to be asking questions and making comments instead of smiling and nodding like a puppet. Hoping there was a residue of interest in her eyes, she held her chin toward him and continued to smile—but only a little—in case what he was remembering was poignant but not happy. Long ago she had given up trying to be deft or profound or anything in the company of people she was not interested in, who didn't thrill her. Gazing at her stem of crystal she knew that whatever he was saying, her response was going to miss the point entirely. Her mind was in automatic park. She played with the little bit of port, gently swirling it around the well of her glass. "Sunday," he was saying with the bell-full voice of ownership like "in the land" or "the whole of London" or "*tout* Paris." He had a smile like Sunday. His Sunday. She wondered what Sunday was to this tall, thin man with eyes like the gloaming. Light? Warmth? A drawing room full of flowers? He was pouring himself a fifth glass of wine, too morose, too preoccupied with Sundays to think of offering her more. The peaches and walnuts were quiet in their silver bowls. She took a cigarette from a crystal cigarette holder. Next to it lay a round matchbox patterned like an Indian carpet. Inside were tiny white matchsticks with speckled gold heads that exploded with a hiss when struck. Three months, no two, and the quiet to which the house succumbed at night still disturbed her. Sunset, three minutes of Titian blue, and deep night. And with it a solid earthbound silence. No crickets, no frogs, no mosquitoes up here. Only the sounds, heard or imagined, that humans made. The hiss of a gold-headed match; the short cascade of wine into a goblet; the faint, very faint, click and clatter of the kitchen being tidied, and now a scream so loud and full of terror it woke the maiden aunts from their sleep in the corners of the room. And when they saw those blue-if-it's-a-boy blue eyes gone white with fear, they fled, pulling their maiden hair behind them.

She stood in the doorway screaming, first at Valerian and then at Jadine, who rushed to her side.

"What? What? What is it?"

But she would not stop. She just balled her beautiful hands into fists and pummeled her own temples, screaming louder. Valerian stared through port-softened eyes at his wife as though he, not she, were in pain.

"What is it, Margaret?" Jadine put her arm around her shoulders. Sydney and Ondine both burst through the other door.

"What's the matter?"

"I don't know."

"She hurt herself?"

"I don't *know*."

"Hold her hands or she will."

"What is it? What happened?"

Then Ondine, fed up, shouted, "Speak, woman!" and Margaret sank to her knees gasping for the breath with which to whisper the words: "In my closet. In my closet."

"Her what?"

"Her closet. Something's in her closet."

"What's in your closet?"

"Black," she whispered, her eyes shut tight.

Jadine dropped to her knees and leaned close to Margaret's face. "You mean it's dark in your closet?"

Margaret shook her head and put the back of her fist in her mouth.

Then Valerian spoke for the first time since she had come screaming into the room. "Margaret, this is not the Met. It's a simple house on a simple island. Michael's not even here yet . . ."

But she was screaming again and Jadine had to shout, "Tell me! Tell me!"

"In my things!" said Margaret. "In all my things!"

"What's she saying?"

"Go look in her closet."

"Take the gun, Sydney." Ondine was the ranking officer, barking instructions.

"Right!" he answered, and ran back through the door to the kitchen.

"And be careful!" Ondine shouted after him.

"Hadn't I better call the harbor, Valerian?" asked Jadine.

"Don't leave me!" shrieked Margaret.

"All right. All right. Nanadine, give her some of that wine."

"Maybe she's had enough of that."

"No. She drank hardly anything."

"I heard her slam up the stairs in the middle of my dinner," said Ondine. "Between then and now she could have killed a quart." Ondine spoke without moving her lips hoping it was enough to keep Valerian from hearing.

"He's in my things, Jade." Margaret was crying softly.

"Okay, okay."

"You have to believe me."

"I don't smell anything on her breath; maybe she just flipped." Ondine was mumbling again.

"Can't you get her to a chair?" asked Valerian. He hated seeing her bent over like that on the floor.

"Come on, honey. Let's sit here," said Jadine.

"What are you doing?" Margaret was screaming again and trying to stand. "Why are you acting like this? He's there. I saw him. Valerian, please. Somebody better . . . go, call the harbor!"

"Let's wait for Sydney before we call the police," said Ondine.

"She's drunk," said Valerian with the wisdom of the drunk, "and nobody's paid her any attention for a whole hour."

"Why don't you believe me?" She looked around at them all. They looked back at her, each thinking why, indeed, he didn't; and then they heard the footsteps of Sydney plus one. Into the light of the sixty-four-bulb chandelier came Sydney pointing a .32 caliber pistol at the shoulder blades of a black man with dreadlock hair.

"It's him!" Margaret screamed.

"Have mercy," said Ondine.

"You can call the harbor now, Mr. Street," said Sydney.

"I'll do it," said Ondine.

Jadine said nothing. She did not dare.

Valerian's mouth was open and he closed it before saying, in a voice made stentorian by port, "Good evening, sir. Would you care for a drink?"

The black man looked at Valerian and it seemed to Jadine that there was a lot of space around his eyes.

4

BEES have no sting on Isle des Chevaliers, nor honey. They are fat and lazy, curious about nothing. Especially at noon. At noon parrots sleep and diamondbacks work down the trees toward the cooler undergrowth. At noon the water in the mouths of orchids left there by the breakfast rain is warm. Children stick their fingers in them and scream as though scalded. People in town go inside because the sky weighs too much at noon. They wait for hot food with lots of pepper so the day will feel cooler by comparison. They drink sweet drinks and swallow bitter coffee to distract their insides from the heat and weight of the sky. But the eaves of the house on Isle des Chevaliers were deep—the curtains light and light-filtering. So the sky did not require the occupants to distract themselves. They were free to concentrate on whichever of their personal problems they wished: the wrapped and shelved ones—the ones they always meant to take down and open one day—or the ones they caressed every hour. Just as on beaches, in summer homes, in watering places, tourists the world over lay under the breeze behind their anti-sunglasses wondering and mulling. So mulled the occupants of L'Arbe de la Croix that noon the day after a man with living hair stayed for dinner. Outwardly everything looked the same. Only the emperor butterflies appeared excited about something. Such vigorous flapping in blazing heat was uncommon for them. They hovered near the bedroom windows but the shutters had remained closed all morning and none of them could see a thing. They knew, however, that the woman was in there. Her blue-if-it's-a-boy blue eyes red-rimmed with longing for a trailer softened by columbine and for her Ma. Leonora, the daily communicant; Leonora, whose head was covered at mass with lace older than Maine itself, who at sixty folded away her stockings and from then on wore white socks with her black Cuban-heeled oxfords. Sweet, darling socks out of which grew strong, wide legs that had never been crossed at the knees.

I have come full circle, Ma, thought Margaret. Now that the breakfast rain was over and cleaned light filtered through the shutters she was amazed to discover how much like the trailer it was. Full circle, she thought, I have come full circle. The trailer had been like this room. All economy and parallel lines. All secret storage and uncluttered surfaces. South Suzanne's idea of luxury back then had been the antique-stuffed houses of old Bangor families: blue bottles and white moldings, soft yellow wallpaper and re-covered Federal chairs. But Margaret loved the trailer best and when she married the non-Catholic over the objections of her parents and moved to Philadelphia, it took years to get rid of the afterboom and now that she had, he'd left it and put her in this room that was "sculpted" he said, not decorated, that for all its Mies van der Rohe and Max whatever reminded her of the trailer in South Suzanne where she had been the envy of her girlfriends for the first dozen years of her life and was fourteen before she discovered that everybody in South Suzanne had not shared that envy. Did not think the little toilet was cute, or the way the tables folded down and beds became sofas was really neat like having your own dollhouse to live in. And when she did discover that most people thought living in a trailer was tacky, it might have crushed the life out of her except that she discovered at the same time that all of South Suzanne was overwhelmed by her astonishing good looks. She agreed, finally, with their evaluation, but it didn't help much because it meant she had to be extra nice to other girls to keep them from getting mad at her. It meant having teachers go fuzzy in her presence (the men with glee, the women with distrust), fighting off cousins in cars, dentists in chairs and feeling apologetic to every woman over thirty. Privately she neither valued it nor enjoyed it and before she could learn to use it properly, she met an older man who was never fuzzy in her presence. She knew that because almost the first thing he said to her was "You really *are* beautiful," as if it could have been fake like the float but wasn't. And she smiled because he seemed surprised. "Is that enough?" she asked, and it was the first honest response she had ever made to a male compliment. "Beauty is never enough," he said. "But you are." The safety she heard in his voice was in his nice square fingernails too. And it was that, not his money, that comforted her and made her feel of consequence under the beauty, back down beneath it where her Margaret-hood lay in the same cup it had always lain in—faceless, silent and trying like hell to please. And now she longed for her mother's trailer so far from Philadelphia and L'Arbe de la Croix but maybe not so far after all since the bedroom she had locked herself into was a high-class duplication, minus the coziness, of the first.

Margaret Lenore stared into the spaces and thought desperately of coffee, but she did not want to ring up Sydney or Ondine, for that would begin the day she was not sure she wanted to participate in. She had had no sleep to speak of, and now, drained of panic, wavering between anger and sorrow, she lay in bed. Things were not getting better. She was not getting better. She could feel it and right smack in the middle of it, with Michael on his way, *this* had to happen: literally, literally a nigger in the woodpile. And of course Valerian had to think up something to shock everybody and actually ask him to dinner. A stranger who was found hiding in his own wife's closet, a bum that even Sydney wanted to shoot, he invited to dinner while she was shaking like a leaf on the floor. In her closet. The end, the living end, but as disgusting as that was, it wasn't as bad as Valerian's insult that it was okay for him to be there. And if it wasn't for the fact that Michael was coming, she would pack up that very day and really leave him this time. Valerian knew it too, knew he could get away with it, because Michael's Christmas visit was so important to her and would keep her from leaving. Now he was playing that boring music in the greenhouse as though nothing had happened. She was so hungry and coffee-starved but she couldn't start things off just yet. And Jade hadn't knocked at all.

Usually when Margaret overslept Jade woke her with a smile, some funny piece of mail or an exciting advertisement. She would sink her cup of chocolate into Margaret's carpet (there were no end tables in the chic sparse sculpture) and they would begin the day with some high-spirited girlish nonsense.

"Look. Chloë has four new parfumes. Four."

"I think Mr. Broughton's lover has gone; you have been invited to dinner. You'd better go, 'cause I think *her* mistress is due to visit them soon. Have you seen the three of them eating together? Ondine says the cook over there said it makes her sick." Long ago when Jade used to come for holiday visits, Margaret found her awkward and pouty, but now that she was grown up, she was pretty and a lot of fun. All those colleges hadn't made her uppity and she was not at all the Mother Superior Ondine had become.

She didn't know how the dinner went. Did Jade stay? When did the man leave? She lifted her hand to press a button. Then changed her mind. Maybe the man killed everybody, and she alone escaped because she had run up to her room and locked herself in. No. If he had, the boring music would not be going. God. Maybe he will come back and do it later. And what could they do to stop him? All the neighbors would have to be told that a black man had been roaming around, and it could happen again. They would have to share security and keep in touch with each other. Each house could post one of the help so that around the clock someone was on guard. She wouldn't mention Valerian's feeding him dinner first and trying to make her stay there and watch him eat it. The neighbors would think he was crazy and blame him for whatever the burglar did. Maybe he was already in jail. He couldn't have gotten off the island last night but, early in the morning, she'd heard the jeep take off and return. Sydney probably drove him to the launch where harbor police shackled him. In any case, she wasn't going to pretend what Valerian did was okay by her. He hadn't even bothered to come in and explain, let alone apologize to her. Just as he never bothered to explain why he wouldn't go back to the States. He really expected her to steam in that jungle, knowing as he did what heat and sun and wind did to her skin. Knowing that after Maine, Philadelphia was the torrid zone for her. That her arms went pimiento with even a little sun and her back burst into pebbles. Still he stayed in this place she had never enjoyed except when Michael was younger and they all vacationed there. Now it was a boiling graveyard made bearable—just bearable—by Jade's company, shopping in Queen of France and lunches with the neighbors. She would never get through Christmas here without Michael. Never. Already the confusion was coming back. The salad things last night, for instance, and earlier at breakfast. But with Michael around she never forgot the names and uses of things.

Margaret Street closed her eyes and turned over on her stomach although she knew she would not sleep again. All night she'd been conscious of the closet door where she had gone to find the poem just to make sure Valerian was making fun of her and that there really was the line "and he glittered when he walked" in the poem Bridges had dedicated to Michael. It was a walk-in closet with dressing room separate from the wardrobe and a tiny storage niche at the very back where she kept things and in there right among all her most private stuff she saw him sitting on the floor as calm as you please and as filthy as could be. He looked at her but never moved and it seemed like hours before she could back out and hours more before she could make sound come from her open mouth and how she got down the stairs she would never in this world know but when she did it was like a dream with them looking at her but not looking as though they believed her and Valerian was worst of all sitting there like some lord or priest who doubted her confession, the completeness of it, and let her know with his eyes that she'd left something important out like the salad things. She had lain there all night with the lights on thinking of her closet as a toilet now where something rotten had been and still was. Only at dawn did she slip into a light and unrefreshing sleep not dreaming something she was supposed to be dreaming. She was exhausted when she woke but, as night disappeared, so did her fear. Among the many things she felt, anger was the most consistent but even that kept sliding away as her thoughts, unharnessed, turned sorrowful and galloped back to Leonora and a trailer sunk in columbine.

It was getting unbearably hot but she would not toss aside the sheet. Her door was locked. Jade would come soon to see about her. Valerian could do what he wished. She herself would not budge. In her things. Actually in her things. Probably jerking off. Black sperm was sticking in clots to her French jeans or down in the toe of her Anne Klein shoes. Didn't men sometimes jerk off in women's shoes? She'd have the whole closetful cleaned. Or better still, she'd throw them all out and buy everything new—from scratch. What a louse Valerian was. What a first-class louse. Wait till Michael hears about it. Just wait. And then she was crying about the night she won the beauty contest in a strapless gown that her mother had to borrow money from Uncle Adolph for and a gold cross that she always wore until her sister-in-law told her only whores wore crosses. The bitch.

She lay there wiping teary cheeks with the top hem of a Vera sheet. There was nothing the cool sculptured spaces could do to keep her from forgetting the fact that she was almost fifty sitting on a hill in the middle of a jungle in the middle of the ocean where the temperature was on broil and not even a TV with anything on it she could understand and where her husband was punishing her for forgetting to put the salad things back and there was no one to talk to except Jade and where her sex life had become such a wreck it was downright interesting. And if that wasn't enough now this nigger he lets in this real live dope addict ape just to get back at her wanting to live near Michael. "We'll see about that," she said. "Just wait till Michael comes." She whispered so nobody would hear and nobody did, not even the emperor butterflies. They were clinging to the windows of another bedroom trying to see for themselves what the angel trumpets had described to them: the hides of ninety baby seals stitched together so nicely you could not tell what part had sheltered their cute little hearts and which had cushioned their skulls. They had not seen the coat at all but a few days ago a bunch of them had heard the woman called Jade telling the woman called Margaret all about it. The butterflies didn't believe it and went to see for themselves. Sure enough, there it was, swirling around the naked body of the woman called Jade, who opened the French windows and greeted the emperor butterflies with a smile, but the heavy one called Ondine said, "Shoo! Shoo!"

"Leave them alone, Nanadine. They don't bother anything."

"They die and have to be swept up. You should put some clothes on and cover yourself up. I thought you asked me to come up and see your coat, not your privates."

"This is the best way to feel it. Here. Feel."

"Well, it's nice enough, no question about that. Mr. Street see it yet?"

"No, just you and Margaret."

"What'd she say?"

"She loved it. Said it was prettier than hers."

"Does this mean you're going to marry him?"

Jadine dug her hands deep into the pockets and spun around. Her hair was as black and shiny as the coat. "Who knows?"

"He must mean business if he fly that out to you all the way from Paris. And he must expect you back there. Lord knows you don't need a sealskin coat down here."

"It's just a Christmas present, Nanadine."

"It's not *just* anything, honey. I could buy a house with what that cost."

"No, you couldn't."

"I'd lock it up somewhere if I were you."

"I have to find a cool place for it. Maybe Valerian will let me use the air-conditioned part of his greenhouse."

"You crazy? Don't you dare leave that coat out there."

"There you go again. Nothing's going to happen, I told you. He'll be out of here by tonight."

"He better be. I'm not going to spend another night underneath the same roof with him."

"Apparently you've spent several. We all have."

"Well, I didn't know it. Although why I didn't, I can't figure. Stuff has been missing for weeks—all my chocolate, the Evian. No telling what else. I'm going to take inventory. Me and Sydney—"

"What for? What he ate, just replace. He'll be out of here tomorrow."

"You said tonight."

"It's not my house, Nanadine. Valerian invited him to dinner."

"Crazy."

"So it's Valerian who has to tell him to go."

"Why'd he put him in the guest room though? Sydney almost had a stroke when Mr. Street told him to take him there."

"Well, if he didn't have a stroke when he said 'Hi' to him, he won't have one at all."

"He said 'Hi'? Sydney didn't tell me about that."

"*Un*believable."

"Well, I can't stay up here gawking at a coat. I have to get the breakfast things cleared up. Did you call Solange yet?"

"No. I'll do it now. How did you manage to place orders before I came?"

"It was a mess, believe me. I can't get my tongue right for that language."

"Three geese, then? And another quart of raspberries?"

"That should do it. I wish they'd tell me things. How can I cook if I don't know how many's eating?" Ondine walked over to Jadine's bed and straightened the sheets. "Now when is he due?"

"Christmas Eve, I think. Just after Michael gets here."

"You sure?"

"No, but if he's a Christmas present, he'll have to be here by Christmas, won't he?"

"I can't believe that. Giving your son a whole human being for a Christmas present."

"Michael worships him. Took all of his courses at college."

"Now he'll own him, I suspect. What money can't buy. I've got to go. I want to fix a nice lunch for Sydney. He's still shook."

"Tell him not to worry."

"I'll try, but you saw him at breakfast. Mean as a tampered rooster."

"It'll be all *right,* now. I'm telling you."

Ondine left, holding her hand to her neck, hoping Jadine was right and that Mr. Street was finished being funny and would get rid of that thieving Negro before it was too late. A crazy white man and a crazy Black is a shake too much, she thought. She glanced quickly down the hall to the door of the room where he had been put. It was closed. Still asleep, she guessed. A night prowler—sleeps all day, prowls all night.

Jadine took off the sealskin coat and wiped her damp neck. She thought of another quick shower before she dressed but decided against it. Hot as it was, the seal-feel was too good to let go. She put the coat back on, sat down and dialed Solange. No response other than a light free-floating buzz. Everybody on Isle des Chevaliers seemed to live rather well without good telephone service. She and Margaret used it more than all the families combined. Since she had come, shopping had become a major part of Margaret's life as it had always been her own. She fondled the hides of ninety baby seals and went to the closet thinking she may as well begin wrapping her gifts.

There were a dozen shirts for Sydney, who loved fine cloth. And a stunning black chiffon dress for Ondine. A little overdone, but Ondine liked that. Zircons on the bodice and the waist, swirls of chiffon skirting. And (the best thing) black suede shoes with zircons studding the heels. Hooker shoes. Ondine wouldn't be able to walk long in them, but how she could reign from a sitting position. She had wanted to get her a tiara too but maybe that *was* pushing it. The dress she packed neatly in a box among layers of tissue paper. The zircon-studded shoes went into a red satin shoe bag. Perspiration was forming on her forehead as she finished, and she blotted it away without ever taking off the coat. Both Sydney's and Ondine's presents were too large for the wrapping paper she had, so she put them aside and wrapped Valerian's record album. Finally she had to admit she was stifling and took the coat off. Naked she walked to the window. The emperor butterflies were gone now. Not one had fallen dead on the Karastan. Only the bougainvillea saw her standing in the window, her head thrown back to catch all the breeze she could in the soft place under her chin. I'm all done, she thought, except for a half-hour or so of finishing Margaret's chain of gold coins. Unless, of course, she was expected to buy something for Michael. Should she? Should the—what?—social secretary buy a present for the son of her employer/patron? She could exchange gifts with the Streets because she had known them so long, and they were like family, almost, and had given her so much. But she wasn't sure if giving a gift to their son was not a presumption. If she were married to Ryk (coat and all) it would be all right. Her status would be unquestioned. But like this? She had seen him only twice. He was always at prep school or camp or some spa when she visited before. A gift would embarrass him, probably, because he wouldn't have gotten one for her. Or would he? What had Margaret told him about the household? Even so, would he be offended by a gift from her, however modest? No, of course not. He was a poet, presumably, and a Socialist, so social awkwardness wouldn't trouble him the way it would have his father. But if she did get him one, it would have to be something earthy and noncapitalistic. She smiled. A loaf of bread maybe?

Footsteps on the gravel interrupted her. That must be Yardman, come to mount the Christmas tree. Jadine stepped away from the window so Yardman shouldn't see her nakedness, wondering what he would think of the black man in the guest room. She went to the bed where the skins of the ninety baby seals sprawled. She lay on top of them and ran her fingertips through the fur. How black. How shiny. Smooth. She pressed her thighs deep into its dark luxury. Then she lifted herself up a little and let her nipples brush the black hairs, back and forth, back and forth. It had frightened Ondine, the coat. She spoke as though the marriage was all right, but Jadine knew Ondine would be heartsick. More and more Sydney and Ondine looked to her for solutions to their problems. They had been her parents since she was twelve and now she was required to parent them—guide them, do the small chores that put them in touch with the outside world, soothe them, allay their fears. Like with that wild man sleeping down the hall. She had to calm them and make them understand Valerian's whimsy. Style. All style. That was Valerian. He had once been mugged on a trip to Miami. He stood there, his arms over his head, while the muggers, some black teenagers with rags around their heads, ran their fingers through his pockets. One of them looked at him and must have seen the disdain in Valerian's eyes. He sneered at Valerian and said, "You don't like us, do you?" "Gentlemen," Valerian had replied, "I don't *know* you." It must have been that same antique grace that made him look at a raggedy black man who had been hiding in his wife's closet (with rape, theft or murder on his mind) and say, "Good evening," and offer him a drink. Then tell Sydney to prepare another place for "our guest."

Jadine smiled as she pushed her nipples into the baby seals' skin. You had to give it to him. He was marvelous. All while the man ate limp salad, flat soufflé, peaches and coffee, Valerian behaved as though it was the most ordinary of incidents. Margaret never left off shaking and would not stay at the table in spite of Valerian's insistence that she do so. (She locked her bedroom door and, according to Sydney, did not come down for breakfast—only Valerian was there with his robust morning appetite.) Jadine and Valerian held up the conversation, and it was Jadine who cautioned Sydney and Ondine with meaningful looks to help them get through the serving with composure. At one point, after the man was seated and when Sydney held the bowl of salad toward him, the man looked up and said, "Hi." For the first time in his life, Sydney had dropped something. He collected the salad greens and righted the bowl expertly, but his anger and frustration were too strong to hide. He tried his best to be no less dignified than his employer, but he barely made it to civility. Valerian, however, was splendid. As soon as the man sat down Valerian was sober. Jadine thought she may have imagined it, but she believed Valerian was comforted, made more secure, by her presence at the table. That she exercised some restraint on the man; that Valerian believed that in her presence the man might be kept manageable. At any rate he sipped his brandy as though the man's odor wasn't there. He didn't even blink when the man poured his demitasse into the saucer and blew on it gently before sipping it through a lump of sugar. More than grace, she thought, Valerian had courage. He could not have known, could not know even now, what that nigger was up to. He didn't even know his real name.

"How long have you been with us, Mister—? I'm sorry, I don't know your name."

The man looked up from his plate. His mouth was full and he chewed silently and swallowed before he answered. "Five days. A week maybe."

"And before that?" asked Valerian.

The man removed the pit of a black olive from his mouth. "Swamp."

"Oh, yes. Sein de Veilles. It couldn't have been very comfortable for you there. The local people avoid it entirely. Spirits live there, I'm told."

The man didn't answer.

"Did you see any ghosts while you were there?" Jadine asked him.

He shook his head but did not look at her. "No, but I guess they saw me."

Valerian laughed heartily. "Are you a believer then?"

"Sometimes," said the man.

"Sometimes? You pick and choose when to believe and when not?"

"In a swamp, I believe," said the man.

"An excellent solution. Excellent." Valerian chuckled. He seemed to be enjoying himself thoroughly. "You're not local, are you? Your accent is American. Am I correct?"

"Yeah."

"Have you just left there?"

"No." The man sopped the salad dressing on his plate with a round of French bread, and gulped it down. Then he wiped his mouth with the back of his hand. "Jumped ship and tried to swim ashore. Couldn't make it so I climbed aboard this boat I thought was going to dock there, but it brought me here. I waited a few days for a way to get back. Nothing. So I came to the first house I saw. I was—" he glanced at Jadine—"good and hungry by then." He was exhausted it seemed, having said so much.

"Reasonable," said Valerian. "But I'm confused. Is there a pantry in my wife's bedroom?" He gazed at the man's profile.

"Huh?"

Valerian smiled, but did not repeat the question.

"He wants to know why you were in the bedroom," said Jadine. "If you were just feeding yourself, that is."

"Oh. I got tired sitting in one spot all day. I was just looking around. I heard footsteps and hid." He looked around at them as though his reply had finally solved everything, and he could now be sociable. "Nice pad you got here," he said smiling, and that was when Jadine felt the first bolt of fear. As long as he burrowed in his plate like an animal, grunting in monosyllables, but not daring to look up, she was without fear. But when he smiled she saw small dark dogs galloping on silver feet.

More to regain her confidence than to get information she asked him, "Why didn't you take the boat?"

"What?" He looked at her quickly and just as quickly looked away.

"You said you were waiting to get to Dominique. The *Seabird* is docked. If you've been to sea, you could have managed the boat."

He stared at his plate and said nothing.

"Boats are highly visible, dear," Valerian said to Jadine, "and call a great deal of attention to themselves." He smiled at the man and went on. "I'm sorry, but I don't know your name."

"That makes us even," said the man with a wide smile. "I don't know yours either."

And they still didn't, but Valerian instructed him to be put up in the guest room anyway. And Sydney's jawbones were still working back and forth the next morning as he told his wife and niece about putting silk pajamas out for him. Jadine laughed and said he would slide out of bed in them, but Sydney couldn't see any humor in that, and Ondine was too concerned about her husband to join the pretty careless girl in laughter.

ONDINE picked up an onion and pressed it for soft spots. Things went back to their natural state so quickly in that place. A layer of slippery skin gave way beneath her thumb, but the onion was firm underneath. At that moment, Yardman scratched the screen door and when Ondine turned to look she saw his bloody shirt first and then his foolish smile.

"Leave it." She turned back to her table and tossed the words over her shoulder. "Put some newspaper down out there."

He broadened his smile and nodded vigorously, but Ondine did not see that; she assumed it and, as an afterthought lest he think she had no manners at all, she said, "Thanks." She put down the onion and turned one eye of the gas range up high. In fact, the "thanks" was sincere for she felt guilty about letting him do what was once a marked skill of her own.

Can't do it anymore, she thought. Have to chase around too much. She didn't like asking Yardman to do it for her, but her feet were too tender and her ankles too swollen to manage, so when he brought four or five young hens tied in a crate, she told him she needed only one at a time—let the others pick around behind the washhouse and to "wring one of them for me while you're at it."

"Yes, madame," he said as he always said.

"Are they young? Tender?" she had asked him.

"Yes, madame."

"Don't look it. Look like brooders."

"No, madame. Pullet every one."

"We'll see," she answered him. "Mind how you go. I don't want to be scrubbing up blood all afternoon." But he was bloody anyway so she said, "Leave it," to let him know that he had killed it wrong and also to remind him that she did not want him in her kitchen. And there it was on the newspaper and wouldn't you know he had not plucked one single feather, heavenly Father? That'll take me forever.

She lifted her head to call him back, come right back here, she was going to say, but suddenly she was too tired. Too tired to fuss, too tired to even have to confront him with his sloppiness. She sighed, picked up the chicken and brought it into the kitchen.

She hoisted a large pot of water onto the burning eye and wondered what he did with the head and feet. When the water was hot enough she dropped the chicken in and held it down with a wooden ladle long enough to loosen the pins. Then she removed it from the hot water and with newspaper spread out, started to pluck. She was still nimble at it but slower than she would have been if she wasn't being careful about where the feathers went. A big nuisance to have to do it herself; it was going to make Sydney's lunch late, but she didn't feel up to seeing Yardman again, or giving him an order angrily, firmly or even sweetly. Yesterday everything was all right. The best it could be and exactly the way she had hoped it would be: a good man whom she trusted; a good and permanent job doing what she was good at for a boss who appreciated it; beautiful surroundings which included her own territory where she alone governed; and now with Jadine back, a "child" whom she could enjoy, indulge, protect and, since this "child" was a niece it was without the stress of a mother-daughter relationship. She was uneasy about the temporary nature of their stay on the island and Margaret's visits always annoyed her—but it was being there that made Jade want to stay with them for a longish spell. Otherwise their niece would light anywhere except back in Philadelphia. She hoped Mr. Street would stay on in spite of his addled wife. Now here come this man upstairs in the guest room. Maybe Jadine was right, she thought, he would be gone today or, certainly, the next and they were making too much of it. Ondine stopped plucking and lifted her eyes slowly to the place where the window shutters did not quite close. A bit of the sky was unhidden by foliage. She thought she heard a small, smooth sound, like a well-oiled gear shifting. Not a sound really—more of an imagined impression, as though she were a dust mote watching an eye blink. There would be the hurricane wind of eyelashes falling through the air and the weighty crash of lid on lid.

Slowly she returned to the white hen in her hands. She was

down to the pinfeathers when Sydney walked in with a small basket of mail.

"Already?" she asked him.

"No. I just thought I'd finish it up in here."

"It'll be at least an hour. Maybe two."

"What are you doing that for?" He pointed at the pile of feathers on the floor.

"That's the way I got it."

"Call him. You want me to call him back here?"

"No. I'm just about finished now."

"He knows better than that. Where is he?" Sydney moved toward the door.

"Sit down, Sydney. Don't bother yourself."

"I'm already bothered. I can't run a house like this with everybody doing whatever comes to mind."

"Sit down, I say. Hen's done."

He sat at the table and began sorting letters, circulars, magazines, and putting them into piles.

"Maybe we should look for somebody else. I'll speak to Mr. Street."

"It's not worth the trouble, Sydney. Unless you can guarantee the next one won't be worse. On balance, he's still reliable and he does keep the place up, you got to give him his due."

"You don't sound like yourself, Ondine." He looked at her heavy white braids sitting on her head like a royal diadem.

"Oh, I'm fine, I guess," but her voice was flat, like a wide river without any undertow at all.

"I never heard you stand up for Yardman when he does something contrary to what you tell him."

"I'm not standing up for him. I just think he's a whole lot better than nobody and a little bit better than most."

"You the one doing the plucking. I'm trying to make it easier for you—not me."

"He *is* easier for me. I was just thinking how I used to be able to get my own yard hens. Not no more. If they tear loose from me, they free. I can't chase em anymore. I don't even know if I got the strength to wring their necks."

"Well, what you don't have the strength for, Yardman is supposed to do. I don't want you running all over the yard after chickens. Killing them neither. We long past that, Ondine. Long past that." He rested his hands on a letter for a minute as he recollected the bloody, long-legged girl in the back of Televettie Poultry sitting with three grown women, ankle deep in feathers among the squawks of crated fowl. At their feet two troughs of dead birds, one for the feathered ones, one for the newly plucked.

"I know, and we're going to stay past it, too."

"Not if you start changing up on me, we won't. Not if you start letting people run over you. Start changing the rules in the middle of the stream." He pushed the stack of magazines to one side.

Ondine laughed lightly. "You mean horse."

"What?"

"Horse. Horse in midstream. Never mind. You know as well as anybody that I can handle Yardman and you also know that I'm not changing up on you. That's not what you're going on about. You're edgy and I understand. That makes two of us. Three, I guess, since the Principal Beauty locked herself in. She call you for anything yet?"

"No. Not a thing."

"Me neither."

"Why three? Jadine ain't bothered?"

"Not as far as I can see. She's laughing and swinging around in that coat."

"Damn."

"She says we're overdoing it. That Mr. Street'll have him out of here today."

"But what'd he do it for? She say anything about that? I been knowing him for fifty-one years and I never would have guessed—not in a million years—he do something like this. Where does he think he is? Main Line? Ain't no police out here. Ain't nobody hardly. He think that nigger came here and hid in his own wife's bedroom just to get a meal? He could have knocked on the back door and got something to eat. Nobody comes in a house and hides in it for days, weeks . . ."

Ondine looked at her husband. Talk about changing up, she hadn't seen him this riled since before they were married. "I know," she said, "I know that, but Jadine says it was a joke; he had too much liquor and him and her had an argument and. . ." she stopped.

". . . and what? Can't finish, can you? No, 'cause it don't make a bit of sense. Not one bit."

"There's no point in gnawing it, Sydney, like a dog with a bone. Swallow it or drop it."

"Can't do either one."

"You have to. It ain't your bone."

"You have taken leave of your senses, woman. It is my bone and right now it's stuck in my craw. I live here too. So do you and so does Jadine. My family lives here—not just his. If that nigger wants to steal something or kill somebody you think he's going to skip us, just 'cause we don't own it? Hell, no. I sat up in that chair all night, didn't I? Mr. Street slept like a log. He was snoring like a hound when I went in there this morning."

"He drank a lot, Jadine says." She reached in the oven and poked a baking potato.

"Ain't that much whiskey in the world make a man sleep with a wife-raper down the hall."

"He didn't rape anybody. Didn't even try."

"Oh? You know what's on his mind, do you?"

"I know he's been here long enough and quiet enough to rape, kill, steal—do whatever he wanted and all he did was eat."

"You amaze me. You really amaze me. All these years I thought I knew you."

"You're tired, honey. You didn't sleep hardly any at all with that gun in your lap, and carrying it around under your coat ain't making things better. You really ought to put it back where it belongs."

"Long as he's in this house, it belongs with me."

"Come on, now. It's barely noon. Mr. Street'll get rid of him just like Jadine said. Then everything will be just like it was."

"Like it was? Like it was, eh? Not by a long shot. When I brought him his coffee and rolls, he never said a word. Just 'More coffee, please.' Ondine, it's more than just being here, you know. I mean, Mr. Street had him stay in the guest room. The guest room. You understand me?"

"Well?"

"What do you mean, 'well'?"

"I don't know what you're driving at."

"Where do we sleep? Ondine?"

"Me and you?"

"You heard me."

"We sleep where we're supposed to."

"Where's that?"

"It's nice down there, Sydney. And you know it is: sitting room, *two* bedrooms, patio, bath . . ."

"But where is it?"

"Over there."

"Over where?"

"Up over the downstairs kitchen."

"Right. Up over the downstairs kitchen."

"Jadine sleeps up there. With them."

"Jadine? Now I am through. You comparing Jadine to a . . . a . . . stinking ignorant swamp nigger? To a wild-eyed pervert who hides in women's closets? Do you know what he said to me?"

" 'Hi'?"

"Before that. When I was bringing him down the stairs under the barrel of my gun?"

"No, what'd he say?"

"Could he take a leak."

"A leak?"

"A leak! I got him with his hands up and the safety off and he wants to stop and pee!"

"That's nerve all right."

"Nerve? He's crazy, that's what. You understand me? Crazy. Liable to do anything. And I have to show him to the guest room and lay him out some fresh pajamas. The guest room, right next to Jadine. I told her to keep that door locked and not to open it up for nobody."

"You should have left it at that. You didn't have to go creeping up there all night to make sure. Scared her to death."

"Wait a minute. Whose side you on?"

"Your side, naturally. Our side. I'm not arguing for him. I told you last night what I thought about it. I just want to calm you down. He's leaving, Sydney. But we're not, and I don't want no big rift between you and Mr. Street about where that Negro slept and why and so forth. I want us to stay here. Like we have been. That old man loves you. Loves us both. Look what he gives us at Christmas."

"I know all that."

"Stock. No slippers. No apron. Stock! And look what he did for Jadine, just because you asked him to. You going to break up with him, lose all that just because he got drunk and let a crazy hobo spend the night. We have a future here, as well as a past, and I tell you I can't pick up and move in with some strange new white folks at my age. I can't do it."

"Nobody's talking about moving."

"If you keep working yourself up, you'll rile him, or do something rash, I don't know."

"If I stay on here, I have to know whether—"

"See there? If. Already you saying if. Keep on and you'll have us over in them shacks in Queen of France. You want me shucking crayfish on a porch like those Marys? Do you?"

"You know I don't."

"Then drop that bone. Drop it before it chokes you. You know your work. Just do what you're supposed to do. Here. Take him his potato. Finish the rest of the mail later. Just give Mr. Street his. He likes to read it while he eats, if you call that eating. And Sydney? Don't worry yourself. Remember, Jadine's here. Nothing can happen to us as long as she's here."

SYDNEY went out with the tray on which a steaming potato in a covered dish was situated to the left of an empty wineglass, a napkin and a stack of mail. As the kitchen door swung on its hinges, Ondine took a deep breath. She had surprised herself. Before Sydney came in she was as nervous as he was. Still tasting her breakfast, too confused to quarrel with Yardman about the unplucked hen. She didn't put any stock in Jadine's assurances, but when Sydney looked like he was falling apart, she'd pulled herself together and talked sense. Good sense. That was what surprised her. She talked sense she didn't know she had about a situation that both frightened and disoriented her. But in talking to Sydney she knew what it was. The man was black. If he'd been a white bum in Mrs. Street's closet, well, she would have felt different. Sydney was right. It was his bone. Whether they liked it or not. But she was right, too. He had to drop it. The man upstairs wasn't a Negro—meaning one of them. He was a stranger. (She had made Sydney understand that.) Mr. Street might keep him for two days, three, for his own amusement. And even if he didn't steal, he was nasty and ignorant and they would have to serve him anyway, if Mr. Street wanted it. Clean his tub, change his bed linen, bring his breakfast to his bed if he wanted it, collect his underwear (Jesus), call him sir, step aside if they met him in the hall, light his cigarettes, hold open his door, see to it there were fresh flowers in his room, books, a dish of mints.

"Shoot," she said aloud. "That nigger's not going nowhere. No matter what they say." Ondine picked up the chicken. Her fingers quickly found the joints they were searching for, and broke each one. Then she removed the wings from its back. The hen's little elbows held a dainty *V* as though protecting its armpits from the cold although it was noon and the water the breakfast rain had left in the mouths of the orchids was so hot it burned the children's fingers—or would have, if any children lived at L'Arbe de la Croix. But none did. So the stamens of the orchids went untickled and the occupants of the lovely breezy house with the perfectly beveled cabinets heard no children's screams and no tramp of red soldier ants marching toward the greenhouse, past the washhouse where a woman sat rubbing the dirt from her feet with one of seventeen Billy Blass towels. Stacked before her in two wicker baskets were the other sixteen, some everyday table napkins and tablecloths, assorted underwear and T-shirts, four white uniforms, four white shirts, a corset, six pairs of black nylon socks and two thin cotton nightgowns. She was happy as she sat there cleaning her calluses. Her laundry load was getting smaller each week and the bundle of clothes that traveled by motorboat to Cecile's in Queen of France was getting bigger and bigger. She knew quite well that she was supposed to be insulted by that, and when the opportunity arose she managed a pout, but in her heart of hearts she was happy.

She put the black socks in a bucket to soak and dropped the corset in a basinful of soapy water and vinegar. She made the Billy Blass towels the first load for the washing machine since they took longest to dry. Once the machine began to agitate she could sit for a while and attend to her own thoughts while she waited for Gideon to come by her. From the pocket of her dress she pulled two wrinkled avocados and some smoked fish and placed them on a piece of newspaper and covered it all against flies with a stained Dior napkin. Then she disconnected the dryer, plugged in her hot plate and set an old drip-pot of coffee on to heat. She had no assigned lunch hour so she ate while the laundry washed itself. It was such a pleasure. Washing for these people was child's play compared to the way she did it on Place de Vent. But at least there she had the pleasure of gossip over the tubs; here there was mostly silence (unless you counted the music that came from the *serre chaude*), which is why she could hear the soldier ants so clearly and why she was so eager for Gideon to finish with the hens and join her on some pretext or other for if the heavy one with the braids crossed like two silver machetes on her head caught them chatting in the washhouse or in the garden behind, she would fly into a rage and her machetes would glitter and clang on her head. The silence was why she often brought Alma, and although the girl's chatter was so young it made her head ache, it was better than listening to soldier ants trying one more time to enter the greenhouse and being thwarted as usual by the muslin dipped in poison and taped to the doorsill.

She was sorry Alma could not come today. Gideon and she had a bet on how long the chocolate eater could last. Gideon said, "Long as he wants. Till New Year," while she said, "No. The chocolate eater's heart would betray him—not his mind or stomach." And as they rowed back to Queen of France she raised the bet to 150,000 francs instead of the 100,000 she began with. She laughed and spat in the sea as she raised him, so confident was she. For she had seen evidence of the man who ate chocolate (in the washhouse, in the trees, in the gazebo, down by the pond, in the toolshed, near the greenhouse). And it was he who brought the soldier ants onto the property with his trail of foil paper containing flecks of chocolate that the ants loved and sought vigorously. She had seen him in a dream smiling at her as he rode away wet and naked on a stallion. So she knew he was in agreement with her and any day now he would be discovered or reveal himself. As soon as she got out of the jeep that very morning, she was convinced that today was the day. A great rush of butterflies was what she noticed first and later, as she stood in the courtyard waiting for machete-hair to bring the baskets of clothes, she instantly saw that the machetes were not clanging now. They, like their owner, were subdued—by fear, she thought. The chocolate man would be the cause of that. She could think of nothing else —hurricane wind, or magic doll, diamondback or monkey teeth— that would quiet those curved and clanging knives. Only the man who ate chocolate in the night and lived like a foraging animal and who was as silent as a star could have done it.

She had eaten the fish and one avocado and still Gideon had not come. She didn't want to start on the coffee, because it ran right through her and not having access to a toilet (she felt unwelcome even in the kitchen) she did not want to run off to the bushes behind the garden in the middle of his visit. She insisted she knew about the man before Gideon—although it was he who actually saw him first. She knew of his presence twelve days ago long before he left the trail of chocolate foil paper (which she mistook for a fabricated attack against herself made up by machete-hair who had asked her point-blank had she been taking chocolate and she had said, No, madame, over her shoulder to every query without allowing her eyes to see the heavy one). Before that mistakable trail, he left the unmistakable one of his smell. Like a beast who loses his animal smell after too long a diet of cooked food, a man's smell is altered by a fast. She caught the scent twelve days ago: the smell of a fasting, or starving, as the case might be, human. It was the smell of human afterbirth that only humans could produce. A smell they reproduced when they were down to nothing for food. So a hungry man was on the grounds, or, as she said to Gideon, "Somebody's starving to death round here." And Gideon said, "Me, Thérèse," and she said, "No, not you. A really starving somebody." And later that day a bug-eyed Gideon crept over to her under the lime tree near the kitchen terrace and whispered that he'd seen a swamp woman dart out from behind some trees near the pond. Thérèse stopped scaling grouper fish and said that what he saw was what she smelled and it couldn't be a swamp woman because they had a pitchlike smell. What he saw must have been a rider. So she took to bringing two avocados instead of one and leaving the second one in the washhouse. But each third day when she returned it was still there, untouched by all but fruit flies. It was Gideon who had the solution: instead of fixing the sash on the window of the pantry as he was ordered, he removed one of its panes and told machete-hair he was having trouble getting another. The heavy one fumed and removed "perishables" and things that attracted flies into the other kitchen until he could repair the window. In the meanwhile, they hoped the horseman would have access to the food left there. And soon they saw bits of folded foil in funny places and they knew he had gotten from the pantry chocolate at the very least. Once Gideon saw an empty Evian bottle in the gazebo. Then they knew he had fresh water too.

Thérèse removed the coffee pot from the stove and put it back five times before she heard Gideon's footsteps. She poked her head out of the doorway, grinned and started to speak.

"Sh," he said, "sh." His finger touched his lips. But Thérèse could not restrain herself.

"Something's going on. I can tell." Then as he stepped inside and came close she saw his shirt. "You slaughter the hen or the hen slaughter you?"

Gideon held up one hand to shush her and with the other pulled the door shut.

"Open the door, man," she complained. "Too hot in here."

Gideon stood fast. "Listen," he said. "He's in the house. *In* it! All out in the open! I saw him!"

"I knew it! I knew it!" Thérèse's whisper was close to a shout. Gideon went to the coffee pot. Two cups were sitting on top of the folding table and he filled them both.

"A little fridge out here wouldn't be a bad idea," he said. "Just one of them little ones, like he got out in the greenhouse. Plug it up right there . . ."

"Talk, man. Stop going on about a fridge."

"Wouldn't you like a little cold beer or chilled wine from time to time?"

"Cold beer?" She looked at him in amazement. "That country ruined you, man. Stop fooling with me. Where did you see him?"

"In the window. Her window." He took the chicken head and feet from his shirt and wrapped them in newspaper.

"Doing what?"

"Looking. Just looking. A sheet or something wrapped around him, but bare naked on top."

"Did he see you see him?"

"No. Don't think so. I pretended I was taking off my cap to scratch my head and looking off up in the trees."

"He didn't do anything? Move?"

"Nope. Just looked around. Then I turned and walked back away."

"Alone? Was she with him?"

"Can't say. But it was in her room. Get what I mean? And I saw her up there before naked as a worm when I was fixing to put up the tree. She jumped back, but didn't do no good. She don't know I got eyes in the top of my head. Then next, about a hour or so later, there *he* was. Naked too, almost. Just a piece of white stuff around his waist. You reckon they got it on?" He had stopped trying to appear uninterested and was openly enjoying the possibilities.

"I told you!" said Thérèse. "He's a horseman come down here to get her. He was just skulking around waiting for his chance."

"Maybe. Maybe." Gideon looked at her milky eyes. "You damn near blind, but I have to hand it to you. Some things you see better than me. Otherwise why would a big strong-looking man be hiding round here like that? Why this house all the time? Why not over the other side, or up the road where those Filipinos are? He must have been looking for somebody specific."

"The chippy. The fast-ass," said Thérèse. "That's why he went straight up to her room. Because he knew she was here, he saw her from the hills. Maybe he'll run her out of here."

"Back to the States, eh?"

"Or France even. Where that big box came from. Maybe he's not a rider. Maybe he's an old boyfriend and he the one sent her the box, Gideon."

"Hold on. You going wild."

"And machete-hair she don't like it. Tried to keep them apart. But it didn't work. He find her, swim the whole ocean big, till he find her, eh? Make machete-hair too mad. Now she tell her bow-tie husband . . ." Thérèse sat on the wooden chair and rocked in the telling, pressing her fingers into Gideon's shoulder as each new sequence presented itself to her. "Bow-tie get mad very. 'Cause he lives near machete-hair's thumb . . ." The more she invented the more she rocked and the more she rocked the more her English crumbled till finally it became dust in her mouth stopping the flow of her imagination and she spat it out altogether and let the story shimmer through the clear cascade of the French of Dominique.

Gideon couldn't stop her, so he tried to gulp coffee while warding off the jabs to his shoulder. When she abandoned English he stopped listening for it was in French that she had tricked him into leaving the States after twenty years and coming back to Dominique to handle family property. So he shut his ears and tried to finish his coffee submitting to the shoulder jabs out of deference to her because she was his mother's baby sister and because of a grudging respect for her magic breasts and because she had been able to trick him (of all people) with thirty-four letters in fifteen years, begging him to come home and take care of the property by which she must have meant herself because when he got there that's all there was left: no land, no hills of coffee bush. Just Thérèse, two years his senior, and a cement house whose roof had to be put back on after every hurricane which meant four times a year. When he looked at the house—one of a dozen scattered over the emerald hill—and discovered that the 130 *arpents* he'd remembered from his childhood belonged, like the emerald hills, to the Frenchman who lived in Guadeloupe and that except for the kitchen garden and the village garden on the riverbank there was no land to care for, only this laughing, lying crone with a craving for apples, he wasn't even angry. Just amazed that he had believed those thirty-four letters written in perfect French by the priest at first and then by an acolyte describing the burden of managing so much property, too much for an old lady who nevertheless always thought of a way to get a ten-dollar money order out of him, and asking over and over again to make sure he brought apples when he came or to send them, and if he would let her know when that would be she would alert a friend at customs because apples were contraband and could not be imported into Dominique which was true because only French-grown fruit and vegetables could arrive at that port or be sold in the stores. And ships unloaded wilted lettuce, thin rusty beans and pithy carrots every month. A hardship for the rich and the middle class, neither of whom would consider working a kitchen garden (except, of course, the American, who made it a hobby) and were dependent on the market but it was of no consequence to the poor who ate splendidly from their gardens, from the sea and from the avocado trees that grew by the side of the road. Only Thérèse had tasted apples once when she was seven and again when she was thirty-five and had a craving for them akin to hysteria. When Gideon appeared in 1973 with twelve apples hidden in the lining of his electric blue leisure suit which Thérèse's friends at customs noticed—but for two dollars U.S. ignored—her gratitude was so complete he didn't get on the next plane back as he threatened. After all he hadn't left much: just U.S. citizenship, the advantage of which was the ability to send an occasional ten-dollar money order, buy a leisure suit and watch TV. Most of the friends of his youth had emigrated to France, but the stories of their lives there were so heartbreaking, he'd chosen Quebec instead although he had to wait until he was twenty-two for a visa and then he arrived in the coat pocket so to speak of a Canadian farmer. And two years later, by much subterfuge (including marriage to an American Negro) got into the States where money orders, leisure suits and TV abounded. Now that he'd come back what was there to do but build a new roof after each hurricane, find a little work, and wait for carnival? At first he was ashamed before his family and friends. Just as Thérèse had lied to him, so had he lied to her about the wealth he had accumulated in the States. Now there he was for all the world to see building another temporary roof, looking for tourist tips, eying women at the bars—just like before. With no suitcase of American dollars. Just twelve apples and a leisure suit. Humiliating. Who but an ass would go back to Dominique with no more than what he had when he left? Those who wished desperately to come back (from France, Quebec, New York City or wherever) could not, would not, unless they were accompanied by the college certificates or money they had gone to find. He spoke English very well, however, and that could have been something of an asset on the island, but at his age with no certificate and out of touch with friends who could make a way for him he could not carry luggage at the airlines, or wait tables at the Old Queen. So he drifted to the docks for a few days' work or got a lucky day collecting fares for a taxi man until, finally, all of his forty years of immigrant labor paid off when an American who owned a house on Isle des Chevaliers came to stay and needed a regular handyman/gardener with boat skills, English and a manner less haughty than that of the local Blacks. For in spite of the fact that they built their houses four times a year the natives of Dominique did not hide the contempt they felt in their hearts for everybody but themselves.

Gideon got over the shame: the work at Isle des Chevaliers, which began for a season and had lasted three years, helped and so did the fact that the jokes and insults heaped on him by his family were nothing compared to the humiliations of immigrant life which U.S. citizenship did not change. Also the thought of being able to die in those coffee-growing hills rather than in those lonely Stateside places gave him so much happiness he could not hold a grudge or sustain anger for more than an hour. Unlike Thérèse whose hatreds were complex and passionate as exemplified by her refusal to speak to the American Negroes, and never even to acknowledge the presence of the white Americans in her world. To effect this she believed all she had to do was not look at them (or rather not look at them while they looked at her) so her face was always turned away when they addressed her and her glance (when it was not on her work) went to a distant point on the horizon which she could not have seen if her life depended on it. What they took for inattentiveness was a miracle of concentration.

"Hush, Thérèse," said Gideon. "They can hear you in the harbor. Finish making up your romance in your head. I have to go." He stood up and rubbed the abused shoulder. "But you forgetting one thing in your story. One important thing. I said I saw him in the house, in the open. Open. Get it? Now there are five people living there. Not three. And two of them is white and the same two is the boss of everything as well. While you making up your story about what this one thinks and this one feels, you have left out the white bosses. What do they feel about it? It's not important who this one loves and who this one hates and what bow-tie do or what machete-hair don't do if you don't figure on the white ones and what they thinking about it all." He tapped her on the chest bone and left her sitting there with a half-finished plot on her tongue.

Thérèse unplugged the hot plate and put the last of the Billy Blass towels in the dryer. Then she put all the white shirts and uniforms into the washing machine. The load was too tight and too much, but she had wasted time gossiping with Gideon so she left it that way. She sat down again on the chair and began sloshing the black socks of the bow-tie husband.

It was true, she thought. She had forgotten the white Americans. How would they fit into the story? She could not imagine them. In her story she knew who the others were: the chocolate-eating man was a lover, the fast-ass a coquette who had turned him down; the other two were the traditional hostile family. She understood that, but now she had to get a grasp of the tall thin

American who played in the greenhouse whom she had never seen clearly and certainly never spoken to. And also the wife with the sunset hair and milk-white skin. What would they feel? She realized then that all her life she thought they felt nothing at all. Oh, well, yes, she knew they talked and laughed and died and had babies. But she had never attached any feeling to any of it. She thought of her priest, the shopkeepers, the gendarmes, the schoolteachers Alma talked about, the two little French girls she took care of one day when the governess ran away, and the hundreds of French babies who used to nurse at her magical breasts. What went on inside them? Inside.

Thérèse resented the problem and the necessity for solving it to get on with the story. "What difference does it make," she murmured. "I don't know what they would think about him, but I know for certain what they would do about him. Kill him. Kill the chocolate-eating black man. Kill him dead. Ah. Poor thing. Poor, poor thing. He dies and the fast-ass is brought low at last. Too late, bitch—too late you discover how wonderful he really was. How gentle, how kind. And you are full of remorse, but too late, cow, too too late; you will never have him now. And you machete-hair and you bow-tie you will think everything is all right now he's dead, but no! you will suffer too, because the fast-ass is grief-stricken and will blame you for his untimely death and hate you forever. So you can go back to the States the whole pack of you and choke to death on your big red apples."

THE SKIN of the baby seals sucked up the dampness of her own. Jadine closed her eyes and imagined the blackness she was sinking into. She lay spread-eagled on the fur, nestling herself into it. It made her tremble. She opened her lips and licked the fur. It made her tremble more. Ondine was right; there was something a little fearful about the coat. No, not fearful, seductive. After a few more moments of nestling she got up and made preparations to take another shower and to get dressed. The clock showed twelve-thirty and she still had to phone Solange, answer letters, and see about Margaret. She would need soothing. Maybe they would take their fruit and cold consommé down by the fish pond or farther up the hill to the gazebo. Because of Margaret's refusal to leave her bedroom, they had already missed their session of exercise and muscle-tightening calisthenics. Valerian would be in the greenhouse through lunch where he usually had a baked potato or some other single item. Only Ondine and Sydney ate a substantial lunch. Both had three very full meals a day and their menu was in no way related to what was served at Valerian's table.

Jadine came out of the shower as moist as she was when she went in, so she dressed as slowly as possible in order to prevent more perspiration.

The emperor butterflies were back now agitating the air. Jadine watched them languidly as she brushed her hair and bound it into a knot at the top of her head. Then she pulled a few strands over her ears and temples to soften the look. On impulse she put on her coat again and she was looking in a full-length mirror judging the effect when the smell hit her. She moved a little to her left to see what the mirror reflected behind her. There he stood in mauve silk pajamas, his skin as dark as a riverbed, his eyes as steady and clear as a thief's.

"Morning," he said, and smiled bringing once more into view the small dark dogs galloping on silver feet. Jadine could not find her tongue. She was staring into the mirror at his hair. Last night, sitting with Valerian in the soft light of the dining room, it had looked merely long and unkempt. Here, alone in her bedroom where there were no shadows, only glimmering unrelieved sunlight, his hair looked overpowering—physically overpowering, like bundles of long whips or lashes that could grab her and beat her to jelly. And would. Wild, aggressive, vicious hair that needed to be put in jail. Uncivilized, reform-school hair. Mau Mau, Attica, chain-gang hair.

"Good morning." He said it again.

She struggled to pull herself away from his image in the mirror and to yank her tongue from the roof of her mouth. She was sober now and the thought that she had not grasped fully the night before, the picture that only Margaret had seen clearly, was framed for her now in the fruitwood of the mirror: this man had been living among them (in their *things*) for days. And they had not known it. What had he seen or heard? What was he doing there?

"Hey. I was saying good morning to you."

She turned, freed at last from the image in the mirror.

"You could knock, you know."

"The door was open." He gestured to the door behind him.

"But it's still a door and can be knocked on."

He seemed to close his eyes to her without shutting the lids, and what was left of his smile disappeared into his beard and the riverbed darkness of his face.

This is wrong, she thought. I shouldn't make him angry.

"I'm sorry, but you startled me. Did you sleep well?"

He nodded but did not return the smile she dredged up to her own lips.

"The shower doesn't work," he said, glancing around the room.

"Oh." She laughed and, to hide her confusion, shed her sealskin coat, throwing it on the bed. "There's no handle. Just push the knob in the center. It'll come on. It took me a while too, at first."

He looked past her to the sealskin coat sprawled on the bed. Jadine flushed as though he could see the print of her nipples and thighs in the pelts. He walked toward the coat and the bed. The pajamas they'd given him were too small—the sleeves ended somewhere between wrist and elbow and the pants leg came to just above his shins. As he stood looking at the coat she could not tell whether he or it was the blacker or the shinier, but she knew she did not want him to touch it.

"I'll get Sydney to get some clothes for you if you like." Then thinking of Sydney's response to that chore she added, "Or Yardman. Yardman can get some things for you."

"Who?" He turned away from the coat.

"Yardman. The gardener."

"That his name?"

"No." She smiled, searching for the leashes of the small dark dogs. "But he answers to it. Which is something, at least. Some people don't have a name of any kind."

He smiled too, moving away from the bed toward her. "What do you like? Billy? Paul? What about Rastus?"

"Don't be funny. What *is* your name?"

"What's yours?"

"Jade."

He shook his head as though he knew better.

"Okay. Jadine. Jadine Childs." She reached for a cigarette.

"Can I have one of those?"

"Sure." She gestured toward the escritoire for him to help himself. He pulled out a Gauloise filter, lit it and began to cough.

"Been a long time," he said, and for the first time looked vulnerable. Jadine grabbed the leashes.

"Keep the pack," she said. "There's plenty more if you want them."

He nodded and took another drag with a little more success.

"Who's the copper Venus?" he asked her.

Jadine dropped the leashes. "Where did you see that?"

"I didn't see it. I heard it."

"Where?" She could not find them, they were gone.

"The woman who comes to work here. She talks to herself out in the washhouse."

Now she had them again, safely back in her fingers. "Mary. It must have been Mary." Jadine laughed. "That was a publicity thing. When I was modeling they called me that. I wonder how Mary knows about it. I don't think she can even read."

"You were a model?" He narrowed his eyes with interest.

Jadine walked over to a large straw chest. As she left the Karastan her gold-thread slippers clicked on the tile. After rummaging awhile she pulled out a fashion magazine with her face on the cover. When she handed it to him he sat down at the desk and made a flute sound between his teeth. And then another as his eyes traveled from the crown of her head to the six centimeters of cleavage supported (more or less) by silver lamé. Her hair in the picture was pressed flat to her head, pulled away from her brow revealing a neat hairline. Her eyes were the color of mink and her lips wet and open. He continued the flute sounds and then opened the magazine. After flipping the pages for a few seconds he came to a four-page spread of her in other poses, other clothes, other hair, but always the same wet and open lips.

"Goddamn," he whispered. "Go-oddamn."

Jadine said nothing, but she held on tight to the leashes. The look on his face made her smile. He examined the pictures closely, whispering "shit" and "goddamn" softly to himself at intervals.

"What does it say?" He put the magazine flat on the desk, turned at an angle so she could read and translate the text.

"Oh, it's just stuff about me." She leaned on the edge of the desk facing him and the magazine. "Where I went to school. Things like that."

"Read it to me."

Jadine leaned over and translated rapidly the important parts of the copy. "Mademoiselle Childs . . . graduate of the Sorbonne . . . an accomplished student of art history . . . a degree in . . . is an expert on cloisonné, having visited and worked with the Master Nape. . . . An American now living in Paris and Rome, where she had a small but brilliantly executed role in a film by . . ." She stopped. The man was tracing her blouse with his forefinger.

"This," he said, lifting his finger from the picture to point at the caption beneath, "what does this say?"

"That's just a description of the dress. Natural raw silk . . . honey-colored . . ."

"Right here it says 'fast lane.' What's that about?"

"Oh, they're trying to be hip. It says, 'If you travel as Jade does in what the Americans call the fast lane, you need elegant but easy-to-pack frocks.' Then it goes on about the jewelry."

"What about the jewelry?" Now he traced the heaps of gold necklaces above the honey-colored silk.

"The total worth of it is—" she calculated quickly from francs into dollars—"thirty-two thousand dollars."

"Thirty-two *thou*sand?"

"Um-hm."

"Shit. And the earrings? Do they talk about the earrings?" He was looking at a facing close-up of her, from the nose down to the first swell of her breasts, which featured earrings, a sculptured piece around her throat and again the wet and open lips.

"Lovely, aren't they? Antiques. They belonged to Catherine the Great."

"Catherine the Great. A queen, huh?"

"Empress. The Empress of all the Russias."

"She give them to you?"

"Stupid! She's been dead for almost two hundred years."

"Oh, yeah?"

"Yeah." She drew out the word and made it as flat and American as she could. But she was smiling at the same time.

"They must be worth a lot, then."

"Quite a lot. Priceless."

"Nothing's priceless. Everything has a price." He was tracing again, circling Catherine's earrings with his forefinger. Jadine felt her earlobes prickle as she watched him.

"Well, half a million, certainly."

"Half a million? Shit."

"Don't you have any other word to express awe?" She tilted her head and fastened her big minky eyes on him.

He nodded. "Goddamn."

She laughed then, and for the first time there was no tension in it at all. He merely smiled and continued fingering the photograph. "Are these your clothes or did they just let you use them for the pictures?"

"They're mine. Some were given to me after I was photographed. A kind of payment."

"And the jewelry? They give you that too?"

"No. That was mine from before—except the earrings. They were on loan from the Russians. But the rest is part of my own collection."

"Collection, huh?"

"Why? Are you a thief?"

"I wish I was. Be a lot easier for me if I could steal."

"If? What do you call what you were doing in this house for days? Or were you planning to give Ondine back her chocolate?"

"You call that stealing?"

"You don't."

He shook his head. "No. I call it eating. If I wanted to steal I had plenty of time and plenty of opportunities."

"But no way to escape with what you took. So maybe there was no point in stealing. *Then.*"

"You think there's a point in my stealing now?"

"There might be. It depends on what you want from us."

"Us? You call yourself 'us'?"

"Of course. I live here."

"But you . . . you're not a member of the family. I mean you don't belong to anybody here, do you?"

"I belong to me. But I live here. I work for Margaret Street. She and Valerian are my . . . patrons. Do you know what that means?"

"They take care of you. Feed you and all."

"They educated me. Paid for my travel, my lodgings, my clothes, my schools. My mother died when I was twelve; my father when I was two. I'm an orphan. Sydney and Ondine are all the family I have, and Valerian did what nobody else even offered to do."

The man was silent, still staring at the pictures. Jadine examined his profile and made sure the leather was knotted tightly around her wrists.

"Why don't you look at me?" she asked him.

"I can't," he said.

"Why can't you?"

"The pictures are easier. They don't move."

Jadine felt a flash of pity. "You want me to be still? Will you look at me if I'm still?"

He didn't answer.

"Look," she said. "I'm still. Very still."

He lifted his head and looked at her. Her eyes were mink-colored just like in the pictures, and her lips were like the pictures too. Not moist, but open a little, the way they were in sleep. The way they were when he used to slip into her room and wait hours, hardly breathing himself, for the predawn light to bring her face out of the shadows and show him her sleeping mouth, and he had thought hard during those times in order to manipulate her dreams, to insert his own dreams into her so she would not wake or stir or turn over on her stomach but would lie still and dream steadily the dreams he wanted her to have about yellow houses with white doors which women opened and shouted Come on in, you honey you! and the fat black ladies in white dresses minding the pie table in the basement of the church and white wet sheets flapping on a line, and the sound of a six-string guitar plucked after supper while children scooped walnuts up off the ground and handed them to her. Oh, he thought hard, very hard during those times to press his dreams of icehouses into hers, and to keep her still and dreaming steadily so that when she woke finally she would long as she had longed for nothing in her life for the sound of a nickel nickelodeon, but after a while he began to smell like an animal in that room with her and he was afraid his smell would waken her before the sun did and before he could adjust his breath to hers and breathe into her open mouth his final dream of the men in magenta slacks who stood on corners under sky-blue skies and sang "If I Didn't Care" like the Ink Spots, and he fought hard against the animal smell and fought hard to regulate his breathing to hers, but the animal smell got worse and her breathing was too light and shallow for his own lungs and the sun always eschewed a lingering dawn in that part of the world and strutted into the room like a gladiator so he barely had time to breathe into her the smell of tar and its shiny consistency before he crept away hoping that she would break wind or believe she had so the animal smell would not alarm her or disturb the dream he had placed there. But now she was not sleeping; now she was awake and even though she was being still he knew that at any moment she might talk back or, worse, press her dreams of gold and cloisonné and honey-colored silk into him and then who would mind the pie table in the basement of the church?

"How much?" he asked her. "Was it a lot?" His voice was quiet.

"What are you talking about? How much what?"

"Dick. That you had to suck, I mean to get all that gold and be in the movies. Or was it pussy? I guess for models it's more pussy than cock." He wanted to go on and ask her was it true what the black whores always said, but she was hitting him in the face and on the top of his head with a badly formed fist and calling him an ignorant motherfucker with the accent on the syllable *ig*.

Jadine jumped away from the desk and leaned forward trying to kill him with her fists while her mind raced to places in the room where there might be a poker or a vase or a sharp pair of shears. He turned his head a little but did not raise his arms to protect himself. All he had to do was what he did: stand up and let his height put his face and head out of her easy reach. She stretched nonetheless trying to tear the whites from his eyes. He caught both her wrists and crossed them in front of her face. She spit full in his face but the saliva fell on the C of his pajama top.

Her gold-thread slippers were no good for kicking but she kicked anyhow. He uncrossed her wrists and swung her around, holding her from behind in the vise of his arms. His chin was in her hair.

Jadine closed her eyes and pressed her knees together. "You smell," she said. "You smell worse than anything I have ever smelled in my life."

"Shh," he whispered in her hair, "before I throw you out the window."

"Valerian will kill you, ape. Sydney will chop you, slice you . . ."

"No, they won't."

"You rape me and they'll feed you to the alligators. Count on it, nigger. You good as dead right now."

"Rape? Why you little white girls always think somebody's trying to rape you?"

"White?" She was startled out of fury. "I'm not . . . you know I'm not white!"

"No? Then why don't you settle down and stop acting like it."

"Oh, God," she moaned. "Oh, good God, I think you better throw me out of the window because as soon as you let me loose I am going to kill you. For that alone. Just for that. For pulling that black-woman-white-woman shit on me. Never mind the rest. What you said before, that was nasty and mean, but if you think you can get away with telling me what a black woman is or ought to be . . ."

"I *can* tell you." He nestled his cheek in her hair as she struggled in his arms.

"You *can't,* you ugly barefoot baboon! Just because you're black you think you can come in here and give me orders? Sydney was right. He should have shot you on the spot. But no. A white man thought you were a human being and should be treated like one. He's civilized and made the mistake of thinking you might be too. That's because he didn't smell you. But I did and I know you're an animal because I smell you."

He rubbed his chin in her hair and blew at the little strand over her ears. "I smell you too," he said, and pressed his loins as far as he could into the muted print of her Madeira skirt. "I smell you too."

His voice was soft, breathy and seemed to her to come from a great height. Someplace far far up, higher than the ceiling, higher than the ake trees even and it frightened her. "Let me go," she said, surprised at the steadiness of her own voice and even more surprised that he did it.

She stood with her back to him, rubbing her wrists. "I'll have to tell Valerian."

He didn't say anything so she turned to face him and repeated, "I'll have to tell Valerian."

He nodded. "Tell him," he said. "All of it or part of it. Whatever you like."

"I will," she said, and started walking toward the door, clicking her gold-thread slippers on the tile.

"Except for one thing," he said. "Leave out one thing. Don't tell him that I smelled you."

She walked out the door and down the hall. She meant to go to the downstairs powder room and clean him off her, but she didn't want to stop walking just yet, so she descended the staircase, crossed the front hall and opened the door. The gravel of the driveway hurt her feet in the little gold-thread slippers, but she went on, rubbing her wrists, feeling frightened and then angry, then frightened then angry again. When she got to the end of the drive, she stepped with relief onto the gravel-free macadam and continued until she came to a large stone by the side of the road. She sat down on it under the eyes of an avocado tree and lifted the hem of her skirt to wipe her face. She would tell Valerian to get rid of him that very afternoon. He would go and that would be that. A minor episode in an otherwise uneventful winter in the Caribbean. Something to chat about at supper, to elaborate on with friends, and laugh and laugh and say, "Can you believe it? He was in the house all that time! And when we found him, we invited him to dinner where he sat down and poured the coffee into his saucer and said 'Hi' to the butler. Ha ha, you should have seen Sydney's face and Margaret was out of her mind, but Valerian was superb, as you might guess, you know Valerian, right? Totally unflappable. Totally! But I was about to wet my pants, right? . . . and later . . ." But no. She would not tell that part, although it was funny, especially about how he asked her did Catherine the Great give her those earrings (he actually believed it, that they had belonged to the empress), and how he kept fingering her pictures, but she couldn't tell about the question he asked her: how much did she have to suck. She would make it some other impudence so she could get to the part about smashing his face and his trying to rape her, and maybe she could say that he was so dumb and country he thought she was white probably because she had a bath that morning and didn't have any hoops in her ears, and that he didn't want to rape her after all, but was content just to smell her. No, she'd leave out the smelling part. She would not mention that part at all.

Jadine felt the fear again and another thing that wasn't fear. Something more like shame. Because he was holding my wrists so tight and pressing himself into my behind? God, what a nasty motherfucker. Really nasty. Stink nasty. Maybe that was it. His smell. Other men had done worse to her and tried worse but she was always able to talk about it and think about it with appropriate disgust and amusement. But not this. He had jangled something in her that was so repulsive, so awful, and he had managed to make her feel that the thing that repelled her was not in him, but in her. That was why she was ashamed. He was the one who smelled. Rife, ripe. But she was the one he wanted to smell. Like an animal. Treating her like another animal and both of them must have looked just like it in that room. One dog sniffing at the hindquarters of another, and the female, her back to him, not moving, but letting herself be sniffed, letting him nuzzle her asshole as the man had nuzzled hers, the bitch never minding that the male never looked in her face or ran by her side or that he had just come up out of nowhere, smelled her ass and stuck his penis in, humping and jerking and grinding away while she stood there bearing, actually *bearing* his whole weight as he pummeled around inside her not even speaking, or barking, his eyes sliced and his mouth open and dripping with saliva, and other dogs too, waiting, circling until the engaged dog was through and then they would mount her also in the street in broad daylight no less, not even under a tree or behind a bush, but right there on Morgan Street in Baltimore with cars running by and children playing and the retired postman coming out of his house in his undershirt shouting get that bitch out of here. She's in heat. Lock that bitch up. Every goddamn dog in town'll be over here and he went back inside to get a mop handle to run the males off and crack the bitch over the back and send her home, she who had done nothing but be "in heat" which she couldn't help but which was her fault just the same so it was she who was beaten and cracked over the head and spine with the mop handle and made to run away and I felt sorry for her and went looking for her to see if she was hurt and when I found her she was behind the gas station standing very quietly while another dog sniffed her ass embarrassing me in the sunlight.

All around her it was like that: a fast crack on the head if you let the hunger show so she decided then and there at the age of twelve in Baltimore never to be broken in the hands of any man. Whatever it took—knife blades or screaming teeth—Never. And yes, she would tap dance, and yes, she would skate, but she would do it with a frown, pugnacious lips and scary eyes, because Never. And anybody who wanted nice from this little colored girl would have to get it with pliers and chloroform, because Never. When her mother died and she went to Philadelphia and then away to school, she was so quick to learn, but no touchee, teacher, and no, I do not smile, because Never. It smoothed out a little as she grew older. The pugnacious lips became a seductive pout—eyes more heated than scary. But beneath the easy manners was a claw always ready to rein in the dogs, because Never.

"Tell him," he said. "Tell him anything but don't tell him I smelled you because then he would understand that there was something in you *to* smell and that I smelled it and if Valerian understands that then he will understand everything and even if he makes me go away he will still know that there is something in you to be smelled which I have discovered and smelled myself. And no sealskin coat or million-dollar earrings can disguise it."

You son of a bitch I need this like a wart. I came here to get some rest and have some peace and find out if I really wanted to kick my legs up on a runway and let buyers with Binaca breath lick my ears or if I wanted to roam around Europe instead, following soccer games for the rest of my life and looking for another Bezzi or if I should buy an Alfa and drive through Rome making the scene where producers and agents can see me and say *Cara mia* is it really you I have just the part!

I came here to do some serious thinking and the fact is that I *can* come here. I belong here. You, motherfucker, do not and you, motherfucker, are leaving now as soon as I tell Valerian what you did to me and the harbor police will be here and return you to the sharks where you belong. Damn Valerian, what does he think he's doing? Playing white people's games? Or what the hell is the matter with him? He sits there and complains about Margaret, practically breaks down thinking about his son and talks about how he loves them both and has sacrificed everything for their happiness and then watches her go crazy, she's so scared. And instead of protecting her or at least getting upset he invites the very thing that scared the shit out of her to dinner and lets him sleep down the hall from us all. Doesn't he know the difference between one Black and another or does he think we're all . . . Some mess this is.

Jadine cupped her elbows in her palms and rocked back and forth on the stone trying hard to pull herself together before she went back to talk to Valerian, to tell him he and his joke had gone too far and might backfire. She sat for a long time, longer than necessary since she had already made up her mind. She started to stand several times, but each time something held her to the rock. Something very like embarrassment. Embarrassment at the possibility of overreacting, as she told her aunt and uncle they were doing. More awful than the fear of danger was the fear of looking foolish—of being excited when others were laid back—of being somehow manipulated, surprised or shook. Sensitive people went into therapy and stayed there when they felt out of control. Was this really a funny story she could tell later or was there real danger? But there was more. She felt a curious embarrassment in the picture of herself telling on a black man to a white man and then watching those red-necked gendarmes zoom him away in a boat. But he was going to rape her; maybe Margaret too, or worse. She couldn't wait for Valerian to get bored or sober or come to his senses and she couldn't risk hanging loose in this place where there was no one really to call on, where they were virtually alone. It would have to be done now, in the light of day. There was no betrayal in that. That nigger knew better and if he didn't he was crazy and needed to be hauled away.

Besides that fear and the fear of fear, there was another authentic loathing that she felt for the man. With him she was in strange waters. She had not seen a Black like him in ten years. Not since Morgan Street. After that in the college she attended the black men were either creeps or so rare and desirable they had every girl in a 150-mile radius at their feet. She was barely noticeable in (and never selected from) that stampede. Later when she traveled her society included Blacks and whites in profusion, but the black people she knew wanted what she wanted—either steadily and carefully like Sydney and Ondine or uproariously and flashily like theater or media types. But whatever their scam, "making it" was on their minds and they played the game with house cards, each deck issued and dealt by the house. With white people the rules were even simpler. She needed only to be stunning, and to convince them she was not as smart as they were. Say the obvious, ask stupid questions, laugh with abandon, look interested, and light up at any display of their humanity if they showed it. Most of it required only charm—occasionally panache. None of it called for this . . . this . . .

"Oh, horseshit!" she said aloud. It couldn't be worth all this rumination, she thought, and stood up. The avocado tree standing by the side of the road heard her and, having really seen a horse's shit, thought she had probably misused the word. Jadine dusted off the back of her skirt and turned toward the house. The avocado tree watched her go then folded its leaves tightly over its fruit. When Jade got near the greenhouse she thought she saw two figures behind the translucent panes. One was gesticulating wildly. Her heart pounding, she raced to the open door and peeped in. There they were. Valerian and the man, both laughing to beat the band.

5

"LAUGHING?" Margaret could not believe her ears.

"I'm telling you! They were in there laughing! I was looking right at them when you called out the window."

"Good God. What's gotten into him?"

"I don't know."

"Are you scared?"

"Not really. Well, sort of."

"You don't know him, do you?"

"*Know* him? How would I know him?"

"I don't know. This is making me crazy. Maybe we should do something."

"What? We're the only women. And Ondine. Should I go to the Broughtons' and . . ." Jadine stopped and sat down on Margaret's bed. She shook her head. "This is too much."

"What did he say?" asked Margaret. "When you all had dinner? Did he say what he was doing here?"

"Oh, he said he was hiding. That he'd been looking for food after he jumped ship a few days ago. That he was trying to get something out of the kitchen and heard footsteps and ran up the stairs to hide. Apparently he didn't know what room he went into, he was just waiting for a chance to get back out."

"Do you believe him?"

"I believe some of it. I mean I don't believe he came here to rape you." (Me, maybe, she thought, but not you.)

"How did he get here?"

"He says he swam."

"That's impossible."

"It's what he said."

"Well, then he can swim back. Now. Today. I'm not going to sleep with him in this house. If I had known that I would have had a heart attack. All night I waited for that bastard Valerian to come up here and tell me what the hell was going on. He never showed."

"And Sydney was patrolling the halls with a gun. I thought he would have killed him by now."

"What does he think?"

"He's angry. Ondine's scared, I think."

"I'm going to have it out with Valerian. He's doing this just to ruin Christmas for me. Michael's coming and he knows I want everything right for him, and look what he does to get me upset. Instead of throwing that . . . that . . ."

"Nigger."

"Right, nigger, instead of throwing him right out of here."

"Maybe we're making something out of nothing."

"Jade. He was in my closet. He had my box of souvenirs in his lap."

"Open?"

"No. Not open. Just sitting there holding it. He must have picked them up from the floor. Oh, God, he scared the shit out of me. He looked like a gorilla!"

Jadine's neck prickled at the description. She had volunteered nigger—but not gorilla. "We were all scared, Margaret," she said calmly. "If he'd been white we would still have been scared."

"I know, I know."

"Look. Valerian let him in. Valerian has to get him out. I'm sure he will anyway but you talk to him and I will too. It will be all right. You want to calm down. Let's do the breathing exercises. Cool out."

"I don't want to breathe, we have to *do* something. We can't leave it up to Valerian. Listen, let's leave: take the boat to town and fly to Miami. We won't come back till he's gone. Oh, but Michael!" She touched her hair. "I'll telephone him. He can meet us in Miami and if Valerian's got his senses back . . ."

"But it's the twenty-second. There isn't time. And what about Sydney and Ondine?"

"You don't think he'd go after Ondine, do you? Well, we'll start. We'll look like we're going and tell Valerian why. We can call the police ourselves when we get to town. Is the boy here?" Margaret asked.

"Yes, but—"

"Jade. Come on, now. You've got to help. There's nobody else."

"Let's see if Valerian will send him away."

"You said they were in there laughing."

"Let's wait and see. Pack just in case. I'll get reservations."

"All right. But I'm not going to leave this room until I know something definite."

"I'll bring you something to eat."

"Yes, and please hurry. I don't want to take a Valium on an empty stomach."

They stayed in their rooms all afternoon, and the next time they saw the stranger he was so beautiful they forgot all about their plans.

WHEN JADINE had clicked out of her bedroom in her gold-thread slippers, the man sat down in her chair and lit another cigarette. He listened to the four/four time of her clicking shoes, tapping it out on the little writing table. The seat was too small for him—like a grade school chair—even though he had lost the ship-food weight and now—after two weeks of scavenging—his body was as lean as a runner's. He glanced around him and was surprised at how uncomfortable-looking her room was. Not at all the way it appeared at dawn when he crouched there watching her sleep and trying to change her dreams. Then it looked mysterious but welcoming. Now in the noon light it looked fragile—like a dollhouse for an absent doll—except for the sealskin coat sprawled on her bed which looked more alive than seals themselves. He had seen them gliding like shadows in water off the coast of Greenland, moving like supple rocks on pebbly shores, and never had they looked so alive as they did now that their insides were gone: lambs, chickens, tuna, children—he had seen them all die by the ton. There was nothing like it in the world, except the slaughter of whole families in their sleep and he had seen that, too.

He took another cigarette and walked to a table to look at the presents she'd started to wrap. Two damp spots formed on the yoke of his pajamas. Still smoking, he left off looking at the packages and walked into her bathroom. Peeping into the shower he saw a fixture exactly like the one in the bathroom down the hall. But her shower had curtains, not sliding doors. Heavy shiny curtains with pictures of old-fashioned ladies all over. Towel material was on the other side, still damp. Water glistened on the tub and wall tile. On the corner of the tub was a bottle of Neutrogena Rainbath Gel and a natural sponge, the same color as her skin. He picked up the sponge and squeezed it. Water gushed from the cavities. Careless, he thought. She should wring it out thoroughly, otherwise it would rot. The sponge was so large he wondered how her small hands held it. He squeezed it again, but lightly this time, loving the juice it gave him. Unbuttoning his pajama top he rubbed it on his chest and under his arms. Then he took the pajamas off altogether and stepped into the shower.

"Pull," she had said. Tepid water hit him full in the face. He pushed the knob in and the water stopped. He adjusted the shower head, pulled again and water peppered his chest. After a moment he noticed that the shower head was removable and he lifted it from its clamps to let it play all over his skin. He never let go the sponge. When he was wet all over, he let the shower head dangle while he picked up the bath gel, pumping the spout above the sponge. He lathered himself generously and rinsed. The water that ran into the drain was dark—charcoal gray. As black as the sea before sunrise.

His feet were impossible. A thick crust scalloped his heels and the balls of both feet. His fingernails were long and caked with dirt. He lathered and rinsed twice before he felt as though he'd accomplished anything. The sponge felt good. He had never used one before. Always he had bathed with his own hands. Now he pumped a dollop of bath gel into his palm and soaped his beard, massaging as best he could with his nails. The beard hair tangled and crackled like lightning. He turned his soapy face up and sprayed water on it. Too hard. He stopped, wiped his eyes and fiddled with the head until he got mist instead of buckshot. He soaped his face again and misted the lather away. Some of it got into his mouth and reminded him of a flavor he could not name. He sprayed more and swallowed it. It did not taste like water; it tasted like milk. He squirted it all around in his mouth before pressing the button to shut off the water.

He got out dripping and looking around for shampoo. He was about to give up, not seeing any medicine cabinets, when he accidentally touched a mirror that gave way to reveal shelf upon shelf of bottles among which were several of shampoo boasting placenta protein among their ingredients. The man chose one and stood before the mirror looking at his hair. It spread like layer upon layer of wings from his head, more alive than the sealskin. It made him doubt that hair was in fact dead cells. Black people's hair, in any case, was definitely alive. Left alone and untended it was like foliage and from a distance it looked like nothing less than the crown of a deciduous tree. He knew perfectly well what it was that had frightened her, paralyzed her for a moment. He could still see those minky eyes frozen wide in the mirror. Now he stuck his head under the shower and wet the hair till it fell like a pelt over his ears and temples. Then he soaped and rinsed, soaped and rinsed until it was as metallic and springy as new wire. After he dried it, he found a toothbrush and brushed his teeth furiously. Rinsing his mouth he noticed blood. He was bleeding from the gums of his perfect teeth. He unscrewed the cap from a bottle of Listerine with instructions in French on the label and gargled. Finally he wrapped a white towel around his waist. He noticed another door in the bathroom and opened it with the easy familiarity of someone who has been there before. It led to a dressing room within an alcove in which stood a table and a mirror circled by lights. Farther along were dresses, shelves of shoe boxes, luggage, and a narrow lingerie chest. On a tiny chair lay shorts and a white tennis visor. The smell of perfume nauseated him—he had not eaten since the gobbling of cold soufflé and peaches the night before. He picked a robe, returned to the bathroom and urinated. Then he stooped to pick up the pajamas, damp and bunched on the floor, but changed his mind, left them there and walked back through the bedroom. The breeze from the open window was sweet and he went to it and stood looking out.

They are frightened, he thought. All but the old man. The old man knows that whatever I jumped ship for it wasn't because I wanted to rape a woman. Women were not on his mind and however strange it looked, he had not followed the women. He didn't even see them properly. When the boat docked, he stayed in the closet. Their voices were as light as their feet pattering on the dock and when he went, at last, to look, all he saw were two slim-backed women floating behind the beam of a flashlight toward what looked like a jeep. They got in, turned on the lights, then the engine (in that order, just like women would) and were gone. It amused him that these tiny women had handled that big boat. Which one had thrown the rope? Who jumped onto the dock and secured the line? He had not seen them clearly at all: just the hand and left side of one as she picked a bottle off the deck, and now their slim backs disappearing into the darkness toward a jeep. He had not followed them. He didn't even know where they were off to. He waited until the sea, the fish, the waves all shut up and the only sound came from the island. When he had eaten mustard, flat bread and the last of the bottled water he too disembarked but not before he looked up at the sky holy with stars and inhaled the land smell sailors always swear they love. Behind him to his right the dim lights of Queen of France. Before him a dark shore. Ahead, under the stars and above the black of the beach he could barely see the hilly outline of the island against the sky.

He walked along the dock and then over forty feet of sand past the shadow of something that looked like a gasoline pump to the road the jeep had taken. He stayed on it and hoped he wouldn't meet anybody, for, having lost his shoes, he was not willing to cut through the bush, fat and tangled, by the side of the road. At every step clouds of mosquitoes surrounded him biting through his shirt and on the back of his neck. An old dread of mines chilled him—stopped him dead and he had to remind himself several times that this was the Caribbean—there were no beautiful pygmies in the trees or spring mines in the road.

He had not followed the women. He didn't even know what they looked like or where they were going. He just walked for an hour on the only road there was and saw nothing to make him stop; nothing that appeared to offer rest. At some point during that hour a foul smell rose about him. But the mosquitoes left him and he supposed it was the fumes coming from a marsh or swamp that he imagined he was passing through. When he emerged from it he saw above him a house with lights in its upper and lower stories. He stopped and rested one hand against a tree. How cool and civilized the house looked. After that hot solitary walk through darkness lined by trees muttering in their sleep, how cool, clean and civilized it looked. They are drinking clear water in there, he thought, with ice cubes in it. He should have stayed on the boat for the night. But he'd been shipbound so long and the land smell was so good, so good. "I'd better go back," he told himself. "Back to the boat where there is a refrigerator and ice cubes and a bunk." He drew his tongue across his lips and felt the cracks. Moving his hand an inch or two up the tree in preparation to go his fingers grazed a breast, the tight-to-breaking breast of a pubescent girl three months pregnant. He snatched his hand away and turned to look. Then he let his breath out in a snort that was more relief than laughter. An avocado was hanging from the tree right at his fingertips and near his cheek. He parted the leaves and stroked it. Saved, he thought. It smelled like an avocado, felt like an avocado. But suppose it wasn't. Suppose it was a variety of ake, the fruit that contained both a pulp that was edible and a poison that killed. No, he thought, ake trees are bigger, taller and their fruit would not grow so close to the trunk. He strained to see the color, but could not. He decided not to chance it and looked again at the house lights—the home lights—beaming like a safe port in front of him. Just then the wind, or perhaps it was the tree herself, lifted the leaves and, precisely as he had done a moment ago, parted wide the leaves. The avocado swung forward and touched his cheek. Why not? he thought, and placed three fingers on either side of the fruit and bit it where it hung. Under the tough bitter skin was the completely tasteless, wholly satisfying meat and it made him thirstier than he was before.

He had not followed the women. He had not even seen them clearly, only their slim backs. What he went toward the house for was a drink of water. To find an outside spigot; a well, a fountain, anything to quench a thirst brought on by mosquitoes, the hot night and the meat of a teenaged avocado.

He approached the house from its northern side, away from the gravel of the driveway and over where the grass was wet and silky under his feet. Through the first window he looked into he saw not the women (for he was not following the women) but the piano. Nothing like Miss Tyler's, but still a piano. It made him tired, weak and tired, as though he had swum seven seas for seven years only to arrive at the place he had started from:

thirsty, barefoot and alone. No water, no shipboard bunk, no ice cubes could fight the fatigue that overwhelmed him at the sight of the piano. He backed away, away from the light and the window into the protection of the trees that were still muttering in their sleep. He would have sunk where he stood and slept under the dreaming trees and the holy sky except for the part of him that never slept and which told him now what it always told him: to hide, to look for cover. So he obeyed the self that never blinked or yawned, and moved farther from the house looking for anything: a hutch, a toolshed, a cloister of shrubbery—and found a gazebo. He crawled under the circular bench where he could sleep safely. But sleep did not join him there at once. What came, what entered the gazebo, what floated through the screen, were the boys who laughed at first when he used to go to Miss Tyler's and teased him about fucking Andrew's auntie when all he was doing was playing her piano, because there wasn't another one in town except behind the altars of the A.M.E. Zion and Good Shepherd Baptist Church. Two churches for fewer than three hundred people. Drake, Soldier and Ernie Paul laughed and pointed their fingers. How it feel? Is she good? But he went anyway because she let him and because nothing else mattered. And after a while she said she would give him lessons if he would weed for her. And a year later Drake, Soldier and Ernie Paul weren't laughing; they were sitting on Miss Tyler's porch steps listening and waiting for him to come out. Cheyenne too listened while he played and waited out front for him. But that was much later and thank God she did not come into the gazebo with Drake, Soldier and Ernie Paul. They kept him up all night, practically, so he thought they were probably alive somewhere. Each of them had been afraid for something different: his balls, eyes, spine. He had been afraid for his hands. All through the war he thought of sitting in a dark and smoky joint—a small place that couldn't pack a hundred and could make it with a steady crowd of thirty—and him hidden behind the piano, surrounded and protected by the bass the drum the brass—taking eight once in a while but mostly letting his hands get to the crowd softly pleasantly. His hands would be doing something nice and human for a change. After he was busted—discharged without honor or humor—he had done it but so badly only the pity of the owner and the absence of a rival kept him there, playing at night while Cheyenne slept at home—waiting.

He had not followed the women. He came to get a drink of water, tarried to bite an avocado, stayed because of the piano, slept all through the next day because Drake, Soldier and Ernie Paul kept him awake in the night. That's how he came to sleep in the day and wander the property at night contrary to common sense and all notions of self-preservation. And he stayed tired. Even at night when he walked around looking for food and trying to think of what his next step should be. To go back to the boat and wait for one of them to sail it again. To examine the island and maybe find a rowboat—something anonymous—and make it to town at night. Get a little work, enough to fly to Miami and then work his way back home? To knock on the door, ask for help and take the risk of being turned in. Each possibility seemed fine and each seemed stupid. But he was so tired in the day and so hungry at night, nothing was clear for days on end. Then he woke up, in a manner of speaking. The first night he entered the house was by accident. The broken pantry window where he was accustomed to look for food and bottled water was boarded up. He tried the door and found it unlocked. He walked in. There in the moonlight was a basket of pineapples, one of which he rammed into his shirt mindless of its prickers. He listened a moment before opening the refrigerator door a crack. Its light cut into the kitchen like a wand. He shielded the opening as best he could while he reached inside. Three chicken wings were wrapped in wax paper. He took them all and closed the door. The silence was startling compared to the noisy night outside. He pushed the swinging doors and looked into a moonlit room with a big table in the middle and a chandelier overhead. It led to a hall which he entered and which led to the front door which he opened and he stepped back outside. The chicken was incredible. He hadn't tasted flesh since the day he went crazy with homesickness and jumped into the sea. He ate the bones even, and had to restrain himself from going right back and raiding the refrigerator again. Later. Wait till tomorrow night, he told himself. And he did. Each tomorrow night he entered the house and it was a week before he ventured upstairs and then it was out of curiosity as well as a sense of familiarity. The door of the first bedroom at the head of the stairs was open, the room itself, empty. The one to the left was not empty. A woman was sleeping in it. He meant to look but not to watch and not to stay because he had not followed the women. Had not even seen them clearly. So the first time he entered her room he stayed only a few seconds, watching her sleep. Anybody could have told him it was only the beginning. Considering the piano and Cheyenne and this sleeping woman he was bound to extend his stay until he was literally spending the night with her gratified beyond belief to be sitting on the floor, his back against the wall, his shirt full of fruit (and meat if he could find any), in the company of a woman asleep. His appetite for her so gargantuan it lost its focus and spread to his eyes, the oranges in his shirt, the curtains, the moonlight. Spread to everything everywhere around her, and let her be.

He spent some part of every night with her and grew to know the house well, for he sneaked out just before dawn when the kitchen came alive. And he had to admit now, standing in the sunlight, that he had liked living in the house that way. It became his, sort of. A nighttime possession complete with a beautiful sleeping woman. Little by little he learned the people. And little by little he forgot that he had not followed the women. He thought he had. Only now did he remember that it was the avocado, the thirst, the piano. And now here he was with the immediate plans of a newborn baby.

He didn't like to think too far in advance anyway, but he supposed he'd have to think up a story to tell them about who he was and what his name was. Oh, he had been alone so long, hiding and running so long. In eight years he'd had seven documented identities and before that a few undocumented ones, so he barely remembered his real original name himself. Actually the name most truly his wasn't on any of the Social Security cards, union dues cards, discharge papers, and everybody who knew it or remembered it in connection with him could very well be dead. Son. It was the name that called forth the true him. The him that he never lied to, the one he tucked in at night and the one he did not want to die. The other selves were like the words he spoke—fabrications of the moment, misinformation required to protect Son from harm and to secure that one reality at least.

THROUGH the window on the ground below he saw the back of a man stooping at some cutting or digging chore. It was the black man he had seen off and on around the grounds. He stared at his back. Yardman, she called him. That was Yardman's back. He knew backs, studied them because backs told it all. Not eyes, not hands, not mouths either, but backs because they were simply there, all open, unprotected and unmanipulable as Yardman's was, stretched like a smokehouse cot where hobos could spend the night. A back where the pain of every canker, every pinched neck nerve, every toothache, every missed train home, empty mailbox, closed bus depot, do-not-disturb and this-seat-taken sign since God made water came to rest. He watched the angle of the old man's spine and for no reason that he could think of tears stung his eyes. It astonished him, those unshed tears, for he knew well the area into which his heart was careening—an area as familiar as the knuckle of his thumb. Not the street of yellow houses with white doors, but the wide lawn places where little boys in Easter white shorts played tennis under their very own sun. A sun whose sole purpose was to light their way, golden their hair and reflect the perfection of their Easter white shorts. He had fingered that image hundreds of times before and it had never produced tears. But now watching Yardman—he was kneeling, chopping at the trunk of a small tree—while he himself was so spanking clean, clean from the roots of his hair to the crevices between his toes, having watched his personal dirt swirl down a drain, while he himself stood wrapped waist-to-thigh in an Easter white towel—now he was as near to crying as he'd been since he'd fled from home. You would have thought something was leaving him and all he could see was its back.

Slowly Yardman stood. He turned around toward the house and for less than a pulse beat glanced at the trees that grew at the edge of the courtyard. Then he lifted his cap, scratched his head with his ring and little finger, and pulled the cap back on. "Thanks," whispered Son. "One more second of your smokehouse cot might have brought me there at last."

WHILE MARGARET had been lying in her sculptured bedroom, fighting hunger, anger and fear, Valerian was in his greenhouse staring out of the one glass window imagining what was not so: that the woman in the washhouse was bending over a scrub board rubbing pillow slips with a bar of orange Octagon soap. He knew perfectly well that a washer and dryer were installed there (he couldn't hear the hum, for the music and the drone of the air conditioner in the greenhouse obliterated it, but he could see the steam puffing from the exhaust pipe) but the scrub board, the pillow slips and the orange soap were major parts of what he wished to see: the back yard of the house of his childhood in Philadelphia; the hydrangea, fat and brown in the September heat. His father, knocked down by a horse-drawn milk truck, lay in bed, the house already funereal. Valerian went out back to the shed where a washerwoman did the family's laundry. She was thin, toothless and looked like a bird. Valerian sometimes visited her, or rather hung around her shed, asking questions and chattering. She was like a pet who would listen agreeably to him and not judge or give orders. The first time he came, she had said, by way of polite conversation—the pointless conversation of an adult without stature to a child who had some —"What your daddy doin today?" And he had answered that his daddy was away on a sales trip to Atlantic City. From then on she greeted him that way. He would wander to the shed door and she would ask, "What your daddy doin today?" and he would tell her, as a preliminary to the conversation, "He's at the factory today" or "He's in New York today." It was a delightful opener to him because she and his father had never laid eyes on each other. A sort of grown-up conversation followed the question that they both took seriously. On one of the Wednesdays she came to work, his father died without regaining consciousness. Valerian was fussed over by his mother and relatives and then left alone while they busied themselves with death arrangements. He wandered out to the washhouse that afternoon and when the woman said, "Hi. What your daddy doin today?" Valerian answered, "He's dead today," as though tomorrow he would be something else. The woman looked up at him and paused for an awkward silence in which he suddenly understood the awfulness of what had happened and that his father would also be dead the next day and the day after that as well. In that instant, while the birdlike colored woman looked at him, he knew limitlessness. The infinity of days in which the answer to her question would be the same. "He's dead today." And each day it would be so. It was too big, too deep, a bottomless bucket of time into which his little boy legs were sinking and his little boy hands were floundering.

Finally she blinked and pointed to a shelf behind him. "Hand me that soap," she said. And he did. "Now unwrap it and stand right over here. Up close. Closer." He did that too and she made him rub soap on the wet pillowcase that clung to the washboard. He scrubbed his heart out, crying all the while, pillowcase after pillowcase, rubbed and rubbed until his knuckles were cherry red and his arms limp with fatigue. And when he could not do another, she patted him on the head and said she would hire him any day. Later George, the butler they had before Sydney, found out about it (he had wondered about those cherry-red knuckles) and told him to stay out of there because that woman drank like a fish and he mustn't let her use him to do her work. Valerian told him to mind his own "beeswax," but they let the woman go and Valerian never again had to say, "He's dead today," but he said it anyway to himself until his little boy legs were strong enough to tread the black water in the bucket that had no bottom. So, inconvenient as it was, he had insisted on a separate washhouse when he built L'Arbe de la Croix, less for an island touch than for the remembrance of having once done something difficult and important while the world was zooming away from him. Now another washerwoman came. It wasn't quite the same. No Octagon soap, no wavy gleaming washboard, but he liked looking at it through his greenhouse window knowing there was a woman in there doing something difficult but useful in peace. A soothing thought to concentrate on while his own house was prickly with tension and unanswered questions.

He had rattled last night to Jade. And why he had ascribed his exile to the Caribbean to the relationship between Margaret and Michael, he couldn't imagine. The fact was he'd become a stranger in his own city and chose not to spend his retirement there at exactly sixty-five (or close to) in order to avoid watching it grow away from him. Sidewalks and thoroughfares were populated by people he did not know; shops were run by keepers who did not know him; familiar houses were bought by bright couples who either updated them or returned them to some era that existed only in their minds. They tore out unfashionable shrubbery for decks and patios; they closed in the wide-open porches and enlarged windows that had been tiny, private and sweet. These new people privatized their houses by turning them backward away from the street, but publicized their lives and talked about wine as though it were a theology instead of a drink. The unending problem of growing old was not how he changed, but how things did. A condition bearable only so long as there were others like him to share that knowledge. But his wife, twenty-two years younger and from another place, did not remember, and his friends were dead and dying. In his heart he was still the thirty-nine-year-old Temple alumnus working in the candy factory about to assume from his uncles control of the company, and who had married a high school beauty queen he was determined to love in order to prove he was capable of it to his first wife—that unlovable shrew who was unlovable to this very day. She had died a year before his retirement in South Carolina, where she had gone to live with her sister. When he heard about it, she was already in the ground. He began to miss her at precisely that point—terribly—and when he settled in the Caribbean she must have missed him too for she started visiting him in the greenhouse with the regularity of a passionate mistress. Funny. He couldn't remember her eyes, but when she came, flitting around his chair and gliding over his seed flats, he recognized her at once. In nine years of marriage she had had two abortions and all she wanted to talk about during these visits was how relieved she was that she'd had at least that foresight. He wished she felt something else. You'd think in death, in the Beyond, she would have felt something else. Or nothing at all.

He was not alarmed by her visits; he knew he conjured them up himself, just as he conjured up old friends and childhood playmates who were clearer to him now than the last thirty years were, and nicer. But he was astonished to see—unconjured—his only living son in the dining room last night. Probably the consequence of describing the sink business to Jade. Michael seemed to be smiling at him last night but not the smile of derision he usually had in the flesh; this was a smile of reconciliation. And Valerian believed that was part of the reason he invited the black man to have a seat, the forepresence of Michael in the dining room. His face smiling at him from the bowl of peaches was both the winsome two-year-old under the sink and the thirty-year-old Socialist. The face in the peaches compelled him to dismiss Margaret's screaming entrance as the tantrum of a spoiled child, the deliberate creation of a scene, which both father and son understood as feminine dementia. Michael had been on his heart if not in his mind since Margaret had announced the certainty of his visit. He could not say to her that he hoped far more than she did that Michael would come. That maybe this time there would be that feeling of rescue between them as it had been when he had taken him from underneath the sink. Thus when the black man appeared, Valerian was already in complicity with an overripe peach, and took on its implicit dare. And he invited the intruder to have a drink. The Michael of the reservation and the Michael of the sink was both surprised and pleased.

It was easy not to believe in Margaret's hysteria; he had seen examples of it many times before and thought she was up to her old combo of masochism plus narcissism that he believed common to exceptionally beautiful women. But when, in a flash too speedy for reflex, he saw his entire household standing there, and in each of their faces disgust and horror, and all together triumphant, and all together anticipating his command, already acting on it in fact, just waiting for the signal from him to call the harbor police and thereby make him acknowledge his mistake in not taking Margaret seriously, having to admit that he was not capable of judgment in a crisis, that he was wrong, that she was right, that his house had been violated and he neither knew it or believed it when it was discovered and it had been Sydney who had the foresight to have a gun and the legs to ferret out the intruder, when he saw Margaret's triumphant face, Jade's frightened one, and Sydney and Ondine looking at the prisoner with faces as black as his but smug, their manner struck him as what Michael meant when he said "bourgeois" in that tone that Valerian always thought meant unexciting, but now he thought meant false, but last night he thought meant Uncle Tom-ish. He had defended his servants vigorously to Michael then, with aphorisms about loyalty and decency and with shouts that the press was ruining with typical carelessness the concept of honor for a people who had a hard enough time achieving any. What he had said to Jade, he believed: that Michael was a purveyor of exotics, a typical anthropologist, a cultural orphan who sought other cultures he could love without risk or pain. Valerian hated them, not from any hatred of the minority or alien culture, but because of what he saw to be the falseness and fraudulence of the anthropological position. The Indian problem, he told Michael, was between Indians, their conscience and their own derring-do. And all of his loving treks from ghetto to reservation to barrio to migrant farm were searches for people in whose company the Michaels could enjoy the sorrow they were embarrassed to feel for themselves. And yet, in the space of that flash he felt not only as Michael must have when he urged Jade to do something for her people (no matter how silly his instruction), but something more. Disappointment nudging contempt for the outrage Jade and Sydney and Ondine exhibited in defending property and personnel that did not belong to them from a black man who was one of their own. As the evening progressed, Valerian thoroughly enjoyed the disarray that his invitation had thrown them into. Margaret ran from the room—foiled. Jade was at least sophisticated about it, but Sydney and Ondine were wrecked while the intruder himself didn't even look "caught." He walked in with his hands raised and clasped behind his head and looked neither right nor left—not at Jade or Ondine or Margaret, but straight at Valerian and in his eyes was neither a question nor a plea. And no threat whatsoever. Valerian was not afraid then and he was not afraid at noon the next day, when Sydney tapped quietly on his door and brought his mail and his baked potato. Valerian could sense the small waiting in Sydney, some expectation or hope that his employer would give him a hint of what had been in his head last night. Valerian felt a twinge of compassion for him, but since he could not tell him about faces that looked up out of peaches, he said nothing at all.

Actually he had no plans. He was curious about the man, but

not all that much. He assumed he was what he'd said he was: a crewman jumping ship, and his roaming about the house and grounds, hiding in Margaret's closet, was more outrageous than threatening. He had looked into the man's eyes and had no fear.

Digesting his potato and sipping wine, he was rewarded for his serenity by an expansive "Howdy" followed by the entrance of the stranger wrapped in a woman's kimono, barefoot with gleaming wrought-iron hair.

Valerian let his eyes travel cautiously down from the hair to the robe to the naked feet. The man smiled broadly. He looked down at himself, back at Valerian and said, "But I don't do no windows."

Valerian laughed, shortly.

"Good morning, Mr. Sheek," said the man.

"Street. Valerian Street," said Valerian. "What did you say your name was?"

"Green. William Green."

"Well, good morning, Willie. Sleep well?"

"Yes, sir. Best sleep I ever had. Your name really Valerian?"

"Yes." Valerian shrugged helplessly and smiled.

"I used to eat a candy called Valerians."

"Ours," said Valerian. "Our candy company made them."

"No kiddin? You named after a candy?"

"The candy was named after me. I was named after an emperor."

"Oh," said the man looking around the greenhouse. Its sudden coldness was delicious after the heat outside. Shady and cool with plants shooting from pots and boxes everywhere. "It's sho pretty in here," he said, still smiling.

"Tell me the truth," said Valerian, "before you get confused by what you see. What were you really doing in my wife's bedroom?"

The man stopped smiling. "The truth?" He looked down at the brick walk in some embarrassment. "The truth is I made a mistake. I thought it was the other one."

"What other one?"

"The other bedroom."

"Jade's?"

"Yes, sir. I uh thought I smelled oyster stew out back yesterday. And it got dark early, the fog I mean. They done left the kitchen and I thought I'd try to get me some, but before I knew it I heard them coming back. I couldn't run out the back door so I run through another one. It was a dinin room. I ran upstairs into the first room I seen. When I got in I seen it was a bedroom but thought it belonged to the one y'all call Jade. I aimed to hide there till I could get out, but then I heard somebody comin and I ducked into the closet. I was just as scared as your wife was when she opened that door and turned that light on me."

"You've been skulking around here for days. Why didn't you ask at the kitchen for something to eat?"

"Scared. I ain't got a passport, I told you. You going to turn me over to the police?"

"Well, not in that get-up certainly."

"Yeah." He glanced at his kimono again and laughed. "They'd give me life. I don't reckon you have an old suit to lend me? Then I can go to jail in style."

"In one of my suits they'd make you governor. I'll tell Sydney to find something for you. But don't be surprised if he bites your head off."

Suddenly the man jumped and stamped his feet on the bricks.

"What's the matter?"

"Ants," he said.

"Oh dear. You've let them in, and I'm out of thalomide." Valerian stood up. "Over there, that can. Spray the doorsill. It won't do much good, but it will help for a while, and tuck that muslin in tighter."

The man did as he was told and then said, "You ought to get mirrors."

"Mirrors for what?"

"Put outside the door. They won't come near a mirror."

"Really?"

"Yeah," he said, and sprayed some of the ant killer on his legs. His kimono came undone at the belt and fell away from his body. Valerian looked at his genitals and the skinny black thighs. "You can't go round like that in front of the ladies. Leave that alone, and go tell Sydney to give you some clothes. Tell him I said so."

The man looked up letting the kimono hang to his sides. "You ain't gonna turn me in?"

"I guess not. You didn't take anything, but we'll have to figure a way to get you some papers. Go on now. Get some clothes." Valerian took the ant spray and set it down near a heavy plant of many shades of green. Its leaves spread out healthily and long stems stood straight up among them. Stems with closed buds. Valerian peered into the plant and frowned.

"What's the matter with it?" asked the man. "Looks sick."

Valerian turned the pot around for a different view. "I don't know. It's been in bud like that for I don't know how long. They won't open no matter what I do."

"Shake it," said the man. "They just need jacking up." And he walked over to the cyclamen and with thumb and middle finger flicked the stems hard as though they were naughty students.

"What the hell are you doing?" Valerian reached out to grab the man's hand.

"Don't worry. They'll be in bloom tomorrow morning."

"If they are I'll buy you a brand-new suit; if they die I'll have Sydney chase you back into the sea."

"Deal!" said the man. "I know all about plants. They like women, you have to jack them up every once in a while. Make em act nice, like they're supposed to." He finished flicking the cyclamen stems and smiled first to himself and then at Valerian. "Did you ever hear the one about the three colored whores who went to heaven?"

"No," said Valerian. "Tell me." And he did and it was a good joke. Very funny and when Jadine ran to the greenhouse certain the noise coming from it was somebody murdering somebody she heard laughter to beat the band.

SYDNEY had put some of his boss's old clothes in the guest room for him, and Valerian sent him off with Gideon to get a haircut, because Sydney refused flat out to cut it. Valerian half expected the man would get into town and not return, since he had given him enough money to buy some underwear and some shoes that fit him better than his did. While Valerian had dinner alone that night served by a silent steeping butler, and while Margaret pouted in her room and Jadine ate with Ondine in the kitchen, Mr. Green alias Son drifted off with Gideon and Thérèse in the *Prix de France.* With country people's pride in a come-from-far guest, they paraded the American Negro through the streets of town like a king. Gideon even got one of his friends to give them a free taxi ride to the outskirts of town, and then they had to walk and walk and walk up into the hills to Place de Vent before they reached the powder pink house where he lived with Thérèse and, sometimes, Alma Estée.

Thérèse was in ecstasy and kept moving her head about the better to see him out of her broken eyes. As soon as they had got ashore she let it be known to every island Black she saw that they had a guest, a visitor from the States, and that he was going to spend the night. Her pride and her message ran all over the streets and up the hillside, and at various times during the evening, heads poked in her doorway, and neighbors dropped by on some pretense or other. Thérèse sent Alma Estée flying back down the hill to the market for a packet of brown sugar, and she went into the bag that hung by her side under her dress for money for goat meat and two onions. Then she brewed black thick coffee while she listened to the men talk and waited her turn. Gideon told her stories on Isle des Chevaliers, but here at home he did not socialize with her—he kept to himself or spent his free time with old cronies. Only at work on the island of the rich Americans did he entertain her. Now she was to be privy to the talk between them, and in her house at that. She would also have a chance to ask the American Black herself whether it was really so that American women killed their babies with their fingernails. She waited until Gideon had cut his hair with clippers he'd borrowed from the man who sold rum. Waited until great clouds of glittering graphite hair fell to the floor and on the bedspread they had wrapped around the man's neck and the front of his whole body. Waited until Gideon was through with his boasts about when he was in the States, boasts about the nurse he had married, the hospital he had worked in, the hatefulness of that nurse and all American women. Waited until Gideon had lied about all the money he made there and why he returned home. Waited until the stranger who ate chocolate and drank bottled water was properly shorn and his neck dusted with baking soda, and Alma Estée was back and the meat was frying on the two-burner stove. Waited till they ate it and drank coffee loaded with sugar. Waited till they opened the bottle of rum and the chocolate eater had coughed like a juvenile with his first taste of it. Thérèse served the two men but did not eat with them. Instead she stood at the portable stove burning the hair she had swept up from the floor, burning it carefully and methodically with many glances at the chocolate eater to show him she meant him no evil. When they had eaten and Thérèse had grown accustomed to the rhythm of their guest's English, she joined them at the table. Alma Estée sat on the cot by the window.

Son smoked Gideon's cigarettes and poured the rest of the rum into his coffee. He stretched his legs and permitted himself a hearthside feeling, comfortable and free of postures and phony accents. The tough goat meat, the smoked fish, the pepper-hot gravy over the rice settled in him. It had been served all on one plate and he knew what the delicacies had cost them: the sweet, thick cookies, the canned milk and especially the rum. The nakedness of his face and head made him vulnerable, but his hosts gave him adoration to cover it. Alma Estée had taken off her short print dress and returned in her best clothes—a school uniform—but Son knew right away that she had not had school tuition for a long time now. The uniform was soiled and frayed. He could feel her waves of desire washing over him and for the first time in years he felt like a well-heeled man. Thérèse urged him on into a feast of plantain and fried avocado, then leaned toward him in the lamplight, her broken eyes cheerful, and asked him, "Is it true? American women reach into their wombs and kill their babies with their fingernails?"

"Close down your mouth," Gideon said to her, and then to Son, "She's gone stupid as well as blind." He explained to Son that he used to tell her what working in an American hospital was like. About free abortions and D & C's. The scraping of the womb. But that Thérèse had her own views of understanding that had nothing to do with the world's views. That however he tried to explain a blood bank to her, or an eye bank, she always twisted it. The word "bank," he thought, confused her. And it was true. Thérèse said America was where doctors took the stomachs, eyes, umbilical cords, the backs of the neck where the hair grew, blood, sperm, hearts and fingers of the poor and froze them in plastic packages to be sold later to the rich. Where children as well as grown people slept with dogs in their beds. Where women took their children behind trees in the park and sold them to strangers. Where everybody on the television set was naked and that even the priests were women. Where for a bar of gold a doctor could put you into a machine and, in a matter of minutes, would change you from a man to a woman or a woman to a man. Where it was not uncommon or strange to see people with both penises and breasts.

"Both," she said, "a man's parts and a woman's on the same person, yes?"

"Yes," said Son.

"And they grow food in pots to decorate their houses? Avocado and banana and potato and limes?"

Son was laughing. "Right," he said. "Right."

"Don't encourage her, man," said Gideon. "She's a mean one and one of the blind race. You can't tell them nothing. They love lies."

Thérèse said she was not of that race. That the blind race lost their sight around forty and she was into her fifties and her vision had not gone dark until a few years ago.

Gideon started to tease her about being "into her fifties." Sixties, more like, he said, and she had faked sight so long she didn't remember herself when she started to go blind.

Son asked who were the blind race so Gideon told him a story about a race of blind people descended from some slaves who went blind the minute they saw Dominique. A fishermen's tale, he said. The island where the rich Americans lived is named for them, he said. Their ship foundered and sank with Frenchmen, horses and slaves aboard. The blinded slaves could not see how or where to swim so they were at the mercy of the current and the tide. They floated and trod water and ended up on that island along with the horses that had swum ashore. Some of them were only partially blinded and were rescued later by the French, and returned to Queen of France and indenture. The others, totally blind, hid. The ones who came back had children who, as they got on into middle age, went blind too. What they saw, they saw with the eye of the mind, and that, of course, was not to be trusted. Thérèse, he said, was one such. He himself was not, since his mother and Thérèse had different fathers.

Son felt dizzy. The cheap rum and the story together made his head light.

"What happened to the ones who hid on the island? Were they ever caught?"

"No, man, still there," said Gideon. "They ride those horses all over the hills. They learned to ride through the rain forest avoiding all sorts of trees and things. They race each other, and for sport they sleep with the swamp women in Sein de Veilles. Just before a storm you can hear them screwing way over here. Sounds like thunder," he said, and burst into derisive laughter.

Son laughed too, then asked, "Seriously, did anybody ever see one of them?"

"No, and they can't stand for sighted people to look at them without their permission. No telling what they'll do if they know you saw them."

"We thought you was one," said Thérèse.

"She thought," said Gideon. "Not me. Personally I think the blindness comes from second-degree syphilis."

Thérèse ignored this remark. "I was the one made him leave the window that way. So you could get the food," said Thérèse.

"You did that?" Son smiled at her.

Thérèse tapped her chest bone with pride.

"Miss Thérèse, love of my life, I thank you from the bottom of my heart." Son took her hand and kissed the knuckles. Thérèse shrieked and cackled with happiness.

"I said you wouldn't ask machete-hair for anything, so I left food for you in the washhouse. You never came for it."

"Machete-hair? The cook?"

"That one. That devil. The one I almost drown myself for twice a week. No matter what the weather I got to drown myself to get there."

"Don't listen to her. She knows those waters just like the fishermen. She doesn't like the Americans for meanness. Just because they a little snooty sometimes. I get along with them okay. When they say to let Thérèse go, I say okay. But I bring her right back and tell them it's a brand-new woman."

"They don't know?"

"Not yet. They don't pay her any attention."

Stimulated by the hand kiss, Thérèse wanted to ask more questions about the women who clawed their wombs, but Gideon grew loud and stopped her. "She was a wet-nurse," he told Son, "and made her living from white babies. Then formula came and she almost starve to death. Fishing kept her alive."

"Enfamil!" said Thérèse, banging her fist on the table. "How can you feed a baby a thing calling itself Enfamil. Sounds like murder and a bad reputation. But my breasts go on giving," she said. "I got milk to this day!"

"Go way, woman, who wants to hear about your wretched teats. Go on out of here." Gideon shooed her and she left the table but not the room. When she was quiet, Gideon waved his arm about the house and told Son, "You welcome here any time you want." His arm took in the cot where Thérèse slept at night, the floor where Alma Estée sometimes slept and the tiny bedroom where he did.

Son nodded. "Thanks."

"I mean it. Any time. Not much life going on over there. Maybe you could find work here. Plenty work here and you young."

Son sipped rum-laced coffee wondering why, if there was plenty work there, Gideon wasn't doing any of it. "How long have you been working over there?"

"Three years steady now. Off and on before. They used to come seasonal."

"Did you become a citizen in the States?"

"Sure. Why you think I marry that crazy nurse woman? Got a passport and everything. But, listen, I don't let on over there that I can read. Too much work they give you. Instructions about how to install this and that. I make out that I can't read at all."

"You've been away so long, you must have lost your citizenship by now."

Gideon shrugged. "The U.S. is a bad place to die in," he said. He didn't regret it. The only thing he regretted was his unemployment insurance. A marvelous, marvelous thing, that was. You had to hand it to the U.S. They knew how to make money and they knew how to give it away. The most generous people on the globe. Now the French were as tight as a virgin, but the Americans, ahhh.

After a while they were quiet. Thérèse was breathing heavily so Son thought she was asleep. He could not see her eyes, but Alma's were bright and on him.

"You going back?" asked Gideon, "to the island?"

"I don't know."

"You want to get in there, don't you, eh? That yalla?" Gideon stroked his chin.

"Man," said Son. "Oh, man." He said it with enthusiasm but he put a period in his voice too. He didn't want her chewed over by Gideon's stone-white teeth. Didn't want her in Gideon's mind, his eye. It unnerved him to think that Gideon had looked at her at all.

The old man heard the period in his voice and turned the conversation to serious advice.

"Your first yalla?" he asked. "Look out. It's hard for them not to be white people. Hard, I'm telling you. Most never make it. Some try, but most don't make it."

"She's not a yalla," said Son. "Just a little light." He didn't want any discussion about shades of black folk.

"Don't fool yourself. You should have seen her two months ago. What you see is tanning from the sun. Yallas don't come to being black natural-like. They have to choose it and most don't choose it. Be careful of the stuff they put down."

"I'll be careful."

"Come on," said Gideon. "Let's go see some of the boys. Let me show you this place. Paradise, boy. Paradise."

They got up to leave and Alma Estée sprang into life. She stood near the door and stretched out her hand. Son stopped and smiled at her.

"You think," she said whispering, "you think you can send to

America for me and buy me a wig? I have the picture of it." And she pulled from the pocket of her school blazer a folded picture which she tried her best to show him before Gideon pushed her away.

"TARZAN mind if I use his piano?"

It was incredible what Hickey Freeman and a little Paco Rabanne could do. He held the jacket by his forefinger over his shoulder. With the other hand he struck the keys. Jadine was startled. In a white shirt unbuttoned at the cuffs and throat, and with a gentle homemade haircut, he was gorgeous. He had preserved his mustache but the kinky beard was gone along with the chain-gang hair.

"If I were wearing Tarzan's suit," she said, "I'd show a little respect."

"That's why I asked. I'm showing respect."

"Then ask him yourself," she answered, and turned to leave. She had been sitting in the living room after lunch waiting for Margaret when he entered and stood at the piano. She was impressed and relieved by his looks, but his behavior in her bedroom was uppermost in her mind.

"Wait," he said. "I want to talk to you—apologize. I'm sorry about yesterday."

"Good," she said, and kept walking.

"You can't forgive me?" he asked.

Jadine stopped and turned around. "Uh-uh."

"Why not?" He stayed near the piano but looked directly at her, the question apparently important to him.

Jadine took a few steps toward him. "I don't have to explain anything to you."

"But I said I'm sorry. You can figure out why I did it, can't you? You were so clean standing in that pretty room, and I was so dirty. I was ashamed kinda so I got mad and tried to dirty you. That's all, and I'm sorry."

"Okay. You're sorry you did it; I'm sorry you did it. Let's just drop it." She turned around once more.

"Wait."

"What for?"

"I want to play you something." He tossed his jacket on the piano lid and sat down on the stool. "Would you believe this is one of the things I used to do for a living?" He played a chord, then another and tried a whole phrase, but his fingers would not go where he directed them. Slowly he took his hands away from the keys and stared at them.

"Couldn't have been much of a living," she said.

"It wasn't. I could barely keep up with the drums when I was cookin my best. Now—" He turned his hands over and looked up at her with a very small smile. "Maybe I'll just do the melody." He tapped out a line.

"I don't like what you did, hear? So don't play any songs for me."

"Hard," he said without looking up. "Hard, hard lady."

"Right."

"Okay. I quit. I just wanted to tell you I was sorry, and that you don't have to be nervous anymore."

"I'm not nervous," she answered. "I was never nervous. I was mad."

"Or mad either."

She walked toward him now and leaned an elbow on the piano, her thumbnail pressed into her bottom teeth. "I suppose Valerian invited you to stay for Christmas?"

"Did he?"

"Didn't he?"

"I don't know. I just got back this minute."

Jadine stepped away from the piano and looked out the sliding glass doors. "He was carrying on this morning about some flower you made bloom."

"Oh, that. He hasn't got enough wind in there. It needed shaking."

"You some sort of farmer?"

"No. Just a country boy."

"Well, listen, country boy, my aunt and uncle are upset. You go and apologize to them. Their name is Childs. Sydney and Ondine Childs. I had to throw the pajamas you left in my bathroom out the window so they wouldn't see them. You don't have to apologize to me; I can take care of myself. But you apologize to them."

"All right," he said, and she sure did look it—like she could take care of herself. He did not know that all the time he tinkled the keys she was holding tight to the reins of dark dogs with silver feet. For she was more frightened of his good looks than she had been by his ugliness the day before. She watched him walk away saying "See you later" and thought that two months in that place with no man at all made even a river rat look good. There was no denying the fact that looking at his face and keeping her voice stern required some concentration. Spaces, mountains, savannas—all those were in his forehead and eyes. Too many art history courses, she thought, had made her not perceptive but simpleminded. She saw planes and angles and missed character. Like the vision in yellow—she should have known that bitch would be the kind to spit at somebody, and now this man with savannas in his eyes was distracting her from the original insult. She wanted to sketch him and get it over with, but when she thought of trying to lay down that space and get the eagle beak of his nose, she got annoyed with herself. And did he have a cleft in his chin? Jadine closed her eyes to see it better, but couldn't remember. She left the room and climbed the stairs quickly. Christmas will be over soon. She had called Air France just as she promised Margaret she would, but she also made a reservation for herself for December 28, standby. Just in case. This winter retreat thing was running out anyway. She had not accomplished anything, was more at loose ends here than anywhere. At least in Paris there was work, excitement. She thought she had better go to New York, do this job, and then return to

Paris and Ryk. The idea of starting a business of her own, she thought, was a fumble. Valerian would lend her the money, she knew, but maybe that was a sidestep, too. It was a silly age, twenty-five; too old for teenaged dreaming, too young for settling down. Every corner was a possibility and a dead end. Work? At what? Marriage? Work and marriage? Where? Who? What can I do with this degree? Do I really want to model? It was nothing like she thought it would be: soft and lovely smiles in soft and lovely clothes. It was knife hard and everybody frowned and screamed all the time, and if ever she wanted to paint a predatory jungle scene she would use the faces of the people who bought the clothes. She was bored and no more together than the river rat. She kept calling him that. River rat. Sydney called him swamp nigger. What the hell did he say his name was and even if she could remember it would she say it out loud without reaching for the leash?

SON WENT immediately from the living room piano to the kitchen and, finding it empty, walked down to the lower kitchen which was empty also. He retraced his steps and noticed a door on the landing to the short flight of stairs separating the kitchens. He rapped shortly and a voice said, "Yes?" He opened the door.

"Mrs. Childs?"

Ondine was soaking her feet in a basin. At first she thought it was Yardman. He alone on the island called her that. Even the Filipinos over at the nearest house called her Ondine. But the clean-shaven man in the doorway was not Yardman.

"Jadine said it was all right if I came to see you," he said.

"What you want?"

"To apologize. I didn't mean to scare everybody." Son did not allow himself a smile.

"Well, I'd hate to think what would be the case if you had meant to."

"I was a little off. From not eating. Drove me a little nuts, ma'am."

"You could have asked," Ondine said. "You could have come to the door decent-like and asked."

"Yes, ma'am, but I'm, like, an outlaw. I jumped ship. I couldn't take a chance and I stayed too hungry to think. I was in a little trouble back in the States too. I'm, you know, just out here trying to hang in."

"What kind of trouble?"

"Car trouble. Wrecked a car, and couldn't pay for it. No insurance, no money. You know."

Ondine was watching him closely. Sitting in a chintz rocker, rubbing one foot against the other in an Epsom salt solution. The difference between this room and the rest of the house was marked. Here were second-hand furniture, table scarves, tiny pillows, scatter rugs and the smell of human beings. It had a tacky permanence to it, but closed. Closed to outsiders. No visitors ever came in here. There were no extra chairs; no display of tea-set. Just the things they used, Sydney and Ondine, and used well. A stack of Philadelphia *Tribune*s piled neatly on the coffee table. Worn house slippers to the left of the door. Photographs of women with their legs crossed at the ankles and men standing behind wicker chairs, touching them lightly with their fingers. Groups of people standing on stairs. One blue-tinted photograph of a man with magnificent handlebar mustaches. All-dressed-up black people of some earlier day who looked like they had serious business at hand.

Ondine sensed his absorption of her apartment.

"Not as grand, I suppose, as where you sleep."

Now he did smile. "Too grand," he said. "Much too grand for me. I feel out of place there."

"I shouldn't wonder."

"I want to apologize to your husband too. Is he here?"

"He'll be back in a minute."

Son thought she sounded like the single woman who answers

the door and wants the caller to think there is a huge, tough male in the next room.

"I'll be gone soon. Mr. Street said he would help me get papers. He has friends in town, he says."

She looked skeptical.

"But even if he doesn't, I've got to make tracks. I just don't want you upset or worried. I didn't come here for no harm."

"Well, I'm more inclined to believe you now that you had a bath. You was one ugly something."

"I know. Don't think I don't know it."

"You went off with Yardman yesterday?"

It bothered him that everybody called Gideon Yardman, as though he had not been mothered. "Yes, ma'am," he said. "Mr. Street told me to. I spent the night there. I started to just stay on there, since that's where I was heading for in the first place. But I didn't want to leave without making peace with you all. My own mama wouldn't forgive me for that."

"Where is your own mama?"

"Dead now. We live in Florida. Just my father, my sister and me. But I don't know if he's alive still."

Ondine saw the orphan in him and rubbed her feet together. "What line of work you in?"

"I've been at sea off and on for eight years. All over. Dry cargo mostly. Wrecks."

"Married?"

"Yes, ma'am, but she's dead, too. It was when she died that I got in that car trouble and had to leave Florida, before they threw me in jail. That's when I started fooling around on docks."

"Huh."

"What's the matter with your feet, Mrs. Childs?"

"Tired. Stand on any feet for thirty years and they might talk back."

"You should put banana leaves in your shoes. Better'n Dr. Scholl's."

"Is that so?"

"Yeah. Want me to get you some?"

"I'll get em if I want to. Later on."

"Well, I'll leave you alone now," and he turned to go just as Sydney walked in. His face zigzagged like lightning as soon as he saw who was standing there talking to his wife.

"What are you doing in my place?"

Ondine held up a hand. "He came to apologize, Sydney."

Son moved aside so he would not be standing between them and said, "Yes, sir . . ."

"Anything you got to say to me or my wife, you say it somewhere else. Don't come in here. You are not invited in here."

"It was Jadine," Son began. "She suggested . . ."

"Jadine can't invite you in here, only I can do that. And let me tell you something now. If this was my house, you would have a bullet in your head. Right there." And he pointed to a spot between Son's eyebrows. "You can tell it's not my house because you are still standing upright. But this here is." He pointed a finger at the floor.

"Mr. Childs, you have to understand me. I was surprised as anybody when he told me to stay—"

Sydney interrupted him again. "You have been lurking around here for days, and a suit and a haircut don't change that."

"I'm not trying to change it. I'm trying to explain it. I was in some trouble and left my ship. I couldn't just knock on the door."

"Don't hand me that mess. Save it for people who don't know better. You know what I'm talking about, you was upstairs!"

"I was wrong, okay? I took to stealing food and started wandering around in here. I got caught, okay? I'm guilty of being hungry and I'm guilty of being stupid, but nothing else. He knows that. Your boss knows that, why don't you know it?"

"Because you are not stupid and because Mr. Street don't know nothing about you, and don't care nothing about you. White folks play with Negroes. It entertained *him,* that's all, inviting you to dinner. He don't give a damn what it does to anybody else. You think he cares about his wife? That you scared his wife? If it entertained him, he'd *hand* her to you!"

"Sydney!" Ondine was frowning.

"It's true!"

"You know him all this time and you think that?" she asked him.

"You tell *me,*" he answered. "You ever see him worry over her?"

Ondine did not answer.

"No. You don't. And he don't worry over us neither. What he wants is for people to do what he says do. Well, it may be his house, but I live here too and I don't want *you* around!" Sydney turned back to Son, pointing at him again.

"Mr. Childs," Son spoke softly, but clearly, "you don't have to be worried over me either."

"But I am. You the kind of man that does worry me. You had a job, you chucked it. You got in some trouble, you say, so you just ran off. You hide, you live in secret, underground, surface when you caught. I know you, but you don't know me. I am a Phil-a-delphia Negro mentioned in the book of the very same name. My people owned drugstores and taught school while yours were still cutting their faces open so as to be able to tell one of you from the other. And if you looking to lounge here and live off the fat of the land, and if you think I'm going to wait on you, think twice! He'll lose interest in you faster than you can blink. You already got about all you can out of this place: a suit and some new shoes. Don't get another idea in your head."

"I'm leaving, Mr. Childs. He said he'd help me get a visa—something—so I can get back home. So . . ."

"You don't need no visa to go home. You a citizen, ain't you?"

"Well, I use another name. I mean I don't want nobody checking me out."

"Take my advice. Clean your life up."

Son sighed. He had told six people in two days all about himself. Had talked more about himself than he had in years and told each of them as much of the truth as he had to. Sydney, he knew from the start, would be the hardest to convince. But he kept calling him Mr. Childs and sir and allowing in gesture as how he was a reprobate, and ended by asking them both if they knew somewhere else he could sleep while he waited for Mr. Street to get the visa and some identification for him. Outside if need be, he said. It would just be one more night, he thought, and he didn't feel comfortable up there on the second floor.

The couple exchanged glances and Sydney said he'd think about it. Maybe on the patio outside the kitchen they could fix something up for him.

"I'd appreciate it," Son said. "And would you do me one more favor? Could you let me eat in the kitchen with you all?"

They nodded, and Son left quickly, pleased, rather, that Sydney thought he was interested in Valerian's generosity.

THE HOUSE locked back together that evening and busied itself for Christmas. In Ondine's kitchen Son ate so much of her food she softened considerably toward him. Sydney was less accommodating than his wife, but he could not doubt the man's hunger and his ways were quiet and respectful, almost erasing the memory of that "Hi." By the time they finished eating and reminiscing about the States, Sydney was calling him Son.

Valerian and Margaret and Jadine had eaten together in the dining room earlier, Sydney serving regally. Margaret was mollified by two telephone calls and a window view of the man who'd been in her closet which made her feel as Jadine apparently did now—that he was harmless. At any rate, he was not sleeping upstairs, she'd been informed by Jadine, nor eating with them, and maybe Michael would enjoy him if he was still on the property then. Especially if B.J. didn't show. The travel agency said the ticket had not been picked up yet. She tried to hang on to her despair about Valerian, but it was hopeless. He was tickled to death by the sight of four cyclamen blossoms, so happy he was considering putting down mirrors for the ants. He'd gone around all morning beating up other plants, especially his miniature orange trees which had come with no blossoms or fruit. He had even drafted a letter to the consulate asking whether a B-class visa could be arranged for a local employee of his. And he spoke of Michael's visit as though it were a reality.

They were amiable that evening. Relaxed. Valerian cracked jokes that were not funny back in the fifties. Margaret chattered and thought up extra niceties for the holidays and ended by insisting that she would cook the Christmas dinner herself. It was to be a really old-fashioned Christmas, and that required the woman of the house to be bustling in the kitchen with an apron roasting turkey and baking apple pies. Valerian should call the consulate. They would have some apples; they always got American produce. Valerian said she'd never made a crust in her life and he wasn't looking forward to an experiment at Christmas. But Margaret wouldn't listen. She was hyper and happy: Michael was on his way. Valerian thought she had gone hog-wild this time—but her cheer cheered him and he encouraged rather than spoiled it.

The quiet amiability lasted the whole evening and there was rest in everybody's sleep that night. Except Son's. He was swinging in a hammock outside in the night wind with that woman on his mind. He had managed a face for everybody but her. The others were seduced by the Hickey Freeman suit and the haircut, but she was not and neither was he. Not seduced at all. He did not always know who he was, but he always knew what he was like.

The soldier ants were not out in the night wind, neither were the bees. But heavy clouds grouped themselves behind the hills as though for a parade. You could almost see the herd assemble but the man swinging in the hammock was not aware of them. He was dwelling on his solitude, rocking in the wind, adrift. A man without human rites: unbaptized, uncircumcised, minus puberty rites or the formal rites of manhood. Unmarried and undivorced. He had attended no funeral, married in no church, raised no child. Propertyless, homeless, sought for but not after. There were no grades given in his school, so how could he know when he had passed? He used to want to go down in blue water, down, down, then to rise and burst from the waves to see before him a single hard surface, a heavy thing, but intricate. He would enclose it, conquer it, for he knew his power then. And it was perhaps because the world knew it too that it did not consider him able. The conflict between knowing his power and the world's opinion of it secluded him, made him unilateral. But he had chosen solitude and the company of other solitary people —opted for it when everybody else had long ago surrendered, because he never wanted to live in the world their way. There was something wrong with the rites. He had wanted another way. Some other way of being in the world that he felt leaving him when he stood in the white towel watching Yardman's—Gideon's —back. But something had come loose in him, like the ball that looped around the roulette wheel, carried as much by its own weight as by the force of the wheel.

In those eight homeless years he had joined that great underclass of undocumented men. And although there were more of his kind in the world than students or soldiers, unlike students or soldiers they were not counted. They were an international legion of day laborers and musclemen, gamblers, sidewalk merchants, migrants, unlicensed crewmen on ships with volatile cargo, part-time mercenaries, full-time gigolos, or curbside musicians. What distinguished them from other men (aside from their terror of Social Security cards and *cédula de identidad*) was their refusal to equate work with life and an inability to stay anywhere for long. Some were Huck Finns; some Nigger Jims. Others were Calibans, Staggerlees and John Henrys. Anarchic, wandering, they read about their hometowns in the pages of out-of-town newspapers.

Since 1971 Son had been seeing the United States through the international edition of *Time,* by way of shortwave radio and the views of other crewmen. It seemed sticky. Loud, red and sticky. Its fields spongy, its pavements slick with the blood of all the best people. As soon as a man or woman did something generous or said something bold, pictures of their funeral lines appeared in the foreign press. It repelled him and made him suspicious of all knowledge he could not witness or feel in his bones. When he thought of America, he thought of the tongue that the Mexican drew in Uncle Sam's mouth: a map of the U.S. as an ill-shaped tongue ringed by teeth and crammed with the corpses of children. The Mexican had presented it to him with a smile the day Son bashed the snapper's head in. *"Americano,"* said the Mexican, and handed him the picture that he'd drawn in prison and kept in his locker. They were close to Argentina and had been fishing off the prow that morning, pulling in snapper so rapidly they seemed to be leaping onto the deck. All but Son. The Swede and the Mexican—the two he was closest to—laughed at his spectacular bad luck. Suddenly a bite and he reeled in a huge glitter of froth and steel. The friends watched admiringly as the fish flopped into death. But when Son bent down to remove the hook, the fish executed a dazzling final arc three feet above the deck and slapped his face. The Mexican and the Swede laughed like children, and Son, holding the tail down with his knee, bashed with his fist the snapper's head. The mouth pulped and a little eye skittered across the deck. The Swede roared but the Mexican was suddenly quiet, and later handed him the drawing saying, *"Americano. Cierto Americano. Es verdad,"* and maybe it was so. In any case, if he was punching dying fish in anger, if he was pricked to fury by the outrageous claim of a snapper on its own life, stunned by its refusal to cooperate with his hook, to want, goddamn it, to surrender itself for his pleasure, then perhaps he was *cierto Americano* and it was time to go home. Not to the sticky-red place, but to his home in it. That separate place that was presided over by wide black women in snowy dresses and was ever dry, green and quiet.

There weren't going to be any impalas or water buffalo; no mating dance, no trophies. There was dice instead of tusk; a job when he wanted a journey. And the lion he believed was exclusive to his past—and his alone—was frozen in stone (can you beat it?) in front of the New York Public Library in a city that had laughed at his private's uniform. Like an Indian seeing his profile diminished on a five-cent piece, he saw the things he imagined to be his, including his own reflection, mocked. Appropriated, marketed and trivialized into decor. He could not give up the last thing left to him—fraternity. On the ocean and in lockups he had it; in tiny bars and shape-up halls he had it, and if he was becoming *cierto Americano,* he'd better go where he could never be deprived of it—home. He wanted to go home but that woman was on his mind. The one whose dreams he had tried to change and whom he had insulted to keep her unhinging beauty from afflicting him and keeping him away from home.

She is on my mind, he thought, but I am not on hers. What must it be like to be on her mind, and he guessed the only way to know was to find out. The next morning he asked her if she would like to eat lunch with him down on the beach, and she said, "Sure, I want to sketch down there before I go, anyway." It surprised him into awkwardness and the word "go" sent a ripple through him, exacerbating the awkwardness. She was getting ready to leave? Go somewhere?

They took the Willys and she drove, saying almost nothing. She sat quietly under the wheel in an expertly crushed white cotton halter and a wide, wide skirt that rich people called "peasant" and peasants called "wedding," her skin damp and glowing against the Easter white cotton—all temptation and dare.

When they got to the dock and parked, she jumped out with her sketch pad and box of pencils. He followed her with the basket for she was leading the way—making little prints in the hard-packed sand. They walked about half a mile to a bend of good clean sand and a clump of pineapple palms. They sat down and she took off her canvas shoes. It was after they ate that carelessly assembled, hurriedly packed lunch that she seemed really aware of him but only because she was opening her sketch pad and fiddling with the wooden box of pencils. She examined him then with an intent but distant eye and asked him a casual question which he answered by saying, "My original dime. That's all. My original dime." The sun was hiding from them and the mosquitoes were held off by a burning can of commercial repellent. The olives, French bread, uncuttable cheese, ham slices, jar of black mushy cherries and wine left them both as hungry as they were when they started.

It was a deliberately unappetizing lunch which she had literally dumped into a beautiful brown and purple Haitian basket as though to disabuse him of any idea that this was a real picnic or that it was important to her. But they ate it all up and wished for more. It was probably that yearning for more that made Jadine ask him, "What do you want out of life?" A tiresome question of monumental ordinariness, the kind artists ask models while they measure the distance between forehead and chin but one which he had apparently given some thought to. "My original dime," he said. "The one San Francisco gave me for cleaning a tub of sheephead." He was half sitting, half lying, propped upon his elbow facing her with the sky-blue sky of the sky behind him. "Nothing I ever earned since was like that dime," he said. "That was the best money in the world and the only real money I ever had. Even better than the seven hundred and fifty dollars I won one time at craps. Now that felt good, you know what I mean, but not like that original dime did. Want to know what I spent it on? Five cigarettes and a Dr Pepper."

"Five cigarettes?"

"Yeah. They used to sell them loose in the country. That was my first personal, store-bought purchase. You believe that? Wish you could have seen how it looked in the palm of my hand. Shining there."

"The Dr Pepper?"

"The dime, girl. The dime. You know I picked up money before. In the street and a quarter once on the riverbank. That was something too, you know. Really great. But nothing, nothing was ever like that sheephead dime. That original dime from Frisco." He paused for a comment from her, but she made none. She just kept busy behind the screen, the wall of her sketch pad. "Just before I left home, I heard he got blown up in a gas explosion. Old Frisco." He murmured the name. "Son of a bitch. I heard about it on my way out of town, and I couldn't wait for the funeral. He worked in the gas field and got blown to bits. I left town crying like a baby. He was a nothing kind of dude, mind you. Treated his wife like a dog and ran other women all over town. But I still cried when he got blown up and I was a full-grown man. It must have been that dime, I mean, no money ever meant much to me after that. I couldn't work just for that—just for money. I like to have it, sure, it feels fine for a while, but there's no magic in it. No sheephead. No Frisco. And nothing to buy worth anything, anyway. I mean nothing like five Chesterfield cigarettes and a Dr Pepper. Talk about good!" He threw his head back and directed his laughter into the sky. He was beautiful, like that; laughing like that: teeth lips mustache perfect and perfectly disarming. Jadine paused. She could not draw his laughing heaven-raised face. "Well, anyway, I guess that's what I want, all I want, in the money line. Something nice and simple and personal, you know? My original original dime."

Jadine's eyes followed the movements of her charcoal. "Lazy. Really lazy. I never thought I'd hear a black man admit it." She rubbed the line with her thumb and frowned.

"Uh-uh. I'm not admitting any such thing." Son's voice cracked with indignation.

"Ah got duh sun in duh mawnin and duh moon at night."

Jadine waggled her charcoal stick and rocked her head like "truckin on down." "Oooooo, Ah got plenty of nuffin and nuffin's plenty fo meeeeeee."

Son laughed in spite of himself. "That's not lazy."

"What is it then?"

"It's not being able to get excited about money."

"*Get* able. *Get* excited."

"What for?"

"For you, for yourself, your future. Money isn't what the scramble's all about. It's what money does, can do."

"What can it do?"

"Please. Don't give me that transcendental, Thoreau crap. Money is—"

"Who's that?"

"Who's who?"

"Thoreau."

"Jesus."

"Don't look disgusted. I'm illiterate."

"You're not illiterate. You're stupid."

"So tell me; educate me. Who is he?"

"Another time, okay? Just hold your head still and stop making excuses about not having anything. Not even your original dime. It's not romantic. And it's not being free. It's dumb. You think you're above it, above money, the rat race and all that. But you're not above it, you're just without it. It's a prison, poverty is. Look at what its absence made you do: run, hide, steal, lie."

"Money didn't have anything to do with that."

"Sure it did. If you had some you could have paid a lawyer, a good lawyer, and he would have gotten you off. You think like a kid."

"Maybe I didn't want to get off."

"Then what did you run away for? You told Ondine you got into some trouble with the law and jumped bail."

"I didn't want to go to prison."

"But–"

"That's not the same thing. I didn't want their punishment. I wanted my own."

"Well, you got it."

"Yeah."

"And you might end up with theirs *and* yours."

"No way."

"You're like a baby. A big country baby. Anybody ever tell you that?"

"No. Nobody ever told me that."

"Well, you are. Like you were just born. Where are your family?"

"Home, I guess."

"You don't know?"

"I haven't been back in a long time."

"Where in Florida are you from?"

"Eloe."

"Eloe? What on earth is that? A town?"

"A town, yeah."

"God. I know it already: gas stations, dust, heat, dogs, shacks, general store with ice coolers full of Dr Pepper."

"No shacks in Eloe."

"Tents, then. Trailer camps."

"Houses. There are ninety houses in Eloe. All black."

"Black houses?"

"Black people. No whites. No white people live in Eloe."

"You're kidding me."

"I'm not."

"Black mayor?"

"No mayor at all, black or white."

"Who runs it?"

"Runs itself."

"Come on. Who pumps the water, hooks up the telephones?"

"Oh, well, white folks do that."

"I'll bet they do."

"But they live in Poncie, Ferris, Sutterfield—off a ways."

"I see. What work do these ninety black people do?"

"Three hundred and eighty-five. Ninety houses, three hundred and eighty-five people."

"Okay. What work do they do?"

"They fish a little."

"Sheephead. Right. Oooooo, Ah got plenty of nuffin . . ."

"Don't laugh. They work in the gas field too, in Poncie and Sutterfield. And they farm a little."

"God. Eloe."

"Where's your home?"

"Baltimore. Philadelphia. Paris."

"City girl."

"Believe it."

"Oh, I believe it."

"Were you ever in Philly?" She put the pad and pencil down and rubbed her fingers together.

"Never."

"Just as well." Jadine dug her fingers in the sand then brushed them.

"Not so hot?"

"Well, better than Eloe."

"Nothing's better than Eloe."

"Oh, sure. When's the last time you were there?"

"Long time. Eight years."

"Eight, huh. You haven't seen your family in eight years. Even your mother must have forgotten your name by now."

"She's *been* dead. My father raised us."

"He know your name?"

"He knows it. Sure, he knows it."

"I don't. What is it?"

"I told you already—everybody calls me Son."

"I want to know what's on your birth certificate."

"No birth certificates in Eloe."

"What about your Social Security card. That says Son?"

"No. That says William Green."

"At last."

"One of them anyway. I got another that says Herbert Robinson. And one says Louis Stover. I got a driver's license that says—"

"Okay. Okay. But I can't call you Son. 'Hi, Son. Come here, Son.' I sound like a grandmother. Give me something else."

"You pick."

"Okay. I will. Let's see. I need something that fits. I know. I'll ask you a question—a question I want to ask anyway and the best name will fit right in. Here I go. 'Why did you have to leave Eloe on the run, leave so fast you couldn't go to Frisco's funeral, uh, uh, Phil?' That's good. That's Anglicized French for son."

"Not Phil. Anything but Phil."

"Well, what then?"

"What about Sugar? 'Why did you have to leave Eloe on the run, Sugar?' "

"All right. 'What did you do to have to leave Eloe on the run, Sugar? So fast, Sugar, you couldn't go to the funeral of the man who gave you your original dime?' "

"I killed somebody."

Actually he didn't look like a baby or even a big old country boy dressed up in a white man's suit. His hair was cut and his nails filed, but he had lived in the house and hid in the closet and pressed his face into her hair and his hips into the back of her skirt and underneath the light cologne was a man with hair like snakes. It was hot. Hazy and hot. A bad day for a picnic.

"Should I be scared?" asked Jadine.

"Not if you have to ask."

"I'm serious."

"So am I."

"Who was he? The man you killed?"

He stood up, untangling himself gracefully but swiftly. They always assume that, he thought. That it was a man. "Let's change the subject," he said. His voice was soft, a little sad, it seemed to her, and he gazed out into the water as he spoke. Fake, she thought. He's faking remorse and he thinks I am impressed by it.

"I hate killers," she said. "All killers. Babies. They don't understand anything but they want everybody to understand them. Lotta nerve, don't you think?"

"Killing doesn't take nerve. It takes no nerve, no nerves at all."

"I don't feel sorry for you, you know. I think you ought to be in jail. So you can stop looking pitifully into the sea and thinking how terrible life's been to you."

He glanced at her, briefly, as though she were a distraction from the major work of looking at the sea. "Sorry," he murmured. "I didn't mean to. I wasn't thinking about me. I was thinking about the person I killed. And that *is* pitiful."

"Then why'd you do it?"

"There is no *why*. The reason doesn't hold. I mean it wasn't a good reason; it was a mistake."

"Sure. You didn't mean to, right?"

"Oh, I meant to, but I didn't mean to. I meant the killing but I didn't mean the death. I went too far."

"That's not so smart. Death frequently follows killing. Definitely unhip."

"Yeah."

"Temper, temper, temper," she sang.

He looked down at her again wishing it had been temper. Something simple like that or something forgivable like that. But he knew better and for eight years wherever he looked—in the molten sea, in shape-up halls, in canneries and on flophouse cots he saw that mouth dying before the eyes did when it should have been the other way around and while he could not regret the fact that she was dead, he was ashamed of having been unable to look her in the eyes as she died. She deserved that. Everybody deserves that. That somebody look at them, with them, as they face death—especially the killer. But he had not had the courage or the sympathy and it shamed him.

He looked at Jadine. Now it was her turn to gaze into the sea. "Who'd you kill?" she said.

"A woman."

"I should have known. That's all you could think of to do with your life? Kill a woman? Was she black?"

"Yes."

"Of course. Of course she was. What did she do? Cheat on you?" She said it ugly. Cheat. Like "Take away your candy?"

He nodded.

"My my my. And you, I suppose, were the faithful boyfriend who never looked at another girl."

"Never. After I got out of the army, never. I played a little—piano, I mean, at night. Nothing much but okay until I could get on at the gas field. I had this gig in Sutterfield. Off and on for about three months. Then one morning I came home and . . ."

"No," sang Jadine, "don't tell me. You found her with somebody else and shot her."

"No. I mean yes, I found her—that way, but I didn't go in. I left. I got in the car. I was just gonna drive off, you know, and I backed the car out in the road, but I couldn't leave, couldn't leave them there so I turned the car around and drove it through the house."

"You ran over them?" Jadine's upper lip was lifted in disgust.

"No, I just busted up the place. But the car exploded and the bed caught on fire. It was a little place we had, just a little box, and I drove through the bedroom wall. I pulled her out of the fire but she never made it. They booked me after that."

"What about the man?"

"It wasn't a man; it was a boy. Thirteen, I heard. Singed him bald, but nothing more. They had me up for Murder Two."

He was still standing and now he looked down at her and noticed that she had folded her legs under her white cotton skirt. She is scared, he thought. In the company of a killer on an island, far away from the house, she is too scared. Suddenly he liked it. Liked her fear. Basked in it like a cat in steam-pipe heat and it made him feel protective and violent at the same time. She was looking into the horizon and kept her legs hidden under her skirt. Does she think I'll cut them off, or is there something under there she is afraid I will take out and kill? The idea both alarmed and pleased him and he dropped down on one knee and said very softly, "I won't kill you. I love you."

Quick like a doe she turned her head. Her eyes stretched wide with the problem of deciding what to be outraged by: the promise or the confession.

"You better not do either one," she said. "I don't want you loving me, and don't threaten me either. Don't ever threaten me again."

"I wasn't threatening you. I said I won't—wouldn't . . ."

"Why would you even say that? What kind of man are you? People don't say things like that. Nobody says that. Where do you think we are, in some jungle? Why would you say you're not going to kill me?"

"Shhhh."

"I won't shhhhh. You can't just sit here on the sand and say something like that. You trying to scare me?"

She's bolting, he thought. I have disgusted her again. And it was true that she was looking at him as though he were a dwarf with a head lopsided and swollen with water. She's right, he thought. I am crazy. Whenever I try to tell the truth it comes out wrong, or dumb or scary and there was no way to hide his helpless naked face. "No, wait a minute. I . . . I wasn't trying to scare you. I was trying to comfort you."

"Comfort me?"

"Yeah. You tucked your legs in like you were scared of me. You don't have to tuck your legs. I mean . . ."

"What are you talking about?"

"You changed the way you were sitting."

"You thought I sat this way because I was afraid?"

"Okay. I was wrong. But I didn't say it to say, 'maybe I could but I won't.' I said it so you wouldn't think that I would or . . . I'm not a killer. Just that one time, accidentally when I was fucked-up. I just didn't want to see your legs folded up like that. I wanted you relaxed, like you were before. You were sassy before and rubbing your ankles with your hands."

Jadine looked at him trying to figure out whether he was the man who understood potted plants or the man who drove through houses.

"Honest," he said. "I didn't mean to scare you. Honest. I can live without a lot of things, but I didn't want you to take your feet away from me just because I didn't go to jail like I was supposed to. I don't have a real life like most people, I've missed a lot. Don't take your feet away from me too."

"You are not well," she said.

"Yes, I am."

"No, you're not."

" 'Cause I like your feet?"

"You can't have my feet."

"I didn't ask to have them. I just asked to see them."

"I can't carry on a conversation like this. This is not a conversation that anybody has."

"Let me see them."

"Stop it."

"Please?"

"Look, Harvey, Henry, Son, Billy Green, maybe we'd just better pack it up and call it a day."

He sat down on the hard-packed sand in front and a little to the right of her and looked at her steadily. He quit. Quit trying to make an impression.

"I'm not crazy, Jadine. Raw, maybe, but not nuts."

"I'm not convinced."

"A man admires your feet and you want to lock him up?"

"You need professional care."

"Put one foot out. Just one. I prefer two, but if you want, you can show me just one, although two is better. Two feet is a pair. They go together, so to speak. One is just–" he shrugged slightly–"one. Alone. Two is better. I want to see them both."

"I don't know about you."

"Take your time, I'll see them anyway when you stand up, but I'd like it better if you showed them to me yourself."

Jadine's feet were warm under her skirt, each one hidden near a thigh.

"I won't touch," he said, "I promise."

She looked past his face and felt wavy. The sun was still hiding in some fuzz in the sky. Gulls with dark hoods rested beyond the surf. They looked like ducks from where she sat. All the gulls she remembered screeched and dived. She'd never seen them quiet before, sitting still in water as though they were listening.

"Come on," he said. "Show me. Please?"

Slowly she started to unfold one leg, carefully, cautiously as though she was about to do something wild.

"Just a little bit more," he urged her. "Come on."

Quickly then, she straightened both legs and stuck them into the air. He looked at them and did not touch. The waviness traveled from her head to her toes pointing up from the sand. He looked at them, and whispered, "Look at that." He leaned down for a better look. "I said I wouldn't touch and I won't. If you object, that is. But I have to tell you how much I want to. Right there." He pointed to the arch. "If you don't want me to, I won't, though, like I said."

He wants to kiss my feet, she thought. He wants to put his mouth on my foot. If he does I'll kick his teeth out. But she didn't move.

"Can I? Can I touch it right there?"

She didn't answer and he didn't say anything more for several pulse beats. Then he did it. Put his forefinger on her sole and held it and held it and held it there.

"Please stop," she said, and he did, but his forefinger stayed where his finger had been in the valley of her naked foot. Even after she laced up the canvas shoes.

"I've got to get back," she said.

He stood quickly so there would be no mistake, and walked ahead of her, leading the way. He drove this time, while Jadine sat quietly going over in her mind the reasons why she was not going to let him make love to her; the reasons it would be impossible to even consider going to bed with him, fingerprint or no fingerprint, laughing into the sky or not. The most important reason was that he expected her to. As hard as she tried, he did not seem convinced that she was unattracted to him. Second, it would trouble Nanadine and Sydney. Third, he wasn't manageable. Afterward. What would he be like afterward? Stake a claim? Try to trade his room for hers? Drive the jeep into the house if she said no? He was whistling now, driving along whistling through closed teeth like he already had it made. Still, she had been there two whole months with nobody. Jadine sighed and set her jaw. Fifteen more minutes and they would be back at the house where she could put the whole business out of her mind, but the jeep slowed down and she couldn't believe it. He must have done something; did he think she would sit still for something as dumb as that? But it was true; he pumped and pumped the accelerator. Nothing happened. The gauge was securely empty. Jadine looked around: jungle muck on both sides; trees close to the road on the left. An uphill walk to the house was longer than a trek back to the pier. Jadine reached into the glove compartment and took out a key. "It unlocks the pump back at the pier," she said.

"Got something to put it in?" he asked.

"In back under the seat, there's a five-liter bottle. Use that."

"I hope you're right. That there's gas in that pump."

"I hope I am too. If not, get some from the boat. I know there's some there."

He nodded. "Twenty minutes about, to get there and another twenty to get back."

She agreed and settled back in the seat crossing her legs.

"You're not coming with me?"

"No," she said, "I'll wait here."

"Alone?"

"Go on, will you? I'll be all right. There's nobody on the island I don't know. If somebody drives down, I'll have them pick you up and bring you back."

He left then and Jadine rummaged around in the basket to see if there was anything left of the awful lunch. Nothing. Nothing at all. She sat for a while under the hateful sun that had come out in full dress when they least needed her. Thank God there were no mosquitoes here, just a funny jungle-rot smell. She waited until the sun burnt a hole in her head. She didn't have a watch on but thought twenty minutes must have passed by. Only twenty more. Then she decided to seek shelter from the sun under the trees to the left of the road, in spite of that unpleasant odor. This was the ugly part of Isle des Chevaliers—the part she averted her eyes from whenever she drove past. Its solitude was heavy and there was something sly about its silence. Her jangled nerves she attributed however to the conversation with Son, the print of his forefinger on her foot, and the silly thoughts she'd had afterward. A fair amount of composure returned quickly once they had gotten back to the jeep where all was familiar, but a tremor had not yet died in her stomach and required the resolutions of a new nun to subdue. It was nothing like the fear-slashed anger she had felt the morning he had held her from behind and pressed into her. Nothing like that. But he was bathed now, clipped and beautiful with spacious tender eyes and a woodsy voice. His smile was always a surprise like a sudden rustle of wind across the savanna of his face. Playful sometimes, sometimes not. Sometimes it made her grab the reins. She took her pad and a stick of charcoal and walked toward the trees, wishing once more that she had had genuine talent in her fingers. She loved to paint and draw so it was unfair not to be good at it. Still she was lucky to know it, to know the difference between the fine and the mediocre, so she'd put that instinct to work and studied art history—there she was never wrong.

The trees were not as close together as she'd thought. Tall bushes had made them seem so. She approached the shade and peeped in between the trees. She almost laughed at what she saw. Young trees ringed and soared above a wavy mossy floor. There was hardly any color; just greens and browns because there was hardly any light and what light there was—a sentimental shaft of sunlight to the left—bunched the brown into deeper shadow. In the center under a roof of greens was a lawn of the same dark green the Dutchmen loved to use. The circle of trees looked like a standing rib of pork. Jadine tucked her pad under her arm and clenched the charcoal stick. It was amazing; the place looked like something by Bruce White or Fazetta—an elegant comic book illustration. She stepped through some bushes that looked like rhododendron and onto the mossy floor. The lawn, the center of the place began only a couple of yards ahead. She walked toward it and sank up to her knees. She dropped the pad and charcoal and grabbed the waist of a tree which shivered in her arms and swayed as though it wished to dance with her. She struggled to lift her feet and sank an inch or two farther down into the moss-covered jelly. The pad with Son's face badly sketched looked up at her and the women hanging in the trees looked down at her. There is an easy way to get out of this, she thought, and every Girl Scout knows what it is but I don't. Movement was not possible. At least not sudden movement. Perhaps she was supposed to lie horizontally. She tightened her arms around the tree and it swayed as though it wished to dance with her. Count, she thought. I will count to fifty and then pull, then count again and pull again. She had only to hang on until Son returned and shout—fifteen minutes, not more. And she would spend it edging up the tree that wanted to dance. No point in looking down at the slime, it would make her think of worms or snakes or crocodiles. Count. Just count. Don't sweat or you'll lose your partner, the tree. Cleave together like lovers. Press together like man and wife. Cling to your partner, hang on to him and never let him go. Creep up on him a millimeter at a time, slower than the slime and cover him like the moss. Caress his bark and finger his ridges. Sway when he sways and shiver with him too. Whisper your numbers from one to fifty into the parts that have been lifted away and left tender skin behind. Love him and trust him with your life because you are up to your kneecaps in rot.

The young tree sighed and swayed. The women looked down from the rafters of the trees and stopped murmuring. They were delighted when first they saw her, thinking a runaway child had been restored to them. But upon looking closer they saw differently. This girl was fighting to get away from them. The women hanging from the trees were quiet now, but arrogant—mindful as they were of their value, their exceptional femaleness; knowing as they did that the first world of the world had been built with their sacred properties; that they alone could hold together the stones of pyramids and the rushes of Moses's crib; knowing their steady consistency, their pace of glaciers, their permanent embrace, they wondered at the girl's desperate struggle down below to be free, to be something other than they were.

Jadine counted to fifty eight times, pulled eight times, then her right knee grazed something hard and she managed to lift her leg and bend it enough to kneel on the hard thing that seemed to be growing out of her partner the tree. It held and she got her other leg up, but the slimy soles of her shoes could find no other footing on the bark. She had to shimmy, using the insides of her knees for leverage. When she was up far enough, she twisted with a giant effort around to the road side of the tree—the part of the trunk that leaned out of solid ground. She slid down on her stomach and when Son came sweating up the hill she was crying a little and cleaning her feet and legs with leaves. The white skirt showed a deep dark and sticky hem and hung over the door of the jeep. She was in halter and panties.

"What the hell happened to you?" He ran to her and put the

bottle on the seat. She didn't look up, just wiped her eyes and said, "I took a walk over there and fell in."

"Over where?"

"There. Behind those trees."

"Fell in what? That looks like oil."

"I don't know. Mud I guess, but it felt like jelly while I was in it. But it doesn't come off like jelly. It's drying and sticking."

Son kneeled down and stroked her skin. The black stuff was shiny in places and where it was dry it was like mucilage. Nothing much was happening with her leaves. He shook some drops of the gasoline onto a clean place in her skirt and handed it to her. She took it and continued to clean herself in silence. He poured the gas into the tank and they waited for a few minutes for it to get into the line, and only when the motor finally caught did Jadine hazard a glance back at the place where she'd gone in. She could not identify the tree that had danced with her.

Son drove slowly up the hill to conserve the gas. He glanced at her from time to time, but could see she was not about to be consoled easily. He decided to tease her gently.

"That's where the swamp women live," he said. "You see any?"

She didn't answer.

"They mate with the horsemen up in the hills."

"Oh, shut up. Just shut up."

"I just thought you might have seen one."

"Look," she said. "I might have died. That mess was up to my knees. Don't try to cheer me up; it's not funny! Just drive, will you, and get me home so I can get this shit off me!"

"Okay, okay," he said, and smiled because he liked her sitting next to him in her underwear. Liked it so much it was hard to look serious when they drove up to the house and Margaret, sitting on the living room patio, came round to see who it was.

"An accident," said Jadine before Margaret could shift her stare from the underwear to Son. "I took a walk and fell in the swamp."

"My God," said Margaret. "You poor thing. You must have

been scared out of your mind. Where was *he?*" She jutted her chin at Son's back as he drove the jeep to the kitchen side of the house.

"At the dock getting gas. We ran out." Jadine was hurrying into the house. Her legs were burning from the gasoline. "I have to get in the tub."

Margaret followed her. "Soap first. Then alcohol. Jesus, what *is* that stuff? It looks like pitch."

In the bedroom Jadine took off halter and panties and tiptoed into the bathroom.

"He's bad luck, Jade. He really is. Any time anybody gets near him, something happens."

"Except Valerian," said Jadine. "He's good luck for Valerian."

"That figures," said Margaret. "Turpentine's better, honey. You have any?"

"No. But it's coming off all right with the soap. I won't be able to wax my legs for a week now. God, it burns."

"He's bad luck, Jade. Really. I just know it."

"Don't worry, Margaret, Michael will show. You'll see."

"I hope so. It's going to be so nice. I'm cooking everything myself, did I tell you?"

"You told me."

"He hasn't been here since he was fourteen. I could like this place if he'd stay. I could like everything about it. He won't spoil it, will he?"

"Who?"

"Him. Willie."

"No. Why would he? He's leaving as soon as Valerian hears from the consulate. What are you afraid of?"

"Well, Jade, he was in my closet."

"He isn't there now. What's the matter, Margaret? You think he wants your bod?"

"I don't know what I think. I'm all nerves. This place makes me crazy and so does he. Look at you, you go off with him, step out of a car and fall in a mudhole."

"Margaret, I fell in, not you. And it was my fault, not his." Jadine surprised herself; she was defending him against her. She thought it was gone—that mistrust, that stupid game she and Margaret used to play. Any minute now, Margaret would be reaching out her hand and saying "What'd ja do to yer hay-er? What'd ja do to yer hay-er?" like white girls all over the world, or telling her about Dorcus, the one black girl she ever looked in the face. But there was a little bit more in her annoyance now. Maybe she should just say it. He doesn't want you, Margaret. He wants me. He's crazy and beautiful and black and poor and beautiful and he killed a woman but he doesn't want you. He wants me and I have the fingerprint to prove it. But she didn't say any of that; she said she wanted to sleep now. Margaret left but her alarm stayed behind. Jadine got into bed and discovered she was jealous of Margaret of all people. Just because he was in her closet, she thought his sole purpose in life was to seduce her. Naturally her. A white woman no matter how old, how flabby, how totally sexless, believed it and she could have shot him for choosing Margaret's closet and giving her reason to believe it was true.

God. Jadine turned over carefully to protect her raw legs. I am competing with her for rape! She thinks this place is driving her crazy; it's making a moron out of me. Certified.

It took some time before she could fall asleep. The soap had done its job. The little feet he wanted so badly to see were clean again, peachy soft again as though they had never been touched and never themselves had touched the ground.

6

CHRISTMAS EVE'S EVE and even the goddamn hydrangea had bloomed!

The whole island was vomiting up color like a drunk and here in the corner, in plastic filtered light, was one spot of sane, refined mauve. Valerian sprayed it with water and aerated the soil around the stem. "Merry Christmas," he said, and toasted the shy violet buds with his wineglass. Maybe Margaret was right: this would be a warm and memorable Christmas. The black man had brought luck to the greenhouse, maybe he'd bring luck to the whole celebration. Michelin would be there; Michael, Michael's friend; that was just enough. And Margaret was sober and busy and cheerfully preoccupied with something outside herself for a change.

Valerian walked away from the hydrangea and looked out the window toward the washhouse. The washerwoman was there, bless her heart, with the yard boy. He couldn't hear them, but they looked as though they were laughing. A nip, he thought. They're already celebrating and have taken a Christmas nip. He liked that. That was the way a holiday ought to begin and since everything was in its place as it should be—Michael coming, Margaret cooking, hydrangea in bloom—he decided to go out there with the servants and wish them a Merry Christmas too. All that was needed was that holiday bread Grandmother Stadt used to make. Ollieballen.

"Ollieballen?"

"Yes. My grandmother used to make it at New Year."

"The Candy Queen?" asked Margaret. "I never heard of it."

"It's not hard," said Valerian. "It's Dutch."

"What's it taste like?"

"Sweet. Like a doughnut."

"We can't serve doughnuts at dinner, Valerian."

"It's not for dinner, it's for afterward. With brandy and coffee."

"This is going to be hard enough without ollieballen."

"Then let's forget the whole thing."

"No. I said I'd do it and I'm going to. Michael will get a kick out of it."

"So will Ondine."

"Maybe. I've never seen her eat anything."

"Nobody ever sees a cook eat anything. Let's go over the menu again. Turkey, mashed potatoes and gravy, green beans—what else?"

"The lemon whip and this ollieballen thing."

"You can use the apples in it. It's easier than pie and it's traditional in our family—or it was. What about something to start? Soup or fish?"

"Valerian."

"Something simple. You can handle it."

"You'll help?"

"I'll be entertaining the guests. I can't do both. And that's not what you said. You said you'd do the whole dinner for everybody."

"So how many is that? Six?"

"Seven. It'll be fun. You'll enjoy it. Don't forget it was your suggestion."

"How do you get seven?"

"B.J. has a girlfriend, doesn't he? So there's me, you and Michael, B.J. and his guest, Jade and Michelin. Seven. The turkey is here—beans, potatoes—nothing to it. You can make the ollieballen ahead of time. Christmas Eve."

"You have the recipe?"

"I have it."

"What do I need?"

"Nothing special: yeast, eggs, milk, sugar, lemon, flour, raisins, apples and butter."

"What about the lemon whip?"

"Just lemon-flavored gelatin beaten to froth and whipped cream on top. Very simple. We can have smoked fish, perhaps, to start. All that needs is parsley. The lemon whip is a light sweet for after a heavy dinner. Then coffee and brandy with the ollieballen." Valerian spread his fingers to show how easy it was. He wanted her occupied the next few days—not sitting around in anxiety about when (or if) Michael would get there.

"Doughnuts and brandy," she said, and shook her head.

"Margaret."

"No, no. It's fine. Just sounded funny that's all."

"They don't have a hole in the middle."

"Too bad," she said. "It might inspire you."

"I'm sorry about last night. That wasn't why I came. I've been hateful and I know it. I shouldn't have behaved that way when you found Willie up there in your closet."

"We've been through all that. Forget it."

"It worked out okay, didn't it?"

"I suppose."

"You should see the greenhouse now. Black magic."

"Really?"

"Really. You should come and see. And I *am* sorry, Margaret. I liked what you did though."

"Sure. We'll do it again sometime."

"Soon?"

"Soon."

"Now."

"Now?"

"Why not?"

"It doesn't work like that, Valerian. I mean I can't just lie down in the middle of the afternoon."

"I can. I can even kneel. Might need help getting back up, but I can do it."

"No. Wait."

"Margie. Marge."

"WHAT KIND of dinner is that? I wouldn't have it for lunch. Does she think she's doing me a favor?"

"Stop grumbling. It's Christmastime and for once in your life you don't have to cook the dinner."

"But I have to do the dishes, I bet."

"No, you don't."

"Who then? You? No Mary. No Yardman. They decide not to show up without telling anybody. Everything's on me. A pile of laundry a mile high in there. Jadine off playing games with that jailbird; guests coming . . ."

"I told you he already called Dr. Michelin, and Dr. Michelin said he'd get us somebody right away. Maybe not right away because they got Christmas there too, but he thinks his housekeeper can find somebody. We'll just have to make do for a day or two. Let the laundry stay there, and get yourself organized. You are worrying the life out of me."

"You can stop riding me any time you please. And if you expect anything at all to go right, you better quit soon."

"You the one riding people. You been hot for days. Nothing can please you."

"The whole house is upset. Hard to think and be nice in a house that's upset."

"The house is not upset. You are. Everybody else is laughing and having a good time but you. Mr. Street slept with his wife last night. You know how long it's been since he did that? Slept in the same bed with her?"

"Slept is the word all right."

"Don't you believe it. They been cooing all morning."

"I don't care. They ought to sleep together. I never did know how he puts up with that. Whoever heard of married folks sleeping any other way but together. They can sleep anywhere they want. It's where Jadine sleeps that bothers me."

"She slept in her own bed."

"I'm going to bring this basin down on your head. You know what I'm talking about."

"Well, what you want me to do about it?"

"Talk to somebody."

"Who?"

"Her."

"Get away from me."

"Sydney, listen here. I don't like it. None of it. What she want to mess with him for? He ain't got a dime and no prospect of one."

"She's just playing. Nothing much else to do out here, you know that. Cleaned him up and he looks fine and even acts all right. Look here. They pack a lunch, go off to the beach and swim a little. What is that? Marriage? First you was screaming because you thought she was going to marry some white boy; now she goes swimming with one of us and you still mad. Jadine's not a fool and he's okay."

"He is not okay."

"When he busted in here you were the one trying to get me to calm down. I was ready to shoot him. Now you the one want the gun."

"I just don't like it."

"What you afraid of? She's not going off with him. Just because you foolish, don't think she is. She's worked hard to make something out of herself, and nothing will make her throw it all away on a swamp nigger."

"It ain't what she thinks that worries me. It's what he thinks."

"You know something I don't?"

"No."

"Well then."

"But I've seen his eyes when nobody's looking. At least when he thinks nobody's looking."

"And what did you see in his eyes, Ondine?"

"Wildness. Plain straight-out wildness. He wants her, Sydney. And he'll do what he has to do to get her and what he has to to keep her."

"Takes two, Ondine. He can't kidnap her."

"Wouldn't put it past him."

"Mr. Street likes him."

"He likes him because Jadine likes him."

"No. He helped him with those plants in there. Made something grow that was dying."

"He wants to keep him here so Jade will stay and if Jadine stays then his wife might stay and if Michael does show up maybe she won't want to go running off after him."

"Well. Maybe he's right."

"Don't rely on it. If that boy gets in she'll be out of here like a shot. She's got a lot of cleaning up to do with Michael. It's sitting on her heart and she's never going to have no peace until she cleans it up. She'll trail him to the end of the world and God himself knows that is exactly where she ought to be."

"You hate that woman, and you want her out of here so you can run everything your way."

"I don't hate her; I feel sorry for her, to tell the truth."

"Want some more hot water in there?"

"No, this is fine."

"It's going to be all right, Ondine. She is coming in the kitchen to cook Christmas dinner. And you have to get out of the way. Maybe it'll taste bad, but it's only for one night. We can behave for one night, can't we? Then it'll be over and everything will be back to normal."

"Everything but my feet."

"Your feet too. Put 'em up here. Let me rub them for you."

"They not going to last much longer, you know. I get the

littlest cut on them now and it don't seem to heal. I have to stand up to do the work I do, if I can't stand then I can't work."

"When you can't stand, girl, sit down. You don't have to work. I can take care of you, you know that."

"We don't have a place of our own. And the little bit of savings went to Jadine. Not that I regret a penny of it; I don't."

"We got a few stocks and Social Security. Years of it. Remember how I tried to get Mr. Street not to take it out, back when we first started, and he wouldn't listen to me? Now I appreciate the fact that he didn't."

"Such a smart little girl, and so pretty. I never minded not having children after we started taking care of her. I would have stood on my feet all day all night to put her through that school. And when my feet were gone, I would have cooked on my knees."

"I know, baby, I know."

"She crowned me, that girl did. No matter what went wrong or how tired I was, she was my crown."

"He helped too, you know. We never could have done it without him."

"And I'm grateful. You know I am. I've never had no problem with him. He's a nuisance, but he stood by us when we needed him to."

"And she never objected to it, Ondine. A lot of wives would have."

"I suppose."

"Lay back. Put your legs up on this pillow. Rest yourself and don't worry about nothing. Nothing's going to change. Everything's going to be all right."

"She wouldn't up and marry some no-count Negro, would she? I don't care how good-looking and sweet-talking he is. You didn't say nothing about stuffin. Is she going to stuff that bird or just roast him empty?"

"Rest, girl."

"And what the devil is lemon whip?"

NOBODY CAME. At least none of the invited. The emperor butterflies flew in the window, but they were not invited, nor were the bees. They were roused by the six-part singing of the tin-tin birds sitting in formation at the top of the bougainvillea. But the maiden aunts weren't there, thank God, with their wispy maiden aunt hair. Still nobody came. Uninvited and emergency guests shared dinner on Christmas Day. First the telephone operator read off the cable from B. J. Bridges: "Boston weather cannot fly okay postpone New Year." Then Dr. Michelin called with regrets saying the crossing would be too rough. Finally customs *contrôle* reported there was no red trunk on the last flight arriving at nine in the morning from Miami, and there was no Houston flight at all that day. More telephone calls. Michael did not answer his telephone. Margaret would have caved in Christmas Eve except for the busy-ness of confirming the disaster: more placing of calls—forty-five-minute waits until they were connected; more cables with "confirm delivery" instructions; Michael's neighbors were summoned, but the number had changed or the neighbors had; his old girlfriends were asked to go to his house and check. Had he left? When? But it was the day before Christmas and people had other things to do. Then there was the wrapping of gifts, the ollieballen to make, the turkey that was really a goose to prepare. Margaret was too tired to feel her sorrow at its deepest point until Christmas Day dawned bright and secular and nobody at all came to L'Arbe de la Croix, and nobody was in his proper place. Ondine was in the bathtub. Margaret was in the kitchen. Sydney was in the greenhouse cutting flowers for the table. Jadine was in the washhouse waiting for a dryer load to conclude. And Valerian was by the telephone placing incomplete calls. Son, who had no place of his own, got in everybody's way. The exchange of gifts, scheduled for Michael's arrival, took place anywhere, furtively and without fanfare or enthusiasm. When it was certain that no one was coming and the day looked as if it belonged to the tin-tin birds and not to family and friends, Valerian, to raise Margaret's spirits probably or simply to get through the day, said, "Let's all sit down and have the dinner among ourselves. Everybody. Jade, Willie, Ondine, Sydney." They would all have a good time, he said. Margaret nodded, and left the kitchen, where the uses of things now eluded her completely. She was in control the night before —enough to wash the fowl whose legs would not stand up as they ought to. But the ollieballen recipe slipped out of reach entirely. Sydney rescued it and now when Valerian called her away from the kitchen she seemed not to care one way or another. It was just another meal now and the dinner she had planned to cook Ondine had to finish, including the lemon whip. Ondine was persuaded to dress up and join Sydney and the others in the dining room partly because she'd had the foresight to bake a ham and a coconut cake and would not be required to eat Margaret's menu and partly because she'd have to eat alone otherwise, but she was deeply unhappy about being thrown out of her kitchen in the first place and then pushed back in when Margaret abandoned the whole thing halfway through because the guests were different. She was also unhappy because she thought Jadine had secret plans to leave right after Christmas. A few days ago she had the humiliation of Alma Estée handing her a pair of recently worn pajamas that she found in the gardenia bushes underneath Jadine's bedroom. Ondine took them and did not mention the find to anyone, but it worried her. Jadine's scurrilous remarks about Son seemed too pointed, too loud. Sydney took the invitation in stride. The suggestion of a special and intimate relationship with his employer pleased him more than it disconcerted him. And what was unthinkable and undesirable in Philadelphia was not so on that island. In addition, it leveled, in a way, the invitation Mr. Street had extended to Son when everybody thought he was a burglar. More than leveled—this invitation was formal and sober although it was an emergency solution to a rapidly deteriorating holiday.

Jadine was enchanted. Wanted everybody dressed up and gave Ondine and Sydney their presents right after breakfast when she heard the plans, exacting a promise from her aunt that she would wear hers to dinner. It was hard to tell what Son felt. Perhaps he did not know himself. For such a long time a Christmas spent on land for him was an extempore dinner or party with miscellaneous people he never expected to see again. This was another, except that the imminent exit of one of those persons alarmed him. She said "before I go" on the beach. Not "before *you* go." And he had had a brief encounter with Margaret that confirmed it. He was still apologizing all around and saw Margaret lying in a canvas-back chair, sunning herself in the shade and away from the wind too, so she could acquire a tan but not the aging of skin that would accompany it. Her place for this was on the patio outside the living room where the piano was, sheltered by the bougainvillea bushes. Next to her chair on a small glass-topped table was a box of stationery, Bain de Soleil, tissues and a half-glass of Evian, ice and lime. She was in a bathing suit and Son thought she was like a marshmallow warming but not toasting itself. That inside the white smooth skin was liquid sugar, no bones, no cartilage—just liquid sugar, soft and a little pully. Quite unlike her tips, where all of her strength was. Direction, focus, aggression, tenacity—all that was tough and survivalist in her lay in the tips of her fingers, the tips of her toes, her nose tip, her chin tip, and he suspected her breast tips were tiny brass knobs like those ornately carved fixtures screwed into the drawers of Jadine's writing table. Even the top of her head was fierce, pulled back as it was into a red foxtail of stamina. She heard him approach and turned her head slowly. The minute she saw him, she reached for her towel. Son picked it up from the flagstones and handed it to her. His gesture was swift and accommodating so she did not fling it over herself as she had probably intended to do but simply held it in her lap.

"I scare you?"

"No. Yes," she said. "I didn't hear you come up."

He did not comment on that so she said, "What is it?"

"Nothing. I just saw you out here and wanted to say hello."

"Hello. Is that all?"

"That's all."

"It shouldn't be. You should have more to say after what you did to me."

"What did I do to you?" He was counting on the liquid sugar. Never mind the tips.

"You know what. You sat in my closet and scared the hell out of me."

He smiled. "You scared the hell out of me too."

"Bullshit," she said.

"It's true. Your husband was right; you were wrong. As soon as he saw me he knew I didn't mean no harm."

"He wasn't there. I was. I was in that closet; I saw you."

"What did you see?"

"I saw a big black man sitting in my closet is what I saw."

"I'm not so big. Your husband's bigger—taller—than I am. Besides, I was sitting down. What made you think I was big?"

"There are no small men in a closet. Unless the closet belongs to them. Any stranger in a closet is big. Big and scary. I thought—"

"You thought what?"

She looked at him out of the corner of her eyes and did not answer.

Son finished her sentence. "That I was going to—that if you hadn't come in and turned on the light, I was going to stay there, wait there, until you went to bed and then I would creep out and GETCHA!" He laughed then, laughed like a ten-year-old at a Three Stooges movie. Mouth wide open, bubbly sounds coming from his chest.

"Cut that out. Don't try to make fun of it."

But he kept on laughing, long enough to make a little anger spread inside her. When he could stop laughing he said, "I'm sorry, I wasn't laughing at you. I was laughing at myself. I was seeing myself do it. Or try to do it, and it looked funny. Me with my raggedy pants down around my ankles trying to get in your bed."

"It's not funny."

"No, it's not, but believe me it wouldn't have been much of a rape. Sex is hard when you're starving, but I thank you for the compliment."

"I don't know what you're talking about." Margaret spread the towel across her knees and picked up the iced glass. "And the part I do understand, I don't believe."

"When your son gets here, ask him. He'll explain it."

Margaret stopped sipping the water and looked at him. "How old are you?"

"About as old as your son."

"My son is twenty-nine going on thirty."

"Okay. Almost as old as your son."

"He'll be thirty March tenth."

"Does he favor you or your husband?"

"Favor?"

"Look like. Does he look like you?"

"People say so. Everybody says so. The hair, of course, and his eyes are blue like mine. Everybody says he looks exactly like me. Nothing like his father."

"He must be good-looking."

"He is. He is. But tall like Valerian. Is that true? You're shorter than Valerian?"

Son nodded. "He's got at least two inches on me."

"Huh," she said, "I wouldn't have thought so. Well, Michael is every bit as tall as Valerian, but he does look more like me. Inside though, that's where he's really beautiful. Do you know what he's been doing? for a year now? He's been working on an Indian reservation. With the young people there, teenagers. There's a lot of suicide among Indian teenagers. The conditions are awful, you know. You would not *believe.* I visited him when he was in Arizona. Well, some of the tribesmen have money but they're just—well, they don't really help their own. Most of them live in terrible conditions and they are very proud people, you know. Very. Michael encourages them to keep their own heritage intact. You'd really like Michael. Everybody does."

He listened. She took sips of the Evian and lime as she talked, her knees covered with the towel. She was looking at him now. Relaxed. Interested in what she was saying. Interested in his hearing it, knowing it, knowing that her son was beautiful, wise and kind. That he loved people, was not selfish, was actually self-sacrificing, committed, that he could have lived practically any kind of life he chose, could be dissolute, reckless, trivial, greedy. But he wasn't. He had not turned out that way. He could have been president of the candy company if he had wanted, but he wanted value in his life, not money. He had turned out fine, just fine. "Jade knows him," she said. "They used to see each other during the summers she spent with us. Oh, he'll be thrilled to see her again. She's not leaving till a couple of days after Christmas so they'll have some time together."

Son did not blink—he took it in and nodded his appreciation of Michael into his mother's face. *She was leaving soon.* Margaret was perspiring a little bit on the forehead. A light glisten on the healthy and cared-for skin. Her blue-if-it's-a-boy blue eyes wide open, not squinting in the sun for it could not get to her under the shade of the bougainvillea. Just the heat, and she was warming and marshmallow soft. But her tips were terribly sharp.

THEY SERVED themselves from the sideboard and drank wine in some haste to hurry the dismal affair along. The forced gaiety was helped into some semblance of naturalness by Jadine with much cheery help from Valerian. Sydney was awkward but subdued. Ondine was irritable, her aching feet encased in high heels with zircons up the back.

"The turkey is very tender, Mrs. Street," said Sydney.

Margaret smiled.

"Not bad at all," said Valerian, who had none of it on his plate. "Geese makes excellent turkey." He glanced at Margaret to see if she would be amused. She seemed not to hear.

"Lot of fat in a goose." Ondine was slicing her ham. "It should be cooked on its breast, not on its back."

"Oh, but I like the juices."

"That ain't juice, Jadine, that's grease," Ondine answered.

Valerian lifted his fork like a toastmaster. "Margaret has a surprise for us. Made it last night."

"What?" asked Jadine.

"You'll see. An old family recipe. Right, Margaret? Margaret?"

"Oh. Yes. Right. It wasn't hard."

"Don't be modest."

Sydney looked at Ondine with what he hoped was a stern gaze. They say it's a surprise, his eyes seemed to be saying, let's agree and be surprised. Ondine kept her eyes on her ham.

"Is that the phone?" Margaret was alert.

"Would you get that, Sydney?"

"I'll get it." Margaret was rising from her chair.

"No, let Sydney."

No one spoke as Sydney left the room.

"Dr. Michelin," said Sydney when he returned, "calling to say Merry Christmas. I suggested he call back later."

"I thought it might be the airport," said Margaret.

"Airport, what for? You heard the final news."

"I asked the office to call if there was going to be a break in the weather."

"The weather is in Boston, not California."

"How do you know that?"

"I think," said Jadine, "that the radio said there were storms all over."

"Downed the telephone lines too, I suppose," said Valerian.

"Probably, yes—" Margaret's voice was a bit shrill.

"Well, he'll be sorry," said Valerian. "He's missing some very good food and some very good company. We should have thought of this before. Give Ondine a day off, and you get to show off in the kitchen, Margaret. It's good to have some plain Pennsylvania food for a change. This *is* an old-fashioned Christmas."

"Too bad Gideon couldn't come." Son, who seemed to be the only one genuinely enjoying the food, had been silent until then.

"Who?" asked Valerian.

"Gideon. Yardman."

"His name is Gideon?" asked Jadine.

"What a beautiful name. Gideon." Valerian smiled.

"Well, at least we knew Mary's name. Mary," said Jadine.

"Nope," said Son.

"No?"

"Thérèse."

"Thérèse? Wonderful," said Valerian. "Thérèse the Thief and Gideon the Get Away Man."

Ondine looked up. "They didn't steal that chocolate, Mr. Street. That was this one here." She nodded her head at Son.

"Chocolate? Who's talking about chocolate? They stole the apples." Valerian got up to go to the sideboard for some more mashed potatoes and gravy.

"Gideon stole apples?" asked Son.

"Yep." Valerian's back was to them. "I caught him red-handed, so to speak. Them, rather. She, Mary, had them stuffed in her blouse. He had some in each pocket."

Sydney and Ondine both stopped eating. "What did he say? When you caught him?" Sydney was frowning.

"Said he was going to put them back." Valerian rejoined them and chuckled.

"So that's why they didn't come back to work. Ashamed."

"Oh, more than that," said Valerian. "Much more than that. I fired him. Her too."

"You what?" Ondine almost shouted.

"Ondine," Sydney whispered.

"You didn't tell us," she said to Valerian.

"Beg pardon?" Valerian looked amused.

"I mean . . . Did you know that, Sydney?"

"No. Nobody told me anything."

"Mr. Street, you could have mentioned it."

"I'll get someone else. I've already spoke to Michelin, I told you that."

"But I thought that was temporary help, until they came back after Christmas, I thought."

"Well, Ondine, it isn't temporary help I'm asking for. It's permanent because they are not coming back."

"Please stop bickering," Margaret said softly. "I'm getting a headache."

"I never bicker, Margaret. I am discussing a domestic problem with my help."

"Well, they are guests tonight."

"The problem is still of interest to everybody at the table, except you."

"Certain things I need to know," Ondine was talking into her plate, "if I'm to get work done right. I took on all sorts of extra work because I thought they were just playing hooky. I didn't know they was fired."

"Ondine, what would you have done differently if you had known? You would have grumbled, and tried to make me keep them on. And since they were obviously stealing, and the whole house was upset anyway, I did what I thought was best."

"I wouldn't have tried any such thing, if they stole. I don't condone that."

"Well, they did and I let them go and that's that."

Son's mouth went dry as he watched Valerian chewing a piece of ham, his head-of-a-coin profile content, approving even of the flavor in his mouth although he had been able to dismiss with a flutter of the fingers the people whose sugar and cocoa had allowed him to grow old in regal comfort; although he had taken the sugar and cocoa and paid for it as though it had no value, as though the cutting of cane and picking of beans was child's play and had no value; but he turned it into candy, the invention of which really was child's play, and sold it to other children and made a fortune in order to move near, but not in the midst of, the jungle where the sugar came from and build a palace with more of their labor and then hire them to do more of the work he was not capable of and pay them again according to some scale of value that would outrage Satan himself and when those people wanted a little of what he wanted, some apples for *their* Christmas, and took some, he dismissed them with a flutter of the fingers, because they were thieves, and nobody knew thieves and thievery better than he did and he probably thought he was a law-abiding man, they all did, and they all always did, because they had not the dignity of wild animals who did not eat where they defecated but they could defecate over a whole people and come there to live and defecate some more by tearing up the land and that is why they loved property so, because they had killed it soiled it defecated on it and they loved more than anything the places where they shit. Would fight and kill to own the cesspools they made, and although they called it architecture it was in fact elaborately built toilets, decorated toilets, toilets surrounded with and by business and enterprise in order to have something to do in between defecations since waste was the order of the day and the ordering principle of the universe. And especially the Americans who were the worst because they were new at the business of defecation spent their whole lives bathing bathing bathing washing away the stench of the cesspools as though pure soap had anything to do with purity.

That was the sole lesson of their world: how to make waste, how to make machines that made more waste, how to make wasteful products, how to talk waste, how to study waste, how to design waste, how to cure people who were sickened by waste so they could be well enough to endure it, how to mobilize waste, legalize waste and how to despise the culture that lived in cloth houses and shit on the ground far away from where they ate. And it would drown them one day, they would all sink into their own waste and the waste they had made of the world and then, finally they would know true peace and the happiness they had been looking for all along. In the meantime this one here would chew a morsel of ham and drink white wine secure in the knowledge that he had defecated on two people who had dared to want some of his apples.

And Jadine had defended him. Poured his wine, offered him a helping of this, a dab of that and smiled when she did not have to. Soothed down any disturbance that might fluster him; quieted even the mild objections her own aunt raised, and sat next to him more alive and responsive and attentive than even his own wife was, basking in the cold light that came from one of the killers of the world.

Jadine who should know better, who had been to schools and seen some of the world and who ought to know better than any of them because she had been made by them, coached by them and should know by heart the smell of their huge civilized latrines.

Sydney closed his knife and fork and said, "Other folks steal and they get put in the guest room."

Jadine shot a look at Son and said, "Uncle Sydney, please."

"It's true, ain't it? We were slighted by taking in one thief and now we are slighted by letting another go."

"We are quarreling about apples," said Margaret with surprise. "We are actually quarreling about apples."

"It is not about apples, Mrs. Street," said Sydney quietly. "I just think we should have been informed. We would have let them go ourselves, probably. This way, well . . ." He looked as if even staying on at the table let alone the job was hopeless.

Valerian, at the head of his Christmas table, looked at the four black people; all but one he knew extremely well, all but one, and even that one was in his debt. Across from him at the bottom of the table sat Son who thought he knew them all very well too, except one and that one was escaping out of his hands, and that one was doing the bidding of her boss and "patron." Keeping the dinner going smoothly, quietly chastising everybody including her own uncle and aunt, soothing Margaret, agreeing with Valerian and calling Gideon Yardman and never taking the trouble to know his name and never calling his own name out loud. He looked at Valerian and Valerian looked back.

The evening eyes met those of the man with savannas in his face. The man who respected industry looked over a gulf at the man who prized fraternity.

So he said to Valerian, in a clear voice, "If they had asked, would you have given them some of the apples?" The whole table looked at Son as if he were crazy.

"Of course," said Valerian. "Some, surely, but they didn't ask; they took. Do you know how many Americans here want special treats and goodies from the consulate? Especially at Christmas. They sent us one crate, and those two, along with that girl they bring, took them, or tried to. I stopped them. Besides, it wasn't the apples alone. It was the way they acted when I caught them. After trying to lie out of it, they didn't even apologize. They got arrogant—the woman called me names I haven't heard since I left the army. So I fired them. Those apples came at great expense and inconvenience from the consulate. I don't see what the problem is."

"Inconvenience for who?" Son asked. "You didn't go and get them. They did. You didn't row eighteen miles to bring them here. They did."

"Surely you don't expect me to explain my actions, defend them to you?"

"You should explain it to somebody. Two people are going to starve so your wife could play American mama and fool around in the kitchen."

"Keep me out of it, please," said Margaret.

"Precisely," said Valerian. His evening eyes had a touch of menace. "You keep my wife out of this. I rather think you have caused her enough mischief." Somewhere in the back of Valerian's mind one hundred French chevaliers were roaming the hills on horses. Their swords were in their scabbards and their epaulets glittered in the sun. Backs straight, shoulders high—alert but restful in the security of the Napoleonic Code.

Somewhere in the back of Son's mind one hundred black men on one hundred unshod horses rode blind and naked through the hills and had done so for hundreds of years. They knew the rain forest when it was a rain forest, they knew where the river began, where the roots twisted above the ground; they knew all there was to know about the island and had not even seen it. They had floated in strange waters blind, but they were still there racing each other for sport in the hills behind this white man's house. Son folded his hands before his jawline and turned his savanna eyes on those calm head-of-a-coin evening ones. "Whatever mischief I did," he said, "it wasn't enough to make you leave the table to find out about it."

"You will leave this house," said Valerian. "Now."

"I don't think so," said Son.

Margaret raised her hand and touched Valerian on the shoulder. "It's all right, Valerian. Let's just . . ."

"It's not all right! Whose house is this?"

"We got them back," she said. "I made the ollieballen with them." Her voice was limp. Maybe if they all just ignored that "I don't think so," it would disappear. It didn't. It clicked like a key opening a lock.

"That's not the point!"

"Well, what is the point, I'd like to know. It's Christmas . . ."

"I am being questioned by these people, as if, as if I *could* be called into question!"

Jadine spoke. "Valerian, Ondine's feelings were hurt. That's all."

"By what, pray? By my removing a pair of thieves from my house?"

"No, by not telling her," said Margaret.

"So what? All of a sudden I'm beholden to a cook for the welfare of two people she hated anyway? I don't understand."

Ondine had been watching the exchanges with too bright eyes, chagrined by Margaret's defense of her interests. Having caused all the trouble, now she was pretending that Ondine was the source of the dispute. "I may be a cook, Mr. Street, but I'm a person too."

"Mr. Street," said Sydney, "my wife is as important to me as yours is to you and should have the same respect."

"More," said Ondine. "I should have more respect. I am the one who cleans up her shit!"

"Ondine!" Both Sydney and Valerian spoke at once.

"This is impossible!" Valerian was shouting.

"I'll tell it," said Ondine. "Don't push me, I'll tell it."

"Nanadine! Get hold of yourself!" Jadine pushed her chair back as though to rise.

"I'll tell it. She wants to meddle in my kitchen, fooling around with pies. And *my* help gets fired!"

"*Your* kitchen? *Your* help?" Valerian was astonished.

"Yes my kitchen and yes my help. If not mine, whose?"

"You are losing your mind!" shouted Valerian.

Ondine was fuming now. "The first time in her life she tries to boil water and I get slapped in the face. Keep that bitch out of my kitchen. She's not fit to enter it. She's no cook and she's no mother."

Valerian stood up. "If you don't leave this room I'll . . ." It was the second time he ordered a dismissal and the second time it held no force.

"What? You'll what?" asked Ondine.

"Leave!" said Valerian.

"Make me," said Ondine.

"You don't work here anymore," he said.

"Oh, yeah? Who's going to feed you? *Her?*" She pointed up-table at Margaret. "You'll be dead in a week! and lucky to be dead. And away from her."

Margaret picked up her glass and threw it. The Evian splashed on the cloth and some got on Ondine's chiffon dress. As the others jumped up from their seats, Ondine slipped out of her zircon-studded shoes and raced around the table at the target of all her anger. The real target, who would not be riled until now when she got fed up with the name-calling and shot her water glass across the table. "Don't you come near me!" Margaret shouted, but Ondine did and with the back of her hand slapped Margaret across the face.

"Call the harbor!" shouted Valerian, but again there was no one to do his bidding. He had played a silly game, and everyone was out of place.

Margaret touched her flaming cheek and then rose up from her chair like a red-topped geyser and grabbed Ondine's braids, forced her head down to the table where she would have banged it except for the woman's fist blows to her waist.

It was Jadine and Son who managed to separate them. Sydney was shaking and saying, "O Lord O Lord." Valerian was shaking and saying nothing—his evening eyes gone dawn with rage.

Held tightly in the arms of Son, Ondine was shouting wildly, "You white freak! You baby killer! I saw you! I saw you! You think I don't know what that apple pie shit is for?"

Jadine had a hard time holding back Margaret, who was shouting, "Shut up! Shut up! You nigger! You nigger bitch! Shut your big mouth, I'll kill you!"

"You cut him up. You cut your baby up. Made him bleed for you. For fun you did it. Made him scream, you, you freak. You crazy white freak. She did," Ondine addressed the others, still shouting. "She stuck pins in his behind. Burned him with cigarettes. Yes, she did, I saw her; I saw his little behind. She burned him!"

Valerian held on to the table edge as though it were the edge of the earth. His face was truly white and his voice cracked a little as he asked, "Burned . . . who?"

"Your son! Your precious Michael. When he was just a baby. A wee wee little bitty baby." Ondine started to cry. "I used to hold him and pet him. He was so scared." Her voice was hardly audible under the sobbing. "All the time scared. And he wanted her to stop. He wanted her to stop so bad. And every time she'd stop for a while, but then I'd see him curled up on his side, staring off. After a while—after a while he didn't even cry. And she wants him home . . . for Christmas and apple pie. A little boy who she hurt so much he can't even cry."

She broke down then and said no more. Sydney put his arms around her. Son let her arms go and picked up a table napkin so she could wipe her streaming eyes with it instead of with the backs and the palms of her hands. Sydney led her barefoot, her diadem braids turned into horns, away from the table. Margaret was standing as still and as straight as a pillar. There were tears in her eyes but her beautiful face was serene. They could hear Ondine's cries all the way into the first kitchen and down the stairs to the apartment of second-hand furniture. "Yes my kitchen. Yes my kitchen. I am the woman in this house. None other. As God is my witness there is none other. Not in this house."

Margaret serene and lovely stared ahead at nobody. "I have always loved my son," she said. "I am not one of those women in the *National Enquirer*."

"THAT WAS AWFUL, awful," said Jadine. She was holding Son's hand as they walked up the stairs. There had been no point in staying or even excusing themselves. Valerian was looking at Margaret and she was looking at nobody. So the two of them left as soon as Ondine and Sydney did. Jadine would not admit to herself that she was rattled, but her fingertips were ice-cold in

Son's hand. She wanted a little human warmth, some unsullied person to be near, someone to be with, so she took his hand without thinking about it and said, "That was awful!"

"Yes," he said.

"What happened? We all went crazy. Do you think it's true? What Nanadine said? She wouldn't make up anything like that." They were at Jadine's bedroom door and went in. Still holding hands. In the center of the room, Jadine stopped, released his hand and turned to face him. She pressed her fingers together in front of her lips. "Awful," she said frowning, looking at the floor.

"Don't think about it. It's over."

Jadine put her head on his chest. "It's not over. They're fired for sure. Tomorrow will be terrible. God, how can I wake up in the morning and face that? I won't be able to sleep at all. Maybe I should go down and see about her?"

"Ondine?"

"Yes."

"Leave her alone with Sydney. You shouldn't bother them now."

"I wish I could figure it out, what got into everybody." Son put his arm around her; she was like a bird in the crook of his arm. "What does it mean?" She closed her eyes.

"It means," he said, talking into her hair, "that white folks and black folks should not sit down and eat together."

"Oh, Son." Jadine looked up at him and smiled a tiny smile.

"It's true," he said. "They should work together sometimes, but they should not eat together or live together or sleep together. Do any of those personal things in life."

She put her head back into his shirt front. "What'll we do now?"

"Sleep," he said.

"I can't sleep. It was so ugly. Did you see the faces?"

Son kissed her cheek, bending his neck down low.

"It's true, isn't it? She stuck pins into Michael, and Ondine knew it and didn't tell anybody all this time. Why didn't she tell somebody?"

"She's a good servant, I guess, or maybe she didn't want to lose her job." He kissed the other cheek.

"I always wondered why she hated Margaret so. Every time she could she would jab at her."

"Sleep," he said, and kissed her eyelids. "You need sleep."

"Will you sleep with me?" she asked.

"I will," he said.

"I mean really sleep. I'm not up to anything else."

"I'll sleep."

"You sure? It was terrible, Son. Terrible. I don't want to think about it, but I know I will and I don't want to do it alone."

"I know. I'll stay with you. You sleep and I'll watch you."

Jadine stepped back from him. "Oh, the hell with it. You won't. You'll start something and I'm not up to it."

"Relax. Stop imagining things. You want somebody to be with tonight, so I'll do it. Don't complicate it."

"You start something and I'll throw you out."

"All right. Take off your dress and get in the bed."

Jadine folded her arms behind her and unzipped the top part of her dress. He reached behind her and pulled it the rest of the way down. Jadine stepped out of it and sat down on the bed. "No foolishness, Son. I'm serious." Her voice sounded small and tired.

"So am I," he said, and began unbuttoning his shirt. Jadine sat on the bed and watched him. Then, for the first time, she saw his huge hands. One hand alone was big enough for two. A finger spread that could reach from hither to yon. The first time she had been aware of his hands they were clasped over his head under Sydney's gun, so she had not really seen them. The second time was at the beach when he touched the bottom of her foot with one finger. She had not looked then either, only felt that fingerprint in the arch of her sole. Now she could not help looking, seeing those hands large enough to sit down in. Large enough to hold your whole head. Large enough, maybe, to put your whole self into.

"I hope you are serious," she said. She left her panties on and got under the sheet. Son undressed completely and Jadine shot him a quick look to see if he had an erection.

"Look at you," she said. "You're going to meddle me and all I want is rest."

"Be quiet," he said. "I'm not meddling you. I can't control that, but I can control whether I meddle you." He walked to the bed and got in next to her.

"Well, how am I supposed to sleep with you taking up half the sheet in that tent?"

"Don't think about it and it'll go away."

"I'll bet. You sound like a character in those blue comics."

"Hush."

Jadine turned round on her stomach and then her side, with her back to him. After a silence during which she listened for but could not hear his breathing, she said, "Have you slept with anybody since you jumped ship?"

"Yes."

"You have?" She raised her head. "Who? I mean where?"

"In town."

"Oh *ho*." She put her head back on the pillow. "Who?"

"Can't remember her name."

"Men. Why can't you remember her name? Didn't Yardman tell you her name?"

"Gideon."

"Gideon. Didn't he introduce you?"

"Go to sleep, Jadine."

"I can't. I'm tired, but not sleepy."

"You're agitated. Calm down."

"You won't bother me? I don't want to wrestle."

"I won't bother you. I'll just be here while you sleep, just like I said I would."

"I'm not up to any fucking."

"For somebody who's not up to it, you sure bring it up a lot."

"I know what's going to happen. I'll fall asleep and then I'll feel something cold on my thigh."

"Nothing cold is going to be on your thigh."

"I just don't want to fuck, that's all."

"I didn't ask you to, did I? If I wanted to make love, I'd ask you."

"I didn't say make love, I said—"

"I know what you said."

"You don't like me to use that word, do you? Men."

"Go to sleep. Nobody's talking about fucking or making love but you."

"Admit it. You don't like me to say fuck."

"No."

"Hypocrite."

Son thought he must have had this conversation two million times. It never varied, this dance. Except when you paid your money and there was no seduction involved. Free stuff was always a pain in the ass, and it annoyed him that this conversation should be taking place with this sponge-colored girl with mink eyes whom he was certain he could not live in the world without. He wished she would either fall asleep, throw him out or jump him. "Listen," he said, "I'm not a hypocrite. Whatever you call it, I'm not doing it."

"What do you call it?" Jadine turned over and lay on her back.

"I don't call it anything. I don't have the language for it."

"Why not?"

"I just don't. It's not love-making and it's not fucking."

"If it's not making love, it's because you don't love me and you said at the beach that you did."

"I said that because I don't know how else to say it. If I had another way, I'd have used it. Whatever I want to do to you—that's not it."

"What do you want to do to me? I mean if you had the language what would you do?"

"I'd make you close your eyes," he said, and when he didn't add anything Jadine raised up on her elbows.

"Is that all?"

"Then I'd ask you what you saw."

She lay back down. "I don't see anything."

"Nothing?"

"Nothing."

"Not even the dark?"

"Oh, yes, that."

"Is it all dark? Nothing else? No lights moving around? No stars? No moon?"

"No. Nothing. Just black."

"Imagine something. Something that fits in the dark. Say the dark is the sky at night. Imagine something in it."

"A star?"

"Yes."

"I can't. I can't see it."

"Okay. Don't try to see it. Try to be it. Would you like to know what it's like to be one? Be a star?"

"A movie star?"

"No, a star star. In the sky. Keep your eyes closed, think about what it feels like to be one." He moved over to her and kissed her shoulder. "Imagine yourself in that dark, all alone in the sky at night. Nobody is around you. You are by yourself, just shining there. You know how a star is supposed to twinkle? We say twinkle because that is how it looks, but when a star feels itself, it's not a twinkle, it's more like a throb. Star throbs. Over and over and over. Like this. Stars just throb and throb and throb and sometimes, when they can't throb anymore, when they can't hold it anymore, they fall out of the sky."

7

THE BLACK GIRLS in New York City were crying and their men were looking neither to the right nor to the left. Not because they were heedless, or intent on what was before them, but they did not wish to see the crying, crying girls split into two parts by their tight jeans, screaming at the top of their high, high heels, straining against the pull of their braids and the fluorescent combs holding their hair. Oh, their mouths were heavy with plum lipstick and their eyebrows were a thin gay line, but nothing could stop their crying and nothing could persuade their men to look to the right or look to the left. They stoked their cocks into bikini underwear and opened their shirts to their tits. But they walked on tippy-toe through the streets looking straight ahead, and Son looked in vain for children. He couldn't find them anywhere There were short people and people under twelve years of age, but they had no child's vulnerability, no unstuck laughter. They cracked into the M2 bus like terrified bison running for their lives, for fear the school at their backs would grab them and eat them up one more time. It wasn't until he caught the downtown A that he saw what they had done with their childhood. They had wrapped it in dark cloth, sneaked it underground and thrown it all over the trains. Like blazing jewels, the subway cars burst from the tunnels to the platforms shining with the recognizable artifacts of childhood: fantasy, magic, ego, energy, humor and paint. They had taken it all underground. Pax and Stay High and the Three Yard Boys. Teen, P-Komet and Popeye. He sat on a bench at the Fifty-ninth Street station watching the childhood flash by. Now all he needed to know was where were the old people. Where were the Thérèses and Gideons of New York? They were not on the subways and they were not in the street. Perhaps they were all in kennels. That must be the reason the men walked that way—on tippy-toe looking neither to the right nor to the left. The old people were in kennels and childhood was underground. But why were all the black girls crying on buses, in Red Apple lines, at traffic lights and behind the counters of Chemical Bank? Crying from a grief so stark you would have thought they'd been condemned to death by starvation in the lobby of Alice Tully Hall. Death by starvation in Mikell's, death by starvation on the campus of C.U.N.Y. And death by starvation at the reception desks of large corporations. It depressed him, all that crying, for it was silent and veiled by plum lipstick and the thin gay lines over their eyes. Who did this to you? Who has done this thing to you? he wondered, as he walked down Columbus Avenue looking first to the right and then to the left. The street was choked with beautiful males who had found the whole business of being black and men at the same time too difficult and so they'd dumped it. They had snipped off their testicles and pasted them to their chests; they put the weighty wigs Alma Estée dreamed of on their heads and feathery eyelashes on their eyes. They flung sharp hips away to the right and away to the left and smiled sweetly at the crying girls and the men on tippy-toe. Only the Hilton whores seemed to him quiet and feeling no pain. He had tried a little television that first day, but the black people in whiteface playing black people in blackface unnerved him. Even their skin had changed through the marvel of color TV. A gray patina covered them all and they were happy. Really happy. Even without looking at their gray, no-color faces, the sound of their televised laughter was enough to tell him so. Different laughter from what he remembered it to be—without irony or defiance or genuine amusement. Now all he heard were shrieks of satisfaction. It made him shiver. How long had he been gone, anyway? If those were the black folks he was carrying around in his heart all those years, who on earth was he? The trouble he'd had the night he checked in was representative of how estranged he felt from these new people. The Hickey Freeman suit passed muster easily enough, and he wadded Jadine's four hundred dollars in his fist as he approached the desk. The clerk was about to give him a very hard time because no, he would not be paying with a credit card, and no, no check either. Cash. Two nights. Cash. Son had chosen that line to wait in because the clerk's little pecan-pie face looked friendly; now he realized the boy was in love with his identification badge. Son was surprised at himself. He seldom misjudged people. He thought the love thing with Jadine must have thrown his sensibilities off, derailed his judgment, so he leaned toward the clerk and whispered, "Brother, do you want to get home tonight? This ain't your fuckin hotel." But now he thought it was less an error in judgment than it was being confronted with a whole new race of people he was once familiar with.

He was heart-weary when he opened the door to his room, and the purple carpet fairly took his breath away. He wanted her in that room with him giving him the balance he was losing, the ballast and counterweight to the stone of sorrow New York City had given him. Jadine would lighten up the purple carpet, soften the tooth-white walls. She'd read the room-service menu as though it were a private message to them both and then choose a corner of the room to make love in. They had spent two whole days following the Christmas dinner in or near each other's arms, and the demoralized house never noticed. But they both understood that Son had to get out fast, so he used Jadine's ticket and Gideon's passport, and split. She was to follow as soon as she could get a flight and had seen what Ondine's and Sydney's situation was—whether they would stay or leave.

He sat down in a plastic tub chair, rested his arms on the windowsill and looked down at Fifty-third Street. How hard this one night's wait would be, shot full already of fallen airplanes and missed connections. Even if he managed to sleep from 6:30 p.m. to 6:30 a.m., what would he do with the morning? Refuse to have breakfast until nine; shave long and shower longer till noon when Air France would glide like a crane into Kennedy. Did she say baggage claim or lobby? Or did she say to wait at the hotel? His mouth went suddenly dry with the possibility of losing her in that city. Was he in the right hotel? Was it the New York Hilton or the Statler Hilton? She just said Hilton. There was no way to call and find out without letting Sydney know. He might answer the phone himself, or Ondine might, and if they knew she was joining him, they both might try to stop her. He could call Gideon. He tried to remember that hillside hut, but all he could summon were the powder pink walls and the record player sitting on a shelf. Gideon had no telephone, but messages got to him via a store halfway down the hill that sold rum and meat pies and lent out hair clippers.

That was foolish. What could Gideon tell him anyway? He was so angry at the Americans, he was actually helping Thérèse prepare all sorts of potions and incantations for their destruction, just in case there was such a thing as magic after all. And he was quite willing to lend his passport to the man who shared his anger at the Americans. He could not understand why Son wanted to return to the country too terrible for dying, but he agreed that one black face would look like another and a difference of twenty years would not be noticed in a black man's five-year-old passport. Thérèse gave Son, as a going-away present, a tiny, dirty bag of good fortune, but he tossed it away—it *looked* like ganja and he didn't want to draw any attention to himself at customs. He took what Jadine gave him and left. Now, on the second day of their separation he would just have to wait and keep on imagining disaster since his emotions were so young that this heavy, grown-up love made him feel fresh-born, unprecedented, surrounded by an extended present loaded with harm.

There was nothing to do; he would have to trust to her city-sense to do the right thing and be in the right places. And this time tomorrow he could smooth back her hair and sweep her eyebrows with his thumb. This time tomorrow the side teeth in her smile would divert him from what she was saying or laughing at. He loved to watch her eyes when she was not watching his. And to listen to the four/four time of her heels. Son sat there wagging his knees back and forth like a schoolboy. Not thinking most of the important things there were to think about: What would they do? Where would they go, live? How would he earn money to take care of her and, later, their children? He smiled at the vigor of his own heartbeat at the thought of her having his baby. Watch her. He would watch her stomach while she slept just the way he had when he'd lived like an animal around the house and spent the hind part of the night at her bedside pressing his dreams into hers. Now those dreams embarrassed him. The mewings of an adolescent brutalized by loneliness for a world he thought he would never see again.

There was a future. A reason for hauling ass in the morning. No more moment to moment play-it-as-it-comes existence. That stomach required planning. Thinking through a move long before it was made. What would he name his son? Son of Son?

He should have thought about that before he left. Perhaps he would have taken things: cash, jewelry and the passport of a stranger instead of a friend. Instead he took the clothes, one piece of luggage and the Bally shoes and his bottle of Paco Rabanne. He saw it all as a rescue: first tearing her mind away from that blinding awe. Then the physical escape from the plantation. His first, hers to follow two days later. Unless . . . he remembered sitting at the foot of the table, gobbling the food, watching her pour *his* wine, listening to her take *his* part, trying to calm Ondine and Sydney to *his* satisfaction. Just as she had done the first night when they found him in the closet. He would not look at her then—refused to lock with those mink-dark eyes that looked at him with more distaste than Valerian's had. The mocking voice, the superior managerial, administrative, clerk-in-a-fucking-loan-office tone she took. Gatekeeper, advance bitch, house-bitch, welfare office torpedo, corporate cunt, tar baby side-of-the-road whore trap, who called a black man old enough to be her father "Yardman" and who couldn't give a shit who he himself was and only wanted his name to file away in her restrung brain so she could remember it when the cops came to fill out the report—five eleven, maybe six feet, black as coal with the breath and table manners of a rhino. But underneath her efficiency and know-it-all sass were wind chimes. Nine rectangles of crystal, rainbowed in the light. Fragile pieces of glass tinkling as long as the breeze was gentle. But in more vigorous weather the thread that held it together would snap. So it would be his duty to keep the climate mild for her, to hold back with his hands if need be thunder, drought and all manner of winterkill, and he would blow with his own lips a gentle enough breeze for her to tinkle in. The bird-like defenselessness he had loved while she slept and saw when she took his hand on the stairs was his to protect. He would have to be alert, feed her with his mouth if he had to, construct a world of steel and down for her to flourish in, for the love thing was already there. He had been looking for her all his life, and even when he thought he had found her, in other ports and other places, he shied away. He stood in her bedroom, a towel wrapped around his waist. Clean as a whistle, having just said the nastiest thing he could think of to her. Staring at a heart-red tree desperately in love with a woman he could not risk loving because he could not afford to lose her. For if he loved and lost this woman whose sleeping face was the limit his eyes could safely behold and whose wakened face threw him into confusion, he would surely lose the world. So he made himself disgusting to her. Insulted and offended her. Gave her sufficient cause to help him keep his love in chains and hoped to God the lock would hold. It snapped like a string.

He stood up, searching for the anger that had shaken him so that first time and again on Christmas Day. But here in this island of crying girls and men on tippy-toe, he could not find it. Even conjuring up that head-of-a-coin profile, the unfleshed skin and evening eyes, was not a vivid enough memory to produce it. He needed the blood-clot heads of the bougainvillea, the simple green rage of the avocado, the fruit of the banana trees puffed up and stiff like the fingers of gouty kings. Here prestressed concrete and steel contained anger, folded it back on itself to become a craving for things rather than vengeance. Still, he thought of it not just as love, but as rescue. He took off his clothes and filled the tub, smiling to think of what the leaden waves of the Atlantic had become in the hands of civilization. The triumph of ingenuity that had transferred the bored treachery of the sea into a playful gush of water that did exactly what it was told. And why not? Wilderness wasn't wild anymore or threatening; wildlife needed human protection to exist at all.

Stretched out in the water, his eyes closed, he thought of this city that he should have remembered. Where was the wavy-seven language on the windows of the butcher shops? The laundries named Hand. What had they done to the Apollo? Where was Michaux's, the awnings on St. Nicholas Avenue? Who were these people on the islands in the middle of Broadway and where were the trees? There used to be trees. Trees coming out of the concrete. But nobody would chop down a tree in New York, so he guessed he must have been wrong. That must have been some other city he had been memorizing.

JADINE sat in the taxi barely able to see over her luggage piled in the seat in front of her. Unlike the anxiety-ridden man in a Hilton bathtub, she wanted to giggle. New York made her feel like giggling, she was so happy to be back in the arms of that barfly with the busted teeth and armpit breath. New York oiled her joints and she moved as though they were oiled. Her legs were longer here, her neck really connected her body to her head. After two months of stingless bees, butterflies and avocado trees, the smart thin trees on Fifty-third Street refreshed her. They were to scale, human-sized, and the buildings did not threaten her like the hills of the island had, for these were full of people whose joints were oiled just like hers. This is home, she thought with an orphan's delight; not Paris, not Baltimore, not Philadelphia. This is home. The city had gone on to something more interesting to it than the black people who had fascinated it a decade ago, but if ever there was a black woman's town, New York was it. No, no, not over there making land-use decisions, or deciding what was or was not information. But there, there, there and there. Snapping whips behind the tellers' windows, kicking ass at Con Edison offices, barking orders in the record companies, hospitals, public schools. They refused loans at Household Finance, withheld unemployment checks and drivers' licenses, issued parking tickets and summonses. Gave enemas, blood transfusions and please lady don't make me mad. They jacked up meetings in boardrooms, turned out luncheons, energized parties, redefined fashion, tipped scales, removed lids, cracked covers and turned an entire telephone company into such a diamondhead of hostility the company paid you for not talking to their operators. The manifesto was simple: "Talk shit. Take none." Jadine remembered and loved it all. This would be her city too, her place, the place she spent a whole summer once in love with Oom. Riding the subways looking for his name, first as a talisman, then as a friend and finally as a lover in the tunnels of New York City. And now she would take it; take it and give it to Son. They would make it theirs. She would show it, reveal it to him, live it with him. They would fall out of Max's Kansas City at 4:00 a.m.; they would promenade Third Avenue from the Fifties to SoHo; they would fight landlords and drink coffee in the Village, eat bean pie on 135th Street, paella on Eighty-first Street; they would laugh in the sex boutiques, eat yogurt on the steps of the Forty-second Street library; listen to RVR and BLS, buy mugs in Azuma's, chocolate chip cookies in Grand Central Station, drink margaritas at Suggs, and shop Spanish and West Indian at the Park Avenue Market. She would look up Dawn and Betty and Aisha and show him off: her fine frame, her stag, her man.

Jadine was so ruttish by the time she got to the Hilton, she could barely stand still for the doorman to take her bags, and when she was checked in, and had gotten his room number from information, she did not call him—she took the elevator to his floor and banged on the door. When he opened it, she jumped on him with her legs around his waist crashing him into the purple carpet.

But he insisted on Eloe. In spite of the Gate and Central Park in the snow. They moved into Dawn's apartment, available to them for four months while she was on the Coast shooting her seventh pilot, the one that was sure to stick. Four months in that apartment of long and bristling winter days when he slowed her down to the speed of a tulip. Murky New York days when she spun him like a top until he slammed into the headboard. He met her women friends—girls who talked with their shoulders, and found them less than she; he met her men friends—alight with success, almost rich—and found them less than he. Everybody was ridiculous, maimed or unhappy to them, so satisfied were they with their mutual adoration. He thought he would have to stamp the ground, paw it and butt horns with every male they came in contact with, but he didn't. Her devotion surprised him; she looked only at him and grew her own horns when other men got out of line. She was startled and pleased to discover that his beauty, so sudden and impressive on Isle des Chevaliers, was volcanic in the city. As if waitresses and the eyes of passersby had not already told her, her own friends altered as well in his presence. Dawn went completely Annie Rooney, falling all over herself with helplessness, and generosity. Betty, who had been "into" bisexuality for six months, couldn't get back into the closet fast enough when Son was in the room, and when Jadine told Son about Betty's range of interests, she was angry enough to fight.

Still he insisted on Eloe. Even after she earned $2,500 for four walks and a picture spread all in two weeks and they bought each other pretty things. Even after he worked the bar three afternoons at a fashion show where he got the drinks mixed up, dropped a fifth of gin, and Leonard, the old man who had taken him on as a favor to Jadine, shook his head in disbelief. Son took six bottles of leftover champagne, the $150, and gave it all to her. They got swinging drunk and Jadine laughed in his ear and called him an unskilled sickle-cell-anemia motherfucker.

They were sober too. And he let her be still and cry after she told him about her mother and the awful hat she'd worn to the funeral. Too big and grown-up for a little girl of twelve. She poured her heart out to him and he to her. Dumb things, secret things, sin and heroism. They told each other all of it. Or all they could. He told her what she wished to hear about the war. He could not speak to her or anyone about it coherently so he told her what she wished to hear: no, he never killed anybody "with his hands"; yes, he was wounded and he showed her a burn on his skin from a burst boiler to prove it; yes, he had been afraid, although in truth he had not been, or had not been properly frightened. He had laughed, in fact, laughed all over Vietnam because at eighteen laughter was his only reliable weapon. It was still early in the war, but when trucks sank in mud and grenades exploded too soon or not at all, laughter was always there, almost always; but one day it ran out too, as unreliable as his fucked-up M-14. The silence in his throat where laughter or tears ought to be blew up in his head and he was stockaded, busted and, when he refused to re-up, discharged without honor or humor. He went to Eloe, married Cheyenne, left the set early when a fistfight broke out and found his sleeping wife sleeping with a teenager. He was silent then too as he ran his car through the house and the bed caught on fire. He pulled them both out—the teenager and Cheyenne—but she didn't make it. He watched her wrappings but not her eyes in the hospital and still no sound. It was hearing about Frisco blowing up in a gas field. Old no-good Frisco who used to pay him to clean fish. That did it. His father told him the news when he met him at the bus stop across the state line with money. Told him to hurry; told him to write; and told him about Frisco. In a tiny toilet at the rear of the bus, Son cried like an infant for all the blowings up in Asia.

Jadine kissed his hands and he asked her why she left the States in the first place. She said she always thought she had three choices: marry a dope king or a doctor, model, or teach art at Jackson High. In Europe she thought there might be a fourth choice. They told each other everything. Yet he insisted on Eloe. She listened to him and nodded, thinking anywhere with him would be all right. She was completely happy. After all those sexually efficient men, all those foreplay experts and acrobats, and the nonverbal equipment men, his wildness and fumbling, his corny unself-conscious joy was like blue-sky water. Show me again what it's like to be shining all alone in the sky. And he did that, and he did more. Regarding her whole self as an ear, he whispered into every part of her stories of icecaps and singing fish, The Fox and the Stork, The Monkey and the Lion, The Spider Goes to Market, and so mingled was their sex with adventure and fantasy that to the end of her life she never heard a reference to Little Red Riding Hood without a tremor.

They thought about Isle des Chevaliers sometimes. He would say "ollieballen" and she would scream with laughter. She wrote two misleading postcards to Ondine and Sydney. Got a short, sorrowful, somewhat accusatory letter back which she refused to let sour her happiness. Her leave-taking had been difficult. She was dependent at last on that mulatto with a leer sent by Dr. Michelin as the new yard boy. The Streets seemed not to notice or mind her going. Only Ondine and Sydney were cut up about it. She promised to send for them as soon as they wanted her to, but she had to take this gig, she told them, and she left the two sullen and confused old people at the kitchen table, their hearts steeled against her leaving, even though her New York trip, she said, was vital if she were to arrange things so all three could live together. She couldn't let them know who waited at the Hilton.

Son and Jadine discussed their situation in Dawn's apartment. Ondine and Sydney seemed unsure of their jobs, but no steps had been taken to let them go, it seemed. Son was less than sympathetic to Ondine's plight because she had acted too shuffle-footed—keeping her white lady's secret "lak it wuz hern" and loving her white lady's baby "lak it wuz hern, too." And much less sympathetic to Sydney because in thirty years he had not split Valerian's skull. Eighty percent of both Sydney's and Ondine's conversation was the caprice and habits of their master.

"You still like that old man, don't you?" Son asked her.

"Who? Valerian?"

"Yes."

"He put me through school, I told you."

"Nothing in return?"

"No. Nothing. Never made a pass, nothing."

"And Margaret?" he asked. "How did she treat you?"

"Okay. She was more distant than he was, but she was nice to me. Nice enough anyway."

"She wasn't very nice to your folks," he said.

"Actually, she was," Jadine answered. "They both were. At least from what I could see of it. That's why I was so took-out that day. I couldn't believe it. They fought like we did in grade school."

"Wild," he said, thinking of rescue.

"Really wild." Jadine let two of her fingers do the Charleston in the hair of his chest. "We'll get rich and send for them and live happily ever after," she said, and thought it was so, but not right this minute, not today, there was so much nestling to do. They had only two months left in the apartment, but they needed more time. Jadine habitually shaved herself all over like a fourth grade Girl Scout and he finally got around to telling her he wanted some body hair. But they needed time for it to grow. Much more time. Time for her to sketch him right for once. But why sketch when she could touch? Time to make a genuine paella; time for her to finish the macramé plant holder, for him to fix the dishwasher. They must have been in love—they never once turned on the television. They forgot to buy cigarettes or alcohol and they didn't even jog in the park.

There wasn't a permanent adult job in the whole of the city for him, so he did teenager's work on occasion and pieces of a grown man's work. He spoke to the men at the shape-up halls. The black men told him Baltimore. Everybody works on the docks in Baltimore. Or Galveston, or San Diego or New Orleans or Savannah. New York—not a chance. There was a little pilfering money—that was about all. Some small-time truckers gave him brute work, look-out work, and sometimes he dropped payoffs when asked. But none of it could hold his attention and one afternoon while he was helping a trucker unload boxes on Broadway and 101st Street, he heard a commotion in the traffic. A young girl with a shaved head and a small ring in her nostril was cursing a man right in the middle of the street. The man, who looked African or West Indian to Son by the innocent confusion in his face, stood watching her in silence. Two or three of his friends leaned on cars, looking elsewhere but obviously waiting for the finale. The girl was in jeans, platform shoes and a thin sweater. She had the voice of a sergeant and her language was nasty enough to be memorable. Cars honked at them before swerving into parallel lanes; pedestrians glanced and then pretended they weren't there. Only Son and people in second-story windows gave them their undivided attention. It was beyond embarrassment. The girl's face was as tight and mean as broccoli, her forefinger shot bullets into the pavement. But inside her narrowed angry eyes were many other eyes—some of them hurt, some brave, some just lonely hollow eyes, and her shaved head reminded Son of his sister. He listened to the abuse, the catalog of shame and rage until the man felt safe enough (his back-up team still leaned on the cars) to turn his back on her and walk away. None of which dulled the glitter of her nose ring or shut her mouth. She word-whipped him on down the street and probably would have followed him to make it stick except Son, made miserable by the eyes inside her eyes, went over and stood in front of her with his arms wide open. She looked at him with hatred older than lava.

"Come here," he said.

She didn't move, so he put his arms around her to shield her from the eyes of the second-story people and bank her fire. The girl bucked, but he wouldn't let her go. "You're going to freeze to death," he said. "Let me buy you a drink." She tipped her forehead onto his chest then, and began to cry.

"Come on," he said. "There's a place down the block." Arm around her shoulder, he led the way to a Chinese restaurant and ordered her gin. She drank and began to tell him about the man, but Son shook his head. "Don't," he said. "Don't think about it. You got a place to stay?"

She said, "Not tonight, I don't," so he left the job hauling boxes and took her home.

All three, Nommo, Jadine and Son, went to a delicatessen where, after much discussion, they bought potato chips, A & W root beer, and three Payday candy bars with Son's last ten-dollar bill. They ate it all in the snow. Cold and giggling they trudged back to the apartment where Son and Jadine slept like puppies and Nommo made off with the change.

Yet he insisted on Eloe. She agreed but before they could make plans, she stubbed her big toe on a metal plate bolted to the middle of Sixth Avenue. By the time she got home, her toe was the size of a plum and very painful. Son made a splint for it out of emery boards and the ribbon from a Valentine candy box. All night he woke at half-hour intervals to bathe her toe in an Epsom salt solution. In the morning, the swelling had decreased and he left for work while she slept. When she woke and hobbled to the bathroom she saw that he had drawn a happily obscene picture under the toilet lid. At his coffee break he called.

"How's your toe?"

"Lonely."

"Mine too."

"Come home for lunch."

"I only have thirty minutes for lunch, baby."

"Come anyway."

"I won't be able to get back in time. I'll lose a half-day's pay."

"I'll make it worth your while."

He came home and didn't report to work again until she could walk effortlessly. In the meantime they ate Chinese food in the tub. She read *True Confessions* stories to him with appropriate "white girl" voices and gestures and he laughed until his chest hurt. She read Césaire to him and he closed his eyes. She read the sexy parts of the Bible and he looked at her.

Gradually she came to feel unorphaned. He cherished and safeguarded her. When she woke in the night from an uneasy dream she had only to turn and there was the stability of his shoulder and his limitless, eternal chest. No part of her was hidden from him. She wondered if she should hold back, keep something in store from him, but he opened the hair on her head with his fingers and drove his tongue through the part. There was nothing to forgive, nothing to win and the future was five minutes away. He unorphaned her completely. Gave her a brand-new childhood. They were the last lovers in New York City—the first in the world—so their passion was inefficient and kept no savings account. They spent it like Texans. When he had a sore throat so bad he could not speak, she put him to bed and drew a checker board on the inside of a Bergdorf box. They played the game with M&M's. It didn't work because the crowns wouldn't stay still, so they used her Enovids instead, partly because of their plane surface and partly to keep her from eating the pieces jumped by her kings. She told him straight brandy was good for his throat and made him drink so much so fast, he passed out. She didn't like his being unconscious without her so she drank the rest and passed out with him. He woke first and vomited the strep away. After bathing and dressing, he watched her sleep. She woke unable to see, speak or move and he put his huge hand on her forehead until she could. They didn't go to parties anymore—other people interfered with their view of each other. They stopped going to Suggs and Across 110th Street. They stopped laughing and began to smile at each other. From across the room, across the mattress, across the table. Their language diminished to code at times, and at others ballooned to monologues delivered while cradled in the other's arms. They never looked at the sky or got up early to see a sunrise. They played no music and hadn't the foggiest notion that spring was on its way. Vaguely aware of such things when they were apart, together they could not concentrate on the given world. They reinvented it, remembered it through the other. He looked at her face in the mirror and was reminded of days at sea when water looked like sky. She surveyed his body and thought of oranges, playing jacks, and casks of green wine. He was still life, babies, cut glass, indigo, hand spears, dew, cadmium yellow, Hansa red, moss green and the recollection of a tree that wanted to dance with her. It was difficult to be sober, to take anything other than themselves seriously, but they managed occasionally. She thought about calling her old professor who said he could always find work for her. But maybe May would be a better time to ring him—after exams. They discussed opening a retail flower shop and boutique that they could call Jade and Son; they discussed bank robbery and an agency for black models; they discussed the New School and Empire State and figured out a way to collect Gideon's unemployment checks.

But Jadine was not worried. She had $1,940 in the bank, $5,000 in Paris and connections. If push came to shove, she'd go permanent with an agency and work her behind off.

The check scheme worked, but he had time to pick up just one check before they left hand-in-hand for Eloe.

8

THE AIR was so charged with pain the angel trumpets could not breathe it. Rows of them wrinkled on the vine and fell unnoticed right in Valerian's sightline. He sat in the greenhouse oblivious to everything but 1950 when he heard for the first time his son's song.

All the years since, he thought she drank, was a not-so-secret alcoholic: the sleeping masks, the clumsiness, the beauty spa vacations, the withdrawals, the hard-to-wake mornings, the night crying, the irritability, the sloppy candy-kisses mother love. He thought she drank—heavily, in private, and that was why she took only wine and sherry in his presence. Nondrinkers take real drinks; only secret drinkers insist on Chablis at every occasion—or so he thought. And he wished it were true. He was devastated knowing that she had never been drunk, had never been "out of her mind," never in a stupor, never hung-over, never manic from being dry too long. Drunkenness he could take, *had* taken, in fact, since he'd always believed it. Anything was better than knowing that a pretty (and pretty nice) sober young woman had loved the bloodying of her own baby. Had loved it dearly. Had once locked herself in the bathroom, a pair of cuticle scissors in her hand, to keep from succumbing to that love. Nothing serious, though. No throwing across the room, or out of the window. No scalding, no fist work. Just a delicious pin-stab in sweet creamy flesh. That was her word, "delicious." "I knew it was wrong, knew it was bad. But something about it was delicious too." She was telling him, saying it aloud at the dinner table after everyone had gone. His knees were trembling and he'd had to sit down again. The Negroes had all gone out of the room, disappeared like bushes, trees, out of his line of vision, and left the two of them in the light of the chandelier. She was standing there next to him, her cheek white again after the blow Ondine had given her, her hair rumpled but lovely. She was serene standing there saying it, and he agreed with that, thought it could be, must be, true—that it was delicious, for at that moment it would have been delicious to him too if he could have picked up the carving knife lying on the platter next to the carcass of the goose and slashed into her lovely Valentine face. Delicious. Conclusive and delicious. But he could not concentrate. His knees were trembling, his fingers shuddering on the tablecloth. He didn't want to see them shaking there, but he did not want to see her face either. He thought about that—how or whether to stop looking at her and look instead at his hands. He couldn't make up his mind and he couldn't shift his gaze. But he thought about it while she was saying it. "It's funny, but I would see the mark and hear him cry but somehow I didn't believe it hurt all that much." "Mark" she called it. She saw the mark. Didn't think it hurt "all that much." Like a laboratory assistant removing the spleen of a cute but comatose mouse.

Suddenly he knew exactly what to do: go to him. Go to Michael. Find him, touch him, rub him, hold him in his arms. Now. He tried to stand but the spastic legs defied him.

"I cannot hear anymore," he said. "I can't."

She stopped then and looked at him with complete understanding and complete patience. Still he could not stand. She understood that too, and without another word walked slowly out of the room, "Later," her footsteps seemed to say, "when you are stronger, I will say it to you. Share it with you. Make it yours as well as mine."

Valerian did not move. I will never be that strong, he thought. I will never be strong enough to hear it. I have to die now or go to him. When I move from this table I will do one or the other, nothing in between. I will never be able to hear it.

It was two in the morning when Sydney returned dressed in robe, slippers and pajama bottoms. Valerian was sitting in the chandelier light—legs and fingers finally at rest.

"You should go on up to bed, Mr. Street."

Valerian gave a small shake of his head. If he went up he might never come down again and if he stood up it would only be to die or go to Michael.

"Get some rest; figure things out in the morning," Sydney said.

Valerian nodded.

The table was precisely as it was when Sydney guided the sobbing Ondine away. No one had moved a thing while he helped Ondine undress, made her lie down and rubbed her feet until she slept. But he could not sleep at all. The sea spread around him and his wife. They were afloat in it and if removed from the island there was nowhere to land. They had no house, no place of their own. Some certificates worth a bit, but no savings. Just the promises of being taken care of in the will of a man whose wife his own wife had slapped. Sydney started to clear the table and stack things on the sideboard. The suspense was too great, so he asked him outright.

"Mr. Street."

Valerian showed him his evening eyes, but did not speak.

"You going to let us go?"

Valerian stared at Sydney trying to focus on, then comprehend, the question.

"What?"

"Me and Ondine. You going to let us go?"

Valerian rested his forehead in his hand. "I don't know. I don't know anything," he said, and Sydney had to be content for now with that answer spoken faintly, remotely, for Valerian, holding on to his head, fell back into the waxen horror Sydney had tried to penetrate. He was still there at six the next morning. His eyes closed at last, his mind slowed to an occasional thud. He woke because nature required him to. Not to die or board an airplane headed for his son, but to go to the bathroom. So he did move from the table and he climbed the stairs on frail new legs. Once attending to that call, it was not unthinkable to attend to another—to rinse his face, clean his teeth, brush back his hair with his hands. He took off his shoes and sat on the bed holding them. The picture of the beautiful boy in the laundry under the sink, singing because he could not speak or cry—because he had no vocabulary for what was happening to him, who sang la la la, la la la instead—that picture had stayed with Valerian all night, through fitful sleep, and was there between his stockinged feet in the morning.

I have to cry about this, Valerian thought. I have got to shed tears about this. But not water, please God, may they be blood. I have to cry blood tears for his wounds. But I will need several lives, life after life after life after life, one for each wound, one for every trickle of blood, for every burn. I will need a lifetime of blood tears for each one of them. And then more. Lives upon lives upon lives for the the the the the. Hurt. The deep-down eternal little boy hurt. The not knowing when, the never knowing why, and never being able to shape the tongue to speak, let alone the mind to cogitate how the one person in the world upon whom he was totally, completely dependent—the one person he could not even choose not to love—could do that to him. Believing at last as a little boy would that he deserved it, must deserve it, otherwise it would not be happening to him. That no world in the world would be imagined, thought up, or even accidentally formed not to say say say say *created* that would permit such a thing to happen. And he is right. No world in the world would allow it. So this is not the world at all. It must be something else. I have lived in it and I will die out of it but it is not the world. This is not life. This is some other thing.

It comforted him a bit, knowing that whatever this was it was not life. He achieved a kind of blank, whited-out, no-feeling-at-all that he hoped would sustain him until the blood tears came. Until his heart, revivified, pumped its way along for a single purpose: to spill out of his eyes throughout the millennia he would have to live. Until then, then.

Margaret awoke very early that morning, having had the dream she ought to have had: it was unspeakable. She rose at once; the wonderful relief of public humiliation, the solid security of the pillory, were upon her. Like the much-sought-after, finally captured, strangler, she wore that look of harmony that in newspaper photos comes across as arrogance, or impenitence at the least. The harmony that comes from the relieved discovery that the jig is up. The parts settle back into their proper places, and the strangler sighs, "Thank God I didn't get away scot-free." She had no idea of what would be next, but that was not a problem to which she had to provide a solution. That was the future, her job at hand was to reveal the past. Right now she had to wash her hair, *hard*. Soap it with mountains of lather, and rinse it over and over again. Then she sat in the sun against every instruction ever given her about the care of her hair, and let it dry.

L'Arbe de la Croix became a house of shadows. Couples locked into each other or away from each other, the murmurings of whose hearts rivaled the dreaming daisy trees. Jadine and Son off together plotting. Sydney and Ondine walking on glass shards, afraid, angry, sullen. Snapping at one another one minute, soothing each other the next. Valerian stayed mostly in his room; the greenhouse remained untended, the mail unread. Silence pressed down on the dahlias and cyclamen—for there was no diet of music anymore. Sydney brought pieces of dinner to the table but no one was there. Jadine and Son foraged in the refrigerator—accomplices. Margaret appeared for breakfast coffee only. Sydney took trays of halfheartedly prepared sandwiches to Valerian's room and brought them back untouched.

Margaret told her husband in pieces. Little by little, she

spooned it out to him a sip here a drop there. A fleeting sentence in midair as they passed on the stairs: "It was not as often as you think and there were long, long periods of happiness between us in between." But he had stepped inside his bedroom door. Another time she said, "Don't try to persuade yourself that I didn't love him. He was more important to me than my life. Than my life." She had to repeat the phrase for his back was receding fast. He never directed those gloaming eyes her way. She told him in bite-sized pieces, small enough for him to swallow quickly because she did not have the vocabulary to describe what she had come to know, remember. So there was no way or reason to describe those long quiet days when the sun was drained and nobody ever on the street. There were magazines, of course, to look forward to, but neither *Life* nor *Time* could fill a morning. It started on a day like that. Just once she did it, a slip, and then once more, and it became the thing to look forward to, to resist, to succumb to, to plan, to be horrified by, to forget, because out of the doing of it came the reason. And she was outraged by that infant needfulness. There were times when she absolutely had to limit its *being there;* stop its implicit and explicit demand for her best and constant self. She could not describe her loathing of its prodigious appetite for security—the criminal arrogance of an infant's conviction that while he slept, someone is there; that when he wakes, someone is there; that when he is hungry, food will somehow magically be provided. So she told him that part that was palatable: that she could not control herself—which was true, for when she felt hostage to that massive insolence, that stupid trust, she could not help piercing it.

Finally, Margaret entered his room one night and locked the door behind her.

"I've just spoken to Michael," she said.

Valerian could not believe it. She could call him? Speak to him? Say his name? Did she think it was business as usual?

"He said he sent two cables telling us he couldn't make it.

Two. Neither one was telephoned to us. I asked him to call B. J. Bridges. Obviously we don't need any guests at New Year's."

Valerian was speechless. She was going to go on about it, chatting about things just as if nothing had happened. The blood had not dropped out of his eyes yet, so this still was not life. He could get through it because it was some other thing he was living.

"How dare you call him?" he asked hoarsely. "How do you dare?"

"He isn't damaged, Valerian. He *isn't*."

Valerian said nothing; he only stared at her. She was even lovelier now that her hair had no spray in it, that it was not tortured into Art Deco, now that it hung according to its own will and the shape of her head. And she wore no make-up. Little charming eyebrows instead of styled ones, and the thin top lip was much nicer than the full one she ritually painted.

"How can you know that? How can you know what is damage and what is not? If you don't know the difference between between between between." He stopped, he could not say it. "How do you know the difference between what is damaged and what is healed?"

"I know; I see him; I visit him. Believe me, he's fine. Finer than most."

They were both silent for a few moments and then Margaret said, "You want to ask me why. Don't. I can't answer that. I can tell you that I was more successful in keeping myself from doing it than not. When it did happen, it was out of my control. I thought at first it was because he was crying or wouldn't sleep. But then sometimes it was in order to make him cry, or to wake him from sleep."

"I can't hear this, Margaret."

"You can. I have *done* it, lived with it. You can hear it."

She seemed strong to him. He was wasting away, filed to nothing by grief, and she was strong, stronger. Talking about it as though it were a case history, an operation, some surgery that had been performed on her that she had survived and she was describing it to him.

"You are disgusting. You are are are are monstrous. You did it because you are monstrous."

"I did it because I could, Valerian, and I stopped doing it or wanting to do it when I couldn't."

"Couldn't?"

"Yes, couldn't. When he was too big, when he could do it back, when he could . . . tell."

"Leave me."

"He's fine, I'm telling you. He's all right."

"Please leave me."

She understood, understood completely, and without another word she unlocked the door and left.

Another time she waited for him at the breakfast table and said, "You are angry because he didn't tell you."

"Why didn't he tell me?" Valerian had not thought of that yet; he had been living with just the picture of the boy under the sink and had only been hearing the la la la, la la la, but now he realized that was part of his anger. "Why didn't he tell me?"

"He was probably too ashamed."

"Oh, God."

"I think he is still ashamed."

Valerian's hands were shuddering again. "Why does he love you?" he asked her over his shuddering fingers. "Why does he love *you?*"

"Because I love him."

Valerian shook his head and asked her a third time, "Why does he love you?"

"He knows I love him," she said, "that I couldn't help it."

Valerian shouted then, at the top of his throat, "Why does he love you?"

Margaret closed her blue-if-it's-a-boy blue eyes. "I don't know."

Now the tears came. Not all at once. Not in the rush of blood he anticipated, longed for; rather a twilight glimmer, a little mercury in the eyes that grew brighter and brighter. That was the beginning and he knew there would be more of them. For now he would settle for this bright burning.

Margaret opened her eyes and looked into his. "Hit me," she said softly. "Hit me, Valerian."

His shuddering fingers went wild at the thought of touching her, making physical contact with that skin. His whole body recoiled. "No," he said. "No."

"Please. Please."

"*No*"

"You have to. Please, you have to."

Now he could see the lines, the ones the make-up had shielded brilliantly. A thread here and there and the roots of her hair were markedly different from the rest. She looked real. Not like a piece of Valerian candy, but like a person on a bus, already formed, fleshed, thick with a life which is not yours and not accessible to you.

"Tomorrow," he said. "Perhaps tomorrow."

Every day she asked him, every day he answered, "Tomorrow, perhaps tomorrow." But he never did and she was hard-pressed to think of a way to ease their mutual sorrow.

ON THE FIRST DAY of the year, Margaret pushed open the kitchen door. Ondine was there as she always was; the braids Margaret had snatched were folded quietly now across her head. Margaret, having had the dream she ought to, felt clean, weightless as she walked through the doors and stood at the oak table. Ondine was napping, her head resting on the back of a chair, her feet resting on another. When she heard the grunt of the door hinges, she woke at once and stood up, alert.

"No, no. Sit back down, Ondine."

Ondine shoved her feet into her moccasins and continued to stand. "Can I get you something?" she asked out of habit and out of a need to do what was wanted of her and get the woman out of the kitchen.

"No. No, thank you." Margaret sat down and did not seem disturbed by the painful silence Ondine was keeping after the refusal. She looked past the black woman's silhouette to a place in the shutters where the sky showed through.

"I knew you knew," she said. "I always knew you knew."

Ondine sat down without answering.

"You loved my son, didn't you?" It was more a statement than a question.

"I love anything small that needs it," said Ondine.

"I suppose I should thank you for not saying anything, but I have to tell you that it would have been better, Ondine, if you had. It's terrible living in the same house with your own witness. But I think I understand it. You wanted me to hate you, didn't you? That's why you never said anything all those years. You wanted me to hate you."

"No, I didn't. You . . . you wasn't a whole lot on my mind."

"Oh, yes I was, and you felt good hating me, didn't you? I could be the mean white lady and you could be the good colored one. Did that make it easier for you?"

Ondine did not answer.

"Anyway, I came in here to tell you that I'm sorry."

Ondine sighed. "Me too."

"We could have been friends, Ondine. Like at first when I used to come in your kitchen and eat your food and we laughed all the time. Didn't we, Ondine? Didn't we use to laugh and laugh. Didn't we? I have it right, don't I?"

"You got it right."

"But you wanted to hate me, so you didn't tell."

"There was nobody to tell. It was woman stuff. I couldn't tell your husband and I couldn't tell mine."

"Why didn't you tell me? I mean why didn't you scream at me, stop me, something. You knew and you never said a word."

"I guess I thought you would let us go. If I told Sydney he

might tell Mr. Street and then we'd be out of a job—a good job. I don't know now what I thought, to tell the truth. But once I started keeping it—then it was like my secret too. Sometimes I thought if you all let me go there won't be anyone around to take the edge off it. I didn't want to leave him there, all by himself."

"You should have stopped me."

"You should have stopped yourself."

"I did. I did stop myself after a while, but you could have stopped me right away, Ondine."

Ondine put the heels of her hands on her eyelids. When she removed them, her eyes were red. She blew out a breath and she was old. "Is that my job too? To stop you?"

"No. It's not your job, Ondine. But I wish it had been your duty. I wish you had liked me enough to help me. I was only nineteen. You were—what—thirty? Thirty-five?"

Ondine tilted her head and looked at her employer sideways. She raised her eyebrows slowly and then squinted. It was as though she saw Margaret for the first time. She shook her head back and forth back and forth in wonder. "No," she said. "I wasn't thirty-five. I was twenty-three. A girl. Just like you."

Margaret put her forehead into her palm. The roots of her sunset hair were brown. She held her head that way for a moment and said, "You have to forgive me for that, Ondine. You have to."

"You forgive you. Don't ask for more."

"You know what, Ondine? You know what? I want to be a wonderful, wonderful old lady." Margaret laughed a rusty little bark that came from a place seldom used. "Ondine? Let's be wonderful old ladies. You and me."

"Huh," said Ondine, but she smiled a little.

"We're both childless now, Ondine. And we're both stuck here. We should be friends. It's not too late."

Ondine looked out of the window and did not answer.

"Is it too late, Ondine?"

"Almost," she said. "Almost."

AT SOME POINT in life the world's beauty becomes enough. You don't need to photograph, paint or even remember it. It is enough. No record of it needs to be kept and you don't need someone to share it with or tell it to. When that happens—that letting go—you let go because you can. The world will always be there—while you sleep it will be there—when you wake it will be there as well. So you can sleep and there is reason to wake. A dead hydrangea is as intricate and lovely as one in bloom. Bleak sky is as seductive as sunshine, miniature orange trees without blossom or fruit are not defective; they are that. So the windows of the greenhouse can be opened and the weather let in. The latch on the door can be left unhooked, the muslin removed, for the soldier ants are beautiful too and whatever they do will be part of it.

Valerian began going back to his greenhouse. Not as early as before; now he waited until after the breakfast rain. He was still telling Margaret, "Tomorrow. Perhaps tomorrow." But he did not change anything in there. Didn't sow or clip or transpose. Things grew or died where and how they pleased. Isle des Chevaliers filled in the spaces that had been the island's to begin with.

He thought about innocence there in his greenhouse and knew that he was guilty of it because he had lived with a woman who had made something kneel down in him the first time he saw her, but about whom he knew nothing; had watched his son grow and talk but also about whom he had known nothing. And there was something so foul in that, something in the crime of innocence so revolting it paralyzed him. He had not known because he had not taken the trouble to know. He was satisfied with what he did know. Knowing more was inconvenient and frightening. Like a bucket of water with no bottom. If you know how to tread, bottomlessness need not concern you. Margaret knew the bottomlessness—she had looked at it, dived in it and pulled herself out—obviously tougher than he. What an awful thing she had done. And how much more awful not to have known it. Which was all he could say in his defense: that he did not know; that the postman passed him by. Perhaps that was why he had never received the message he'd been waiting for: his innocence made him unworthy of it. The instinct of kings was always to slay the messenger, and they were right. A real messenger, a worthy one, is corrupted by the message he brings. And if he is noble he should accept that corruption. Valerian had received no message, but after waiting so long, to receive, know and deliver its contents, imperceptibly he had made it up. Made up the information he was waiting for. Preoccupied himself with the construction of the world and its inhabitants according to this imagined message. But had chosen not to know the real message that his son had mailed to him from underneath the sink. And all he could say was that he did not know. He was guilty, therefore, of innocence. Was there anything so loathsome as a willfully innocent man? Hardly. An innocent man is a sin before God. Inhuman and therefore unworthy. No man should live without absorbing the sins of his kind, the foul air of his innocence, even if it did wilt rows of angel trumpets and cause them to fall from their vines.

9

"THIS IS a town?" Jadine shouted. "It looks like a block. A city block. In Queens."

"Hush up," he said squeezing her waist. "This is not only a town, it's the county seat. We call it the city."

"This is Eloe?"

"No. This is Poncie. Eloe is a little town. We got fourteen miles to go yet."

Now she understood why he wanted to rent a car and drive to Florida. There was no way to fly to Eloe. They had to go to Tallahassee or Pensacola, then get a bus or train to Poncie, *then* bum a ride to Eloe for no buses went out there, and as for taxis—well, he doubted if either one would take them. Bumming a ride didn't seem to be a problem in his mind. Her luggage held all he had and when they got off the bus she saw eight or ten black men lounging there in front of the depot, as Son called it. Son talked to one of them for at least five minutes. They waited another thirty minutes at the candy machine until a black man named Carl appeared driving a four-door Plymouth.

He drove them to Eloe asking pointed questions all the way. Son said he was an army buddy of a man named Soldier—that they were out of Brewton on their way to Gainesville. Thought he'd look in on old Soldier, he said. Carl said he knew of Soldier but had never met him. He had never seen a cashmere sweater with a cowl neckline, or Chacrel boots, and didn't know they could make jeans that tight or if they did who but a child would wear them since no honest work could be done in them. So he looked in the rear-view mirror with disbelief. Nobody dressed like that in Brewton, Alabama, and he suspected they didn't in Montgomery either.

He followed Son's directions and dropped them off in front of a house Jadine supposed was in Eloe since Son paid the man and got out.

"Where are the ninety houses? I see four," asked Jadine, looking around.

"They're here."

"Where?"

"Spread out. Folks don't live all crunched up together in Eloe. Come on, girl." He picked up the luggage and, grinning like a groom, led her up the steps. A frame door was open to the still March morning. They both stood in front of a screen door through which they could see a man sitting at a table with his back to them. Son didn't knock or move, he simply looked at the back of the man's head. Slowly the man turned his head and stared at them. Then he got up from the table. Son opened the screen door and stepped in with Jadine just behind him. He didn't move closer to the man; he just stopped and smiled. The man did not speak and did not smile; he kept on staring. Then he raised his hands, clenching them into fists, and began to jump up and down on both feet, stamping the floor like a kid jumping rope. Son was laughing soundlessly. A woman ran in, but the man kept on jumping—pounding the floor. The woman looked at Son and Jadine with a little confused smile. The man jumped higher and faster. Son kept watching and laughing. The man was still jumping rope, but not smiling or laughing as Son was. Finally when the stamping shook a lamp to the table's edge and a window banged down, and the children were peering in the doorway, the man shouted at the top of his lungs Son! Son! Son! to the beat of his crazy feet, and kept on until Son grabbed his head and pressed it into his chest. "It's me, Soldier. It's me."

Soldier wrenched away, looked him in the face, then ran to the back window. "Wahoo! Wahoo!" he shouted, and came back to march four-step around the room. Two men came to the front door and looked in at the marcher and then at the visitors.

"Soldier's clownin," said the woman.

"Soldier's clownin," said the children.

"Good God a' mighty, that's Son," whispered one of the men. And then it stopped. Son and Soldier hit each other on the head, the hands, the shoulders.

"Who bought you them skinny shoes?"

"Where's your hair, nigger?"

HE ASKED HER if she would mind staying at Soldier's house with his wife, Ellen, while he went to see his father. Jadine demurred; she had run out of conversation with Ellen ten minutes after it started, but Son urged her, saying he had not seen Old Man in eight years and that he didn't want to bring someone his father didn't know into his house the first time they met in all that time. Could she understand that? She said yes, out in Soldier's yard near the mimosa, but she didn't understand at all, no more than she understood the language he was using when he talked to Soldier and Drake and Ellen and the others who stopped by; no more than she could understand (or accept) her being shunted off with Ellen and the children while the men grouped on the porch and, after a greeting, ignored her; or why he seemed so shocked and grateful at the same time by news that some woman named Brown, Sarah or Sally or Sadie—from the way they pronounced it she couldn't tell—was dead. But she agreed. God. Eloe.

He left her there and walked alone to the house he was born in. The yellow brick front looked tiny. It had seemed so large and sturdy compared to the Sutterfield shack he and Cheyenne had—the one he drove a car through. It wasn't as big as Ondine's kitchen. The door was unlocked, but no one was home. In the kitchen a pepper pot was simmering, so he knew Old Man wasn't far and wouldn't be long. His father, Franklin G. Green, had been called Old Man since he was seven years old and when he grew up, got married, had a baby boy, the baby was called Old Man's son until the second child was born and the first became simply Son. They all used to be here—all of them. Horace who lived in Gainesville, Frank G. who died in Korea, his sister Francine who was in a mental home in Jacksonville, and the baby girl Porky Green who still lived in Eloe, so Soldier said, but went to Florida A and M on a track scholarship. They had all been in this house together at one time—with his mother.

Only a few minutes had passed when Old Man climbed the porch steps. Son waited, standing in the middle of the room. The door opened, Old Man looked at Son and dropped his onions on the floor.

"Hey, Old Man, how you been doing?"

"Save me, you got back."

They didn't touch. They didn't know how. They fooled around with the onions and each asked the other about his condition until Old Man said, "Come on in here and let me fix you something to eat. Not much in here but it ain't like I had notice."

"I ate something over to Soldier's."

"You was over there?"

"I wanted to hear about you before I came by," said Son.

"Oh, I ain't dead, Son. I ain't dead," he chuckled.

"I see you ain't."

"Them money orders sure helped."

"You got them?"

"Oh, yeah. Every one. I had to use some of em though."

"*Some* of em? They were all for you. Why didn't you use them all?"

"I couldn't do that. I didn't want to raise no suspicions. I just cashed a few when I couldn't help it."

"Shit, Old Man, don't tell me you still got some?"

"They in there." He nodded toward one of the two bedrooms. "Porky in school, you know. I had to help her out, too."

They went in the bedroom and Old Man took a White Owl

cigar box from under his bed and opened it. There was a thin pile of envelopes bound by a rubber band; some postal money orders held together with a paper clip, and a few ten and twenty dollar bills. Eight years of envelopes.

"These were for you, Old Man. To take care of you."

"They did. They did. But you know I didn't want to be going over there to the Post Office every month, cashin em. Might set folks to talkin and turn the law out on account of that other business. So I just took a few in every now and then. Quiet, you know."

"Old Man, you one crazy old man."

"You been to Sutterfield yet?"

"No. Straight here."

"Well, you know Sally Brown died here a while back."

"They told me."

"Be at peace."

"Hope so."

"She slept with a shotgun every night."

"Huh."

"Every night. Well, she burnin up down there now, her and her nasty daughter . . ."

"Don't say it, Old Man."

"Yeah. You right. Shouldn't rile the dead. But you know I was more scared of Sally than the law."

"So was I."

"Law don't care about no dead colored gal, but Sally Brown, she slept with that shotgun every night waitin for you. Made my skin crinkle to walk past her. And she just about lived in church moanin. Stopped me from vespers altogether. I couldn't sit there listenin to her berate you. Can you feature that? Pray every Sunday and hold on to a shotgun every night?"

"Where's the boy?"

"Gone away from here, his folks too."

"He get his eyebrows back?"

"Never did. Guess his folks figured he couldn't hide nowhere around here lookin like that. Sally was lookin for him too."

"I didn't see his face. All I saw was his asshole."

"That didn't have no eyebrows either I bet."

"I should have made him some with a razor." They laughed together then and an hour or so passed while Son told what all he'd been doing for the last eight years. It was almost four when Son said, "I didn't come by myself."

"You with a woman?"

"Yeah."

"Where is she?"

"Over to Soldier's. Can she stay here?"

"You all married?"

"No, Old Man."

"Better take her to your Aunt Rosa's then."

"She won't like that."

"I can't help it. You be gone. I have to live here."

"Come on, Old Man."

"Uh-uh. Go see your Aunt Rosa. She be mad anyway you don't stop by."

"Scripture don't say anything about two single people sleeping under the same roof." Son was laughing.

"What you know bout Scripture?"

"I could have lied and said we were married."

"But you didn't lie. You told the truth and so you got to live by the truth."

"Oh, shit."

"That's right. Shit. She's welcome in my house all day in the day. Bring her back so I can meet her."

"She's special, Old Man."

"So am I, Son. So am I."

"All right. All right. I'll go get her and bring her by. Cook up something, then I'll take her by Aunt Rosa. That suit you?"

"Suit me fine."

Son stood up to go, and his father walked him to the door. When Son said, "Be right back," Old Man said, "Wait a minute. Can I ask you somethin?"

"Sure. Ask it."

"How come you never put no note or nothin in them envelopes? I kept on lookin for a note."

Son stopped. How hurried all those money order purchases had been. Most of the time he sent a woman out to both buy and mail them. He'd done it as often as he could and sometimes five would be sent from one city and none from any place for six months. How hurried he had been.

"I guess I didn't want nobody to read em and know where I was . . ." But it was too lame an excuse to continue with. "Is that why you kept the empty envelopes too?"

"Yeah. They had your handwritin on em, you know. You wrote it, that part anyway. 'Franklin Green.' You got a nice handwritin. Pretty. Like your mama."

"See you, Old Man."

"Go by Rosa. Tell her you comin."

JADINE was squatting down in the middle of the road, the afternoon sun at her back. The children were happy to pose, and so were some of the younger women. Only the old folks refused to smile and glared into her camera as though looking at hell with the lid off. The men were enjoying the crease in her behind so clearly defined in the sunlight, click, click. Jadine had remembered her camera just before she thought she would go nuts, trying to keep a conversation going with Ellen and the neighbor women who came in to see Son's Northern girl. They looked at her with outright admiration, each one saying, "I was in Baltimore once," or, "My cousin she live in New York." They did not ask her what they really wanted to know: where did she know Son from and how much did her boots cost. Jadine smiled, drank glasses of water and tried to talk "down home" like Ondine.

But their worshipful stares and nonconversation made Son's absence seem much too long. She was getting annoyed when she remembered her camera. Now she was having a ball photographing everybody. Soldier's yard was full. "Beautiful," she said. "Fantastic. Now over here," click click. "Hey, what'd you say your name was? Okay, Beatrice, could you lean up against the tree?" click, click. "This way. Beautiful. Hold it. Hooooold it. Heaven," click click click click.

Son didn't mean to snatch it. Just to end it somehow. Stop the crease, the sunlight, the click click click. And when he did she looked at him with confusion at first, then with evolved anger. "What's the matter with you?"

It wasn't nice. To snatch the camera and then to have to tell her about the sleeping arrangements—it wasn't nice. Not nice at all.

He took her to Old Man's, and after supper there to Rosa's. Drake and Soldier picked them up and drove them to a joint in Poncie called Night Moves, where there was live music, Bar B Que sandwiches and unrestrained dancing under four blue lights that neither flashed or strobed. They even managed some snatch in the car—Jadine under the impression that nobody knew; he aware that everybody did. The back seat turned her volume up, but the beer and the bad whiskey made her so sleepy there was no problem when he left her at Rosa's. She slept like a boulder for three hours, then woke missing him and suffocating in that little bedroom without windows. She sat up naked, for she never wore nightgowns, and held her shoulders. The room had a door to the living room and one that opened to the back yard. She opened the latter and looked out into the blackest nothing she had ever seen. Blacker and bleaker than Isle des Chevaliers, and loud. Loud with the presence of plants and field life. If she was wanting air, there wasn't any. It's not possible, she thought, for anything to be this black. Maybe if she stood there long enough light would come from somewhere, and she could see shadows, the outline of something, a bush, a tree, a line between earth and sky, a heavier darkness to show where this very house stopped and space began. She remembered the blackness she saw when Son told her to close her eyes, and to put a star in it. That would be the only way it would get there, she thought, for the world in the direction of the sky, in that place where the sky ought to be, was starless. Haze, she guessed; there must be haze in the sky. Otherwise there would be a moon, at the least. The loudness of the plants was not audible, but it was strong nonetheless. She might as well have been in a cave, a grave, the dark womb of the earth, suffocating with the sound of plant life moving, but deprived of its sight. She could see nothing and could not remember what she had seen when it was daylight. A movement behind made her jump and turn around. Rosa was standing in the inner doorway, lit from behind by a lamp.

"Anything the matter? I heard you moving around."

Jadine closed the back door. The lamplight from the other door was weak but it was healthy enough to spotlight her nakedness. Rosa gazed down Jadine's body with a small bowing of her head, and then up again. Her eyes traveled slowly, moving like one of those growing plants Jadine could not see, but whose presence was cracking loud.

"Why didn't you tell me you didn't have no nightclothes. I got somethin I can let you have," Rosa said.

"I . . . I forgot," said Jadine. "I forgot to bring anything."

"I'll get you something."

When Rosa came back, Jadine was in the bed. Rosa handed her a kind of slip, wrinkled but clean-smelling.

"You all right, daughter?"

"Oh, I'm fine. I just got too warm and wanted some air," Jadine answered.

"This used to be a porch. I made it into a extra room, but it does heat up. I didn't feel like buyin no windows."

"Can you leave the back door open?" asked Jadine.

"I wouldn't advise it. Anything at all might come in here out of those trees. I got a little old electric fan I'll get you."

"No. No. Don't bother."

"You sure?"

"Yes."

"It's beat up, but it stirs the air around."

"It's okay."

"Well, I'll leave this here door open." Rosa propped a wooden slatback chair against the inner door. "Sorry," she said. "That gown ain't much, but it'll cover you."

"Thanks," said Jadine, but it didn't cover her. She lay down in the slip under the sheet and her nakedness before Rosa lay down with her. No man had made her feel that naked, that unclothed. Leerers, lovers, doctors, artists—none of them had made her feel exposed. More than exposed. Obscene.

God. Eloe.

They were leaving Sunday. Surely she could get through a Sunday and then she and Son would be back on the train holding hands, and then on the airplane playing with each other under the Delta Airlines blanket—their faces serene as passengers, their hands devious and directed. She fell asleep on that thought and woke at ten-thirty with Rosa's fingertips tapping her on the shoulder.

"Son's in there," she said. "You all goin to eat with me, ain't you?"

Jadine got up and dressed quickly. He was sitting at the table looking more beautiful than after the first haircut on Isle des Chevaliers, more beautiful than when he stood at the piano with his coat over his shoulder and she saw savannas in his face, more beautiful than on the beach when he touched her foot, than when he opened the door to his room at the Hilton. She wanted to sit in his lap, but Drake and Soldier were at the table too, so she just walked over and put her hand on his head. He smiled up at her and kissed the palm of her other hand. Drake and Soldier looked bathed and glittery. They beamed at Son with the same adoration she did, but they didn't compete. They sat back and enjoyed his presence and his prize woman. They looked at him with love and looked at her like she was a Cadillac he had won, or stolen, or even bought for all they knew.

"YOU ALL gettin hitched?" Soldier asked. They were alone in the house while Son and Drake drove Rosa to church.

"I guess so," Jadine answered. "We haven't talked about it."

"He's good. You ought to snatch him."

She laughed. "Should I?"

"Damn right. You don't, somebody else sure will. He was married before, you know."

"I know."

"Never should have married that woman. That Cheyenne. Every one of us told him that, or tried to. But he did it anyway to his grief and sorrow."

"Was she pretty?" asked Jadine. She didn't want to ask it, but it seemed extremely important to know the answer.

"Naw. I wouldn't say pretty. Not bad-lookin, mind, but nothin like pretty."

"He must have loved her, though."

"That could be what it was." Soldier sounded as though there were some doubts. "Naw," he said. "She wasn't pretty, but you had to hand it to her though. She had the best pussy in Florida, the absolute best," and he turned his eyes on Jadine as if to say Now top that!

It wasn't nice. Not nice at all. Son embarrassed her in the road with the camera; Rosa made her feel like a slut; and now Soldier was trying to make her feel like a virgin competing with . . . She didn't answer him so he went on.

"You ever been married?"

"No," she said, and looked squarely in his face thinking, if he says "Good-lookin woman like you ought to be able . . ." she would smack him in the mouth. But all he said was "Too bad," and that didn't seem definite enough to break his face for.

"Any children?"

"You ask too many questions," she said. "Anything you want to know about me ask Son."

Soldier smiled at that and shook his head. "Son don't talk about his women and don't let nobody else talk about em either."

"I'm glad of that," she said.

"I ain't. Keeps him dumb. He wouldn't know a good woman from a snake and he won't let nobody point out the difference."

"Can he tell the difference between a good man and a snake?"

"Oh, yeah. Son knows people. He just gets confused when it comes to women. With most everything else he thinks with his heart. But when it comes to women he thinks with his dick, you know what I mean?"

"Some people think with their mouths."

"Yeah. I guess you right about that." Soldier smiled. "But maybe it's better'n not thinkin at all."

"How would *you* know?" she asked him.

He laughed. "You a hot one, ain't you?"

"Yes, I'm a hot one."

"Yeah." He ran his fingers over the place on his head where his hair was thinning. "A hot one all right and a live one too."

"Believe it." She got up to pour herself more coffee.

Soldier scanned her hips. "Can I ask you somethin?"

"What?"

"Who's controllin it?"

"Controlling what?"

"The thing. The thing between you two. Who's in control?"

"Nobody. We're together. Nobody controls anybody," she said.

"Good," he said. "That's real good. Son, he don't like control. Makes him, you know wildlike."

"We don't have that kind of relationship. I don't like to be controlled either."

"But you like to have it, don't you?"

"Not with him."

"Good. Good."

"Did Cheyenne have control?" She sat down and stirred air into her coffee.

"Cheyenne? Naw. She didn't control nothin. At least not during the day. But good God she sure did run the nights." He laughed and then, since she did not join in, he sobered quickly and asked, "How long you all plannin to stay around?"

Jadine repressed a smile. He'd lost, and wanted her out of town. "We're leaving today."

"Today? You can't leave today."

"Why not?"

"Ernie Paul is coming. We called him up. He left from Montgomery already, be here Monday." Soldier was alarmed.

"Who's Ernie Paul?"

"He's one of us. Grew up with Son and Drake and me. He takin off work to come down and see Son and all of us."

TKO, thought Jadine, but she didn't hang up her gloves. When Son got back she showed him the train schedule.

"One more night, baby," he said.

"I can't. Not in that room. Not alone."

"Come on."

"No, Son. Not unless you stay with me."

"I can't do that."

"Then I'm leaving. I'm long past fourteen."

"Okay. Look. After church, when Rosa gets back, we'll go for a ride."

"Son."

"Listen now. Let me show you this county. Bring your camera. Then tonight you go back to Rosa's . . ."

"Son."

"Wait. Leave the back door open. I'll come in and stay with you all night. And in the morning I'll go round the front like I just got there."

"You promise."

"I promise."

Paleolithic, she thought. I am stuck here with a pack of Neanderthals who think sex is dirty or strange or something and he is standing here almost thirty years old doing it too. Stupid. "Stupid," she said aloud.

"I know, but that's the way they are. What do you want me to do? You think anything we do is going to change them?"

"I want us to be honest."

"Can't we be gentle first, and honest later?"

Accommodating beyond all belief. Because it was his hometown and his people, she supposed. She photographed everything during the ride until she was out of film. They found sheds and orchards to make love in and an open window of a schoolhouse with a teacher's desk wide enough for two. They got back to Eloe at eight and stayed out as late as they could—when Night Moves closed—then gave everybody a ride home. When Jadine got to Rosa's she put on the wrinkled slip to amuse him when he returned, unlatched the door and got in the bed. Half an hour later he was there. She had been listening carefully so she heard the swing of the door.

"Son?"

"Yeah."

"Hurry up."

He hurried. Something was in his hand as he knelt by the bed, leaves or fern or something. He made her take the slip off and he brushed her all over with the fern and she tried not to moan or laugh or cry out while he was saying Sssh, sssh. He undressed and climbed in. Jadine opened her arms to this man accustomed to the best pussy in Florida. It must have been that thought, put there by Soldier, that made her competitive, made her struggle to outdo Cheyenne and surpass her legendary gifts. She was thinking of her, whipped on by her, and that, perhaps, plus the fact that she had left the door unlatched and Son had opened it on its hinges and after it was open on its hinges it stayed wide open but they had not noticed because they were paying attention only to each other so that must have been why and how Cheyenne got in, and then the rest: Rosa and Thérèse and Son's dead mother and Sally Sarah Sadie Brown and Ondine and Soldier's wife Ellen and Francine from the mental institution and her own dead mother and even the woman in yellow. All there crowding into the room. Some of them she did not know, recognize, but they were all there spoiling her love-making, taking away her sex like succubi, but not his. He fell asleep and didn't see the women in the room and she didn't either but they were there crowding each other and watching her. Pushing each other—nudging for space, they poured out of the dark like ants out of a hive. She shook Son and he woke saying "Huh?" and she said "Shouldn't you close the door" because she didn't want to say there are women in the room; I can't see them, but this room is full of women. He said, "Yeah," and went back to sleep. She just lay there, too frightened to do it herself for then she would have to walk through the crowd of women standing in the pitch-dark room whom she could not see but would have to touch to get through them. And she felt them nudging each other for a better look at her, until finally being frightened was worse than anything they could do to her so she got mad and sat up. Her voice was half as loud as her heart.

"What do you want with me, goddamn it!"

They looked as though they had just been waiting for that question and they each pulled out a breast and showed it to her. Jadine started to tremble. They stood around in the room, jostling each other gently, gently—there wasn't much room—revealing one breast and then two and Jadine was shocked. This was not the dream of hats for in that she was asleep, her eyes closed. Here she was wide-awake, but in total darkness looking at her own mother for God's sake and *Nan*adine!

"I have breasts too," she said or thought or willed, "I have breasts too." But they didn't believe her. They just held their own higher and pushed their own farther out and looked at her. All of them revealing both their breasts except the woman in yellow. She did something more shocking—she stretched out a long arm and showed Jadine her three big eggs. It scared her so, she began to cry. Her back pressed hard, hard into the wall, her right hand in a ball over her stomach, she shook Son and shook him some more. When he stirred and woke she slammed her face into his shoulder crying.

"What is it? What's going on?"

"Tell them to leave me alone."

"What?"

"Hold me."

"Jadine."

"Shut the door. No, don't move. Hold me."

"Those hats again?"

"No."

"What?"

"*Hold* me."

And he did. Till morning. Even while he slept and she didn't and the women finally went away—sighing—he did not let her go.

Nobody was fooled by that little charade. Old Man guessed, the men knew and Rosa heard them as clear as the radio.

She couldn't shake it. Not because Rosa fried eggs in the morning, or even the camera business or Soldier's big mouth or Old Man's phony biblical conversation, or the wrinkled slip and the stuffy room, but the possibility of more plant sounds in the cave and the certainty of the night women kept her nervous. She couldn't shake it. The women in the night had killed the whole weekend. Eloe was rotten and more boring than ever. A burnt-out place. There was no life there. Maybe a past but definitely no future and finally there was no interest. All that Southern small-town country romanticism was a lie, a joke, kept secret by people who could not function elsewhere. An excuse to fish. Ernie Paul could come to New York—faster, even, if he flew. She needed air, and taxicabs and conversation in a language she understood. She didn't want to have any more discussions in which the silences meant more than the words did. And no, she didn't want to party at Night Moves, Son, please, get me out of here.

You know I have things to do. Take me back, or I'll go back and you stay, or go. But Son, I'm not spending another night here.

"I'll come to you again tonight."

"It doesn't help."

"We'll stay out all night."

"No. Just get me to the train on time."

Son closed the eyes inside his eyes to her for a minute—the way he had in the bedroom when he had come in without knocking—closed them without shutting them. She was making him choose. But he opened them again and asked her, "You love me?"

"I love you," she said.

"Will you be there when I get there?"

"I'll be there. Of course I'll be there. Waiting."

"Ernie Paul has a car. I'll go back to Montgomery with him tomorrow and fly from there to New York."

"Okay. No longer?"

"No longer."

"I love you."

"I love you."

They got to the train on time, but he didn't get to New York on time. Four days passed and he still had not come. Jadine was not disturbed—there was so much to do, errands, and lunches, and hair appointments and jobs. She had to call Dawn to see if she was coming back as planned. Did she have to find another place? On the fifth day, she was feeling orphaned again. He could have called. She imagined him carousing with Ernie Paul and Soldier. Then another weekend rolled by and still no Son. Apparently he knew how to call Ernie Paul but not how to call her. She thought of calling Eloe; there was a telephone in Night Moves, but she couldn't remember whether she'd seen one in any of the houses. Now she was biting mad. At his carelessness, his indifference. Then she got desperate. In her heart she knew he would come, sometime, and that he would have either a good excuse or no excuse at all; but she knew that he would come. The desperation came from the sense she had of his being down there with all those women with their breasts and eggs, the bitches. All the women in his life and in hers were down there—well, not *all* the women in her life. Dawn wasn't there, and neither was Aisha, or Felicité, or Betty. They wouldn't have done that to her anyway. They were her friends. They were like her. Not like old Cheyenne with the statewide pussy, or Rosa with the witness eyes, or Nanadine with the tight-fisted braids looking sorrowful at the kitchen table and accusatory in that room. And not like Francine attacked by dogs and driven crazy, or even like her own mother how could you Mama how could you be with them. You left me you died you didn't care enough about me to stay alive you knew Daddy was gone and you went too. But she had rerun that movie so many times its zazz was gone leaving only technique to admire. Of course her mother was with them, showing her boobs; of course she would be there. But what made them think they could all get together to do that to her? They didn't even know each other. What did they have in common even, besides the breasts. She had breasts; so did Dawn, and Aisha and Felicité and Betty. But she couldn't shake it and it kept her angry and the anger was good for the photographers and the agency and the telephone company and the apartment managers. Everybody took notice and got out of the way.

Dawn said May 15, she would be back then. Jadine asked around about another sublet, and found two—one a house for one month, June; another an apartment for six months, but it was way uptown. Then a loft she could share for two weeks and keep for the summer. . . . Every night she went to bed too exhausted to worry, only on waking did it come back—fresher each time, heavier, till finally she sat with a glass of grapefruit juice in her hand in the morning and since she could not shake it, she decided to reel it in. Cut off its head, slice it open and see what lay in its belly. The women had looked awful to her: onion heels, potbellies, hair surrendered to rags and braids. And the breasts they thrust at her like weapons were soft, loose bags closed at the tip with a brunette eye. Then the slithery black arm of the woman in yellow, stretching twelve feet, fifteen, toward her and the fingers that fingered eggs. It hurt, and part of the hurt was in having the vision at all—at being the helpless victim of a dream that chose you. Some was the frontal sorrow of being publicly humiliated by those you had loved or thought kindly toward. A little bitty hurt that was always gleaming when you looked at it. So you covered it over with a lid until the next time. But most of the hurt was dread. The night women were not merely against her (and her alone—not him), not merely looking superior over their sagging breasts and folded stomachs, they seemed somehow in agreement with each other about her, and were all out to get her, tie her, bind her. Grab the person she had worked hard to become and choke it off with their soft loose tits.

Jadine sipped the grapefruit juice. Its clean, light acid dissolved the morning cloud from her tongue. "No, Rosa. I am not your daughter, and he is not your son."

WHEN SON got back, she fought him. In between the sweet times—she fought him. He thought she was fighting him about Ernie Paul and being late and not calling. She thought so too, part of the time—but most of the time she knew she was fighting the night women. The mamas who had seduced him and were trying to lay claim to her. It would be the fight of their lives to get away from that coven that had nothing to show but breasts.

He needed a job, a degree, she said. They should go in business for themselves. He should enroll in business school. He had two semesters of Florida A and M, maybe he could pass the LSAT; he should take the SAT the GRE the CEE. "You can go to law school," she said.

"I don't want to be a lawyer," he said.

"Why?" she asked.

"Think," he said.

"Why?"

"Think."

"Why?"

"I can't hassle nobody that looks like me, or you either."

"Oh, shit. There's other kinds of law."

"No, there isn't. Besides I don't want to know *their* laws; I want to know mine."

"You don't *have* any."

"Then that's the problem with it."

She fought him, but she never mentioned the night women. They fought instead about Valerian Street. He would lend them the money to open a shop or start an agency.

Son said, "No way and I am not about to sit here and argue about that white man."

"Who cares what color he is?"

"I care. And he cares. He cares what color he is."

"He's a person, not a white man. He put me through school."

"You have told me that a million times. Why *not* educate you? You did what you were told, didn't you? Ondine and Sydney were obedient, weren't they? White people love obedience—love it! Did he do anything hard for you? Did he give up anything important for you?"

"He wasn't required to. But maybe he would have since he was not *required* to educate me."

"That was toilet paper, Jadine. He *should* have wiped his ass after he shit all over your uncle and aunt. He *was* required to; he still is. His debt is big, woman. He can't never pay it off!"

"He educated me!" Jadine was shouting, "and you can't make me think that was not an important thing to do. Because nobody else did! No. Body. Else. Did. *You* didn't!"

"What do you mean, *I* didn't?"

"I mean you *didn't! You didn't!*" She slapped him and before he could turn his head back she was choking him with both hands around his neck, screaming all the while, "*You* didn't *you* didn't." He pulled her hair until she let go and when she tried another blow, he dropped her as carefully as he could. She fell back on her behind, turned over and crawled on all fours to jump him again. He held her arms behind her back and she bit him to his teeth. The pain was so powerful he had to put out her light with his fist.

When she came to and touched her jaw he went wild thinking he had loosened one of the side teeth so precious to him. Jadine dressed the bite marks on his face; and they said, "Ollieballen," laughing as best they could with the bruises.

Sometimes they argued about school. Maybe that was the problem.

"It's bullshit, Jadine."

"It is not. When will you listen to the truth?"

"What truth?"

"The truth that while you were playing the piano in the Night Moves Café, I was in school. The truth is that while you were driving your car into your wife's bed I was being educated. While you were hiding from a small-town sheriff or some insurance company, hiding from a rap a two-bit lawyer could have gotten you out of, I was being educated, I was working, I was making something out of my life. I was learning how to make it in *this* world. The one we live in, not the one in your head. Not that dump Eloe; *this* world. And the truth is I could not have done that without the help and care of some poor old white dude who thought I had brains enough to learn something! Stop loving your ignorance—it isn't lovable."

Son picked her up and took her to the window. After a violent struggle he actually held her out of it by her wrists shouting, "The truth is that whatever you learned in those colleges that didn't include me ain't shit. What did they teach you about me? What tests did they give? Did they tell you what I was like, did they tell you what was on my mind? Did they describe me to you? Did they tell you what was in my heart? If they didn't teach you that, then they didn't teach you nothing, because until you know about me, you don't know nothing about yourself. And you don't know anything, anything at all about your children and anything at all about your mama and your papa. You find out about *me,* you educated nitwit!"

It was only ten feet off the ground and she wet her pants, but still she hollered loud enough for him to hear as well as the few people gathered on the sidewalk to watch, "You want to be a yardman all your life?"

"His name is Gideon! Gideon! Not Yardman, and Mary Thérèse Foucault, you hear me! Why don't you ask me to help you buy a house and put your aunt and uncle in it and take that woman off her feet. Her feet are killing her, killing her, and let them live like people for a change, like the people you never studied, like the people you can't photograph. *They* are the ones who put you through school, woman, they are the ones. Not him. They worked for him all their lives. And you left them down there with him not knowing if they had a job or not. You should cook for *them.* What the hell kind of education is it that didn't teach you about Gideon and Old Man and me. Nothing about me!"

When he pulled her back in, her arms were so sore she could not move them. But she was curled up teary-eyed in his lap an hour later when the doorbell rang. Son was massaging her shoulders, and begging forgiveness. They both went to the door and looked so lovey-dovey the police thought they had the wrong apartment, it must have been somebody else throwing a woman out of the window.

Other times they fought about work; surely *that* was the problem.

He mentioned once wanting to go back to the boats.

"You can't; you're blacklisted. You jumped ship, remember?"

"That don't mean nothing."

"You'll be away all the time. Why do you want to leave me?"

"I don't. But we don't have to live here. We can live anywhere."

"You mean Eloe."

"I mean anywhere. I can get good work in other places."

"Where?"

"Houston, Montgomery, Atlanta, San Diego."

"I can't live there."

"Why do you want to *change* me?"

"Why do you want to change *me?*"

"I want to live, not change. I can't live just for this goddamn city."

"Is it because you're afraid? Because you can't make it in New York?"

"Make it in New York. Make it in New York. I'm tired of hearing that shit. What the fuck is it? If I make it in New York, then that's all I do: 'Make it in New York.' That's not life; that's making it. I don't want to *make* it; I want to *be* it. New York ain't hard, baby. Not really hard. It's just sad, and what you need to make it here is the easy stuff I got rid of a long time ago. I've lived all over the world, Jadine. I can live anywhere."

"You've never lived anywhere."

"And you? Where have you lived? Anybody ask you where you from, you give them five towns. You're not *from* anywhere. I'm from Eloe."

"I hate Eloe and Eloe hates me. Never was any feeling more mutual."

She kept him on the defensive; demanded clarity, precision, very specific solutions to open-ended problems, and any furry notion he had in mind of what to do or where to do it matted before her rakelike intellect. He wanted to do things in time—she wanted them done on time. So he let her make private appointments, did take the SAT and scored in the 400s; the LET and was below the 13th percentile; the IRE and ranked above the 80th percentile; the CEE and scored in the 600s. "That proves," he told her, "that I can sit still for three hours at a clip, but I always knew that."

"One of two things," she said finally. "Either you go to school while I work or we ask Valerian to invest in a business."

"Will you marry me?"

"Yes."

"Okay."

"Okay what?"

"I'll go to school."

"Ooo-wee!" She grabbed him around the neck and pulled him to the floor.

"But not here."

"Why?"

"We're living in other people's space. This is not our crib. Let's go someplace else."

"How many times do I have to tell you—I can't work someplace else. You can, but I can't."

"What the hell do you do that's so jive you can't take it out of the city and do it there?"

"I pay the bills is what I do."

It was August. Jadine had sent for applications to C.U.N.Y. and S.U.N.Y. When they came, she sat down and filled them out. She was tired and looking tired. So much so the agency people were skipping her. That twenty-five-year-old face looked twenty-six and she had not been keeping up the regimen that held her at the twenty-year-old peak. Seventeen-year-old girls were getting the jobs. In Europe they liked older-looking black models, but in the U.S. the look was twelve. Soon she would really have to call her old professor. The modeling thing was going bust fast—she'd make all she could as fast as she could since it was seven times what teaching would bring. She sat at the table, perspiring a little, filling out Son's application. You'd think he would at least do *that.*

Son was watching her—she was a model of industry and planning. Every now and then she asked him a question and they agreed on whether to lie or tell the truth. He watched her. There is the power, he thought, right there. That is all the power there is or ever will be and I don't want any of it. She always referred to Eloe as his cradle. As though living there was child's play, easy. As though living anywhere outside the First Cities of the World was kiddy stuff. Well, it hadn't been easy for Francine and it hadn't been easy for Rosa or his mother. Not easy at all. It was hard and he believed it scared her to think of how hard. She thought this was hard, New York. She was scared of being still, of not being busy, scared to have to be quiet, scared to have children alone. He tried to imagine what kind of woman she would be in fifty years. Would she be Thérèse? Or Ondine? Or Rosa or Sally Brown, or maybe even Francine, frail as a pick tearing all her hair out in the state hospital? Bald, bald Francine. Some cradle. It took all the grown-up strength you had to stay there and stay alive and keep a family together. They didn't know about state aid in Eloe; there were no welfare lines in Eloe and unemployment insurance was a year of trouble with no rewards. She kept barking at him about equality, sexual equality, as though he thought women were inferior. He couldn't understand that. Before Francine was attacked by the dogs, she gave him ten points on the court and still beat him. It was her athletic skill that caused her trouble. She was running in the fields and went too far. Some dogs tracking an escaped convict, frustrated at having lost the scent, attacked her. Sixty seconds later the police got them off her and took her home. She stayed nervous after that, well, "nervous" was what they all called it. But God that girl could run. Cheyenne was driving a beat-up old truck at age nine, four years before he could even shift gears, and she could drop a pheasant like an Indian. His mother's memory was kept alive by those who remembered how she roped horses when she was a girl. His grandmother built a whole cowshed with only Rosa to help. In fact the room Jadine had slept in, Rosa built herself which was why it didn't have any windows. Anybody who thought women were inferior didn't come out of north Florida.

ON SEPTEMBER 16, two weeks before registration, a dividend came in the mail, $1,246 from the four municipal bond certificates Valerian had given her one Christmas when she was sixteen. She was delighted; it would take care of the school expenses. Son said no. Valerian educated her, all right; there was nothing to be done about that, but he would not let him finance his own education. Jadine dropped her hands to her side with sheer exhaustion.

"Valerian is not the problem." Her voice was faint, gooey with repetition.

This rescue was not going well. She thought she was rescuing him from the night women who wanted him for themselves, wanted him feeling superior in a cradle, deferring to him; wanted her to settle for wifely competence when she could be almighty, to settle for fertility rather than originality, nurturing instead of building. He thought he was rescuing her from Valerian, meaning *them,* the aliens, the people who in a mere three hundred years had killed a world millions of years old. From Micronesia to Liverpool, from Kentucky to Dresden, they killed everything they touched including their own coastlines, their own hills and forests. And even when some of them built something nice and human, they grew vicious protecting it from their own predatory children, let alone an outsider. Each was pulling the other away from the maw of hell—its very ridge top. Each knew the world as it was meant or ought to be. One had a past, the other a future and each one bore the culture to save the race in his hands. Mama-spoiled black man, will you mature with me? Culture-bearing black woman, whose culture are you bearing?

"Correct," he said. "The problem is not Valerian. The problem is me. Solve it. With me or without me, but solve it because it ain't going anywhere. You sweep me under the rug and your children will cut your throat. That fucker in Europe, the one you were thinking about marrying? Go have his children. That should suit you. Then you can do exactly what you bitches have always done: take care of white folks' children. Feed, love and care for white people's children. That's what you were born for; that's what you have waited for all your life. So have that white man's baby, that's your job. You have been doing it for two hundred years, you can do it for two hundred more. There are no 'mixed' marriages. It just looks that way. People don't mix races; they abandon them or pick them. But I want to tell you something: if you have a white man's baby, you have *chosen* to be just another mammy only you are the *real* mammy 'cause you had it in your womb and you are still taking care of white folks' children. Fat or skinny, head rag or wig, cook or model, you take care of white folks' babies—that's what you do and when you don't have any white man's baby to take care of you make one—out of the babies black men give you. You turn little black babies into little white ones; you turn your black brothers into white brothers; you turn your men into white men and when a black woman treats me like what I am, what I really am, you say she's spoiling me. You think I won't do all that company shit because I don't know how? I can do anything! Anything! But I'll be goddamn if I'll do that!"

She looked at him and when he saw the sheen gone from her minky eyes and her wonderful mouth fat with disgust, he tore open his shirt, saying, "I got a story for you."

"Get out of my face."

"You'll like it. It's short and to the point."

"Don't touch me. Don't you touch me."

"Once upon a time there was a farmer—a white farmer . . ."

"Quit! Leave me *alone!*"

"And he had this bullshit bullshit bullshit farm. And a rabbit. A rabbit came along and ate a couple of his . . . ow . . . cabbages."

"You better kill me. Because if you don't, when you're through, I'm going to kill you."

"Just a few cabbages, you know what I mean?"

"I am going to kill you. *Kill* you."

"So he got this great idea about how to get him. How to, to trap . . . this rabbit. And you know what he did? He made him a tar baby. He made it, you hear me? He made it!"

"As sure as I live," she said. "I'm going to kill you."

But she didn't. After he banged the bedroom door, she lay in wrinkled sheets, slippery, gutted, not thinking of killing him. Thinking instead that it would soon be Thanksgiving and there was no place to go for dinner. Then she thought of a towering brass beech—the biggest and oldest in the state. It stood on the north side of the campus and near it was a well. In April the girls met their mothers there to sing and hold hands and sway in the afternoon light. Some of the girls hated it—the well, the beech, the mother-daughter day, and sat around in jeans and no shoes smoking herb to show their contempt for bourgeoisie sentiment and alumni hustling. But the girls who did not hate it surrounded the beech and in long pastel skirts swayed in the spring light. Pale sulfur light sprinkled so softly with lilac it made her want to cry. Jadine joined the barefoot ones, of course, but her tears were not because there was no one to sing with under the biggest beech in the state, but because of the light, pale sulfur sprinkled with lilac.

A piece of her hair was in her mouth and she tried to extricate it with her tongue for her hands weighed a ton apiece. This is familiar, she thought. I know what this is; it's familiar. I am twenty-five and this feeling is too old for me.

Four hours later he was back—repentant, terrified that he had gone too far. But Jadine was solemn—a closed-away orphan in a Cheech and Chong T-shirt with no place to go at Thanksgiving.

Son sat at the foot of the bed and covered his knees with his hands. Jadine spoke very quietly to him.

"I can't let you hurt me again. You stay in that medieval slave basket if you want to. You will stay there by yourself. Don't ask me to do it with you. I won't. There is nothing any of us can do about the past but make our own lives better, that's all I've been trying to help you do. That is the only revenge, for us to get over. *Way* over. But no, you want to talk about white babies; you don't know how to forget the past and do better."

His budding repentance decomposed into a steaming compost.

"If I wanted the editorial page of the Atlanta *Constitution* I would have bought it."

"With what?" Jadine's voice was slick with danger.

"With the money you got from Valerian. The money you fucked your way across Europe for!"

"Well, buy it then. Here, here it is." She picked her wallet up from the night table and opened it. "Here it is. Your original dime. The one you cleaned sheephead for, right? The one you loved? The *only* one you loved. All you want 'in the money line.' Take it. Now you know where it came from, your original dime: some black woman like me fucked a white man for it and then *gave* it to Frisco who made you work your ass off for it. That's your original dime." She threw it on the floor. "Pick it up."

He stared at her. The Cheech and Chong T-shirt was up around her waist and her nakedness below embarrassed him now. He had produced that nakedness and having soiled it, it shamed him.

"Pick it up." She said it again and didn't even sit up. She just lay there, stroking her raw silk thighs the color of natural honey. There was sealskin in her eyes and the ladies minding the pie table vanished like shadows under a noon gold sun.

He thought it would be hard to do, but it wasn't. He thought it would be cold, too. Cold and hard. But it wasn't. It was warm, almost soft, and quite round.

He put it in his pocket and having no place to put himself left the apartment again. He came back the next night to empty rooms and a door key for each of the several locks. He sat down on the sofa and looked at the keys. A pile of mail was on the coffee table too and in it a heavy yellow envelope. He stared at it awhile and then opened it. Out came the photos she had taken in the middle of the road in Eloe. Beatrice, pretty Beatrice, Soldier's daughter. She looked stupid. Ellen, sweet cookie-faced Ellen, the one he always thought so pretty. She looked stupid. They all looked stupid, backwoodsy, dumb, dead . . .

Son put down the photos. I have to find her, he thought. Whatever she wants, I have to do it, want it. But first I have to find her.

10

AFTER THIRTY YEARS of shame the champion daisy trees were marshaling for war. The wild parrots that had escaped the guns of Dominique could feel menace in the creeping of their roots. During the day they tossed their branches; at night they walked the hills. At dawn their new formations challenged the wit of the chevaliers. Their brothers over on Dominique knew nothing of the battle plans for they were in a rain forest tamed for tourists that came by bus from the Old Queen Hotel, gallant and royal since 1927. Now she was dying from behind. Her front on Rue Madelaine was still seacap white and the columns at her entrance showed no signs of wear. Yet at her great round-skirted rear among breadfruit trees and lime, the cells of a motel were growing. A concrete *Y*-shaped thing with patios the size of a card table extended from the dining room from whose forty-seven windows diners once gazed at breadfruit trees and lawn. Now they looked at workmen, concrete and patios the size of a card table. Beyond that were the hills of black Dominiques, and beyond that spectacular mountains of rain forest. The road that cuts through the mountains is a regular tourist attraction. Breathlessly steep and winding, without benefit of guardrails, it offers a view of God's hair, hibiscus, magnolia and oleander, poinsettia and jacaranda. Away in the distance under pink immortelles is an occasional dead plantation, now a hotel with marble dolphins and air conditioning pumping purity into two-hundred-year-old stone. The mountain road descends on the other side of the island to a coastline of cliffs and grottos where fishing villages lay. No marinas here, no golf courses, for here the winds do not trade. They are hot and capricious and the fishermen design strange sails to accommodate them so they can sell their grouper, tuna and bonito to the dead plantations, and the Old Queen Hotel where Jadine sat alone at a table for four.

"Crème de menthe," she had said because the words seemed nice and right and she wanted to say them aloud. And when the waiter returned she regretted it immediately and ordered vermouth. She had called L'Arbe de la Croix. Ondine had answered.

"Where are you?"

"Queen of France, but I missed the ferry, Nanadine. Can somebody come?"

"Well, yes, I reckon so. But it might take awhile."

"I'll wait. Tell him to come to the Old Queen. If I'm not in the lobby, ask for me in the dining room."

"You by yourself?"

"Of course. Hurry, please, Nanadine?"

Of course I'm by myself. When haven't I been by myself. She was alone at a table for four, proud of having been so decisive, so expert at the leaving. Of having refused to be broken in the big ugly hands of any man. Now *she* felt lean and male, having left quickly with no peeping back just in case—no explanatory, loophole-laden note. No last supper. New York had agreed with her exit. A cab right at the door, an uncommunicative driver who took her directly to the place she was going to; Raymond at home; his studio available for the night; a short line at Chemical Bank and Air France ready to go. Aloneness tasted good and even at a table set for four she was grateful to be far away from his original-dime ways, his white-folks-black-folks primitivism. How could she make a life with a cultural throwback, she asked herself, and answered No way. Eloe. No way. Not for all the cadmium yellow and Hansa red in the world. So what if she was alone. So what if when she went away, no one stayed home and remained there all while she was gone and was waiting when she got back.

But he had put his finger on the very bottom of her foot. He had opened the hair on her head with his hands and drove his tongue through the part.

THE MULATTO didn't talk; he hummed a Creole hit and drummed a little on the steering wheel. As they passed Sein de Veilles, Jadine's legs burned with the memory of tar. She could hardly see L'Arbe de la Croix when they got to it, the trees leaned so close to the house. She dashed into Ondine's kitchen, kissed her and said, "Let me get my stuff together first. I'll be right back down and we can talk. Is Margaret here?"

"Upstairs," said Ondine.

No one answered her knock at Margaret's door, but she saw a brighter-than-hallway light falling from Valerian's door and went toward it. Inside, heaped on the twin beds, on the dresser, the chairs and even on the bed table were clothes. Suits, ties, shirts, socks, sweaters and pair after pair of men's shoes.

"Valerian?" she called out.

Margaret stepped from the closet-dressing room, her hands full of empty hangers.

"Well," she said, genuinely surprised. "The prodigal daughter. What did you do to your hair?" Margaret looked flushed and sparkly, her movements directed and sure.

"Something different."

"It's wonderful looking," said Margaret coming toward her, hand outstretched to touch Jadine's hair. Then she stopped and snapped her fingers twice. "We used to call it . . . oh dear . . ." She closed her eyes. "Poodle-cut! That's it. Poodle-cut," and she laughed with such pleasure that Jadine had to smile.

"I'm sorry about leaving you with so little notice. I don't want you to think I didn't appreciate your helping me out last winter."

Margaret waved her hand. "Don't mention it. It was a lousy time for everybody." She sat down on a cluttered bed and began to unbunch the hangers.

"Are you all leaving?" asked Jadine.

"Leaving? No. Why?"

Jadine looked at the clothes.

"Oh, no. I'm just straightening out this unbelievable mess. You wouldn't believe the things that man has accumulated. Eight shoe trees in his closet and only two of them actually in shoes. And look. Linen slacks. Linen. Never worn and so yellow now they can't be. I never knew what a clotheshorse the man was. See here?" Margaret fingered the garment label. "Silk, and here, virgin wool. Look here, one hundred percent cotton. All his undershirts too. He won't wear nylon or tricot. None of the man-made fibers. Everything he owns has to be made by Mother Nature. But what a mess. It'll take me days to get it all sorted. I can't expect Sydney to do this. It's not his job really. Ondine's either. I really could use you now, Jade, but I don't suppose you're staying."

"No. I'm going back tomorrow."

"France?"

"Yes."

"Will you marry that fellow? Mr. Sealskin?"

Jadine sighed. "No."

"Oh? Why not?" Margaret folded the slacks over padded hangers and laid them carefully on the bed. Now she was sorting shirts, smelling them for mildew, examining them for tears, missing buttons, frayed collars. She didn't seem interested in an answer to her question so Jadine didn't give her one, didn't tell her that she hardly knew what the word meant. Instead she asked how Valerian was.

"Better," said Margaret.

"He's not sick, is he?" asked Jadine.

"He says he isn't, but he trembles sometimes and won't go in to town to see a doctor."

"This is no place to be sick in, Margaret. Maybe you should get him back to Philadelphia."

"Of course I will, if it gets really bad." She looked at Jadine as though hurt that her judgment about what was best for her husband was doubted.

"And Michael, how is he?"

"Oh, you don't know, do you? He got in. Berkeley, I mean. The semester begins next week."

"Then you're not going out there?"

"Oh, no. Michael's an adult, Jade. Thirty. I can't go traipsing around the world looking after him when there's so much to do here. You see the mess these clothes are in." She had finished separating the shirts into three piles and had begun on the sweaters. "Jade," she said; she held a blue *V*-necked sweater to her chest. It was nothing like the blue of her eyes. "Sometimes in the morning he can't do everything he used to. You know: buttons, zippers. I have to tie his shoes even. Yesterday I washed his hair"—she smiled—"with Kirk's Original Castile Soap. He doesn't like Breck."

Jadine stared.

"Sydney's going to teach me how to shave him and maybe together we can get him to let us cut his hair. God, is he stubborn. Worse than a child." She laughed lightly, indulgently, and went on sorting, piling, like a confident curator who knew the names of everything in his museum, while Jadine watched saying to herself, And he thinks Valerian made *me*.

ONDINE picked up a screaming lobster and threw him into a pot of boiling water. She held it down with a wooden ladle to make it die faster for she was in the mood for death. It had been an hour since Jadine had come in and kissed her, all smiles and speed. Ondine didn't like her new hairdo: fluffy, frothy as though it was important to look like a schoolgirl. Now she was back in the kitchen, looking subdued.

"What's come over Margaret?" asked Jadine. "She's working her butt off."

"Do her good. Him too."

"But she talks about Valerian like he was a patient, or a baby."

"People do what they have to, I guess, and take payment where they can."

"What's she mad at him for? She's the one who stuck pins in her baby."

Ondine wiped sweat from her forehead with her free hand. "She didn't stick pins in her baby. She stuck em in his baby. Her baby she loved."

"That's a description, maybe, but not a reason. He gave her everything she ever wanted. Remember that little Triumph? And what about—"

"He kept her stupid; kept her idle. That always spells danger."

"Now she's the master, not him?"

"Master, patient, baby—it don't matter. He's still the center of everything." Ondine withdrew the lobster and got right down to it. "You ran off with him, didn't you?"

"It's over, Nanadine. I don't know what got into me."

"You could have told us."

"Maybe. But everything was so messed up here. I mean that was some Christmas."

"You still could have told us."

"Well, if it will make you any happier, it was a mistake. A mistake of the first order, believe me. You know I never worked so hard in my life to keep something going. I'd never done that before. I never cared whether a relationship worked or not, you know. I mean if it worked, it worked; if it didn't—later. But this time I worked my butt off and all I got for it was a black eye and the rent. So—" Jadine slapped the table with her palm marking the end of the affair. "That's that."

"He hit you?"

"Yes, among other things."

"He actually *hit* you?"

"It's over, Nanadine, besides, I hit him too."

"I should hope so. I should damn well hope so. Oh, baby, baby, how could you run off with a . . ."

"Let's don't talk about it. I left and that's that. One thing though. If he calls here, you don't know where I am, and if he comes here . . ."

"Comes here?"

"Well, I don't know, he might. Anyhow, don't tell him where I am."

"Where are you?" asked Ondine.

"I'm going to get my stuff and go back to Paris."

Stuff, thought Ondine, meant mainly the fur coat. She wondered if her niece would even have come to say goodbye had it not been that the sealskin coat was there. "Then what?" she asked.

Jadine shrugged and changed the subject. "How's Valerian?"

"Hanging on."

"Did she really do all of that to her baby?"

"She really did."

"Wow. And she's not bugging you anymore?"

"Not at all."

"So what's your situation here?" Jadine's voice was serious, but there was pleading in it too. (Please don't need me now, not now. I can't parent now. I cannot be needed now. Another time, please. I have spent it all. Please don't need me now.)

"Same. They want us to stay. Mrs. Street does anyway, and he don't say much one way or the other. Sits in that greenhouse all day listening to music."

"Do you want to stay?"

"Do we have a choice?" asked Ondine, looking carefully at the ringlets on Jadine's head.

"Sure you have a choice. You can work other places or not at all. You want to come with me to Paris?" Jadine's shoulder ached for a second as she remembered hanging out of a second-story window on Ninety-third Street.

"Girl, don't play with me."

"I'm serious."

"Jadine, we done what we could for you because—well, what

I mean to say is you don't owe us nothing. But, well, I never told you nothing. I never told you nothing at all and I take full responsibility for that. But I have to tell you something now."

Jadine lifted her head and looked in her aunt's eyes.

"Jadine, a girl has got to be a daughter first. She have to learn that. And if she never learns how to be a daughter, she can't never learn how to be a woman. I mean a real woman: a woman good enough for a child; good enough for a man—good enough even for the respect of other women. Now you didn't have a mother long enough to learn much about it and I thought I was doing right by sending you to all them schools and so I never told you it and I should have. You don't need your own natural mother to be a daughter. All you need is to feel a certain way, a certain careful way about people older than you are. Don't mistake me now. I don't mean you have to love all kinds of mean old people, and if it's in your mind that I'm begging you for something, get it out. I ain't."

"Yes, you are, Ondine." Jadine's voice was steady. "You are asking me to parent you. Please don't. I can't do that now."

"I am not asking you that. I'm just saying what a daughter is. A daughter is a woman that cares about where she come from and takes care of them that took care of her. No, I don't want you to be what you call a parent. Not me, and not Sydney either. What I want from you is what I want for you. I don't want you to care about me for my sake. I want you to care about me for yours." She reached out to touch her niece's hand, but something made her stop short of it.

When Ondine said, "You didn't have a mother long enough," blood rushed to Jadine's skin the way it always did when her motherlessness was mentioned. But she spoke gently and steadily to Ondine. "No, you don't, Nanadine. You want me to pay you back. You worked for me and put up with me. Now it's my turn to do it for you, that's all you're saying."

"Turn? Turn? This ain't no game a bid whist . . ."

"There are other ways to be a woman, Nanadine," Jadine

went on. "Your way is one, I guess it is, but it's not my way. I don't want to be . . . like you. Wait. Don't look at me like that. I'm being honest with you now and you have to listen! I don't want to learn how to be the kind of woman you're talking about because I don't want to be that kind of woman."

"There ain't but one kind. Just one, and if you say another hateful word to me, I'll . . ." She stopped.

"What? Hit me? Would you, Nanadine? You'd hit me too?"

The older woman was quiet. Her niece, her baby, her crown had put her in the same category as that thing she ran off with. And now she was going on talking, explaining, saying, but Ondine never heard anymore. The volume of her heart was up too loud.

When Jadine went off to finish packing, Ondine sat patting the table with her right hand, her chin resting on the fist of her left. She didn't know what she expected. What she was expecting her niece to do or think or feel. But something more than she had seen. Maybe she's right. Maybe I just wanted her to feel sorry for us, she thought, maybe that's what I expected and that's a lowdown wish if ever I had one.

Sydney came in and stopped her thoughts. "That her?" he asked.

"Yes."

"Off again?"

"Yep. Paris."

"Where's he?"

"She dumped him."

"I could have told him that."

"So could I. Go up and say goodbye to her. She's making tracks tomorrow if she can."

Sydney sat down and unclasped his bow tie. "She ask you for any money?"

"Nothing dangerous. Just a few francs for the shuttle. She had a thing full of those what you call traveling checks. Go on up and see her. I'll take him his tray."

"She wants to say goodbye, she knows where I am."

"Sydney, don't be like that."

"But I *am* like that. She didn't do well by us, Ondine."

"She's young. She'll settle."

"Age ain't got nothing to do with it."

"She's not a savings account, Sydney. You don't get interest back."

"Ought to."

"It's more different for them than it was for us. There's a whole bunch of stuff they can do that we never knew nothing about."

"And a whole bunch they don't know nothing about," he answered.

"Well, maybe you right. Maybe it don't pay to love nothing. I loved that little boy like he was mine, so he wouldn't grow up and kill somebody. And instead of thanks, I get meanness. Disrespect."

"Let's not go into that no more."

"He's okay now. Doin fine. But I'm not responsible for that, no. I'm responsible for not telling nobody. She accused me of not liking her enough to stop her. You go figure that out. Then I take another one in my heart, your brother's baby girl. Another one not from my womb, and I stand on my feet thirty years so she wouldn't have to. And did without so she wouldn't have to. And she couldn't think of nothing better to do than buy me some shoes I can't wear, a dress I shouldn't, and run off with the first pair of pants that steps in the door. Now explain me that."

"I can't explain nothing no more. It didn't used to be this way. Seem like folks used to take care of folks once upon a time. Old black people must be a worrisome thing to the young ones these days."

Ondine went to the oven and removed a baked potato. She put it on a plate and the plate on a tray. Then she went to the refrigerator and removed a wineglass that had been chilling there. Sydney watched her movements.

Ondine got out a napkin. "She said she didn't think he would, but if he did call or come looking for her we shouldn't let him know where she is."

"He better not set foot on this place."

"From what she says he beat her up some."

"Then I hope he does come," said Sydney. "I'll put that bullet in him for sure."

"No, you won't."

"You mistake me if you don't think so. I'll shoot him the same minute I see him and explain later."

"This is not your property, Sydney."

"No, but it's my home. If this ain't my home, then nothing is but the grave."

"Well, we'll be there soon enough."

Sydney thought about that. "You think she'll bury us, Ondine?"

"I think we're going to have to bury ourselves, Sydney."

"Well, in that case the shroud may as well be comfy." He picked up the rattan tray and, since he was a genuine Philadelphia Negro mentioned in the book of that name, he reclasped his bow tie and adjusted his cuff links before he left the kitchen and went to the greenhouse. He noticed that the bricks that edged the courtyard were popping up out of the ground, leaning every which way. Urged, it seemed to him, out of the earth, like they were poked from beneath. Cement, he thought, is all that will keep this earth still. This place dislocates everything. I'll get that mulatto to fix them right this time. And something serious had to be done about the ants. They had already eaten through the loudspeaker wires and he had had to transfer the entire system to the greenhouse: turntable, receiver, records. Sydney was grateful to the ants because he really hated vacuuming or polishing doorknobs while the music boomed through the house. He preferred silence for his work. Now he was free of it and Mr. Street had it all to himself. Still, if ants will eat copper—something serious had to be done. If it's not one thing it's another, he thought, and either he was shrinking in his old age or the trees were jumping up overnight. The roof of the washhouse was completely obscured by a heavy branch. That mulatto may buck if I tell him to cut it down, he thought. Better get somebody from town.

The greenhouse was sunk in violins and Valerian, seated at a seed bench, did not hear Sydney enter. He was drenched in music and although his fingers shuddered occasionally, his head-of-a-coin profile moved accurately to the tempo. Sydney tapped him on the shoulder and he turned.

"Your lunch, Mr. Street."

Valerian motioned for him to put the tray down, his fingers describing a wavy arc in the air.

"You letting this place run down, Mr. Street."

"What's that?" asked Valerian.

Sydney walked over to the record player and lifted the arm away. "I said you letting this place run down. Used to be pretty in here. You letting it go to pieces."

"It's my place," said Valerian. "Turn the music back on."

Sydney did not move, but said, "You don't grow nothing in here anymore."

"I like it this way, Sydney. Put the music back."

"Then you should take care of it."

"That'll do, Sydney. Hand me the mail."

Sydney picked up the stack of letters, circulars and catalogs and held them out to Valerian, but the dancing hands could not receive them. "Want me to open them for you?" asked Sydney.

"No. Yes."

Sydney pulled up a stepping stool and sat down next to Valerian. "You should take care of yourself, too. You need a haircut."

"I prefer it long," said Valerian.

"No, you don't. You just don't want to go into town. The mulatto's here today. If you won't let me cut it, let him take you over."

"What mulatto?"

Sydney slit open a letter with a penknife. "The one Dr. Michelin sent over. A mulatto. Been coming awhile now. He can take you over to get your hair cut."

"Not today," said Valerian. "Not today; later, Sydney." Valerian turned toward the tray and tried to pick up the knife and fork. He succeeded but could not manage to make them do anything else but wave there in his hands. Sydney put aside the mail, and stood up. He took the knife and fork from Valerian, broke open the steaming potato, and scooped out a forkful. He blew on it and then held it in front of Valerian's mouth. Valerian closed his lips and looked into Sydney's eyes. He tried as best he could to see what was there, what was really there. He wasn't sure, but he believed he saw kindness. He opened his lips and swallowed.

"Good," said Sydney. "That's good. It's not too hot, is it?"

Valerian shook his head and opened his mouth for more. He chewed for a little while and then said, "Sydney?"

"Yes, sir?"

"Did you . . . ah . . ."

"No, sir, I didn't. I heard about it same time you did."

"Ondine never told you?"

"Not a word."

"I hear them in the kitchen. Talking, like they used to."

"Yes, sir."

"Remember? How they used to gossip in the kitchen back then?"

"I remember."

"He's all right, isn't he?"

"Michael? Oh, yes, sir. He's fine."

"I'm thinking of going back. I think I should leave this place and go back to Philadelphia."

"What for?"

"I don't like it here anymore. No reason to be here now."

"No reason to be anywhere, Mr. Street. But I'd think carefully on it if I was you. Ondine and me, we like it down here.

Philadelphia winters can be hard on old people. It's nice and warm down here. Quiet too. We like it fine. Would you like a sip of Chablis now?" He put down the fork and went to the small refrigerator for a bottle of wine.

"No," said Valerian. "Not now."

"I would," said Sydney. "I'd like a glass myself." He worked the screw into the cork. "You sure you don't want any?"

"I said no."

"How are your bunions, Mr. Street?"

"Corns. I don't have bunions. I have corns."

"How are they?"

"Sydney, you are drinking my wine."

"Next time that mulatto comes, I'll tell him to bring you back a pair of huaraches."

"I don't want any huaraches."

"Sure you do. Nice pair of huaraches be good for you. Make your feet feel good. This time next year, you'll thank me for em."

"What do you mean, this time next year? I'm going back."

"I figure we're going to be here a long time, Mr. Street. A good long time."

"What's happening here. Something's happening here."

"Don't agitate yourself. Rest your mind." Sydney put down the wineglass, and went to the record player. He held the arm over the record and turned to Valerian. "We'll give you the best of care. Just like we always done. That's something you ain't never got to worry about." He placed the arm carefully in the groove and turned the volume up high. Valerian smiled then, and his fingers danced lightly in the air.

THE AIRPORT in Dominique is a long building made of pale yellow concrete blocks. If you didn't know you were in the Caribbean, the paper in the ladies' room would tell you. To an American the contempt in which the rest of the world holds toilet paper is incomprehensible. It is treated as though it were, in fact, toilet paper. Jadine stepped out of the stall and stood before the tiny mirror over the sink. She sudsed her hands generously with a piece of her own soap and rinsed them carefully. She wrapped the soap in a piece of wax paper, returned it to her traveling bag, from which she took a tube of hand lotion. She creamed her palms and the backs of her hands, then with tissue wiped away the lotion that had gotten under her fingernails. Unhurried at last, with thirty minutes before flight time. The frantic scampering over with. She had run away from New York City with the same speed she had run toward it. New York was not her home after all. The dogs were leashed in the city but the reins were not always secure. Sometimes walking with their owners they met other dogs and if they were unspayed and unchecked you could see a female standing quietly under the paws of a male who had not even spoken to her, just sniffed for purposes of identification. She thought it could be a shelter for her because there the night women could be beaten, reduced to shadows and confined to the brier patch where they belonged. But she could not beat them alone. There were no shelters anyway; it was adolescent to think that there were. Every orphan knew that and knew also that mothers however beautiful were not fair. No matter what you did, the diaspora mothers with pumping breasts would impugn your character. And an African woman, with a single glance from eyes that had burned away their own lashes, could discredit your elements.

She still had plenty of time to take two Dramamines, comb her hair, check her make-up, but this ladies' lounge was not designed for lingering. She was doing her eyes when a girl came out of the stall next to the one she had used. She had a short mop and a plastic pail of various cleansers in her hands. She wore a green uniform which looked even greener beneath her russet wig. Jadine glanced at the wig in the mirror and then back to her own lashes. The girl stopped dead and did not take her eyes off Jadine, who was flattered but wished she would not stare so. Then the girl approached her.

"You don't remember me?" she asked.

Jadine turned around. The wig was so overwhelming it was awhile before she recognized her.

"L'Arbe de la Croix," said the girl.

"Oh, wow." Jadine smiled. "I didn't recognize you. What are you doing here? You work here now?"

The girl nodded. "You took the chocolate eater away," she said.

Jadine closed her smile and turned back to the mirror. There was nothing like an islander; they never had any chat—or manners for that matter. Conversation with them was always an interrogation and she was not about to explain anything to this child.

"He was going to send me a wig, he said."

"Looks like he did," said Jadine.

"Not this one. I have a picture of the other one. It's at home. Is he coming back? Can you get it for me?"

"No," Jadine answered.

"You kill him?" asked the girl in a very matter-of-fact tone.

Jadine slung the huge, lightweight traveling bag over her shoulder and removed her coat from the top of the stall where it hung. "I have to go now," she said.

"Thérèse said you kill him," the girl insisted.

"Tell Thérèse *she* killed him."

"No," said the girl, perplexed. "Thérèse has magic breasts. They still give milk."

"I bet they do," said Jadine.

"But there is nobody to nurse them."

"She's not looking in the right places," said Jadine. Black pearls of hair were visible at the wig's edge. The girl's eyes were wide, still, the curiosity in them was the only thing that kept them from looking like an animal's. A deer, thought Jadine. She has the eyes of a curious deer. She wished once more that she had had real talent—she'd like to draw her—deer eyes, wig and all. Suddenly she reached into the side pocket of her traveling bag. A few francs were shoved in there and she dropped the whole lot into the girl's plastic pail. "Bye, Mary, I have to go. Good luck." Jadine pushed open the door and was gone.

"Alma," whispered the girl. "Alma Estée."

ABOARD the 707 Jadine had free use of the seat next to her. Not many passengers in first class. She checked her five luggage claim tickets stapled to the envelope that held a copy of her one-way ticket to Orly. Everything was in order. As soon as the plane was airborne, she reached above her head to adjust the air flow. Bringing her hand down she noticed a tiny irregularity in the nail of her forefinger. She opened her purse and took out an emery board. Two swift strokes and it was gone. Her nail was perfect again. She turned her sealskin coat lining side out and folded it carefully into the empty seat beside her. Then she adjusted the headrest. The same sixteen answers to the question What went wrong? kicked like a chorus line. Having sixteen answers meant having none. So none it was. Zero. She would go back to Paris and begin at Go. Let loose the dogs, tangle with the woman in yellow—with her and with all the night women who had *looked* at her. No more shoulders and limitless chests. No more dreams of safety. No more. Perhaps that was the thing—the thing Ondine was saying. A grown woman did not need safety or its dreams. She *was* the safety she longed for.

The plane lifted itself gracefully over the island; its tail of smoke widened, then dispersed. It was evening and the stars were already brilliant. The hills below crouched on all fours under the weight of the rain forest where liana grew and soldier ants marched in formation. Straight ahead they marched, shamelessly single-minded, for soldier ants have no time for dreaming. Almost all of them are women and there is so much to do—the work is literally endless. So many to be born and fed, then found and buried. There is no time for dreaming. The life of their world requires organization so tight and sacrifice so complete there is little need for males and they are seldom produced.

When they are needed, it is deliberately done by the queen who surmises, by some four-million-year-old magic she is heiress to, that it is time. So she urges a sperm from the private womb where they were placed when she had her one, first and last copulation. Once in life, this little Amazon trembled in the air waiting for a male to mount her. And when he did, when he joined a cloud of others one evening just before a summer storm, joined colonies from all over the world gathered for the marriage flight, he knew at last what his wings were for. Frenzied, he flies into the humming cloud to fight gravity and time in order to do, just once, the single thing he was born for. Then he drops dead, having emptied his sperm into his lady-love. Sperm which she keeps in a special place to use at her own discretion when there is need for another dark and singing cloud of ant folk mating in the air. Once the lady has collected the sperm, she too falls to the ground, but unless she breaks her back or neck or is eaten by one of a thousand things, she staggers to her legs and looks for a stone to rub on, cracking and shredding the wings she will never need again. Then she begins her journey searching for a suitable place to build her kingdom. She crawls into the hollow of a tree, examines its walls and corners. She seals herself off from all society and eats her own wing muscles until she bears her eggs. When the first larvae appear, there is nothing to feed them so she gives them their unhatched sisters until they are old enough and strong enough to hunt and bring their prey back to the kingdom. That is all. Bearing, hunting, eating, fighting, burying. No time for dreaming, although sometimes, late in life, somewhere between the thirtieth and fortieth generation she might get wind of a summer storm one day. The scent of it will invade her palace and she will recall the rush of wind on her belly—the stretch of fresh wings, the blinding anticipation and herself, there, airborne, suspended, open, trusting, frightened, determined, vulnerable—girlish, even, for an entire second and then another and another. She may lift her head then, and point her wands toward the place where the summer storm is entering her palace and in the weariness that ruling queens alone know, she may wonder whether his death was sudden. Or did he languish? And if so, if there was a bit of time left, did he think how mean the world was, or did he fill that space of time thinking of her? But soldier ants do not have time for dreaming. They are women and have much to do. Still it would be hard. So very hard to forget the man who fucked like a star.

THE MAN sat on the stone wall that separated Rue Madelaine from the sea. His legs hung over the ledge below which were rocks and a thin strip of dirty sand. To the left a rickety pier extended some two hundred feet into the water where black boys leaped, splashed, screamed and climbed back up to leap again. The garbage on the sand was mostly paper and bottles. No food garbage down here. Here, away from the tourist shops, away from the restaurants and offices, was that part of the boulevard where the sea threw up what it could not digest. Whatever life there is on the sand is desperate. A gull negotiated the breeze and swooped down on a black starfish. The gull pecked it, flew away and returned to peck again and again until finally the starfish yielded the magenta string that was its heart. The man watched the gull tear it out with a great deal of interest. Then he swung his legs over the wall and stood up. Shielding his eyes from the sun with his arm, he looked toward the market crowd: a half-block of cloth roofs, tables, baskets, pots, boxes and trays. His jacket was draped across his forearm—both hands in his pockets—as he started toward the market looking for Thérèse. Earlier he had taken the shuttle bus from the airport to the Old Queen Hotel and gone directly from there up the hill to the powder pink house, climbing slowly, carefully, keeping to the edge of the road where the dust gave way to grass. He moved like a man saving his strength, or one suspicious of trip mines.

No one was in the pink house. The door was latched although the windows were open; a print skirt ripped down the back seam hung from one of the front windows and served it as both curtain and shade. He poked his head through and tossed a piece of hand luggage into the room. Then he walked back down the hill, nodding to a few passersby, and stopped at the house that sold meat pies and rum and sometimes lent hair clippers. He didn't even try the little tin-can French he'd learned in Vietnam, he simply said Gideon? Thérèse? The owner and another man told him something he could not understand about Thérèse, and mentioned Gideon's name in connection with "taxi." He nodded and smiled as though it was all brilliantly clear and continued down the hill. The morning he spent walking the streets, looking at the elegant houses turned into restaurants or offices, and the colonial administration buildings built like castles to last. Away from the town to the north and east were the frightened houses of the whites, hiding on sloped roads behind hedges of tropical flora. South was the business district collected mainly on Rue Madelaine and the tributaries running from it. The Blacks lived in the western hills in shacks and cement-block houses or along narrow streets on the west side of town where the sea spit up what it could not digest. It was unusually cool and his weather eye saw that a rainstorm might be due announcing the hurricane season. He walked the streets of Queen of France, glancing at the drivers of the taxis in case Gideon might be one. Three hours of walking and he was not tired. Had not been tired for days now. Being still was the problem. In the apartment in New York he could not sit for long—except to look again and again at the photographs she had taken in Eloe. A fat yellow envelope of pictures had lain unopened on the coffee table along with the keys. Having nothing quiet to do with his huge hands except finger his original dime, he opened the envelope and looked at the pictures of all the places and people he had loved. Then he could be still. Gazing at the photos one by one trying to find in them what it was that used to comfort him so, used to reside with him, in him like royalty in his veins. Used to people his dreams, and anchor his floating days. When danger was most imminent and he fell asleep in spite of himself they were there—the yellow houses with white doors, the ladies at the pie table at Good Shepherd—Aunt Rosa; Soldier's mother May Downing whom they called Mama May; Drake's grandmother Winnie Boon who switched them every spring; Miss Tyler who had taught him how to play piano, and the younger women: Beatrice, Ellen, and the children who had been born while he was away. The men: Old Man, Rascal, Turner and Soldier and Drake and Ernie Paul who left the service a first lieutenant and now had his own mortuary in Montgomery, Alabama, and doin fine. There were no photos of them, but they were there in the pictures of trees behind their houses, the fields where they worked, the river they fished, the church where they testified, the joints where they drank. It all looked miserable in the photographs, sad, poor and even poor-spirited.

When he was not looking at the pictures, he had telephoned her friends and acquaintances. Her women friends knew nothing but suggested he come over and talk about it; the men he would not call. So he paced, walked the streets, listened to the telephone that did not ring, waited for the mail and finally made up his mind to go back to Isle des Chevaliers. Start there in order to find her. He left the keys with the super and the photos on the table, and it was hard to sit still on the airplane; hard to sit still on the sea wall, so he stood up and walked toward the market. Maybe Thérèse was there.

The afternoon sun had knocked away the earlier chill and the air was damp and much too warm. A smallish crowd of local buyers and tourists milled about the stalls and stands. There were more people selling than buying. He stopped before a tray of meat tarts thinking to buy one, but the smell turned his stomach and he moved away. Farther down he could see crates of bright red bottles of soda. Something cold to drink, he thought, might be better. As he turned in that direction, he bumped into two young Germans with cameras. Automatically he looked toward where their cameras were focused. There she was, hat intact, mouth moving a mile a minute, her broken eyes cheerfully evil.

He stepped in front of the cameras and said No to the Germans. No, and shook his head. The young men looked angry for a second and then, glancing at each other, shrugged and moved on. He stood close to Thérèse for a full minute before she recognized him and shrieked, "Chocolate eater! Chocolate eater!" almost knocking her tray of smoked eels to the ground.

"This place is closed," she said to a would-be customer, "*fermé,* madame, *fermé,*" and packed up her eels, her folding camp stool and her wooden crate—none of which she would let him carry as they made their way up to the powder pink house. Thérèse laughed and chattered about the weather and her girlhood all the way but once in the house she became shy and formal, making him uncomfortable and unable to sit. To break the awkward atmosphere he initiated a pointed conversation.

"Have you been back over there?" he asked her.

She spit on the floor for an answer and added nothing to it.

He smiled. "What work does Gideon do now?"

"Hires out," she said. "To taxi men."

Drumming up business, he guessed, at airports and hotels for the men who owned their taxis. They would tip him for the fares he got them. Thérèse grew silent and formal again. Like a duenna she avoided his eyes but watched him nonetheless. Quietly (all she needed was lace in her hands) guarding some virtue that was only in her mind. The atmosphere of starch returned until he remembered something. He'd put his plastic-wrapped airplane snack in his hand luggage: a pastrami on a roll, a tiny packet of pasteurized cheese, one of mustard and an apple. He opened the bag and presented it to Thérèse, whose happiness, instead of being cheerful, was so deep it was solemn.

"Eat," he told her, but she wouldn't. She left everything just as it was, patting the Saran Wrap fondly. Then she turned to him and said, "I was a pretty girl." He looked at her and thought perhaps it was so. Perhaps. He couldn't tell, and didn't care. "Pretty" was inapplicable to what he liked about her. She repeated it. "I was a pretty girl."

"I'm sure you were," he said smiling.

"No one remembers now how I was. I was a pretty girl. A pretty girl." She patted the snack package and he could see that there was some relationship between the present he had given her and her recollections of her youth and beauty. He thought she was going to go on about it, but she stopped and lingered with that thought, patting the plastic wrap tenderly. He had decided to excuse himself from the awkwardness and walk around outside when Gideon came in. The day's disappointment ran from his face as soon as he saw Son. He put the paper bag he was carrying on the table and encircled Son in his arms.

"What you doing back here?" he wanted to know.

"I got a little business to attend to."

"Isle des Chevaliers?"

"Yes."

"Murder, I hope." Gideon took off his shirt and walked to the sink.

Son shook his head. "I need some information."

Gideon leaned over the sink washing his hands and face. When he had rinsed, Thérèse took a cloth from a nail and handed it to him.

"What you want to know?" Gideon asked, drying his ears.

"If she's there. If she's not, I need an address."

"Christ," said Gideon, and snapped his cloth in disgust. "I knew it. The yalla. What did I tell you? Huh?"

"I have to find her." Son's voice was flat, stale.

Thérèse sitting by the record player was rocking her head as though she were at a wake. When Son said "I have to find her" in that emotionless voice, she began to accompany the rocking with soft grunts, "Unh, unh, unh, unh."

"Stop that!" said Gideon. "Fix some food, for Christ's sake!"

Thérèse stood up slowly, caressing her airplane food and, after placing it on top of the dead record player, put a pot of water on to boil. She busied herself picking stones out of the rice while Gideon told Son that the yalla was gone.

"She was here? How do you know?" asked Son.

"What black girl can take a plane here I don't know about? Besides Alma Estée saw her go. She cleans up at the airport. She saw her and spoke to her in the toilet there. Thérèse, go call Alma Estée."

"I don't know where she is." Thérèse was reluctant to leave.

"At her mama's. Go on now." Then he said to Son, "A week ago, maybe less, Alma saw her leave. *Let* her leave, man. *Let* her go."

Son looked at Thérèse as if to question why she tarried. She saw his impatience and, leaving her rice half-picked, left the house. Son was deeply depressed at that news. He had waited in New York too long before coming here. But he had been convinced that she was not really gone as in "never coming back." He thought before long she'd come banging in as she had done before. So he couldn't leave the apartment except for short spells. She'd call and he would not be there. She'd ring the bell and he would not be there. It took a week of silent pacing—of sleeplessness for him—to decide to go looking, and from what Gideon said it was a week ago that she was here; she must have left almost immediately.

Gideon opened his paper bag and took out a bottle of beer. He sat down next to Son and offered it to him.

"You can get used to it," he said. "After all those years in the States I thought that was the only way, cold. Ice-cold. I still prefer it that way. But now I can drink it warm again. Like before."

Son looked at it. The very notion of warm beer in his empty stomach sickened him. He refused.

"You sick, man. Not just your head either. Why can't you let her go?"

"Let her go?" asked Son, and he smiled a crooked smile. Let go the woman you had been looking for everywhere just because she was difficult? Because she had a temper, energy, ideas of her own and fought back? Let go a woman whose eyebrows were a study, whose face was enough to engage your attention all your life? Let go a woman who was not only a woman but a sound, all the music he had ever wanted to play, a world and a way of being in it? Let *that* go? "I can't," he said. "I can't."

Gideon swallowed his beer and they were both quiet until Thérèse returned and the girl stepped in the door. Son grew dizzy as soon as he saw her. He looked at the red-brown wig on her head and the blood ran away from his own. It was all mixed up. He had it straight before: the pie ladies and the six-string banjo and then he was seduced, corrupted by cloisonné and raw silk the color of honey and he was willing to change, to love the cloisonné, to abandon the pie ladies and the nickel nickelodeon and Eloe itself and Frisco too because she had given him back his original dime, the pretty one, the shiny one, the romantic ten-cent piece, and made him see it the way it was, the way it really was, not just a dazzling coin, but a piece of currency with a history rooted in gold and cloisonné and humiliation and death, so what was he doing loving Frisco and his dime when it had no value and didn't belong to Frisco anyway? And what was he doing thinking that Drake and Soldier and Ernie Paul were more precious than Catherine the Great's earrings or that the pie ladies were in danger unless he alone protected them and kept them alive. So he had changed, given up fraternity, or believed he had, until he saw Alma Estée in a wig the color of dried blood. Her sweet face, her midnight skin mocked and destroyed by the pile of synthetic dried blood on her head. It was all mixed up. But he could have sorted it out if she had just stood there like a bougainvillea in a girdle, like a baby jaguar with lipstick on, like an avocado with earrings, and let him remove it.

"Oh, baby baby baby baby," he said, and went to her to take off the wig, to lift it, tear it, throw it far from her midnight skin and antelope eyes. But she jumped back, howled and resecured it on her head with clenched fingers. It was all mixed up. He did not know what to think or feel. The dizziness increased and played a middle ear drone in his head.

Gideon tapped him on the shoulder and he sat down.

"Leave her be," he said. "She want to look the fool, let her. Ask her about the American girl. Alma, tell him."

Alma told him, but from a distance so he could not get his hands on her head again, so he could not deprive her of the red wig which she had to buy herself because he had not sent her one as he promised to do, and had not brought her one either when he came back, but had come, in fact, looking for the American girl whom he loved and remembered, but not her. He had forgotten all about her and forgotten to bring her the one thing she had asked for. Oh, she was good enough to run to the store for him, and good enough to clean the toilet for American black girls to pee in, and to be tipped by them but not have her name remembered by them and not good enough to be remembered at all by the chocolate eater who did go to the trouble of knowing her name. She told him then that she worked in the airport cleaning, and that she had seen the American girl getting on a plane bound for Paris with a huge bag on her shoulder and a black fur coat and that she had been met by a young man with yellow hair and blue eyes and white skin and they had laughed and kissed and laughed in the corridor outside the ladies' room and had held hands and walked to the plane and she had her head on his shoulder the whole time they walked to the plane. She had seen it, and Son saw it too: the mink-dark eyes staring greedily into blue ones, another hand on the inside of her raw silk knee the color of honey. Not being able to go further with those pictures, he diverted his mind to the irrelevant. Who was it? Was it Michael who met her, Valerian's son, the one that didn't show up for Christmas, but who came later? Was that the Ryk who sent her the coat? Or was it someone in New York who had come to the island with her? Or was it someone she met in the airport? It was all mixed up, like when he ran out of laughter ammunition and kicked an M.P. in the groin, but the thing that was clear was the thing he knew when he stood wrapped in a towel gazing out of the window at this same man's back: he had not wanted to love her because he could not survive losing her. But it was done.

Already done and he was in it; stuck in it and revolted by the possibility of being freed.

Gideon interrupted his questions. "What will you do?"

"Find her. Go to Paris and find her." He pressed his temples with his fingers to stop the drone.

"But if she's with another?"

"I'll take her away from him."

"A woman, man. Just a woman," said Gideon patiently.

"I have to find her."

"How? Paris is a big place."

"I'll get her address."

"Where?"

"From over there."

"They won't give it to you."

"They will. I'll make them. Make them tell me who the man is. Where she went." He was standing now. Nervous. Eager to get going.

"You not going for the address, you going to cause mayhem."

"Let him," said Thérèse. "Kill them, chocolate eater."

"Don't be crazy. It's just a woman, man."

It was true. He wanted to find her but he wanted to smash something too. Smash the man who took the woman he had loved while she slept, and smash where they had first made love, where she took his hand and was afraid and needed him and they walked up the stairs holding hands, just like she walked to the plane holding somebody else's hand. She should not have done that if she was going to get on an airplane and put her head on another man's shoulder.

"Get me there," he said to Gideon. "Now, while there is still light."

Gideon ran his tongue over his stone-white teeth. "No. I'm not doing that. Take you to smash up the place?"

"I only want her address. That's all."

"You won't be welcome there and neither me."

"I will only talk to them."

"And if they won't talk to you?"

"They will. They'll tell me."

"No, man. That's final."

"All right. I'll take the launch."

"Good," said Gideon. "Take the launch. In two days maybe you'll be cooler."

"Two days?"

"Two, yes. Launch don't go again till Monday. Today is market day. Saturday."

"I can't wait that long."

"Telephone them."

"They won't tell me anything on the telephone. Take me."

"This is crazy-mad shit, man. You can't go there."

"I don't have a choice. There's nothing else for me to do. You think I'd choose this if I had a choice?"

Thérèse turned around and looked at him. Then she looked at the airplane food on the record player. "I can take you," she said.

"You not taking him nowhere. You blind as a bat."

"I can take you," she repeated.

"The sun's going down. You'll drown!" said Gideon. "We'll fish you off the beach in the morning."

"I can see better in the dark and I know that crossing too well."

"Don't trust her, man. Don't. I'm telling you."

Son looked at Thérèse and nodded. "Get me there, Thérèse."

"Two big fools," said Gideon. "One blind, the other gone mad!"

"Eat," said Thérèse to Son. "I'll take you when it's time."

Son stood up. "I can't eat," he said. "And I've been awake for days. Sleep won't come and I can't get hungry."

"Come with me then," said Gideon. "Let's go out. Go to Grande Cinq, have a drink and relax a little."

"No," he said. "I don't want a woman."

"Christ!" Gideon was disgusted. He never got over being amazed at that kind of passion, though he had seen it enough. "Well, rum's good anywhere. I resign from the sober world tonight." He went into the bedroom and returned with a pint of rum, the bottle half-full. He poured and passed a cup to Son who took it in tiny sips with much time in between. All three sat at the table, Son alone not eating the fish and rice. Gideon told stories about women he had known: their "wiles" and their "ways" till he settled on the nurse he'd married in the States. His grievances about the lady were trotted out one by one for show: her children by a former marriage; her ailments; her habits of dress; her laugh; her relatives; her food; her looks. He allowed as how she was faithful, but that's all she was. Had she been otherwise he swore he would never have left her out of gratitude. As it was, she was insatiable: mean, arrogant and insatiable. He went to bed fully clothed on that note: the abnormal sexual hunger of black American nurses.

Son lay down on the cot Alma Estée sometimes used while Thérèse got ready and he did not know he slept until she woke him. He sat up relieved that the jaw's harp in his head had stopped. She brought a flashlight, but they did not need it to walk down the hill or to find the *Prix de France*. They checked the gas and agreed there was enough for a round trip. They rowed away from the dock until they were far enough out to start a motor without attracting the attention of any gendarmes who might be on contraband patrol. It was raining a little, getting foggier, but the sea was not high. Thérèse insisted on steering for she knew the way, she said, and could not talk the directions to him. The feel of the current was what she went by. She only prayed no larger boats were out there, as hampered in vision as she was in the fog.

He remembered the trip over as half an hour, forty-five minutes at most, but this trip seemed longer. They'd been out at least an hour. The boat rocked and skipped, rocked and skipped to a regular beat. The jaw's harp was back like a nuthouse lullaby and he dozed a little and woke; dozed a little and woke. Each time his eyes opened they rested on the shadow of Marie Thérèse Foucault. Each time her shoulders and profile grew darker—her outline fainter. Till finally he could barely make her out at all, he simply felt her feet against his. Even her breathing could not be heard over the motor's breath and the insistent harp in his head. The light rain stopped and the clouds descended to examine that party of two. One tranquil, dozing, weakly fighting sleep—the other, head turned landward intent on a horizon she could not possibly see even if she were not as blind as justice. Her hands on the lever were nimble, steady. The upper part of her body leaned forward straining as if to hear fish calling from the sea. Behind the curious clouds, hills crouched on all fours and at their knees were rocks and the permanent sea. Thérèse cut the motor and dropped one oar to guide with. The tide carried them and the little boat seemed to be floating on its own. She held the oar midships until it struck a rock, split and slowed the boat to a half turn and then a rocking on baby waves. Son stirred and opened his eyes. There was nothing to see—not sky or island or Marie Thérèse. The sea was very still as in a lagoon or a cove.

"Here," she said. "We are here."

"Where?" All he could see was mist. "Where's the dock?"

"On the other side. We are at the back of Isle des Chevaliers. You can climb here on the rocks. They are all together here, like a bridge. You can crawl them all the way to shore."

"It's too foggy," he said. "I can't see my way."

"Don't be afraid. This is the place. On the far side."

"I can't see shit. I can hardly see you."

"Don't see; feel," she said. "You can feel your way, but hurry, hurry. I have to get back."

"This doesn't make sense. Why don't you go to the other side, where the dock is?"

"No," she said. "This is the place."

"Isle des Chevaliers?"

"Yes. Yes. The far side."

"Are you sure?"

"Positive."

Son took his tie out of his jacket pocket and began to knot it around the handle of his traveling bag. "I don't get it, Thérèse. You bring me here as a favor, but before I can say thanks, you make it hard for me to land and even harder to get to the house. What'd you do that for?"

"This is the place. Where you can take a choice. Back there you say you don't. Now you do."

"What the hell are you talking about? If I get off these rocks without drowning, I have to stomp all around in those hills to get to the other side. It must be, good God, ten miles. I'll be all night and half the day . . ."

"Hurry! Get out. I have to get away before the water is too small."

He attached the tie to his waist so the bag hung from behind him. Then he moved over to negotiate the rocks.

"It's easy," she said. "Climb to it and the next one is right behind, then another and another like a road. Then the land."

"You sure, Thérèse?"

"Yes. Yes," she said, then as he turned toward the rocks she touched his back. "Wait. Tell me. If you cannot find her what will you do? Live in the garden of some other white people house?"

He looked around to tell her to mind her own business, but the inability to see her face in the fog stopped him.

"Small boy," she said, "don't go to L'Arbe de la Croix." Her voice was a calamitous whisper coming out of the darkness toward him like jaws. "Forget her. There is nothing in her parts for you. She has forgotten her ancient properties."

He swallowed and, saying nothing, turned back to the rocks, kneeling, stretching his hand to feel them. He touched one. It was dry above the water line and rough, but large enough, it seemed to him, to hold a grown man.

He leaned out of the boat tipping it so it took a little water. The bag knocked clumsily against his thigh. He sat back down and undid the knot. "Keep it for me," he said. Then he grabbed with both hands the surface of the rock and heaved himself onto it. He lay there for a bit, then stretched his arm again and felt the sister rock at his fingertips. Now he could smell the land.

"Hurry," she urged him. "They are waiting."

"Waiting? Who's waiting?" Suddenly he was alarmed.

"The men. The men are waiting for you." She was pulling the oars now, moving out. "You can choose now. You can get free of her. They are waiting in the hills for you. They are naked and they are blind too. I have seen them; their eyes have no color in them. But they gallop; they race those horses like angels all over the hills where the rain forest is, where the champion daisy trees still grow. Go there. Choose them." She was far from him now, but her voice was near like skin.

"Thérèse!" he shouted, turning his head around to the place where the urging of her jaws had come from. "Are you sure?"

If she answered, he could not hear it, and he certainly couldn't see her, so he went. First he crawled the rocks one by one, one by one, till his hands touched shore and the nursing sound of the sea was behind him. He felt around, crawled off and then stood up. Breathing heavily with his mouth open he took a few tentative steps. The pebbles made him stumble and so did the roots of trees. He threw out his hands to guide and steady his going. By and by he walked steadier, now steadier. The mist lifted and the trees stepped back a bit as if to make the way easier for a certain kind of man. Then he ran. Lickety-split. Lickety-split. Looking neither to the left nor to the right. Lickety-split. Lickety-split. Lickety-lickety-lickety-split.

A NOTE ON THE TYPE

THE TEXT of this book was set on the Linotype in Fairfield, a type face designed by the distinguished American artist and engraver, Rudolph Ruzicka. This type displays the sober and sane qualities of a master craftsman whose talent has long been dedicated to clarity.

Rudolph Ruzicka was born in Bohemia in 1883 and came to America in 1894. He has designed and illustrated many books and has created a considerable list of individual prints in a variety of techniques.

Composed by
American–Stratford Graphic Services, Inc.,
Brattleboro, Vermont.

HB 4 Z